Hugo and Nebula Award Winners From Asimov's Science Fiction

HUGO and NEBULA

Award Winners from
ASIMOV'S® SCIENCE FICTION

Edited by
Sheila Williams

WINGS BOOKS
New York • Avenel, New Jersey

We are grateful to the following for permission to reprint their copyrighted material:

"Hardfought" by Greg Bear, copyright © 1982 Greg Bear, reprinted by permission of the author; "Bears Discover Fire" by Terry Bisson, copyright © 1990 by Davis Publications, Inc., reprinted by permission of Susan Ann Protter, Literary Agent; "Speech Sounds" by Octavia Butler, copyright © 1983 by Davis Publications, Inc., reprinted by permission of the author; "Boobs" by Suzy McKee Charnas, copyright © 1989 by Davis Publications, Inc., reprinted by permission of the author; "The Peacemaker" by Gardner Dozois, copyright © 1983 by Gardner Dozois, reprinted by permission of the author and the author's agent, Virginia Kidd; "The Nutcracker Coup" by Janet Kagan, copyright © 1992 by Janet Kagan, reprinted by permission of the author; "Beggars in Spain" by Nancy Kress, copyright © 1991 by Davis Publications, Inc., reprinted by permission of the author; "Ripples in the Dirac Sea" by Geoffrey A. Landis, copyright © 1988 by Davis Publications, Inc., reprinted by permission of the author; "Portraits of His Children" by George R. R. Martin, copyright © 1985 by Davis Publications, Inc., reprinted by permission of the author; "Rachel in Love" by Pat Murphy, copyright © 1987 by Davis Publications, Inc., reprinted by permission of the author; "The Manamouki" by Mike Resnick, copyright © 1990 by Davis Publications, Inc., reprinted by permission of the author; "Danny Goes to Mars" by Pamela Sargent, copyright © 1992 by Bantam Doubleday Dell Magazines, reprinted by permission of the author; "Barnacle Bill the Spacer" by Lucius Shepard, copyright © 1992 by Bantam Doubleday Dell Magazines, reprinted by permission of the author; "Press Enter■" by John Varley, copyright © 1984 by Davis Publications, Inc., reprinted by permission of the author; "Why I Left Harry's All-Night Hamburgers" by Lawrence Watt-Evans, copyright © 1987 by Davis Publications, Inc., reprinted by permission of the author; "Fire Watch" by Connie Willis, copyright © 1982 by Connie Willis, reprinted by permission of the author; "Unicorn Variations" by Roger Zelazny, copyright © 1981 by Davis Publications, Inc., reprinted by permission of the author. All stories have previously appeared in ASIMOV'S SCIENCE FICTION, published by Bantam Doubleday Dell Magazines.

This 1995 edition is published by Wings Books, distributed by Random House Value Publishing, Inc., 40 Engelhard Avenue, Avenel, New Jersey 07001, by arrangement with Dell Magazines, Inc.
Random House
New York • Toronto • London • Sydney • Auckland

Printed and bound in the United States of America

Library of Congress Cataloging-in-Publication Data

Hugo and Nebula award winners from Asimov's science fiction / edited
    by Sheila Williams.
            p.   cm.
      ISBN 0-517-12410-6
      1. Science fiction, American.   I. Williams, Sheila.
PS648.S3H79   1995
813'.0876208—dc20   95-37246
                                                 CIP

8 7 6 5 4 3 2 1

ACKNOWLEDGMENTS

I would like to thank the present editor of *Asimov's Science Fiction* magazine, Gardner Dozois, and past editors Shawna McCarthy and George Scithers. Their combined good taste is amply demonstrated by the quality of the award-winning stories published here. In addition, I'd like to thank Sharah Thomas, Scott L. Towner, and Kathleen Halligan, who helped me with the detail work; Constance Scarborough, who cleared the permissions; and Cynthia Manson, who made this book possible. Special thanks are due my husband, David Bruce, for his help and support.

Dedication

To Irene,
My Evening and My Morning Star

CONTENTS

INTRODUCTION: THE AWARD WINNERS

by SHEILA WILLIAMS

Striking new concepts: artificial satellites replicating African savannas, bears discover fire; unforgettable characters: a teenage werewolf, a distraught chimpanzee; and enthralling plots: uprisings on distant planets, horrifying entities coming through the phone lines, are all to be found in science fiction's most distinguished stories. We try to publish as many tales of this caliber at *Asimov's Science Fiction* as we possibly can. Still, only a few will seek out our night terrors, fill us with awe, or remind us how often the human spirit triumphs in adversity. These are the stories that are recognized with the field's most precious honors, the Hugo, the Nebula, or both. These are the stories that make up this anthology.

The Hugo and the Nebula Awards are selected by two distinct groups of readers. The older, and more inclusive award is the Hugo. First founded in 1954, it is officially known (though hardly ever referred to) as the Science Fiction Achievement Award. The award is voted on by attending and supporting members of the annual World Science Fiction Convention. The convention has been held throughout the United States and Canada, and in The Netherlands, Australia, and Great Britain. It usually takes place over Labor Day weekend, and its membership is open to the public. Anyone familiar with the science fiction field is encouraged to vote.

The award is shaped like a rocketship standing upright on fins. It is presented in a number of categories. The fiction awards are for Best Novel, Best Novella, Best Novelette, and Best Short Story of the previous calendar year, but the award is dated by the year in which it is given. A short story is usually defined as any work up to 7,500 words; a novelette is from 7,500 to 17,500 words; a novella falls from 17,500 words to 40,000; while a novel is any work over 40,000 words. The professional awards also include Best Editor, Best Artist, Best Nonfiction Book, and Best Dramatic Presentation. The latter award generally goes to the best science fiction movie or television episode—*Star Trek's* "City on the Edge of Forever" in 1968, *Jurassic Park* in 1994—but in 1970, the award went to television for its news coverage of Apollo XI, and the moon landing. The Hugo Award is presented in several amateur and special categories as well.

While the convention is heavily attended by professionals— authors, editors, publishers, agents, and artists—the membership is primarily made up of thousands of people who simply like to read science fiction. Since anyone who has paid the nominal fee for a supporting membership can vote, writers and publishers see this award as coming directly from the reading public. The Hugo indicates who is, and who is about to become, immensely popular. Readers who haven't had the chance to catch every story and novel as they appear have found the Hugo Award a reliable indicator of highly entertaining and enjoyable material.

The earliest Hugo-Award winner in this anthology is Roger Zelazny. In 1966, his book, *. . . And Call Me Conrad*, tied with Frank Herbert's *Dune* for Best Novel. *Dune* went on to win the first Nebula Award for Best Novel, but that same year Roger Zelazny won two of the very first Nebula Awards for best short fiction. His story, "He Who Shapes," tied with Brian W. Aldiss for Best Novella, and he won Best Novelette with "The Doors of His Face, the Lamps of His Mouth." This new award had been created by an organization that is now known as the Science Fiction and Fantasy Writers of America (SFWA).

The Nebula Award is limited to the same four fiction categories as the Hugo and an occasional Grand Master Award. The fiction awards differ from the Hugos in that they are usually dated by the year of publication. This means that while a novel published in 1965 might receive a 1966 Hugo, it could also be the winner of the 1965 Nebula Award. Both awards would be distributed in 1966. In addition, the Nebulas more closely resemble the movie industry's Oscars, because they can only be bestowed by one's peers. Only active members of SFWA—writers who have published at least one novel or three short stories—can vote for these awards. Although they don't all cast their votes, SFWA presently has about nine hundred active members.

The Grand Master Nebula Award for life-time achievement is selected by a small Nebula jury of active SFWA members. This honor must go to a living author, and it can only be awarded six times in ten years. The Grand Master and the other four awards are all presented in the spring at the annual Nebula Awards Banquet.

The Nebula is a physically beautiful award. Embedded in clear Lucite, a metallic-glitter spiral nebula is usually suspended over a rock crystal. The Nebula is sometimes perceived as a more literary award than the Hugo. The literary tastes of professional authors and the general readership, however, is often not too different. The final ballots for the two awards frequently resemble each other, and there is a great deal of crossover between the winners of the Nebula and the Hugo. Science fiction authors and readers regard both awards as major triumphs for the victor.

Asimov's Science Fiction magazine was founded in 1977 under the directorship of Isaac Asimov. In 1978 its first editor, George H. Scithers, won the Best Professional Editor Hugo. Barry B. Longyear's novella, "Enemy Mine" (September 1979), which won the Hugo and the Nebula, brought the magazine its first two fiction awards. That story was later made into a movie by 20th Century Fox, starring Dennis Quaid and Louis Gossett, Jr.

Although George Scithers picked up another Hugo for Best Editor, two more years went by before Roger Zelazny won the Hugo Award for "Unicorn Variations" (April 1981). That novelette is the first story featured in this book, and its award marked the beginning of a trend. Since then, *Asimov's Science Fiction* magazine's award winners and finalists have been well represented at the Nebula and Hugo Award ceremonies.

In 1983, I attended my first Nebula Awards Banquet, which was held in New York City at the Warwick Hotel. I sat at the *Asimov's* table with Shawna McCarthy, the magazine's new editor, and Connie Willis. Connie's short story, "A Letter from the Cleary's" (July 1982), and her novella, "Fire Watch" (February 1982), were both up for Nebula Awards. I was ecstatic when they both won, but I came back to Earth in a hurry when an editor from another magazine leaned over and told me this wouldn't happen every year. Although the editor was right in the long run, her powers of prediction were off for the short term. For the next five years, for six years in a row, stories from the magazine won two out of three of the short fiction Nebulas. During that same period of time, *Asimov's* won seven short fiction Hugos, and Shawna and the magazine's subsequent editor, Gardner Dozois, were presented with Hugos of their own.

Connie Willis has become the magazine and the field's leading award winner. While her stories can be funny or tragic, they are always complex and compassionate. "Fire Watch," which is as at home in an Oxford of the future as it is in London during the Blitz, is a brilliant example of her finest work. It is a time travel story that brings history to life. It shows us what we all lose when war and terrorism try to destroy our culture, and what we gain when we see the brave response of the ordinary person.

"Fire Watch" is followed in this anthology by Greg Bear's stunning 1983 novella, "Hardfought." The story begins in the distant future, and moves on even farther into time. Although the tale's scope is truly awesome, it too is about war. Those who wage it can only be redeemed as long as they hold on to some vague trace of humanity. "Hardfought" won its author a Nebula the same year that Gardner Dozois won a Nebula for "The Peacemaker"—a deceptively quiet story that takes place much closer to home.

This book includes another tale from 1983, Octavia Butler's explosive Hugo-Award winning short story, "Speech Sounds." This is a gripping tale of a Los Angeles, and the country at large, that has lost the means to communicate and to reason. While the consequences are frightening, hope again lies in the actions of ordinary people.

Hope is in short supply, however, in John Varley's terrifying 1984 novella, "PRESS ENTER■." This electrifying story is an early example of why we shouldn't take our household computers too lightly. This Hugo- and Nebula-Award-winning hard science fiction story about the dangers of machine intelligence complemented George R.R. Martin's dark psychological look at "Portraits of His Children." The 1984 Nebula-Award winning novelette took a disturbing look at the artist whose art exposes even the most sacred moments of his life.

In 1986, *Asimov's* began its own annual Readers' Award Poll. The winners of this poll are chosen by the readers. Anyone with a ballot from the magazine can vote. Like the Hugos and the Nebulas, the awards go to stories that were published during the previous year. The poll closes around the first of February, and the results are made public over the Nebula Awards weekend. The Nebula ballot is finalized around the middle of February, and the Hugo ballot comes out in the spring. The readers' preferences are not influenced by the stories that make it on to the major award ballots, and our own poll has no effect on the Nebulas or on the list of stories that constitute the Hugo ballot. We have found, though, that a strong correlation does exist among the stories that win the Readers' Award Poll and those that are finalists for science fiction's two most prestigious awards.

The two tales in this anthology from 1987—Pat Murphy's Nebula-Award-winning novelette, "Rachel in Love," and Lawrence Watt-Evans's Hugo-Award-winning short story, "Why I Left Harry's All-Night Hamburgers"—were both winners of the 2nd Annual Readers' Award Poll. Pat Murphy's story takes a wry look at the consequences that may arise when we augment the intelligence of other life forms. Lawrence Watt-Evans's tale is a gentle reminder of why many of us first fell in love with science fiction. All the wonder and adventure in the universe can be found in Harry's diner around the corner.

The book's sole representative from 1988 is the Nebula-Award-winning short story, "Ripples in the Dirac Sea," by Geoffrey A. Landis. As in Connie Willis's "Fire Watch," the character travels in time, but this trip is to a personal past. In a brief few pages, the author brutally reveals the tragic immutability of time. Suzy McKee Charnas's Hugo-Award-winning short story from 1989, "Boobs," offers us one teenage girl's sweet revenge on her chief tormentor. The denouement may be cruel, but it is one that any current or ex-teenager can understand.

Stories from *Asimov's* did not lack for recognition in 1990. Mike Resnick's controversial tale, "The Manamouki," won the Hugo Award for Best Novelette. This powerful story is part of a series of tales set on an artificial satellite that has been modified to resemble the African plains before the arrival of the Europeans. How far a modern settler must go to reclaim the "simplicity" of the past, is chillingly revealed in this unforgettable story. Terry Bisson's 1990 short story, "Bears Discover Fire," won the Hugo, the Nebula, and the *Asimov's* Readers' Award Poll. This charming, bittersweet tale suggests life is held in balance by miracles and privations.

Asimov's 1991 Hugo- and Nebula-Award-winning novella, "Beggars in Spain," was also a winner of the Readers' Award Poll. Nancy Kress's forceful novella takes on the unsettling questions of bio-engineering: What does it mean to design our own children? What if we really do design children that seem superior to ourselves? Will we nurture them or attempt to destroy them?

The final crop of stories in this anthology come from 1992. Lucius Shepard's spectacular novella, "Barnacle Bill the Spacer," shows us the beauty of space and the ugly side of humanity. This Hugo-Award-winning story also reveals the difference one person can make in the lives of others. "Barnacle Bill the Spacer" tied with one of Isaac Asimov's last stories for first place in the 7th annual Readers' Award Poll. The 1992 Nebula Award for Best Novelette went to Pamela Sargent's odd look at the United States' space program, "Danny Goes to Mars."

Janet Kagan's uplifting 1992 novelette, "The Nutcracker Coup," is the last story in this book. It was no surprise to us when this tale came in first in the *Asimov's* Readers' Award Poll. Janet Kagan had been delighting our readers for years. She'd won in the novelette category so many times (even forcing "The Manamouki" into second place in 1992) that we had virtually renamed the award for her. We were thrilled, though, when she was awarded the Hugo by the rest of the voting public. Set on a distant planet, "The Nutcracker Coup" is an amusing and seemingly light-hearted tale. Yet, like so many stories in this anthology, it demonstrates the difference ordinary people can make when they have the courage to take action. Civil rights may never be as easily enacted in real life as they are on Rejoicing, but the drive to try, the need to save others in a Los Angeles gone mad, or to save St. Paul's from burning, is the drive that makes us human, and one of the themes that makes these stories so powerful.

The magazine continues to look for the uplifting story, the spell-binding adventure, the dramatic tragedy, and the terrifying tale. We are still a strong awards' contender. In 1993, all three short fiction Hugos went to stories from *Asimov's Science Fiction* magazine, and Gardner Dozois won his sixth Best Editor Hugo. The 1994 World Science Fiction Convention brought Connie Willis another Hugo Award for a short story from *Asimov's*. We will continue to look for the tales that live up to the grand tradition established by the seventeen Hugo- and Nebula-Award-winning stories appearing in this exciting anthology.

UNICORN VARIATIONS

by ROGER ZELAZNY

The late Roger Zelazny was one of science fiction's most re-spected authors. He was awarded at least six Hugos and three Nebu-las. His most famous works include *A Rose for Ecclesiastics, The Doors of His Face, The Lamps of His Mouth, and Other Stories, . . . And Call Me Conrad, Lord of Light*, and the Amber series of novels. While it bears little resemblance to his riveting post-apocalyptic tale, his novel about *Damnation Alley* was filmed by 20th Century Fox. The movie's cast was headed by Jan-Michael Vincent, George Peppard, and Dominique Sanda.

The author's novelette, "Unicorn Variations" (April 1981), re-ceived one of *Asimov's Science Fiction* magazine's earliest Hugos. Four years later his novella, "24 Views of Mt. Fuji" (July 1985), captured another Hugo for the magazine.

A bizarrerie of fires, cunabulum of light, it moved with a deft, almost dainty deliberation, phasing into and out of existence like a storm-shot piece of evening; or perhaps the darkness between the flares was more akin to its truest nature—swirl of black ashes assembled in prancing cadence to the lowing note of desert wind down the arroyo behind buildings as empty yet filled as the pages of unread books or stillnesses between the notes of a song.

Gone again. Back again. Again.

Power, you said? Yes. It takes considerable force of identity to manifest before or after one's time. Or both.

As it faded and gained it also advanced, moving through the warm afternoon, its tracks erased by the wind. That is, on those occasions when there were tracks.

A reason. There should always be a reason. Or reasons.

It knew why it was there—but not why it was *there*, in that particular locale.

It anticipated learning this shortly, as it approached the desolation-bound line of the old street. However, it knew that the reason may also come before, or after. Yet again, the pull was there and the force of its being was such that it had to be close to something.

The buildings were worn and decayed and some of them fallen and all of them drafty and dusty and empty. Weeds grew among floorboards. Birds nested upon rafters. The droppings of wild things were everywhere; and it knew them all as they would have known it, were they to meet face to face.

It froze, for there had come the tiniest unanticipated sound from somewhere ahead and to the left. At that moment, it was again phasing into existence and it released its outline which faded as quickly as a rainbow in hell, but the naked presence remained beyond subtraction.

Invisible, yet existing, strong, it moved again. The clue. The cue. Ahead. *A gauche.* Beyond the faded word **SALOON** on weathered board above. Through the swinging doors. (One of them pinned alop.)

Pause and assess.

Bar to the right, dusty. Cracked mirror behind it. Empty bottles. Broken bottles. Brass rail, black, encrusted. Tables to the left and rear. In various states of repair.

Man seated at the best of the lot. His back to the door. Levis. Hiking boots. Faded blue shirt. Green backpack leaning against the wall to his left.

Before him, on the tabletop, is the faint, painted outline of a chessboard, stained, scratched, almost obliterated.

The drawer in which he had found the chessmen is still partly open.

He could no more have passed up a chess set without working out a problem or replaying one of his better games than he could have gone without breathing, circulating his blood or maintaining a relatively stable body temperature.

It moved nearer, and perhaps there were fresh prints in the dust behind it, but none noted them.

It, too, played chess.

It watched as the man replayed what had perhaps been his finest game, from the world preliminaries of seven years past. He had blown up after that—surprised to have gotten even as far as he had—for he never could perform well under pressure. But he had always been proud of that one game, and he relived it as all sensitive beings do certain turning points in their lives. For perhaps twenty minutes, no one could have touched him. He had been shining and pure and hard and clear. He had felt like the best.

It took up a position across the board from him and stared. The man completed the game, smiling. Then he set up the board again, rose and fetched a can of beer from his pack. He popped the top.

When he returned, he discovered that White's King's Pawn had been advanced to K4. His brow furrowed. He turned his head, searching the bar, meeting his own puzzled gaze in the grimy mirror. He looked under the table. He took a drink of beer and seated himself.

He reached out and moved his Pawn to K4. A moment later, he saw White's King's Knight rise slowly into the air and drift forward to settle upon KB3. He stared for a long while into the emptiness across the table before he advanced his own Knight to his KB3.

White's Knight moved to take his Pawn. He dismissed the novelty of the situation and moved his Pawn to Q3. He all but forgot the absence of a tangible opponent as the White Knight dropped back to its KB3. He paused to take a sip of beer, but no sooner had he placed the can upon the tabletop than it rose again, passed across the board and was upended. A gurgling noise followed. Then the can fell to the floor, bouncing, ringing with an empty sound.

"I'm sorry," he said, rising and returning to his pack. "I'd have offered you one if I'd thought you were something that might like it."

He opened two more cans, returned with them, placed one near the far edge of the table, one at his own right hand.

"Thank you," came a soft, precise voice from a point beyond it.

The can was raised, tilted slightly, returned to the tabletop.

"My name is Martin," the man said.

"Call me Tlingel," said the other. "I had thought that perhaps your kind was extinct. I am pleased that you at least have survived to afford me this game."

"Huh?" Martin said. "We were all still around the last time that I looked—a couple of days ago."

"No matter. I can take care of that later," Tlingel replied. "I was misled by the appearance of this place."

"Oh. It's a ghost town. I backpack a lot."

"Not important. I am near the proper point in your career as a species. I can feel that much."

"I am afraid that I do not follow you."

"I am not at all certain that you would wish to. I assume that you intend to capture that pawn?"

"Perhaps. Yes, I do wish to. What are you talking about?"

The beer can rose. The invisible entity took another drink.

"Well," said Tlingel, "to put it simply, your—successors—grow anxious. Your place in the scheme of things being such an important one, I had sufficient power to come and check things out."

" 'Successors'? I do not understand."

"Have you seen any griffins recently?"

Martin chuckled.

"I've heard the stories," he said, "seen the photos of the one supposedly shot in the Rockies. A hoax, of course."

"Of course it must seem so. That is the way with mythical beasts."

"You're trying to say that it was real?"

"Certainly. Your world is in bad shape. When the last grizzly bear died recently, the way was opened for the griffins—just as the death of the last aepyornis brought in the yeti, the dodo the Loch Ness creature, the passenger pigeon the sasquatch, the blue whale the kraken, the American eagle the cockatrice—"

"You can't prove it by me."

"Have another drink."

Martin began to reach for the can, halted his hand and stared.

A creature approximately two inches in length, with a human face, a lion-like body and feathered wings was crouched next to the beer can.

"A mini-sphinx," the voice continued. "They came when you killed off the last smallpox virus."

"Are you trying to say that whenever a natural species dies out a mythical one takes its place?" he asked.

"In a word—yes. Now. It was not always so, but you have destroyed the mechanisms of evolution. The balance is now redressed by those others of us from the morning land—we, who have never truly been endangered. We return, in our time."

"And you—whatever you are, Tlingel—you say that humanity is now endangered?"

"Very much so. But there is nothing that you can do about it, is there? Let us get on with the game."

The sphinx flew off. Martin took a sip of beer and captured the Pawn.

"Who," he asked then, "are to be our successors?"

"Modesty almost forbids," Tlingel replied. "In the case of a species as prominent as your own, it naturally has to be the loveliest, most intelligent, most important of us all."

"And what are you? Is there any way that I can have a look?"

"Well—yes. If I exert myself a trifle."

The beer can rose, was drained, fell to the floor. There followed a series of rapid rattling sounds retreating from the table. The air began to flicker over a large area opposite Martin, darkening within the growing flamework. The outline continued to brighten, its interior growing jet black. The form moved, prancing about the saloon, multitudes of tiny, cloven hoof-prints scoring and cracking the floor-boards. With a final, near-blinding flash it came into full view and Martin gasped to behold it.

A black unicorn with mocking, yellow eyes sported before him, rising for a moment onto its hind legs to strike a heraldic pose. The fires flared about it a second longer, then vanished.

Martin had drawn back, raising one hand defensively.

"Regard me!" Tlingel announced. "Ancient symbol of wisdom, valor, and beauty, I stand before you!"

"I thought your typical unicorn was white," Martin finally said.

"I am archetypical," Tlingel responded, dropping to all fours, "and possessed of virtues beyond the ordinary."

"Such as?"

"Let us continue our game."

"What about the fate of the human race? You said—"

". . . And save the small talk for later."

"I hardly consider the destruction of humanity to be small talk."

"And if you've any more beer . . ."

"All right," Martin said, retreating to his pack as the creature advanced, its eyes like a pair of pale suns. "There's some lager."

Something had gone out of the game. As Martin sat before the ebon horn on Tlingel's bowed head, like an insect about to be pinned, he realized that his playing was off. He had felt the pressure the moment he had seen the beast—and there was all that talk about an imminent doomsday. Any run-of-the-mill pessimist could say it without troubling him, but coming from a source as peculiar as this . . .

His earlier elation had fled. He was no longer in top form. And Tlingel was good. Very good. Martin found himself wondering whether he could manage a stalemate.

After a time, he saw that he could not and resigned.

The unicorn looked at him and smiled.

"You don't really play badly—for a human," it said.

"I've done a lot better."

"It is no shame to lose to me, mortal. Even among mythical creatures there are very few who can give a unicorn a good game."

"I am pleased that you were not wholly bored," Martin said. "Now will you tell me what you were talking about concerning the destruction of my species?"

"Oh, that," Tlingel replied. "In the morning land where those such as I dwell, I felt the possibility of your passing come like a gentle wind to my nostrils, with the promise of clearing the way for us—"

"How is it supposed to happen?"

Tlingel shrugged, horn writing on the air with a toss of the head.

"I really couldn't say. Premonitions are seldom specific. In fact, that is what I came to discover. I should have been about it already, but you diverted me with beer and good sport."

"Could you be wrong about this?"

"I doubt it. That is the other reason I am here."

"Please explain."

"Are there any beers left?"

"Two, I think."

"Please."

Martin rose and fetched them.

"Damn! The tab broke off this one," he said.

"Place it upon the table and hold it firmly."

"All right."

Tlingel's horn dipped forward quickly, piercing the can's top.

". . . Useful for all sorts of things," Tlingel observed, withdrawing it.

"The other reason you're here . . ." Martin prompted.

"It is just that I am special. I can do things that the others cannot."

"Such as?"

"Find your weak spot and influence events to exploit it, to—hasten matters. To turn the possibility into a probability, and then—"

"*You* are going to destroy us? Personally?"

"That is the wrong way to look at it. It is more like a game of chess. It is as much a matter of exploiting your opponent's weaknesses as of exercising your own strengths. If you had not already laid the groundwork I would be powerless. I can only influence that which already exists."

"So what will it be? World War III? An ecological disaster? A mutated disease?"

"I do not really know yet, so I wish you wouldn't ask me in that fashion. I repeat that at the moment I am only observing. I am only an agent—"

"It doesn't sound that way to me."

Tlingel was silent. Martin began gathering up the chessmen.

"Aren't you going to set up the board again?"

"To amuse my destroyer a little more? No thanks."

"That's hardly the way to look at it—"

"Besides, those are the last beers."

"Oh." Tlingel stared wistfully at the vanishing pieces, then remarked, "I would be willing to play you again without additional refreshment . . ."

"No thanks."

"You are angry."

"Wouldn't you be, if our situations were reversed?"

"You are anthropomorphizing."

"Well?"

"Oh, I suppose I would."

"You could give us a break, you know—at least, let us make our own mistakes."

"You've hardly done that yourself, though, with all the creatures my fellows have succeeded."

Martin reddened.

"Okay. You just scored one. But I don't have to like it."

"You are a good player. I know that. . . ."

"Tlingel, if I were capable of playing at my best again, I think I could beat you."

The unicorn snorted two tiny wisps of smoke.

"Not *that* good," Tlingel said.

"I guess you'll never know."

"Do I detect a proposal?"

"Possibly. What's another game worth to you?"

Tlingel made a chuckling noise.

"Let me guess: You are going to say that if you beat me you want my promise not to lay my will upon the weakest link in mankind's existence and shatter it."

"Of course."

"And what do I get for winning?"

"The pleasure of the game. That's what you want, isn't it?"

"The terms sound a little lopsided."

"Not if you are going to win anyway. You keep insisting that you will."

"All right. Set up the board."

"There is something else that you have to know about me first."

"Yes?"

"I don't play well under pressure, and this game is going to be a terrific strain. You want my best game, don't you?"

"Yes, but I'm afraid I've no way of adjusting your own reactions to the play."

"I believe I could do that myself if I had more than the usual amount of time between moves."

"Agreed."

"I mean a lot of time."

"Just what do you have in mind?"

"I'll need time to get my mind off it, to relax, to come back to the positions as if they were only problems . . ."

"You mean to go away from here between moves?"

"Yes."

"All right. How long?"

"I don't know. A few weeks, maybe."

"Take a month. Consult your experts, put your computers onto it. It may make for a slightly more interesting game."

"I really didn't have that in mind."

"Then it's time that you're trying to buy."

"I can't deny that. On the other hand, I will need it."

"In that case, I have some terms. I'd like this place cleaned up, fixed up, more lively. It's a mess. I also want beer on tap."

"Okay. I'll see to that."

"Then I agree. Let's see who goes first."

Martin switched a black and a white pawn from hand to hand beneath the table. He raised his fists then and extended them. Tlingel leaned forward and tapped. The black horn's tip touched Martin's left hand.

"Well, it matches my sleek and glossy hide," the unicorn announced.

Martin smiled, setting up the white for himself, the black pieces for his opponent. As soon as he had finished, he pushed his Pawn to K4.

Tlingel's delicate, ebon hoof moved to advance the Black King's Pawn to K4.

"I take it that you want a month now, to consider your next move?"

Martin did not reply but moved his Knight to KB3. Tlingel immediately moved a Knight to QB3.

Martin took a swallow of beer and then moved his Bishop to N5. The unicorn moved the other Knight to B3. Martin immediately castled and Tlingel moved the Knight to take his Pawn.

"I think we'll make it," Martin said suddenly, "if you'll just let us alone. We do learn from our mistakes, in time."

"Mythical beings do not exactly exist in time. Your world is a special case."

"Don't you people ever make mistakes?"

"Whenever we do they're sort of poetic."

Martin snarled and advanced his Pawn to Q4. Tlingel immediately countered by moving the Knight to Q3.

"I've got to stop," Martin said, standing. "I'm getting mad, and it will affect my game."

"You will be going, then?"

"Yes."

He moved to fetch his pack.

"I will see you here in one month's time?"

"Yes."

"Very well."

The unicorn rose and stamped upon the floor and lights began to play across its dark coat. Suddenly, they blazed and shot outward in all directions like a silent explosion. A wave of blackness followed.

Martin found himself leaning against the wall, shaking. When he lowered his hand from his eyes, he saw that he was alone, save for the knights, the bishops, the kings, the queens, their castles and both the kings' men.

He went away.

*   *   *

Three days later Martin returned in a small truck, with a generator, lumber, windows, power tools, paint, stain, cleaning compounds, wax. He dusted and vacuumed and replaced rotted wood. He installed the windows. He polished the old brass until it shone. He stained and rubbed. He waxed the floors and buffed them. He plugged holes and washed glass. He hauled all the trash away.

It took him the better part of a week to turn the old place from a wreck back into a saloon in appearance. Then he drove off, returned all of the equipment he had rented and bought a ticket for the Northwest.

The big, damp forest was another of his favorite places for hiking, for thinking. And he was seeking a complete change of scene, a total revision of outlook. Not that his next move did not seem obvious, standard even. Yet, something nagged. . . .

He knew that it was more than just the game. Before that he had been ready to get away again, to walk drowsing among shadows, breathing clean air.

Resting, his back against the bulging root of a giant tree, he withdrew a small chess set from his pack, set it up on a rock he'd moved into position nearby. A fine, mist-like rain was settling, but the tree sheltered him, so far. He reconstructed the opening through Tlingel's withdrawal of the Knight to Q3. The simplest thing would be to take the Knight with the Bishop. But he did not move to do it.

He watched the board for a time, felt his eyelids drooping, closed them and drowsed. It may only have been for a few minutes. He was never certain afterwards.

Something aroused him. He did not know what. He blinked several times and closed his eyes again. Then he reopened them hurriedly.

In his nodded position, eyes directed downward, his gaze was fixed upon an enormous pair of hairy, unshod feet—the largest pair of feet that he had ever beheld. They stood unmoving before him, pointed toward his right.

Slowly—very slowly—he raised his eyes. Not very far, as it turned out. The creature was only about four and a half feet in height. As it was looking at the chessboard rather than at him, he took the opportunity to study it.

It was unclothed but very hairy, with a dark brown pelt, obviously masculine, possessed of low brow ridges, deep-set eyes that matched its hair, heavy shoulders, five-fingered hands that sported opposing thumbs.

It turned suddenly and regarded him, flashing a large number of shining teeth.

"White's pawn should take the pawn," it said in a soft, nasal voice.

"Huh? Come on," Martin said. "Bishop takes knight."

"You want to give me black and play it that way? I'll walk all over you."

Martin glanced again at its feet.

". . . Or give me white and let me take that pawn. I'll still do it."

"Take white," Martin said, straightening. "Let's see if you know what you're talking about." He reached for his pack. "Have a beer?"

"What's a beer?"

"A recreational aid. Wait a minute."

Before they had finished the six-pack, the sasquatch—whose name, he had learned, was Grend—had finished Martin. Grend had quickly entered a ferocious midgame, backed him into a position of dwindling security and pushed him to the point where he had seen the end and resigned.

"That was one hell of a game," Martin declared, leaning back and considering the ape-like countenance before him.

"Yes, we Bigfeet are pretty good, if I do say it. It's our one big recreation, and we're so damned primitive we don't have much in the way of boards and chessmen. Most of the time, we just play it in our heads. There're not many can come close to us."

"How about unicorns?" Martin asked.

Grend nodded slowly.

"They're about the only ones can really give us a good game. A little dainty, but they're subtle. Awfully sure of themselves, though, I must say. Even when they're wrong. Haven't seen any since we left the morning land, of course. Too bad. Got any more of that beer left?"

"I'm afraid not. But listen, I'll be back this way in a month. I'll bring some more if you'll meet me here and play again."

"Martin, you've got a deal. Sorry. Didn't mean to step on your toes."

He cleaned the saloon again and brought in a keg of beer which he installed under the bar and packed with ice. He moved in some bar stools, chairs and tables which he had obtained at a Goodwill store. He hung red curtains. By then it was evening. He set up the board, ate a light meal, unrolled his sleeping bag behind the bar and camped there that night.

The following day passed quickly. Since Tlingel might show up at any time, he did not leave the vicinity, but took his meals there and sat about working chess problems. When it began to grow dark, he lit a number of oil lamps and candles.

He looked at his watch with increasing frequency. He began to pace. He couldn't have made a mistake. This was the proper day. He—

He heard a chuckle.

Turning about, he saw a black unicorn head floating in the air above the chessboard. As he watched, the rest of Tlingel's body materialized.

"Good evening, Martin." Tlingel turned away from the board. "The place looks a little better. Could use some music . . ."

Martin stepped behind the bar and switched on the transistor radio he had brought along. The sounds of a string quartet filled the air. Tlingel winced.

"Hardly in keeping with the atmosphere of the place."

He changed stations, located a Country & Western show.

"I think not," Tlingel said. "It loses something in transmission."

He turned it off.

"Have we a good supply of beverage?"

Martin drew a gallon stein of beer—the largest mug that he could locate, from a novelty store—and set it upon the bar. He filled a much smaller one for himself. He was determined to get the beast drunk if it were at all possible.

"Ah! Much better than those little cans," said Tlingel, whose muzzle dipped for but a moment. "Very good."

The mug was empty. Martin refilled it.

"Will you move it to the table for me?"

"Certainly."

"Have an interesting month?"

"I suppose I did."

"You've decided upon your next move?"

"Yes."

"Then let's get on with it."

Martin seated himself and captured the Pawn.

"Hm. Interesting."

Tlingel stared at the board for a long while, then raised a cloven hoof which parted in reaching for the piece.

"I'll just take that bishop with this little knight. Now I suppose you'll be wanting another month to decide what to do next."

Tlingel leaned to the side and drained the mug.

"Let me consider it," Martin said, "while I get you a refill."

Martin sat and stared at the board through three more refills. Actually, he was not planning. He was waiting. His response to Grend had been Knight takes Bishop, and he had Grend's next move ready.

"Well?" Tlingel finally said. "What do you think?"

Martin took a small sip of beer.

"Almost ready," he said. "You hold your beer awfully well."

Tlingel laughed.

"A unicorn's horn is a detoxicant. Its possession is a universal remedy. I wait until I reach the warm-glow stage, then I use my horn to burn off any excess and keep me right there."

"Oh," said Martin. "Neat trick, that."

". . . If you've had too much, just touch my horn for a moment and I'll put you back in business."

"No, thanks. That's all right. I'll just push this little pawn in front of the queen's rook two steps ahead."

"Really . . ." said Tlingel. "That's interesting. You know, what this place really needs is a piano—rinkytink, funky . . . Think you could manage it?"

"I don't play."

"Too bad."

"I suppose I could hire a piano player."

"No. I do not care to be seen by other humans."

"If he's really good, I suppose he could play blindfolded."

"Never mind."

"I'm sorry."

"You are also ingenious. I am certain that you will figure something out by next time."

Martin nodded.

"Also, didn't these old places used to have sawdust all over the floors?"

"I believe so."

"That would be nice."

"Check."

Tlingel searched the board frantically for a moment.

"Yes. I meant 'yes'. I said 'check'. It means 'yes' sometimes, too."

"Oh. Rather. Well, while we're here . . ."

Tlingel advanced the Pawn to Q3.

Martin stared. That was not what Grend had done. For a moment, he considered continuing on his own from here. He had tried to think of Grend as a coach up until this point. He had forced away the notion of crudely and crassly pitting one of them against the other. Until P–Q3. Then he recalled the game he had lost to the sasquatch.

"I'll draw the line here," he said, "and take my month."

"All right. Let's have another drink before we say good night. Okay?"

"Sure. Why not?"

They sat for a time and Tlingel told him of the morning land, of primeval forests and rolling plains, of high craggy mountains and purple seas, of magic and mythic beasts.

Martin shook his head.

"I can't quite see why you're so anxious to come here," he said, "with a place like that to call home."

Tlingel sighed.

"I suppose you'd call it keeping up with the griffins. It's the thing to do these days. Well. Till next month . . ."

Tlingel rose and turned away.

"I've got complete control now. Watch!"

The unicorn form faded, jerked out of shape, grew white, faded again, was gone, like an afterimage.

Martin moved to the bar and drew himself another mug. It was a shame to waste what was left. In the morning, he wished the unicorn were there again. Or at least the horn.

It was a gray day in the forest and he held an umbrella over the chessboard upon the rock. The droplets fell from the leaves and made dull, plopping noises as they struck the fabric. The board was set up again through Tlingel's P–Q3. Martin wondered whether Grend had remembered, had kept proper track of the days . . .

"Hello," came the nasal voice from somewhere behind him and to the left.

He turned to see Grend moving about the tree, stepping over the massive roots with massive feet.

"You remembered," Grend said. "How good! I trust you also remembered the beer?"

"I've lugged up a whole case. We can set up the bar right here."

"What's a bar?"

"Well, it's a place where people go to drink—in out of the rain— a bit dark, for atmosphere—and they sit up on stools before a big counter, or else at little tables—and they talk to each other—and sometimes there's music—and they drink."

"We're going to have all that here?"

"No. Just the dark and the drinks. Unless you count the rain as music. I was speaking figuratively."

"Oh. It does sound like a very good place to visit, though."

"Yes. If you will hold this umbrella over the board, I'll set up the best equivalent we can have here."

"All right. Say, this looks like a version of that game we played last time."

"It is. I got to wondering what would happen if it had gone this way rather than the way that it went."

"Hmm. Let me see . . ."

Martin removed four six-packs from his pack and opened the first.

"Here you go."

"Thanks."

Grend accepted the beer, squatted, passed the umbrella back to Martin.

"I'm still white?"

"Yeah."

"Pawn to King six."

"Really?"

"Yep."

"About the best thing for me to do would be to take this pawn with this one."

"I'd say. Then I'll just knock off your knight with this one."

"I guess I'll just pull this knight back to K2."

". . . And I'll take this one over to B3. May I have another beer?"

An hour and a quarter later, Martin resigned. The rain had let up and he had folded the umbrella.

"Another game?" Grend asked.

The afternoon wore on. The pressure was off. This one was just for fun. Martin tried wild combinations, seeing ahead with great clarity, as he had that one day. . . .

"Stalemate," Grend announced much later. "That was a good one, though. You picked up considerably."

"I was more relaxed. Want another?"

"Maybe in a little while. Tell me more about bars now."

So he did. Finally, "How is all that beer affecting you?" he asked.

"I'm a bit dizzy. But that's all right. I'll still cream you the third game."

And he did.

"Not bad for a human, though. Not bad at all. You coming back next month?"

"Yes."

"Good. You'll bring more beer?"

"So long as my money holds out."

"Oh. Bring some plaster of Paris then. I'll make you some nice footprints and you can take casts of them. I understand they're going for quite a bit."

"I'll remember that."

Martin lurched to his feet and collected the chess set.

"Till then."

"Ciao."

Martin dusted and polished again, moved in the player piano and scattered sawdust upon the floor. He installed a fresh keg. He hung some reproductions of period posters and some atrocious old paintings he had located in a junk shop. He placed cuspidors in strategic locations. When he was finished, he seated himself at the bar and opened a bottle of mineral water. He listened to the New Mexico wind moaning as it passed, to grains of sand striking against the windowpanes. He wondered whether the whole world would have that dry, mournful sound to it if Tlingel found a means for doing away with humanity, or—disturbing thought—whether the successors to his own kind might turn things into something resembling the mythical morning land.

This troubled him for a time. Then he went and set up the board through Black's P–Q3. When he turned back to clear the bar he saw a line of cloven hoofprints advancing across the sawdust.

"Good evening, Tlingel," he said. "What is your pleasure?"

Suddenly, the unicorn was there, without preliminary pyrotechnics. It moved to the bar and placed one hoof upon the brass rail.

"The usual."

As Martin drew the beer, Tlingel looked about.

"The place has improved, a bit."

"Glad you think so. Would you care for some music?"

"Yes."

Martin fumbled at the back of the piano, locating the switch for the small, battery-operated computer which controlled the pumping mechanism and substituted its own memory for rolls. The keyboard immediately came to life.

"Very good," Tlingel stated. "Have you found your move?"

"I have."

"Then let us be about it."

He refilled the unicorn's mug and moved it to the table.

"Pawn to King six," he said, executing it.

"What?"

"Just that."

"Give me a minute. I want to study this."

"Take your time."

"I'll take the pawn," Tlingel said, after a long pause and another mug.

"Then I'll take this knight."

Later, "Knight to K2," Tlingel said.

"Knight to B3."

An extremely long pause ensued before Tlingel moved the Knight to N3.

The hell with asking Grend, Martin suddenly decided. He'd been through this part any number of times already. He moved his Knight to N5.

"Change the tune on that thing!" Tlingel snapped.

Martin rose and obliged.

"I don't like that one either. Find a better one or shut it off!"

After three more tries, Martin shut it off.

"And get me another beer!"

He refilled their mugs.

"All right."

Tlingel moved the Bishop to K2.

Keeping the unicorn from castling had to be the most important thing at the moment. So Martin moved his Queen to R5. Tlingel made a tiny, strangling noise, and when Martin looked up smoke was curling from the unicorn's nostrils.

"More beer?"

"If you please."

As he returned with it, he saw Tlingel move the Bishop to capture the Knight. There seemed no choice for him at that moment, but he studied the position for a long while anyhow.

Finally, "Bishop takes bishop," he said.

"Of course."

"How's the warm glow?"

Tlingel chuckled.

"You'll see."

The wind rose again, began to howl. The building creaked.

"Okay," Tlingel finally said, and moved the Queen to Q2.

Martin stared. What was he doing? So far, it had gone all right, but—He listened again to the wind and thought of the risk he was taking.

"That's all, folks," he said, leaning back in his chair. "Continued next month."

Tlingel sighed.

"Don't run off. Fetch me another. Let me tell you of my wanderings in your world this past month."

"Looking for weak links?"

"You're lousy with them. How do you stand it?"

"They're harder to strengthen than you might think. Any advice?"

"Get the beer."

They talked until the sky paled in the east, and Martin found himself taking surreptitious notes. His admiration for the unicorn's analytical abilities increased as the evening advanced.

When they finally rose, Tlingel staggered.

"You all right?"

"Forgot to detox, that's all. Just a second. Then I'll be fading."

"Wait!"

"Whazzat?"

"I could use one, too."

"Oh. Grab hold, then."

Tlingel's head descended and Martin took the tip of the horn between his fingertips. Immediately, a delicious, warm sensation flowed through him. He closed his eyes to enjoy it. His head cleared. An ache which had been growing within his frontal sinus vanished. The tiredness went out of his muscles. He opened his eyes again.

"Thank—"

Tlingel had vanished. He held but a handful of air.

"—you."

"Rael here is my friend," Grend stated. "He's a griffin."

"I'd noticed."

Martin nodded at the beaked, golden-winged creature.

"Pleased to meet you, Rael."

"The same," cried the other in a high-pitched voice. "Have you got the beer?"

"Why—uh—yes."

"I've been telling him about beer," Grend explained, half-apologetically. "He can have some of mine. He won't kibitz or anything like that."

"Sure. All right. Any friend of yours—"

"The beer!" Rael cried. "Bars!"

"He's not real bright," Grend whispered. "But he's good company. I'd appreciate your humoring him."

Martin opened the first six-pack and passed the griffin and the sasquatch a beer apiece. Rael immediately punctured the can with his beak, chugged it, belched and held out his claw.

"Beer!" he shrieked. "More beer!"

Martin handed him another.

"Say, you're still into that first game, aren't you?" Grend observed, studying the board. "Now, *that* is an interesting position."

Grend drank and studied the board.

"Good thing it's not raining," Martin commented.

"Oh, it will. Just wait a while."

"More beer!" Rael screamed.

Martin passed him another without looking.

"I'll move my pawn to N6," Grend said.

"You're kidding."

"Nope. Then you'll take that pawn with your bishop's pawn. Right?"

"Yes . . ."

Martin reached out and did it.

"Okay. Now I'll just swing this knight to Q5."

Martin took it with the Pawn.

Grend moved his Rook to K1.

"Check," he announced.

"Yes. That *is* the way to go," Martin observed.

Grend chuckled.

"I'm going to win this game another time," he said.

"I wouldn't put it past you."

"More beer?" Rael said softly.

"Sure."

As Martin passed him another, he noticed that the griffin was now leaning against the tree trunk.

After several minutes, Martin pushed his King to B1.

"Yeah, that's what I thought you'd do," Grend said. "You know something?"

"What?"

"You play a lot like a unicorn."

"Hm."

Grend moved his Rook to R3.

Later, as the rain descended gently about them and Grend beat him again, Martin realized that a prolonged period of silence had prevailed. He glanced over at the griffin. Rael had tucked his head beneath his left wing, balanced upon one leg, leaned heavily against the tree and gone to sleep.

"I told you he wouldn't be much trouble," Grend remarked.

Two games later, the beer was gone, the shadows were lengthening, and Rael was stirring.

"See you next month?"

"Yeah."

"You bring any plaster of Paris?"

"Yes, I did."

"Come on, then. I know a good place pretty far from here. We don't want people beating about *these* bushes. Let's go make you some money."

"To buy beer?" Rael said, looking out from under his wing.

"Next month," Grend said.

"You ride?"

"I don't think you could carry both of us," said Grend, "and I'm not sure I'd want to right now if you could."

"Bye-bye then," Rael shrieked, and he leaped into the air, crashing into branches and tree trunks, finally breaking through the overhead cover and vanishing.

"There goes a really decent guy," said Grend. "He sees everything and he never forgets. Knows how everything works—in the woods, in the air—even in the water. Generous, too, whenever he has anything."

"Hm," Martin observed.

"Let's make tracks," Grend said.

"Pawn to N6? Really?" Tlingel said. "All right. The bishop's pawn will just knock off the pawn."

Tlingel's eyes narrowed as Martin moved the Knight to Q5.

"At least this is an interesting game," the unicorn remarked. "Pawn takes knight."

Martin moved the rook.

"Check."

"Yes, it is. This next one is going to be a three-flagon move. Kindly bring me the first."

Martin thought back as he watched Tlingel drink and ponder. He almost felt guilty for hitting it with a powerhouse like the sasquatch behind its back. He was convinced now that the unicorn was going to lose. In every variation of this game that he'd played with Black against Grend, he'd been beaten. Tlingel was very good, but the sasquatch was a wizard with not much else to do but mental chess. It was unfair. But it was not a matter of personal honor, he kept telling himself. He was playing to protect his species against a supernatural force which might well be able to precipitate World War III by some arcane mind-manipulation or magically induced computer foulup. He didn't dare give the creature a break.

"Flagon number two, please."

He brought it another. He studied it as it studied the board. It was beautiful, he realized for the first time. It was the loveliest living thing he had ever seen. Now that the pressure was on the verge of evaporating and he could regard it without the overlay of fear which had always been there in the past, he could pause to admire it. If something *had* to succeed the human race, he could think of worse choices. . . .

"Number three now."

"Coming up."

Tlingel drained it and moved the King to B1.

Martin leaned forward immediately and pushed the Rook to R3.

Tlingel looked up, stared at him.

"Not bad."

Martin wanted to squirm. He was struck by the nobility of the creature. He wanted so badly to play and beat the unicorn on his own, fairly. Not this way.

Tlingel looked back at the board, then almost carelessly moved the Knight to K4.

"Go ahead. Or will it take you another month?"

Martin growled softly, advanced the Rook, and captured the Knight.

"Of course."

Tlingel captured the Rook with the Pawn. This was not the way that the last variation with Grend had run. Still . . .

He moved his Rook to KB3. As he did, the wind seemed to commence a peculiar shrieking, above, amid the ruined buildings.

"Check," he announced.

The hell with it! he decided. I'm good enough to manage my own endgame. Let's play this out.

He watched and waited and finally saw Tlingel move the King to N1.

He moved his Bishop to R6. Tlingel moved the Queen to K2. The shrieking came again, sounding nearer now. Martin took the Pawn with the Bishop.

The unicorn's head came up and it seemed to listen for a moment. Then Tlingel lowered it and captured the Bishop with the King.

Martin moved his Rook to KN3.

"Check."

Tlingel returned the King to B1.

Martin moved the Rook to KB3.

"Check."

Tlingel pushed the King to N2.

Martin moved the Rook back to KN3.

"Check."

Tlingel returned the King to B1, looked up and stared at him, showing teeth.

"Looks as if we've got a drawn game," the unicorn stated. "Care for another one?"

"Yes, but not for the fate of humanity."

"Forget it. I'd given up on that a long time ago. I decided that I wouldn't care to live here after all. I'm a little more discriminating than that.

"Except for this bar." Tlingel turned away as another shriek sounded just beyond the door, followed by strange voices. "What is that?"

"I don't know," Martin answered, rising.

The doors opened and a golden griffin entered.

"Martin!" it cried. "Beer! Beer!"

"Uh—Tlingel, this is Rael, and, and—"

Three more griffins followed him in. Then came Grend, and three others of his own kind.

"—and that one's Grend," Martin said lamely. "I don't know the others."

They all halted when they beheld the unicorn.

"Tlingel," one of the sasquatches said. "I thought you were still in the morning land."

"I still am, in a way. Martin, how is it that you are acquainted with my former countrymen?"

"Well—uh—Grend here is my chess coach."

"Aha! I begin to understand."

"I am not sure that you really do. But let me get everyone a drink first."

Martin turned on the piano and set everyone up.

"How did you find this place?" he asked Grend as he was doing it. "And how did you get here?"

"Well . . ." Grend looked embarrassed. "Rael followed you back."

"Followed a jet?"

"Griffins are supernaturally fast."

"Oh."

"Anyway, he told his relatives and some of my folks about it. When we saw that the griffins were determined to visit you, we decided that we had better come along to keep them out of trouble. They brought us."

"I—see. Interesting . . ."

"No wonder you played like a unicorn, that one game with all the variations."

"Uh—yes."

Martin turned away, moved to the end of the bar.

"Welcome, all of you," he said. "I have a small announcement. Tlingel, a while back you had a number of observations concerning possible ecological and urban disasters and lesser dangers. Also, some ideas as to possible safeguards against some of them."

"I recall," said the unicorn.

"I passed them along to a friend of mine in Washington who used to be a member of my old chess club. I told him that the work was not entirely my own."

"I should hope so."

"He has since suggested that I turn whatever group was involved into a think tank. He will then see about paying something for its efforts."

"I didn't come here to save the world," Tlingel said.

"No, but you've been very helpful. And Grend tells me that the griffins, even if their vocabulary is a bit limited, know almost all that there is to know about ecology."

"That is probably true."

"Since they have inherited a part of the Earth, it would be to their benefit as well to help preserve the place. Inasmuch as this many of us are already here, I can save myself some travel and suggest right now that we find a meeting place—say here, once a month—and that you let me have your unique viewpoints. You must know more about how species become extinct than anyone else in the business."

"Of course," said Grend, waving his mug, "but we really should ask the yeti, also. I'll do it, if you'd like. Is that stuff coming out of the big box music?"

"Yes."

"I like it. If we do this think-tank thing, you'll make enough to keep this place going?"

"I'll buy the whole town."

Grend conversed in quick gutturals with the griffins, who shrieked back at him.

"You've got a think tank," he said, "and they want more beer."

Martin turned toward Tlingel.

"They were your observations. What do you think?"

"It may be amusing," said the unicorn, "to stop by occasionally." Then, "So much for saving the world. Did you say you wanted another game?"

"I've nothing to lose."

Grend took over the tending of the bar while Tlingel and Martin returned to the table.

He beat the unicorn in thirty-one moves and touched the extended horn.

The piano keys went up and down. Tiny sphinxes buzzed about the bar, drinking the spillage.

FIRE WATCH

by CONNIE WILLIS

Connie Willis has the honor of holding the most Nebula Awards in science fiction. She won her first Nebula and Hugo Awards for her poignant novelette, "Fire Watch" (*Asimov's*, February 1982). That same year, she picked up her second Nebula for her short story, "A Letter from the Clearys" (*Asimov's*, July 1982). In 1989, her heart-breaking novella, "The Last of the Winnebagos" (*Asimov's*, July 1988), brought the author one more Nebula and Hugo. In 1990, her only award-winning short fiction not to appear in *Asimov's*, "At the Rialto," received another Nebula for Best Novelette. Two years later, Connie Willis's short story, "Even the Queen" (*Asimov's*, April 1992), and her novel, *Doomsday Book*, were both awarded Hugos and Nebulas. This feat made her the first person to possess a Hugo and a Nebula in each of the four fiction categories. "Death on the Nile," a short story from the March 1993 issue of *Asimov's*, was Connie Willis's most recent Hugo Award winner.

Doomsday Book, the author's beautiful novel about time travel and the plague year, has some of the same characters as the equally compelling novelette, "Fire Watch," that is presented here.

"History hath triumphed over time, which besides it nothing but eternity hath triumphed over."

—Sir Walter Raleigh

September 20—Of course the first thing I looked for was the fire-watch stone. And of course it wasn't there yet. It wasn't dedicated until 1951, accompanying speech by the Very Reverend Dean Walter Matthews, and this is only 1940. I knew that. I went to see the fire-watch stone only yesterday, with some kind of misplaced notion that seeing the scene of the crime would somehow help. It didn't.

The only things that would have helped were a crash course in London during the Blitz and a little more time. I had not gotten either.

"Travelling in time is not like taking the tube, Mr. Bartholomew," the esteemed Dunworthy had said, blinking at me through those antique spectacles of his. "Either you report on the twentieth or you don't go at all."

"But I'm not ready," I'd said. "Look, it took me four years to get ready to travel with St. Paul. *St. Paul.* Not St. Paul's. You can't expect me to get ready for London in the Blitz in two days."

"Yes," Dunworthy had said. "We can." End of conversation.

"Two days!" I had shouted at my roommate Kivrin. "All because some computer adds an apostrophe s. And the esteemed Dunworthy doesn't even bat an eye when I tell him. 'Time travel is not like taking the tube, young man,' he says. 'I'd suggest you get ready. You're leaving day after tomorrow.' The man's a total incompetent."

"No," she said. "He isn't. He's the best there is. He wrote the book on St. Paul's. Maybe you should listen to what he says."

I had expected Kivrin to be at least a little sympathetic. She had been practically hysterical when she got her practicum changed from fifteenth to fourteenth century England, and how did either century qualify as a practicum? Even counting infectious diseases they couldn't have been more than a five. The Blitz is an eight, and St. Paul's itself is, with my luck, a ten.

"You think I should go see Dunworthy again?" I said.

"Yes."

"And then what? I've got two days. I don't know the money, the language, the history. Nothing."

"He's a good man," Kivrin said. "I think you'd better listen to him while you can." Good old Kivrin. Always the sympathetic ear.

The good man was responsible for my standing just inside the propped-open west doors, gawking like the country boy I was supposed to be, looking for a stone that wasn't there. Thanks to the good man, I was about as unprepared for my practicum as it was possible for him to make me.

I couldn't see more than a few feet into the church. I could see a candle gleaming feebly a long way off and a closer blur of white moving toward me. A verger, or possibly the Very Reverend Dean himself. I pulled out the letter from my clergyman uncle in Wales that was supposed to gain me access to the Dean, and patted my back pocket to make sure I hadn't lost the microfiche *Oxford English Dictionary, Revised, with Historical Supplements*, I'd smuggled out of the Bodleian. I couldn't pull it out in the middle of the conversation, but with luck I could muddle through the first encounter by context and look up the words I didn't know later.

"Are you from the ayarpee?" he said. He was no older than I am, a head shorter and much thinner. Almost ascetic looking. He reminded me of Kivrin. He was not wearing white, but clutching it to his chest. In other circumstances I would have thought it was a pillow. In other circumstances I would know what was being said to me, but there had been no time to unlearn sub-Mediterranean Latin and Jewish law and learn Cockney and air-raid procedures. Two days, and the esteemed Dunworthy, who wanted to talk about the sacred burdens of the historian instead of telling me what the ayarpee was.

"Are you?" he demanded again.

I considered slipping out the *OED* after all on the grounds that Wales was a foreign country, but I didn't think they had microfilm in 1940. Ayarpee. It could be anything, including a nickname for the fire watch, in which case the impulse to say no was not safe at all. "No," I said.

He lunged suddenly toward and past me and peered out the open doors. "Damn," he said, coming back to me. "Where are they then? Bunch of lazy bourgeois tarts!" And so much for getting by on context.

He looked at me closely, suspiciously, as if he thought I was only pretending not to be with the ayarpee. "The church is closed," he said finally.

I held up the envelope and said, "My name's Bartholomew. Is Dean Matthews in?"

He looked out the door a moment longer, as if he expected the lazy bourgeois tarts at any moment and intended to attack them with the white bundle, then he turned and said, as if he were guiding a tour, "This way; please," and took off into the gloom.

He led me to the right and down the south aisle of the nave. Thank God I had memorized the floor plan or at that moment, heading into total darkness, led by a raving verger, the whole bizarre metaphor of my situation would have been enough to send me out the west doors and back to St. John's Wood. It helped a little to know where I was. We should have been passing number twenty-six: Hunt's painting of "The Light of the World"—Jesus with his lantern—but it was too dark to see it. We could have used the lantern ourselves.

He stopped abruptly ahead of me, still raving. "We weren't asking for the bloody Savoy, just a few cots. Nelson's better off than we are—at least he's got a pillow provided." He brandished the white bundle like a torch in the darkness. It was a pillow after all. "We asked for them over a fortnight ago, and here we still are, sleeping on the bleeding generals from Trafalgar because those bitches want to play tea and crumpets with the tommies at Victoria and the Hell with us!"

He didn't seem to expect me to answer his outburst, which was good, because I had understood perhaps one key word in three. He stomped on ahead, moving out of sight of the one pathetic altar candle and stopping again at a black hole. Number twenty-five: stairs to the Whispering Gallery, the Dome, the library (not open to the public). Up the stairs, down a hall, stop again at a medieval door and knock. "I've got to go wait for them," he said. "If I'm not there they'll likely take them over to the Abbey. Tell the Dean to ring them up again, will you?" and he took off down the stone steps, still holding his pillow like a shield against him.

He had knocked, but the door was at least a foot of solid oak, and it was obvious the Very Reverend Dean had not heard. I was going to have to knock again. Yes, well, and the man holding the pinpoint had to let go of it, too, but even knowing it will all be over in a moment and you won't feel a thing doesn't make it any easier to say, "Now!" So I stood in front of the door, cursing the history department and the esteemed Dunworthy and the computer that had made the mistake and brought me here to this dark door with only a letter from a fictitious uncle that I trusted no more than I trusted the rest of them.

Even the old reliable Bodleian had let me down. The batch of research stuff I cross-ordered through Balliol and the main terminal is probably sitting in my room right now, a century out of reach. And Kivrin, who had already done her practicum and should have been bursting with advice, walked around as silent as a saint until I begged her to help me.

"Did you go to see Dunworthy?" she said.

"Yes. You want to know what priceless bit of information he had for me? 'Silence and humility are the sacred burdens of the historian.' He also told me I would love St. Paul's. Golden gems from the master. Unfortunately, what I need to know are the times and places of the bombs so one doesn't fall on me." I flopped down on the bed. "Any suggestions?"

"How good are you at memory retrieval?" she said.

I sat up. "I'm pretty good. You think I should assimilate?"

"There isn't time for that," she said. "I think you should put everything you can directly into long-term."

"You mean endorphins?" I said.

The biggest problem with using memory-assistance drugs to put information into your long-term memory is that it never sits, even for a micro-second, in your short-term memory, and that makes retrieval complicated, not to mention unnerving. It gives you the most unsettling sense of *déjà vu* to suddenly know something you're positive you've never seen or heard before.

The main problem, though, is not eerie sensations but retrieval. Nobody knows exactly how the brain gets what it wants out of storage, but short-term is definitely involved. That brief, sometimes microscopic, time information spends in short-term is apparently used for something besides tip-of-the-tongue availability. The whole complex sort-and-file process of retrieval is apparently centered in short-term; and without it, and without the help of the drugs that put it there or artificial substitutes, information can be impossible to retrieve. I'd used endorphins for examinations and never had any difficulty with retrieval, and it looked like it was the only way to store all the information I needed in anything approaching the time I had left, but it also meant that I would *never* have known any of the things I needed to know, even for long enough to have forgotten them. If and when I could retrieve the information, I would know it. Till then I was as ignorant of it as if it were not stored in some cobwebbed corner of my mind at all.

"You can retrieve without artificials, can't you?" Kivrin said, looking skeptical.

"I guess I'll have to."

"Under stress? Without sleep? Low body endorphin levels?" What exactly had her practicum been? She had never said a word about it, and undergraduates are not supposed to ask. Stress factors in the Middle Ages? I thought everybody slept through them.

"I hope so," I said. "Anyway, I'm willing to try this idea if you think it will help."

She looked at me with that martyred expression and said, "Nothing will help." Thank you, St. Kivrin of Balliol.

But I tried it anyway. It was better than sitting in Dunworthy's rooms having him blink at me through his historically accurate eyeglasses and tell me I was going to love St. Paul's. When my Bodleian requests didn't come, I overloaded my credit and bought out Blackwell's. Tapes on World War II, Celtic literature, history of mass transit, tourist guidebooks, everything I could think of. Then I rented a high-speed recorder and shot up. When I came out of it, I was so panicked by the feeling of not knowing any more than I had when I started that I took the tube to London and raced up Ludgate Hill to see if the firewatch stone would trigger any memories. It didn't.

"Your endorphin levels aren't back to normal yet," I told myself and tried to relax, but that was impossible with the prospect of the practicum looming up before me. And those are real bullets, kid. Just because you're a history major doing his practicum doesn't mean you can't get killed. I read history books all the way home on the tube and right up until Dunworthy's flunkies came to take me to St. John's Wood this morning.

Then I jammed the microfiche *OED* in my back pocket and went off feeling as if I would have to survive by my native wit and hoping I could get hold of artificials in 1940. Surely I could get through the first day without mishap, I thought; and now here I was, stopped cold by almost the first word that was spoken to me.

Well, not quite. In spite of Kivrin's advice that I not put anything in short-term, I'd memorized the British money, a map of the tube system, a map of my own Oxford. It had gotten me this far. Surely I would be able to deal with the Dean.

Just as I had almost gotten up the courage to knock, he opened the door, and as with the pinpoint, it really was over quickly and without pain. I handed him my letter, and he shook my hand and said something understandable like, "Glad to have another man, Bartholomew." He looked strained and tired and as if he might collapse if I told him the Blitz had just started. I know, I know: Keep your mouth shut. The sacred silence, etc.

He said, "We'll get Langby to show you round, shall we?" I assumed that was my Verger of the Pillow, and I was right. He met us at the foot of the stairs, puffing a little but jubilant.

"The cots came," he said to Dean Matthews. "You'd have thought they were doing us a favor. All high heels and hoity-toity. 'You made us miss our tea, luv,' one of them said to me. 'Yes, well, and a good thing, too,' I said. 'You look as if you could stand to lose a stone or two.' "

Even Dean Matthews looked as though he did not completely understand him. He said, "Did you set them up in the crypt?" and then introduced us. "Mr. Bartholomew's just got in from Wales," he said. "He's come to join our volunteers." Volunteers, not fire watch.

Langby showed me around, pointing out various dimnesses in the general gloom and then dragged me down to see the ten folding canvas cots set up among the tombs in the crypt, also in passing Lord Nelson's black marble sarcophagus. He told me I didn't have to stand a watch the first night and suggested I go to bed, since sleep is the most precious commodity in the raids. I could well believe it. He was clutching that silly pillow to his breast like his beloved.

"Do you hear the sirens down here?" I asked, wondering if he buried his head in it.

He looked round at the low stone ceilings. "Some do, some don't. Brinton has to have his Horlich's. Bence-Jones would sleep if the roof fell in on him. I have to have a pillow. The important thing is to get your eight in no matter what. If you don't, you turn into one of the walking dead. And then you get killed."

On that cheering note he went off to post the watches for tonight, leaving his pillow on one of the cots with orders for me to let nobody touch it. So here I sit, waiting for my first air-raid siren and trying to get all this down before I turn into one of the walking or non-walking dead.

I've used the stolen *OED* to decipher a little Langby. Middling success. A tart is either a pastry or a prostitute (I assume the latter, although I was wrong about the pillow). Bourgeois is a catchall term for all the faults of the middle class. A Tommy's a soldier. Ayarpee I could not find under any spelling and I had nearly given up when something in long-term about the use of acronyms and abbreviations in wartime popped forward (bless you, St. Kivrin) and I realized it must be an abbreviation. ARP. Air Raid Precautions. Of course. Where else would you get the bleeding cots from?

September 21—Now that I'm past the first shock of being here, I realize that the history department neglected to tell me what I'm supposed to do in the three-odd months of this practicum. They handed me this journal, the letter from my uncle, and a ten-pound note, and sent me packing into the past. The ten pounds (already depleted by train and tube fares) is supposed to last me until the end of December and get me back to St. John's Wood for pickup when the second letter calling me back to Wales to sick uncle's bedside comes. Till then I live here in the crypt with Nelson, who, Langby tells me, is pickled in alcohol inside his coffin. If we take a direct hit, will he burn like a torch or simply trickle out in a decaying stream onto the crypt floor, I wonder. Board is provided by a gas ring, over which are cooked wretched tea and indescribable kippers. To pay for all this luxury I am to stand on the roofs of St. Paul's and put out incendiaries.

I must also accomplish the purpose of this practicum, whatever it may be. Right now the only purpose I care about is staying alive until the second letter from uncle arrives and I can go home.

I am doing makework until Langby has time to "show me the ropes." I've cleaned the skillet they cook the foul little fishes in, stacked wooden folding chairs at the altar end of the crypt (flat instead of standing because they tend to collapse like bombs in the middle of the night), and tried to sleep.

I am apparently not one of the lucky ones who can sleep through the raids. I spent most of the night wondering what St. Paul's risk rating is. Practica have to be at least a six. Last night I was convinced this was a ten, with the crypt as ground zero, and that I might as well have applied for Denver.

The most interesting thing that's happened so far is that I've seen a cat. I am fascinated, but trying not to appear so since they seem commonplace here.

September 22—Still in the crypt. Langby comes dashing through periodically cursing various government agencies (all abbreviated) and promising to take me up on the roofs. In the meantime, I've run out of makework and taught myself to work a stirrup pump. Kivrin was overly concerned about my memory retrieval abilities. I have not had any trouble so far. Quite the opposite. I called up fire-fighting information and got the whole manual with pictures, including instructions on the use of the stirrup pump. If the kippers set Lord Nelson on fire, I shall be a hero.

Excitement last night. The sirens went early and some of the chars who clean offices in the City sheltered in the crypt with us. One of them woke me out of a sound sleep, going like an air raid siren. Seems she'd seen a mouse. We had to go whacking at tombs and under the cots with a rubber boot to persuade her it was gone. Obviously what the history department had in mind: murdering mice.

September 24—Langby took me on rounds. Into the choir, where I had to learn the stirrup pump all over again, assigned rubber boots and a tin helmet. Langby says Commander Allen is getting us asbestos firemen's coats, but hasn't yet, so it's my own wool coat and muffler and very cold on the roofs even in September. It feels like November and looks it, too, bleak and cheerless with no sun. Up to the dome and onto the roofs which should be flat, but in fact are littered with towers, pinnacles, gutters, and statues, all designed expressly to catch and hold incendiaries out of reach. Shown how to smother an incendiary with sand before it burns through the roof and sets the church on fire. Shown the ropes (literally) lying in a heap at the base of the dome in case somebody has to go up one of the west towers or over the top of the dome. Back inside and down to the Whispering Gallery.

Langby kept up a running commentary through the whole tour, part practical instruction, part church history. Before we went up into the Gallery he dragged me over to the south door to tell me how Christopher Wren stood in the smoking rubble of Old St. Paul's and asked a workman to bring him a stone from the graveyard to mark the cornerstone. On the stone was written in Latin, "I shall rise again," and Wren was so impressed by the irony that he had the words inscribed above the door. Langby looked as smug as if he had not told me a story every first-year history student knows, but I suppose without the impact of the firewatch stone, the other is just a nice story.

Langby raced me up the steps and onto the narrow balcony circling the Whispering Gallery. He was already halfway round to the other side, shouting dimensions and acoustics at me. He stopped facing the wall opposite and said softly, "You can hear me whispering because of the shape of the dome. The sound waves are reinforced around the perimeter of the dome. It sounds like the very crack of doom up here during a raid. The dome is one hundred and seven feet across. It is eighty feet above the nave."

I looked down. The railing went out from under me and the black-and-white marble floor came up with dizzying speed. I hung onto something in front of me and dropped to my knees, staggered and sick at heart. The sun had come out, and all of St. Paul's seemed drenched in gold. Even the carved wood of the choir, the white stone pillars, the leaden pipes of the organ, all of it golden, golden.

Langby was beside me, trying to pull me free. "Bartholomew," he shouted, "What's wrong? For God's sake, man."

I knew I must tell him that if I let go, St. Paul's and all the past would fall in on me, and that I must not let that happen because I was an historian. I said something, but it was not what I intended because Langby merely tightened his grip. He hauled me violently free of the railing and back onto the stairway, then let me collapse limply on the steps and stood back from me, not speaking.

"I don't know what happened in there," I said. "I've never been afraid of heights before."

"You're shaking," he said sharply. "You'd better lie down." He led me back to the crypt.

September 25—Memory retrieval: ARP manual. Symptoms of bombing victims. Stage one—shock; stupefaction; unawareness of injuries; words may not make sense except to victim. Stage two—shivering; nausea; injuries, losses felt; return to reality. Stage three—talkativeness that cannot be controlled; desire to explain shock behavior to rescuers.

Langby must surely recognize the symptoms, but how does he account for the fact there was no bomb? I can hardly explain my shock behavior to him, and it isn't just the sacred silence of the historian that stops me.

He has not said anything, in fact assigned me my first watches for tomorrow night as if nothing had happened, and he seems no more preoccupied than anyone else. Everyone I've met so far is jittery (one thing I had in short-term was how calm everyone was during the raids) and the raids have not come near us since I got here. They've been mostly over the East End and the docks.

There was a reference tonight to a UXB, and I have been thinking about the Dean's manner and the church being closed when I'm almost sure I remember reading it was open through the entire Blitz. As soon as I get a chance, I'll try to retrieve the events of September. As to retrieving anything else, I don't see how I can hope to remember the right information until I know what it is I am supposed to do here, if anything.

There are no guidelines for historians, and no restrictions either. I could tell everyone I'm from the future if I thought they would believe me. I could murder Hitler if I could get to Germany. Or could I? Time paradox talk abounds in the history department, and the graduate students back from their practica don't say a word one way or the other. Is there a tough, immutable past? Or is there a new past every day and do we, the historians, make it? And what are the consequences of what we do, if there are consequences? And how do we dare do anything without knowing them? Must we interfere boldly, hoping we do not bring about all our downfalls? Or must we do nothing at all, not interfere, stand by and watch St. Paul's burn to the ground if need be so that we don't change the future?

All those are fine questions for a late-night study session. They do not matter here. I could no more let St. Paul's burn down than I could kill Hitler. No, that is not true. I found that out yesterday in the Whispering Gallery. I could kill Hitler if I caught him setting fire to St. Paul's.

* * *

September 26—I met a young woman today. Dean Matthews has opened the church, so the watch have been doing duties as chars and people have started coming in again. The young woman reminded me of Kivrin, though Kivrin is a good deal taller and would never frizz her hair like that. She looked as if she had been crying. Kivrin has looked like that since she got back from her practicum. The Middle Ages were too much for her. I wonder how she would have coped with this. By pouring out her fears to the local priest, no doubt, as I sincerely hoped her lookalike was not going to do.

"May I help you?" I said, not wanting in the least to help. "I'm a volunteer."

She looked distressed. "You're not paid?" she said, and wiped at her reddened nose with a handkerchief. "I read about St. Paul's and the fire watch and all and I thought, perhaps there's a position there for me. In the canteen, like, or something. A paying position." There were tears in her red-rimmed eyes.

"I'm afraid we don't have a canteen," I said as kindly as I could, considering how impatient Kivrin always makes me, "and it's not actually a real shelter. Some of the watch sleep in the crypt. I'm afraid we're all volunteers, though."

"That won't do, then," she said. She dabbed at her eyes with the handkerchief. "I love St. Paul's, but I can't take on volunteer work, not with my little brother Tom back from the country." I was not reading this situation properly. For all the outward signs of distress, she sounded quite cheerful and no closer to tears than when she had come in. "I've got to get us a proper place to stay. With Tom back, we can't go on sleeping in the tubes."

A sudden feeling of dread, the kind of sharp pain you get sometimes from involuntary retrieval, went over me. "The tubes?" I said, trying to get at the memory.

"Marble Arch, usually," she went on. "My brother Tom saves us a place early and I go—" She stopped, held the handkerchief close to her nose, and exploded into it. "I'm sorry," she said, "this awful cold!"

Red nose, watering eyes, sneezing. Respiratory infection. It was a wonder I hadn't told her not to cry. It's only by luck that I haven't made some unforgivable mistake so far, and this is not because I can't get at the long-term memory. I don't have half the information I need even stored: cats and colds and the way St. Paul's looks in full sun. It's only a matter of time before I am stopped cold by something I do not know. Nevertheless, I am going to try for retrieval tonight after I come off watch. At least I can find out whether and when something is going to fall on me.

I have seen the cat once or twice. He is coal-black with a white patch on his throat that looks as if it were painted on for the blackout.

September 27—I have just come down from the roofs. I am still shaking.

Early in the raid the bombing was mostly over the East End. The view was incredible. Searchlights everywhere, the sky pink from the fires and reflecting in the Thames, the exploding shells sparkling like fireworks. There was a constant, deafening thunder broken by the occasional droning of the planes high overhead, then the repeating stutter of the ack-ack guns.

About midnight the bombs began falling quite near with a horrible sound like a train running over me. It took every bit of will I had to keep from flinging myself flat on the roof, but Langby was watching. I didn't want to give him the satisfaction of watching a repeat performance of my behavior in the dome. I kept my head up and my sand-bucket firmly in hand and felt quite proud of myself.

The bombs stopped roaring past about three, and there was a lull of about half an hour, and then a clatter like hail on the roofs. Everybody except Langby dived for shovels and stirrup pumps. He was watching me. And I was watching the incendiary.

It had fallen only a few meters from me, behind the clock tower. It was much smaller than I had imagined, only about thirty centimeters long. It was sputtering violently, throwing greenish-white fire almost to where I was standing. In a minute it would simmer down into a molten mass and begin to burn through the roof. Flames and the frantic shouts of firemen, and then the white rubble stretching for miles, and nothing, nothing left, not even the firewatch stone.

It was the Whispering Gallery all over again. I felt that I had said something, and when I looked at Langby's face he was smiling crookedly.

"St. Paul's will burn down," I said. "There won't be anything left."

"Yes," Langby said. "That's the idea, isn't it? Burn St. Paul's to the ground? Isn't that the plan?"

"Whose plan?" I said stupidly.

"Hitler's, of course," Langby said. "Who did you think I meant?" and, almost casually, picked up his stirrup pump.

The page of the ARP manual flashed suddenly before me. I poured the bucket of sand around the still sputtering bomb, snatched up another bucket and dumped that on top of it. Black smoke billowed up in such a cloud that I could hardly find my shovel. I felt for the smothered bomb with the tip of it and scooped it into the empty bucket, then shovelled the sand in on top of it. Tears were streaming down my face from the acrid smoke. I turned to wipe them on my sleeve and saw Langby.

He had not made a move to help me. He smiled. "It's not a bad plan, actually. But of course we won't let it happen. That's what the fire watch is here for. To see that it doesn't happen. Right, Bartholomew?"

I know now what the purpose of my practicum is. I must stop Langby from burning down St. Paul's.

September 28—I try to tell myself I was mistaken about Langby last night, that I misunderstood what he said. Why would he want to burn down St. Paul's unless he is a Nazi spy? How can a Nazi spy have gotten on the fire watch? I think about my faked letter of introduction and shudder.

How can I find out? If I set him some test, some fatal thing that only a loyal Englishman in 1940 would know, I fear I am the one who would be caught out. I *must* get my retrieval working properly.

Until then, I shall watch Langby. For the time being at least that should be easy. Langby has just posted the watches for the next two weeks. We stand every one together.

September 30—I know what happened in September. Langby told me.

Last night in the choir, putting on our coats and boots, he said, "They've already tried once, you know."

I had no idea what he meant. I felt as helpless as that first day when he asked me if I was from the ayarpee.

"The plan to destroy St. Paul's. They've already tried once. The tenth of September. A high explosive bomb. But of course you didn't know about that. You were in Wales."

I was not even listening. The minute he had said, "high explosive bomb," I had remembered it all. It had burrowed in under the road and lodged on the foundations. The bomb squad had tried to defuse it, but there was a leaking gas main. They decided to evacuate St. Paul's, but Dean Matthews refused to leave, and they got it out after all and exploded it in Barking Marshes. Instant and complete retrieval.

"The bomb squad saved her that time," Langby was saying. "It seems there's always somebody about."

"Yes," I said. "There is," and walked away from him.

* * *

October 1—I thought last night's retrieval of the events of September tenth meant some sort of breakthrough, but I have been lying here on my cot most of the night trying for Nazi spies in St. Paul's and getting nothing. Do I have to know exactly what I'm looking for before I can remember it? What good does that do me?

Maybe Langby is not a Nazi spy. Then what is he? An arsonist? A madman? The crypt is hardly conducive to thought, being not at all as silent as a tomb. The chars talk most of the night and the sound of the bombs is muffled, which somehow makes it worse. I find myself straining to hear them. When I did get to sleep this morning, I dreamed about one of the tube shelters being hit, broken mains, drowning people.

October 4—I tried to catch the cat today. I had some idea of persuading it to dispatch the mouse that has been terrifying the chars. I also wanted to see one up close. I took the water bucket I had used with the stirrup pump last night to put out some burning shrapnel from one of the anti-aircraft guns. It still had a bit of water in it, but not enough to drown the cat, and my plan was to clamp the bucket over him, reach under, and pick him up, then carry him down to the crypt and point him at the mouse. I did not even come close to him.

I swung the bucket, and as I did so, perhaps an inch of water splashed out. I thought I remembered that the cat was a domesticated animal, but I must have been wrong about that. The cat's wide complacent face pulled back into a skull-like mask that was absolutely terrifying, vicious claws extended from what I had thought were harmless paws, and the cat let out a sound to top the chars.

In my surprise I dropped the bucket and it rolled against one of the pillars. The cat disappeared. Behind me, Langby said, "That's no way to catch a cat."

"Obviously," I said, and bent to retrieve the bucket.

"Cats hate water," he said, still in that expressionless voice.

"Oh," I said, and started in front of him to take the bucket back to the choir. "I didn't know that."

"Everybody knows it. Even the stupid Welsh."

October 8—We have been standing double watches for a week—bomber's moon. Langby didn't show up on the roofs, so I went looking for him in the church. I found him standing by the west doors talking to an old man. The man had a newspaper tucked under his arm and he handed it to Langby, but Langby gave it back to him. When the man saw me, he ducked out. Langby said, "Tourist. Wanted to know where the Windmill Theater is. Read in the paper the girls are starkers."

I know I looked as if I didn't believe him because he said, "You look rotten, old man. Not getting enough sleep, are you? I'll get somebody to take the first watch for you tonight."

"No," I said coldly. "I'll stand my own watch. I like being on the roofs," and added silently, *where I can watch you.*

He shrugged and said, "I suppose it's better than being down in the crypt. At least on the roofs you can hear the one that gets you."

October 10—I thought the double watches might be good for me, take my mind off my inability to retrieve. The watched pot idea. Actually, it sometimes works. A few hours of thinking about something else, or a good night's sleep, and the fact pops forward without any prompting, without any artificials.

The good night's sleep is out of the question. Not only do the chars talk constantly, but the cat has moved into the crypt and sidles up to everyone, making siren noises and begging for kippers. I am moving my cot out of the transept and over by Nelson before I go on watch. He may be pickled, but he keeps his mouth shut.

October 11—I dreamed Trafalgar, ships' guns and smoke and falling plaster and Langby shouting my name. My first waking thought was that the folding chairs had gone off. I could not see for all the smoke.

"I'm coming," I said, limping toward Langby and pulling on my boots. There was a heap of plaster and tangled folding chairs in the transept. Langby was digging in it. "Bartholomew!" he shouted, flinging a chunk of plaster aside. "Bartholomew!"

I still had the idea it was smoke. I ran back for the stirrup pump and then knelt beside him and began pulling on a splintered chair back. It resisted, and it came to me suddenly, There is a body under here. I will reach for a piece of the ceiling and find it is a hand. I leaned back on my heels, determined not to be sick, then went at the pile again.

Langby was going far too fast, jabbing with a chair leg. I grabbed his hand to stop him, and he struggled against me as if I were a piece of rubble to be thrown aside. He picked up a large flat square of plaster, and under it was the floor. I turned and looked behind me. Both chars huddled in the recess by the altar. "Who are you looking for?" I said, keeping hold of Langby's arm.

"Bartholomew," he said, and swept the rubble aside, his hands bleeding through the coating of smoky dust.

"I'm here," I said. "I'm all right." I choked on the white dust. "I moved my cot out of the transept."

He turned sharply to the chars and then said quite calmly, "What's under here?"

"Only the gas ring," one of them said timidly from the shadowed recess, "and Mrs. Galbraith's pocketbook." He dug through the mess until he had found them both. The gas ring was leaking at a merry rate, though the flame had gone out.

"You've saved St. Paul's and me after all," I said, standing there in my underwear and boots, holding the useless stirrup pump. "We might all have been asphyxiated."

He stood up. "I shouldn't have saved you," he said.

Stage one: shock, stupefaction, unawareness of injuries, words may not make sense except to victim. He would not know his hand was bleeding yet. He would not remember what he had said. He had said he shouldn't have saved my life.

"I shouldn't have saved you," he repeated. "I have my duty to think of."

"You're bleeding," I said sharply. "You'd better lie down." I sounded just like Langby in the Gallery.

October 13—It was a high explosive bomb. It blew a hole in the choir roof; and some of the marble statuary is broken; but the ceiling of the crypt did not collapse, which is what I thought at first. It only jarred some plaster loose.

I do not think Langby has any idea what he said. That should give me some sort of advantage, now that I am sure where the danger lies, now that I am sure it will not come crashing down from some other direction. But what good is all this knowing, when I do not know what he will do? Or when?

Surely I have the facts of yesterday's bomb in long-term, but even falling plaster did not jar them loose this time. I am not even trying for retrieval now. I lie in the darkness waiting for the roof to fall in on me. And remembering how Langby saved my life.

October 15—The girl came in again today. She still has the cold, but she has gotten her paying position. It was a joy to see her. She was wearing a smart uniform and open-toed shoes, and her hair was in an elaborate frizz around her face. We are still cleaning up the mess from the bomb, and Langby was out with Allen getting wood to board up the choir, so I let the girl chatter at me while I swept. The dust made her sneeze, but at least this time I knew what she was doing.

She told me her name is Enola and that she's working for the WVS, running one of the mobile canteens that are sent to the fires.

She came, of all things, to thank me for the job. She said that after she told the WVS that there was no proper shelter with a canteen for St. Paul's, they gave her a run in the City. "So I'll just pop in when I'm close and let you know how I'm making out, won't I just?"

She and her brother Tom are still sleeping in the tubes. I asked her if that was safe and she said probably not, but at least down there you couldn't hear the one that got you and that was a blessing.

October 18—I am so tired I can hardly write this. Nine incendiaries tonight and a land mine that looked as though it was going to catch on the dome till the wind drifted its parachute away from the church. I put out two of the incendiaries. I have done that at least twenty times since I got here and helped with dozens of others, and still it is not enough. One incendiary, one moment of not watching Langby, could undo it all.

I know that is partly why I feel so tired. I wear myself out every night trying to do my job and watch Langby, making sure none of the incendiaries falls without my seeing it. Then I go back to the crypt and wear myself out trying to retrieve something, anything, about spies, fires, St. Paul's in the fall of 1940, anything. It haunts me that I am not doing enough, but I do not know what else to do. Without the retrieval, I am as helpless as these poor people here, with no idea what will happen tomorrow.

If I have to, I will go on doing this till I am called home. He cannot burn down St. Paul's so long as I am here to put out the incendiaries. "I have my duty," Langby said in the crypt.

And I have mine.

October 21—It's been nearly two weeks since the blast and I just now realized we haven't seen the cat since. He wasn't in the mess in the crypt. Even after Langby and I were sure there was no one in there, we sifted through the stuff twice more. He could have been in the choir, though.

Old Bence-Jones says not to worry. "He's all right," he said. "The jerries could bomb London right down to the ground and the cats would waltz out to greet them. You know why? They don't love anybody. That's what gets half of us killed. Old lady out in Stepney got killed the other night trying to save her cat. Bloody cat was in the Anderson."

"Then where is he?"

"Someplace safe, you can bet on that. If he's not around St. Paul's, it means we're for it. That old saw about the rats deserting a sinking ship, that's a mistake, that is. It's cats, not rats."

* * *

October 25—Langby's tourist showed up again. He cannot still be looking for the Windmill Theatre. He had a newspaper under his arm again today, and he asked for Langby, but Langby was across town with Allen, trying to get the asbestos firemen's coats. I saw the name of the paper. It was *The Worker.* A Nazi newspaper?

November 2—I've been up on the roofs for a week straight, helping some incompetent workmen patch the hole the bomb made. They're doing a terrible job. There's still a great gap on one side a man could fall into, but they insist it'll be all right because, after all, you wouldn't fall clear through but only as far as the ceiling, and "the fall can't kill you." They don't seem to understand it's a perfect hiding place for an incendiary.

And that is all Langby needs. He does not even have to set a fire to destroy St. Paul's. All he needs to do is let one burn uncaught until it is too late.

I could not get anywhere with the workmen. I went down into the church to complain to Matthews, and saw Langby and his tourist behind a pillar, close to one of the windows. Langby was holding a newspaper and talking to the man. When I came down from the library an hour later, they were still there. So is the gap. Matthews says we'll put planks across it and hope for the best.

November 5—I have given up trying to retrieve. I am so far behind on my sleep I can't even retrieve information on a newspaper whose name I already know. Double watches the permanent thing now. Our chars have abandoned us altogether (like the cat), so the crypt is quiet, but I cannot sleep.

If I do manage to doze off, I dream. Yesterday I dreamed Kivrin was on the roofs, dressed like a saint. "What was the secret of your practicum?" I said. "What were you supposed to find out?"

She wiped her nose with a handkerchief and said, "Two things. One, that silence and humility are the sacred burdens of the historian. Two," she stopped and sneezed into the handkerchief. "Don't sleep in the tubes."

My only hope is to get hold of an artificial and induce a trance. That's a problem. I'm positive it's too early for chemical endorphins and probably hallucinogens. Alcohol is definitely available, but I need something more concentrated than ale, the only alcohol I know by name. I do not dare ask the watch. Langby is suspicious enough of me already. It's back to the *OED*, to look up a word I don't know.

* * *

November 11—The cat's back. Langby was out with Allen again, still trying for the asbestos coats, so I thought it was safe to leave St. Paul's. I went to the grocer's for supplies and hopefully, an artificial. It was late, and the sirens sounded before I had even gotten to Cheapside, but the raids do not usually start until after dark. It took awhile to get all the groceries and to get up my courage to ask whether he had any alcohol—he told me to go to a pub—and when I came out of the shop, it was as if I had pitched suddenly into a hole.

I had no idea where St. Paul's lay, or the street, or the shop I had just come from. I stood on what was no longer the sidewalk, clutching my brown-paper parcel of kippers and bread with a hand I could not have seen if I held it up before my face. I reached up to wrap my muffler closer about my neck and prayed for my eyes to adjust, but there was no reduced light to adjust to. I would have been glad of the moon, for all St. Paul's watch curses it and calls it a fifth columnist. Or a bus, with its shuttered headlights giving just enough light to orient myself by. Or a searchlight. Or the kickback flare of an ack-ack gun. Anything.

Just then I did see a bus, two narrow yellow slits a long way off. I started toward it and nearly pitched off the curb. Which meant the bus was sideways in the street, which meant it was not a bus. A cat meowed, quite near, and rubbed against my leg. I looked down into the yellow lights I had thought belonged to the bus. His eyes were picking up light from somewhere, though I would have sworn there was not a light for miles, and reflecting it flatly up at me.

"A warden'll get you for those lights, old tom," I said, and then as a plane droned overhead, "Or a jerry."

The world exploded suddenly into light, the searchlights and a glow along the Thames seeming to happen almost simultaneously, lighting my way home.

"Come to fetch me, did you, old tom?" I said gaily. "Where've you been? Knew we were out of kippers, didn't you? I call that loyalty." I talked to him all the way home and gave him half a tin of the kippers for saving my life. Bence-Jones said he smelled the milk at the grocer's.

November 13—I dreamed I was lost in the blackout. I could not see my hands in front of my face, and Dunworthy came and shone a pocket torch at me, but I could only see where I had come from and not where I was going.

"What good is that to them?" I said. "They need a light to show them where they're going."

"Even the light from the Thames? Even the light from the fires and the ack-ack guns?" Dunworthy said.

"Yes. Anything is better than this awful darkness." So he came closer to give me the pocket torch. It was not a pocket torch, after all, but Christ's lantern from the Hunt picture in the south nave. I shone it on the curb before me so I could find my way home, but it shone instead on the firewatch stone and I hastily put the light out.

November 20—I tried to talk to Langby today. "I've seen you talking to the old gentleman," I said. It sounded like an accusation. I meant it to. I wanted him to think it was and stop whatever he was planning.

"Reading," he said. "Not talking." He was putting things in order in the choir, piling up sandbags.

"I've seen you reading then," I said belligerently, and he dropped a sandbag and straightened.

"What of it?" he said. "It's a free country. I can read to an old man if I want, same as you can talk to that little WVS tart."

"What do you read?" I said.

"Whatever he wants. He's an old man. He used to come home from his job, have a bit of brandy and listen to his wife read the papers to him. She got killed in one of the raids. Now I read to him. I don't see what business it is of yours."

It sounded true. It didn't have the careful casualness of a lie, and I almost believed him, except that I had heard the tone of truth from him before. In the crypt. After the bomb.

"I thought he was a tourist looking for the Windmill," I said.

He looked blank only a second, and then he said, "Oh, yes, that. He came in with the paper and asked me to tell him where it was. I looked it up to find the address. Clever, that. I didn't guess he couldn't read it for himself." But it was enough. I knew that he was lying.

He heaved a sandbag almost at my feet. "Of course you wouldn't understand a thing like that, would you? A simple act of human kindness?"

"No," I said coldly. "I wouldn't."

None of this proves anything. He gave away nothing, except perhaps the name of an artificial, and I can hardly go to Dean Matthews and accuse Langby of reading aloud.

I waited till he had finished in the choir and gone down to the crypt. Then I lugged one of the sandbags up to the roof and over to the chasm. The planking has held so far, but everyone walks gingerly around it, as if it were a grave. I cut the sandbag open and spilled the loose sand into the bottom. If it has occurred to Langby that this is the perfect spot for an incendiary, perhaps the sand will smother it.

* * *

November 21—I gave Enola some of "uncle's" money today and asked her to get me the brandy. She was more reluctant than I thought she'd be so there must be societal complications I am not aware of, but she agreed.

I don't know what she came for. She started to tell me about her brother and some prank he'd pulled in the tubes that got him in trouble with the guard, but after I asked her about the brandy, she left without finishing the story.

November 25—Enola came today, but without bringing the brandy. She is going to Bath for the holidays to see her aunt. At least she will be away from the raids for awhile. I will not have to worry about her. She finished the story of her brother and told me she hopes to persuade this aunt to take Tom for the duration of the Blitz but is not at all sure the aunt will be willing.

Young Tom is apparently not so much an engaging scapegrace as a near-criminal. He has been caught twice picking pockets in the Bank tube shelter, and they have had to go back to Marble Arch. I comforted her as best I could, told her all boys were bad at one time or another. What I really wanted to say was that she needn't worry at all, that young Tom strikes me as a true survivor type, like my own tom, like Langby, totally unconcerned with anybody but himself, well-equipped to survive the Blitz and rise to prominence in the future.

Then I asked her whether she had gotten the brandy.

She looked down at her open-toed shoes and muttered unhappily, "I thought you'd forgotten all about that."

I made up some story about the watch taking turns buying a bottle, and she seemed less unhappy, but I am not convinced she will not use this trip to Bath as an excuse to do nothing. I will have to leave St. Paul's and buy it myself, and I don't dare leave Langby alone in the church. I made her promise to bring the brandy today before she leaves. But she is still not back, and the sirens have already gone.

November 26—No Enola, and she said their train left at noon. I suppose I should be grateful that at least she is safely out of London. Maybe in Bath she will be able to get over her cold.

Tonight one of the ARP girls breezed in to borrow half our cots and tell us about a mess over in the East End where a surface shelter was hit. Four dead, twelve wounded. "At least it wasn't one of the tube shelters!" she said. "Then you'd see a real mess, wouldn't you?"

* * *

November 30—I dreamed I took the cat to St. John's Wood.

"Is this a rescue mission?" Dunworthy said.

"No, sir," I said proudly. "I know what I was supposed to find in my practicum. The perfect survivor. Tough and resourceful and selfish. This is the only one I could find. I had to kill Langby, you know, to keep him from burning down St. Paul's. Enola's brother has gone to Bath, and the others will never make it. Enola wears open-toed shoes in the winter and sleeps in the tubes and puts her hair up on metal pins so it will curl. She cannot possibly survive the Blitz."

Dunworthy said, "Perhaps you should have rescued her instead. What did you say her name was?"

"Kivrin," I said, and woke up cold and shivering.

December 5—I dreamed Langby had the pinpoint bomb. He carried it under his arm like a brown-paper parcel, coming out of St. Paul's Station and up Ludgate Hill to the west doors.

"This is not fair," I said, barring his way with my arm. "There is no fire watch on duty."

He clutched the bomb to his chest like a pillow. "That is your fault," he said, and before I could get to my stirrup pump and bucket, he tossed it in the door.

The pinpoint was not even invented until the end of the twentieth century, and it was another ten years before the dispossessed Communists got hold of it and turned it into something that could be carried under your arm. A parcel that could blow a quarter-mile of the City into oblivion. Thank God that is one dream that cannot come true.

It was a sunlit morning in the dream, and this morning when I came off watch the sun was shining for the first time in weeks. I went down to the crypt and then came up again, making the rounds of the roofs twice more, then the steps and the grounds and all the treacherous alleyways between where an incendiary could be missed. I felt better after that, but when I got to sleep I dreamed again, this time of fire and Langby watching it, smiling.

December 15—I found the cat this morning. Heavy raids last night, but most of them over towards Canning Town and nothing on the roofs to speak of. Nevertheless the cat was quite dead. I found him lying on the steps this morning when I made my own, private rounds. Concussion. There was not a mark on him anywhere except the white blackout patch on his throat, but when I picked him up, he was all jelly under the skin.

I could not think what to do with him. I thought for one mad moment of asking Matthews if I could bury him in the crypt. Honorable death in war or something. Trafalgar, Waterloo, London, died in battle. I ended by wrapping him in my muffler and taking him down Ludgate Hill to a building that had been bombed out and burying him in the rubble. It will do no good. The rubble will be no protection from dogs or rats, and I shall never get another muffler. I have gone through nearly all of uncle's money.

I should not be sitting here. I haven't checked the alleyways or the rest of the steps, and there might be a dud or a delayed incendiary or something that I missed.

When I came here, I thought of myself as the noble rescuer, the savior of the past. I am not doing very well at the job. At least Enola is out of it. I wish there were some way I could send St. Paul's to Bath for safekeeping. There were hardly any raids last night. Bence-Jones said cats can survive anything. What if he was coming to get me, to show me the way home? All the bombs were over Canning Town.

December 16—Enola has been back a week. Seeing her, standing on the west steps where I found the cat, sleeping in Marble Arch and not safe at all, was more than I could absorb. "I thought you were in Bath," I said stupidly.

"My aunt said she'd take Tom but not me as well. She's got a houseful of evacuation children, and what a noisy lot. Where is your muffler?" she said. "It's dreadful cold up here on the hill."

"I . . ." I said, unable to answer, "I lost it."

"You'll never get another one," she said. "They're going to start rationing clothes. And wool, too. You'll never get another one like that."

"I know," I said, blinking at her.

"Good things just thrown away," she said. "It's absolutely criminal, that's what it is."

I don't think I said anything to that, just turned and walked away with my head down, looking for bombs and dead animals.

December 20—Langby isn't a Nazi. He's a Communist. I can hardly write this. A Communist.

One of the chars found *The Worker* wedged behind a pillar and brought it down to the crypt as we were coming off the first watch.

"Bloody Communists," Bence-Jones said. "Helping Hitler, they are. Talking against the king, stirring up trouble in the shelters. Traitors, that's what they are."

"They love England same as you," the char said.

"They don't love nobody but themselves, bloody selfish lot. I wouldn't be surprised to hear they were ringing Hitler up on the telephone," Bence-Jones said. " ''Ello, Adolf, here's where to drop the bombs.' "

The kettle on the gas ring whistled. The char stood up and poured the hot water into a chipped tea pot, then sat back down. "Just because they speak their minds don't mean they'd burn down old St. Paul's, does it now?"

"Of course not," Langby said, coming down the stairs. He sat down and pulled off his boots, stretching his feet in their wool socks. "Who wouldn't burn down St. Paul's?"

"The Communists," Bence-Jones said, looking straight at him, and I wondered if he suspected Langby, too.

Langby never batted an eye. "I wouldn't worry about them if I were you," he said. "It's the jerries that are doing their bloody best to burn her down tonight. Six incendiaries so far, and one almost went into that great hole over the choir." He held out his cup to the char, and she poured him a cup of tea.

I wanted to kill him, smashing him to dust and rubble on the floor of the crypt while Bence-Jones and the char looked on in helpless surprise, shouting warnings to them and the rest of the watch. "Do you know what the Communists did?" I wanted to shout. "Do you? We have to stop him." I even stood up and started toward him as he sat with his feet stretched out before him and his asbestos coat still over his shoulders.

And then the thought of the Gallery drenched in gold, the Communist coming out of the tube station with the package so casually under his arm, made me sick with the same staggering vertigo of guilt and helplessness, and I sat back down on the edge of my cot and tried to think what to do.

They do not realize the danger. Even Bence-Jones, for all his talk of traitors, thinks they are capable only of talking against the king. They do not know, cannot know, what the Communists will become. Stalin is an ally. Communists mean Russia. They have never heard of Karinsky or the New Russia or any of the things that will make "Communist" into a synonym for "monster." They will never know it. By the time the Communists become what they became, there will be no fire watch. Only I know what it means to hear the name "Communist" uttered here, so carelessly, in St. Paul's.

A Communist. I should have known. I should have known.

December 22—Double watches again. I have not had any sleep, and I am getting very unsteady on my feet. I nearly pitched into the chasm this morning, only saved myself by dropping to my knees. My endorphin levels are fluctuating wildly, and I know I must get some sleep soon or I will become one of Langby's walking dead; but I am afraid to leave him alone on the roofs, alone in the church with his Communist party leader, alone anywhere. I have taken to watching him when he sleeps.

If I could just get hold of an artificial, I think I could induce a trance, in spite of my poor condition. But I cannot even go out to a pub. Langby is on the roofs constantly, waiting for his chance. When Enola comes again, I must convince her to get the brandy for me. There are only a few days left.

December 28—Enola came this morning while I was on the west porch, picking up the Christmas tree. It has been knocked over three nights running by concussion. I righted the tree and was bending down to pick up the scattered tinsel when Enola appeared suddenly out of the fog like some cheerful saint. She stooped quickly and kissed me on the cheek. Then she straightened up, her nose red from her perennial cold, and handed me a box wrapped in colored paper.

"Merry Christmas," she said. "Go on then, open it. It's a gift."

My reflexes are almost totally gone. I knew the box was far too shallow for a bottle of brandy. Nevertheless, I believed she had remembered, had brought me my salvation. "You darling," I said, and tore it open.

It was a muffler. Gray wool. I stared at it for fully half a minute without realizing what it was. "Where's the brandy?" I said.

She looked shocked. Her nose got redder and her eyes started to blur. "You need this more. You haven't any clothing coupons and you have to be outside all the time. It's been so dreadful cold."

"I *needed* the brandy," I said angrily.

"I was only trying to be kind," she started, and I cut her off.

"Kind?" I said. "I asked you for brandy. I don't recall ever saying I needed a muffler." I shoved it back at her and began untangling a string of colored lights that had shattered when the tree fell.

She got that same holy martyr look Kivrin is so wonderful at. "I worry about you all the time up here," she said in a rush. "They're *trying* for St. Paul's, you know. And it's so close to the river. I didn't think you should be drinking. I . . . it's a crime when they're trying so hard to kill us all that you won't take care of yourself. It's like you're in it with them. I worry someday I'll come up to St. Paul's and you won't be here."

"Well, and what exactly am I supposed to do with a muffler? Hold it over my head when they drop the bombs?"

She turned and ran, disappearing into the gray fog before she had gone down two steps. I started after her, still holding the string of broken lights, tripped over it, and fell almost all the way to the bottom of the steps.

Langby picked me up. "You're off watches," he said grimly.

"You can't do that," I said.

"Oh, yes, I can. I don't want any walking dead on the roofs with me."

I let him lead me down here to the crypt, make me a cup of tea, put me to bed, all very solicitous. No indication that this is what he has been waiting for. I will lie here till the sirens go. Once I am on the roofs he will not be able to send me back without seeming suspicious. Do you know what he said before he left, asbestos coat and rubber boots, the dedicated fire watcher? "I want you to get some sleep." As if I could sleep with Langby on the roofs. I would be burned alive.

December 30—The sirens woke me, and old Bence-Jones said, "That should have done you some good. You've slept the clock round."

"What day is it?" I said, going for my boots.

"The twenty-ninth," he said, and as I dived for the door, "No need to hurry. They're late tonight. Maybe they won't come at all. That'd be a blessing, that would. The tide's out."

I stopped by the door to the stairs, holding onto the cool stone. "Is St. Paul's all right?"

"She's still standing," he said. "Have a bad dream?"

"Yes," I said, remembering the bad dreams of all the past weeks— the dead cat in my arms in St. John's Wood, Langby with his parcel and his *Worker* under his arm, the fire-watch stone garishly lit by Christ's lantern. Then I remembered I had not dreamed at all. I had slept the kind of sleep I had prayed for, the kind of sleep that would help me remember.

Then I remembered. Not St. Paul's, burned to the ground by the Communists. A headline from the dailies. "Marble Arch hit. Eighteen killed by blast." The date was not clear except for the year. 1940. There were exactly two more days left in 1940. I grabbed my coat and muffler and ran up the stairs and across the marble floor.

"Where the hell do you think you're going?" Langby shouted to me. I couldn't see him.

"I have to save Enola," I said, and my voice echoed in the dark sanctuary. "They're going to bomb Marble Arch."

"You can't leave now," he shouted after me, standing where the firewatch stone would be. "The tide's out. You dirty . . ."

I didn't hear the rest of it. I had already flung myself down the steps and into a taxi. It took almost all the money I had, the money I had so carefully hoarded for the trip back to St. John's Wood. Shelling started while we were still in Oxford Street, and the driver refused to go any farther. He let me out into pitch blackness, and I saw I would never make it in time.

Blast. Enola crumpled on the stairway down to the tube, her open-toed shoes still on her feet, not a mark on her. And when I try to lift her, jelly under the skin. I would have to wrap her in the muffler she gave me, because I was too late. I had gone back a hundred years to be too late to save her.

I ran the last blocks, guided by the gun emplacement that had to be in Hyde Park, and skidded down the steps into Marble Arch. The woman in the ticket booth took my last shilling for a ticket to St. Paul's Station. I stuck it in my pocket and raced toward the stairs.

"No running," she said placidly. "To your left, please." The door to the right was blocked off by wooden barricades, the metal gates beyond pulled to and chained. The board with names on it for the stations was X-ed with tape, and a new sign that read, "All trains," was nailed to the barricade, pointing left.

Enola was not on the stopped escalators or sitting against the wall in the hallway. I came to the first stairway and could not get through. A family had set out, just where I wanted to step, a communal tea of bread and butter, a little pot of jam sealed with waxed paper, and a kettle on a ring like the one Langby and I had rescued out of the rubble, all of it spread on a cloth embroidered at the corners with flowers. I stood staring down at the layered tea, spread like a waterfall down the steps.

"I . . . Marble Arch . . ." I said. Another twenty killed by flying tiles. "You shouldn't be here."

"We've as much right as anyone," the man said belligerently, "and who are you to tell us to move on?"

A woman lifting saucers out of a cardboard box looked up at me, frightened. The kettle began to whistle.

"It's you that should move on," the man said. "Go on then." He stood off to one side so I could pass. I edged past the embroidered cloth apologetically.

"I'm sorry," I said. "I'm looking for someone. On the platform."

"You'll never find her in there, mate," the man said, thumbing in that direction. I hurried past him, nearly stepping on the teacloth, and rounded the corner into hell.

It was not hell. Shopgirls folded coats and leaned back against them, cheerful or sullen or disagreeable, but certainly not damned. Two boys scuffled for a shilling and lost it on the tracks. They bent over the edge, debating whether to go after it, and the station guard yelled to them to back away. A train rumbled through, full of people. A mosquito landed on the guard's hand and he reached out to slap it and missed. The boys laughed. And behind and before them, stretching in all directions down the deadly tile curves of the tunnel like casualties, backed into the entrance-ways and onto the stairs, were people. Hundreds and hundreds of people.

I stumbled back into the hall, knocking over a teacup. It spilled like a flood across the cloth.

"I told you, mate," the man said cheerfully. "It's Hell in there, ain't it? And worse below."

"Hell," I said. "Yes." I would never find her. I would never save her. I looked at the woman mopping up the tea, and it came to me that I could not save her either. Enola or the cat or any of them, lost here in the endless stairways and cul-de-sacs of time. They were already dead a hundred years, past saving. The past is beyond saving. Surely that was the lesson the history department sent me all this way to learn. Well, fine, I've learned it. Can I go home now?

Of course not, dear boy. You have foolishly spent all your money on taxicabs and brandy, and tonight is the night the Germans burn the City. (Now it is too late, I remember it all. Twenty-eight incendiaries on the roofs.) Langby must have his chance, and you must learn the hardest lesson of all and the one you should have known from the beginning. You cannot save St. Paul's.

I went back out onto the platform and stood behind the yellow line until a train pulled up. I took my ticket out and held it in my hand all the way to St. Paul's Station. When I got there, smoke billowed toward me like an easy spray of water. I could not see St. Paul's.

"The tide's out," a woman said in a voice devoid of hope, and I went down in a snake pit of limp cloth hoses. My hands came up covered with rank-smelling mud, and I understood finally (and too late) the significance of the tide. There was no water to fight the fires.

A policeman barred my way and I stood helplessly before him with no idea what to say. "No civilians allowed up there," he said. "St. Paul's is for it." The smoke billowed like a thundercloud, alive with sparks, and the dome rose golden above it.

"I'm fire watch," I said, and his arm fell away, and then I was on the roofs.

My endorphin levels must have been going up and down like an air raid siren. I do not have any short-term from then on, just moments that do not fit together: the people in the church when we brought Langby down, huddled in a corner playing cards, the whirlwind of burning scraps of wood in the dome, the ambulance driver who wore open-toed shoes like Enola and smeared salve on my burned hands. And in the center, the one clear moment when I went after Langby on a rope and saved his life.

I stood by the dome, blinking against the smoke. The City was on fire and it seemed as if St. Paul's would ignite from the heat, would crumble from the noise alone. Bence-Jones was by the northwest tower, hitting at an incendiary with a spade. Langby was too close to the patched place where the bomb had gone through, looking toward me. An incendiary clattered behind him. I turned to grab a shovel, and when I turned back, he was gone.

"Langby!" I shouted, and could not hear my own voice. He had fallen into the chasm and nobody saw him or the incendiary. Except me. I do not remember how I got across the roof. I think I called for a rope. I got a rope. I tied it around my waist, gave the ends of it into the hands of the fire watch, and went over the side. The fires lit the walls of the hole almost all the way to the bottom. Below me I could see a pile of whitish rubble. He's under there, I thought, and jumped free of the wall. The space was so narrow there was nowhere to throw the rubble. I was afraid I would inadvertently stone him, and I tried to toss the pieces of planking and plaster over my shoulder, but there was barely room to turn. For one awful moment I thought he might not be there at all, that the pieces of splintered wood would brush away to reveal empty pavement, as they had in the crypt.

I was numbed by the indignity of crawling over him. If he was dead I did not think I could bear the shame of stepping on his helpless body. Then his hand came up like a ghost's and grabbed my ankle, and within seconds I had whirled and had his head free.

He was the ghastly white that no longer frightens me. "I put the bomb out," he said. I stared at him, so overwhelmed with relief I could not speak. For one hysterical moment I thought I would even laugh, I was so glad to see him. I finally realized what it was I was supposed to say.

"Are you all right?" I said.

"Yes," he said, and tried to raise himself on one elbow. "So much the worse for you."

He could not get up. He grunted with pain when he tried to shift his weight to his right side and lay back, the uneven rubble crunching sickeningly under him. I tried to lift him gently so I could see where he was hurt. He must have fallen on something.

"It's no use," he said, breathing hard. "I put it out."

I spared him a startled glance, afraid that he was delirious, and went back to rolling him onto his side.

"I know you were counting on this one," he went on, not resisting me at all. "It was bound to happen sooner or later with all these roofs. Only I went after it. What'll you tell your friends?"

His asbestos coat was torn down the back in a long gash. Under it his back was charred and smoking. He had fallen on the incendiary. "Oh, my God," I said, trying frantically to see how badly he was burned without touching him. I had no way of knowing how deep the burns went, but they seemed to extend only in the narrow space where the coat had torn. I tried to pull the bomb out from under him, but the casing was as hot as a stove. It was not melting, though. My sand and Langby's body had smothered it. I had no idea if it would start up again when it was exposed to the air. I looked around, a little wildly, for the bucket and stirrup pump Langby must have dropped when he fell.

"Looking for a weapon?" Langby said, so clearly it was hard to believe he was hurt at all. "Why not just leave me here? A bit of over-exposure and I'd be done for by morning. Or would you rather do your dirty work in private?"

I stood up and yelled to the men on the roof above us. One of them shone a pocket torch down at us, but its light didn't reach.

"Is he dead?" somebody shouted down to me.

"Send for an ambulance," I said. "He's been burned."

I helped Langby up, trying to support his back without touching the burn. He staggered a little and then leaned against the wall, watching me as I tried to bury the incendiary, using a piece of the planking as a scoop. The rope came down and I tied Langby to it. He had not spoken since I helped him up. He let me tie the rope around his waist, still looking steadily at me. "I should have let you smother in the crypt," he said.

He stood leaning easily, almost relaxed against the wood supports, his hands holding him up. I put his hands on the slack rope and wrapped it once around them for the grip I knew he didn't have. "I've been onto you since that day in the Gallery. I knew you weren't afraid of heights. You came down here without any fear of heights when you thought I'd ruined your precious plans. What was it? An attack of conscience? Kneeling there like a baby, whining, 'What have we done? What have we done?' You made me sick. But you know what gave you away first? The cat. Everybody knows cats hate water. Everybody but a dirty Nazi spy."

There was a tug on the rope. "Come ahead," I said, and the rope tautened.

"That WVS tart? Was she a spy, too? Supposed to meet you in Marble Arch? Telling me it was going to be bombed. You're a rotten spy, Bartholomew. Your friends already blew it up in September. It's open again."

The rope jerked suddenly and began to lift Langby. He twisted his hands to get a better grip. His right shoulder scraped the wall. I put up my hands and pushed him gently so that his left side was to the wall.

"You're making a big mistake, you know," he said. "You should have killed me. I'll tell."

I stood in the darkness, waiting for the rope. Langby was unconscious when he reached the roof. I walked past the fire watch to the dome and down to the crypt.

This morning the letter from my uncle came and with it a ten-pound note.

December 31—Two of Dunworthy's flunkies met me in St. John's Wood to tell me I was late for my exams. I did not even protest. I shuffled obediently after them without even considering how unfair it was to give an exam to one of the walking dead. I had not slept in—how long? Since yesterday when I went to find Enola. I had not slept in a hundred years.

Dunworthy was at his desk, blinking at me. One of the flunkies handed me a test paper and the other one called time. I turned the paper over and left an oily smudge from the ointment on my burns. I stared uncomprehendingly at them. I had grabbed at the incendiary when I turned Langby over, but these burns were on the backs of my hands. The answer came to me suddenly in Langby's unyielding voice. "They're rope burns, you fool. Don't they teach you Nazi spies the proper way to come up a rope?"

I looked down at the test. It read, "Number of incendiaries that fell on St. Paul's. Number of land mines. Number of high explosive bombs. Method most commonly used for extinguishing incendiaries. Land mines. High explosive bombs. Number of volunteers on first watch. Second watch. Casualties. Fatalities." The questions made no sense. There was only a short space, long enough for the writing of a number, after any of the questions. Method most commonly used for extinguishing incendiaries. How would I ever fit what I knew into that narrow space? Where were the questions about Enola and Langby and the cat?

I went up to Dunworthy's desk. "St. Paul's almost burned down last night," I said. "What kind of questions are these?"

"You should be answering questions, Mr. Bartholomew, not asking them."

"There aren't any questions about the people," I said. The outer casing of my anger began to melt.

"Of course there are," Dunworthy said, flipping to the second page of the test. "Number of casualties, 1940. Blast, shrapnel, other."

"Other?" I said. At any moment the roof would collapse on me in a shower of plaster dust and fury. "Other? Langby put out a fire with his own body. Enola has a cold that keeps getting worse. The cat . . ."

I snatched the paper back from him and scrawled "one cat" in the narrow space next to "blast." "Don't you care about them at all?"

"They're important from a statistical point of view," he said, "but as individuals, they are hardly relevant to the course of history."

My reflexes were shot. It was amazing to me that Dunworthy's were almost as slow. I grazed the side of his jaw and knocked his glasses off. "Of course they're relevant!" I shouted. "They *are* the history, not all these bloody numbers!"

The reflexes of the flunkies were very fast. They did not let me start another swing at him before they had me by both arms and were hauling me out of the room.

"They're back there in the past with nobody to save them. They can't see their hands in front of their faces and there are bombs falling down on them and you tell me they aren't important? You call that being an historian?"

The flunkies dragged me out the door and down the hall. "Langby saved St. Paul's. How much more important can a person get? You're no historian! You're nothing but a . . ." I wanted to call him a terrible name, but the only curses I could summon up were Langby's. "You're nothing but a dirty Nazi spy!" I bellowed. "You're nothing but a lazy bourgeois tart!"

They dumped me on my hands and knees outside the door and slammed it in my face. "I wouldn't be an historian if you paid me!" I shouted, and went to see the firewatch stone.

December 31—I am having to write this in bits and pieces. My hands are in pretty bad shape, and Dunworthy's boys didn't help matters much. Kivrin comes in periodically, wearing her St. Joan look, and smears so much salve on my hands that I can't hold a pencil.

St. Paul's Station is not there, of course, so I got out at Holborn and walked, thinking about my last meeting with Dean Matthews on the morning after the burning of the City. This morning.

"I understand you saved Langby's life," he said. "I also understand that between you, you saved St. Paul's last night."

I showed him the letter from my uncle and he stared at it as if he could not think what it was. "Nothing stays saved forever," he said, and for a terrible moment I thought he was going to tell me Langby had died. "We shall have to keep on saving St. Paul's until Hitler decides to bomb the countryside."

The raids on London are almost over, I wanted to tell him. He'll start bombing the countryside in a matter of weeks. Canterbury, Bath, aiming always at the cathedrals. You and St. Paul's will both outlast the war and live to dedicate the firewatch stone.

"I am hopeful, though," he said. "I think the worst is over."

"Yes, sir." I thought of the stone, its letters still readable after all this time. No, sir, the worst is not over.

I managed to keep my bearings almost to the top of Ludgate Hill. Then I lost my way completely, wandering about like a man in a grave-yard. I had not remembered that the rubble looked so much like the white plaster dust Langby had tried to dig me out of. I could not find the stone anywhere. In the end I nearly fell over it, jumping back as if I had stepped on a grave.

It is all that's left. Hiroshima is supposed to have had a handful of untouched trees at ground zero, Denver the capitol steps. Neither of them says, "Remember the men and women of St. Paul's Watch who by the grace of God saved this cathedral." The grace of God.

Part of the stone is sheared off. Historians argue there was another line that said, "for all time", but I do not believe that, not if Dean Matthews had anything to do with it. And none of the watch it was dedicated to would have believed it for a minute. We saved St. Paul's every time we put out an incendiary, and only until the next one fell. Keeping watch on the danger spots, putting out the little fires with sand and stirrup pumps, the big ones with our bodies, in order to keep the whole vast complex structure from burning down. Which sounds to me like a course description for History Practicum 401. What a fine time to discover what historians are for when I have tossed my chance for being one out the windows as easily as they tossed the pinpoint bomb in! No, sir, the worst is not over.

There are flash burns on the stone, where legend says the Dean of St. Paul's was kneeling when the bomb went off. Totally apocryphal, of course, since the front door is hardly an appropriate place for prayers. It is more likely the shadow of a tourist who wandered in to ask the whereabouts of the Windmill Theatre, or the imprint of a girl bringing a volunteer his muffler. Or a cat.

Nothing is saved forever, Dean Matthews; and I knew that when I walked in the west doors that first day, blinking into the gloom, but it is pretty bad nevertheless. Standing here knee-deep in rubble out of which I will not be able to dig any folding chairs or friends, knowing that Langby died thinking I was a Nazi spy, knowing that Enola came one day and I wasn't there. It's pretty bad.

But it is not as bad as it could be. They are both dead, and Dean Matthews too; but they died without knowing what I knew all along, what sent me to my knees in the Whispering Gallery, sick with grief and guilt: that in the end none of us saved St. Paul's. And Langby can-not turn to me, stunned and sick at heart, and say, "Who did this? Your friends the Nazis?" And I would have to say, "No. The Communists." That would be the worst.

I have come back to the room and let Kivrin smear more salve on my hands. She wants me to get some sleep. I know I should pack and get gone. It will be humiliating to have them come and throw me out, but I do not have the strength to fight her. She looks so much like Enola.

January 1—I have apparently slept not only through the night, but through the morning mail drop as well. When I woke up just now, I found Kivrin sitting on the end of the bed holding an envelope. "Your grades came," she said.

I put my arm over my eyes. "They can be marvelously efficient when they want to, can't they?"

"Yes," Kivrin said.

"Well, let's see it," I said, sitting up. "How long do I have before they come and throw me out?"

She handed the flimsy computer envelope to me. I tore it along the perforation. "Wait," she said. "Before you open it, I want to say something." She put her hand gently on my burns. "You're wrong about the history department. They're very good."

It was not exactly what I expected her to say. "Good is not the word I'd use to describe Dunworthy," I said and yanked the inside slip free.

Kivrin's look did not change, not even when I sat there with the printout on my knees where she could surely see it.

"Well," I said.

The slip was hand-signed by the esteemed Dunworthy. I have taken a first. With honors.

January 2—Two things came in the mail today. One was Kivrin's assignment. The history department thinks of everything—even to keeping her here long enough to nursemaid me, even to coming up with a prefabricated trial by fire to send their history majors through.

I think I wanted to believe that was what they had done, Enola and Langby only hired actors, the cat a clever android with its clockwork innards taken out for the final effect, not so much because I wanted to believe Dunworthy was not good at all, but because then I would not have this nagging pain at not knowing what had happened to them.

"You said your practicum was England in 1300?" I said, watching her as suspiciously as I had watched Langby.

"1349," she said, and her face went slack with memory. "The plague year."

"My God," I said. "How could they do that? The plague's a ten."

"I have a natural immunity," she said, and looked at her hands.

Because I could not think of anything to say, I opened the other piece of mail. It was a report on Enola. Computer-printed, facts and dates and statistics, all the numbers the history department so dearly loves, but it told me what I thought I would have to go without knowing: that she had gotten over her cold and survived the Blitz. Young Tom had been killed in the Baedaker raids on Bath, but Enola had lived until 2006, the year before they blew up St. Paul's.

I don't know whether I believe the report or not, but it does not matter. It is, like Langby's reading aloud to the old man, a simple act of human kindness. They think of everything.

Not quite. They did not tell me what happened to Langby. But I find as I write this that I already know: I saved his life. It does not seem to matter that he might have died in hospital next day; and I find, in spite of all the hard lessons the history department has tried to teach me, I do not quite believe this one: that nothing is saved forever. It seems to me that perhaps Langby is.

January 3—I went to see Dunworthy today. I don't know what I intended to say—some pompous drivel about my willingness to serve in the firewatch of history, standing guard against the falling incendiaries of the human heart, silent and saintly.

But he blinked at me nearsightedly across his desk, and it seemed to me that he was blinking at that last bright image of St. Paul's in sunlight before it was gone forever and that he knew better than anyone that the past cannot be saved, and I said instead, "I'm sorry that I broke your glasses, sir."

"How did you like St. Paul's?" he said, and like my first meeting with Enola, I felt I must be somehow reading the signals all wrong, that he was not feeling loss, but something quite different.

"I loved it, sir," I said.

"Yes," he said. "So do I."

Dean Matthews is wrong. I have fought with memory my whole practicum only to find that it is not the enemy at all, and being an historian is not some saintly burden after all. Because Dunworthy is not blinking against the fatal sunlight of the last morning, but into the gloom of that first afternoon, looking in the great west doors of St. Paul's at what is, like Langby, like all of it, every moment, in us, saved forever.

HARDFOUGHT

by GREG BEAR

When Greg Bear won the 1995 Nebula Award for his novel, *Moving Mars* (Tor), he became the second person to hold the award in every category. In 1987, Greg Bear won the Hugo and the Nebula for his short story, "Tangents." His 1983 novelette, "Blood Music," also won the Nebula and the Hugo. In February of that same year, *Asimov's Science Fiction* published the brilliant Nebula-Award-winning novella featured here.

The author has distinguished himself in a number of other ways. In the early part of his career, he worked as a professional illustrator as well as a writer, and he was a founding member of the Association of Science Fiction Artists. He has held several positions for the Science Fiction Writers of America, and from 1988–1990, he served as the organization's president. His other acclaimed works include, *The Forge of God*, *Eon*, and *Anvil of Stars*. Greg Bear, his wife Astrid, and their two children, live in the state of Washington.

Humans called it the Medusa. Its long twisted ribbons of gas strayed across fifty parsecs, glowing blue, yellow, and carmine. Its central core was a ghoulish green flecked with watery black. Half a dozen protostars circled the core, and as many more dim conglomerates pooled in dimples in the nebula's magnetic field. The Medusa was a huge womb of stars—and disputed territory.

Whenever Prufrax looked at it in displays or through the ship's ports, it seemed malevolent, like a zealous mother displaying an ominous face to protect her children. Prufrax had never had a mother, but she had seen them in some of the fibs.

At five, Prufrax was old enough to know the *Mellangee*'s mission and her role in it. She had already been through four ship-years of indoctrination. Until her first battle she would be educated in both the Know and the Tell. She would be exercised and trained in the Mocks; in sleep she would dream of penetrating the huge red-and-white Senexi seedships and finding the brood mind. "Zap, Zap," she went with her lips, silent so the tellman wouldn't think her thoughts were straying.

The tellman peered at her from his position in the center of the spherical classroom. Her mates stared straight at the center, all focusing somewhere around the tellman's spiderlike teaching desk, waiting for the trouble, some fidgeting. "How many branch individuals in the Senexi brood mind?" he asked. He looked around the classroom. Peered face by face. Focused on her again. "Pru?"

"Five," she said. Her arms ached. She had been pumped full of moans the wake before. She was already three meters tall, in elfstate, with her long, thin limbs not nearly adequately fleshed out and her fingers still crisscrossed with the surgery done to adapt them to the gloves.

"What will you find in the brood mind?" the tellman pursued, his impassive face stretched across a hammerhead as wide as his shoulders. Some of the fems thought tellmen were attractive. Not many—and Pru was not one of them.

"Yoke," she said.

"What is in the brood-mind yoke?"

"Fibs."

"More specifically? And it really isn't all fib, you know."

"Info. Senexi data."

"What will you do?"

"Zap," she said, smiling.

"Why, Pru?"

"Yoke has team gens-memory. Zap yoke, spill the life of the team's five branch inds."

"Zap the brood, Pru?"

"No," she said solemnly. That was a new instruction, only in effect since her class's inception. "Hold the brood for the supreme overs." The tellmen did not say what would be done with the Senexi broods. That was not her concern.

"Fine," said the tellman. "You tell well, for someone who's always half-journeying."

She was already five, soon six. Old. Some saw Senexi by the time they were four.

"Zap, Zap," she went with her lips.

Aryz skidded through the thin layer of liquid ammonia on his broadest pod, considering his new assignment. He knew the Medusa by another name, one that conveyed all the time and effort the Senexi had invested in it. The protostar nebula held few mysteries for him. He and his four branch-mates, who along with the all-important brood mind made up one of the six teams aboard the seedship, had patrolled the nebula for ninety-three orbits, each orbit—including the timeless periods outside status geometry—taking some one hundred and thirty human years. They had woven in and out of the tendrils of gas, charting the infalling masses and exploring the rocky accretion disks of stars entering the main sequence. With each measure and update, the brood minds refined their view of the nebula as it would be a hundred generations hence when the Senexi plan would finally mature.

The Senexi were nearly as old as the galaxy. They had achieved spaceflight during the time of the starglobe when the galaxy had been a sphere. They had not been a quick or brilliant race. Each great achievement had taken thousands of generations, and not just because of their intellectual handicaps. In those times elements heavier than helium had been rare, found only around stars that had greedily absorbed huge amounts of primeval hydrogen, burned fierce and blue, and exploded early, permeating the ill-defined galactic arms with carbon and nitrogen, lithium and oxygen. Elements heavier than iron had been almost nonexistent. The biologies of cold gas-giant worlds had developed with a much smaller palette of chemical combinations in producing the offspring of the primary Population II stars.

Aryz, even with the limited perspective of a branch ind, was aware that, on the whole, the humans opposing the seedship were more adaptable, more vital. But they were not more experienced. The Senexi with their billions of years had often matched them. And Aryz's perspective was expanding with each day of his new assignment.

In the early generations of the struggle, Senexi mental stasis and cultural inflexibility had made them avoid contact with the Population I species. They had never begun a program of extermination of the younger, newly life-forming worlds; the task would have been monumental and probably useless. So when spacefaring cultures developed, the Senexi had retreated, falling back into the redoubts of old stars even before engaging with the new kinds. They had retreated for three generations, about thirty thousand human years, raising their broods on cold nestworlds around red dwarfs, conserving, holding back for the inevitable conflicts.

As the Senexi had anticipated, the younger Population I races had found need of even the aging groves of the galaxy's first stars. They had moved in savagely, voraciously, with all the strength and mutability of organisms evolved from a richer soup of elements. Biology had, in some ways, evolved in its own right and superseded the Senexi.

Aryz raised the upper globe of his body, with its five silicate eyes arranged in a cross along the forward surface. He had memory of those times, and times long before, though his team hadn't existed then. The brood mind carried memories selected from the total store of nearly twelve billion years' experience, an awesome amount of knowledge, even to a Senexi. He pushed himself forward with his rear pods.

Through the brood mind Aryz could share the memories of a hundred thousand past generations, yet the brood mind itself was younger than its branch individuals. For a time in their youth, in their liquid-dwelling larval form, the branch inds carried their own sacs of data, each a fragment of the total necessary for complete memory. The branch inds swam through ammonia seas and wafted through thick warm gaseous zones, protoplasmic blobs three to four meters in diameter, developing their personalities under the weight of the past—and not even a complete past. No wonder they were inflexible, Aryz thought. Most branch inds were aware enough to see that—especially when they were allowed to compare histories with the Population I species, as he was doing—but there was nothing to be done. They were content the way they were. To change would be unspeakably repugnant. Extinction was preferable . . . almost.

But now they were pressed hard. The brood mind had begun a number of experiments. Aryz's team had been selected from the seedship's contingent to oversee the experiments, and Aryz had been chosen as the chief investigator. Two orbits past, they had captured six human embryos in a breeding device, as well as a highly coveted memory storage center. Most Senexi engagements had been with humans for the past three or four generations. Just as the Senexi dominated Population II species, humans were ascendant among their kind.

Experiments with the human embryos had already been conducted. Some had been allowed to develop normally; others had been tampered with, for reasons Aryz was not aware of. The tamperings had not been very successful.

The newer experiments, Aryz suspected, were going to take a different direction, and the seedship's actions now focused on him; he believed he would be given complete authority over the human shapes. Most branch inds would have dissipated under such a burden, but not Aryz. He found the human shapes rather interesting, in their own horrible way. They might, after all, be the key to Senexi survival.

The moans were toughening her elfstate. She lay in pain for a wake, not daring to close her eyes; her mind was changing and she feared sleep would be the end of her. Her nightmares were not easily separated from life; some, in fact, were sharper.

Too often in sleep she found herself in a Senexi trap, struggling uselessly, being pulled in deeper, her hatred wasted against such power. . . .

When she came out of the rigor, Prufrax was given leave by the subordinate tellman. She took to the *Mellangee*'s greenroads, walking stiffly in the shallow gravity. Her hands itched. Her mind seemed almost empty after the turmoil of the past few wakes. She had never felt so calm and clear. She hated the Senexi double now; once for their innate evil, twice for what they had made her overs put her through to be able to fight them. She was growing more mature wake by wake. Fight-budding, the tellman called it, hate coming out like blooms, synthesizing the sunlight of his teaching into pure fight.

The greenroads rose temporarily beyond the labyrinth shields and armor of the ship. Simple transparent plastic-and-steel geodesic surfaces formed a lacework over the gardens, admitting radiation necessary to the vegetation growing along the paths.

Prufrax looked down on the greens to each side of the paths without much comprehension. They were *beautiful.* Yes, one should say that, think that, but what did it mean? Pleasing? She wasn't sure what being pleased meant, outside of thinking Zap. She sniffed a flower that, the signs explained, bloomed only in the light of young stars not yet fusing. They were near such a star now, and the greenroads were shiny black and electric green with the blossoms. Lamps had been set out for other plants unsuited to such darkened conditions. Some technic allowed suns to appear in selected plastic panels when viewed from certain angles. Clever, the technicals.

She much preferred the looks of a technical to a tellman, but she was common in that. She wished a technical were on the greenroads with her. The moans had the effect of making her receptive—what she saw, looking in mirrors, was a certain shine in her eyes—but there was no chance of a breeding liaison. She was quite unreproductive in this moment of elfstate.

She looked up and saw a figure at least a hundred meters away, sitting on an allowed patch near the path. She walked casually, as gracefully as possible with the stiffness. Not a technical, she saw soon, but she was not disappointed. Too calm.

"Over," he said as she approached.

"Under," she replied. But not by much—he was probably six or seven ship-years old and not easily classifiable.

"Such a fine elfstate," he commented. His hair was black. He was shorter than she, but something in his build reminded her of the glovers. He motioned for her to sit, and she did so with a whuff, massaging her knees.

"Moans?" he asked.

"Bad stretch," she said.

"You're a glover." He was looking at the fading scars on her hands.

"Can't tell what you are," she said.

"Noncombat," he said. "Tuner of the mandates."

She knew very little about the mandates, except that law decreed every ship carry one, and few of the crew were ever allowed to peep. "Noncombat, hm?" She mused. She didn't despise him for that; one never felt strong negatives for a crew member.

"Been working on ours this wake," he said. "Too hard, I guess. Told to talk." Overzealousness in work was considered an erotic trait aboard the *Mellangee.* Still, she didn't feel too receptive toward him.

"Glovers walk after a rough growing," she said.

He nodded. "My name's Clevo."

"Prufrax."

"Combat soon?"

"Hoping. Waiting forever."

"I know. Just been allowed access to the mandate for a half-dozen wakes. All new to me. Very happy."

"Can you talk about it?" she asked. Information about the ship not accessible in certain rates was excellent barter.

"Not sure," he said, frowning. "I've been told caution."

"Well, I'm listening."

He could come from glover stock, she thought, but probably not from technical. He wasn't very muscular, but he wasn't as tall as a glover, or as thin, either.

"If you'll tell me about gloves."

With a smile she held up her hands and wriggled the short, stumpy fingers. "Sure."

The brood mind floated weightless in its tank, held in place by buffered carbon rods. Metal was at a premium aboard the Senexi ships, more out of tradition than actual material limitations.

Aryz floated before the brood mind, all these thoughts coursing through his tissues. He had no central nervous system, no truly differentiated organs except those that dealt with the outside world—limbs, eyes, permea. The brood mind, however, was all central nervous system, a thinly buffered sac of viscous fluids about ten meters wide.

"Have you investigated the human memory device yet?" the brood mind asked.

"I have."

"Is communication with the human shapes possible for us?"

"We have already created interfaces for dealing with their machines. Yes, it seems likely we can communicate."

"Does it strike you that in our long war with humans, we have made no attempt to communicate before?"

This was a complicated question. It called for several qualities that Aryz, as a branch ind, wasn't supposed to have. Inquisitiveness, for one. Branch inds did not ask questions. They exhibited initiative only as offshoots of the brood mind.

He found, much to his dismay, that the question had occurred to him. "We have never captured a human memory store before," he said, by way of incomplete answer. "We could not have communicated without such an extensive source of information."

"Yet, as you say, even in the past we have been able to use human machines."

"The problem is vastly more complex."

The brood mind paused. "Do you think the teams have been prohibited from communicating with humans?"

Aryz felt the closest thing to anguish possible for a branch ind. Was he being considered unworthy? Accused of conduct inappropriate to a branch ind? His loyalty to the brood mind was unshakeable. "Yes."

"And what might our reasons be?"

"Avoidance of pollution."

"Correct. We can no more communicate with them and remain untainted than we can walk on their worlds, breathe their atmosphere." Again, silence. Aryz lapsed into a mode of inactivity. When the brood mind readdressed him, he was instantly aware.

"Do you know how you are different?" it asked.

"I am not . . ." Again, hesitation. Lying to the brood mind was impossible for him. He signaled his distress.

"You are useful to the team," the brood mind said. Aryz calmed instantly. His thoughts became sluggish, receptive. There was a possibility of redemption. But how was he different? "You are to attempt communication with the shapes yourself. You will not engage in any discourse with your fellows while you are so involved." He was banned. "And after completion of this mission and transfer of certain facts to me, you will dissipate."

Aryz struggled with the complexity of the orders. "How am I different, worthy of such a commission?"

The surface of the brood mind was as still as an undisturbed pool. The indistinct black smudges that marked its radiating organs circulated slowly within the interior, then returned, one above the other, to focus on him. "You will grow a new branch ind. It will not have your flaws, but, then again, it will not be useful to me should such a situation come a second time. Your dissipation will be a relief, but it will be regretted."

"How am I different?"

"I think you know already," the brood mind said. "When the time comes, you will feed the new branch ind all your memories but those of human contact. If you do not survive to that stage of its growth, you will pick your fellow who will perform that function for you."

A small pinkish spot appeared on the back of Aryz's globe. He floated forward and placed his largest permeum against the brood mind's cool surface. The key and command were passed, and his body became capable of reproduction. Then the signal of dismissal was given. He left the chamber.

Flowing through the thin stream of liquid ammonia lining the corridor, he felt ambiguously stimulated. His was a position of privilege and anathema. He had been blessed—and condemned. Had any other branch ind experienced such a thing?

Then he knew the brood mind was correct. He was different from his fellows. None of them would have asked such questions. None of them could have survived the suggestion of communicating with human shapes. If this task hadn't been given to him, he would have had to dissipate anyway.

The pink spot grew larger, then began to make grayish flakes. It broke through the skin, and casually, almost without thinking, Aryz scraped it off against a bulkhead. It clung, made a radio-frequency emanation something like a sigh, and began absorbing nutrients from the ammonia.

Aryz went to inspect the shapes.

She was intrigued by Clevo, but the kind of interest she felt was new to her. She was not particularly receptive. Rather, she felt a mental gnawing as if she were hungry or had been injected with some kind of brain moans. What Clevo told her about the mandates opened up a topic she had never considered before. How did all things come to be—and how did she figure in them?

The mandates were quite small, Clevo explained, each little more than a cubic meter in volume. Within them was the entire history and culture of the human species, as accurate as possible, culled from all existing sources. The mandate in each ship was updated whenever the ship returned to a contact station.

Clevo had been assigned small tasks—checking data and adding ship records—that had allowed him to sample bits of the mandate. "It's mandated that we have records," he explained, "and what we have, you see, is *man-data*." He smiled. "That's a joke," he said. "Sort of."

Prufrax nodded solemnly. "So where do we come from?"

"Earth, of course," Clevo said. "Everyone knows that."

"I mean, where do *we* come from—you and I, the crew."

"Breeding division. Why ask? You know."

"Yes." She frowned, concentrating. "I mean, we don't come from the same place as the Senexi. The same way."

"No, that's foolishness."

She saw that it was foolishness—the Senexi were different all around. What was she struggling to ask? "Is their fib like our own?"

"Fib? History's not a fib. Not most of it, anyway. Fibs are for unreal. History is over fib."

She knew, in a vague way, that fibs were unreal. She didn't like to have their comfort demeaned, though. "Fibs are fun," she said. "They teach Zap."

"I suppose," Clevo said dubiously. "Being noncombat, I don't see Zap fibs."

Fibs without Zap were almost unthinkable to her. "Such dull," she said.

"Well, of course you'd say that. I might find Zap fibs dull—think of that?"

"We're different," she said. "Like Senexi are different."

Clevo's jaw hung open. "No way. We're crew. We're human. Senexi are . . ." He shook his head as if fed bitters.

"No, I mean . . ." She paused, uncertain whether she was entering unallowed territory. "You and I, we're fed different, given different moans. But in a big way we're different from Senexi. They aren't made, nor act, as you and I. But . . ." Again it was difficult to express. She was irritated. "I don't want to talk to you anymore."

A tellman walked down the path, not familiar to Prufrax. He held out his hand for Clevo, and Clevo grasped it. "It's amazing," the tellman said, "How you two gravitate to each other. Go, elfstate," he addressed Prufrax. "You're on the wrong greenroad."

She never saw the young researcher again. With glover training under way, the itches he aroused soon faded, and Zap resumed its overplace.

The Senexi had ways of knowing humans were near. As information came in about fleets and individual cruisers less than one percent nebula diameter distant, the seedship seemed warmer, less hospitable. Everything was UV with anxiety, and the new branch ind on the wall had to be shielded by a special silicate cup to prevent distortion. The brood mind grew a corniculum automatically, though the toughened outer membrane would be of little help if the seedship was breached.

Aryz had buried his personal confusion under a load of work. He had penetrated the human memory store deeply enough to find instructions on its use. It called itself a *mandate* and even the simple preliminary directions were difficult for Aryz. It was like swimming in another family's private sea, though of course infinitely more alien; how could he connect with experiences never had, problems and needs never encountered by his kind?

He observed the new branch ind once or twice each watch period. Never before had he seen an induced replacement. The normal process was for two brood minds to exchange plasm and form new team buds, then to exchange and nurture the buds. The buds were later cast free to swim as individual larvae. While the larvae swam through the liquid and gas atmosphere of a Senexi world often for thousands, even tens of thousands of kilometers, inevitably they returned to gather with the other buds of their team. Replacements were selected from a separately created pool of "generic" buds only if one or more originals had been destroyed during their wanderings. The destruction of a complete team meant reproductive failure.

In a mature team, only when a branch ind was destroyed did the brood mind induce a replacement. In essence, then, Aryz was already considered dead.

Yet he was still useful. That amused him, if the Senexi emotion could be called amusement. Restricting himself from his fellows was difficult, but he filled the time by immersing himself, through the interface, in the mandate.

The humans were also connected with the mandate through their surrogate parent, and in this manner they were quiescent.

He reported infrequently to the brood mind. Until he had established communication, there was little to report.

And throughout his turmoil, like the others he could sense a fight was coming. It could determine the success or failure of all their work in the nebula. In the grand scheme, failure here might not be crucial. But the Senexi had taken the long view too often in the past.

And he knew himself well enough to doubt he would fail.

He could feel an affinity for the humans already, peering at them through the thick glass wall in their isolated chamber, his skin paling at the thought of their heat, their poisonous chemistry. A diseased affinity. He hated himself for it. And reveled in it. It was what made him particularly useful to the team. If he was defective, and this was the only way he could serve, then so be it.

The other branch inds observed his passings from a distance, making no judgments. Aryz was dead, though he worked and moved. His sacrifice had been fearful. Yet he would not be a hero. His kind could never be emulated.

It was a horrible time, a horrible conflict.

She floated in language, learned it in a trice; there were no distractions. She floated in history and picked up as much as she could, for the source seemed inexhaustible. She tried to distinguish between eyes-open—the barren, pale gray-brown chamber with the thick green wall, beyond which floated a murky roundness—and eyes-shut, when she dropped back into language and history with no fixed foundation.

Eyes-open, she saw the Mam with its comforting limbs and its soft voice, its tubes and extrusions of food and its hissings and removal of waste. Through Mam's wires she learned. Mam also tended another like herself, and another unlike either of them, more like the shape beyond the green wall.

She was very young, and it was all a mystery.

At least she knew her name. And what she was supposed to do. She took small comfort in that.

They fitted Prufrax with her gloves, and she went into the practice chamber, dragged by her gloves almost, for she hadn't yet knitted the plug-in nerves in her right index digit and her pace control was uncertain.

There, for six wakes straight, she flew with the other glovers back and forth across the dark spaces like elfstate comets. Constellations and nebula aspects flashed at random on the distant walls, and she oriented to them like a night-flying bird. Her glovemates were Ornin, an especially slender male, and Ban, a red-haired female, and the special-projects sisters Ya, Trice, and Damu, new from the breeding division.

When she let the gloves have their way, she was freer than she had ever felt before. Control was somewhere uncentered, behind her eyes and beyond her fingers, as if she were drawn on a beautiful silver wire where it was best to go. Doing what was best to do. She barely saw the field that flowed from the grip of the thick, solid gloves or felt its caressing, life-sustaining influence. Truly, she hardly saw or felt anything but situations, targets, opportunities, the success or failure of the Zap. Failure was an acute pain. She was never reprimanded for failure; the reprimand was in her blood, and she felt as if she wanted to die. But then the opportunity would improve, the Zap would succeed, and everything around her—stars, Senexi seedship, the *Mellangee*, everything—seemed part of a beautiful dream all her own.

She was intense in the Mocks.

Their initial practice over, the entry play began.

One by one, the special-projects sisters took their hyperbolic formation. Their glove fields threw out extensions, and they combined force. In they went, the mock Senexi seedship brilliant red and white and UV and radio and hateful before them. Their tails swept through the seedship's outer shields and swirled like long silky hair laid on water; they absorbed fantastic energies, grew bright like violent little stars against the seedship outline. They were engaged in the drawing of the shields, and sure as topology, the spirals of force had to have a dimple on the opposite side that would iris wide enough to let in glovers. The sisters twisted the forces, and Prufrax could see the dimple stretching out under them—

The exercise ended. The elfstate glovers were cast into sudden dark. Prufrax came out of the mock unprepared, her mind still bent on the Zap. The lack of orientation drove her as mad as a moth suddenly flipped from night to day. She careened until gently mitted and channeled. She flowed down a tube, the field slowly neutralizing, and came to a halt still gloved, her body jerking and tingling.

"What the breed happened?" she screamed, her hands beginning to hurt.

"Energy conserve," a mechanical voice answered. Behind Prufrax the other elfstate glovers lined up in the catch tube, all but the special-projects sisters. Ya, Trice, and Damu had been taken out of the exercise early and replaced by simulations. There was no way their functions could be mocked. They entered the tube ungloved and helped their comrades adjust to the overness of the real.

As they left the mock chamber, another batch of glovers, even younger and fresher in elfstate, passed them. Ya held her hands up, and they saluted in return. "Breed more every day," Prufrax grumbled. She worried about having so many crew she'd never be able to conduct a satisfactory Zap herself. Where would the honor of being a glover go if everyone was a glover?

She wriggled into her cramped bunk, feeling exhilarated and irritated. She replayed the mocks and added in the missing Zap, then stared gloomily at her small narrow feet.

Out there the Senexi waited. Perhaps they were in the same state as she—ready to fight, testy at being reined in. She pondered her ignorance, her inability to judge whether such things were even possible among the enemy. She thought of the researcher, Clevo. "Blank," she murmured. "Blank, blank." Such thoughts were unnecessary, and humanizing Senexi was unworthy of a glover.

Aryz looked at the instrument, stretched a pod into it, and willed. Vocal human language came out the other end, thin and squeaky in the helium atmosphere. The sound disgusted and thrilled him. He removed the instrument from the gelatinous strands of the engineering wall and pushed it into his interior through a stretched permeum. He took a thick draft of ammonia and slid to the human-shapes chamber again.

He pushed through the narrow port into the observation room. Adjusting his eyes to the heat and bright light beyond the transparent wall, he saw the round mutated shape first—the result of their unsuccessful experiments. He swung his sphere around and looked at the others.

For a time he couldn't decide which was uglier—the mutated shape or the normals. Then he thought of what it would be like to have humans tamper with Senexi and try to make them into human forms. . . .

He looked at the round human and shrank as if from sudden heat. Aryz had had nothing to do with the experiments. For that, at least, he was grateful.

Aryz placed the tip of the vocalizer against a sound-transmitting plate and spoke.

"Zello," came the sound within the chamber. The mutated shape looked up. It lay on the floor, great bloated stomach backed by four almost useless pods. It usually made high-pitched sounds continuously. Now it stopped and listened, straining on the tube that connected it to the breed-supervising device.

"Hello," replied the *male*. It sat on a ledge across the chamber, having unhooked itself.

The machine that served as surrogate parent and instructor stood in one corner, an awkward parody of a human, with limbs too long and head too small. Aryz could see the unwillingness of the designing engineers to examine human anatomy too closely.

"I am called—" Aryz said, his name emerging as a meaningless stretch of white noise. He would have to do better than that. He compressed and adapted the frequencies. "I am called Aryz."

"Hello," the young female said.

"What are your names?" He knew them well enough, having listened many times to their conversations.

"Prufrax," the female said. "I'm a glover."

The human shapes contained very little genetic memory. As a kind of brood marker, Aryz supposed, they had been equipped with their name, occupation, and the rudiments of environmental knowledge.

"I'm a teacher, Prufrax," Aryz said.

"I don't understand you," the female replied.

"You teach me, I teach you."

"We have the Mam," the male said, pointing to the machine. "She teaches us." The Mam, as they called it, was hooked into the mandate.

"Do you know where you are?" Aryz asked.

"Where we live," Prufrax said. "Eyes-open."

"Don't talk to it," the male said. "Mam talks to us." Aryz consulted the mandate for some understanding of the name they had given to the breed-supervising machine. Mam, it explained, was probably a natural expression for womb-carrying parent. Aryz severed the machine's power.

"Mam is no longer functional," he said. He would have the engineering wall put together another less identifiable machine to link them to the mandate and to their nutrition. He wanted them to associate comfort and completeness with nothing but himself.

The machine slumped, and the female shape pulled herself free of the hookup. She started to cry, a reaction quite mysterious to Aryz. His link with the mandate had not been intimate enough to answer questions about the wailing and moisture from the eyes. After a time the male and female lay down and became dormant.

The mutated shape made more soft sounds and tried to approach the transparent wall. It held up its thin arms as if beseeching. The others would have nothing to do with it; now it wished to go with him. Perhaps the biologists had partially succeeded in their attempt at transformation; perhaps it was more Senexi than human.

Aryz quickly backed out through the port, into the cool and security of the corridor beyond.

It was an endless orbital dance, this detection and matching of course, moving away and swinging back, deceiving and revealing, between the *Mellangee* and the Senexi seedship.

Filled with her skill and knowledge, Prufrax waited, feeling like a ripe fruit about to fall from the tree. At this point in their training, just before the application, elfstates were most receptive. She was allowed to take a lover, and they were assigned small separate quarters near the outer greenroads.

The contact was satisfactory, as far as it went. Her mate was an older glover named Kumnax, and as they lay back in the cubicle, soothed by air-dance fibs, he told her stories about past battles, special tactics, how to survive.

"Survive?" she asked, puzzled.

"Of course." His long brown face was intent on the view of the greenroads through the cubicle's small window.

"I don't understand," she said.

"Most glovers don't make it," he said patiently.

"I will."

He turned to her. "You're six," he said. "You're very young. I'm ten. I've seen. You're about to be applied for the first time, you're full of confidence. But most glovers won't make it. They breed thousands of us. We're expendable. We're based on the best glovers of the past but even the best don't survive."

"I will," Prufrax repeated, her jaw set.

"You always say that," he murmured.

Prufrax stared at him for a moment.

"Last time I knew you," he said, "you kept saying that. And here you are, fresh again."

"What last time?"

"Master Kumnax," a mechanical voice interrupted.

He stood, looking down at her. "We glovers always have big mouths. They don't like us knowing, but once we know, what can they do about it?"

"You are in violation," the voice said. "Please report to S."

"But now, if you last, you'll know more than the tellman tells."

"I don't understand," Prufrax said slowly, precisely, looking him straight in the eye.

"I've paid my debt," Kumnax said. "We glovers stick. Now I'm going to go get my punishment." He left the cubicle. Prufrax didn't see him again before her first application.

The seedship buried itself in a heating protostar, raising shields against the infalling ice and stone. The nebula had congealed out of a particularly rich cluster of exploded fourth- and fifth-generation stars, thick with planets, the detritus of which now fell on Aryz's ship like hail.

Aryz had never been so isolated. No other branch ind addressed him; he never even saw them now. He made his reports to the brood mind, but even there the reception was warmer and warmer, until he could barely endure to communicate. Consequently—and he realized this was part of the plan—he came closer to his charges, the human shapes.

The brood mind was interested in one question: how successfully could they be planted aboard a human ship? Would they be accepted until they could carry out their sabotage, or would they be detected? Already Senexi instructions were being coded into their teachings.

"I think they will be accepted in the confusion of an engagement," Aryz answered. He had long since guessed the general outlines of the brood mind's plans. Communication with the human shapes was for one purpose only, to use them as decoys, insurgents. They were weapons. Knowledge of human activity and behavior was not an end in itself; seeing what was happening to him, Aryz fully understood why the brood mind wanted such study to proceed no further.

He would lose them soon, he thought, and his work would be over. He would be much too human-tainted. He would end, and his replacement would start a new existence, very little different from Aryz's—but, he reasoned, adjusted. The replacement would not have Aryz's peculiarity.

He approached his last meeting with the brood mind, preparing himself for his final work, for the ending. In the cold liquid-filled chamber, the great red-and-white sac waited, the center of his team, his existence. He adored it. There was no way he could criticize its action.

Yet—

"We are being sought," the brood mind radiated. "Are the shapes ready?"

"Yes," Aryz said. "The new teaching is firm. They believe they are fully human." And, except for the new teaching, they were. "They defy sometimes." He said nothing about the mutated shape. It would not be used. If they won this encounter, it would probably be placed with Aryz's body in a fusion torch for complete purging.

"Then prepare them," the brood mind said. "They will be delivered to the vector for positioning and transfer."

Darkness and waiting. Prufrax nested in her delivery tube like a freshly chambered round. Through her gloves she caught distant communications murmurs that resembled voices down hollow pipes. The *Mellangee* was coming to full readiness.

Huge as her ship was, Prufrax knew that it would be dwarfed by the seedship. She could recall some hazy details about the seedship's structure, but most of that information was stored securely away from interference by her conscious mind.

More information would be fed to her just before the launch, but she knew the general procedure. The seedship was deep in a protostar, hiding behind the distortion of geometry and the complete hash of electromagnetic energy. The *Mellangee* would approach, collide if need be. Penetrate. Release. Find. Zap. Her fingers ached. Sometime before the launch she would also be fed her final moans—the tempers—and she would be primed to leave elfstate. She would be a mature glover. She would be a woman.

If she returned

will return.

Her fingers ached worse.

The tempers came, moans tiding in, then the battle data. As it passed into her subconscious, she caught a flash of—

Rocks and ice, a thick cloud of dust and gas glowing red but seeming dark, no stars, no constellation guides this time. The beacon came on. That would be her only way to orient once the gloves stopped inertial and locked onto the target.

The seedship
was like
a shadow within a shadow
twenty-two kilometers across, yet
carrying

only six
teams
LAUNCH *she flies!*
Data: The *Mellangee* has buried herself in the seedship, plowed deep into the interior like a carnivore's muzzle looking for vitals

Instruction a swarm of seeks is dashing through the seedship, looking for the brood minds, for the brood chambers, for branch inds. The glovers will follow.

Prufrax sees herself clearly now. She is the great avenging comet, bringer of omen and doom, like a knife moving through the glass and ice and thin, cold helium as if they weren't there, the chambered round fired and tearing at hundreds of kilometers an hour through the Senexi vessel, following the seeks.

The seedship cannot withdraw into higher geometries now. It is pinned by the *Mellangee*. It is hers.

Information floods her, pleases her immensely. She swoops down orange-and-gray corridors, buffeting against the walls like a ricocheting bullet. Almost immediately she comes across a branch ind, sliding through the ammonia film against the out-rushing wind, trying to reach an armored cubicle. Her first Zap is too easy, not satisfying, nothing like what she thought. In her wake the branch ind becomes scattered globules of plasma. She plunges deeper.

Aryz delivers his human charges to the vectors that will launch them. They are equipped with simulations of the human weapons, their hands encased in the hideous gray gloves.

The seedship is in deadly peril; the battle has almost been lost at one stroke. The seedship cannot remain whole. It must self-destruct, taking the human ship with it, leaving only a fragment with as many teams as can escape.

The vectors launch the human shapes. Aryz tries to determine which part of the ship will be elected to survive; he must not be there. His job is over, and he must die.

The glovers fan out through the seedship's central hollow, demolishing the great cold drive engines, bypassing the shielded fusion flare and the reprocessing plant, destroying machinery built before their Earth was formed.

The special-projects sisters take the lead. Suddenly they are confused. They have found a brood mind, but it is not heavily protected. They surround it, prepare for the Zap—

It is sacrificing itself, drawing them into an easy kill and away from another portion of the seedship. Power is concentrating elsewhere. Sensing that, they kill quickly and move on.

Aryz's brood mind prepares for escape. It begins to wrap itself in flux bind as it moves through the ship toward the frozen fragment.

Already three of its five branch inds are dead; it can feel other brood minds dying. Aryz's bud replacement has been killed as well.

Following Aryz's training, the human shapes rush into corridors away from the main action. The special-projects sisters encounter the decoy male, allow it to fly with them . . . until it aims its weapons. One Zap almost takes out Trice. The others fire on the shape immediately. He goes to his death weeping, confused from the very moment of his launch.

The fragment in which the brood mind will take refuge encompasses the chamber where the humans had been nurtured, where the mandate is still stored. All the other brood minds are dead, Aryz realizes; the humans have swept down on them so quickly. What shall he do?

Somewhere, far off, he feels the distressed pulse of another branch ind dying. He probes the remains of the seedship. He is the last. He cannot dissipate now; he must ensure the brood mind's survival.

Prufrax, darting through the crumbling seedship, searching for more opportunities, comes across an injured glover. She calls for a mediseek and pushes on.

The brood mind settles into the fragment. Its support system is damaged; it is entering the time-isolated state, the flux bind, more rapidly than it should. The seals of foamed electric ice cannot quite close off the fragment before Ya, Trice, and Damu slip in. They frantically call for bind cutters and preservers; they have instructions to capture the last brood mind, if possible.

But a trap falls upon Ya, and snarling fields tear her from her gloves. She is flung down a dark disintegrating shaft, red cracks opening all around as the seedship's integrity fails. She trails silver dust and freezes, hits a barricade, shatters.

The ice seals continue to close. Trice is caught between them and pushes out frantically, blundering into the region of the intensifying flux bind. Her gloves break into hard bits, and she is melded into an ice wall like an insect trapped on the surface of a winter lake.

Damu sees that the brood mind is entering the final phase of flux bind. After that they will not be able to touch it. She begins a desperate Zap.

and is too late.

Aryz directs the subsidiary energy of the flux against her. Her Zap deflects from the bind region, she is caught in an interference pattern and vibrates until her tiniest particles stop their knotted whirlpool spins and she simply becomes

space and searing light.

The brood mind, however, has been damaged. It is losing information from one portion of its anatomy. Desperate for storage, it looks for places to hold the information before the flux bind's last wave.

Aryz directs an interface onto the brood mind's surface. The silvery pools of time binding flicker around them both. The brood mind's damaged sections transfer their data into the last available storage device—the human mandate.

Now it contains both human and Senexi information.

The silvery pools unite, and Aryz backs away. No longer can he sense the brood mind. It is out of reach but not yet safe. He must propel the fragment from the remains of the seedship. Then he must wrap the fragment in its own flux bind, cocoon it in physics to protect it from the last ravages of the humans.

Aryz carefully navigates his way through the few remaining corridors. The helium atmosphere has almost completely dissipated, even there. He strains to remember all the procedures. Soon the seedship will explode, destroying the human ship. By then they must be gone.

Angry red, Prufrax follows his barely sensed form, watching him behind barricades of ice, approaching the moment of a most satisfying Zap. She gives her gloves their way

and finds a shape behind her, wearing gloves that are not gloves, not like her own, but capable of grasping her in tensed fields, blocking the Zap, dragging them together. The fragment separates, heat pours in from the protostar cloud. They are swirled in their vortex of power, twin locked comets—one red, one sullen gray.

"Who are you?" Prufrax screams as they close in on each other in the fields. Their environments meld. They grapple. In the confusion, the darkening, they are drawn out of the cloud with the fragment, and she sees the other's face.

her own.

The seedship self-destructs. The fragment is propelled from the protostar, above the plane of what will become planets in their orbits, away from the crippled and dying *Mellangee*.

Desperate, Prufrax uses all her strength to drill into the fragment. Helium blows past them, and bits of dead branch inds.

Aryz catches the pair immediately in the shapes chamber, rearranging the fragment's structure to enclose them with the mutant shape and mandate. For the moment he has time enough to concentrate on them. They are dangerous. They are almost equal to each other, but his shape is weakening faster than the true glover. They float, bouncing from wall to wall in the chamber, forcing the mutant to crawl into a corner and howl with fear.

There may be value in saving the one and capturing the other. Involved as they are, the two can be carefully dissected from their fields and induced into a crude kind of sleep before the glover has a chance to free her weapons. He can dispose of the gloves—fake and real—and hook them both to the Mam, reattach the mutant shape as well. Perhaps something can be learned from the failure of the experiment.

The dissection and capture occur faster than the planning. His movement slows under the spreading flux bind. His last action, after attaching the humans to the Mam, is to make sure the brood mind's flux bind is properly nested within that of the ship.

The fragment drops into simpler geometries.

It is as if they never existed.

The battle was over. There were no victors. Aryz became aware of the passage of time, shook away the sluggishness, and crawled through painfully dry corridors to set the environmental equipment going again. Throughout the fragment, machines struggled back to activity.

How many generations? The constellations were unrecognizable. He made star traces and found familiar spectra and types, but advanced in age. There had been a malfunction in the overall flux bind. He couldn't find the nebula where the battle had occurred. In its place were comfortably middle-aged stars surrounded by young planets.

Aryz came down from the makeshift observatory. He slid through the fragment, established the limits of his new home, and found the solid mirror surface of the brood mind's cocoon. It was still locked in flux bind, and he knew of no way to free it. In time the bind would probably wear off—but that might require life spans. The seedship was gone. They had lost the brood chamber, and with it the stock.

He was the last branch ind of his team. Not that it mattered now; there was nothing he could initiate without a brood mind. If the flux bind was permanent, then he might as well be dead.

He closed his thoughts around him and was almost completely submerged when he sensed an alarm from the shapes chamber. The interface with the mandate had turned itself off; the new version of the Mam was malfunctioning. He tried to repair the equipment, but without the engineer's wall he was almost helpless. The best he could do was rig a temporary nutrition supply through the old human-form Mam. When he was done, he looked at the captive and the two shapes, then at the legless, armless Mam that served as their link to the interface and life itself.

She had spent her whole life in a room barely eight by ten meters, and not much taller than her own height. With her had been Grayd and the silent round creature whose name—if it had any—they had never learned. For a time there had been Mam, then another kind of Mam not nearly as satisfactory. She was hardly aware that her entire existence had been miserable, cramped, in one way or another incomplete.

Separated from them by a transparent partition, another round shape had periodically made itself known by voice or gesture.

Grayd had kept her sane. They had engaged in conspiracy. Removing themselves from the interface—what she called "eyes-shut"—they had held onto each other, tried to make sense out of what they knew instinctively, what was fed them through the interface, and what the being beyond the partition told them.

First they knew their names, and they knew that they were glovers. They knew that glovers were fighters. When Aryz passed instruction through the interface on how to fight, they had accepted it eagerly but uneasily. It didn't seem to jibe with instructions locked deep within their instincts.

Five years under such conditions had made her introspective. She expected nothing, sought little beyond experience in the eyes-shut. Eyes-open with Grayd seemed scarcely more than a dream. They usually managed to ignore the peculiar round creature in the chamber with them; it spent nearly all its time hooked to the mandate and the Mam.

Of one thing only was she completely sure. Her name was Prufrax. She said it in eyes-open and eyes-shut, her only certainty.

Not long before the battle, she had been in a condition resembling dreamless sleep, like a robot being given instructions. The part of Prufrax that had taken on personality during eyes-shut and eyes-open for five years had been superseded by the fight instructions Aryz had programmed. She had flown as glovers must fly (though the gloves didn't seem quite right). She had fought, grappling (she thought) with herself, but who could be certain of anything?

She had long since decided that reality was not to be sought too avidly. After the battle she fell back into the mandate—into eyes-shut—all too willingly.

But a change had come to eyes-shut, too. Before the battle, the information had been selected. Now she could wander through the mandate at will. She seemed to smell the new information, completely unfamiliar, like a whiff of ocean. She hardly knew where to begin. She stumbled across:

—that all vessels carry one, no matter what their size or class, just as every individual carries the map of a species. The mandate shall contain all the information of our kind, including accurate and uncensored history, for if we have learned anything, it is that censored and untrue accounts distort the eyes of the leaders. Unders are told lies. Leaders must seek and be provided with accounts as accurate as possible, or we will be weakened and fall—

What wonderful dreams the *leaders* must have had. And they possessed some intrinsic gift called *truth*, through the use of the *mandate*. Prufrax could hardly believe that. As she made her tentative explorations through the new fields of eyes-shut, she began to link the word *mandate* with what she experienced. That was where she was.

And she was alone. Once, she had explored with Grayd. Now there was no sign of Grayd.

She learned quickly. Soon she walked along a beach on Earth, then a beach on a world called Myriadne, and other beaches, fading in and out. By running through the entries rapidly, she came up with a blurred *eidos* and so learned what a beach was in the abstract. It was a boundary between one kind of eyes-shut and another, between water and land, neither of which had any corollary in eyes-open.

Some beaches had sand. Some had clouds—the *eidos* of clouds was quite attractive. And one—

had herself running scared, screaming.

She called out, but the figure vanished. Prufrax stood on a beach under a greenish-yellow star, on a world called Kyrene, feeling lonelier than ever.

She explored further, hoping to find Grayd, if not the figure that looked like herself. Grayd wouldn't flee from her. Grayd would—

The round thing confronted her, its helpless limbs twitching. Now it was her turn to run, terrified. Never before had she met the round creature in eyes-shut. It was mobile; it had a purpose. Over land, clouds, trees, rocks, wind, air, equations, and an edge of physics she fled. The farther she went, the more distant from the round one with hands and small head, the less afraid she was.

She never found Grayd.

The memory of the battle was fresh and painful. She remembered the ache of her hands, clumsily removed from the gloves. Her environment had collapsed and been replaced by something indistinct. Prufrax had fallen into a deep slumber and had dreamed.

The dreams were totally unfamiliar to her. If there was a left-turning in her arc of sleep, she dreamed of philosophies and languages and other things she couldn't relate to. A right-turning led to histories and sciences so incomprehensible as to be nightmares.

It was a most unpleasant sleep, and she was not at all sorry to find she wasn't really asleep.

The crucial moment came when she discovered how to slow her turnings and the changes of dream subject. She entered a pleasant place of which she had no knowledge but which did not seem threatening. There was a vast expanse of water, but it didn't terrify her. She couldn't even identify it as water until she scooped up a handful. Beyond the water was a floor of shifting particles. Above both was an open expanse, not black but obviously space, drawing her eyes into intense pale blue-green. And there was that figure she had encountered in the seedship. Herself. The figure pursued. She fled.

Right over the boundary into Senexi information. She knew then that what she was seeing couldn't possibly come from within herself. She was receiving data from another source. Perhaps she had been taken captive. It was possible she was now being forcibly debriefed. The tellman had discussed such possibilities, but none of the glovers had been taught how to defend themselves in specific situations. Instead it had been stated—in terms that brooked no second thought—that self-destruction was the only answer. So she tried to kill herself.

She sat in the freezing cold of a red-and-white room, her feet meeting but not touching a fluid covering on the floor. The information didn't fit her senses—it seemed blurred, inappropriate. Unlike the other data, this didn't allow participation or motion. Everything was locked solid.

She couldn't find an effective means of killing herself. She resolved to close her eyes and simply will herself into dissolution. But closing her eyes only moved her into a deeper or shallower level of deception—other categories, subjects, visions. She couldn't sleep, wasn't tired, couldn't die.

Like a leaf on a stream, she drifted. Her thoughts untangled, and she imagined herself floating on the water called ocean. She kept her eyes open. It was quite by accident that she encountered:

Instruction. Welcome to the introductory use of the mandate. As a noncombat processor, your duties are to maintain the mandate, provide essential information for your overs, and, if necessary, protect or destroy the mandate. The mandate is your immediate over. If it requires maintenance, you will oblige. Once linked with the mandate, as you are now, you may explore any aspect of the information by requesting delivery. To request delivery, indicate the core of your subject—

Prufrax! she shouted silently. What is Prufrax?

A voice with different tone immediately took over.

Ah, now that's quite a story. I was her biographer, the organizer of her life tapes (ref. GEORGE MACKNAX), and knew her well in the last years of her life. She was born in the Ferment 26468. Here are selected life tapes. Choose emphasis. Analyses follow.

—Hey! Who are you? There's someone here with me. . . .

—Shh! Listen. Look at her. Who is she?

They looked, listened to the information.

—Why, she's *me* . . . sort of.

—She's *us*.

She stood two and a half meters tall. Her hair was black and thick, though cut short; her limbs well muscled though drawn out by the training and hormonal treatments. She was seventeen years old, one of the few birds born in the solar system, and for the time being she had a chip on her shoulder. Everywhere she went, the birds asked about her mother, Jay-ax. "You better than her?"

Of course not! Who could be? But she was good; the instructors said so. She was just about through training, and whether she graduated to hawk or remained bird she would do her job well. Asking Prufrax about her mother was likely to make her set her mouth tight and glare.

On Mercior, the Grounds took up four thousand hectares and had its own port. The Grounds was divided into Land, Space, and Thought, and training in each area was mandatory for fledges, those birds embarking on hawk training. Prufrax was fledge three. She had passed Land—though she loathed downbound fighting—and was two years into Space. The tough part, everyone said, was not passing Space, but lasting through four years of Thought after the action in nearorbit and planetary.

Since she had been a little girl, no more than five—

—Five! Five what?

and had seen her mother's ships and fightsuits and fibs, she had known she would never be happy until she had ventured far out and put a seedship in her sights, had convinced a Senexi of the overness of end—

—The Zap! She's talking the Zap!

—What's that?

—You're me, you should know.

—I'm not you, and we're not her.

The Zap, said the mandate, and the data shifted.

"Tomorrow you receive your first implants. These will allow you to coordinate with the zero-angle phase engines and find your targets much more rapidly than you ever could with simple biologic. Are there any questions?"

"Yes, sir." Prufrax stood at the top of the spherical classroom, causing the hawk instructor to swivel his platform. "I'm having problems with the zero-angle phase maths. Reduction of the momenta of the real."

Other fledge threes piped up that they, too, had had trouble with those maths. The hawk instructor sighed. "We don't want to install cheaters in all of you. It's bad enough needing implants to supplement biologic. Individual learning is much more desirable. Do you request cheaters?" That was a challenge. They all responded negatively, but Prufrax had a secret smile. She knew the subject. She just took delight in having the maths explained again. She could reinforce an already thorough understanding. Others not so well versed would benefit. She wasn't wasting time. She was in the pleasure of her weapon—the weapon she would be using against the Senexi.

"Zero-angle phase is the temporary reduction of the momenta of the real." Equations and plexes appeared before each student as the instructor went on. "Nested unreals can conflict if a barrier is placed between the participator princip and the assumption of the real. The effectiveness of the participator can be determined by a convenience model we call the angle of phase. Zero-angle phase is achieved by an opaque probability field according to modified Fourier of the separation of real waves. This can also be caused by the reflection of the beam—an effective counter to zero-angle phase, since the beam is always compoundable and the compound is always time-reversed. Here are the true gedanks—"

—Zero-angle phase. She's learning the Zap.

—She hates them a lot, doesn't she?

—The Senexi? They're Senexi.

—I think . . . eyes-open is the world of the Senexi. What does that mean?

—That we're prisoners. You were caught before me.

—Oh.

The news came as she was in recovery from the implant. Seed-ships had violated human space again, dropping cuckoos on thirty-five worlds. The worlds had been young colonies, and the cuckoos had wiped out all life, then tried to reseed with Senexi forms. The overs had reacted by sterilizing the planets' surfaces. No victory, loss to both sides. It was as if the Senexi were so malevolent they didn't care about success, only about destruction.

She hated them. She could imagine nothing worse.

Prufrax was twenty-three. In a year she would be qualified to hawk on a cruiser/raider. She would demonstrate her hatred.

Aryz felt himself slipping into endthought, the mind set that always preceded a branch ind's self-destruction. What was there for him to do? The fragment had survived, but at what cost, to what purpose? Nothing had been accomplished. The nebula had been lost, or he supposed it had. He would likely never know the actual outcome.

He felt a vague irritation at the lack of a spectrum of responses. Without a purpose, a branch ind was nothing more than excess plasm.

He looked in on the captive and the shapes, all hooked to the mandate, and wondered what he would do with them. How would humans react to the situation he was in? More vigorously, probably. They would fight on. They always had. Even without leaders, with no discernible purpose, even in defeat. What gave them such stamina? Were they superior, more deserving? If they were better, then was it right for the Senexi to oppose their triumph?

Aryz drew himself tall and rigid with confusion. He had studied them too long. They had truly infected him. But here at least was a hint of purpose. A question needed to be answered.

He made preparations. There were signs the brood mind's flux bind was not permanent, was in fact unwinding quite rapidly. When it emerged, Aryz would present it with a judgment, an answer.

He realized, none too clearly, that by Senexi standards he was now a raving lunatic.

He would hook himself into the mandate, improve the somewhat isolating interface he had used previously to search for selected answers. He, the captive, and the shapes would be immersed in human history together. They would be like young suckling on a Population I mother-animal—just the opposite of the Senexi process, where young fed nourishment and information into the brood mind.

The mandate would nourish, or poison. Or both.

—Did she love?
—What—you mean, did she receive?
—No, did she—we—I—give?
—I don't know what you mean.
—I wonder if *she* would know what I mean. . . .
Love, said the mandate, and the data proceeded.

Prufrax was twenty-nine. She had been assigned to a cruiser in a new program where superior but untested fighters were put into thick action with no preliminary.

The Cruiser was a million-ton raider, with a hawk contingent of fifty-three and eighty regular crew. She would be used in a secondwave attack, following the initial hardfought.

She was scared. That was good; fright improved basic biologic, if properly managed. The cruiser would make a raid into Senexi space and retaliate for past cuckoo-seeding programs. They would come up against thornships and seedships, probably.

The fighting was going to be fierce.

The raider made its final denial of the overness of the real and pipsqueezed into an arduous, nasty sponge space. It drew itself together again and emerged far above the galactic plane.

Prufrax sat in the hawks wardroom and looked at the simulated rotating snowball of stars. Red-coded numerals flashed along the borders of known Senexi territory, signifying where they had first come to power when the terrestrial sun had been a mist-wrapped youngster. A green arrow showed the position of the raider.

She drank sponge-space supplements with the others but felt isolated because of her firstness, her fear. Everyone seemed so calm. Most were fours or fives—on their fourth or fifth battle call. There were ten ones and an upper scatter of experienced hawks with nine to twenty-five battles behind them. There were no thirties. Thirties were rare in combat; the few that survived so many engagements were plucked off active and retired to PR service under the polinstructors. They often ended up in fibs, acting poorly, looking unhappy.

Still, when she had been more naive, Prufrax's heros had been a man-and-woman thirty team she had watched in fib after fib—Kumnax and Arol. They had been better actors than most.

Day in, day out, they drilled in their fightsuits. While the crew bustled, hawks were put through implant learning, what slang was already calling the Know, as opposed to the Tell, of classroom teaching. Getting background, just enough to tickle her curiosity, not enough to stimulate morbid interest.

—There it is again. Feel?

—I know it. Yes. The round one, part of eyes-open . . .

—Senexi?

—No, brother without name.

—Your . . . brother?

—No . . . I don't know.

Still, there were items of information she had never received before, items privileged only to the fighters, to assist them in their work. Older hawks talked about the past, when data had been freely available. Stories circulated in the wardroom about the Senexi, and she managed to piece together something of their origins and growth.

Senexi worlds, according to a twenty, had originally been large, cold masses of gas circling bright young suns nearly metal-free. Their gas-giant planets had orbited the suns at hundreds of millions of kilometers and had been dusted by the shrouds of neighboring dead stars; the essential elements carbon, nitrogen, silicon, and fluorine had gathered in sufficient quantities on some of the planets to allow Population II biology.

In cold ammonia seas, lipids had combined in complex chains. A primal kind of life had arisen and flourished. Across millions of years, early Senexi forms had evolved. Compared with evolution on Earth, the process at first had moved quite rapidly. The mechanisms of procreation and evolution had been complex in action, simple in chemistry.

There had been no competition between life forms of different genetic bases. On Earth, much time had been spent selecting between the plethora of possible ways to pass on genetic knowledge.

And among the early Senexi, outside of predation there had been no death. Death had come about much later, self-imposed for social reasons. Huge colonies of protoplasmic individuals had gradually resolved into the team-forms now familiar.

Soon information was transferred through the budding of branch inds; cultures quickly developed to protect the integrity of larvae, to allow them to regroup and form a new brood mind. Technologies had been limited to the rare heavy materials available, but the Senexi had expanded for a time with very little technology. They were well adapted to their environment, with few predators and no need to hunt, absorbing stray nutrients from the atmosphere and from layers of liquid ammonia. With perceptions attuned to the radio and microwave frequencies, they had before long turned groups of branch inds into radio telescope chains, piercing the heavy atmosphere and probing the universe in great detail, especially the very active center of the young galaxy. Huge jets of matter, streaming from other galaxies and emitting high-energy radiation, had provided laboratories for their vicarious observations. Physics was a primitive science to them.

Since little or no knowledge was lost in breeding cycles, cultural growth was rapid at times; since the dead weight of knowledge was often heavy, cultural growth often slowed to a crawl.

Using water as a building material, developing techniques that humans still understood imperfectly, they prepared for travel away from their birthworlds.

Prufrax wondered, as she listened to the older hawks, how humans had come to know all this. Had Senexi been captured and questioned? Was it all theory? Did anyone really know—anyone she could ask?

—She's weak.

—Why weak?

—Some knowledge is best for glovers to ignore. Some questions are best left to the supreme overs.

—Have you thought that in here, you can answer her questions, our questions?

—No. No. Learn about me—us—first.

In the hour before engagement, Prufrax tried to find a place alone. On the raider, this wasn't difficult. The ship's size was overwhelming for the number of hawks and crew aboard. There were many areas where she could put on an environs and walk or drift in silence, surrounded by the dark shapes of equipment wrapped in plexerv.

She pulled herself through the cold G-less tunnels, feeling slightly awed by the loneness, the quiet. One tunnel angled outboard, toward the hull of the cruiser. She hesitated, peering into its length with her environs beacon, when a beep warned her she was near another crew member. She was startled to think someone else might be as curious as she. She scooted expertly up the tunnel, spreading her arms and tucking her legs as she would in a fightsuit.

The tunnel was filled with a faint milky green mist, absorbing her environs beam. It couldn't be much more than a couple of hundred meters long, however, and it was quite straight. The signal beeped louder.

Ahead she could make out a dismantled weapons blister. That explained the fog: a plexerv aerosol diffused in the low pressure. Sitting in the blister was a man, his environs glowing a pale violet. He had deopaqued a section of the blister and was staring out at the stars. He swiveled as she approached and looked her over dispassionately. He seemed to be a hawk—he had fightform, tall, thin with brown hair above hull-white skin, large eyes with pupils so dark she might have been looking through his head into space beyond.

"Under," she said as their environs met and merged.

"Over. What are you doing here?"

"I was about to ask you the same."

"You should be getting ready for the fight," he admonished.

"I am. I need to be alone for a while."

"Yes." He turned back to the stars. "I used to do that, too."

"You don't fight now?"

He shook his head. "Retired. I'm a researcher."

She tried not to look impressed. Crossing rates was almost impossible. A bitalent was unusual in the service.

"What kind of research?" she asked.

"I'm here to correlate enemy finds."

"Won't find much of anything, after we're done with the zero phase."

It would have been polite for him to say, "Power to that," or offer some other encouragement. He said nothing.

"Why would you want to research them?"

"To fight an enemy properly, you have to know what they are. Ignorance is defeat."

"You research tactics?"

"Not exactly."

"What, then?"

"You'll be in tough hardfought this wake. Make you a proposition. You fight well, observe, come to me, and tell me what you see. Then I'll answer your questions."

"Brief you before my immediate overs?"

"I have the authority," he said. No one had ever lied to her; she didn't even suspect he would. "You're eager?"

"Very."

"You'll be doing what?"

"Engaging Senexi fighters, then hunting down branch inds and brood minds."

"How many fighters going in?"

"Twelve."

"Big target, eh?"

She nodded.

"While you're there, ask yourself—what are they fighting for? Understand?"

"I—"

"Ask, what are they fighting for. Just that. Then come back to me."

"What's your name?"

"Not important," he said. "Now go."

She returned to the prep center as the sponge-space warning tones began. Overhawks went among the fighters in the lineup, checking gear and giveaway body points for mental orientation. Prufrax submitted to the molded sensor mask being slipped over her face. "Ready!" the over-hawk said. "Hardfought!" He clapped her on the shoulder. "Good luck."

"Thank you, sir." She bent down and slid into her fightsuit. Along the launch line, eleven other hawks did the same. The overs and other crew left the chamber, and twelve red beams delineated the launch tube. The fightsuits automatically lifted and aligned on their individual beams. Fields swirled around them like silvery tissue in moving water, then settled and hardened into cold scintillating walls, pulsing as the launch energy built up.

The tactic came to her. The ship's sensors became part of her information net. She saw the Senexi thornship—twelve kilometers in diameter, cuckoos lacing its outer hull like maggots on red fruit, snakes waiting to take them on.

She was terrified and exultant, so worked up that her body temperature was climbing. The fightsuit adjusted her balance.

At the count of ten and nine, she switched from biologic to cyber. The implant—after absorbing much of her thought processes for weeks—became Prufrax.

For a time there seemed to be two of her. Biologic continued, and in that region she could even relax a bit, as if watching a fib.

With almost dreamlike slowness, in the electronic time of cyber, her fightsuit followed the beam. She saw the stars and oriented herself to the cruiser's beacon, using both for reference, plunging in the sword-flower formation to assault the thornship. The cuckoos retreated in the vast red hull like worms withdrawing into an apple. Then hundreds of tiny black pinpoints appeared in the quadrant closest to the sword flower.

Snakes shot out, each piloted by a Senexi branch ind. "Hardfought!" she told herself in biologic before that portion gave over completely to cyber.

Why were we flung out of dark
through ice and fire, a shower
of sparks? a puzzle;
Perhaps to build hell.

We strike here, there;
Set brief glows, fall through
and cross round again.

By our dimming, we see what
Beatitude we have.
In the circle, kindling
together, we form an
exhausted Empyrean.
We feel the rush of
igniting winds but still
grow dull and wan.

New rage flames, new light,
dropping like sun through muddy
ice and night and fall
Close, spinning blue and bright.

In time they, too,
Tire. Redden.
We join, compare pasts
cool in huddled paths,
turn gray.

And again.
We are a companion flow

of ash, in the slurry,
out and down.
We sleep.

Rivers form above and below.
Above, iron snakes twist,
clang and slice, chime,
helium eyes watching, seeing
Snowflake hawks,
signaling adamant muscles and
energy teeth. What hunger
compels our venom spit?

It flies, strikes the crystal
flight, making mist gray-green
with ammonia rain.

Sleeping we glide,
and to each side
unseen shores wait
with the moans of an
unseen tide.

—She wrote that. We. One of her—our—poems.
—Poem?
—A kind of fib, I think.
—I don't see what it says.
—Sure you do! She's talking hardfought.
—Do you understand it?
—Not all . . .

She lay back in the bunk, legs crossed, eyes closed, feeling the receding dominance of the implant—the overness of cyber—and the almost pleasant ache in her back. She had survived her first. The thornship had retired, severely damaged, its surface seared and scored so heavily it would never release cuckoos again.

It would become a hulk, a decoy. Out of action. *Satisfaction/out of action/Satisfaction . . .*

Still, with eight of the twelve fighters lost, she didn't quite feel the exuberance of the rhyme. The snakes had fought very well. Bravely, she might say. They lured, sacrificed, cooperated, demonstrating teamwork as fine as that in her own group. Strategy was what made the cruiser's raid successful. A superior approach, an excellent tactic. And perhaps even surprise, though the final analysis hadn't been posted yet.

Without those advantages, they might have all died.

She opened her eyes and stared at the pattern of blinking lights in the ceiling panel, lights with their secret codes that repeated every second, so that whenever she looked at them, the implant deep inside was debriefed, reinstructed. Only when she fought would she know what she was now seeing.

She returned to the tunnel as quickly as she was able. She floated up toward the blister and found him there, surrounded by packs of information from the last hardfought. She waited until he turned his attention to her.

"Well?" he said.

"I asked myself what they are fighting for. And I'm very angry."

"Why?"

"Because I don't know. I *can't* know. They're Senexi."

"Did they fight well?"

"We lost eight. Eight." She cleared her throat.

"Did they fight well?" he repeated, an edge in his voice.

"Better than I was ever told they could."

"Did they die?"

"Enough of them."

"How many did you kill?"

"I don't know." But she did. Eight.

"You killed eight," he said, pointing to the packs. "I'm analyzing the battle now."

"You're behind what we read, what gets posted?" she asked.

"Partly," he said. "You're a good hawk."

"I knew I would be," she said, her tone quiet, simple.

"Since they fought bravely—"

"How can Senexi be brave?" she asked sharply.

"Since," he repeated, "they fought bravely, why?"

"They want to live, to do their . . . work. Just like me."

"No," he said. She was confused, moving between extremes in her mind, first resisting, then giving in too much. "They're Senexi. They're not like us."

"What's your name?" she asked, dodging the issue.

"Clevo."

Her glory hadn't even begun yet, and already she was well into her fall.

Aryz made his connection and felt the brood mind's emergency cache of knowledge in the mandate grow up around him like ice crystals on glass. He stood in a static scene. The transition from living memory to human machine memory had resulted in either a coding of data or a reduction of detail; either way, the memory was cold, not dynamic. It would have to be compared, recorrelated, if that would ever be possible.

How much human data had had to be dumped to make space for this?

He cautiously advanced into the human memory, calling up topics almost at random.

He backed away from sociological data, trying to remain within physics and mathematics. There he could make conversions to fit his understanding without too much strain.

Then something unexpected happened. He felt the brush of another mind, a gentle inquiry from a source made even stranger by the hint of familiarity. It made what passed for a Senexi greeting, but not in the proper form, using what one branch ind of a team would radiate to a fellow; a gross breach, since it was obviously not from his team or even from his family. Aryz tried to withdraw. How was it possible for minds to meet in the mandate? As he retreated, he pushed into a broad region of incomprehensible data. It had none of the characteristics of the other human regions he had examined.

—This is for machines, the other said. —Not all cultural data are limited to biologic. You are in the area where programs and cyber designs are stored. They are really accessible only to a machine hooked into the mandate.

—What is your family? Aryz asked, the first step-question in the sequence Senexi used for urgent identity requests.

—I have no family. I am not a branch ind. No access to active brood minds. I have learned from the mandate.

—Then what are you?

—I don't know, exactly. Not unlike you.

It was the mind of the mutated shape, the one that had remained in the chamber, beseeching when he approached the transparent barrier.

—I must go now, the shape said. Aryz was alone again in the incomprehensible jumble. He moved slowly, carefully, into the Senexi sector, calling up subjects familiar to him. If he could encounter one shape, doubtless he could encounter the others—perhaps even the captive.

The idea was dreadful—and fascinating. So far as he knew, such intimacy between Senexi and human had never happened before. Yet there was something very Senexi-like in the method, as if branch inds attached to the brood mind were to brush mentalities while searching in the ageless memories.

The dread subsided. There was little worse that could happen to him, with his fellows dead, his brood mind in flux bind, his purpose uncertain.

What Aryz was feeling, for the first time, was a small measure of *freedom*.

The story of the original Prufrax continued.

In the early stages she visited Clevo with a barely concealed anger. His method was aggravating, his goals never precisely spelled out. What did he want with her, if anything?

And she with him? Their meetings were clandestine, though not precisely forbidden. She was a hawk one now with considerable personal liberty between exercises and engagements. There were no monitors in the closed-off reaches of the cruiser, and they could do whatever they wished. The two met in areas close to the ship's hull, usually in weapons blisters that could be opened to reveal the stars; there they talked.

Prufrax was not accustomed to prolonged conversation. Hawks were neither raised to be voluble, nor selected for their curiosity. Yet the exhawk Clevo talked a great deal and was the most curious person she had met, herself included, and she regarded herself as uncharacteristically curious.

Often he was infuriating, especially when he played the "leading game," as she called it. Leading her from one question to the next, like an instructor, but without the trappings or any clarity of purpose. "What do you think of your mother?"

"Does that matter?"

"Not to me."

"Then why ask?"

"Because you matter."

Prufrax shrugged. "She was a fine mother. She bore me with a well-chosen heritage. She raised me as a hawk candidate. She told me her stories."

"Any hawk I know would envy you for listening at Jay-ax's knee."

"I was hardly at her knee."

"A speech tactic."

"Yes, well, she was important to me."

"She was a preferred single?"

"Yes."

"So you have no father."

"She selected without reference to individuals."

"Then you are really not that much different from a Senexi."

She bristled and started to push away. "There! You insult me again."

"Not at all. I've been asking one question all this time, and you haven't even heard. How well do you know the enemy?"

"Well enough to destroy them." She couldn't believe that was the only question he'd been asking. His speech tactics were very odd.

"Yes, to win battles, perhaps. But who will win the war?"

"It'll be a long war," she said softly, floating a few meters from him. He rotated in the blister, blocking out a blurred string of stars. The cruiser was preparing to shift out of status geometry again. "They fight well."

"They fight with conviction. Do you believe them to be evil?"

"They destroy us."

"We destroy them."

"So the question," she said, smiling at her cleverness, "is who began to destroy?"

"Not at all," Clevo said. "I suspect there's no longer a clear answer to that. We are the new, they are the old. The old must be superseded."

"That's the only way we're different? They're old, we're not so old? I don't understand."

"Nor do I, entirely."

"Well, finally!"

"The Senexi," Clevo continued, unperturbed, "long ago needed only gas-giant planets like their homeworlds. They lived in peace for billions of years before our world was formed. But as they moved from star to star, they learned uses for other types of worlds. We were most interested in rocky Earth-like planets. Gradually we found uses for gas giants, too. By the time we met, each of us encroached on the other's territory. Their technology is so improbable, so unlike ours, that when we first encountered them we thought they must come from another geometry."

"Where did you learn all this?" Prufrax squinted at him suspiciously.

"I'm no longer a hawk," he said, "but I was too valuable just to discard. My experience was too broad, my abilities too useful. So I was placed in research. It seems a safe place for me. Little contact with my comrades." He looked directly at her. "We must try to know our enemy, at least a little."

"That's dangerous," Prufrax said, almost instinctively.

"Yes, it is. What you know, you cannot hate."

"We must hate," she said. "It makes us strong. Senexi hate."

"They might," he said. "But, sometime, wouldn't you like to . . . sit down and talk with one, after a battle? Talk with a fighter? Learn its tactic, how it bested you in one move, compare—"

"No!" Prufrax shoved off rapidly down the tube. "We're shifting now. We have to get ready."

—She's smart. She's leaving him. He's crazy.

—Why do you think that?

—He would stop the fight, end the Zap.

—But he was a hawk.

—And hawks became glovers, I guess. But glovers go wrong, too. Like you.

—?

—Did you know they used you? How you were used?

—That's all blurred now.

—She's doomed if she stays around him. Who's that?

—Someone is listening with us.

The next battle was bad enough to fall into the hellfought. Prufrax was in her fightsuit, legs drawn up as if about to kick off. The cruiser exited sponge space and plunged into combat before sponge space supplements could reach full effectiveness. She was dizzy, disoriented. The overhawks could only hope that a switch from biologic to cyber would cure the problem.

She didn't know what they were attacking. Tactic was flooding the implant, but she was only receiving the wash of that; she hadn't merged yet. She sensed that things were confused. That bothered her. Overs did not feel confusion.

The cruiser was taking damage. She could sense at least that, and she wanted to scream in frustration. Then she was ordered to merge with the implant. Biologic became cyber. She was in the Know.

The cruiser had reintegrated above a gas-giant planet. They were seventy-nine thousand kilometers from the upper atmosphere. The damage had come from ice mines—chunks of Senexi-treated water ice, altered to stay in sponge space until a human vessel integrated near by. Then they emerged, packed with momentum and all the residual instability of an unsuccessful return to status geometry. Unsuccessful for a ship, that is—very successful for a weapon.

The ice mines had given up the overness of the real within range of the cruiser and had blasted out whole sections of the hull. The launch lanes had not been damaged. The fighters lined up on their beams and were peppered out into space, spreading in the famous sword flower.

The planet was a cold nest. Over didn't know what the atmosphere contained, but Senexi activity had been high in the star system, concentrating on this world. Over had decided to take a chance. Fighters headed for the atmosphere. The cruiser began planting singularity eggs. The eggs went ahead of the fighters, great black grainy ovoids that seemed to leave a trail of shadow—the wake of a birthing disruption in status geometry that could turn a gas giant into a short-lived sun.

Their time was limited. The fighters would group on entry sleds and descend to the liquid water regions where Senexi commonly kept their upwelling power plants. The fighters would first destroy any plants, loop into the liquid ammonia regions to search for hidden cuckoos, then see what was so important about the world.

She and five other fighters mounted the sled. Growing closer, the hazy clear regions of the atmosphere sparkled with Senexi sensors. Spiderweb beams shot from the six sleds to down the sensors. Buffet began. Scream, heat, then a second flower from the sled at a depth of two hundred kilometers. The sled slowed and held station. It would be their only way back. The fightsuits couldn't pull out of such a large gravity well.

She descended deeper. The pale, bloated beacon of the red star was dropping below the second cloudtops, limning the strata in orange and purple. At the liquid ammonia level she was instructed to key in permanent memory of all she was seeing. She wasn't "seeing" much, but other sensors were recording a great deal, all of it duly processed in her implant. "There's life here," she told herself. Indigenous life. Just another example of Senexi disregard for basic decency: they were interfering with a world developing its own complex biology.

The temperature rose to ammonia vapor levels, then to liquid water. The pressure on the fightsuit was enormous, and she was draining her stores much more rapidly than expected. At this level the atmosphere was particularly thick with organics.

Senexi snakes rose from below, passed them in altitude, then doubled back to engage. Prufrax was designated the deep diver; the others from her sled would stay at this level in her defense. As she fell, another sled group moved in behind her to double the cover.

She searched for the characteristic radiation curve of an upwelling plant. At the lower boundary of the liquid water level, below which her suit could not safely descend, she found it.

The Senexi were tapping the gas giant's convection from greater depths than usual. Above the plant, almost indetectable, was another object with an uncharacteristic curve. They were separated by ten kilometers. The power plant was feeding its higher companion with tight energy beams.

She slowed. Two other fighters, disengaged from the brief skirmish above, took positions as backups a few dozen kilometers higher than she. Her implant searched for an appropriate tactic. She would avoid the zero-angle phase for the moment, go in for reconnaissance. She could feel sound pouring from the plant and its companion—rhythmic, not waste noise, but deliberate. And homing in on that sound were waves of large vermiform organisms, like chains of gas-filled sausage. They were dozens of meters long, two meters at their greatest thickness, shaped vaguely like the Senexi snake fighters. The vermiforms were native, and they were being lured into the uppermost floating structure. None were emerging. Her backups spread apart, descended, and drew up along her flanks.

She made her decision almost immediately. She could see a pattern in the approach of the natives. If she fell into the pattern, she might be able to enter the structure unnoticed.

—It's a grinder. She doesn't recognize it.

—What's a grinder?

—She should make the Zap! It's an ugly thing; Senexi use them all the time. Net a planet with grinders, like a cuckoo, but for larger operations.

The creatures were being passed through separator fields. Their organics fell from the bottom of the construct, raw material for new growth—Senexi growth. Their heavier elements were stored for later harvest.

With Prufrax in their midst, the vermiforms flew into the separator. The interior was hundreds of meters wide, lead-white walls with flat gray machinery floating in a dust haze, full of hollow noise, the distant bleats of vermiforms being slaughtered. Prufrax tried to retreat, but she was caught in a selector field. Her suit bucked and she was whirled violently, then thrown into a repository for examination. She had been screened from the separator; her plan to record, then destroy, the structure had been foiled by an automatic filter.

"Information sufficient." Command logic programmed into the implant before launch was now taking over. "Zero-angle phase both plant and adjunct." She was drifting in the repository, still slightly stunned. Something was fading. Cyber was hissing in and out; the over logic-commands were being scrambled. Her implant was malfunctioning and was returning control to biologic. The selector fields had played havoc with all cyber functions, down to the processors in her weapons.

Cautiously she examined the down systems one by one, determining what she could and could not do. This took as much as thirty seconds—an astronomical time on the implant's scale.

She still could use the phase weapon. If she was judicious and didn't waste her power, she could cut her way out of the repository, maneuver and work with her escorts to destroy both the plant and the separator. By the time they returned to the sleds, her implant might have rerouted itself and made sufficient repairs to handle defense. She had no way of knowing what was waiting for her if—when—she escaped, but that was the least of her concerns for the moment.

She tightened the setting of the phase beam and swung her fight-suit around, knocking a cluster of junk ice and silty phosphorescent dust. She activated the beam. When she had a hole large enough to pass through, she edged the suit forward, beamed through more walls and obstacles, and kicked herself out of the repository into free fall. She swiveled and laid down a pattern of wide-angle beams, at the same time relaying a message on her situation to the escorts.

The escorts were not in sight. The separator was beginning to break up, spraying debris through the almost opaque atmosphere. The rhythmic sound ceased, and the crowds of vermiforms began to disperse.

She stopped her fall and thrust herself several kilometers higher—directly ito a formation of Senexi snakes. She had barely enough power to reach the sled, much less fight and turn her beams on the upwelling plant.

Her cyber was still down.

The sled signal was weak. She had no time to calculate its direction from the inertial guidance cyber. Besides, all cyber was unreliable after passing through the separator.

Why do they fight so well? Clevo's question clogged her thoughts. Cursing, she tried to blank and keep all her faculties available for running the fightsuit. *When evenly matched, you cannot win against your enemy unless you understand them. And if you truly understand, why are you fighting and not talking?* Clevo had never told her that—not in so many words. But it was part of a string of logic all her own.

Be more than an automaton with a narrow range of choices. Never underestimate the enemy. Those were old Grounds dicta, not entirely lost in the new training, but only emphasized by Clevo.

If they fight as well as you, perhaps in some ways they fightthink like you do. Use that.

Isolated, with her power draining rapidly, she had no choice. They might disregard her if she posed no danger. She cut her thrust and went into a diving spin. Clearly she was on her way to a high-pressure grave. They would sense her power levels, perhaps even pick up the lack of field activity if she let her shields drop. She dropped the shields. If they let her fall and didn't try to complete the kill—if they concentrated on active fighters above—she had enough power to drop into the water vapor regions, far below the plant, and silently ride a thermal into range. With luck, she could get close enough to lay a web of zero-angle phase and take out the plant.

She had minutes in which to agonize over her plan. Falling, buffeted by winds that could knock her kilometers out of range, she spun like a vagrant flake of snow.

She couldn't even expend the energy to learn if they were scanning her, checking out her potential.

Perhaps she underestimated them. Perhaps they would be that much more thorough and take her out just to be sure. Perhaps they had unwritten rules of conduct like the ones she was using, taking hunches into account. Hunches were discouraged in Grounds training—much less reliable than cyber.

She fell. Temperature increased. Pressure on her suit began to constrict her air supply. She used fighter trancing to cut back on her breathing.

Fell.

And broke the trance. Pushed through the dense smoke of exhaustion. Planned the beam web. Counted her reserves. Nudged into an updraft beneath the plant. The thermal carried her, a silent piece of paper in a storm, drifting back and forth beneath the objective. The huge field intakes pulsed above, lightning outlining their invisible extension. She held back on the beam.

Nearly faded out. Her suit interior was almost unbearably hot.

She was only vaguely aware of laying down the pattern. The beams vanished in the murk. The thermal pushed her through a layer of haze, and she saw the plant, riding high above clear-atmosphere turbulence. The zero-angle phase had pushed through the field intakes, into their source nodes and the plant body, surrounding it with bright blue Tcherenkov. First the surface began to break up, then the middle layers, and finally key supports. Chunks vibrated away with the internal fury of their molecular, then atomic, then particle disruption. Paraphrasing Grounds description of beam action, the plant became less and less convinced of its reality. "Matter dreams," an instructor had said a decade before. "Dreams it is real, maintains the dream by shifting rules with constant results. Disturb the dreams, the shifting of the rules results in inconstant results. Things cannot hold."

She slid away from the updraft, found another, wondered idly how far she would be lifted. Curiosity at the last. Let's just see, she told herself; a final experiment.

Now she was cold. The implant was flickering, showing signs of reorganization. She didn't use it. No sense expanding the amount of time until death. No sense at all.

The sled, maneuvered by one remaining fighter, glided up beneath her almost unnoticed.

Aryz waited in the stillness of a Senexi memory, his thinking temporarily reduced to a faint susurrus. What he waited for was not clear.

—Come.

The form of address was wrong, but he recognized the voice. His thoughts stirred, and he followed the nebulous presence out of Senexi territory.

—Know your enemy.

Prufrax . . . the name of one of the human shapes sent out against their own kind. He could sense her presence in the mandate, locked into a memory store. He touched on the store and caught the essentials—the grinder, the updraft plant, the fight from Prufrax's viewpoint.

—Know how your enemy knows you.

He sensed a second presence, similar to that of Prufrax. It took him some time to realize that the human captive was another form of the shape, a reproduction of the . . .

Both were reproductions of the female whose image was in the memory store. Aryz was not impressed by threes—Senexi mysticism, what had ever existed of it, had been preoccupied with fives and sixes—but the coincidence was striking.

—Know how your enemy sees you.

He saw the grinder processing organics—the vermiform natives—in preparation for a widespread seeding of deuterium gatherers. The operation had evidently been conducted for some time; the vermiform populations were greatly reduced from their usual numbers. Vermiforms were a common type-species on gas giants of the sort depicted. The mutated shape nudged him into a particular channel of the memory, that which carried the original Prufrax's emotions. She had reacted with *disgust* to the Senexi procedure. It was a reaction not unlike what Aryz might feel when coming across something forbidden in Senexi behavior. Yet eradication was perfectly natural, analogous to the human cleansing of *food* before *eating*.

—It's in the memory. The vermiforms are intelligent. They have their own kind of civilization. Human action on this world prevented their complete extinction by the Senexi.

—So what matter they were *intelligent?* Aryz responded. They did not behave or think like Senexi, or like any species Senexi find compatible. They were therefore not desirable. Like humans.

—You would make humans extinct?

—We would protect ourselves from them.

—Who damages the other most?

Aryz didn't respond. The line of questioning was incomprehensible. Instead he flowed into the memory of Prufrax, propelled by another aspect of complete freedom, confusion.

The implant was replaced. Prufrax's damaged limbs and skin were repaired or regenerated quickly, and within four wakes, under intense treatment usually reserved only for overs, she regained all her reflexes and speed. She requested liberty of the cruiser while it returned for repairs. Her request was granted.

She first sought Clevo in the designated research area. He wasn't there, but a message was, passed on to her by a smiling young crew member. She read it quickly:

"You're free and out of action. Study for a while, then come find me. The old place hasn't been damaged. It's less private, but still good. Study! I've marked highlights."

She frowned at the message, then handed it to the crew member, who duly erased it and returned to his duties. She wanted to talk with Clevo, not study.

But she followed his instructions. She searched out highlighted entries in the ship's memory store. It was not nearly as dull as she had expected. In fact, by following the highlights, she felt she was learning more about Clevo and about the questions he asked.

Old literature was not nearly as graphic as fibs, but it was different enough to involve her for a time. She tried to create imitations of what she read, but erased them. Nonfib stories were harder than she suspected. She read about punishment, duty; she read about places called heaven and hell, from a writer who had died tens of thousands of years before. With ed supplement guidance, she was able to comprehend most of what she read. Plugging the store into her implant, she was able to absorb hundreds of volumes in an hour.

Some of the stores were losing definition. They hadn't been used in decades, perhaps centuries.

Halfway through, she grew impatient. She left the research area. Operating on another hunch, she didn't go to the blister as directed, but straight to memory central, two decks inboard the research area. She saw Clevo there, plugged into a data pillar, deep in some aspect of ship history. He noticed her approach, unplugged, and swiveled on his chair. "Congratulations," he said, smiling at her.

"Hardfought," she acknowledged, smiling.

"Better than that, perhaps," he said.

She looked at him quizzically. "What do you mean, better?"

"I've been doing some illicit tapping on over channels."

"So?"

—He *is dangerous!*

"For what?"

"You may have a valuable genetic assortment. Overs think you behaved remarkably well under impossible conditions."

"Did I?"

He nodded. "Your type may be preserved."

"Which means?"

"There's a program being planned. They want to take the best fighters and reproduce them—clone them—to make uniform top-grade squadrons. It was rumored in my time—you haven't heard?"

She shook her head.

"It's not new. It's been done, off and on, for tens of thousands of years. This time they believe they can make it work."

"You were a fighter, once," she said. "Did they preserve your type?"

Clevo nodded. "I had something that interested them, but not, I think, as a fighter."

Prufrax looked down at her stubby-fingered hands. "It was grim," she said. "You know what we found?"

"An extermination plant."

"You want me to understand them better. Well, I can't. I refuse. How could they do such things?" She looked disgusted and answered her own question. "Because they're Senexi."

"Humans," Clevo said, "have done much the same, sometimes worse."

"No!"

—No!

"Yes," he said firmly. He sighed. "We've wiped Senexi worlds, and we've even wiped worlds with intelligent species like our own. Nobody is innocent. Not in this universe."

"We were never taught that."

"It wouldn't have made you a better hawk. But it might make a better human of you to know. Greater depth of character. Do you want to be more aware?"

"You mean, study more?"

He nodded.

"What makes you think *you* can teach me?"

"Because you thought about what I asked you. About how Senexi thought. And you survived where some other hawk might not have. The overs think it's in your genes. It might be. But it's also in your head."

"Why not tell the overs?"

"I have," he said. He shrugged.

"They wouldn't want me to learn from you?"

"I don't know," Clevo said. "I suppose they're aware you're talking to me. They could stop it if they wanted."

"And if I learn from you?"

"Not from me, actually. From the past. From history, what other people have thought. I'm really not any more capable than you . . . but I know history, small portions of it. I won't teach you so much as guide."

"I did use your questions," Prufrax said. "But will I ever need to use them—think that way—again?"

Clevo nodded. "Of course."

—You're quiet.

—She's giving in to him.

—She gave in a long time ago.

—She should be afraid.

—Were you—we—ever really afraid of a challenge?

—No.

—Not Senexi, not forbidden knowledge.

Clevo first led her through the history of past wars, judging that was appropriate considering her occupation. She was attentive enough, though her mind wandered; sometimes he was didactic, but she found she didn't mind that much.

She saw that in all wars, the first stage was to dehumanize the enemy, reduce the enemy to a lower level so that he might be killed without compunction. When the enemy was not human to begin with, the task was easier. As wars progressed, this tactic frequently led to an underestimation of the enemy, with disastrous consequences. "We aren't exactly underestimating the Senexi," Clevo said. "The overs are too smart for that. But we refuse to understand them, and that could make the war last indefinitely."

"Then why don't the overs see that?"

"Because we're being locked into a pattern. We've been fighting for so long, we've begun to lose ourselves. And it's getting worse." He assumed his didactic tone, and she knew he was reciting something he'd formulated years before and repeated to himself a thousand times. "There is no war so important that, to win it, we must destroy our minds."

She didn't agree with that; losing the war with the Senexi would mean extinction, as she understood things.

Most often they met in the single unused weapons blister that had not been damaged. They met when the ship was basking in the real between sponge-space jaunts. He brought memory stores with him in portable modules, and they read, listened, experienced together. She never placed a great deal of importance in the things she learned; her interest was focused on Clevo. Still, she learned.

The rest of her time she spent training. She was aware of a growing isolation from the hawks, which she attributed to her uncertain rank status. Was her genotype going to be preserved or not? The decision hadn't been made. The more she learned, the less she wanted to be singled out for honor. Attracting that sort of attention might be dangerous, she thought. Dangerous to whom, or what, she could not say.

Clevo showed her how hero images had been used to indoctrinate birds and hawks in a standard of behavior that was ideal, not realistic.

The results were not always good; some tragic blunders had been made by fighters trying to be more than anyone possibly could or refusing to be flexible.

The war was certainly not a fib. Yet more and more the overs seemed to be treating it as one. Unable to bring about strategic victories against the Senexi, the overs had settled in for a long war of attrition and were apparently bent on adapting all human societies to the effort.

"There are overs we never hear of, who make decisions that shape our entire lives. Soon they'll determine whether or not we're even born, if they don't already."

"That sounds paranoid," she said, trying out a new word and concept she had only recently learned.

"Maybe so."

"Besides, it's been like that for ages—not knowing all our overs."

"But it's getting worse," Clevo said. He showed her the projections he had made. In time, if trends continued unchanged, fighters and all other combatants would be treated more and more mechanically, until they became the machines the overs wished them to be.

—No.

—Quiet. How does he feel toward her?

It was inevitable that as she learned under his tutelage, he began to feel responsible for her changes. She was an excellent fighter. He could never be sure that what he was doing might reduce her effectiveness. And yet he had fought well—despite similar changes—until his billet switch. It had been the overs who had decided he would be more effective, less disruptive, elsewhere.

Bitterness over that decision was part of his motive. The overs had done a foolish thing, putting a fighter into research. Fighters were tenacious. If the truth was to be hidden, then fighters were the ones likely to ferret it out. And pass it on. There was a code among fighters, seldom revealed to their immediate overs, much less to the supreme overs parsecs distant in their strategospheres. What one fighter learned that could be of help to another had to be passed on, even under penalty. Clevo was simply following that unwritten rule.

Passing on the fact that, at one time, things had been different. That war changed people, governments, societies, and that societies could effect an enormous change on their constituents, especially now—change in their lives, their thinking. Things could become even more structured. Freedom of fight was a drug, an illusion—

—No!

used to perpetuate a state of hatred.

"Then why do they keep all the data in stores?" she asked. "I mean, you study the data, everything becomes obvious."

"There are still important people who think we may want to find our way back someday. They're afraid we'll lose our roots, but—" His face suddenly became peaceful. She reached out to touch him, and he jerked slightly, turning toward her in the blister. "What is it?" she asked.

"It's not organized. We're going to lose the information. Ship overs are going to restrict access more and more. Eventually it'll decay, like some already has in these stores. I've been planning for some time to put it all in a single unit—"

—*He* built the mandate!

"and have the overs place one on every ship, with researchers to tend it. Formalize the loose scheme still in effect, but dying. Right now I'm working on the fringes. At least I'm allowed to work. But soon I'll have enough evidence that they won't be able to argue. Evidence of what happens to societies that try to obscure their histories. They go quite mad. The overs are still rational enough to listen; maybe I'll push it through." He looked out the transparent blister. The stars were smudging to one side as the cruiser began probing for entrances to sponge space. "We'd better get back."

"Where are you going to be when we return? We'll all be transferred."

"That's some time removed. Why do you want to know?"

"I'd like to learn more."

He smiled. "That's not your only reason."

"I don't need someone to tell me what my reasons are," she said testily.

"We're so reluctant," he said. She looked at him sharply, irritated and puzzled. "I mean," he continued, "we're hawks. Comrades. Hawks couple like *that*." He snapped his fingers. "But you and I sneak around it all the time."

Prufrax kept her face blank.

"Aren't you receptive toward me?" he asked, his tone almost teasing.

"It's just that that's not all," she said, her tone softening.

"Indeed," he said in a barely audible whisper.

In the distance they heard the alarms.

—It was never any different.

—What?

—Things were never any different before me.

—Don't be silly. It's all here.

—If Clevo made the mandate, then he put it here. It isn't true.

—Why are you upset?

—I don't like hearing that everything I believe is a . . . fib.

—I've never known the difference, I suppose. Eyes-open was never all that real to me. This isn't real, you aren't . . . this is eyes-shut.

So why be upset? You and I . . . we aren't even whole people. I feel you. You wish the Zap, you fight, not much else. I'm just a shadow, even compared to you. But she is whole. She loves him. She's less a victim than either of us. So something has to have changed.

—You're saying things have gotten worse.

—If the mandate is a lie, that's all I am. You refuse to accept. I *have* to accept, or I'm even less than a shadow.

—I don't refuse to accept. It's just hard.

—You started it. You thought about love.

—You did!

—Do you know what love is?

—Reception.

They first made love in the weapons blister. It came as no surprise; if anything, they approached it so cautiously they were clumsy. She had become more and more receptive, and he had dropped his guard. It had been quick, almost frantic, far from the orchestrated and drawn-out ballet the hawks prided themselves for. There was no pretense. No need to play the roles of artists interacting. They were depending on each other. The pleasure they exchanged was nothing compared to the emotions involved.

"We're not very good with each other," Prufrax said.

Clevo shrugged. "That's because we're shy."

"Shy?"

He explained. In the past—at various times in the past, because such differences had come and gone many times—making love had been more than a physical exchange or even an expression of comradeship. It had been the acknowledgment of a bond between people.

She listened, half-believing. Like everything else she had heard, that kind of love seemed strange, distasteful. What if one hawk was lost, and the other continued to love? It interfered with the hard-fought, certainly. But she was also fascinated. Shyness—the fear of one's presentation to another. The hesitation to present truth, or the inward confusion of truth at the awareness that another might be important, more important than one thought possible.

Complex emotion was not encouraged either at the Grounds or among hawks on station. Complex emotion degraded complex performance. The simple and direct was desirable.

"But all we seem to do is talk—until now," Prufrax said, holding his hand and examining his fingers one by one. They were very little different from her own, though extended a bit from hawk fingers to give greater versatility with key instruction.

"Talking is the most human thing we can do."

She laughed. "I know what you are," she said, moving up until her eyes were even with his chest. "You're an instructor at heart. You make love by telling." She felt peculiar, almost afraid, and looked up at his face. "Not that I don't enjoy your lovemaking, like this. Physical."

"You receive well," he said. "Both ways."

"What we're saying," she whispered, "is not truth-speaking. It's amenity." She turned into the stroke of his hand through her hair. "Amenity is supposed to be decadent. That fellow who wrote about heaven and hell. He would call it a sin."

"Amenity is the recognition that somebody may see or feel differently than you do. It's the recognition of individuals. You and I, we're part of the end of all that."

"Even if you convince the overs?"

He nodded. "They want to repeat success without risk. New individuals are risky, so they duplicate past success. There will be more and more people, fewer individuals. More of you and me, less of others. The fewer individuals, the fewer stories to tell. The less history. We're part of the death of history."

She floated next to him, trying to blank her mind as she had done before, to drive out the nagging awareness that he was right. She thought she understood the social structure around her. Things seemed new. She said as much.

"It's a path we're taking," Clevo said. "Not a place we're at."

—It's a place *we're* at. How different are *we*?

—But there's so much history in here. How can it be over for us?

—I've been thinking. Do we know the last event recorded in the mandate?

—Don't, we're drifting from Prufrax now. . . .

Aryz felt himself drifting with them. They swept over countless millennia, then swept back the other way. And it became evident that as much change had been wrapped in one year of the distant past as in a thousand years of the closing entries in the mandate. Clevo's voice seemed to follow them, though they were far from his period, far from Prufrax's record.

"Tyranny is the death of history. We fought the Senexi until we became like them. No change, youth at an end, old age coming upon us. There is no important change, merely elaborations in the pattern."

—How many times have we been here, then? How many times have we died?

Aryz wasn't sure, now. *Was* this the first time humans had been captured? Had he been told everything by the brood mind? Did the Senexi have no *history*, whatever that was—

The accumulated lives of living, thinking beings. Their actions, thoughts, passions, hopes.

The mandate answered even his confused, nonhuman requests. He could understand action, thought, but not passion or hope. Perhaps without those there was no *history*.

—You have no history, the mutated shape told him. There have been millions like you, even millions like the brood mind. What is the last event recorded in the brood mind that is not duplicated a thousand times over, so close they can be melded together for convenience?

—How do you understand that—because we made you between human and Senexi?

—Not only that.

The requests of the twin captives and shape were moving them back once more into the past, through the dim gray millennia of repeating ages. History began to manifest again, differences in the record.

On the way back to Mercior, four skirmishes were fought. Prufrax did well in each. She carried something special with her, a thought she didn't even tell Clevo, and she carried the same thought with her through their last days at the Grounds.

Taking advantage of hawk liberty, she opted for a posthardfought residence just outside the Grounds, in the relatively uncrowded Daughter of Cities zone. She wouldn't be returning to fight until several issues had been decided—her status most important among them.

Clevo began making his appeal to the middle overs. He was given Grounds duty to finish his proposals. They could stay together for the time being.

The residence was sixteen square meters in area, not elegant—*natural*, as rentOpts described it.

On the last day she lay in the crook of Clevo's arm. They had done a few hours of nature sleep. He hadn't come out yet, and she looked up at his face, reached up with a hand to feel his arm.

It was different from the arms of others she had been receptive toward. It was unique. The thought amused her. There had never been a reception like theirs. This was the beginning. And if both were to be duplicated, this love, this reception, would be repeated an infinite number of times. Clevo meeting Prufrax, teaching her, opening her eyes.

Somehow, even though repetition contributed to the death of history, she was pleased. This was the secret thought she carried into fight. Each time she would survive, wherever she was, however many duplications down the line. She would receive Clevo, and he would teach her. If not now—if one or the other died—then in the future. The death of history might be a good thing. Love could go on forever.

She had lost even a rudimentary apprehension of death, even with present pleasure to live for. Her functions had sharpened. She would please him by doing all the things he could not. And if he was to enter that state she frequently found him in, that state of introspection, of reliving his own battles and of envying her activity, then that wasn't bad. All they did to each other was good.

—*Was* good

—*Was*

She slipped from his arm and left the narrow sleeping quarter, pushing through the smoke-colored air curtain to the lounge. Two hawks and an over she had never seen before were sitting there. They looked up at her.

"Under," Prufrax said.

"Over," the woman returned. She was dressed in tan and green, Grounds colors, not ship.

"May I assist?"

"Yes."

"My duty, then?"

The over beckoned her closer. "You have been receiving a researcher."

"Yes," Prufrax said. The meetings could not have been a secret on the ship, and certainly not their quartering near the Grounds. "Has that been against duty?"

"No." The over eyed Prufrax sharply, observing her perfected fightform, the easy grace with which she stood, naked, in the middle of the small compartment. "But a decision has been reached. Your status is decided now."

She felt a shiver.

"Prufrax," said the elder hawk. She recognized him from fibs, and his companion: Kumnax and Arol. Once her heroes. "You have been accorded an honor, just as your partner has. You have a valuable genetic assortment—"

She barely heard the rest. They told her she would return to fight, until they deemed she had had enough experience and background to be brought into the polinstruc division. Then her fighting would be over. She would serve better as an example, a hero.

Heroes never partnered out of function. Hawk heroes could not even partner with exhawks.

Clevo emerged from the air curtain. "Duty," the over said. "The residence is disbanded. Both of you will have separate quarters, separate duties."

They left. Prufrax held out her hand, but Clevo didn't take it. "No use," he said.

Suddenly she was filled with anger. "You'll give it up? Did I expect too much? *How strongly?*"

"Perhaps even more strongly than you," he said. "I knew the order was coming down. And still I didn't leave. That may hurt my chances with the supreme overs."

"Then at least I'm worth more than your breeding history?"

"Now you are history. History the way they make it."

"I feel like I'm dying," she said, amazement in her voice. "What is that, Clevo? What did you do to me?"

"I'm in pain, too," he said.

"You're hurt?"

"I'm confused."

"I don't believe that," she said, her anger rising again. "You knew, and you didn't do anything?"

"That would have been counter to duty. We'll be worse off if we fight it."

"So what good is your great, exalted history?"

"History is what you have," Clevo said. "I only record."

—Why did they separate them?

—I don't know. You didn't like him, anyway.

—Yes, but now . . .

—I don't understand.

—We don't. Look what happens to her. They took what was best out of her. Prufrax

went into battle eighteen more times before dying as heroes often do, dying in the midst of what she did best. The question of what made her better before the separation—for she definitely was not as fine a fighter after—has not been settled. Answers fall into an extinct classification of knowledge, and there are few left to interpret, none accessible to this device.

—So she went out and fought and died. They never even made fibs about her. This killed her?

—I don't think so. She fought well enough. She died like other hawks died.

—And she might have lived otherwise.

—How can I know that, any more than you?

—They—we—met again, you know. I met a Clevo once, on my ship. They didn't let me stay with him long.

—How did you react to him?

—There was so little time, I don't know.

—Let's ask. . . .

In thousands of duty stations, it was inevitable that some of Prufrax's visions would come true, that they should meet now and then. Clevos were numerous, as were Prufraxes. Every ship

carried complements of several of each. Though Prufrax was never quite as successful as the original, she was a fine type. She—

—She was never quite as successful. They took away her edge. They didn't even know it!

—They must have known.

—Then they didn't want to win!

—We don't know that. Maybe there were more important considerations.

—Yes, like killing history.

Aryz shuddered in his warming body, dizzy as if about to bud, then regained control. He had been pulled from the mandate, called to his own duty.

He examined the shapes and the human captive. There was something different about them. How long had they been immersed in the mandate? He checked quickly, frantically, before answering the call. The reconstructed Mam had malfunctioned. None of them had been nourished. They were thin, pale, cooling.

Even the bloated mutant shape was dying; lost, like the others, in the mandate.

He turned his attention away. Everything was confusion. Was he human or Senexi now? Had he fallen so low as to understand them? He went to the origin of the call, the ruins of the temporary brood chamber. The corridors were caked with ammonia ice, burning his pod as he slipped over them. The brood mind had come out of flux bind. The emergency support systems hadn't worked well; the brood mind was damaged.

"Where have you been?" it asked.

"I assumed I would not be needed until your return from the flux bind."

"You have not been watching!"

"Was there any need? We are so advanced in time, all our actions are obsolete. The nebula is collapsed, the issue is decided."

"We do not know that. We are being pursued."

Aryz turned to the sensor wall—what was left of it—and saw that they were, indeed, being pursued. He had been lax.

"It is not your fault," the brood mind said. "You have been set a task that tainted you and ruined your function. You will dissipate."

Aryz hesitated. He had become so different, so tainted, that he actually *hesitated* at a direct command from the brood mind. But it was damaged. Without him, without what he had learned, what could it do? It wasn't reasoning correctly.

"There are facts you must know, important facts—"

Aryz felt a wave of revulsion, uncomprehending fear, and something not unlike human anger radiate from the brood mind. Whatever he had learned and however he had changed, he could not withstand that wave.

Willingly, and yet against his will—it didn't matter—he felt himself liquefying. His pod slumped beneath him, and he fell over, landing on a pool of frozen ammonia. It burned, but he did not attempt to lift himself. Before he ended, he saw with surprising clarity what it was to be a branch ind, or a brood mind, or a human. Such a valuable insight, and it leaked out of his permea and froze on the ammonia.

The brood mind regained what control it could of the fragment. But there were no defenses worthy of the name. Calm, preparing for its own dissipation, it waited for the pursuit to conclude.

The Mam set off an alarm. The interface with the mandate was severed. Weak, barely able to crawl, the humans looked at each other in horror and slid to opposite corners of the chamber.

They were confused: which of them was the captive, which the decoy shape? It didn't seem important. They were both bone-thin, filthy with their own excrement. They turned with one motion to stare at the bloated mutant. It sat in its corner, tiny head incongruous on the huge thorax, tiny arms and legs barely functional even when healthy. It smiled wanly at them.

"We felt you," one of the Prufraxes said. "You were with us in there." Her voice was a soft croak.

"That was my place," it replied. "My only place."

"What function, what name?"

"I'm . . . I know that. I'm a researcher. In there, I knew myself in there."

They squinted at the shape. The head. Something familiar, even now. "You're a Clevo . . ."

There was noise all around them, cutting off the shape's weak words. As they watched, their chamber was sectioned like an orange, and the wedges peeled open. The illumination ceased. Cold enveloped them.

A naked human female, surrounded by tiny versions of herself, like an angel circled by fairy kin, floated into the chamber. She was thin as a snake. She wore nothing but silver rings on her wrists and a thin torque around her waist. She glowed blue-green in the dark.

The two Prufraxes moved their lips weakly but made no sound in the near vacuum. *Who are you?*

She surveyed them without expression, then held out her arms as if to fly. She wore no gloves, but she was of their type.

As she had done countless times before on finding such Senexi experiments—though this seemed older than most—she lifted one arm higher. The blue-green intensified, spread in waves to the mangled walls, surrounded the freezing, dying shapes. Perfect, angelic, she left the debris behind to cast its fitful glow and fade.

They destroyed every portion of the fragment but one. They left the mandate behind unharmed.

Then they continued, millions of them thick like mist, working the spaces between the stars, their only master the overness of the real.

They needed no other masters. They would never malfunction.

The mandate drifted in the dark and cold, its memory going on, but its only life the rapidly fading tracks where minds had once passed through it. The trails writhed briefly, almost as if alive, but only following the quantum rules of diminished energy states. Briefly, a small memory was illuminated.

Prufrax's last poem, explained the mandate reflexively.

> How the fires grow! Peace passes
> All memory lost.
> Somehow we always miss that single door,
> Dooming ourselves to circle.
>
> Ashes to stars, lies to souls,
> Let's spin 'round the sinks and holes.
>
> Kill the good, eat the young.
> Forever and more
> You and I are never done.

The track faded into nothing. Around the mandate, the universe grew old very quickly.

THE PEACEMAKER

by GARDNER DOZOIS

Gardner Dozois's Nebula-Award-winning short story, "The Peacemaker" was purchased by Shawna McCarthy and published in the August 1983 issue of *Asimov's*. Two and a half years later, Gardner Dozois became the editor of the magazine, and he has held that position ever since. In addition to his work at the *Asimov's*, he edits the highly respected Years' Best Science Fiction Anthology Series. He has been awarded seven Hugos for Best Editor, and another Nebula Award for his short story "Morning Child."

Some of his other major publications are *Strangers, Slow Dancing Through Time*, and *The Fiction of James Tiptree, Jr.* He lives in Philadelphia, Pennsylvania, with his wife, the author Susan Casper.

Roy had dreamed of the sea, as he often did. When he woke up that morning, the wind was sighing through the trees outside with a sound like the restless murmuring of surf, and for a moment he thought that he was home, back in the tidy brick house by the beach, with everything that had happened undone, and hope opened hotly inside him, like a wound.

"Mom?" he said. He sat up, straightening his legs, expecting his feet to touch the warm mass that was his dog Toby. Toby always slept curled at the foot of his bed, but already everything was breaking up and changing, slipping away, and he blinked through sleep-gummed eyes at the thin blue light coming in through the attic window, felt the hardness of the old Army cot under him, and realized that he wasn't home, that there was no home anymore, that for him there could never be a home again.

He pushed the blankets aside and stood up. It was bitterly cold in the big attic room—winter was dying hard, the most terrible winter he could remember—and the rough wood planking burned his feet like ice, but he couldn't stay in bed anymore, not now.

None of the other kids were awake yet; he threaded his way through the other cots—accidently bumping against one of them so that its occupant tossed and moaned and began to snore in a higher register—and groped through cavernous shadows to the single high window. He was just tall enough to reach it, if he stood on tiptoe. He forced the window open, the old wood of its frame groaning in protest, plaster dust puffing, and shivered as the cold dawn wind poured inward, hitting him in the face, tugging with ghostly fingers at his hair, sweeping past him to rush through the rest of the stuffy attic like a restless child set free to play.

The wind smelled of pine resin and wet earth, not of salt flats and tides, and the bird-sound that rode in on that wind was the burbling of wrens and the squawking of bluejays, not the raucous shrieking of seagulls . . . but even so, as he braced his elbows against the window frame and strained up to look out, his mind still full of the broken fragments of dreams, he half-expected to see the ocean below, stretched out to the horizon, sending patient wavelets to lap against the side of the house. Instead he saw the nearby trees holding silhouetted arms up against the graying sky, the barn and the farmyard, all still lost in shadow, the surrounding fields, the weathered macadam line of the road, the forested hills rolling away into distance. Silver mist lay in pockets of low ground, retreated in wraithlike streamers up along the ridges.

Not yet. The sea had not chased him here—yet.

Somewhere out there to the east, still invisible, were the mountains, and just beyond those mountains was the sea that he had dreamed of, lapping quietly at the dusty Pennsylvania hill towns, coal towns, that were now, suddenly, seaports. There the Atlantic waited, held at bay, momentarily at least, by the humpbacked wall of the Appalachians, still perhaps forty miles from here, although closer now by leagues of swallowed land and drowned cities than it had been only three years before.

He had been down by the seawall that long-ago morning, playing some forgotten game, watching the waves move in slow oily swells, like some heavy, dull metal in liquid form, watching the tide come in . . . and come in . . . and come *in* . . . He had been excited at first, as the sea crept in, way above the high-tide line, higher than he had ever seen it before, and then, as the sea swallowed the beach entirely and began to lap patiently against the base of the seawall, he had become uneasy, and *then*, as the sea continued to rise up toward the top of the seawall itself, he had begun to be afraid. . . . The sea had just kept coming in, rising slowly and inexorably, swallowing the land at a slow walking pace, never stopping, always coming *in*, always rising higher. . . . By the time the sea had swallowed the top of the seawall and begun to creep up the short grassy slope toward his house, sending glassy fingers probing almost to his feet, he had started to scream, and as the first thin sheet of water rippled up to soak his sneakers, he had whirled and run frantically up the slope, screaming hysterically for his parents, and the sea had followed patiently at his heels. . . .

A "marine transgression," the scientists called it. Ordinary people called it, inevitably, the Flood. Whatever you called it, it had washed away the old world forever. Scientists had been talking about the possibility of such a thing for years—some of them even pointing out that it was already as warm as it had been at the peak of the last interglacial, and getting warmer—but few had suspected just how *fast* the Antarctic ice could melt. Many times during those chaotic weeks, one scientific King Canute or another had predicted that the worst was over, that the tide would rise this high and no higher . . . but each time the sea had come inexorably on, pushing miles and miles further inland with each successive high-tide, rising almost 300 feet in the course of one disastrous summer, drowning lowlands around the globe until there *were* no lowlands anymore. In the United States alone, the sea had swallowed most of the East Coast east of the Appalachians, the West Coast west of the Sierras and the Cascades, much of Alaska and Hawaii, Florida, the Gulf Coast, East Texas, taken a big wide scoop out of the lowlands of the Mississippi Valley, thin fingers of water penetrating north to Iowa and Illinois, and caused the St. Lawrence and the Great Lakes to overflow and drown their shorelines. The Green Mountains, the White Mountains, the Adirondacks, the Poconos and the Catskills, the Ozarks, the Pacific Coast Ranges—all had been transformed to archipelagos, surrounded by the invading sea.

The funny thing was . . . that as the sea pursued them relentlessly inland, pushing them from one temporary refuge to another, he had been unable to shake the feeling that *he* had caused the Flood: that he had done something that day while playing atop the seawall, inadvertently stumbled on some magic ritual, some chance combination of gesture and word that had untied the bonds of the sea and sent it sliding up over the land . . . that it was chasing *him*, personally. . . .

A dog was barking out there now, somewhere out across the fields toward town, but it was not *his* dog. His dog was dead, long since dead, and its whitening skull was rolling along the ocean floor with the tides that washed over what had once been Brigantine, New Jersey, three hundred feet down.

Suddenly he was covered with gooseflesh, and he shivered, rubbing his hands over his bare arms. He returned to his cot and dressed hurriedly—no point in trying to go back to bed, Sara would be up to kick them all out of the sack in a minute or two anyway. The day had begun; he would think no further ahead than that. He had learned in the refugee camps to take life one second at a time.

As he moved around the room, he thought that he could feel hostile eyes watching him from some of the other bunks. It was much colder in here now that he had opened the window, and he had inevitably made a certain amount of noise getting dressed, but although they all valued every second of sleep they could scrounge, none of the other kids would dare to complain. The thought was bittersweet, bringing both pleasure and pain, and he smiled at it, a thin, brittle smile that was almost a grimace. No, they would watch sullenly from their bunks, and pretend to be asleep, and curse him under their breath, but they would say nothing to anyone about it. Certainly they would say nothing to *him*.

He went down through the still-silent house like a ghost, and out across the farmyard, through fugitive streamers of mist that wrapped clammy white arms around him and beaded his face with dew. His uncle Abner was there at the slit-trench before him. Abner grunted a greeting, and they stood pissing side by side for a moment in companionable silence, their urine steaming in the gray morning air.

Abner stepped backward and began to button his pants. "You start playin' with yourself yet, boy?" he said, not looking at Roy.

Roy felt his face flush. "No," he said, trying not to stammer, "no sir."

"You growin' hair already," Abner said. He swung himself slowly around to face Roy, as if his body was some ponderous machine that could only be moved and aimed by the use of pulleys and levers. The hard morning light made his face look harsh as stone, but also sallow and old. Tired, Roy thought. Unutterably weary, as though it took almost more effort than he could sustain just to stand there. Worn out, like the overtaxed fields around them. Only the eyes were alive in the eroded face; they were hard and merciless as flint, and they looked at you as if they were looking right through you to some distant thing that nobody else could see. "I've tried to explain to you about remaining pure," Abner said, speaking slowly. "About how important it is for you to keep yourself pure, not to let yourself be sullied in any way. I've tried to explain that, I hope you could understand—"

"Yes, sir," Roy said.

Abner made a groping hesitant motion with his hand, fingers spread wide, as though he were trying to sculpt meaning from the air itself. "I mean—it's important that you understand, Roy. Everything has to be *right*. I mean, everything's got to be just . . . *right* . . . or nothing else will mean anything. You got to be right in your *soul*, boy. You got to let the Peace of God into your soul. It all depends on *you* now— you got to let that Peace inside yourself, no one can do it for you. And it's so important . . ."

"Yes, sir," Roy said quietly, "I understand."

"I wish . . ." Abner said, and fell silent. They stood there for a minute, not speaking, not looking at each other. There was wood-smoke in the air now, and they heard a door slam somewhere on the far side of the house. They had instinctively been looking out across the open land to the east, and now, as they watched, the sun rose above the mountains, splitting the plum-and-ash sky open horizontally with a long wedge of red, distinguishing the rolling horizon from the lowering clouds. A lance of bright white sunlight hit their eyes, thrusting straight in at them from the edge of the world.

"You're going to make us proud, boy, I know it," Abner said, but Roy ignored him, watching in fascination as the molten disk of the sun floated free of the horizon-line, squinting against the dazzle until his eyes watered and his sight blurred. Abner put his hand on the boy's shoulder. The hand felt heavy and hot, proprietary, and Roy shook it loose in annoyance, still not looking away from the horizon. Abner sighed, started to say something, thought better of it, and instead said, "Come on in the house, boy, and let's get some breakfast inside you."

Breakfast—when they finally did get to sit down to it, after the usual rambling grace and invocation by Abner—proved to be unusually lavish. For the brethren, there were hickory-nut biscuits, and honey, and cups of chicory, and even the other refugee kids—who on occasion during the long bitter winter had been fed as close to nothing at all as law and appearances would allow—got a few slices of fried fatback along with their habitual cornmeal mush. Along with his biscuits and honey, Roy got wild turkey eggs, Indian potatoes, and a real pork chop. There was a good deal of tension around the big table that morning: Henry and Luke were stern-faced and tense, Raymond was moody and preoccupied, Albert actually looked frightened; the refugee kids were round-eyed and silent, doing their best to make themselves invisible; the jolly Mrs. Crammer was as jolly as ever, shoveling her food in with gusto, but the grumpy Mrs. Zeigler, who was feared and disliked by all the kids, had obviously been crying, and ate little or nothing; Abner's face was set like rock, his eyes were hard and bright, and he looked from one to another of the brethren, as if daring them to question his leadership and spiritual guidance. Roy ate with good appetite, unperturbed by the emotional convection currents that were swirling around him, calmly but deliberately concentrating on mopping up every morsel of food on his plate—in the last couple of months he had put back some of the weight he had lost, although by the old standards, the ones his Mom would have applied four years ago, he was still painfully thin. At the end of the meal, Mrs. Reardon came in from the kitchen and, beaming with the well-justified pride of someone who is about to do the impossible, presented Roy with a small, rectangular object wrapped in shiny brown paper. He was startled for a second, but yes, by God, it *was:* a Hershey bar, the first one he'd seen in years. A black market item, of course, difficult to get hold of in the impoverished East these days, and probably expensive as hell. Even some of the brethren were looking at him enviously now, and the refugee kids were frankly gaping. As he picked up the Hershey bar and slowly and caressingly peeled the wrapper back, exposing the pale chocolate beneath, one of the other kids actually began to drool.

After breakfast, the other refugee kids—"wetbacks," the townspeople sometimes called them, with elaborate irony—were divided into two groups. One group would help the brethren work Abner's farm that day, while the larger group would be loaded onto an ox-drawn dray (actually an old flatbed truck, with the cab knocked off) and sent out around the countryside to do what pretty much amounted to slave labor: road work, heavy farm work, helping with the quarrying or the timbering, rebuilding houses and barns and bridges damaged or destroyed in the chaotic days after the Flood. The federal government—or what was left of the federal government, trying desperately, and not always successfully, to keep a battered and Balkanizing country from flying completely apart, struggling to put the Humpty Dumpty that was America back together again—the federal government paid Abner (and others like him) a yearly allowance in federal scrip or promise-of-merchandise notes for giving room and board to refugees from the drowned lands . . . but times being as tough as they were, no one was going to complain if Abner also helped ease the burden of their upkeep by hiring them out locally to work for whomever could come up with the scrip, or sufficient barter goods, or an attractive work-swap offer; what was left of the state and town governments also used them on occasion (and the others like them, adult or child), gratis, for work-projects "for the common good, during this time of emergency . . ."

Sometimes, hanging around the farm with little or nothing to do, Roy almost missed going out on the work-crews, but only almost: he remembered too well the back-breaking labor performed on scanty rations . . . the sickness, the accidents, the staggering fatigue . . . the blazing sun and the swarms of mosquitoes in summer, the bitter cold in winter, the snow, the icy wind . . . He watched the dray go by, seeing the envious and resentful faces of kids he had once worked beside—Stevie, Enrique, Sal—turn toward him as it passed, and, reflexively, he opened and closed his hands. Even two months of idleness and relative luxury had not softened the thick and roughened layers of callus that were the legacy of several seasons spent on the crews. . . . No, boredom was infinitely preferable.

By mid-morning, a small crowd of people had gathered in the road outside the farmhouse. It was hotter now; you could smell the promise of summer in the air, in the wind, and the sun that beat down out of a cloudless blue sky had a real sting to it. It must have been uncomfortable out there in the open, under that sun, but the crowd made no attempt to approach—they just stood there on the far side of the road and watched the house, shuffling their feet, occasionally muttering to each other in voices that, across the road, were audible only as a low wordless grumbling.

Roy watched them for a while from the porch door; they were townspeople, most of them vaguely familiar to Roy, although none of them belonged to Abner's sect, and he knew none of them by name. The refugee kids saw little of the townspeople, being kept carefully segregated for the most part. The few times that Roy had gotten into town he had been treated with icy hostility—and God help the wet-back kid who was caught by the town kids on a deserted stretch of road! For that matter, even the brethren tended to keep to themselves, and were snubbed by certain segments of town society, although the sect had increased its numbers dramatically in recent years, nearly tripling in strength during the past winter alone; there were new chapters now in several of the surrounding communities.

A gaunt-faced woman in the crowd outside spotted Roy, and shook a thin fist at him. "Heretic!" she shouted. "Blasphemer!" The rest of the crowd began to buzz ominously, like a huge angry bee. She spat at Roy, her face contorting and her shoulders heaving with the ferocity of her effort, although she must have known that the spittle had no chance of reaching him. "Blasphemer!" she shouted again. The veins stood out like cords in her scrawny neck.

Roy stepped back into the house, but continued to watch from behind the curtained front windows. There was shouting inside the house as well as outside—the brethren had been cloistered in the kitchen for most of the morning, arguing, and the sound and ferocity of their argument carried clearly through the thin plaster walls of the crumbling old house. At last the sliding door to the kitchen slammed open, and Mrs. Zeigler strode out into the parlor, accompanied by her two children and her scrawny, pasty-faced husband, and followed by two other families of brethren—about nine people altogether. Most of them were carrying suitcases, and a few had backpacks and bindles. Abner stood in the kitchen doorway and watched them go, his anger evident only in the whiteness of his knuckles as he grasped the door-frame. "*Go*, then," Abner said scornfully. "We spit you up out of our mouths! Don't ever think to come back!" He swayed in the doorway, his voice tremulous with hate. "We're better off without you, you hear? You *hear* me? We don't *need* the weak-willed and the short-sighted."

Mrs. Zeigler said nothing, and her steps didn't slow or falter, but her homely hatchet-face was streaked with tears. To Roy's astonishment—for she had a reputation as a harridan—she stopped near the porch door and threw her arms around him. "Come with us," she said, hugging him with smothering tightness, "Roy, *please* come with us! You can, you know—we'll find a place for you, everything will work out fine." Roy said nothing, resisting the impulse to squirm—he was uncomfortable in her embrace; in spite of himself, it touched some sleeping corner of his soul he had thought was safely bricked-over years before, and for a moment he felt trapped and panicky, unable to breathe, as though he were in sudden danger of wakening from a comfortable dream into a far more terrible and less desirable reality. "Come *with* us," Mrs. Zeigler said again, more urgently, but Roy shook his head gently and pulled away from her. "You're a goddamned fool then!" she blazed, suddenly angry, her voice ringing harsh and loud, but Roy only shrugged, and gave her his wistful, ghostly smile. "Damn it—" she started to say, but her eyes filled with tears again, and she whirled and hurried out of the house, followed by the other members of her party. The children—wetbacks were kept pretty much segregated from the children of the brethren as well, and he had seen some of these kids only at meals—looked at Roy with wide, frightened eyes as they passed.

Abner was staring at Roy now, from across the room; it was a hard and challenging stare, but there was also a trace of desperation in it, and in that moment Abner seemed uncertain and oddly vulnerable. Roy stared back at him serenely, unblinkingly meeting his eyes, and after a while some of the tension went out of Abner, and he turned and stumbled out of the room, listing to one side like a church steeple in the wind.

Outside, the crowd began to buzz again as Mrs. Zeigler's party filed out of the house and across the road. There was much discussion and arm-waving and head-shaking when the two groups met, someone occasionally gesturing back toward the farmhouse. The buzzing grew louder, then gradually died away. At last, Mrs. Zeigler and her group set off down the road for town, accompanied by some of the locals. They trudged away dispiritedly down the center of the dusty road, lugging their shabby suitcases, only a few of them looking back.

Roy watched them until they were out of sight, his face still and calm, and continued to stare down the road after them long after they were gone.

About noon, a carload of reporters arrived outside, driving up in one of the bulky new methane-burners that were still rarely seen east of Omaha. They circulated through the crowd of townspeople, pausing briefly to take photographs and ask questions, working their way toward the house, and Roy watched them as if they were unicorns, strange remnants from some vanished cycle of creation. Most of the reporters were probably from State College or the new state capital at Altoona—places where a few small newspapers were again being produced—but one of them was wearing an armband that identified him as a bureau man for one of the big Denver papers, and that was probably where the money for the car had come from. It was strange to be reminded that there were still areas of the country that were . . . not unchanged, no place in the world could claim that . . . and not rich, not by the old standards of affluence anyway . . . but, at any rate, better off than *here*. The whole western part of the country—from roughly the

95th meridian on west to approximately the 122nd—had been untouched by the flooding, and although the west had also suffered severely from the collapse of the national economy and the consequent social upheavals, at least much of their industrial base had remained intact. Denver—one of the few large American cities built on ground high enough to have been safe from the rising waters—was the new federal capital, and, if poorer and meaner, it was also bigger and busier than ever.

Abner went out to herd the reporters inside and away from the unbelievers, and after a moment or two Roy could hear Abner's voice going out there, booming like a church organ. By the time the reporters came in, Roy was sitting at the dining room table, flanked by Raymond and Aaron, waiting for them.

They took photographs of him sitting there, while he stared calmly back at them, and they took photographs of him while he politely refused to answer questions, and then Aaron handed him the pre-prepared papers, and he signed them, and repeated the legal formulas that Aaron had taught him, and they took photographs of that too. And then—able to get nothing more out of him, and made slightly uneasy by his blank composure and the remoteness of his eyes—they left.

Within a few more minutes, as though everything were over, as though the departure of the reporters had drained all possible significance from anything else that might still happen, most of the crowd outside had drifted away also, only one or two people remaining behind to stand quietly waiting, like vultures, in the once-again empty road.

Lunch was a quiet meal. Roy ate heartily, taking seconds of everything, and Mrs. Crammer was as jovial as ever, but everyone else was subdued, and even Abner seemed shaken by the schism that had just sundered his church. After the meal, Abner stood up and began to pray aloud. The brethren sat resignedly at the table, heads partially bowed, some listening, some not. Abner was holding his arms up toward the big blackened rafters of the ceiling, sweat runneling his face, when Peter came hurriedly in from outside and stood hesitating in the doorway, trying to catch Abner's eye. When it became obvious that Abner was going to keep right on ignoring him, Peter shrugged, and said in a loud flat voice, "Abner, the sheriff is here."

Abner stopped praying. He grunted, a hoarse, exhausted sound, the kind of sound a baited bear might make when, already pushed beyond the limits of endurance, someone jabs it yet again with a spear. He slowly lowered his arms and was still for a long moment, and then he shuddered, seeming to shake himself back to life. He glanced speculatively—and, it almost seemed, beseechingly—at Roy, and then straightened his shoulders and strode from the room.

They received the sheriff in the parlor, Raymond and Aaron and Mrs. Crammer sitting in the battered old armchairs, Roy sitting unobtrusively to one side on the stool from a piano that no longer worked, Abner standing a little to the fore with his arms locked behind him and his boots planted solidly on the oak planking, as if he were on the bridge of a schooner that was heading into a gale. County Sheriff Sam Braddock glanced at the others—his gaze lingering on Roy for a moment—and then ignored them, addressing himself to Abner as if they were alone in the room. "Mornin', Abner," he said.

"Mornin', Sam," Abner said quietly. "You here for some reason other than just t'say hello, I suppose."

Braddock grunted. He was a short, stocky, grizzled man with iron-gray hair and a tired face. His uniform was shiny and old and patched in a dozen places, but clean, and the huge old revolver strapped to his hip looked worn but serviceable. He fidgeted with his shapeless old hat, turning it around and around in his fingers—he was obviously embarrassed, but he was determined as well, and at last he said, "The thing of it is, Abner, I'm here to talk you out of this damned tomfoolery."

"Are you, now?" Abner said.

"We'll do whatever we damn well want to do—" Raymond burst out, shrilly, but Abner waved him to silence. Braddock glanced lazily at Raymond, then looked back at Abner, his tired old face settling into harder lines. "I'm not going to allow it," he said, more harshly. "We don't want this kind of thing going on in this county."

Abner said nothing.

"There's not a thing you can do about it, sheriff," Aaron said, speaking a bit heatedly, but keeping his melodious voice well under control. "It's all perfectly legal, all the way down the line."

"Well, now," Braddock said, "I don't know about that . . ."

"Well, I *do* know, sheriff," Aaron said calmly. "As a legally sanctioned and recognized church, we are protected by law all the way down the line. There is ample precedent, most of it recent, most of it upheld by appellate decisions within the last year: Carlton *versus* the State of Vermont, Trenholm *versus* the State of West Virginia, the Church of Souls *versus* the State of New York. There was that case up in Tylersville, just last year. Why, the Freedom of Worship Act *alone* . . ."

Braddock sighed, tacitly admitting that he knew Aaron was right—perhaps he had hoped to bluff them into obeying. "The 'Flood Congress' of '93," Braddock said, with bitter contempt. "They were so goddamned panic-stricken and full of sick chatter about Armageddon that you could've rammed *any* nonsense down their throats. That's a bad law, a pisspoor law . . ."

"Be that as it may, sheriff, you have no authority whatsoever—"

Abner suddenly began to speak, talking with a slow heavy deliberateness, musingly, almost reminiscently, ignoring the conversation he was interrupting—and indeed, perhaps he had not even been listening to it. "My grandfather lived right here on this farm, and *his* father before him—you know that, Sam? *They* lived by the old ways, and they survived and prospered. Greatgranddad, there wasn't hardly anything he needed from the outside world, anything he needed to *buy*, except maybe nails and suchlike, and he couldv'e made them himself too, if he'd needed to. Everything they needed, everything they ate, or wore, or used, they got from the woods, or from out of the soil of this farm, right here. *We* don't know how to do that anymore. We forgot the old ways, we turned our faces away, which is why the Flood came on us as a Judgement, a Judgement and a scourge, a scouring, a winnowing. The Old Days have come back again, and we've forgotten so goddamned *much*, we're almost helpless now that there's no goddamned K-mart down the goddamned street. We've got to go back to the old ways, or we'll pass from the earth, and be seen no more in it . . ." He was sweating now, staring earnestly at Braddock, as if to compel him by force of will alone to share the vision. "But it's so *hard*, Sam. . . . We have to *work* at relearning the old ways, we have to reinvent them as we go, step by step . . ."

"Some things we were better off without," Braddock said grimly.

"Up at Tylersville, they *doubled* their yield last harvest. Think what that could mean to a county as hungry as this one has been—"

Braddock shook his iron-gray head, and held up one hand, as if he were directing traffic. "I'm telling you, Abner, the town won't stand for this—I'm bound to warn you that some of the boys just might decide to go outside the law to deal with this thing." He paused. "And, unofficially of course, I just might be inclined to give them a hand . . ."

Mrs. Crammer laughed. She had been sitting quietly and taking all of this in, smiling good-naturedly from time to time, and her laugh was a shocking thing in that stuffy little room, harsh as a crow's caw. "You'll do *nothing*, Sam Braddock," she said jovially. "And neither will anybody else. More than half the county's with us already, nearly all the country folk, and a good part of the town, too." She smiled pleasantly at him, but her eyes were small and hard. "Just you remember, we *know* where *you* live, Sam Braddock. And we know where your sister lives, too, and your sister's child, over to Framington . . ."

"Are you threatening an officer of the law?" Braddock said, but he said it in a weak voice, and his face, when he turned it away to stare at the floor, looked sick and old. Mrs. Crammer laughed again, and then there was silence.

Braddock kept his face turned down for another long moment, and then he put his hat back on, squashing it down firmly on his head, and when he looked up he pointedly ignored the brethren and addressed his next remark to Roy. "You don't have to stay with these people, son," he said. "*That's* the law, too." He kept his eyes fixed steadily on Roy. "You just say the word, son, and I'll take you straight out of here, right now." His jaw was set, and he touched the butt of his revolver, as if for encouragement. "They can't stop us. How about it?"

"No, thank you," Roy said quietly. "I'll stay."

That night, while Abner wrung his hands and prayed aloud, Roy sat half-dozing before the parlor fire, unconcerned, watching the firelight throw Abner's gesticulating shadow across the whitewashed walls. There was something in the wine they kept giving him, Roy knew, maybe somebody's saved-up Quaaludes, but he didn't need it. Abner kept exorting him to let the Peace of God into his heart, but he didn't need that either. He didn't need anything. He felt calm and self-possessed and remote, disassociated from everything that went on around him, as if he were looking down on the world through the wrong end of a telescope, feeling only a mild scientific interest as he watched the tiny mannequins swirl and pirouette. . . . Like watching television with the sound off. If this was the Peace of God, it had settled down on him months ago, during the dead of that terrible winter, while he had struggled twelve hours a day to load foundation-stone in the face of icestorms and the razoring wind, while they had all, wetbacks and brethren alike, come close to starving. About the same time that word of the goings-on at Tylersville had started to seep down from the brethren's parent church upstate, about the same time that Abner, who until then had totally ignored their kinship, had begun to talk to him in the evenings about the old ways. . . .

Although perhaps the great dead cold had started to settle in even earlier, that first day of the new world, while they were driving off across foundering Brigantine, the water already up over the hubcaps of the Toyota, and he had heard Toby barking frantically somewhere behind them. . . . His dad had died that day, died of a heart-attack as he fought to get them onto an overloaded boat that would take them across to the "safety" of the New Jersey mainland. His mother had died months later in one of the sprawling refugee camps, called "Floodtowns," that had sprung up on high ground everywhere along the new coastlines. She had just given up—sat down in the mud, rested her head on her knees, closed her eyes, and died. Just like that. Roy had seen the phenomenon countless times in the Floodtowns, places so festeringly horrible that even life on Abner's farm, with its Dickensian bleakness, forced labor, and short rations, had seemed—and was—a distinct change for the better. It was odd, and wrong, and sometimes it bothered him a little, but he hardly ever thought of his mother and father anymore—it was as if his mind shut itself off every time he came to those memories; he had never even cried for them, but all he had to do was close his eyes and he could see Toby, or his cat Basil running toward him and meowing with his tail held up over his back like a flag, and grief would come up like black bile at the back of his throat. . . .

It was still dark when they left the farmhouse. Roy and Abner and Aaron walked together, Abner carrying a large tattered carpetbag. Hank and Raymond ranged ahead with shotguns, in case there was trouble, but the last of the afternoon's gawkers had been driven off hours before by the cold, and the road was empty, a dim charcoal line through the slowly-lightening darkness. No one spoke, and there was no sound other than the sound of boots crunching on gravel. It was chilly again that morning, and Roy's bare feet burned against the macadam, but he trudged along stoically, ignoring the bite of cinders and pebbles. Their breath steamed faintly against the paling stars. The fields stretched dark and formless around them to either side of the road, and once they heard the rustling of some unseen animal fleeing away from them through the stubble. Mist flowed slowly down the road to meet them, sending out gleaming silver fingers to curl around their legs.

The sky was graying to the east, where the sea slept behind the mountains. Roy could imagine the sea rising higher and higher until it found its patient way around the roots of the hills and came spilling into the tableland beyond, flowing steadily forward like the mist, spreading out into a placid sheet of water that slowly swallowed the town, the farmhouse, the fields, until only the highest branches of the trees remained, held up like the beckoning arms of the drowned, and then they too would slide slowly, peacefully, beneath the water. . . .

A bird was crying out now, somewhere in the darkness, and they were walking through the fields, away from the road, cold mud squelching underfoot, the dry stubble crackling around them. Soon it would be time to sow the spring wheat, and after that, the corn. . . .

They stopped. Wind sighed through the dawn, muttering in the throat of the world. Still no one had spoken. Then hands were helping him remove the old bathrobe he'd been wearing. . . . Before leaving the house, he had been bathed, and annointed with a thick fragrant oil, and with a tiny silver scissors Mrs. Reardon had clipped a lock of his hair for each of the brethren.

Suddenly he was naked, and he was being urged forward again, his feet stumbling and slow.

They had made a wide ring of automobile flares here, the flares spitting and sizzling luridly in the wan dawn light, and in the center of the ring, they had dug a hollow in the ground.

He lay down in the hollow, feeling his naked back and buttocks settle into the cold mud, feeling it mat the hair on the back of his head. The mud made little sucking noises as he moved his arms and legs, settling in, and then he stretched out and lay still. The dawn breeze was cold, and he shivered in the mud, feeling it take hold of him like a giant's hand, tightening around him, pulling him down with a grip old and cold and strong . . .

They gathered around him, seeming, from his low perspective, to tower miles into the sky. Their faces were harsh and angular, gouged with lines and shadows that made them look like something from a stark old woodcut. Abner bent down to rummage in the carpetbag, his harsh woodcut face close to Roy's for a moment, and when he straightened up again he had the big fine-honed hunting knife in his hand.

Abner began to speak now, groaning out the words in a loud, harsh voice, but Roy was no longer listening. He watched calmly as Abner lifted the knife high into the air, and then he turned his head to look east, as if he could somehow see across all the intervening miles of rock and farmland and forest to where the sea waited behind the mountains . . .

Is this enough? he thought disjointedly, ignoring the towering scarecrow figures that were swaying in closer over him, straining his eyes to look east, to where the Presence lived . . . speaking now only to that Presence, to the sea, to that vast remorseless deity, bargaining with it cannily, hopefully, shrewdly, like a country housewife at market, proffering it the fine rich red gift of his death. Is this enough? Will this do?

Will you stop now?

SPEECH SOUNDS

by OCTAVIA BUTLER

"Speech Sounds," Octavia Butler's brutal depiction of a world almost entirely deprived of its reason, was published in the Mid-December 1983 issue of *Asimov's*. This harrowing tale won the Hugo Award for Best Short Story. In June 1984, *Asimov's* published her equally disturbing, Nebula- and Hugo-Award-winning novelette, "Bloodchild." Since then, and much to the magazine's dismay, the author has primarily concentrated on her novels. Her esteemed works include "The Evening and the Morning and the Night," *Patternmaster*, *Clay's Ark*, *Kindred*, and *Parable of the Sower*. She says she's "comfortably asocial—a hermit in the middle of Los Angeles." At *Asimov's*, we only wish that meant she had more time to turn out her brilliant short fiction.

There was trouble aboard the Washington Boulevard bus. Rye had expected trouble sooner or later in her journey. She had put off going until loneliness and hopelessness drove her out. She believed she might have one group of relatives left alive—a brother and his two children twenty miles away in Pasadena. That was a day's journey one-way, if she were lucky. The unexpected arrival of the bus as she left her Virginia Road home had seemed to be a piece of luck—until the trouble began.

Two young men were involved in a disagreement of some kind, or, more likely, a misunderstanding. They stood in the aisle, grunting and gesturing at each other, each in his own uncertain "T" stance as the bus lurched over the potholes. The driver seemed to be putting some effort into keeping them off balance. Still, their gestures stopped just short of contact—mock punches, hand-games of intimidation to replace lost curses.

People watched the pair, then looked at each other and made small anxious sounds. Two children whimpered.

Rye sat a few feet behind the disputants and across from the back door. She watched the two carefully, knowing the fight would begin when someone's nerve broke or someone's hand slipped or someone came to the end of his limited ability to communicate. These things could happen any time.

One of them happened as the bus hit an especially large pothole and one man, tall, thin, and sneering, was thrown into his shorter opponent.

Instantly, the shorter man drove his left fist into the disintegrating sneer. He hammered his larger opponent as though he neither had nor needed any weapon other than his left fist. He hit quickly enough, hard enough to batter his opponent down before the taller man could regain his balance or hit back even once.

People screamed or squawked in fear. Those nearby scrambled to get out of the way. Three more young men roared in excitement and gestured wildly. Then, somehow, a second dispute broke out between two of these three—probably because one inadvertently touched or hit the other.

As the second fight scattered frightened passengers, a woman shook the driver's shoulder and grunted as she gestured toward the fighting.

The driver grunted back through bared teeth. Frightened, the woman drew away.

Rye, knowing the methods of bus drivers, braced herself and held on to the crossbar of the seat in front of her. When the driver hit the brakes, she was ready and the combatants were not. They fell over seats and onto screaming passengers, creating even more confusion. At least one more fight started.

The instant the bus came to a full stop, Rye was on her feet, pushing the back door. At the second push, it opened and she jumped out, holding her pack in one arm. Several other passengers followed, but some stayed on the bus. Buses were so rare and irregular now, people rode when they could, no matter what. There might not be another bus today—or tomorrow. People started walking, and if they saw a bus they flagged it down. People making intercity trips like Rye's from Los Angeles to Pasadena made plans to camp out, or risked seeking shelter with locals who might rob or murder them.

The bus did not move, but Rye moved away from it. She intended to wait until the trouble was over and get on again, but if there was shooting, she wanted the protection of a tree. Thus, she was near the curb when a battered, blue Ford on the other side of the street made a U-turn and pulled up in front of the bus. Cars were rare these days—as rare as a severe shortage of fuel and of relatively unimpaired mechanics could make them. Cars that still ran were as likely to be used as weapons as they were to serve as transportation. Thus, when the driver of the Ford beckoned to Rye, she moved away warily. The driver got out—a big man, young, neatly bearded with dark, thick hair. He wore a long overcoat and a look of wariness that matched Rye's. She stood several feet from him, waiting to see what he would do. He looked at the bus, now rocking with the combat inside, then at the small cluster of passengers who had gotten off. Finally he looked at Rye again.

She returned his gaze, very much aware of the old forty-five automatic her jacket concealed. She watched his hands.

He pointed with his left hand toward the bus. The dark-tinted windows prevented him from seeing what was happening inside.

His use of the left hand interested Rye more than his obvious question. Left-handed people tended to be less impaired, more reasonable and comprehending, less driven by frustration, confusion, and anger.

She imitated his gesture, pointing toward the bus with her own left hand, then punching the air with both fists.

The man took off his coat revealing a Los Angeles Police Department uniform complete with baton and service revolver.

Rye took another step back from him. There was no more LAPD, no more *any* large organization, governmental or private. There were neighborhood patrols and armed individuals. That was all.

The man took something from his coat pocket, then threw the coat into the car. Then he gestured Rye back, back toward the rear of the bus. He had something made of plastic in his hand. Rye did not understand what he wanted until he went to the rear door of the bus and beckoned her to stand there. She obeyed mainly out of curiosity. Cop or not, maybe he could do something to stop the stupid fighting.

He walked around the front of the bus, to the street side where the driver's window was open. There, she thought she saw him throw something into the bus. She was still trying to peer through the tinted glass when people began stumbling out the rear door, choking and weeping. Gas.

Rye caught an old woman who would have fallen, lifted two little children down when they were in danger of being knocked down and trampled. She could see the bearded man helping people at the front door. She caught a thin old man shoved out by one of the combatants. Staggered by the old man's weight, she was barely able to get out of the way as the last of the young men pushed his way out. This one, bleeding from nose and mouth, stumbled into another and they grappled blindly, still sobbing from the gas.

The bearded man helped the bus driver out through the front door, though the driver did not seem to appreciate his help. For a moment, Rye thought there would be another fight. The bearded man stepped back and watched the driver gesture threateningly, watched him shout in wordless anger.

The bearded man stood still, made no sound, refused to respond to clearly obscene gestures. The least impaired people tended to do this—stand back unless they were physically threatened and let those with less control scream and jump around. It was as though they felt it beneath them to be as touchy as the less comprehending. This was an attitude of superiority and that was the way people like the bus driver preceived it. Such "superiority" was frequently punished by beatings, even by death. Rye had had close calls of her own. As a result, she never went unarmed. And in this world where the only likely common language was body language, being armed was often enough. She had rarely had to draw her gun or even display it.

The bearded man's revolver was on constant display. Apparently that was enough for the bus driver. The driver spat in disgust, glared at the bearded man for a moment longer, then strode back to his gas-filled bus. He stared at it for a moment, clearly wanting to get in, but the gas was still too strong. Of the windows, only his tiny driver's window actually opened. The front door was open, but the rear door would not stay open unless someone held it. Of course, the air conditioning had failed long ago. The bus would take some time to clear. It was the driver's property, his livelihood. He had pasted old magazine pictures of items he would accept as fare on its sides. Then he would use what he collected to feed his family or to trade. If his bus did not run, he did not eat. On the other hand, if the inside of his bus were torn apart by senseless fighting, he would not eat very well either. He was apparently unable to preceive this. All he could see was that it would be some time before he could use his bus again. He shook his fist at the bearded man and shouted. There seemed to be words in his shout, but Rye could not understand them. She did not know whether this was his fault or hers. She had heard so little coherent human speech for the past three years, she was no longer certain how well she recognized it, no longer certain of the degree of her own impairment.

The bearded man sighed. He glanced toward his car, then beckoned to Rye. He was ready to leave, but he wanted something from her first. No. No, he wanted her to leave with him. Risk getting into his car when, in spite of his uniform, law and order were nothing—not even words any longer.

She shook her head in a universally understood negative, but the man continued to beckon.

She waved him away. He was doing what the less-impaired rarely did—drawing potentially negative attention to another of his kind. People from the bus had begun to look at her.

One of the men who had been fighting tapped another on the arm, then pointed from the bearded man to Rye, and finally held up the first two fingers of his right hand as though giving two-thirds of a Boy Scout salute. The gesture was very quick, its meaning obvious even at a distance. She had been grouped with the bearded man. Now what?

The man who had made the gesture started toward her.

She had no idea what she intended, but she stood her ground. The man was half-a-foot taller than she was and perhaps ten years younger. She did not imagine she could outrun him. Nor did she expect anyone to help her if she needed help. The people around her were all strangers.

She gestured once—a clear indication to the man to stop. She did not intend to repeat the gesture. Fortunately, the man obeyed. He gestured obscenely and several other men laughed. Loss of verbal language had spawned a whole new set of obscene gestures. The man, with stark simplicity, had accused her of sex with the bearded man and had suggested she accommodate the other men present—beginning with him.

Rye watched him wearily. People might very well stand by and watch if he tried to rape her. They would also stand and watch her shoot him. Would he push things that far?

He did not. After a series of obscene gestures that brought him no closer to her, he turned contemptuously and walked away.

And the bearded man still waited. He had removed his service revolver, holster and all. He beckoned again, both hands empty. No doubt his gun was in the car and within easy reach, but his taking it off impressed her. Maybe he was all right. Maybe he was just alone. She had been alone herself for three years. The illness had stripped her, killing her children one by one, killing her husband, her sister, her parents. . . .

The illness, if it was an illness, had cut even the living off from one another. As it swept over the country, people hardly had time to lay blame on the Soviets (though they were falling silent along with the rest of the world), on a new virus, a new pollutant, radiation, divine retribution. . . . The illness was stroke-swift in the way it cut people down and strokelike in some of its effects. But it was highly specific. Language was always lost or severely impaired. It was never regained. Often there was also paralysis, intellectual impairment, death.

Rye walked toward the bearded man, ignoring the whistling and applauding of two of the young men and their thumbs-up signs to the bearded man. If he had smiled at them or acknowledged them in any way, she would almost certainly have changed her mind. If she had let herself think of the possible deadly consequences of getting into a stranger's car, she would have changed her mind. Instead, she thought of the man who lived across the street from her. He rarely washed since his bout with the illness. And he had gotten into the habit of urinating wherever he happened to be. He had two women already—one tending each of his large gardens. They put up with him in exchange for his protection. He had made it clear that he wanted Rye to become his third woman.

She got into the car and the bearded man shut the door. She watched as he walked around to the driver's door—watched for his sake because his gun was on the seat beside her. And the bus driver and a pair of young men had come a few steps closer. They did nothing, though, until the bearded man was in the car. Then one of them threw a rock. Others followed his example, and as the car drove away, several rocks bounced off it harmlessly.

When the bus was some distance behind them, Rye wiped sweat from her forehead and longed to relax. The bus would have taken her more than halfway to Pasadena. She would have had only ten miles to walk. She wondered how far she would have to walk now—and wondered if walking a long distance would be her only problem.

At Figuroa and Washington where the bus normally made a left turn, the bearded man stopped, looked at her, and indicated that she should choose a direction. When she directed him left and he actually turned left, she began to relax. If he was willing to go where she directed, perhaps he was safe.

As they passed blocks of burned, abandoned buildings, empty lots, and wrecked or stripped cars, he slipped a gold chain over his head and handed it to her. The pendant attached to it was a smooth, glassy, black rock. Obsidian. His name might be Rock or Peter or Black, but she decided to think of him as Obsidian. Even her sometimes useless memory would retain a name like Obsidian.

She handed him her own name symbol—a pin in the shape of a large golden stalk of wheat. She had bought it long before the illness and the silence began. Now she wore it, thinking it was as close as she was likely to come to Rye. People like Obsidian who had not known her before probably thought of her as Wheat. Not that it mattered. She would never hear her name spoken again.

Obsidian handed her pin back to her. He caught her hand as she reached for it and rubbed his thumb over her calluses.

He stopped at First Street and asked which way again. Then, after turning right as she had indicated, he parked near the Music Center. There, he took a folded paper from the dashboard and unfolded it. Rye recognized it as a street map, though the writing on it meant nothing to her. He flattened the map, took her hand again, and put her index finger on one spot. He touched her, touched himself, pointed toward the floor. In effect, "We are here." She knew he wanted to know where she was going. She wanted to tell him, but she shook her head sadly. She had lost reading and writing. That was her most serious impairment and her most painful. She had taught history at UCLA. She had done freelance writing. Now she could not even read her own manuscripts. She had a house full of books that she could neither read nor bring herself to use as fuel. And she had a memory that would not bring back to her much of what she had read before.

She stared at the map, trying to calculate. She had been born in Pasadena, had lived for fifteen years in Los Angeles. Now she was near L.A. Civic Center. She knew the relative positions of the two cities, knew streets, directions, even knew to stay away from freeways which might be blocked by wrecked cars and destroyed overpasses. She ought to know how to point out Pasadena even though she could not recognize the word.

Hesitantly, she placed her hand over a pale orange patch in the upper right corner of the map. That should be right. Pasadena.

Obsidian lifted her hand and looked under it, then folded the map and put it back on the dashboard. He could read, she realized belatedly. He could probably write, too. Abruptly, she hated him—deep, bitter hatred. What did literacy mean to him—a grown man who played cops and robbers? But he was literate and she was not. She never would be. She felt sick to her stomach with hatred, frustration, and jealousy. And only a few inches from her hand was a loaded gun.

She held herself still, staring at him, almost seeing his blood. But her rage crested and ebbed and she did nothing.

Obsidian reached for her hand with hesitant familiarity. She looked at him. Her face had already revealed too much. No person still living in what was left of human society could fail to recognize that expression, that jealousy.

She closed her eyes wearily, drew a deep breath. She had experienced longing for the past, hatred of the present, growing hopelessness, purposelessness, but she had never experienced such a powerful urge to kill another person. She had left her home, finally, because she had come near to killing herself. She had found no reason to stay alive. Perhaps that was why she had gotten into Obsidian's car. She had never before done such a thing.

He touched her mouth and made chatter motions with thumb and fingers. Could she speak?

She nodded and watched his milder envy come and go. Now both had admitted what it was not safe to admit, and there had been no violence. He tapped his mouth and forehead and shook his head. He did not speak or comprehend spoken language. The illness had played with them, taking away, she suspected, what each valued most.

She plucked at his sleeve, wondering why he had decided on his own to keep the LAPD alive with what he had left. He was sane enough otherwise. Why wasn't he at home raising corn, rabbits, and children? But she did not know how to ask. Then he put his hand on her thigh and she had another question to deal with.

She shook her head. Disease, pregnancy, helpless, solitary agony . . . no.

He massaged her thigh gently and smiled in obvious disbelief.

No one had touched her for three years. She had not wanted anyone to touch her. What kind of world was this to chance bringing a child into even if the father were willing to stay and help raise it? It was too bad, though. Obsidian could not know how attractive he was to her—

young, probably younger than she was, clean, asking for what he wanted rather than demanding it. But none of that mattered. What were a few moments of pleasure measured against a lifetime of consequences?

He pulled her closer to him and for a moment she let herself enjoy the closeness. He smelled good—male and good. She pulled away reluctantly.

He sighed, reached toward the glove compartment. She stiffened, not knowing what to expect, but all he took out was a small box. The writing on it meant nothing to her. She did not understand until he broke the seal, opened the box, and took out a condom. He looked at her and she first looked away in surprise. Then she giggled. She could not remember when she had last giggled.

He grinned, gestured toward the back seat, and she laughed aloud. Even in her teens, she had disliked back seats of cars. But she looked around at the empty streets and ruined buildings, then she got out and into the back seat. He let her put the condom on him, then seemed surprised at her eagerness.

Sometime later, they sat together, covered by his coat, unwilling to become clothed near-strangers again just yet. He made rock-the-baby gestures and looked questioningly at her.

She swallowed, shook her head. She did not know how to tell him her children were dead.

He took her hand and drew a cross in it with his index finger, then made his baby-rocking gesture again.

She nodded, held up three fingers, then turned away, trying to shut out a sudden flood of memories. She had told herself that the children growing up now were to be pitied. They would run through the downtown canyons with no real memory of what the buildings had been or even how they had come to be. Today's children gathered books as well as wood to be burned as fuel. They ran through the streets chasing each other and hooting like chimpanzees. They had no future. They were now all they would ever be.

He put his hand on her shoulder and she turned suddenly, fumbling for his small box, then urging him to make love to her again. He could give her forgetfulness and pleasure. Until now, nothing had been able to do that. Until now, every day had brought her closer to the time when she would do what she had left home to avoid doing: putting her gun in her mouth and pulling the trigger.

She asked Obsidian if he would come home with her, stay with her.

He looked surprised and pleased once he understood. But he did not answer at once. Finally he shook his head as she had feared he might. He was probably having too much fun playing cops and robbers and picking up women.

She dressed in silent disappointment, unable to feel any anger toward him. Perhaps he already had a wife and a home. That was likely. The illness had been harder on men than on women—had killed more men, had left male survivors more severely impaired. Men like Obsidian were rare. Women either settled for less or stayed alone. If they found an Obsidian, they did what they could to keep him. Rye suspected he had someone younger, prettier keeping him.

He touched her while she was strapping her gun on and asked with a complicated series of gestures whether it was loaded.

She nodded grimly.

He patted her arm.

She asked once more if he would come home with her, this time using a different series of gestures. He had seemed hesitant. Perhaps he could be courted.

He got out and into the front seat without responding.

She took her place in front again, watching him. Now he plucked at his uniform and looked at her. She thought she was being asked something, but did not know what it was.

He took off his badge, tapped it with one finger, then tapped his chest. Of course.

She took the badge from his hand and pinned her wheat stalk to it. If playing cops and robbers was his only insanity, let him play. She would take him, uniform and all. It occurred to her that she might eventually lose him to someone he would meet as he had met her. But she would have him for a while.

He took the street map down again, tapped it, pointed vaguely northeast toward Pasadena, then looked at her.

She shrugged, tapped his shoulder then her own, and held up her index and second fingers tight together, just to be sure.

He grasped the two fingers and nodded. He was with her.

She took the map from him and threw it onto the dashboard. She pointed back southwest—back toward home. Now she did not have to go to Pasadena. Now she could go on having a brother there and two nephews—three right-handed males. Now she did not have to find out for certain whether she was as alone as she feared. Now she was not alone.

Obsidian took Hill Street south, then Washington west, and she leaned back, wondering what it would be like to have someone again. With what she had scavenged, what she had preserved, and what she grew, there was easily enough food for him. There was certainly room enough in a four-bedroom house. He could move his possessions in. Best of all, the animal across the street would pull back and possibly not force her to kill him.

Obsidian had drawn her closer to him and she had put her head on his shoulder when suddenly he braked hard, almost throwing her off the seat. Out of the corner of her eye, she saw that someone had run across the street in front of the car. One car on the street and someone had to run in front of it.

Straightening up, Rye saw that the runner was a woman, fleeing from an old frame house to a boarded-up storefront. She ran silently, but the man who followed her a moment later shouted what sounded like garbled words as he ran. He had something in his hand. Not a gun. A knife, perhaps.

The woman tried a door, found it locked, looked around desperately, finally snatched up a fragment of glass broken from the storefront window. With this she turned to face her pursuer. Rye thought she would be more likely to cut her own hand than to hurt anyone else with the glass.

Obsidian jumped from the car, shouting. It was the first time Rye had heard his voice—deep and hoarse from disuse. He made the same sound over and over the way some speechless people did, "Da, da, da!"

Rye got out of the car as Obsidian ran toward the couple. He had drawn his gun. Fearful, she drew her own and released the safety. She looked around to see who else might be attracted to the scene. She saw the man glance at Obsidian, then suddenly lunge at the woman. The woman jabbed his face with her glass, but he caught her arm and managed to stab her twice before Obsidian shot him.

The man doubled, then toppled, clutching his abdomen. Obsidian shouted, then gestured Rye over to help the woman.

Rye moved to the woman's side, remembering that she had little more than bandages and antiseptic in her pack. But the woman was beyond help. She had been stabbed with a long, slender, boning knife.

She touched Obsidian to let him know the woman was dead. He had bent to check the wounded man who lay still and also seemed dead. But as Obsidian looked around to see what Rye wanted, the man opened his eyes. Face contorted, he seized Obsidian's just-holstered revolver and fired. The bullet caught Obsidian in the temple and he collapsed.

It happened just that simply, just that fast. An instant later, Rye shot the wounded man as he was turning the gun on her.

And Rye was alone—with three corpses.

She knelt beside Obsidian, dry-eyed, frowning, trying to understand why everything had suddenly changed. Obsidian was gone. He had died and left her—like everyone else.

Two very small children came out of the house from which the man and woman had run—a boy and girl perhaps three years old. Holding hands, they crossed the street toward Rye. They stared at her, then edged past her and went to the dead woman. The girl shook the woman's arm as though trying to wake her.

This was too much. Rye got up, feeling sick to her stomach with grief and anger. If the children began to cry, she thought she would vomit.

They were on their own, those two kids. They were old enough to scavenge. She did not need any more grief. She did not need a stranger's children who would grow up to be hairless chimps.

She went back to the car. She could drive home, at least. She remembered how to drive.

The thought that Obsidian should be buried occurred to her before she reached the car, and she did vomit.

She had found and lost the man so quickly. It was as though she had been snatched from comfort and security and given a sudden, inexplicable beating. Her head would not clear. She could not think.

Somehow, she made herself go back to him, look at him. She found herself on her knees beside him with no memory of having knelt. She stroked his face, his beard. One of the children made a noise and she looked at them, at the woman who was probably their mother. The children looked back at her, obviously frightened. Perhaps it was their fear that reached her finally.

She had been about to drive away and leave them. She had almost done it, almost left two toddlers to die. Surely there had been enough dying. She would have to take the children home with her. She would not be able to live with any other decision. She looked around for a place to bury three bodies. Or two. She wondered if the murderer were the children's father. Before the silence, the police had always said some of the most dangerous calls they went out on were domestic disturbance calls. Obsidian should have known that—not that the knowledge would have kept him in the car. It would not have held her back either. She could not have watched the woman murdered and done nothing.

She dragged Obsidian toward the car. She had nothing to dig with here, and no one to guard for her while she dug. Better to take the bodies with her and bury them next to her husband and her children. Obsidian would come home with her after all.

When she had gotten him onto the floor in the back, she returned for the woman. The little girl, thin, dirty, solemn, stood up and unknowingly gave Rye a gift. As Rye began to drag the woman by her arms, the little girl screamed, "No!"

Rye dropped the woman and stared at the girl.

"No!" the girl repeated. She came to stand beside the woman. "Go away!" she told Rye.

"Don't talk," the little boy said to her. There was no blurring or confusing of sounds. Both children had spoken and Rye had understood. The boy looked at the dead murderer and moved farther from him. He took the girl's hand. "Be quiet," he whispered.

Fluent speech! Had the woman died because she could talk and had taught her children to talk? Had she been killed by a husband's festering anger or by a stranger's jealous rage? And the children . . . they must have been born after the silence. Had the disease run its course, then? Or were these children simply immune? Certainly they had had time to fall sick and silent. Rye's mind leaped ahead. What if children of three or fewer years were safe and able to learn language? What if all they needed were teachers? Teachers and protectors.

Rye glanced at the dead murderer. To her shame, she thought she could understand some of the passions that must have driven him, whoever he was. Anger, frustration, hopelessness, insane jealousy . . . how many more of him were there—people willing to destroy what they could not have?

Obsidian had been the protector, had chosen that role for who knew what reason. Perhaps putting on an obsolete uniform and patrolling the empty streets had been what he did instead of putting a gun into his mouth. And now that there was something worth protecting, he was gone.

She had been a teacher. A good one. She had been a protector, too, though only of herself. She had kept herself alive when she had no reason to live. If the illness let these children alone, she could keep them alive.

Somehow she lifted the dead woman into her arms and placed her on the back seat of the car. The children began to cry, but she knelt on the broken pavement and whispered to them, fearful of frightening them with the harshness of her long unused voice.

"It's all right," she told them. "You're going with us, too. Come on." She lifted them both, one in each arm. They were so light. Had they been getting enough to eat?

The boy covered her mouth with his hand, but she moved her face away. "It's all right for me to talk," she told him. "As long as no one's around, it's all right." She put the boy down on the front seat of the car and he moved over without being told to, to make room for the girl. When they were both in the car Rye leaned against the window, looking at them, seeing that they were less afraid now, that they watched her with at least as much curiosity as fear.

"I'm Valerie Rye," she said, savoring the words. "It's all right for you to talk to me."

PRESS ENTER■

by JOHN VARLEY

John Varley's terrifying novella about the horrors that might be released once you "PRESS ENTER■," was published in the May 1984 issue of *Asimov's* and went on to win the Hugo and the Nebula Awards. The author possesses two other Hugos and a Nebula, and he has written a number of seminal science fiction works. These include shorter pieces such as "Air Raid," "Blue Champagne," "The Barbie Murders," and "The Persistence of Vision," and such novels as *The Ophiuchi Hotline* and *Titan*. He recently co-edited an anthology, *Superheroes* (Berkley, 1995), with Ricia Mainhardt, and he is at work on a novel titled *The Golden Globe*. *Steel Beach*, Varley's last novel and a finalist for the Hugo Award, was published by Putnam in 1992.

"This is a recording. Please do not hang up until—"

I slammed the phone down so hard it fell onto the floor. Then I stood there, dripping wet and shaking with anger. Eventually, the phone started to make that buzzing noise they make when a receiver is off the hook. It's twenty times as loud as any sound a phone can normally make, and I always wondered why. As though it was such a terrible disaster: "Emergency! Your telephone is off the hook!!!"

Phone answering machines are one of the small annoyances of life. Confess, do you really *like* talking to a machine? But what had just happened to me was more than a petty irritation. I had just been called by an automatic dialing machine.

They're fairly new. I'd been getting about two or three such calls a month. Most of them come from insurance companies. They give you a two-minute spiel and then a number to call if you are interested. (I called back, once, to give them a piece of my mind, and was put on hold, complete with Muzak.) They use lists. I don't know where they get them.

I went back to the bathroom, wiped water droplets from the plastic cover of the library book, and carefully lowered myself back into the water. It was too cool. I ran more hot water and was just getting my blood pressure back to normal when the phone rang again.

So I sat there through fifteen rings, trying to ignore it.

Did you ever try to read with the phone ringing?

On the sixteenth ring I got up. I dried off, put on a robe, walked slowly and deliberately into the living room. I stared at the phone for a while.

On the fiftieth ring I picked it up.

"This is a recording. Please do not hang up until the message has been completed. This call originates from the house of your next-door neighbor, Charles Kluge. It will repeat every ten minutes. Mister Kluge knows he has not been the best of neighbors, and apologizes in advance for the inconvenience. He requests that you go immediately to his house. The key is under the mat. Go inside and do what needs to be done. There will be a reward for your services. Thank you."

Click. Dial tone.

I'm not a hasty man. Ten minutes later, when the phone rang again, I was still sitting there thinking it over. I picked up the receiver and listened carefully.

It was the same message. As before, it was not Kluge's voice. It was something synthesized, with all the human warmth of a Speak'n'Spell.

I heard it out again, and cradled the receiver when it was done.

I thought about calling the police. Charles Kluge had lived next door to me for ten years. In that time I may have had a dozen conversations with him, none lasting longer than a minute. I owed him nothing.

I thought about ignoring it. I was still thinking about that when the phone rang again. I glanced at my watch. Ten minutes. I lifted the receiver and put it right back down.

I could disconnect the phone. It wouldn't change my life radically.

But in the end I got dressed and went out the front door, turned left, and walked toward Kluge's property.

My neighbor across the street, Hal Lanier, was out mowing the lawn. He waved to me, and I waved back. It was about seven in the evening of a wonderful August day. The shadows were long. There was the smell of cut grass in the air. I've always liked that smell. About time to cut my own lawn, I thought.

It was a thought Kluge had never entertained. His lawn was brown and knee-high and choked with weeds.

I rang the bell. When nobody came I knocked. Then I sighed, looked under the mat, and used the key I found there to open the door.

"Kluge?" I called out as I stuck my head in.

I went along the short hallway, tentatively, as people do when unsure of their welcome. The drapes were drawn, as always, so it was dark in there, but in what had once been the living room ten television screens gave more than enough light for me to see Kluge. He sat in a chair in front of a table, with his face pressed into a computer keyboard and the side of his head blown away.

* * *

Hal Lanier operates a computer for the L.A.P.D., so I told him what I had found and he called the police. We waited together for the first car to arrive. Hal kept asking if I'd touched anything, and I kept telling him no, except for the front door knob.

An ambulance arrived without the siren. Soon there were police all over, and neighbors standing out in their yards or talking in front of Kluge's house. Crews from some of the television stations arrived in time to get pictures of the body, wrapped in a plastic sheet, being carried out. Men and women came and went. I assumed they were doing all the standard police things, taking fingerprints, collecting evidence. I would have gone home, but had been told to stick around.

Finally I was brought in to see Detective Osborne, who was in charge of the case. I was led into Kluge's living room. All the television screens were still turned on. I shook hands with Osborne. He looked me over before he said anything. He was a short guy, balding. He seemed very tired until he looked at me. Then, though nothing really changed in his face, he didn't look tired at all.

"You're Victor Apfel?" he asked. I told him I was. He gestured at the room. "Mister Apfel, can you tell if anything has been taken from this room?"

I took another look around, approaching it as a puzzle.

There was a fireplace and there were curtains over the windows. There was a rug on the floor. Other than those items, there was nothing else you would expect to find in a living room.

All the walls were lined with tables, leaving a narrow aisle down the middle. On the tables were monitor screens, keyboards, disc drives—all the glossy bric-a-brac of the new age. They were interconnected by thick cables and cords. Beneath the tables were still more computers, and boxes full of electronic items. Above the tables were shelves that reached the ceiling and were stuffed with boxes of tapes, discs, cartridges . . . there was a word for it which I couldn't recall just then. It was software.

"There's no furniture, is there? Other than that . . ."

He was looking confused.

"You mean there was furniture here before?"

"How I would I know?" Then I realized what the misunderstanding was. "Oh. You thought I'd been here before. The first time I ever set foot in this room was about an hour ago."

He frowned, and I didn't like that much.

"The medical examiner says the guy had been dead about three hours. How come you came over when you did, Victor?"

I didn't like him using my first name, but didn't see what I could do about it. And I knew I had to tell him about the phone call.

He looked dubious. But there was one easy way to check it out, and we did that. Hal and Osborne and I and several others trooped over to my house. My phone was ringing as we entered.

Osborne picked it up and listened. He got a very sour expression on his face. As the night wore on, it just got worse and worse.

We waited ten minutes for the phone to ring again. Osborne spent the time examining everything in my living room. I was glad when the phone rang again. They made a recording of the message, and we went back to Kluge's house.

Osborne went into the back yard to see Kluge's forest of antennas. He looked impressed.

"Mrs. Madison down the street thinks he was trying to contact Martians," Hal said, with a laugh. "Me, I just thought he was stealing HBO." There were three parabolic dishes. There were six tall masts, and some of those things you see on telephone company buildings for transmitting microwaves.

Osborne took me to the living room again. He asked me to describe what I had seen. I didn't know what good that would do, but I tried.

"He was sitting in that chair, which was here in front of this table. I saw the gun on the floor. His hand was hanging down toward it."

"You think it was suicide?"

"Yes, I guess I did think that." I waited for him to comment, but he didn't. "Is that what you think?"

He sighed. "There wasn't any note."

"They don't always leave notes," Hal pointed out.

"No, but they do often enough that my nose starts to twitch when they don't." He shrugged. "It's probably nothing."

"That phone call," I said. "That might be a kind of suicide note."

Osborne nodded. "Was there anything else you noticed?"

I went to the table and looked at the keyboard. It was made by Texas Instruments, model TI-99/4A. There was a large bloodstain on the right side of it, where his head had been resting.

"Just that he was sitting in front of this machine." I touched a key, and the monitor screen behind the keyboard immediately filled with words. I quickly drew my hand back, then stared at the message there.

PROGRAM NAME: GOODBYE REAL WORLD
DATE: 8/20
CONTENTS: LAST WILL AND TESTAMENT; MISC. FEATURES
PROGRAMMER: "CHARLES KLUGE"

TO RUN
PRESS ENTER■

The black square at the end flashed on and off. Later I learned it was called a cursor.

Everyone gathered around. Hal, the computer expert, explained how many computers went blank after ten minutes of no activity, so the words wouldn't be burned into the television screen. This one had been green until I touched it, then displayed black letters on a blue background.

"Has this console been checked for prints?" Osborne asked. Nobody seemed to know, so Osborne took a pencil and used the eraser to press the ENTER key.

The screen cleared, stayed blue for a moment, then filled with little ovoid shapes that started at the top of the screen and descended like rain. There were hundreds of them in many colors.

"Those are pills," one of the cops said, in amazement. "Look, that's gotta be a Quaalude. There's a Nembutal." Other cops pointed out other pills. I recognized the distinctive red stripe around the center of a white capsule that had to be a Dilantin. I had been taking them every day for years.

Finally the pills stopped falling, and the damn thing started to play music at us. "Nearer My God To Thee," in three-part harmony.

A few people laughed. I don't think any of us thought it was funny—it was creepy as hell listening to that eerie dirge—but it sounded like it had been scored for pennywhistle, calliope, and kazoo. What could you do but laugh?

As the music played, a little figure composed entirely of squares entered from the left of the screen and jerked spastically toward the center. It was like one of those human figures from a video game, but not as detailed. You had to use your imagination to believe it was a man.

A shape appeared in the middle of the screen. The "man" stopped in front of it. He bent in the middle, and something that might have been a chair appeared under him.

"What's that supposed to be?"

"A computer. Isn't it?"

It must have been, because the little man extended his arms, which jerked up and down like Liberace at the piano. He was typing. The words appeared above him.

SOMEWHERE ALONG THE LINE I MISSED SOMETHING. I SIT HERE, NIGHT AND DAY, A SPIDER IN THE CENTER OF A COAXIAL WEB,

MASTER OF ALL I SURVEY . . . AND IT IS NOT ENOUGH. THERE
MUST BE MORE.

ENTER YOUR NAME HERE■

"Jesus Christ," Hal said. "I don't believe it. An interactive suicide
note."

"Come on, we've got to see the rest of this."

I was nearest the keyboard, so I leaned over and typed my name.
But when I looked up, what I had typed was VICT9R.

"How do you back this up?" I asked.

"Just enter it," Osborne said. He reached around me and pressed
enter.

DO YOU EVER GET THAT FEELING, VICT9R? YOU HAVE WORKED
ALL YOUR LIFE TO BE THE BEST THERE IS AT WHAT YOU DO, AND
ONE DAY YOU WAKE UP TO WONDER WHY YOU ARE DOING IT?
THAT IS WHAT HAPPENED TO ME.

DO YOU WANT TO HEAR MORE, VICT9R? Y/N■

The message rambled from that point. Kluge seemed to be aware
of it, apologetic about it, because at the end of each forty or fifty-word
paragraph the reader was given the Y/N option.

I kept glancing from the screen to the keyboard, remembering
Kluge slumped across it. I thought about him sitting here alone, writing this.

He said he was despondent. He didn't feel like he could go on. He
was taking too many pills (more of them rained down the screen at this
point), and he had no further goal. He had done everything he set out
to do. We didn't understand what he meant by that. He said he no
longer existed. We thought that was a figure of speech.

ARE YOU A COP, VICT9R? IF YOU ARE NOT, A COP WILL BE HERE
SOON. SO TO YOU OR THE COP: I WAS NOT SELLING NARCOTICS.
THE DRUGS IN MY BEDROOM WERE FOR MY OWN PERSONAL
USE. I USED A LOT OF THEM. AND NOW I WILL NOT NEED THEM
ANYMORE.

PRESS ENTER■

Osborne did, and a printer across the room began to chatter,
scaring the hell out of all of us. I could see the carriage zipping back

and forth, printing in both directions, when Hal pointed at the screen and shouted.

"Look! Look at that!"

The compugraphic man was standing again. He faced us. He had something that had to be a gun in his hand, which he now pointed at his head.

"Don't do it!" Hal yelled.

The little man didn't listen. There was a denatured gunshot sound, and the little man fell on his back. A line of red dripped down the screen. Then the green background turned to blue, the printer shut off, and there was nothing left but the little black corpse lying on its back and the word **DONE** at the bottom of the screen.

I took a deep breath, and glanced at Osborne. It would be an understatement to say he did not look happy.

"What's this about drugs in the bedroom?" he said.

We watched Osborne pulling out drawers in dressers and bedside tables. He didn't find anything. He looked under the bed, and in the closet. Like all the other rooms in the house, this one was full of computers. Holes had been knocked in walls for the thick sheaves of cables.

I had been standing near a big cardboard drum, one of several in the room. It was about thirty gallon capacity, the kind you ship things in. The lid was loose, so I lifted it. I sort of wished I hadn't.

"Osborne," I said. "You'd better look at this."

The drum was lined with a heavy-duty garbage bag. And it was two-thirds full of Quaaludes.

They pried the lids off the rest of the drums. We found drums of amphetamines, of Nembutals, of Valium. All sorts of things.

With the discovery of the drugs a lot more police returned to the scene. With them came the television camera crews.

In all the activity no one seemed concerned about me, so I slipped back to my own house and locked the door. From time to time I peeked out the curtains. I saw reporters interviewing the neighbors. Hal was there, and seemed to be having a good time. Twice crews knocked on my door, but I didn't answer. Eventually they went away.

I ran a hot bath and soaked in it for about an hour. Then I turned the heat up as high as it would go and got in bed, under the blankets.

I shivered all night.

Osborne came over about nine the next morning. I let him in. Hal followed, looking very unhappy. I realized they had been up all night. I poured coffee for them.

"You'd better read this first," Osborne said, and handed me the sheet of computer printout. I unfolded it, got out my glasses, and started to read.

It was in that awful dot-matrix printing. My policy is to throw any such trash into the fireplace, un-read, but I made an exception this time.

It was Kluge's will. Some probate court was going to have a lot of fun with it.

He stated again that he didn't exist, so he could have no relatives. He had decided to give all his worldly property to somebody who deserved it.

But who was deserving? Kluge wondered. Well, not Mr. and Mrs. Perkins, four houses down the street. They were child abusers. He cited court records in Buffalo and Miami, and a pending case locally.

Mrs. Radnor and Mrs. Polonski, who lived across the street from each other five houses down, were gossips.

The Anderson's oldest son was a car thief.

Marian Flores cheated on her high school algebra tests.

There was a guy nearby who was diddling the city on a freeway construction project. There was one wife in the neighborhood who made out with door-to-door salesmen, and two having affairs with men other than their husbands. There was a teenage boy who got his girlfriend pregnant, dropped her, and bragged about it to his friends.

There were no fewer than nineteen couples in the immediate area who had not reported income to the IRS, or who had padded their deductions.

Kluge's neighbors in back had a dog that barked all night.

Well, I could vouch for the dog. He'd kept me awake often enough. But the rest of it was *crazy!* For one thing, where did a guy with two hundred gallons of illegal narcotics get the right to judge his neighbors so harshly? I mean, the child abusers were one thing, but was it right to tar a whole family because their son stole cars? And for another . . . how did he *know* some of this stuff?

But there was more. Specifically, four philandering husbands. One was Harold "Hal" Lanier, who for three years had been seeing a woman named Toni Jones, a co-worker at the L.A.P.D. Data Processing facility. She was pressuring him for a divorce; he was "waiting for the right time to tell his wife."

I glanced up at Hal. His red face was all the confirmation I needed.

Then it hit me. What had Kluge found out about *me?*

I hurried down the page, searching for my name. I found it in the last paragraph.

". . . for thirty years Mr. Apfel has been paying for a mistake he did not even make. I won't go so far as to nominate him for sainthood, but by default—if for no other reason—I hereby leave all deed and title to my real property and the structure thereon to Victor Apfel."

I looked at Osborne, and those tired eyes were weighing me.

"But I don't *want* it!"

"Do you think this is the reward Kluge mentioned in the phone call?"

"It must be," I said. "What else could it be?"

Osborne sighed, and sat back in his chair. "At least he didn't try to leave you the drugs. Are you still saying you didn't know the guy?"

"Are you accusing me of something?"

He spread his hands. "Mister Apfel, I'm simply asking a question. You're never one hundred percent sure in a suicide. Maybe it was a murder. If it was, you can see that, so far, you're the only one we know of that's gained by it."

"He was almost a stranger to me."

He nodded, tapping his copy of the computer printout. I looked back at my own, wishing it would go away.

"What's this . . . mistake you didn't make?"

I was afraid that would be the next question.

"I was a prisoner of war in North Korea," I said.

Osborne chewed that over for a while.

"They brainwash you?"

"Yes." I hit the arm of my chair, and suddenly had to be up and moving. The room was getting cold. "No. I don't . . . there's been a lot of confusion about that word. Did they 'brainwash' me? Yes. Did they succeed? Did I offer a confession of my war crimes and denounce the U.S. Government? No."

Once more, I felt myself being inspected by those deceptively tired eyes.

"You still seem to have . . . strong feelings about it."

"It's not something you forget."

"Is there anything you want to say about it?"

"It's just that it was all so . . . no. No, I have nothing further to say. Not to you, not to anybody."

"I'm going to have to ask you more questions about Kluge's death."

"I think I'll have my lawyer present for those." Christ. Now I am going to have to get a lawyer. I didn't know where to begin.

Osborne just nodded again. He got up and went to the door.

"I was ready to write this one down as a suicide," he said. "The only thing that bothered me was there was no note. Now we've got a note." He gestured in the direction of Kluge's house, and started to look angry.

"This guy not only writes a note, he programs the fucking thing into his computer, complete with special effects straight out of Pac-Man.

"Now, I know people do crazy things. I've seen enough of them. But when I heard the computer playing a hymn, that's when I knew this was murder. Tell you the truth, Mr. Apfel, I don't think you did it. There must be two dozen motives for murder in that printout. Maybe he was blackmailing people around here. Maybe that's how he bought all those machines. And people with that amount of drugs usually die violently. I've got a lot of work to do on this one, and I'll find who did it." He mumbled something about not leaving town, and that he'd see me later, and left.

"Vic . . ." Hal said. I looked at him.

"About that printout," he finally said. "I'd appreciate it . . . well, they said they'd keep it confidential. If you know what I mean." He had eyes like a basset hound. I'd never noticed that before.

"Hal, if you'll just go home, you have nothing to worry about from me."

He nodded, and scuttled for the door.

"I don't think any of that will get out," he said.

It all did, of course.

It probably would have even without the letters that began arriving a few days after Kluge's death, all postmarked Trenton, New Jersey, all computer-generated from a machine no one was ever able to trace. The letters detailed the matters Kluge had mentioned in his will.

I didn't know about any of that at the time. I spent the rest of the day after Hal's departure lying in my bed, under the electric blanket. I couldn't get my feet warm. I got up only to soak in the tub or to make a sandwich.

Reporters knocked on the door but I didn't answer. On the second day I called a criminal lawyer—Martin Abrams, the first in the book—and retained him. He told me they'd probably call me down to the police station for questioning. I told him I wouldn't go, popped two Dilantin, and sprinted for the bed.

A couple of times I heard sirens in the neighborhood. Once I heard a shouted argument down the street. I resisted the temptation to look. I'll admit I was a little curious, but you know what happened to the cat.

I kept waiting for Osborne to return, but he didn't. The days turned into a week. Only two things of interest happened in that time.

The first was a knock on my door. This was two days after Kluge's death. I looked through the curtains and saw a silver Ferrari parked at the curb. I couldn't see who was on the porch, so I asked who it was.

"My name's Lisa Foo," she said. "You asked me to drop by."

"I certainly don't remember it."

"Isn't this Charles Kluge's house?"

"That's next door."

"Oh. Sorry."

I decided I ought to warn her Kluge was dead, so I opened the door. She turned around and smiled at me. It was blinding.

Where does one start in describing Lisa Foo? Remember when newspapers used to run editorial cartoons of Hirohito and Tojo, when the *Times* used the word "Jap" without embarrassment? Little guys with faces wide as footballs, ears like jug handles, thick glasses, two big rabbity buck teeth, and pencil-thin moustaches . . .

Leaving out only the moustache, she was a dead ringer for a cartoon Tojo. She had the glasses, and the ears, and the teeth. But her teeth had braces, like piano keys wrapped in barbed wire. And she was five-eight or five-nine and couldn't have weighed more than a hundred and ten. I'd have said a hundred, but added five pounds each for her breasts, so improbably large on her scrawny frame that all I could read of the message on her T-shirt was "POCK LIVE." It was only when she turned sideways that I saw the esses before and after.

She thrust out a slender hand.

"Looks like I'm going to be your neighbor for a while," she said. "At least until we get that dragon's lair next door straightened out." If she had an accent, it was San Fernando Valley.

"That's nice."

"Did you know him? Kluge, I mean. Or at least that's what he called himself."

"You don't think that was his name?"

"I doubt it. 'Klug' means clever in German. And it's hacker slang for being tricky. And he sure was a tricky bugger. Definitely some glitches in the wetware." She tapped the side of her head meaningfully. "Viruses and phantoms and demons jumping out every time they try to key in, Software rot, bit buckets overflowing onto the floor . . ."

She babbled on in that vein for a time. It might as well have been Swahili.

"Did you say there were demons in his computers?"

"That's right."

"Sounds like they need an exorcist."

She jerked her thumb at her chest and showed me another half-acre of teeth.

"That's me. Listen, I gotta go. Drop in and see me anytime."

The second interesting event of the week happened the next day. My bank statement arrived. There were three deposits listed. The first was the regular check from the V.A., for $487.00. The second was for $392.54, interest on the money my parents had left me fifteen years ago.

The third deposit had come in on the twentieth, the day Charles Kluge died. It was for $700,083.04.

A few days later Hal Lanier dropped by.

"Boy, what a week," he said. Then he flopped down on the couch and told me all about it.

There had been a second death on the block. The letters had stirred up a lot of trouble, especially with the police going house to house questioning everyone. Some people had confessed to things when they were sure the cops were closing in on them. The woman who used to entertain salesmen while her husband was at work had admitted her infidelity, and the guy had shot her. He was in the County Jail. That was the worst incident, but there had been others, from fist-fights to rocks thrown through windows. According to Hal, the IRS was thinking of setting up a branch office in the neighborhood, so many people were being audited.

I thought about the seven hundred thousand and eighty-three dollars.

And four cents.

I didn't say anything, but my feet were getting cold.

"I suppose you want to know about me and Betty," he said, at last. I didn't. I didn't want to hear *any* of this, but I tried for a sympathetic expression.

"That's all over," he said, with a satisfied sigh. "Between me and Toni, I mean. I told Betty all about it. It was real bad for a few days, but I think our marriage is stronger for it now." He was quiet for a moment, basking in the warmth of it all. I had kept a straight face under worse provocation, so I trust I did well enough then.

He wanted to tell me all they'd learned about Kluge, and he wanted to invite me over for dinner, but I begged off on both, telling him my war wounds were giving me hell. I just about had him to the door when Osborne knocked on it. There was nothing to do but let him in. Hal stuck around, too.

I offered Osborne coffee, which he gratefully accepted. He looked different. I wasn't sure what it was at first. Same old tired expression . . . no, it wasn't. Most of that weary look had been either an act or a cop's built-in cynicism. Today it was genuine. The tiredness had moved from his face to his shoulders, to his hands, to the way he walked and the way he slumped in the chair. There was a sour aura of defeat around him.

"Am I still a suspect?" I asked.

"You mean should you call your lawyer? I'd say don't bother. I checked you out pretty good. That will ain't gonna hold up, so your motive is pretty half-assed. Way I figure it, every coke dealer in the Marina had a better reason to snuff Kluge than you." He sighed. "I got a couple questions. You can answer them or not."

"Give it a try."

"You remember any unusual visitors he had? People coming and going at night?"

"The only visitors I *ever* recall were deliveries. Post office. Federal Express, freight companies . . . that sort of thing. I suppose the drugs could have come in any of those shipments."

"That's what we figure, too. There's no way he was dealing nickel and dime bags. He must have been a middle man. Ship it in, ship it out." He brooded about that for a while, and sipped his coffee.

"So are you making any progress?" I asked.

"You want to know the truth? The case is going in the toilet. We've got too many motives, and not a one of them that works. As far as we can tell, nobody on the block had the slightest idea Kluge had all that information. We've checked bank accounts and we can't find evidence of blackmail. So the neighbors are pretty much out of the picture. Though if he were alive, most people around here would like to kill him *now*."

"Damn straight," Hal said.

Osborne slapped his thigh. "If the bastard was alive, *I'd* kill him," he said. "But I'm beginning to think he never *was* alive."

"I don't understand."

"If I hadn't seen the goddam body . . ." He sat up a little straighter. "He said he didn't exist. Well, he practically didn't. PG&E never heard of him. He's hooked up to their lines and a meter reader came by every month, but they never billed him for a single kilowatt. Same with the phone company. He had a whole exchange in that house that was *made* by the phone company, and delivered by them, and installed by them, but they have no record of him. We talked to the guy who hooked it all up. He turned in his records, and the computer swallowed them. Kluge didn't have a bank account anywhere in California, and apparently he didn't need one. We've tracked down a hundred companies that sold things to him, shipped them out, and then either marked his account paid or forgot they ever sold him anything. Some of them have check numbers and account numbers in their books, for accounts or even *banks* that don't exist."

He leaned back in his chair, simmering at the perfidy of it all.

"The only guy we've found who ever heard of him was the guy who delivered his groceries once a month. Little store down on Sepulveda. They don't have a computer, just paper receipts. He paid by check. Wells Fargo accepted them and the checks never bounced. But Wells Fargo never heard of him."

I thought it over. He seemed to expect something of me at this point, so I made a stab at it.

"He was doing all this by computers?"

"That's right. Now, the grocery store scam I understand, almost. But more often than not, Kluge got right into the basic programming of the computers and wiped himself out. The power company was never paid, by check or any other way, because as far as they were concerned, they weren't selling him anything.

"No government agency has ever heard of him. We've checked him with everybody from the post office to the CIA."

"Kluge was probably an alias, right?" I offered.

"Yeah. But the FBI doesn't have his fingerprints. We'll find out who he was, eventually. But it doesn't get us any closer to whether or not he was murdered."

He admitted there was pressure to simply close the felony part of the case, label it suicide, and forget it. But Osborne would not believe it. Naturally, the civil side would go on for some time, as they attempted to track down all Kluge's deceptions.

"It's all up to the dragon lady," Osborne said. Hal snorted.

"Fat chance," Hal said, and muttered something about boat people.

"That girl? She's still over there? Who is she?"

"She's some sort of giant brain from Cal Tech. We called out there and told them we were having problems, and she's what they sent." It was clear from Osborne's face what he thought of any help she might provide.

I finally managed to get rid of them. As they went down the walk I looked over at Kluge's house. Sure enough, Lisa Foo's silver Ferrari was sitting in his driveway.

I had no business going over there. I knew that better than anyone.

So I set about preparing my evening meal. I made a tuna casserole—which is not as bland as it sounds, the way I make it—put it in the oven and went out to the garden to pick the makings for a salad. I was slicing cherry tomatoes and thinking about chilling a bottle of white wine when it occurred to me that I had enough for two.

Since I never do anything hastily, I sat down and thought it over for a while. What finally decided me was my feet. For the first time in a week, they were warm. So I went to Kluge's house.

The front door was standing open. There was no screen. Funny how disturbing that can look, the dwelling wide open and unguarded. I stood on the porch and leaned in, but all I could see was the hallway.

"Miss Foo?" I called. There was no answer.

The last time I'd been here I had found a dead man. I hurried in.

Lisa Foo was sitting on a piano bench before a computer console. She was in profile, her back very straight, her brown legs in lotus position, her fingers poised at the keys as words sprayed rapidly onto the screen in front of her. She looked up and flashed her teeth at me.

"Somebody told me your name was Victor Apfel," she said.

"Yes. Uh, the door was open . . ."

"It's hot," she said, reasonably, pinching the fabric of her shirt near her neck and lifting it up and down like you do when you're sweaty. "What can I do for you?"

"Nothing, really." I came into the dimness, and stumbled on something. It was a cardboard box, the large flat kind used for delivering a jumbo pizza.

"I was just fixing dinner, and it looks like there's plenty for two, so I was wondering if you . . ." I trailed off, as I had just noticed something else. I had thought she was wearing shorts. In fact, all she had on was the shirt and a pair of pink bikini underpants. This did not seem to make her uneasy.

". . . would you like to join me for dinner?"

Her smile grew even broader.

"I'd love to," she said. She effortlessly unwound her legs and bounced to her feet, then brushed past me, trailing the smells of perspiration and sweet soap. "Be with you in a minute."

I looked around the room again but my mind kept coming back to her. She liked Pepsi with her pizza; there were dozens of empty cans. There was a deep scar on her knee and upper thigh. The ashtrays were empty . . . and the long muscles of her calves bunched strongly as she walked. Kluge must have smoked, but Lisa didn't, and she had fine, downy hairs in the small of her back just visible in the green computer light. I heard water running in the bathroom sink, looked at a yellow notepad covered with the kind of penmanship I hadn't seen in decades, and smelled soap and remembered tawny brown skin and an easy stride.

She appeared in the hall, wearing cut-off jeans, sandals, and a new T-shirt. The old one had advertised BURROUGHS OFFICE SYS-

TEMS. This one featured Mickey Mouse and Snow White's Castle and smelled of fresh bleached cotton. Mickey's ears were laid back on the upper slopes of her incongruous breasts.

I followed her out the door. Tinkerbell twinkled in pixie dust from the back of her shirt.

"I like this kitchen," she said.

You don't really look at a place until someone says something like that.

The kitchen was a time capsule. It could have been lifted bodily from an issue of *Life* in the early fifties. There was the hump-shouldered Frigidaire, of a vintage when that word had been a generic term, like kleenex or coke. The counter tops were yellow tile, the sort that's only found in bathrooms these days. There wasn't an ounce of Formica in the place. Instead of a dishwasher I had a wire rack and a double sink. There was no electric can opener, Cuisinart, trash compacter, or microwave oven. The newest thing in the whole room was a fifteen-year-old blender.

I'm good with my hands. I like to repair things.

"This bread is terrific," she said.

I had baked it myself. I watched her mop her plate with a crust, and she asked if she might have seconds.

I understand cleaning one's plate with bread is bad manners. Not that I cared; I do it myself. And other than that, her manners were impeccable. She polished off three helpings of my casserole and when she was done the plate hardly needed washing. I had a sense of ravenous appetite barely held in check.

She settled back in her chair and I refilled her glass with white wine.

"Are you sure you wouldn't like some more peas?"

"I'd bust." She patted her stomach contentedly. "Thank you so much, Mister Apfel. I haven't had a home-cooked meal in ages."

"You can call me Victor."

"I just love American food."

"I didn't know there was such a thing. I mean, not like Chinese or . . . you *are* American, aren't you?" She just smiled. "What I mean—"

"I know what you meant, Victor. I'm a citizen, but not native-born. Would you excuse me for a moment? I know it's impolite to jump right up, but with these braces I find I have to brush *instantly* after eating."

I could hear her as I cleared the table. I ran water in the sink and started doing the dishes. Before long she joined me, grabbed a dish towel, and began drying the things in the rack, over my protests.

"You live alone here?" she asked.

"Yes. Have ever since my parents died."

"Ever married? If it's none of my business, just say so."

"That's all right. No, I never married."

"You do pretty good for not having a woman around."

"I've had a lot of practice. Can I ask you a question?"

"Shoot."

"Where are you from? Taiwan?"

"I have a knack for languages. Back home, I spoke pidgin American, but when I got here I cleaned up my act. I also speak rotten French, illiterate Chinese in four or five varieties, gutter Vietnamese, and enough Thai to holler, 'Me wanna see American Consul, pretty-damn-quick, you!' "

I laughed. When she said it, her accent was thick.

"I been here eight years now. You figured out where home is?"

"Vietnam?" I ventured.

"The sidewalks of Saigon, fer shure. Or Ho Chi Minh's Shitty, as the pajama-heads renamed it, may their dinks rot off and their butts be filled with jagged punjee-sticks. Pardon my French."

She ducked her head in embarrassment. What had started out light had turned hot very quickly. I sensed a hurt at least as deep as my own, and we both backed off from it.

"I took you for a Japanese," I said.

"Yeah, ain't it a pisser? I'll tell you about it some day. Victor, is that a laundry room through that door there? With an electric washer?"

"That's right."

"Would it be too much trouble if I did a load?"

It was no trouble at all. She had seven pairs of faded jeans, some with the legs cut away, and about two dozen T-shirts. It could have been a load of boys' clothing except for the frilly underwear.

We went into the back yard to sit in the last rays of the setting sun, then she had to see my garden. I'm quite proud of it. When I'm well, I spend four or five hours a day working out there, year-round, usually in the morning hours. You can do that in southern California. I have a small greenhouse I built myself.

She loved it, though it was not in its best shape. I had spent most of the week in bed or in the tub. As a result, weeds were sprouting here and there.

"We had a garden when I was little," she said. "And I spent two years in a rice paddy."

"That must be a lot different than this."

"Damn straight. Put me off rice for *years*."

She discovered an infestation of aphids, so we squatted down to pick them off. She had that double-jointed Asian peasant's way of sitting that I remembered so well and could never imitate. Her fingers were long and narrow, and soon the tips of them were green from squashed bugs.

We talked about this and that. I don't remember quite how it came up, but I told her I had fought in Korea. I learned she was twenty-five. It turned out we had the same birthday, so some months back I had been exactly twice her age.

The only time Kluge's name came up was when she mentioned how she liked to cook. She hadn't been able to at Kluge's house.

"He has a freezer in the garage full of frozen dinners," she said. "He had one plate, one fork, one spoon, and one glass. He's got the best microwave oven on the market. And that's *it*, man. Ain't nothing else in his kitchen at *all*." She shook her head, and executed an aphid. "He was one weird dude."

When her laundry was done it was late evening, almost dark. She loaded it into my wicker basket and we took it out to the clothesline. It got to be a game. I would shake out a T-shirt and study the picture or message there. Sometimes I got it, and sometimes I didn't. There were pictures of rock groups, a map of Los Angeles, Star Trek tie-ins . . . a little of everything.

"What's the L5 Society?" I asked her.

"Guys that want to build these great big farms in space. I asked 'em if they were gonna grow rice, and they said they didn't think it was the best crop for zero gee, so I bought the shirt."

"How many of these things do you have?"

"Wow, it's gotta be four or five hundred. I usually wear 'em two or three times and then put them away."

I picked up another shirt, and a bra fell out. It wasn't the kind of bra girls wore when I was growing up. It was very sheer, though somehow functional at the same time.

"You like, Yank?" Her accent was very thick. "You oughtta see my sister!"

I glanced at her, and her face fell.

"I'm sorry, Victor," she said. "You don't have to blush." She took the bra from me and clipped it to the line.

She must have mis-read my face. True, I had been embarrassed, but I was also pleased in some strange way. It had been a long time since anybody had called me anything but Victor or Mr. Apfel.

The next day's mail brought a letter from a law firm in Chicago. It was about the seven hundred thousand dollars. The money had come from a Delaware holding company which had been set up in 1933 to provide for me in my old age. My mother and father were listed as the founders. Certain long-term investments had matured, resulting in my recent windfall. The amount in my bank was *after* taxes.

It was ridiculous on the face of it. My parents had never had that kind of money. I didn't want it. I would have given it back if I could find out who Kluge had stolen it from.

I decided that, if I wasn't in jail this time next year, I'd give it all to some charity. Save the Whales, maybe, or the L5 Society.

I spent the morning in the garden. Later I walked to the market and bought some fresh ground beef and pork. I was feeling good as I pulled my purchases home in my fold-up wire basket. When I passed the silver Ferrari I smiled.

She hadn't come to get her laundry. I took it off the line and folded it, then knocked on Kluge's door.

"It's me. Victor."

"Come on in, Yank."

She was where she had been before, but decently dressed this time. She smiled at me, then hit her forehead when she saw the laundry basket. She hurried to take it from me.

"I'm sorry, Victor. I meant to get this—"

"Don't worry about it," I said. "It was no trouble. And it gives me the chance to ask if you'd like to dine with me again."

Something happened to her face which she covered quickly. Perhaps she didn't like "American" food as much as she professed to. Or maybe it was the cook.

"Sure, Victor, I'd love to. Let me take care of this. And why don't you open those drapes? It's like a tomb in here."

She hurried away. I glanced at the screen she had been using. It was blank, but for one word: intercourse-p. I assumed it was a typo.

I pulled the drapes open in time to see Osborne's car park at the curb. Then Lisa was back, wearing a new T-shirt. This one said A CHANGE OF HOBBIT, and had a picture of a squat, hairy-footed creature. She glanced out the window and saw Osborne coming up the walk.

"I say, Watson," she said. "It's Lestrade of the Yard. Do show him in."

That wasn't nice of her. He gave me a suspicious glance as he entered. I burst out laughing. Lisa sat on the piano bench, pokerfaced. She slumped indolently, one arm resting near the keyboard.

"Well, Apfel," Osborne started. "We've finally found out who Kluge really was."

"Patrick William Gavin," Lisa said.

Quite a time went by before Osborne was able to close his mouth. Then he opened it right up again.

"How the hell did you find that out?"

She lazily caressed the keyboard beside her.

"Well, of course I got it when it came into your office this morning. There's a little stoolie program tucked away in your computer that whispers in my ear every time the name Kluge is mentioned. But I didn't need that. I figured it out five days ago."

"Then why the . . . why didn't you tell me?"

"You didn't ask me."

They glared at each other for a while. I had no idea what events had led up to this moment, but it was quite clear they didn't like each other even a little bit. Lisa was on top just now, and seemed to be enjoying it. Then she glanced at her screen, looked surprised, and quickly tapped a key. The word that had been there vanished. She gave me an inscrutable glance, then faced Osborne again.

"If you recall, you brought me in because all your own guys were getting was a lot of crashes. This system was brain-damaged when I got here, practically catatonic. Most of it was down and your guys couldn't get it up." She had to grin at that.

"You decided I couldn't do any worse than your guys were doing. So you asked me to try and break Kluge's codes without frying the system. Well, I did it. All you had to do was come by and interface and I would have downloaded N tons of wallpaper right in your lap."

Osborne listened quietly. Maybe he even knew he had made a mistake.

"What did you get? Can I see it now?"

She nodded, and pressed a few keys. Words started to fill her screen, and one close to Osborne. I got up and read Lisa's terminal.

It was a brief bio of Kluge/Gavin. He was about my age, but while I was getting shot at in a foreign land, he was cutting a swath through the infant computer industry. He had been there from the ground up, working at many of the top research facilities. It surprised me that it had taken over a week to identify him.

"I compiled this anecdotally," Lisa said, as we read. "The first thing you have to realize about Gavin is that he exists nowhere in any computerized information system. So I called people all over the country—interesting phone system he's got, by the way; it generates a new number for each call, and you can't call back or trace it—and started asking who the top people were in the fifties and sixties. I got a lot of names. After that, it was a matter of finding out who no longer existed in the files. He faked his death in 1967. I located one account of it in a newspaper file. Everybody I talked to who had known him knew of his death. There is a paper birth certificate in Florida. That's the only other evidence I found of him. He was the only guy so many people in the field knew who left no mark on the world. That seemed conclusive to me."

Osborne finished reading, then looked up.

"All right, Ms. Foo. What else have you found out?"

"I've broken some of his codes. I had a piece of luck, getting into a basic rape-and-plunder program he'd written to attack *other* people's programs, and I've managed to use it against a few of his own. I've unlocked a file of passwords with notes on where they came from. And I've learned a few of his tricks. But it's the tip of the iceberg."

She waved a hand at the silent metal brains in the room.

"What I haven't gotten across to anyone is just what this *is*. This is the most devious electronic weapon ever devised. It's armored like a battleship. It has to be; there's a lot of very slick programs out there that grab an invader and hang on like a terrier. If they ever got this far Kluge could deflect them. But usually they never even knew they'd been burgled. Kluge'd come in like a cruise missile, low and fast and twisty. And he'd route his attack through a dozen cut-offs.

"He had a lot of advantages. Big systems these days are heavily protected. People use passwords and very sophisticated codes. But Kluge helped *invent* most of them. You need a damn good lock to keep out a locksmith. He helped *install* a lot of the major systems. He left informants behind, hidden in the software. If the codes were changed, the computer *itself* would send the information to a safe system that Kluge could tap later. It's like you buy the biggest, meanest, best-trained watchdog you can. And that night, the guy who *trained* the dog comes in, pats him on the head, and robs you blind."

There was a lot more in that vein. I'm afraid that when Lisa began talking about computers, ninety percent of my head shut off.

"I'd like to know something, Osborne," Lisa said.

"What would that be?"

"What is my status here? Am I supposed to be solving your crime for you, or just trying to get this system back to where a competent user can deal with it?"

Osborne thought it over.

"What worries me," she added, "is that I'm poking around in a lot of restricted data banks. I'm worried about somebody knocking on the door and handcuffing me. *You* ought to be worried, too. Some of these agencies wouldn't like a homicide cop looking into their affairs."

Osborne bridled at that. Maybe that's what she intended.

"What do I have to do?" he snarled. "Beg you to stay?"

"No. I just want your authorization. You don't have to put it in writing. Just say you're behind me."

"Look. As far as L.A. County and the State of California are concerned, this house doesn't exist. There is no lot here. It doesn't appear in the assessor's records. This place is in a legal limbo. If anybody can authorize you to use this stuff, it's me, because I believe a murder was committed in it. So you just keep doing what you've been doing."

"That's not much of a commitment," she mused.

"It's all you're going to get. Now, what else have you got?"

She turned to her keyboard and typed for a while. Pretty soon a printer started, and Lisa leaned back. I glanced at her screen. It said: osculate posterior-p. I remembered that osculate meant kiss. Well, these people have their own language. Lisa looked up at me and grinned.

"Not you," she said, quietly. *"Him."*

I hadn't the faintest notion of what she was talking about.

Osborne got his printout and was ready to leave. Again, he couldn't resist turning at the door for final orders.

"If you find anything to indicate he didn't commit suicide, let me know."

"Okay. He didn't commit suicide."

Osborne didn't understand for a moment.

"I want proof."

"Well, I have it, but you probably can't use it. He didn't write that ridiculous suicide note."

"How do you know that?"

"I knew that my first day here. I had the computer list the program. Then I compared it to Kluge's style. No *way* he could have written it. It's tighter'n a bug's ass. Not a spare line in it. Kluge didn't pick his alias for nothing. You know what it means?"

"Clever," I said.

"Literally. But it means . . . a Rube Goldberg device. Something overly complex. Something that works, but for the wrong reason. You 'kluge around' bugs in a program. It's the hacker's vaseline."

"So?" Osborne wanted to know.

"So Kluge's programs were really crocked. They were full of bells and whistles he never bothered to clean out. He was a genius, and his programs worked, but you wonder why they did. Routines so bletcherous they'd make your skin crawl. Real crufty bagbiters. But good programming's so rare, even his diddles were better than most people's super-moby hacks."

I suspect Osborne understood about as much of that as I did.

"So you base your opinion on his programming style."

"Yeah. Unfortunately, it's gonna be ten years or so before that's admissable in court, like graphology or fingerprints. But if you know anything about programming you can look at it and see it. Somebody else wrote that suicide note—somebody damn good, by the way. That program called up his last will and testament as a sub-routine. And he definitely *did* write that. It's got his fingerprints all over it. He spent the last five years spying on the neighbors as a hobby. He tapped into military records, school records, work records, tax files and bank accounts. And he turned every telephone for three blocks into a listening device. He was one hell of a snoop."

"Did he mention anywhere why he did that?" Osborne asked.

"I think he was more than half crazy. Possibly he was suicidal. He sure wasn't doing himself any good with all those pills he took. But he was preparing himself for death, and Victor was the only one he found worthy of leaving it all to. I'd have *believed* he committed suicide if not for that note. But he didn't write it. I'll swear to that."

We eventually got rid of him, and I went home to fix the dinner. Lisa joined me when it was ready. Once more she had a huge appetite.

I fixed lemonade and we sat on my small patio and watched evening gather around us.

I woke up in the middle of the night, sweating. I sat up, thinking it out, and I didn't like my conclusions. So I put on my robe and slippers and went over to Kluge's.

The front door was open again. I knocked anyway. Lisa stuck her head around the corner.

"Victor? Is something wrong?"

"I'm not sure," I said. "May I come in?"

She gestured, and I followed her into the living room. An open can of Pepsi sat beside her console. Her eyes were red as she sat on her bench.

"What's up?" she said, and yawned.

"You should be asleep, for one thing," I said.

She shrugged, and nodded.

"Yeah. I can't seem to get in the right phase. Just now I'm in day mode. But Victor, I'm used to working odd hours, and long hours, and you didn't come over here to lecture me about that, did you?"

"No. You say Kluge was murdered."

"He didn't write his suicide note. That seems to leave murder."

"I was wondering why someone would kill him. He never left the house, so it was for something he did here with his computers. And now you're . . . well, I don't know *what* you're doing, frankly, but you seem to be poking into the same things. Isn't there a danger the same people will come after you?"

"People?" She raised an eyebrow.

I felt helpless. My fears were not well-formed enough to make sense.

"I don't know . . . you mentioned agencies . . ."

"You notice how impressed Osborne was with that? You think there's some kind of conspiracy Kluge tumbled to, or you think the CIA killed him because he found out too much about something, or—"

"I don't know, Lisa. But I'm worried the same thing could happen to you."

Surprisingly, she smiled at me.

"Thank you so much, Victor. I wasn't going to admit it to Osborne, but I've been worried about that, too."

"Well, what are you going to do?"

"I want to stay here and keep working. So I gave some thought to what I could do to protect myself. I decided there wasn't anything."

"Surely there's something."

"Well, I got a gun, if that's what you mean. But think about it. Kluge was offed in the middle of the day. Nobody saw anybody enter or leave the house. So I asked myself, who can walk into a house in broad daylight, shoot Kluge, program that suicide note, and walk away, leaving no traces he'd ever been there?"

"Somebody very good."

"Goddam good. So good there's not much chance one little gook's gonna be able to stop him if he decides to waste her."

She shocked me, both by her words and by her apparent lack of concern for her own fate. But she had said she was worried.

"Then you have to stop this. Get out of here."

"I won't be pushed around that way," she said. There was a tone of finality to it. I thought of things I might say, and rejected them all.

"You could at least . . . lock your front door," I concluded, lamely.

She laughed, and kissed my cheek.

"I'll do that, Yank. And I appreciate your concern. I really do."

I watched her close the door behind me, listened to her lock it, then trudged through the moonlight toward my house. Halfway there I stopped. I could suggest she stay in my spare bedroom. I could offer to stay with her at Kluge's.

No, I decided. She would probably take that the wrong way.

I was back in bed before I realized, with a touch of chagrin and more than a little disgust at myself, that she had every reason to take it the wrong way.

And me exactly twice her age.

* * *

I spent the morning in the garden, planning the evening's menu. I have always liked to cook, but dinner with Lisa had rapidly become the high point of my day. Not only that, I was already taking it for granted. So it hit me hard, around noon, when I looked out the front and saw her car gone.

I hurried to Kluge's front door. It was standing open. I made a quick search of the house. I found nothing until the master bedroom, where her clothes were stacked neatly on the floor.

Shivering, I pounded on the Laniers' front door. Betty answered, and immediately saw my agitation.

"The girl at Kluge's house," I said. "I'm afraid something's wrong. Maybe we'd better call the police."

"What happened?" Betty asked, looking over my shoulder. "Did she call you? I see she's not back yet."

"Back?"

"I saw her drive away about an hour ago. That's quite a car she has."

Feeling like a fool, I tried to make nothing of it, but I caught a look in Betty's eye. I think she'd have liked to pat me on the head. It made me furious.

But she'd left her clothes, so surely she was coming back.

I kept telling myself that, then went to run a bath, as hot as I could stand it.

When I answered the door she was standing there with a grocery bag in each arm and her usual blinding smile on her face.

"I wanted to do this yesterday but I forgot until you came over, and I know I should have asked first, but then I wanted to surprise you, so I just went to get one or two items you didn't have in your garden and a couple of things that weren't in your spice rack . . ."

She kept talking as we unloaded the bags in the kitchen. I said nothing. She was wearing a new T-shirt. There was a big V, and under it a picture of a screw, followed by a hyphen and a small case "p." I thought it over as she babbled on. V, screw-p. I was determined not to ask what it meant.

"Do you like Vietnamese cooking?"

I looked at her, and finally realized she was very nervous.

"I don't know," I said. "I've never had it. But I like Chinese, and Japanese, and Indian. I like to try new things." The last part was a lie, but not as bad as it might have been. I do try new recipes, and my tastes in food are catholic. I didn't expect to have much trouble with southeast Asian cuisine.

"Well, when I get through you *still* won't know," she laughed. "My momma was half-Chinese. So what you're gonna get here is a mongrel meal." She glanced up, saw my face, and laughed.

"I forgot. You've been to Asia. No, Yank, I ain't gonna serve any dog meat."

There was only one intolerable thing, and that was the chopsticks. I used them for as long as I could, then put them aside and got a fork.

"I'm sorry," I said. "Chopsticks happen to be a problem for me."

"You use them very well."

"I had plenty of time to learn how."

It was very good, and I told her so. Each dish was a revelation, not quite like anything I had ever had. Toward the end, I broke down halfway.

"Does the V stand for victory?" I asked.

"Maybe."

"Beethoven? Churchill? World War Two?"

She just smiled.

"Think of it as a challenge, Yank."

"Do I frighten you, Victor?"

"You did at first."

"It's my face, isn't it?"

"It's a generalized phobia of Orientals. I suppose I'm a racist. Not because I want to be."

She nodded slowly, there in the dark. We were on the patio again, but the sun had gone down a long time ago. I can't recall what we had talked about for all those hours. It had kept us busy, anyway.

"I have the same problem," she said.

"Fear of Orientals?" I had meant it as a joke.

"Of Cambodians." She let me take that in for a while, then went on. "When Saigon fell, I fled to Cambodia. It took me two years with stops when the Khmer Rouge put me in labor camps. I'm lucky to be alive, really."

"I thought they called it Kampuchea now."

She spat. I'm not even sure she was aware she had done it.

"It's the People's Republic of Syphilitic Dogs. The North Koreans treated you very badly, didn't they, Victor?"

"That's right."

"Koreans are pus suckers." I must have looked surprised, because she chuckled.

"You Americans feel so guilty about racism. As if you had invented it and nobody else—except maybe the South Africans and the Nazis—had ever practiced it as heinously as you. And you can't tell one yellow face from another, so you think of the yellow races as one homogeneous block. When in fact Orientals are among the most racist people on the earth. The Vietnamese have hated the Cambodians for a thousand years. The Chinese hate the Japanese. The Koreans hate everybody. And *everybody* hates the 'ethnic Chinese.' The Chinese are the Jews of the East."

"I've heard that."

She nodded, lost in her own thoughts.

"And I hate all Cambodians," she said, at last. "Like you, I don't wish to. Most of the people who suffered in the camps were Cambodians. It was the genocidal leaders, the Pol Pot scum, who I should hate." She looked at me. "But sometimes we don't get a lot of choice about things like that, do we, Yank?"

The next day I visited her at noon. It had cooled down, but was still warm in her dark den. She had not changed her shirt.

She told me a few things about computers. When she let me try some things on the keyboard I quickly got lost. We decided I needn't plan on a career as a computer programmer.

One of the things she showed me was called a telephone modem, whereby she could reach other computers all over the world. She "interfaced" with someone at Stanford who she had never met, and who she knew only as "Bubble Sorter." They typed things back and forth at each other.

At the end, Bubble Sorter wrote "bye-p." Lisa typed T.

"What's T?" I asked.

"True. Means yes, but yes would be too straightforward for a hacker."

"You told me what a byte is. What's a byep?"

She looked up at me seriously.

"It's a question. Add p to a word, and make it a question. So bye-p means Bubble Sorter was asking if I wanted to log out. Sign off."

I thought that over.

"So how would you translate 'osculate posterior-p'?"

" 'You wanna kiss my ass?' But remember, that was for Osborne."

I looked at her T-shirt again, then up to her eyes, which were quite serious and serene. She waited, hands folded in her lap.

Intercourse-p.

"Yes," I said. "I would."

She put her glasses on the table and pulled her shirt over her head.

We made love in Kluge's big waterbed.

I had a certain amount of performance anxiety—it had been a long, *long* time. After that, I was so caught up in the touch and smell and taste of her that I went a little crazy. She didn't seem to mind.

At last we were done, and bathed in sweat. She rolled over, stood, and went to the window. She opened it, and a breath of air blew over me. Then she put one knee on the bed, leaned over me, and got a pack of cigarettes from the bedside table. She lit one.

"I hope you're not allergic to smoke," she said.

"No. My father smoked. But I didn't know you did."

"Only afterwards," she said, with a quick smile. She took a deep drag. "Everybody in Saigon smoked, I think." She stretched out on her back beside me and we lay like that, soaking wet, holding hands. She opened her legs so one of her bare feet touched mine. It seemed enough contact. I watched the smoke rise from her right hand.

"I haven't felt warm in thirty years," I said. "I've been hot, but I've never been warm. I feel warm now."

"Tell me about it," she said.

So I did, as much as I could, wondering if it would work this time. At thirty years remove, my story does not sound so horrible. We've seen so much in that time. There were people in jails at that very moment, enduring conditions as bad as any I encountered. The paraphernalia of oppression is still pretty much the same. Nothing physical happened to me that would account for thirty years lived as a recluse.

"I *was* badly injured," I told her. "My skull was fractured. I still have . . . problems from that. Korea can get very cold, and I was never warm enough. But it was the other stuff. What they call brain-washing now.

"We didn't know what it was. We couldn't understand that even after a man had told them all he knew they'd keep on at us. Keeping us awake. Disorienting us. Some guys signed confessions, made up all sorts of stuff, but even that wasn't enough. They'd just keep on at you.

"I never did figure it out. I guess I couldn't understand an evil that big. But when they were sending us back and some of the prisoners wouldn't go . . . they really didn't *want* to go, they really believed . . ."

I had to pause there. Lisa sat up, moved quietly to the end of the bed, and began massaging my feet.

"We got a taste of what the Vietnam guys got, later. Only for us it was reversed. The G.I.'s were heroes, and the prisoners were . . ."

"You didn't break," she said. It wasn't a question.

"No, I didn't."

"That would be worse."

I looked at her. She had my foot pressed against her flat belly, holding me by the heel while her other hand massaged my toes.

"The country was shocked," I said. "They didn't understand what brainwashing was. I tried telling people how it was. I thought they were looking at me funny. After a while, I stopped talking about it. And I didn't have anything else to talk about.

"A few years back the Army changed its policy. Now they don't expect you to withstand psychological conditioning. It's understood you can say anything or sign anything."

She just looked at me, kept massaging my foot, and nodded slowly. Finally she spoke.

"Cambodia was hot," she said. "I kept telling myself when I finally got to the U.S. I'd live in Maine or someplace, where it snowed. And I did go to Cambridge, but I found out I didn't like snow."

She told me about it. The last I heard, a million people had died over there. It was a whole country frothing at the mouth and snapping at anything that moved. Or like one of those sharks you read about that, when its guts are ripped out, bends in a circle and starts devouring itself.

She told me about being forced to build a pyramid of severed heads. Twenty of them working all day in the hot sun finally got it ten feet high before it collapsed. If any of them stopped working, their own heads were added to the pile.

"It didn't mean anything to me. It was just another job. I was pretty crazy by then. I didn't start to come out of it until I got across the Thai border."

That she had survived it at all seemed a miracle. She had gone through more horror than I could imagine. And she had come through it in much better shape. It made me feel small. When I was her age, I was well on my way to building the prison I have lived in ever since. I told her that.

"Part of it is preparation," she said, wryly. "What you expect out of life, what your life has been so far. You said it yourself. Korea was new to you. I'm not saying I was ready for Cambodia, but my life up to that point hadn't been what you'd call sheltered. I hope you haven't been thinking I made a living in the streets by selling apples."

She kept rubbing my feet, staring off into scenes I could not see.

"How old were you when your mother died?"

"She was killed during Tet, 1968. I was ten."

"By the Viet Cong?"

"Who knows? Lot of bullets flying, lot of grenades being thrown."

She sighed, dropped my foot, and sat there, a scrawny Buddha without a robe.

"You ready to do it again, Yank?"

"I don't think I can, Lisa. I'm an old man."

She moved over me and lowered herself with her chin just below my sternum, settling her breasts in the most delicious place possible.

"We'll see," she said, and giggled. "There's an alternative sex act I'm pretty good at, and I'm pretty sure it would make you a young man again. But I haven't been able to do it for about a year on account of these." She tapped her braces. "It'd be sort of like sticking it in a buzz saw. So now I do this instead. I call it 'touring the silicone valley.' " She started moving her body up and down, just a few inches at a time. She blinked innocently a couple times, then laughed.

"At last, I can see you," she said. "I'm awfully myopic."

I let her do that for a while, then lifted my head.

"Did you say silicone?"

"Uh-huh. You didn't think they were real, did you?"

I confessed that I had.

"I don't think I've ever been so happy with anything I ever bought. Not even the car."

"Why did you?"

"Does it bother you?"

It didn't, and I told her so. But I couldn't conceal my curiosity.

"Because it was safe to. In Saigon I was always angry that I never developed. I could have made a good living as a prostitute, but I was always too tall, too skinny, and too ugly. Then in Cambodia I was lucky. I managed to pass for a boy some of the time. If not for that I'd have been raped a lot more than I was. And in Thailand I knew I'd get to the West one way or another, and when I got there, I'd get the best car there was, eat anything I wanted any time I wanted to, and purchase the best tits money could buy. You can't imagine what the West looks like from the camps. A place where you can buy tits!"

She looked down between them, then back at my face.

"Looks like it was a good investment," she said.

"They do seem to work okay," I had to admit.

We agreed that she would spend the nights at my house. There were certain things she had to do at Kluge's, involving equipment that had to be physically loaded, but many things she could do with a remote terminal and an armload of software. So we selected one of Kluge's best computers and about a dozen peripherals and installed her at a cafeteria table in my bedroom.

I guess we both knew it wasn't much protection if the people who got Kluge decided to get her. But I know I felt better about it, and I think she did, too.

The second day she was there a delivery van pulled up outside, and two guys started unloading a king-size waterbed. She laughed and laughed when she saw my face.

"Listen, you're not using Kluge's computers to—"

"Relax, Yank. How'd you think I could afford a Ferrari?"

"I've been curious."

"If you're really good at writing software you can make a lot of money. I own my own company. But every hacker picks up tricks here and there. I used to run a few Kluge scams, myself."

"But not anymore?"

She shrugged. "Once a thief, always a thief, Victor. I told you I couldn't make ends meet selling my bod."

Lisa didn't need much sleep.

We got up at seven, and I made breakfast every morning. Then we would spend an hour or two working in the garden. She would go to Kluge's and I'd bring her a sandwich at noon, then drop in on her several times during the day. That was for my own peace of mind; I never stayed more than a minute. Sometime during the afternoon I would shop or do household chores, then at seven one of us would cook dinner. We alternated. I taught her "American" cooking, and she taught me a little of everything. She complained about the lack of vital ingredients in American markets. No dogs, of course, but she claimed to know great ways of preparing monkey, snake, and rat. I never knew how hard she was pulling my leg, and didn't ask.

After dinner she stayed at my house. We would talk, make love, bathe.

She loved my tub. It is about the only alteration I have made in the house, and my only real luxury. I put it in—having to expand the bathroom to do so—in 1975, and never regretted it. We would soak for twenty minutes or an hour, turning the jets and bubblers on and off, washing each other, giggling like kids. Once we used bubble bath and made a mountain of suds four feet high, then destroyed it, splashing water all over the place. Most nights she let me wash her long black hair.

She didn't have any bad habits—or at least none that clashed with mine. She was neat and clean, changing her clothes twice a day and never so much as leaving a dirty glass on the sink. She never left a mess in the bathroom. Two glasses of wine was her limit.

I felt like Lazarus.

* * *

Osborne came by three times in the next two weeks. Lisa met him at Kluge's and gave him what she had learned. It was getting to be quite a list.

"Kluge once had an account in a New York bank with nine *trillion* dollars in it," she told me after one of Osborne's visits. "I think he did it just to see if he could. He left it in for one day, took the interest and fed it to a bank in the Bahamas, then destroyed the principal. Which never existed anyway."

In return, Osborne told her what was new on the murder investigation—which was nothing—and on the status of Kluge's property, which was chaotic. Various agencies had sent people out to look the place over. Some FBI men came, wanting to take over the investigation. Lisa, when talking about computers, had the power to cloud men's minds. She did it first by explaining exactly what she was doing, in terms so abstruse that no one could understand her. Sometimes that was enough. If it wasn't, if they started to get tough, she just moved out of the driver's seat and let them try to handle Kluge's contraption. She let them watch in horror as dragons leaped out of nowhere and ate up all the data on a disc, then printed "You Stupid Putz!" on the screen.

"I'm cheating them," she confessed to me. "I'm giving them stuff I *know* they're gonna step in, because I already stepped in it myself. I've lost about forty percent of the data Kluge had stored away. But the others lose a hundred percent. You ought to see their faces when Kluge drops a logic bomb into their work. That second guy threw a three thousand printer clear across the room. Then tried to bribe me to be quiet about it."

When some federal agency sent out an expert from Stanford, and he seemed perfectly content to destroy everything in sight in the firm belief that he was *bound* to get it right sooner or later, Lisa showed him how Kluge entered the IRS main computer in Washington and neglected to mention how Kluge had gotten out. The guy tangled with some watchdog program. During his struggles, it seemed he had erased all the tax records from the letter S down into the W's. Lisa let him think that for half an hour.

"I thought he was having a heart attack," she told me. "All the blood drained out of his face and he couldn't talk. So I showed him where I had—with my usual foresight—arranged for that data to be recorded, told him how to put it back where he found it, and how to pacify the watchdog. He couldn't get out of that house fast enough. Pretty soon he's gonna realize you *can't* destroy that much information with anything short of dynamite because of the backups and the limits of how much can be running at any one time. But I don't think he'll be back."

"It sounds like a very fancy video game," I said.

"It is, in a way. But it's more like Dungeons and Dragons. It's an endless series of closed rooms with dangers on the other side. You don't dare take it a step at a time. You take it a *hundredth* of a step at a time. Your questions are like, 'Now this isn't a question, but if it entered my mind to *ask* this question—which I'm not about to do—concerning what might happen if I looked at this door here—and I'm not touching it, I'm not even in the next room—what do you suppose you might do?' And the program crunches on that, decides if you fulfilled the conditions for getting a great big cream pie in the face, then either throws it or allows as how it *might* just move from step A to step A Prime. Then you say, 'Well, maybe I *am* looking at that door.' And sometimes the program says 'You looked, you looked, you dirty crook!' And the fireworks start."

Silly as all that sounds, it was very close to the best explanation she was ever able to give me about what she was doing.

"Are you telling everything, Lisa?" I asked her.

"Well, not *everything*. I didn't mention the four cents."

Four cents? Oh my god.

"Lisa, I didn't want that, I didn't ask for it, I wish he'd never—"

"Calm down, Yank. It's going to be all right."

"He kept records of all that, didn't he?"

"That's what I spend most of my time doing. Decoding his records."

"How long have you known?"

"About the seven hundred thousand dollars? It was in the first disc I cracked."

"I just want to give it back."

She thought that over, and shook her head.

"Victor, it'd be more dangerous to get rid of it now than it would be to keep it. It was imaginary money at first. But now it's got a history. The IRS thinks it knows where it came from. The taxes are paid on it. The State of Delaware is convinced that a legally chartered corporation disbursed it. An Illinois law firm has been paid for handling it. Your bank has been paying you interest on it. I'm not saying it would be impossible to go back and wipe all that out, but I wouldn't like to try. I'm good, but I don't have Kluge's touch."

"How could he *do* all that? You say it was imaginary money. That's not the way I thought money worked. He could just pull it out of thin air?"

Lisa patted the top of her computer console, and smiled at me.

"This is money, Yank," she said, and her eyes glittered.

* * *

At night she worked by candlelight so she wouldn't disturb me. That turned out to be my downfall. She typed by touch, and needed the candle only to locate software.

So that's how I'd go to sleep every night, looking at her slender body bathed in the glow of the candle. I was always reminded of melting butter dripping down a roasted ear of corn. Golden light on golden skin.

Ugly, she had called herself. Skinny. It was true she was thin. I could see her ribs when she sat with her back impossibly straight, her tummy sucked in, her chin up. She worked in the nude these days, sitting in lotus position. For long periods she would not move, her hands lying on her thighs, then she would poise, as if to pound the keys. But her touch was light, almost silent. It looked more like yoga than programming. She said she went into a meditative state for her best work.

I had expected a bony angularity, all sharp elbows and knees. She wasn't like that. I had guessed her weight ten pounds too low, and still didn't know where she put it. But she was soft and rounded, and strong beneath.

No one was ever going to call her face glamorous. Few would even go so far as to call her pretty. The braces did that, I think. They caught the eye and held it, drawing attention to that unsightly jumble.

But her skin was wonderful. She had scars. Not as many as I had expected. She seemed to heal quickly, and well.

I thought she was beautiful.

I had just completed my nightly survey when my eye was caught by the candle. I looked at it, then tried to look away.

Candles do that sometimes. I don't know why. In still air, with the flame perfectly vertical, they begin to flicker. The flame leaps up then squats down, up and down, up and down, brighter and brighter in regular rhythm, two or three beats to the second—

—and I tried to call out to her, wishing the candle would stop its regular flickering, but already I couldn't speak—

—I could only gasp, and I tried once more, as hard as I could, to yell, to scream, to tell her not to worry, and felt the nausea building . . .

I tasted blood. I took an experimental breath, did not find the smells of vomit, urine, feces. The overhead lights were on.

Lisa was on her hands and knees leaning over me, her face very close. A tear dropped on my forehead. I was on the carpet, on my back.

"Victor, can you hear me?"

I nodded. There was a spoon in my mouth. I spit it out.

"What happened? Are you going to be all right?"

I nodded again, and struggled to speak.

"You just lie there. The ambulance is on its way."

"No. Don't need it."

"Well, it's on its way. You just take it easy and—"

"Help me up."

"Not yet. You're not ready."

She was right. I tried to sit up, and fell back quickly. I took deep breaths for a while. Then the doorbell rang.

She stood up and started to the door. I just managed to get my hand around her ankle. Then she was leaning over me again, her eyes as wide as they would go.

"What is it? What's wrong now?"

"Get some clothes on," I told her. She looked down at herself, surprised.

"Oh. Right."

She got rid of the ambulance crew. Lisa was a lot calmer after she made coffee and we were sitting at the kitchen table. It was one o'clock, and I was still pretty rocky. But it hadn't been a bad one.

I went to the bathroom and got the bottle of Dilantin I'd hidden when she moved in. I let her see me take one.

"I forgot to do this today," I told her.

"It's because you hid them. That was stupid."

"I know." There must have been something else I could have said. It didn't please me to see her look hurt. But she was hurt because I wasn't defending myself against her attack, and that was a bit too complicated for me to dope out just after a grand mal.

"You can move out if you want to," I said. I was in rare form.

So was she. She reached across the table and shook me by the shoulders. She glared at me.

"I won't take a lot more of that kind of shit," she said, and I nodded, and began to cry.

She let me do it. I think that was probably best. She could have babied me, but I do a pretty good job of that myself.

"How long has this been going on?" she finally said. "Is that why you've stayed in your house for thirty years?"

I shrugged. "I guess it's part of it. When I got back they operated, but it just made it worse."

"Okay. I'm mad at you because you didn't tell me about it, so I didn't know what to do. I want to stay, but you'll have to tell me how. Then I won't be mad anymore."

I could have blown the whole thing right there. I'm amazed I didn't. Through the years I'd developed very good methods for doing things like that. But I pulled through when I saw her face. She really did want to stay. I didn't know why, but it was enough.

"The spoon was a mistake," I said. "If there's time, and if you can do it without risking your fingers, you could jam a piece of cloth in there. Part of a sheet, or something. But nothing hard." I explored my mouth with a finger. "I think I broke a tooth."

"Serves you right," she said. I looked at her, and smiled, then we were both laughing. She came around the table and kissed me, then sat on my knee.

"The biggest danger is drowning. During the first part of the seizure, all my muscles go rigid. That doesn't last long. Then they all start contracting and relaxing at random. It's *very* strong."

"I know. I watched, and I tried to hold you."

"Don't do that. Get me on my side. Stay behind me, and watch out for flailing arms. Get a pillow under my head if you can. Keep me away from things I could injure myself on." I looked her square in the eye. "I want to emphasize this. Just *try* to do all those things. If I'm getting too violent, it's better you stand off to the side. Better for both of us. If I knock you out, you won't be able to help me if I start strangling on vomit."

I kept looking at her eyes. She must have read my mind, because she smiled slightly.

"Sorry, Yank. I am not freaked out. I mean, like, it's totally gross, you know, and it barfs me out to the max, you could—"

"—gag me with a spoon, I know. Okay, right, I know I was dumb. And that's about it. I might bite my tongue or the inside of my cheek. Don't worry about it. There is one more thing."

She waited, and I wondered how much to tell her. There wasn't a lot she could do, but if I died on her I didn't want her to feel it was her fault.

"Sometimes I have to go to the hospital. Sometimes one seizure will follow another. If that keeps up for too long, I won't breathe, and my brain will die of oxygen starvation."

"That only takes about five minutes," she said, alarmed.

"I know. It's only a problem if I start having them frequently, so we could plan for it if I do. But if I don't come out of one, start having another right on the heels of the first, or if you can't detect any breathing for three or four minutes, you'd better call an ambulance."

"Three or four minutes? You'd be dead before they got here."

"It's that or live in a hospital. I don't like hospitals."

"Neither do I."

* * *

The next day she took me for a ride in her Ferrari. I was nervous about it, wondering if she was going to do crazy things. If anything, she was too slow. People behind her kept honking. I could tell she hadn't been driving long from the exaggerated attention she put into every movement.

"A Ferrari is wasted on me, I'm afraid," she confessed at one point. "I never drive it faster than fifty-five."

We went to an interior decorator in Beverly Hills and she bought a low-watt gooseneck lamp at an outrageous price.

I had a hard time getting to sleep that night. I suppose I was afraid of having another seizure, though Lisa's new lamp wasn't going to set it off.

Funny about seizures. When I first started having them, everyone called them fits. Then, gradually, it was seizures, until fits began to sound dirty.

I guess it's a sign of growing old, when the language changes on you.

There were rafts of new words. A lot of them were for things that didn't even exist when I was growing up. Like software. I always visualized a limp wrench.

"What got you interested in computers, Lisa?" I asked her.

She didn't move. Her concentration when sitting at the machine was pretty damn good. I rolled onto my back and tried to sleep.

"It's where the power is, Yank." I looked up. She had turned to face me.

"Did you pick it all up since you got to America?"

"I had a head start. I didn't tell you about my Captain, did I?"

"I don't think you did."

"He was strange. I knew that. I was about fourteen. He was an American, and he took an interest in me. He got me a nice apartment in Saigon. And he put me in school."

She was studying me, looking for a reaction. I didn't give her one.

"He was surely a pedophile, and probably had homosexual tendencies, since I looked so much like a skinny little boy."

Again the wait. This time she smiled.

"He was good to me. I learned to read well. From there on, anything is possible."

"I didn't actually ask you about your Captain. I asked why you got interested in computers."

"That's right. You did."

"Is it just a living?"

"It started that way. It's the future, Victor."

"God knows I've read that enough times."

"It's true. It's already here. It's power, if you know how to use it. You've seen what Kluge was able to do. You can make money with one of these things. I don't mean earn it, I mean *make* it, like if you had a printing press. Remember Osborne mentioned that Kluge's house didn't exist? Did you think what that means?"

"That he wiped it out of the memory banks."

"That was the first step. But the lot exists in the county plat books, wouldn't you think? I mean, this country hasn't *entirely* given up paper."

"So the county really does have a record of that house."

"No. That page was torn out of the records."

"I don't get it. Kluge never left the house."

"Oldest way in the world, friend. Kluge looked through the L.A.P.D. files until he found a guy known as Sammy. He sent him a cashier's check for a thousand dollars, along with a letter saying he could earn twice that if he'd go to the hall of records and do something. Sammy didn't bite, and neither did McGee, or Molly Unger. But Little Billy Phipps did, and he got a check just like the letter said, and he and Kluge had a wonderful business relationship for many years. Little Billy drives a new Cadillac now, and hasn't the faintest notion who Kluge was or where he lived. It didn't matter to Kluge how much he spent. He just pulled it out of thin air."

I thought that over for a while. I guess it's true that with enough money you can do just about anything, and Kluge had all the money in the world.

"Did you tell Osborne about Little Billy?"

"I erased that disc, just like I erased your seven hundred thousand. You never know when you might need somebody like Little Billy."

"You're not afraid of getting into trouble over it?"

"Life is risk, Victor. I'm keeping the best stuff for myself. Not because I intend to use it, but because if I ever needed it badly and didn't have it, I'd feel like such a fool."

She cocked her head and narrowed her eyes, which made them practically disappear.

"Tell me something, Yank. Kluge picked you out of all your neighbors because you'd been a Boy Scout for thirty years. How do you react to what I'm doing?"

"You're cheerfully amoral, and you're a survivor, and you're basically decent. And I pity anybody who gets in your way."

She grinned, stretched, and stood up.

" 'Cheerfully amoral.' I like that." She sat beside me, making a great sloshing in the bed. "You want to be amoral again?"

"In a little bit." She started rubbing my chest. "So you got into computers because they were the wave of the future. Don't you ever worry about them . . . I don't know, I guess it sounds corny . . . do you think they'll take over?"

"Everybody thinks that until they start to use them," she said. "You've got to realize just how stupid they are. Without programming they are good for nothing, literally. Now, what I do believe is that the people who *run* the computers will take over. They already have. That's why I study them."

"I guess that's not what I meant. Maybe I can't say it right."

She frowned. "Kluge was looking into something. He'd been eavesdropping in artificial intelligence labs, and reading a lot of neuro-logical research. I think he was trying to find a common thread."

"Between human brains and computers?"

"Not quite. He was thinking of computers and neurons. Brain cells." She pointed to her computer. "That thing, or any other computer, is light-years away from being a human brain. It can't general-ize, or infer, or categorize, or invent. With good programming it can appear to do some of those things, but it's an illusion.

"There's an old speculation about what would happen if we finally built a computer with as many transistors as the human brain has neurons. Would there be a self-awareness? I think that's baloney. A transistor isn't a neuron, and a quintillion of them aren't any better than a dozen.

"So Kluge—who seems to have felt the same way—started look-ing into the possible similarities between a neuron and an 8-bit com-puter. That's why he had all that consumer junk sitting around his house, those Trash-80's and Atari's and TI's and Sinclair's, for chris-sake. He was used to *much* more powerful instruments. He ate up the home units like candy."

"What did he find out?"

"Nothing, it looks like. An 8-bit unit is more complex than a neu-ron, and no computer is in the same galaxy as an organic brain. But see, the words get tricky. I said an Atari is more complex than a neuron, but it's hard to really compare them. It's like comparing a direction with a distance, or a color with a mass. The units are different. Except for one similarity."

"What's that?"

"The connections. Again, it's different, but the concept of net-working is the same. A neuron is connected to a lot of others. There are trillions of them, and the way messages pulse through them determines what we are and what we think and what we remember. And with that computer I can reach a million others. It's bigger than the human brain, really, because the information in that network is more than all human-ity could cope with in a million years. It reaches from Pioneer Ten, out beyond the orbit of Pluto, right into every living room that has a tele-phone in it. With that computer you can tap tons of data that has been collected but nobody's even had the time to look at.

"That's what Kluge was interested in. The old 'critical mass com-puter' idea, the computer that becomes aware, but with a new angle. Maybe it wouldn't be the size of the computer, but the *number* of com-puters. There used to be thousands of them. Now there's millions. They're putting them in cars. In wristwatches. Every home has several, from the simple timer on a microwave oven up to a video game or home terminal. Kluge was trying to find out if critical mass could be reached that way."

"What did he think?"

"I don't know. He was just getting started." She glanced down at me. "But you know what, Yank? I think you've reached critical mass while I wasn't looking."

"I think you're right." I reached for her.

Lisa liked to cuddle. I didn't, at first, after fifty years of sleeping alone. But I got to like it pretty quickly.

That's what we were doing when we resumed the conversation we had been having. We just lay in each others' arms and talked about things. Nobody had mentioned love yet, but I knew I loved her. I didn't know what to do about it, but I would think of something.

"Critical mass," I said. She nuzzled my neck, and yawned.

"What about it?"

"What would it be like? It seems like it would be such a vast intel-ligence. So quick, so omniscient. God-like."

"Could be."

"Wouldn't it . . . run our lives? I guess I'm asking the same ques-tions I started off with. Would it take over?"

She thought about it for a long time.

"I wonder if there would be anything to take over. I mean, why should it care? How could we figure what its concerns would be? Would it want to be worshipped, for instance? I doubt it. Would it want to 'rationalize all human behavior, to eliminate all emotion,' as I'm sure some sci-fi film computer must have told some damsel in dis-tress in the 'fifties.

"You can use a word like awareness, but what does it mean? An amoeba must be aware. Plants probably are. There may be a level of awareness in a neuron. Even in an integrated circuit chip. We don't even know what our own awareness really is. We've never been able to shine a light on it, dissect it, figure out where it comes from or where it goes when we're dead. To apply human values to a thing like this hypothetical computer-net consciousness would be pretty stupid. But I don't see how it could interact with human awareness at all. It might not even notice us, any more than we notice cells in our bodies, or neutrinos passing through us, or the vibrations of the atoms in the air around us."

So she had to explain what a neutrino was. One thing I always provided her with was an ignorant audience. And after that, I pretty much forgot about our mythical hyper-computer.

"What about your Captain?" I asked, much later.

"Do you really want to know, Yank?" she mumbled, sleepily.

"I'm not afraid to know."

She sat up and reached for her cigarettes. I had come to know she sometimes smoked them in times of stress. She had told me she smoked after making love, but that first time had been the only time. The lighter flared in the dark. I heard her exhale.

"My Major, actually. He got a promotion. Do you want to know his name?"

"Lisa, I don't want to know any of it if you don't want to tell it. But if you do, what I want to know is did he stand by you."

"He didn't marry me, if that's what you mean. When he knew he had to go, he said he would, but I talked him out of it. Maybe it was the most noble thing I ever did. Maybe it was the most stupid.

"It's no accident I look Japanese. My grandmother was raped in '42 by a Jap soldier of the occupation. She was Chinese, living in Hanoi. My mother was born there. They went south after Dien Bien Phu. My grandmother died. My mother had it hard. Being Chinese was tough enough, but being half Chinese and half Japanese was worse. My father was half French and half Annamese. Another bad combination. I never knew him. But I'm sort of a capsule history of Vietnam."

The end of her cigarette glowed brighter once more.

"I've got one grandfather's face and the other grandfather's height. With tits by Goodyear. About all I missed was some American genes, but I was working on that for my children.

"When Saigon was falling I tried to get to the American Embassy. Didn't make it. You know the rest, until I got to Thailand, and when I finally got Americans to notice me, it turned out my Major was still looking for me. He sponsored me over here, and I made it in time to watch him die of cancer. Two months I had with him, all of it in the hospital."

"My god." I had a horrible thought. "That wasn't the war, too, was it? I mean, the story of your life—"

"—is the rape of Asia. No, Victor. Not that war, anyway. But he was one of those guys who got to see atom bombs up close, out in Nevada. He was too Regular Army to complain about it, but I think he knew that's what killed him."

"Did you love him?"

"What do you want me to say? He got me out of hell."

Again the cigarette flared, and I saw her stub it out.

"No," she said. "I didn't love him. He knew that. I've never loved anybody. He was very dear, very special to me. I would have done almost anything for him. He was fatherly to me." I felt her looking at me in the dark. "Aren't you going to ask how old he was?"

"Fiftyish," I said.

"On the nose. Can I ask you something?"

"I guess it's your turn."

"How many girls have you had since you got back from Korea?"

I held up my hand and pretended to count on my fingers.

"One," I said, at last.

"How many before you went?"

"One. We broke up before I left for the war."

"How many in Korea?"

"Nine. All at Madame Park's jolly little whorehouse in Pusan."

"So you've made love to one white and ten Asians. I bet none of the others were as tall as me."

"Korean girls have fatter cheeks, too. But they all had your eyes."

She nuzzled against my chest, took a deep breath, and sighed.

"We're a hell of a pair, aren't we?"

I hugged her, and her breath came again, hot on my chest. I wondered how I'd lived so long without such a simple miracle as that.

"Yes. I think we really are."

Osborne came by again about a week later. He seemed subdued. He listened to the things Lisa had decided to give him without much interest. He took the printout she handed him, and promised to turn it over to the departments that handled those things. But he didn't get up to leave.

"I thought I ought to tell you, Apfel," he said, at last. "The Gavin case has been closed."

I had to think a moment to remember Kluge's real name had been Gavin.

"The coroner ruled suicide a long time ago. I was able to keep the case open quite a while on the strength of my suspicions." He nodded toward Lisa. "And on what she said about the suicide note. But there was just no evidence at all."

"It probably happened quickly," Lisa said. "Somebody caught him, tracked him back—it can be done; Kluge was lucky for a long time—and did him the same day."

"You don't think it was suicide?" I asked Osborne.

"No. But whoever did it is home free unless something new turns up."

"I'll tell you if it does," Lisa said.

"That's something else," Osborne said. "I can't authorize you to work over there any more. The county's taken possession of house and contents."

"Don't worry about it," Lisa said, softly.

There was a short silence as she leaned over to shake a cigarette from the pack on the coffee table. She lit it, exhaled, and leaned back beside me, giving Osborne her most inscrutable look. He sighed.

"I'd hate to play poker with you, lady," he said. "What do you mean, 'Don't worry about it'?"

"I bought the house four days ago. And its contents. If anything turns up that would help you re-open the murder investigation, I will let you know."

Osborne was too defeated to get angry. He studied her quietly for a while.

"I'd like to know how you swung that."

"I did nothing illegal. You're free to check it out. I paid good cash money for it. The house came onto the market. I got a good price at the Sheriff's sale."

"How'd you like it if I put my best men on the transaction? See if they can dig up some funny money? Maybe fraud. How about I get the F.B.I. in to look it all over?"

She gave him a cool look.

"You're welcome to. Frankly, Detective Osborne, I could have stolen that house, Griffith Park, and the Harbor Freeway and I don't think you could have caught me."

"So where does that leave me?"

"Just where you were. With a closed case, and a promise from me."

"I don't like you having all that stuff, if it can do the things you say it can do."

"I didn't expect you would. But that's not your department, is it? The county owned it for a while, through simple confiscation. They didn't know what they had, and they let it go."

"Maybe I can get the Fraud detail out here to confiscate your software. There's criminal evidence on it."

"You could try that," she agreed.

They stared at each other for a while. Lisa won. Osborne rubbed his eyes and nodded. Then he heaved himself to his feet and slumped to the door.

Lisa stubbed out her cigarette. We listened to him going down the walk.

"I'm surprised he gave up so easy," I said. "Or did he? Do you think he'll try a raid?"

"It's not likely. He knows the score."

"Maybe you could tell it to me."

"For one thing, it's not his department, and he knows it."

"Why did you buy the house?"

"You ought to ask *how*."

I looked at her closely. There was a gleam of amusement behind the poker face.

"Lisa. What did you do?"

"That's what Osborne asked himself. He got the right answer, because he understands Kluge's machines. And he knows how things get done. It was no accident that house going on the market, and no accident I was the only bidder. I used one of Kluge's pet councilmen."

"You bribed him?"

She laughed, and kissed me.

"I think I finally managed to shock you, Yank. That's gotta be the biggest difference between me and a native-born American. Average citizens don't spend much on bribes over here. In Saigon, everybody bribes."

"Did you bribe him?"

"Nothing so indelicate. One has to go in the back door over here. Several entirely legal campaign contributions appeared in the accounts of a State Senator, who mentioned a certain situation to someone, who happened to be in the position to do legally what I happened to want done." She looked at me askance. "Of *course* I bribed him, Victor. You'd be amazed to know how cheaply. Does that bother you?"

"Yes," I admitted. "I don't like bribery."

"I'm indifferent to it. It happens, like gravity. It may not be admirable, but it gets things done."

"I assume you covered yourself."

"Reasonably well. You're never entirely covered with a bribe, because of the human element. The councilman might geek if they got him in front of a grand jury. But they won't, because Osborne won't pursue it. That's the second reason he walked out of here without a fight. *He* knows how the world wobbles, he knows what kind of force I now possess, and he knows he can't fight it."

There was a long silence after that. I had a lot to think about, and I didn't feel good about most of it. At one point Lisa reached for the pack of cigarettes, then changed her mind. She waited for me to work it out.

"It is a terrific force, isn't it," I finally said.

"It's frightening," she agreed. "Don't think it doesn't scare me. Don't think I haven't had fantasies of being superwoman. Power is an awful temptation, and it's not easy to reject. There's so much I could do."

"Will you?"

"I'm not talking about stealing things, or getting rich."

"I didn't think you were."

"This is political power. But I don't know how to wield it . . . it sounds corny, but to use it for good. I've seen so much evil come from good intentions. I don't think I'm wise enough to do any good. And the chances of getting torn up like Kluge did are large. But I'm not wise enough to walk away from it. I'm still a street urchin from Saigon, Yank. I'm smart enough not to use it unless I have to. But I can't give it away, and I can't destroy it. Is that stupid?"

I didn't have a good answer for that one. But I had a bad feeling.

My doubts had another week to work on me. I didn't come to any great moral conclusions. Lisa knew of some crimes, and she wasn't reporting them to the authorities. That didn't bother me much. She had at her fingertips the means to commit more crimes, and that bothered me a lot. Yet I really didn't think she planned to do anything. She was smart enough to use the things she had only in a defensive way—but with Lisa that could cover a lot of ground.

When she didn't show up for dinner one evening, I went over to Kluge's and found her busy in the living room. A nine-foot section of shelving had been cleared. The discs and tapes were stacked on a table. She had a big plastic garbage can and a magnet the size of a softball. I watched her wave a tape near the magnet, then toss it in the garbage can, which was almost full. She glanced up, did the same operation with a handful of discs, then took off her glasses and wiped her eyes.

"Feel any better now, Victor?" she asked.

"What do you mean? I feel fine."

"No you don't. And I haven't felt right, either. It hurts me to do it, but I have to. You want to go get the other trash can?"

I did, and helped her pull more software from the shelves.

"You're not going to wipe it all, are you?"

"No. I'm wiping records, and . . . something else."

"Are you going to tell me what?"

"There are things it's better not to know," she said, darkly.

I finally managed to convince her to talk over dinner. She had said little, just eating and shaking her head. But she gave in.

"Rather dreary, actually," she said. "I've been probing around some delicate places the last couple days. These are places Kluge visited at will, but they scare the hell out of me. Dirty places. Places where they know things I thought I'd like to find out."

She shivered, and seemed reluctant to go on.

"Are you talking about military computers? The CIA?"

"The CIA is where it starts. It's the easiest. I've looked around at NORAD—that's the guys who get to fight the next war. It makes me shiver to see how easy Kluge got in there. He cobbled up a way to start World War Three, just as an exercise. That's one of the things we just erased. The last two days I was nibbling around the edges of the big boys. The Defense Intelligence Agency and the National Security . . . something. DIA and NSA. Each of them is bigger than the CIA. Something knew I was there. Some watchdog program. As soon as I realized that I got out quick, and I've spent the last five hours being sure it didn't follow me. And now I'm sure, and I've destroyed all that, too."

"You think they're the ones who killed Kluge?"

"They're surely the best candidates. He had tons of their stuff. I know he helped design the biggest installations at NSA, and he'd been poking around in there for years. One false step is all it would take."

"Did you get it all? I mean, are you sure?"

"I'm sure they didn't track me. I'm not sure I've destroyed all the records. I'm going back now to take a last look."

"I'll go with you."

We worked until well after midnight. Lisa would review a tape or a disc, and if she was in any doubt, toss it to me for the magnetic treatment. At one point, simply because she was unsure, she took the magnet and passed it in front of an entire shelf of software.

It was amazing to think about it. With that one wipe she had randomized billions of bits of information. Some of it might not exist anywhere else in the world. I found myself confronted by even harder questions. Did she have the right to do it? Didn't knowledge exist for everyone? But I confess I had little trouble quelling my protests. Mostly I was happy to see it go. The old reactionary in me found it easier to believe There Are Things We Are Not Meant To Know.

We were almost through when her monitor screen began to malfunction. It actually gave off a few hisses and pops, so Lisa stood back from it for a moment, then the streen started to flicker. I stared at it for a while. It seemed to me there was an image trying to form in the screen. Something three-dimensional. Just as I was starting to get a picture of it I happened to glance at Lisa, and she was looking at me. Her face was flickering. She came to me and put her hands over my eyes.

"Victor, you shouldn't look at that."

"It's okay," I told her. And when I said it, it was, but as soon as I had the words out I knew it wasn't. And that is the last thing I remembered for a long time.

I'm told it was a very bad two weeks. I remember very little of it. I was kept under high dosage of drugs, and my few lucid periods were always followed by a fresh seizure.

The first thing I recall clearly was looking up at Doctor Stuart's face. I was in a hospital bed. I later learned it was in Cedars-Sinai, not the Veteran's Hospital. Lisa had paid for a private room.

Stuart put me through the usual questions. I was able to answer them, though I was very tired. When he was satisfied as to my condition he finally began to answer some of my questions. I learned how long I had been there, and how it had happened.

"You went into consecutive seizures," he confirmed. "I don't know why, frankly. You haven't been prone to them for a decade. I was thinking you were well under control. But nothing is ever really stable, I guess."

"So Lisa got me here in time."

"She did more than that. She didn't want to level with me at first. It seems that after the first seizure she witnessed she read everything she could find. From that day, she had a syringe and a solution of Valium handy. When she saw you couldn't breathe she injected you with 100 milligrams, and there's no doubt it saved your life."

Stuart and I had known each other a long time. He knew I had no prescription for Valium, though we had talked about it the last time I was hospitalized. Since I lived alone, there would be no one to inject me if I got in trouble.

He was more interested in results than anything else, and what Lisa did had the desired result. I was still alive.

He wouldn't let me have any visitors that day. I protested, but soon was asleep. The next day she came. She wore a new T-shirt. This one had a picture of a robot wearing a gown and mortarboard, and said "Class of 11111000000." It turns out that was 1984 in binary notation.

She had a big smile and said "Hi, Yank!" and as she sat on the bed I started to shake. She looked alarmed and asked if she should call the doctor.

"It's not that," I managed to say. "I'd like it if you just held me."

She took off her shoes and got under the covers with me. She held me tightly. At some point a nurse came in and tried to shoo her out. Lisa gave her profanities in Vietnamese, Chinese, and a few startling ones in English, and the nurse left. I saw Doctor Stuart glance in later.

I felt much better when I finally stopped crying. Lisa's eyes were wet, too.

"I've been here every day," she said. "You look awful, Victor."

"I feel a lot better."

"Well, you look better than you did. But your doctor says you'd better stick around another couple of days, just to make sure."

"I think he's right."

"I'm planning a big dinner for when you get back. You think we should invite the neighbors?"

I didn't say anything for a while. There were so many things we hadn't faced. Just how long could it go on between us? How long before I got sour about being so useless? How long before she got tired of being with an old man? I don't know just when I had started to think of Lisa as a permanent part of my life. And I wondered how I could have thought that.

"Do you want to spend more years waiting in hospitals for a man to die?"

"What do you want, Victor? I'll marry you if you want me to. Or I'll live with you in sin. I prefer sin, myself, but if it'll make you happy—"

"I don't know why you want to saddle yourself with an epileptic old fart."

"Because I love you."

It was the first time she had said it. I could have gone on questioning—bringing up her Major again, for instance—but I had no urge to. I'm very glad I didn't. So I changed the subject.

"Did you get the job finished?"

She knew which job I was talking about. She lowered her voice and put her mouth close to my ear.

"Let's don't be specific about it here, Victor. I don't trust any place I haven't swept for bugs. But, to put your mind at ease, I did finish, and it's been a quiet couple of weeks. No one is any wiser, and I'll never meddle in things like that again."

I felt a lot better. I was also exhausted. I tried to conceal my yawns, but she sensed it was time to go. She gave me one more kiss, promising many more to come, and left me.

It was the last time I ever saw her.

At about ten o'clock that evening Lisa went into Kluge's kitchen with a screwdriver and some other tools and got to work on the microwave oven.

The manufacturers of those appliances are very careful to insure they can't be turned on with the door open, as they emit lethal radiation. But with simple tools and a good brain it is possible to circumvent the safety interlocks. Lisa had no trouble with them. About ten minutes after she entered the kitchen she put her head in the oven and turned it on.

It is impossible to say how long she held her head in there. It was long enough to turn her eyeballs to the consistency of boiled eggs. At some point she lost voluntary muscle control and fell to the floor, pulling the microwave down with her. It shorted out, and a fire started.

The fire set off the sophisticated burglar alarm she had installed a month before. Betty Lanier saw the flames and called the fire department as Hal ran across the street and into the burning kitchen. He dragged what was left of Lisa out onto the grass. When he saw what the fire had done to her upper body, and in particular her breasts, he threw up.

She was rushed to the hospital. The doctors there amputated one arm and cut away the frightful masses of vulcanized silicone, pulled all her teeth, and didn't know what to do about the eyes. They put her on a respirator.

It was an orderly who first noticed the blackened and bloody T-shirt they had cut from her. Some of the message was unreadable, but it began, "I can't go on this way anymore . . ."

There is no other way I could have told all that. I discovered it piecemeal, starting with the disturbed look on Doctor Stuart's face when Lisa didn't show up the next day. He wouldn't tell me anything, and I had another seizure shortly after.

The next week is a blur. I remember being released from the hospital, but I don't remember the trip home. Betty was very good to me. They gave me a tranquilizer called Tranxene, and it was even better. I ate them like candy. I wandered in a drugged haze, eating only when Betty insisted, sleeping sitting up in my chair, coming awake not knowing where or who I was. I returned to the prison camp many times. Once I recall helping Lisa stack severed heads.

When I saw myself in the mirror, there was a vague smile on my face. It was Tranxene, caressing my frontal lobes. I knew that if I was to live much longer, me and Tranxene would have to become very good friends.

I eventually became capable of something that passed for rational thought. I was helped along somewhat by a visit from Osborne. I was trying, at that time, to find reasons to live, and wondered if he had any.

"I'm very sorry," he started off. I said nothing. "This is on my own time," he went on. "The department doesn't know I'm here."

"Was it suicide?" I asked him.

"I brought along a copy of the . . . the note. She ordered it from a shirt company in Westwood, three days before the . . . accident."

He handed it to me, and I read it. I was mentioned, though not by name. I was "the man I love." She said she couldn't cope with my problems. It was a short note. You can't get too much on a T-shirt. I read it through five times, then handed it back to him.

"She told you Kluge didn't write his note. I tell you she didn't write this."

He nodded reluctantly. I felt a vast calm, with a howling nightmare just below it. Praise Tranxene.

"Can you back that up?"

"She saw me in the hospital shortly before she died. She was full of life and hope. You say she ordered the shirt three days before. I would have felt that. And that note is pathetic. Lisa was never pathetic."

He nodded again.

"Some things I want to tell you. There were no signs of a struggle. Mrs. Lanier is sure no one came in the front. The crime lab went over the whole place and we're sure no one was in there with her. I'd stake my life on the fact that no one entered or left that house. Now, *I* don't believe it was suicide, either, but do you have any suggestions?"

"The NSA," I said.

I explained about the last things she had done while I was still there. I told him of her fear of the government spy agencies. That was all I had.

"Well, I guess they're the ones who could do a thing like that, if anyone could. But I'll tell you, I have a hard time swallowing it. I don't know why, for one thing. Maybe you believe those people kill like you and I'd swat a fly." His look made it into a question.

"I don't know what I believe."

"I'm not saying they wouldn't kill for national security, or some such shit. But they'd have taken the computers, too. They wouldn't have left her alone, they wouldn't even have let her *near* that stuff after they killed Kluge."

"What you're saying makes sense."

He muttered on about it for quite some time. Eventually I offered him some wine. He accepted thankfully. I considered joining him—it would be a quick way to die—but did not. He drank the whole bottle, and was comfortably drunk when he suggested we go next door and look it over one more time. I was planning on visiting Lisa the next day, and knew I had to start somewhere building myself up for that, so I agreed to go with him.

We inspected the kitchen. The fire had blackened the counters and melted some linoleum, but not much else. Water had made a mess of the place. There was a brown stain on the floor which I was able to look at with no emotion.

So we went back to the living room, and one of the computers was turned on. There was a short message on the screen.

IF YOU WISH TO KNOW MORE

PRESS ENTER■

"Don't do it," I told him. But he did. He stood, blinking solemnly, as the words wiped themselves out and a new message appeared.

YOU LOOKED

The screen started to flicker and I was in my car, in darkness, with a pill in my mouth and another in my hand. I spit out the pill, and sat for a moment, listening to the old engine ticking over. In my other hand was the plastic pill bottle. I felt very tired, but opened the car door and shut off the engine. I felt my way to the garage door and opened it. The air outside was fresh and sweet. I looked down at the pill bottle and hurried into the bathroom.

When I got through what had to be done there were a dozen pills floating in the toilet that hadn't even dissolved. There were the wasted shells of many more, and a lot of other stuff I won't bother to describe. I counted the pills in the bottle, remembered how many there had been, and wondered if I would make it.

I went over to Kluge's house and could not find Osborne. I was getting tired, but I made it back to my house and stretched out on the couch to see if I would live or die.

* * *

The next day I found the story in the paper. Osborne had gone home and blown out the back of his head with his revolver. It was not a big story. It happens to cops all the time. He didn't leave a note.

I got on the bus and rode out to the hospital and spent three hours trying to get in to see Lisa. I wasn't able to do it. I was not a relative and the doctors were quite firm about her having no visitors. When I got angry they were as gentle as possible. It was then I learned the extent of her injuries. Hal had kept the worst from me. None of it would have mattered, but the doctors swore there was nothing left in her head. So I went home.

She died two days later.

She had left a will, to my surprise. I got the house and contents. I picked up the phone as soon as I learned of it, and called a garbage company. While they were on the way I went for the last time into Kluge's house.

The same computer was still on, and it gave the same message.

PRESS ENTER■

I cautiously located the power switch, and turned it off. I had the garbage people strip the place to the bare walls.

I went over my own house very carefully, looking for anything that was even the first cousin to a computer. I threw out the radio. I sold the car, and the refrigerator, and the stove, and the blender, and the electric clock. I drained the waterbed and threw out the heater.

Then I bought the best propane stove on the market, and hunted a long time before I found an old icebox. I had the garage stacked to the ceiling with firewood. I had the chimney cleaned. It would be getting cold soon.

One day I took the bus to Pasadena and established the Lisa Foo Memorial Scholarship fund for Vietnamese refugees and their children. I endowed it with seven hundred thousand eighty-three dollars and four cents. I told them it could be used for any field of study except computer science. I could tell they thought me eccentric.

And I really thought I was safe, until the phone rang.

I thought it over for a long time before answering it. In the end, I knew it would just keep on going until I did. So I picked it up.

For a few seconds there was a dial tone, but I was not fooled. I kept holding it to my ear, and finally the tone turned off. There was just silence. I listened intently. I heard some of those far-off musical tones that live in phone wires. Echoes of conversations taking place a thousand miles away. And something infinitely more distant and cool.

I do not know what they have incubated out there at the NSA. I don't know if they did it on purpose, or if it just happened, or if it even has anything to do with them, in the end. But I know it's out there, because I heard its soul breathing on the wires. I spoke very carefully.

"I do not wish to know any more," I said. "I won't tell anyone anything. Kluge, Lisa, and Osborne all committed suicide. I am just a lonely man, and I won't cause you any trouble."

There was a click, and a dial tone.

Getting the phone taken out was easy. Getting them to remove all the wires was a little harder, since once a place is wired they expect it to be wired forever. They grumbled, but when I started pulling them out myself, they relented, though they warned me it was going to cost.

PG&E was harder. They actually seemed to believe there was a regulation requiring each house to be hooked up to the grid. They were willing to shut off my power—though hardly pleased about it— but they just weren't going to take the wires away from my house. I went up on the roof with an axe and demolished four feet of eaves as they gaped at me. Then they coiled up their wires and went home.

I threw out all my lamps, all things electrical. With hammer, chisel, and handsaw I went to work on the drywall just above the baseboards.

As I stripped the house of wiring I wondered many times why I was doing it. Why was it worth it? I couldn't have very many more years before a final seizure finished me off. Those years were not going to be a lot of fun.

Lisa had been a survivor. She would have known why I was doing this. She had once said I was a survivor, too. I survived the camp. I survived the death of my mother and father and managed to fashion a solitary life. Lisa survived the death of just about everything. No survivor expects to live through it all. But while she was alive, she would have worked to stay alive.

And that's what I did. I got all the wires out of the walls, went over the house with a magnet to see if I had missed any metal, then spent a week cleaning up, fixing the holes I had knocked in the walls, ceiling, and attic. I was amused trying to picture the real-estate agent selling this place after I was gone.

It's a great little house, folks. No electricity . . .

* * *

Now I live quietly, as before.

I work in my garden during most of the daylight hours. I've expanded it considerably, and even have things growing in the front yard now.

I live by candlelight, and kerosene lamp. I grow most of what I eat.

It took a long time to taper off the Tranxene and the Dilantin, but I did it, and now take the seizures as they come. I've usually got bruises to show for it.

In the middle of a vast city I have cut myself off. I am not part of the network growing faster than I can conceive. I don't even know if it's dangerous, to ordinary people. It noticed me, and Kluge, and Osborne. And Lisa. It brushed against our minds like I would brush away a mosquito, never noticing I had crushed it. Only I survived.

But I wonder.

It would be very hard . . .

Lisa told me how it can get in through the wiring. There's something called a carrier wave that can move over wires carrying household current. That's why the electricity had to go.

I need water for my garden. There's just not enough rain here in southern California, and I don't know how else I could get the water.

Do you think it could come through the pipes?

PORTRAITS OF HIS CHILDREN

by GEORGE R.R. MARTIN

George R.R. Martin's work has brought him his share of science fiction awards. Hugos were bestowed on his novella, "A Song for Lya;" his short story, "The Way of Cross and Dragon;" and his terrifying novelette, "Sandkings" (which also picked up the Nebula Award). His deeply disturbing tale, "Portraits of His Children," appeared in the November 1985 issue of *Asimov's*. It brought the author his second Nebula for Best Novelette. Martin's short fiction has also received the Bram Stoker Award for best horror, and the World Fantasy Award. He is the editor of the Wild Cards series of anthologies, and his best known novels include *Fevre Dream* and *The Armageddon Rag*.

In recent years, George Martin's work has shown up in the television industry. He was story editor for *Twilight Zone* and the producer of *Beauty and the Beast*, and he wrote several of their episodes. The author lives in Santa Fe, New Mexico.

Richard Cantling found the package leaning up against his front door, one evening in late October when he was setting out for his walk. It annoyed him. He had told his postman repeatedly to ring the bell when delivering anything too big to fit through the mail slot, yet the man persisted in abandoning the packages on the porch, where any passerby could simply walk off with them. Although, to be fair, Cantling's house was rather isolated, sitting on the river bluffs at the end of a cul de sac, and the trees effectively screened it off from the street. Still, there was always the possibility of damage from rain or wind or snow.

Cantling's displeasure lasted only an instant. Wrapped in heavy brown paper and carefully sealed with tape, the package had a shape that told all. Obviously a painting. And the hand that had block-printed his address in heavy green marker was unmistakably Michelle's. Another self-portrait then. She must be feeling repentant.

He was more surprised than he cared to admit, even to himself. He had always been a stubborn man. He could hold grudges for years, even decades, and he had the greatest difficulty admitting any wrong. And Michelle, being his only child, seemed to take after him in all of that. He hadn't expected this kind of gesture from her. It was . . . well, sweet.

He set aside his walking stick to lug the package inside, where he could unwrap it out of the damp and the blustery October wind. It was about three feet tall, and unexpectedly heavy. He carried it awkwardly, shutting the door with his foot and struggling down the long foyer toward his den. The brown drapes were tightly closed; the room was dark, and heavy with the smell of dust. Cantling had to set down the package to fumble for the light.

He hadn't used his den much since that night, two months ago, when Michelle had gone storming out. Her self-portrait was still sitting up above the wide slate mantle. Below, the fireplace badly wanted cleaning, and on the built-in bookshelves his novels, all bound in handsome dark leather, stood dusty and disarrayed. Cantling looked at the old painting and felt a brief wash of anger return to him, followed by depression. It had been such a nasty thing for her to do. The portrait had been quite good, really. Much more to his taste than the tortured abstractions that Michelle liked to paint for her own pleasure, or the trite paperback covers she did to make her living. She had done it when she was twenty, as a birthday gift for him. He'd always been fond of it. It captured her as no photograph had ever done, not just the lines of her face, the high angular cheekbones and blue eyes and tangled ash-blond hair, but the personality inside. She looked so young and fresh and confident, and her smile reminded him so much of Helen, and the way she had smiled on their wedding day. He'd told Michelle more than once how much he'd liked that smile.

And so, of course, it had been the smile that she'd started on. She used an antique dagger from his collection, chopped out the mouth with four jagged slashes. She'd gouged out the wide blue eyes next, as if intent on blinding the portrait, and when he came bursting in after her, she'd been slicing the canvas into ribbons with long angry crooked cuts. Cantling couldn't forget the moment. So ugly. And to do something like that to her own work . . . he couldn't imagine it. He had tried to picture himself mutilating one of his books, tried to comprehend what might drive one to such an act, and he had failed utterly. It was unthinkable, beyond even imagination.

The mutilated portrait still hung in its place. He'd been too stubborn to take it down, and yet he could not bear to look at it. So he had taken to avoiding his den. It wasn't hard. The old house was a huge, rambling place, with more rooms than he could possibly need or want, living alone as he did. It had been built a century ago, when Perrot had been a thriving river town, and they said that a succession of steamer captains had lived there. Certainly the steamboat gothic architecture and all the gingerbread called up visions of the glory days on the river, and he had a fine view of the Mississippi from the third-story windows and the widow's walk. After the incident, Cantling had moved his desk and his typewriter to one of the unused bedrooms and settled in there, determined to let the den remain as Michelle had left it until she came back with an apology.

He had not expected that apology quite so soon, however, nor in quite this form. A tearful phone call, yes—but not another portrait. Still, this was nicer somehow, more personal. And it was a gesture, the first step toward a reconciliation. Richard Cantling knew too well that he was incapable of taking that step himself, no matter how lonely he might become. And he had been lonely, he did not try to fool himself on that score. He had left all his New York friends behind when he moved out to this Iowa river town, and had formed no local friendships to replace them. That was nothing new. He had never been an outgoing sort. He had a certain shyness that kept him apart, even from those few friends he did make. Even from his family, really. Helen had often accused him of caring more for his characters than for real people, an accusation that Michelle had picked up on by the time she was in her teens. Helen was gone too. They'd divorced ten years ago, and she'd been dead for five. Michelle, infuriating as she could be, was really all he had left. He had missed her, missed even the arguments.

He thought about Michelle as he tore open the plain brown paper. He would call her, of course. He would call her and tell her how good the new portrait was, how much he liked it. He would tell her that he'd missed her, invite her to come out for Thanksgiving. Yes, that would be the way to handle it. No mention of their argument, he didn't want to start it all up again, and neither he nor Michelle was the kind to back down gracefully. A family trait, that stubborn willful pride, as ingrained as the high cheekbones and squarish jaw. The Cantling heritage.

It was an antique frame, he saw. Wooden, elaborately carved, very heavy, just the sort of thing he liked. It would mesh with his Victorian decor much better than the thin brass frame on the old portrait. Cantling pulled the wrapping paper away, eager to see what his daughter had done. She was nearly thirty now—or was she past thirty already? He never could keep track of her age, or even her birthdays. Anyway, she was a much better painter than she'd been at twenty. The new portrait ought to be striking. He ripped away the last of the wrappings and turned it around.

His first reaction was that it was a fine, fine piece of work, maybe the best thing that Michelle Cantling had ever done.

Then, belatedly, the admiration washed away, and was replaced by anger. It wasn't her. It wasn't Michelle. Which meant it wasn't a replacement for the portrait she had so willfully vandalized. It was . . . something else.

Someone else.

It was a face he had never before laid eyes on. But it was a face he recognized as readily as if he had looked on it a thousand times. Oh, yes.

The man in the portrait was young. Twenty, maybe even younger, though his curly brown hair was already well-streaked with gray. It was unruly hair, disarrayed as if the man had just come from sleep, falling forward into his eyes. Those eyes were a bright green, lazy eyes somehow, shining with some secret amusement. He had high Cantling cheekbones, but the jawline was all wrong for a relative. Beneath a wide, flat nose, he wore a sardonic smile; his whole posture was somehow insolent. The portrait showed him dressed in faded dungarees and a ravelled WMCA Good Guy sweatshirt, with a half-eaten raw onion in one hand. The background was a brick wall covered with graffiti.

Cantling had created him.

Edward Donohue. Dunnahoo, that's what they'd called him, his friends and peers, the other characters in Richard Cantling's first novel, *Hangin' Out*. Dunnahoo had been the protagonist. A wise guy, a smart mouth, too damn bright for his own good. Looking down at the portrait, Cantling felt as if he'd known him for half his life. As indeed he had, in a way. Known him and, yes, cherished him, in the peculiar way a writer can cherish one of his characters.

Michelle had captured him true. Cantling stared at the painting and it all came back to him, all the events he had bled over so long ago, all the people he had fashioned and described with such loving care. He remembered Jocko, and the Squid, and Nancy, and Ricci's Pizzeria where so much of the book's action had taken place (he could see it vividly in his mind's eye), and the business with Arthur and the motorcycle, and the climactic pizza fight. And Dunnahoo. Dunnahoo especially. Smarting off, fooling around, hanging out, coming of age. "Fuck 'em if they can't take a joke," he said. A dozen times or so. It was the book's closing line.

For a moment, Richard Cantling felt a vast, strange affection well up inside him, as if he had just been reunited with an old, lost friend.

And then, almost as an afterthought, he remembered all the ugly words that he and Michelle had flung at each other that night, and suddenly it made sense. Cantling's face went hard. "Bitch," he said aloud. He turned away in fury, helpless without a target for his anger. "Bitch," he said again, as he slammed the door of the den behind him.

"Bitch," he had called her.

She turned around with the knife in her hand. Her eyes were raw and red from crying. She had the smile in her hand. She balled it up and threw it at him. "Here, you bastard, you like the damned smile so much, here it is."

It bounced off his cheek. His face was reddening. "You're just like your mother," he said. "She was always breaking things too."

"You gave her good reason, didn't you?"

Cantling ignored that. "What the hell is wrong with you? What the hell do you think you're going to accomplish with this stupid melodramatic gesture? That's all it is, you know. Bad melodrama. Who the hell do you think you are, some character in a Tennessee Williams play? Come off it, Michelle. If I wrote a scene like this in one of my books, they'd laugh at me."

"*This isn't one of your goddamned books!*" she screamed. "This is real life. *My* life. I'm a real person, you son of a bitch, not a character in some damned book." She whirled, raised the knife, slashed and slashed again.

Cantling folded his arms against his chest as he stood watching. "I hope you're enjoying this pointless exercise."

"I'm enjoying the hell out of it," Michelle yelled back.

"Good. I'd hate to think it was for nothing. This is all very revealing, you know. That's your own face you're working on. I didn't think you had that much self-hate in you."

"If I do, we know who put it there, don't we?" She was finished. She turned back to him, and threw down the knife. She had begun to cry again, and her breath was coming hard. "I'm leaving. Bastard. I hope you're ever so fucking happy here, really I do."

"I haven't done anything to deserve this," Cantling said awkwardly. It was not much of an apology, not much of a bridge back to understanding, but it was the best he could do. Apologies had never come easily to Richard Cantling.

"You deserve a thousand times worse," Michelle had screamed back at him. She was such a pretty girl, and she looked so ugly. All that nonsense about anger making people beautiful was a dreadful cliche, and wrong as well; Cantling was glad he'd never used it. "You're supposed to be my father," Michelle said. "You're supposed to love me. You're supposed to be my father, and you *raped* me, you bastard."

Cantling was a light sleeper. He woke in the middle of the night, and sat up in bed shivering, with the feeling that something was wrong.

The bedroom seemed dark and quiet. What was it? A noise? He was very sensitive to noise. Cantling slid out from under the covers and donned his slippers. The fire he'd enjoyed before retiring for the night had burned down to embers, and the room was chilly. He felt for his tartan robe, hanging from the foot of the big antique four-poster, slipped into it, cinched the belt, and moved quietly to the bedroom door. The door creaked a little at times, so he opened it very slowly, very cautiously. He listened.

Someone was downstairs. He could hear them moving around.

Fear coiled in the pit of his stomach. He had no gun up here, nothing like that. He didn't believe in that. Besides, he was supposed to be safe. This wasn't New York. He was supposed to be safe here in quaint old Perrot, Iowa. And now he had a prowler in his house, something he had never faced in all of his years in Manhattan. What the hell was he supposed to do?

The police, he thought. He'd lock the door and call the police. He moved back to the bedside, and reached for the phone.

It rang.

Richard Cantling stared at the telephone. He had two lines; a business number hooked up to his recording machine, and an unlisted personal number that he gave only to very close friends. Both lights were lit. It was his private number ringing. He hesitated, then scooped up the receiver. "Hello."

"The man himself," the voice said. "Don't get weird on me, Dad. You were going to call the cops, right? Stupid. It's only me. Come down and talk."

Cantling's throat felt raw and constricted. He had never heard that voice before, but he knew it, he knew it. "Who is this?" he demanded.

"Silly question," the caller replied. "You know who it is."

He did. But he said, "Who?"

"Not who. Dunnahoo." Cantling had written that line.

"You're not real."

"There were a couple of reviewers who said that too. I seem to remember how it pissed you off, back then."

"You're not *real*," Cantling insisted.

"I'm cut to the goddamned quick," Dunnahoo said. "If I'm not real, it's your fault. So quit getting on my case about it, OK? Just get your ass in gear and hustle it downstairs so we can hang out together." He hung up.

The lights went out on the telephone. Richard Cantling sat down on the edge of his bed, stunned. What was he supposed to make of this? A dream? It was no dream. What could he do?

He went downstairs.

Dunnahoo had built a fire in the living room fireplace, and was settled into Cantling's big leather recliner, drinking Pabst Blue Ribbon from a bottle. He smiled lazily when Cantling appeared under the entry arch. "The man," he said. "Well, don't you look half-dead. Want a beer?"

"Who the hell are you?" Cantling demanded.

"Hey, we been round that block already. Don't bore me. Grab a beer and park your ass by the fire."

"An actor," Cantling said. "You're some kind of goddamned actor. Michelle put you up to this, right?"

Dunnahoo grinned. "An actor? Well, that's fuckin' unlikely, ain't it? Tell me, would you stick something that weird in one of your novels? No way, José. You'd never do it yourself and if somebody else did it, in one of them workshops or a book you were reviewing, you'd rip his fuckin' liver out."

Richard Cantling moved slowly into the room, staring at the young man sprawled in his recliner. It was no actor. It was Dunnahoo, the kid from his book, the face from the portrait. Cantling settled into a high, overstuffed armchair, still staring. "This makes no sense," he said. "This is like something out of Dickens."

Dunnahoo laughed. "This ain't no fucking Christmas Carol, old man, and I sure ain't no ghost of Christmas past."

Cantling frowned; whoever he was, that line was out of character. "That's wrong," he snapped. "Dunnahoo didn't read Dickens. Batman and Robin, yes, but not Dickens."

"I saw the movie, dad," Dunnahoo said. He raised the beer bottle to his lips and had a swallow.

"Why do you keep calling me Dad?" Cantling said. "That's wrong too. Anachronistic. Dunnahoo was a street kid, not a beatnik."

"You're telling me? Like I don't know or something?" He laughed. "Shit man, what the hell else should I call you?" He ran his fingers through his hair, pushing it back out of his eyes. "After all, I'm still your fuckin' first-born."

She wanted to name it Edward, if it turned out to be a boy. "Don't be ridiculous, Helen," he told her.

"I thought you liked the name Edward," she said.

He didn't know what she was doing in his office anyway. He was working, or trying to work. He'd told her never to come into his office when he was at the typewriter. When they were first married, Helen was very good about that, but there had been no dealing with her since she'd gotten pregnant. "I do like the name Edward," he told her, trying hard to keep his voice calm. He hated being interrupted. "I like the name Edward a lot. I love the goddamned name Edward. That's why I'm using it for my protagonist. Edward, that's his name. Edward Donohue. So we can't use it for the baby because I've already used it. How many times do I have to explain that?"

"But you never *call* him Edward in the book," Helen protested.

Cantling frowned. "Have you been reading the book again? Damn it, Helen, I *told* you I don't want you messing around with the manuscript until it's done."

She refused to be distracted. "You never call him Edward," she repeated.

"No," he said. "That's right. I never call him Edward. I call him Dunnahoo, because he's a street kid, and because that's his street name, and he doesn't like to be called Edward. Only it's still his name, you see. Edward is his name. He doesn't like it, but it's his fucking *name*, and at the end he tells someone that his name is Edward, and that's real damned important. So we can't name the kid Edward, because *he's* named Edward, and I'm tired of this discussion. If it's a boy, we can name it Lawrence, after my grandfather."

"But I don't *want* to name him Lawrence," she whined. "It's so old-fashioned, and then people will call him Larry, and I hate the name Larry. Why can't you call the character in your book Lawrence?"

"Because his name is Edward."

"This is our baby I'm carrying," she said. She put a hand on her swollen stomach, as if Cantling needed a visual reminder.

He was tired of arguing. He was tired of discussing. He was tired of being interrupted. He leaned back in his chair. "How long have you been carrying the baby?"

Helen looked baffled. "You know. Seven months now. And a week."

Cantling leaned forward and slapped the stack of manuscript pages piled up beside his typewriter. "Well, I've been carrying *this* baby for three damned years now. This is the fourth fucking draft, and the last one. He was named Edward on the first draft, and on the second draft, and on the third draft, and he's damn well going to be named Edward when the goddamned book comes out. He'd been named Edward for *years* before that night of fond memory when you decided to surprise me by throwing away your diaphragm, and thereby got yourself knocked up."

"It's not fair," she complained. "He's only a character. This is our baby."

"Fair? You want fair? OK. I'll make it fair. Our first-born son will get named Edward. How's that for fair?"

Helen's face softened. She smiled shyly.

He held up a hand before she had a chance to say anything. "Of course, I figure I'm only about a month away from finishing this damn thing, if you ever stop interrupting me. You've got a little further to go. But that's as fair as I can make it. You pop before I type THE END and you got the name. Otherwise, my baby here—" he slapped the manuscript again "is—first-born."

"You can't," she started.

Cantling resumed his typing.

"My first-born," Richard Cantling said.

"In the flesh," Dunnahoo said. He raised his beer bottle in salute, and said, "To fathers and sons, hey!" He drained it with one long swallow and flipped the bottle across the room end over end. It smashed in the fireplace.

"This is a dream," Cantling said.

Dunnahoo gave him a raspberry. "Look, old man, face it, I'm here." He jumped to his feet. "The prodigal returns," he said, bowing. "So where the fuck is the fatted calf and all that shit? Least you coulda done was order a pizza."

"I'll play the game," Cantling said. "What do you want from me?"

Dunnahoo grinned. "Want? Who, me? Who the fuck knows? I never knew what I wanted, you know that. Nobody in the whole fucking book knew what they wanted."

"That was the point," Cantling said.

"Oh, I get it," Dunnahoo said. "I'm not dumb. Old Dicky Cantling's boy is anything but dumb, right?" He wandered off toward the kitchen. "There's more beer in the fridge. Want one?"

"Why not?" Cantling asked. "It's not every day my oldest son comes to visit. Dos Equis with a slice of lime, please."

"Drinking fancy spic beer now, huh? Shit. What ever happened to Piels? You could suck up Piels with the best of them, once upon a time." He vanished through the kitchen door. When he returned he was carrying two bottles of Dos Equis, holding them by the necks with his fingers jammed down into the open mouths. In his other hand he had a raw onion. The bottles clanked together as he carried them. He gave one to Cantling. "Here. I'll suck up a little culture myself."

"You forgot the lime," Cantling said.

"Get your own fuckin' lime," Dunnahoo said. "Whatcha gonna do, cut off my allowance?" He grinned, tossed the onion lightly into the air, caught it, and took a big bite. "Onions," he said. "I owe you for that one, Dad. Bad enough I have to eat raw onions, I mean, shit, but you fixed it so I don't even *like* the fucking things. You even said so in the damned book."

"Of course," Cantling said. "The onion had a dual function. On one level, you did it just to prove how tough you were. It was something none of the others hanging out at Ricci's could manage. It gave you a certain status. But on a deeper level, when you bit into an onion you were making a symbolic statement about your appetite for life, your hunger for it all, the bitter and the sharp parts as well as the sweet."

Dunnahoo took another bite of onion. "Horseshit," he said. "I ought to make you eat a fucking onion, see how you like it."

Cantling sipped at his beer. "I was young. It was my first book. It seemed like a nice touch at the time."

"Eat it raw," Dunnahoo said. He finished the onion.

Richard Cantling decided this cozy domestic scene had gone on long enough. "You know, Dunnahoo or whoever you are," he said in a conversational tone, "you're not what I expected."

"What did you expect, old man?"

Cantling shrugged. "I made you with my mind instead of my sperm, so you've got more of me in you than any child of my flesh could ever have. You're me."

"Hey," said Dunnahoo, "not fucking guilty. I wouldn't be you on a bet."

"You have no choice. Your story was built from my own adolescence. First novels are like that. Ricci's was really Pompeii Pizza in Newark. Your friends were my friends. And you were me."

"That so?" Dunnahoo replied, grinning.

Richard Cantling nodded.

Dunnahoo laughed. "You should be so fuckin' lucky, Dad."

"What does that mean?" Cantling snapped.

"You live in a dream world, old man, you know that? Maybe you like to pretend you were like me, but there ain't no way it's true. I was the big man at Ricci's. At Pompeii, you were the four-eyes hanging out back by the pinball machine. You had me balling my brains out at sixteen. You never even got bare tit till you were past twenty, off in that college of yours. It took you weeks to come up with the wisecracks you had me tossing off every fuckin' time I turned around. All those wild, crazy things I did in that book, some of them happened to Dutch and some of them happened to Joey and some of them never happened at all, but none of them happened to you, old man, so don't make me laugh."

Cantling flushed a little. "I was writing fiction. Yes, I was a bit of a misfit in my youth, but . . ."

"A nerd," Dunnahoo said. "Don't fancy it up."

"I was not a nerd," Cantling said, stung. "*Hangin' Out* told the truth. It made sense to use a protagonist who was more central to the action than I'd been in real life. Art draws on life but it has to shape it, rearrange it, give it structure, it can't simply replicate it. That's what I did."

"Nah. What *you* did was to suck off Dutch and Joey and the rest. You helped yourself to their lives, man, and took credit for it all yourself. You even got this weird fuckin' idea that I was based on you, and you been thinking that so long you believe it. You're a leech, Dad. You're a goddamned thief."

Richard Cantling was furious. "Get out of here!" he said.

Dunnahoo stood up, stretched. "I'm fuckin' wounded. Throwing your baby boy out into the cold Ioway night, old man? What's wrong? You liked me well enough when I was in your damn book, when you could control everything I did and said, right? Don't like it so well now that I'm real, though. That's your problem. You never did like real life half as well as you liked books."

"I like life just fine, thank you," Cantling snapped.

Dunnahoo smiled. Standing there, he suddenly looked washed out, insubstantial. "Yeah?" he said. His voice seemed weaker than it had been.

"Yeah!" Cantling replied.

Now Dunnahoo was fading visibly. All the color had drained from his body, and he looked almost transparent. "Prove it," he said. "Go into your kitchen, old man, and take a great big bite out of your fuckin' raw onion of life." He tossed back his hair, and laughed, and laughed, and laughed, until he was quite gone.

Richard Cantling stood staring at the place where he had been for a long time. Finally, very tired, he climbed upstairs to bed.

He made himself a big breakfast the next morning: orange juice and fresh-brewed coffee, English muffins with lots of butter and blackberry preserves, a cheese omelette, six strips of thick-sliced bacon. The cooking and the eating were supposed to distract him. It didn't work. He thought of Dunnahoo all the while. A dream, yes, some crazy sort of dream. He had no ready explanation for the broken glass in the fireplace or the empty beer bottles in his living room, but finally he found one. He had experienced some sort of insane, drunken, somnambulist episode, Cantling decided. It was the stress of the ongoing quarrel with Michelle, of course, triggered by the portrait she'd sent him. Perhaps he ought to see someone about it, a doctor or a psychologist or someone.

After breakfast, Cantling went straight to his den, determined to confront the problem directly and resolve it. Michelle's mutilated portrait still hung above the fireplace. A festering wound, he thought; it had infected him, and the time had come to get rid of it. Cantling built a fire. When it was going good, he took down the ruined painting, dismantled the metal frame—he was a thrifty man, after all—and burned the torn, disfigured canvas. The oily smoke made him feel clean again.

Next there was the portrait of Dunnahoo to deal with. Cantling turned to consider it. A good piece of work, really. She had captured the character. He could burn it, but that would be playing Michelle's own destructive game. Art should never be destroyed. He had made his mark on the world by creation, not destruction, and he was too old to change. The portrait of Dunnahoo had been intended as a cruel taunt, but Cantling decided to throw it back in his daughter's teeth, to make a splendid celebration of it. He would hang it, and hang it prominently. He knew just the place for it.

Up at the top of the stairs was a long landing; an ornate wooden bannister overlooked the first floor foyer and entry hall. The landing was fifteen feet long, and the back wall was entirely blank. It would make a splendid portrait gallery, Cantling decided. The painting would be visible to anyone entering the house, and you would pass right by it on the way to any of the second floor rooms. He found a hammer and some nails and hung Dunnahoo in a place of honor. When Michelle came back to make peace, she would see him there, and no doubt leap to the conclusion that Cantling had totally missed the point of her gift. He'd have to remember to thank her effusively for it.

Richard Cantling was feeling much better. Last night's conversation was receding into a bad memory. He put it firmly out of his mind and spent the rest of the day writing letters to his agent and publisher. In the late afternoon, pleasantly weary, he enjoyed a cup of coffee and some butter streusel he'd hidden away in the refrigerator. Then he went out on his daily walk, and spent a good ninety minutes hiking along the river bluffs with a fresh, cold wind in his face.

When he returned, a large square package was waiting on his porch.

He leaned it up against an armchair, and settled into his recliner to study it. It made him uneasy. It had an effect, no doubt of it. He could feel an erection stirring against his leg, pressing uncomfortably against his trousers.

The portrait was . . . well, frankly erotic.

She was in bed, a big old antique four-poster, much like his own. She was naked. She was half-turned in the painting, looking back over her right shoulder; you saw the smooth line of her backbone, the curve of her right breast. It was a large, shapely, and very pretty breast; the aureole was a pale pink and very large, and her nipple was erect. She was clutching a rumpled sheet up to her chin, but it did little to conceal her. Her hair was red-gold, her eyes green, her smile playful. Her smooth young skin had a flush to it, as if she had just risen from a bout of lovemaking. She had a peace symbol tattooed high on the right cheek of her ass. She was obviously very young. Richard Cantling knew just how young: she was eighteen, a child-woman, caught in that precious time between innocence and experience when sex is just a wonderfully exciting new toy. Oh yes, he knew a lot about her. He knew her well.

Cissy.

He hung her portrait next to Dunnahoo.

Dead Flowers was Cantling's title for the book. His editor changed it to *Black Roses;* more evocative, he said, more romantic, more upbeat. Cantling fought the change on artistic grounds, and lost. Afterwards, when the novel made the bestseller lists, he managed to work up the grace to admit that he'd been wrong. He sent Brian a bottle of his favorite wine.

It was his fourth novel, and his last chance. *Hangin' Out* had gotten excellent reviews and had sold decently, but his next two books had been panned by the critics and ignored by the readers. He had to do something different, and he did. *Black Roses* turned out to be highly controversial. Some reviewers loved it, some loathed it. But it sold and sold and sold, and the paperback sale and the film option (they never made the movie) relieved him of financial worries for the first time in his life. They were finally able to afford a down payment on a house, transfer Michelle to a private school and get her those braces; the rest of the money Cantling invested as shrewdly as he was able. He was proud of *Black Roses* and pleased by its success. It made his reputation.

Helen hated the book with a passion.

On the day the novel finally fell off the last of the lists, she couldn't quite conceal her satisfaction. "I knew it wouldn't last forever," she said.

Cantling slapped down the newspaper angrily. "It lasted long enough. What the hell's wrong with you? You didn't like it before, when we were barely scraping by. The kid needs braces, the kid needs a better school, the kid shouldn't have to eat goddamn peanut butter and jelly sandwiches every day. Well, that's all behind us. And you're more pissed off than ever. Give me a little credit. Did you like being married to a failure?"

"I don't like being married to a pornographer," Helen snapped at him.

"Fuck you," Cantling said.

She gave him a nasty smile. "When? You haven't touched me in weeks. You'd rather be fucking your Cissy."

Cantling stared at her. "Are you crazy, or what? She's a character in a book I wrote. That's all."

"Oh, go to hell," Helen said furiously. "You treat me like I'm a goddamned idiot. You think I can't read? You think I don't know? I read your shitty book. I'm not stupid. The wife, Marsha, dull ignorant boring Marsha, cud-chewing mousy Marsha, that cow, that nag, that royal pain-in-the-ass, that's me. You think I can't tell? I can tell, and so can my friends. They're all very sorry for me. You love me as much as Richardson loved Marsha. Cissy's just a character, right, like hell, like bloody hell." She was crying now. "You're in love with her, damn you. She's your own little wet dream. If she walked in the door right now you'd dump me as fast as Richardson dumps good old Marsha. Deny it. Go on, deny it, I dare you!"

Cantling regarded his wife incredulously. "I don't believe you. You're jealous of a character in my book. You're jealous of someone who doesn't exist."

"She exists in your head, and that's the only place that matters with you. Of course your damned book was a big seller. You think it was because of your writing? It was on account of the sex, on account of *her!*"

"Sex is an important part of life," Cantling said defensively. "It's a perfectly legitimate subject for art. You want me to pull down a curtain every time my characters go to bed, is that it? Coming to terms with sexuality, that's what *Black Roses* is all about. Of course it had to be written explicitly. If you weren't such a damned prude you'd realize that."

"I'm not a prude!" Helen screamed at him. "Don't you dare call me one, either." She picked up one of the breakfast plates and threw it at him. Cantling ducked; the plate shattered on the wall behind him. "Just because I don't like your goddamned filthy book doesn't make me a prude."

"The novel has nothing to do with it," Cantling said. He folded his arms against his chest but kept his voice calm. "You're a prude because of the things you do in bed. Or should I say the things you won't do?" He smiled.

Helen's face was red; beet red, Cantling thought, and rejected it, too old, too trite. "Oh, yes, but she'll do them, won't she?" Her voice was pure acid. "Cissy, your cute little Cissy. She'll get a sexy little tattoo on her ass if you ask her to, right? She'll do it outdoors, she'll do it in all kinds of strange places, with people all around. She'll wear kinky underwear, she thinks it's fun. She's always ready and she doesn't have any stretch marks and she has eighteen-year-old tits, and she'll *always* have eighteen-year-old tits, won't she? How the hell do I compete with that, huh? How? *HOW?*"

Richard Cantling's own anger was a cold, controlled, sarcastic thing. He stood up in the face of fury and smiled sweetly. "Read the book," he said. "Take notes."

He woke suddenly, in darkness, to the light touch of skin against his foot.

Cissy was perched on top of the footboard, a red satin sheet wrapped around her, a long slim leg exploring under his blankets. She was playing footsie with him, and smiling mischievously. "Hi, Daddy," she said.

Cantling had been afraid of this. It had been in his mind all evening. Sleep had not come easily. He pulled his foot away and struggled to a sitting position.

Cissy pouted. "Don't you want to play?" she asked.

"I," he said, "don't believe this. This can't be real."

"It can still be fun," she said.

"What the hell is Michelle doing to me? How can this be happening?"

She shrugged. The sheet slipped a little; one perfect pink-tipped eighteen-year-old breast peeked out.

"You still have eighteen-year-old tits," Cantling said numbly. "You'll always have eighteen-year-old tits."

Cissy laughed. "Sure. You can borrow them, if you like, Daddy. I'll bet you can think of something interesting to do with them."

"Stop calling me Daddy," Cantling said.

"Oh, but you *are* my Daddy," Cissy said in her little-girl voice.

"Stop that!" Cantling said.

"Why? You want to, Daddy, you want to play with your little girl, don't you?" She winked. "Vice is nice but incest is best. The families that play together stay together." She looked around. "I like four-posters. You want to tie me up, Daddy? I'd like that."

"No," Cantling said. He pushed back the covers, got out of bed, found his slippers and robe. His erection throbbed against his leg. He had to get away, he had to put some distance between him and Cissy, otherwise . . . he didn't want to think about otherwise. He busied himself making a fire.

"I like that," Cissy said when he got it going. "Fires are so romantic."

Cantling turned around to face her again. "Why you?" he asked, trying to stay calm. "Richardson was the protagonist of *Black Roses*, not you. And why skip to my fourth book? Why not somebody from *Family Tree* or *Rain?*"

"Those gobblers?" Cissy said. "Nobody real there. You didn't really want Richardson, did you? I'm a lot more fun." She stood up and let go of the satin sheet. It puddled about her ankles, the flames reflected off its shiny folds. Her body was soft and sweet and young. She kicked free of the sheet and padded toward him.

"Cut it out, Cissy," Cantling barked.

"I won't bite," Cissy said. She giggled. "Unless you want me to. Maybe I should tie *you* up, huh?" She put her arms around him, gave him a hug, turned up her face for a kiss.

"Let go of me," he said, weakly. Her arms felt good. She felt good as she pressed up against him. It had been a long time since Richard Cantling had held a woman in his arms; he didn't like to think about how long. And he had never had a woman like Cissy, never, never. But he was frightened. "I can't do this," he said. "I can't. I don't want to."

Cissy reached through the folds of his robe, shoved her hand inside his briefs, squeezed him gently. "Liar," she said. "You want me. You've always wanted me. I'll bet you used to stop and jack off when you were writing the sex scenes."

"No," Cantling said. "Never."

"Never?" She pouted. Her hand moved up and down. "Well, I bet you wanted to. I bet you got hard, anyway. I bet you got hard every time you described me."

"I," he said. The denial would not come. "Cissy, please."

"Please," she murmured. Her hand was busy. "Yes, please." She tugged at his briefs and they fluttered to the floor. "Please," she said. She untied his robe and helped him out of it. "Please." Her hand moved along his side, played with his nipples; she stepped closer, and her breasts pressed lightly against his chest. "Please," she said, and she looked up at him. Her tongue moved between her lips.

Richard Cantling groaned and took her in his trembling arms.

She was like no woman he had ever had. Her touch was fire and satin, electric, and her secret places were sweet as honey.

In the morning she was gone.

Cantling woke late, too exhausted to make himself breakfast. Instead he dressed and walked into town, to a small cafe in a quaint hundred-year-old brick building at the foot of the bluffs. He tried to sort things out over coffee and blueberry pancakes.

None of it made any sense. It could not be happening, but it was; denial accomplished nothing. Cantling forked down a mouthful of home-made blueberry pancake, but the only taste in his mouth was fear. He was afraid for his sanity. He was afraid because he did not understand, did not want to understand. And there was another, deeper, more basic fear.

He was afraid of what would come next. Richard Cantling had published nine novels.

He thought of Michelle. He could phone her, beg her to call it off before he went mad. She was his daughter, his flesh and blood, surely she would listen to him. She loved him. Of course she did. And he loved her too, no matter what she might think. Cantling knew his faults. He had examined himself countless times, under various guises, in the pages of his books. He was impossibly stubborn, willful, opinionated. He could be rigid and unbending. He could be cold. Still, he thought of himself as a decent man. Michelle . . . she had inherited some of his perversity, she was furious at him, hate was so very close to love, but surely she did not mean to do him serious harm.

Yes, he could phone Michelle, ask her to stop. Would she? If he begged her forgiveness, perhaps. That day, that terrible day, she'd told him that she would never forgive him, never, but she couldn't have meant that. She was his only child. The only child of his flesh, at any rate.

Cantling pushed away his empty plate and sat back. His mouth was set in a hard rigid line. Beg for mercy? He did not like that. What had he done, after all? Why couldn't they understand? Helen had never understood and Michelle was as blind as her mother. A writer must live for his work. What had he done that was so terrible? What had he done that required forgiveness? Michelle ought to be the one phoning him.

The hell with it, Cantling thought. He refused to be cowed. He was right; she was wrong. Let Michelle call him if she wanted a rapprochement. She was not going to terrify him into submission. What was he so afraid of, anyway? Let her send her portraits, all the portraits she wanted to paint. He'd hang them up on his walls, display the paintings proudly (they were really an *hommage* to his work, after all), and if the damned things came alive at night and prowled through his house, so be it. He'd enjoy their visits. Cantling smiled. He'd certainly enjoyed Cissy, no doubt of that. Part of him hoped she'd come back. And even Dunnahoo, well, he was an insolent kid, but there was no real harm in him, he just liked to mouth off.

Why, now that he stopped to consider it, Cantling found that the possibilities had a certain intoxicating charm. He was uniquely privileged. Scott Fitzgerald never attended one of Gatsby's fabulous parties, Conan Doyle could never really sit down with Holmes and Watson, Nabokov never actually tumbled Lolita. What would they have said to the idea?

The more he considered things, the more cheerful he became. Michelle was trying to rebuke him, to frighten him, but she was really giving him a delicious experience. He could play chess with Sergei Tederenko, the cynical emigré hustler from *En Passant*. He could argue politics with Frank Corwin, the union organizer from his Depression novel, *Times Are Hard*. He might flirt with beautiful Beth McKenzie, go dancing with crazy old Miss Aggie, seduce the Danzinger twins and fulfill the one sexual fantasy that Cissy had left untouched, yes, certainly, what the hell had he been afraid of? They were his own creations, his characters, his friends and family.

Of course, there was the new book to consider. Cantling frowned. That was a disturbing thought. But Michelle was his daughter, she loved him, surely she wouldn't go that far. No, of course not. He put the idea firmly aside and picked up his check.

* * *

He expected it. He was almost looking forward to it. And when he returned from his evening constitutional, his cheeks red from the wind, his heart beating just a little faster in anticipation, it was there waiting for him, the familiar rectangle wrapped in plain brown paper. Richard Cantling carried it inside carefully. He made himself a cup of coffee before he unwrapped it, deliberately prolonging the suspense to savor the moment, delighting in the thought of how deftly he'd turned Michelle's cruel little plan on its head.

He drank his coffee, poured a refill, drank that. The package stood a few feet away. Cantling played a little game with himself, trying to guess whose portrait might be within. Cissy had said something about none of the characters from *Family Tree* or *Rain* being real enough. Cantling mentally reviewed his life's work, trying to decide which characters seemed most real. It was a pleasant speculation, but he could reach no firm conclusions. Finally he shoved his coffee cup aside and moved to undo the wrappings. And there it was.

Barry Leighton.

Again, the painting itself was superb. Leighton was seated in a newspaper city room, his elbow resting on the gray metal case of an old manual typewriter. He wore a rumpled brown suit and his white shirt was open at the collar and plastered to his body by perspiration. His nose had been broken more than once, and was spread all across his wide, homely, somehow comfortable face. His eyes were sleepy. Leighton was overweight and jowly and rapidly losing his hair. He'd given up smoking but not cigarettes; an unlit Camel dangled from one corner of his mouth. "As long as you don't light the damned things, you're safe," he'd said more than once in Cantling's novel *ByeLine*.

The book hadn't done very well. It was a depressing book, all about the last week of a grand old newspaper that had fallen on bad times. It was more than that, though. Cantling was interested in people, not newspapers; he had used the failing paper as a metaphor for failing lives. His editor had wanted to work in some kind of strong, sensational subplot, have Leighton and the others on the trail of some huge story that offered the promise of redemption, but Cantling had rejected that idea. He wanted to tell a story about small people being ground down inexorably by time and age, about the inevitability of loneliness and defeat. He produced a novel as gray and brittle as newsprint. He was very proud of it.

No one read it.

Cantling lifted the portrait and carried it upstairs, to hang beside those of Dunnahoo and Cissy. Tonight should be interesting, he thought. Barry Leighton was no kid, like the others; he was a man of Cantling's own years. Very intelligent, mature. There was a bitterness in Leighton, Cantling knew very well; a disappointment that life had, after all, yielded so little, that all his bylines and big stories were forgotten the day after they ran. But the reporter kept his sense of humor through all of it, kept off the demons with nothing but a mordant wit and an unlit Camel. Cantling admired him, would enjoy talking to him. Tonight, he decided, he wouldn't bother going to bed. He'd make a big pot of strong black coffee, lay in some Seagram's, and wait.

It was past midnight and Cantling was rereading the leather-bound copy of *ByeLine* when he heard ice cubes clinking together in the kitchen. "Help yourself, Barry," he called out.

Leighton came through the swinging door, tumbler in hand. "I did," he said. He looked at Cantling through heavily-lidded eyes, and gave a little snort. "You look old enough to be my father," he said. "I didn't think anybody could look *that* old."

Cantling closed the book and set it aside. "Sit down," he said. "As I recall, your feet hurt."

"My feet always hurt," Leighton said. He settled himself into an armchair and swallowed a mouthful of whisky. "Ah," he said, "that's better."

Cantling tapped the novel with a fingertip. "My eighth book," he said. "Michelle skipped right over three novels. A pity. I would have liked to meet some of those people."

"Maybe she wants to get to the point," Leighton suggested.

"And what is the point?"

Leighton shrugged. "Damned if I know. I'm only a newspaperman. Five Ws and an H. You're the novelist. You tell me the point."

"My ninth novel," Cantling suggested. "The new one."

"The last one?" said Leighton.

"Of course not. Only the most recent. I'm working on something new right now."

Leighton smiled. "That's not what my sources tell me."

"Oh? What do your sources say?"

"That you're an old man waiting to die," Leighton said. "And that you're going to die alone."

"I'm fifty-two," Cantling said crisply. "Hardly old."

"When your birthday cake has got more candles than you can blow out, you're old," said Leighton drily. "Helen was younger than you, and she died five years ago. It's in the mind, Cantling. I've seen young octogenarians and old adolescents. And you, you had liver spots on your brain before you had hair on your balls."

"That's unfair," Cantling protested.

Leighton drank his Seagram's. "Fair?" he said. "You're too old to believe in fair, Cantling. Young people live life. Old people sit and watch it. You were born old. You're a watcher, not a liver." He frowned. "Not a liver, jeez, what a figure of speech. Better a liver than a gall bladder, I guess. You were never a gall bladder either. You've been full of piss for years, but you don't have any gall at all. Maybe you're a kidney."

"You're reaching, Barry," Cantling said. "I'm a writer. I've always been a writer. That's my life. Writers observe life, they report on life. It's in the job description. You ought to know."

"I do know," Leighton said. "I'm a reporter, remember? I've spent a lot of long gray years writing up other people's stories. I've got no story of my own. You know that, Cantling. Look what you did to me in *ByeLine*. The *Courier* croaks and I decide to write my memoirs and what happens?"

Cantling remembered. "You blocked. You rewrote your old stories, twenty-year-old stories, thirty-year-old stories. You had that incredible memory. You could recall all the people you'd ever reported on, the dates, the details, the quotes. You could recite the first story you'd had bylined word for word, but you couldn't remember the name of the first girl you'd been to bed with, couldn't remember your ex-wife's phone number, you couldn't . . . you couldn't. . . ." His voice failed.

"I couldn't remember my daughter's birthday," Leighton said. "Where do you get those crazy ideas, Cantling?"

Cantling was silent.

"From life, maybe?" Leighton said gently. "I was a good reporter. That was about all you could say about me. You, well, maybe you're a good novelist. That's for the critics to judge, and I'm just a sweaty newspaperman whose feet hurt. But even if you are a good novelist, even if you're one of the great ones, you were a lousy husband, and a miserable father."

"No," Cantling said. It was a weak protest.

Leighton swirled his tumbler; the ice cubes clinked and clattered. "When did Helen leave you?" he asked.

"I don't . . . ten years ago, something like that. I was in the middle of the final draft of *En Passant*."

"When was the divorce final?"

"Oh, a year later. We tried a reconciliation, but it didn't take. Michelle was in school, I remember. I was writing *Times Are Hard*."

"You remember her third grade play?"

"Was that the one I missed?"

"The one you missed? You sound like Nixon saying, 'Was that the time I lied?' That was the one Michelle had the lead in, Cantling."

"I couldn't help that," Cantling said. "I wanted to come. They were giving me an award. You don't skip the National Literary League dinner. You can't."

"Of course not," said Leighton. "When was it that Helen died?"

"I was writing *ByeLine*," Cantling said.

"Interesting system of dating you've got there. You ought to put out a calendar." He swallowed some whisky.

"All right," Cantling said. "I'm not going to deny that my work is important to me. Maybe too important, I don't know. Yes, the writing has been the biggest part of my life. But I'm a decent man, Leighton, and I've always done my best. It hasn't all been like you're implying. Helen and I had good years. We loved each other once. And Michelle . . . I loved Michelle. When she was a little girl, I used to write stories just for her. Funny animals, space pirates, silly poems. I'd write them up in my spare time and read them to her at bedtime. They were something I did just for Michelle, for love."

"Yeah," Leighton said cynically. "You never even thought about getting them published."

Cantling grimaced. "That . . . you're implying . . . that's a distortion. Michelle loved the stories so much, I thought maybe other kids might like them too. It was just an idea. I never did anything about it."

"Never?"

Cantling hesitated. "Look, Bert was my friend as well as my agent. He had a little girl of his own. I showed him the stories once. Once!"

"I can't be pregnant," Leighton said. "I only let him fuck me once. Once!"

"He didn't even like them," Cantling said.

"Pity," replied Leighton.

"You're laying this on me with a trowel, and I'm not guilty. No, I wasn't father of the year, but I wasn't an ogre either. I changed her diaper plenty of times. Before *Black Roses*, Helen had to work, and I took care of the baby every day, from nine to five."

"You hated it when she cried and you had to leave your typewriter."

"Yes," Cantling said. "Yes, I hated being interrupted, I've always hated being interrupted, I don't care if it was Helen or Michelle or my mother or my roommate in college, when I'm writing I don't like to be interrupted. Is that a fucking capital crime? Does that make me inhuman? When she cried, I went to her. I didn't like it, I hated it, I resented it, but I *went to her*."

"When you heard her," said Leighton. "When you weren't in bed with Cissy, dancing with Miss Aggie, beating up scabs with Frank Corwin, when your head wasn't full of their voices, yeah, sometimes you heard, and when you heard you went. Congratulations, Cantling."

"I taught her to read," Cantling said. "I read her *Treasure Island* and *Wind in the Willows* and *The Hobbit* and *Tom Sawyer*, all kinds of things."

"All books you wanted to reread anyway," said Leighton. "Helen did the real teaching, with Dick and Jane."

"*I hate Dick and Jane!*" Cantling shouted.

"So?"

"You don't know what you're talking about," Richard Cantling said. "You weren't there. Michelle was there. She loved me, she still loves me. Whenever she got hurt, scraped her knee or got her nose bloodied, whatever it was, it was me she'd run to, never Helen. She'd come crying to me and I'd hug her and dry her tears and I'd tell her . . . I used to tell her. . . ." But he couldn't go on. He was close to tears himself; he could feel them hiding the corners of his eyes.

"I know what you used to tell her," said Barry Leighton in a sad, gentle voice.

"She remembered it," Cantling said. "She remembered it all those years. Helen got custody, they moved away, I didn't see her much, but Michelle always remembered, and when she was all grown up, after Helen was gone and Michelle was on her own, there was this time she got hurt, and I . . . I . . . ."

"Yes," said Leighton. "I know."

The police were the ones that phoned him. Detective Joyce Brennan, that was her name, he would never forget that name. "Mister Cantling?" she said.

"Yes?"

"Mister Richard Cantling?"

"Yes," he said. "Richard Cantling the writer." He had gotten strange calls before. "What can I do for you?"

She identified herself. "You'll have to come down to the hospital," she said to him. "It's your daughter, Mister Cantling. I'm afraid she's been assaulted."

He hated evasion, hated euphemism. Cantling's characters never passed away, they died; they never broke wind, they farted. And Richard Cantling's daughter . . . "Assaulted?" he said. "Do you mean she's been assaulted or do you mean she's been raped?"

There was a silence on the other end of the line. "Raped," she said at last. "She's been raped, Mister Cantling."

"I'll be right down," he said.

She had in fact been raped repeatedly and brutally. Michelle had been as stubborn as Helen, as stubborn as Cantling himself. She wouldn't take his money, wouldn't take his advice, wouldn't take the help he offered her through his contacts in publishing. She was going to make it on her own. She waitressed in a coffee house in the Village, and lived in a large, drafty, and run-down warehouse loft down by the docks. It was a terrible neighborhood, a dangerous neighborhood, and Cantling had told her so a hundred times, but Michelle would not listen. She would not even let him pay to install good locks and a security system. It had been very bad. The man had broken in before dawn on a Friday morning. Michelle was alone. He had ripped the phone from the wall and held her prisoner there through Monday night. Finally one of the busboys from the coffee house had gotten worried and come by, and the rapist had left by the fire escape.

When they let him see her, her face was a huge purple bruise. She had burn marks all over her, where the man had used his cigarette, and three of her ribs were broken. She was far beyond hysteria. She screamed when they tried to touch her; doctors, nurses, it didn't matter, she screamed as soon as they got near. But she let Cantling sit on the edge of her bed, and take her in his arms, and hold her. She cried for hours, cried until there were no more tears in her. Once she called him "Daddy," in a choked sob. It was the only word she spoke; she seemed to have lost the capacity for speech. Finally they tranquilized her to get her to sleep.

Michelle was in the hospital for two weeks, in a deep state of shock. Her hysteria waned day by day, and she finally became docile, so they were able to fluff her pillows and lead her to the bathroom. But she still would not, or could not, speak. The psychologist told Cantling that she might never speak again. "I don't accept that," he said. He arranged Michelle's discharge. Simultaneously he decided to get them both out of this filthy hellhole of a city. She had always loved big old spooky houses, he remembered, and she used to love the water, the sea, the river, the lake. Cantling consulted realtors, considered a big place on the coast of Maine, and finally settled on an old steamboat gothic mansion high on the bluffs of Perrot, Iowa. He supervised every detail of the move.

Little by little, recovery began.

She was like a small child again, curious, restless, full of sudden energy. She did not talk, but she explored everything, went everywhere. In spring she spent hours up on the widow's walk, watching the big towboats go by on the Mississippi far below. Every evening they would walk together on the bluffs, and she would hold his hand. One day she turned and kissed him suddenly, impulsively, on his cheek. "I love you, Daddy," she said, and she ran away from him, and as Cantling watched her run, he saw a lovely, wounded woman in her mid-twenties, and saw too the gangling, coltish tomboy she had been.

The dam was broken after that day. Michelle began to talk again. Short, childlike sentences at first, full of childish fears and childish naivete. But she matured rapidly, and in no time at all she was talking politics with him, talking books, talking art. They had many a fine conversation on their evening walks. She never talked about the rape, though; never once, not so much as a word.

In six months she was cooking, writing letters to friends back in New York, helping with the household chores, doing lovely things in the garden. In eight months she had started to paint again. That was very good for her; now she seemed to blossom daily, to grow more and more radiant. Richard Cantling didn't really understand the abstractions his daughter liked to paint, he preferred representational art, and best of all he loved the self-portrait she had done for him when she was still an art major in college. But he could feel the pain in these new canvases of hers, he could sense that she was engaged in an exorcism of sorts, trying to squeeze the pus from some wound deep inside, and he approved. His writing had been a balm for his own wounds more than once. He envied her now, in a way. Richard Cantling had not written a word for more than three years. The crashing commercial failure of *ByeLine*, his best novel, had left him blocked and impotent. He'd thought perhaps the change of scene might restore him as well as Michelle, but that had been a vain hope. At least one of them was busy.

Finally, late one night after Cantling had gone to bed, his door opened and Michelle came quietly into his bedroom and sat on the edge of his bed. She was barefoot, dressed in a flannel nightgown covered with tiny pink flowers. "Daddy," she said, in a slurred voice.

Cantling had woken when the door opened. He sat up and smiled for her. "Hi," he said. "You've been drinking."

Michelle nodded. "I'm going back," she said. "Needed some courage, so's I could tell you."

"Going back?" Cantling said. "You don't mean to New York? You can't be serious!"

"I got to," she said. "Don't be mad. I'm better now."

"Stay here. Stay with me. New York is uninhabitable, Michelle."

"I don't want to go back. It scares me. But I got to. My friends are there. My work is there. My life is back there, Daddy. My friend Jimmy, you remember Jimmy, he's art director for this little paperback house, he can get me some cover assignments, he says. He wrote. I won't have to wait tables any more."

"I don't believe I'm hearing this," Richard Cantling said. "How can you go back to that damned city after what happened to you there?"

"That's why I have to go back," Michelle insisted. "That guy, what he did . . . what he did to me . . ." Her voice caught in her throat. She drew in her breath, got hold of herself. "If I don't go back, it's like he ran me out of town, took my whole life away from me, my friends, my art, everything. I can't let him get away with that, can't let him scare me off. I got to go back and take up what's mine, prove that I'm not afraid."

Richard Cantling looked at his daughter helplessly. He reached out, gently touched her long, soft hair. She had finally said something that made sense in his terms. He would do the same thing, he knew. "I understand," he said. "It's going to be lonely here without you, but I understand, I do."

"I'm scared," Michelle said. "I bought plane tickets. For tomorrow."

"So soon?"

"I want to do it quickly, before I lose my nerve," she said. "I don't think I've ever been this scared. Not even . . . not even when it was happening. Funny, huh?"

"No," said Cantling. "It makes sense."

"Daddy, hold me," Michelle said. She pressed herself into his arms. He hugged her and felt her body tremble.

"You're shaking," he said.

She wouldn't let go of him. "You remember, when I was real little, I used to have those nightmares, and I'd come bawling into your bedroom in the middle of the night and crawl into bed between you and Mommy."

Cantling smiled. "I remember," he said.

"I want to stay here tonight," Michelle said, hugging him even more tightly. "Tomorrow I'll be back there, alone. I don't want to be alone tonight. Can I, Daddy?"

Cantling disengaged gently, looked her in the eyes. "Are you sure?"

She nodded; a tiny, quick, shy nod. A child's nod.

He threw back the covers and she crept in next to him. "Don't go away," she said. "Don't even go to the bathroom, okay? Just stay right here with me."

"I'm here," he said. He put his arms around her, and Michelle curled up under the covers with her head on his shoulder. They lay together that way for a long time. He could feel her heart beating inside her chest. It was a soothing sound; soon Cantling began to drift back to sleep.

"Daddy?" she whispered against his chest.

He opened his eyes. "Michelle?"

"Daddy, I have to get rid of it. It's inside me and it's poison. I don't want to take it back with me. I have to get rid of it."

Cantling stroked her hair, long slow steady motions, saying nothing.

"When I was little, you remember, whenever I fell down or got in a fight, I'd come running to you, all teary, and show you my booboo. That's what I used to call it when I got hurt, remember, I'd say I had a booboo."

"I remember," Cantling said.

"And you, you'd always hug me and you'd say, 'Show me where it hurts,' and I would and you'd kiss it and make it better, you remember that? Show me where it hurts?"

Cantling nodded. "Yes," he said softly.

Michelle was crying quietly. He could feel the wetness soaking through the top of his pajamas. "I can't take it back with me, Daddy. I want to show you where it hurts. Please. Please."

He kissed the top of her head. "Go on."

She started at the beginning, in a halting whisper.

When dawn light broke through the bedroom windows, she was still talking. They never slept. She cried a lot, screamed once or twice, shivered frequently despite the weight of the blankets; Richard Cantling never let go of her, not once, not for a single moment. She showed him where it hurt.

Barry Leighton sighed. "It was a far, far better thing you did than you had ever done," he said. "Now if you'd only gone off to that far, far better rest right then and there, that very moment, everything would have been fine." He shook his head. "You never did know when to write Thirty, Cantling."

"Why?" Cantling demanded. "You're a good man, Leighton, tell me. Why is this happening. Why?"

The reporter shrugged. He was beginning to fade now. "That was the W that always gave me the most trouble," he said wearily. "Pick the story, and let me loose, and I could tell you the who and the what and the when and the where and even the how. But the why . . . ah, Cantling, you're the novelist, the whys are your province, not mine. The only Y that I ever really got on speaking terms with was the one goes with MCA."

Like the Cheshire cat, his smile lingered long after the rest of him was gone. Richard Cantling sat staring at the empty chair, at the abandoned tumbler, watching the whisky-soaked ice cubes melt slowly.

He did not remember falling asleep. He spent the night in the chair, and woke stiff and achey and cold. His dreams had been dark and shapeless and full of fear. He had slept well into the afternoon; half the day was gone. He made himself a tasteless breakfast in a kind of fog. He seemed distant from his own body, and every motion was slow and clumsy. When the coffee was ready, he poured a cup, picked it up, dropped it. The mug broke into a dozen pieces. Cantling stared down at it stupidly, watching rivulets of hot brown liquid run between the tiles. He did not have the energy to clean it up. He got a fresh mug, poured more coffee, managed to get down a few swallows.

The bacon was too salty; the eggs were runny, disgusting. Cantling pushed the meal away half-eaten, and drank more of the black, bitter coffee. He felt hung-over, but he knew that booze was not the problem.

Today, he thought. It will end today, one way or the other. She will not go back. *ByeLine* was his eighth novel, the next to last. Today the final portrait would arrive. A character from his ninth novel, his last novel. And then it would be over.

Or maybe just beginning.

How much did Michelle hate him? How badly had he wronged her? Cantling's hand shook; coffee slopped over the top of the mug, burning his fingers. He winced, cried out. Pain was so inarticulate. Burning. He thought of smoldering cigarettes, their tips like small red eyes. His stomach heaved. Cantling lurched to his feet, rushed to the bathroom. He got there just in time, gave his breakfast to the bowl. Afterwards he was too weak to move. He lay slumped against the cold white porcelain, his head swimming. He imagined somebody coming up behind him, taking him by the hair, forcing his face down into the water, flushing, flushing, laughing all the while, saying dirty, dirty, I'll get you clean, you're so dirty, flushing, flushing so the toilet ran and ran, holding his face down so the water and the vomit filled his mouth, his nostrils, until he could hardly breathe, until the world was almost black, until it was almost over, and then up again, laughing while he sucked in air, and then pushing him down again, flushing again, and again and again and again. But it was only his imagination. There was no one there. No one. Cantling was alone in the bathroom.

He forced himself to stand. In the mirror his face was gray and ancient, his hair filthy and unkempt. Behind him, leering over his shoulder, was another face. A man's face, pale and drawn, with black hair parted in the middle and slicked back. Behind a pair of small round glasses were eyes the color of dirty ice, eyes that moved constantly, frenetically, wild animals caught in a trap. They would chew off their own limbs to be free, those eyes. Cantling blinked and the face was gone. He turned on the cold tap, plunged his cupped hands under the stream, splashed water on his face. He could feel the stubble of his beard. He needed to shave. But there wasn't time, it wasn't important, he had to . . . he had to . . .

He had to do something. Get out of there. Get away, get to someplace safe, somewhere his children couldn't find him.

But there was nowhere safe, he knew.

He had to reach Michelle, talk to her, explain, plead. She loved him. She *would* forgive him, she had to. She would call it off, she would tell him what to do.

Frantic, Cantling rushed back to the living room, snatched up the phone. He couldn't remember Michelle's number. He searched around, found his address book, flipped through it wildly. There, there; he punched in the numbers.

The phone rang four times. Then someone picked it up.

"Michelle—" he started.

"Hi," she said. "This is Michelle Cantling, but I'm not in right now. If you'll leave your name and number when you hear the tone, I'll get back to you, unless you're selling something."

The beep sounded. "Michelle, are you there?" Cantling said. "I know you hide behind the machine sometimes, when you don't want to talk. It's me. Please pick up. Please."

Nothing.

"Call me back, then," he said. He wanted to get it all in; his words tumbled over each other in their haste to get out. "I, you, you can't do it, please, let me explain, I never meant, I never meant, please . . ." There was the beep again, and then a dial tone. Cantling stared at the phone, hung up slowly. She would call him back. She had to, she was his daughter, they loved each other, she had to give him the chance to explain.

Of course, he had tried to explain before.

His doorbell was the old-fashioned kind, a brass key that projected out of the door. You had to turn it by hand, and when you did it produced a loud, impatient metallic rasp. Someone was turning it furiously, turning it and turning it and turning it. Cantling rushed to the door, utterly baffled. He had never made friends easily, and it was even harder now that he had become so set in his ways. He had no real friends in Perrot, a few acquaintances perhaps, no one who would come calling so unexpectedly, and twist the bell with such energetic determination.

He undid his chain and flung the door open, wrenching the bell key out of Michelle's fingers.

She was dressed in a belted raincoat, a knitted ski cap, a matching scarf. The scarf and a few loose strands of hair were caught in the wind, moving restlessly. She was wearing high, fashionable boots and carrying a big leather shoulder bag. She looked good. It had been almost a year since Cantling had seen her, on his last Christmas visit to New York. It had been two years since she'd moved back east.

"Michelle," Cantling said. "I didn't . . . this is quite a surprise. All the way from New York and you didn't even tell me you were coming?"

"No," she snapped. There was something wrong with her voice, her eyes. "I didn't want to give you any warning, you bastard. You didn't give me any warning."

"You're upset," Cantling said. "Come in, let's talk."

"I'll come in all right." She pushed past him, kicked the door shut behind her with so much force that the buzzer sounded again. Out of the wind, her face got even harder. "You want to know why I came? I am going to tell you what I think of you. Then I'm going to turn around and leave, I'm going to walk right out of this house and out of your fucking life, just like Mom did. She was the smart one, not me. I was dumb enough to think you loved me, crazy enough to think you cared."

"Michelle, don't," Cantling said. "You don't understand. I do love you. You're my little girl, you—"

"Don't you *dare!*" she screamed at him. She reached into her shoulder bag. "You call this *love*, you rotten bastard!" She pulled it out and flung it at him.

Cantling was not as quick as he'd been. He tried to duck, but it caught him on the side of his neck, and it hurt. Michelle had thrown it hard, and it was a big, thick, heavy hardcover, not some flimsy paperback. The pages fluttered as it tumbled to the carpet; Cantling stared down at his own photograph on the back of the dust-wrapper. "You're just like your mother," he said, rubbing his neck where the book had hit. "She always threw things too. Only you aim better." He smiled weakly.

"I'm not interested in your jokes," Michelle said. "I'll never forgive you. Never. Never ever. All I want to know is how you could do this to me, that's all. You tell me. You tell me now."

"I," Cantling said. He held his hands out helplessly. "Look, I . . . you're upset now, why don't we have some coffee or something, and talk about it when you calm down a little. I don't want a big fight."

"I don't give a fuck what you want," Michelle screamed. "I want to talk about it right now!" She kicked the fallen book.

Richard Cantling felt his own anger building. It wasn't right for her to yell at him like that, he didn't deserve this attack, he hadn't done anything. He tried not to say anything for fear of saying the wrong thing and escalating the situation. He knelt and picked up his book. Without thinking, he brushed it off, turned it over almost tenderly. The title glared up at him; stark, twisted red letters against a black background, the distorted face of a pretty young woman, mouth open in a scream. *Show Me Where It Hurts.*

"I was afraid you'd take it the wrong way," Cantling said.

"The *wrong way!*" Michelle said. A look of incredulity passed across her face. "Did you think I'd *like* it?"

"I, I wasn't sure," said Cantling. "I hoped . . . I mean, I was uncertain of your reaction, and so I thought it would be better not to mention what I was working on, until, well . . ."

"Until the fucking thing was in the bookstore windows," Michelle finished for him.

Cantling flipped past the title page. "Look," he said, holding it out, "I dedicated it to you." He showed her:

To Michelle, who knew the pain.

Michelle swung at it, knocked it out of Cantling's hands. "You bastard," she said. "You think that makes it better? You think your stinking dedication excuses what you did? Nothing excuses it. I'll never forgive you."

Cantling edged back a step, retreating in the face of her fury. "I didn't do anything," he said stubbornly. "I wrote a book. A novel. Is that a crime?"

"You're my *father*," she shrieked. "You knew . . . you knew, you bastard, you knew I couldn't bear to talk about it, to talk about what happened. Not to my lovers or my friends or even my therapist. I can't, I just *can't*, I can't even think about it. You knew. I told you, I told only you, because you were my daddy and I trusted you and I had to get it out, and I told you, it was private, it was just between us, you knew, but what did you do? You wrote it all up in a goddamned book and *published* it for millions of people to read! Damn you, damn you. Were you planning to do that all along, you sonofabitch? Were you? That night in bed, were you memorizing every word?"

"I," said Cantling. "No, I didn't memorize anything, I just, well, I just remembered it. You're taking it all wrong, Michelle. The book's not about what happened to you. Yes, it's inspired by that, that was the starting point, but it's fiction, I changed things, it's just a novel."

"Oh yeah, Daddy, you changed things all right. Instead of Michelle Cantling it's all about Nicole Mitchell, and she's a fashion designer instead of an artist, and she's also kind of stupid, isn't she? Was that a change or is that what you think, that I was stupid to live there, stupid to let him in like that? It's all fiction, yeah. It's just a coincidence that it's about this girl that gets held prisoner and raped and tortured and terrorized and raped some more, and that you've got a daughter who was held prisoner and raped and tortured and terrorized and raped some more, right, just a fucking coincidence!"

"You don't understand," Cantling said helplessly.

"No, *you* don't understand. You don't understand what it's like. This is your biggest book in years, right? Number one best-seller, you've never been number one before, haven't even been on the lists since *Times Are Hard*, or was it *Black Roses*? And why not, why not number one, this isn't no boring story about a has-been newspaper, this is *rape*, hey, what could be hotter? Lots of sex and violence, torture and fucking and terror, and doncha know, *it really happened*, yeah." Her mouth twisted and trembled. "It was the worst thing that ever happened to me. It was all the nightmares that have ever been. I still wake up screaming sometimes, but I was getting better, it was behind me. And now it's there in every bookstore window, and all my friends know, everybody knows, strangers come up to me at parties and tell me how sorry they are." She choked back a sob; she was halfway between anger and tears. "And I pick up your book, your fucking no-good book, and there it is again, in black and white, all written down. You're such a fucking *good* writer, Daddy, you make it all so real. A book you can't put down. Well, I put it down but it didn't help, it's all there, now it will always be there, won't it? Every day somebody in the world will pick up your book and read it and I'll get raped again. That's what you did. You finished the job for him, Daddy. You violated me, took me without my consent, just like he did. You raped me. You're my own father and you *raped* me!"

"You're not being fair," Cantling said. "I never meant to hurt you. The book . . . Nicole is strong and smart. It's the man who's the monster. He uses all those different names because fear has a thousand names, but only one face, you see. He's not just a man, he's the darkness made flesh, the mindless violence that waits out there for all of us, the gods that play with us like flies, he's a symbol of all—"

"He's the man who raped me! He's not a symbol!"

She screamed it so loudly that Richard Cantling had to retreat in the face of her fury. "No," he said. "He's just a character. He's . . . Michelle, I know it hurts, but what you went through, it's something people should know about, should think about, it's a part of life. Telling about life, making sense of it, that's the job of literature, that's my job. Someone had to tell your story. I tried to make it true, tried to do my—"

His daughter's face, red and wet with tears, seemed almost feral for a moment, unrecognizable, inhuman. Then a curious calm passed across her features. "You got one thing right," she said. "Nicole didn't have a father. When I was a little kid I'd come to you crying and my daddy would say show me where it hurts, and it was a private thing, a special thing, but in the book Nicole doesn't have a father, he says it, you gave it to him, he says show me where it hurts, he says it all the time. You're so ironic. You're so clever. The way he said it, it made him so real, more real than when he *was* real. And when you wrote it, you were right. That's what the monster says. Show me where it hurts. That's the monster's line. Nicole doesn't have a father, he's dead, yes, that was right too. I don't have a father. No I don't."

"Don't you talk to me like that," Richard Cantling said. It was terror inside him; it was shame. But it came out anger. "I won't have that, no matter what you've been through. I'm your father."

"No," Michelle said, grinning crazy now, backing away from him. "No, I don't have a father, and you don't have any children, no, unless it's in your books. Those are your children, your only children. Your books, your damned fucking books, those are your children, those are your children, those are your children." Then she turned and ran past him, down the foyer. She stopped at the door to his den. Cantling was afraid of what she might do. He ran after her.

When he reached the den, Michelle had already found the knife and set to work.

Richard Cantling sat by his silent phone and watched his grandfather clock tick off the hours toward darkness.

He tried Michelle's number at three o'clock, at four, at five. The machine, always the machine, speaking in a mockery of her voice. His messages grew more desperate. It was growing dim outside. His light was fading.

Cantling heard no steps on his porch, no knock on his door, no rasping summons from his old brass bell. It was an afternoon as silent as the grave. But by the time evening had fallen, he knew it was out there. A big square package, wrapped in brown paper, addressed in a hand he had known well. Inside a portrait.

He had not understood, not really, and so she was teaching him.

The clock ticked. The darkness grew thicker. The sense of a waiting presence beyond his door seemed to fill the house. His fear had been growing for hours. He sat in the armchair with his legs pulled up under him, his mouth hanging open, thinking, remembering. Heard cruel laughter. Saw the dim red tips of cigarettes in the shadows, moving, circling. Imagined their small hot kisses on his skin. Tasted urine, blood, tears. Knew violence, knew violation, of every sort there was. His hands, his voice, his face, his face, his face. The character with a dozen names, but fear had only a single face. The youngest of his children. His baby. His monstrous baby.

He had been blocked for so long, Cantling thought. If only he could make her understand. It was a kind of impotence, not writing. He had been a writer, but that was over. He had been a husband, but his wife was dead. He had been a father, but she got better, went back to New York. She left him alone, but that last night, wrapped in his arms, she told him the story, she showed him where it hurt, she gave him all that pain. What was he to do with it?

Afterwards he could not forget. He thought of it constantly. He began to reshape it in his head, began to grope for the words, the scenes, the symbols that would make sense of it. It was hideous, but it was life, raw strong life, the grist for Cantling's mill, the very thing he needed.

She had showed him where it hurt; he could show them all. He did resist, he did try. He began a short story, an essay, finished some reviews. But it returned. It was with him every night. It would not be denied.

He wrote it.

"Guilty," Cantling said in the darkened room. And when he spoke the word, a kind of acceptance seemed to settle over him, banishing the terror. He was guilty. He had done it. He would accept the punishment, then. It was only right.

Richard Cantling stood and went to his door.

The package was there.

He lugged it inside, still wrapped, carried it up the stairs. He would hang him beside the others, beside Dunnahoo and Cissy and Barry Leighton, all in a row, yes. He went for his hammer, measured carefully, drove the nail. Only then did he unwrap the portrait, and look at the face within.

It captured her as no other artist had ever done, not just the lines of her face, the high angular cheekbones and blue eyes and tangled ash-blond hair, but the personality inside. She looked so young and fresh and confident, and he could see the strength there, the courage, the stubbornness. But best of all he liked her smile. It was a lovely smile, a smile that illuminated her whole face. The smile seemed to remind him of someone he had known once. He couldn't remember who.

Richard Cantling felt a strange, brief sense of relief, followed by an even greater sense of loss, a loss so terrible and final and total that he knew it was beyond the power of the words he worshipped.

Then the feeling was gone.

Cantling stepped back, folded his arms, studied the four portraits. Such excellent work; looking at the paintings, he could almost feel their presence in his house.

Dunnahoo, his first-born, the boy he wished he'd been.

Cissy, his true love.

Barry Leighton, his wise and tired alter-ego.

Nicole, the daughter he'd never had.

His people. His characters. His children.

A week later, another, much smaller, package arrived. Inside the carton were copies of four of his novels, a bill, and a polite note from the artist inquiring if there would be any more commissions.

Richard Cantling said no, and paid the bill by check.

RACHEL IN LOVE

by PAT MURPHY

Pat Murphy's unusual coming-of-age tale about "Rachel in Love" (*Asimov's*, April 1994) hit SF with a splash. The story won the 1987 Nebula Award for Best Novelette, the Theodore Sturgeon Memorial Award for Short Fiction, and the *Asimov's* Readers' Poll. That same year, she won the Nebula for her novel, *The Falling Woman*. The author's other esteemed works include the novellas "Bones" and "Traveling West;" the short story collection *The City, Not Long After*; and her novel *Points of Departure*.

When she's not writing science fiction, Pat writes for Exploratorium, San Francisco's museum of science, art, and human perception. The work she's published as part of the Exploratorium staff includes *By Nature's Design*, a book of photos and text about recurring natural patterns, and *Bending Light*, a book of optic activities for kids. Pat also holds a black belt in Kenpo Karate, and she has traveled from Mexico to Nepal to research her exotic science fiction and fantasy stories.

It is a Sunday morning in summer and a small brown chimpanzee named Rachel sits on the living room floor of a remote ranch house on the edge of the Painted Desert. She is watching a Tarzan movie on television. Her hairy arms are wrapped around her knees and she rocks back and forth with suppressed excitement. She knows that her father would say that she's too old for such childish amusements—but since Aaron is still sleeping, he can't chastise her.

On the television, Tarzan has been trapped in a bamboo cage by a band of wicked Pygmies. Rachel is afraid that he won't escape in time to save Jane from the ivory smugglers who hold her captive. The movie cuts to Jane, who is tied up in the back of a jeep, and Rachel whimpers softly to herself. She knows better than to howl: she peeked into her father's bedroom earlier, and he was still in bed. Aaron doesn't like her to howl when he is sleeping.

When the movie breaks for a commercial, Rachel goes to her father's room. She is ready for breakfast and she wants him to get up. She tiptoes to the bed to see if he is awake.

His eyes are open and he is staring at nothing. His face is pale and his lips are a purplish color. Dr. Aaron Jacobs, the man Rachel calls father, is not asleep. He is dead, having died in the night of a heart attack.

When Rachel shakes him, his head rocks back and forth in time with her shaking, but his eyes do not blink and he does not breathe. She places his hand on her head, nudging him so that he will waken and stroke her. He does not move. When she leans toward him, his hand falls limply to dangle over the edge of the bed.

In the breeze from the open bedroom window, the fine wisps of grey hair that he had carefully combed over his bald spot each morn-

ing shift and flutter, exposing the naked scalp. In the other room, elephants trumpet as they stampede across the jungle to rescue Tarzan.
Rachel whimpers softly, but her father does not move.

Rachel backs away from her father's body. In the living room,
Tarzan is swinging across the jungle on vines, going to save Jane.
Rachel ignores the television. She prowls through the house as if
searching for comfort—stepping into her own small bedroom, wandering through her father's laboratory. From the cages that line the
walls, white rats stare at her with hot red eyes. A rabbit hops across its
cage, making a series of slow dull thumps, like a feather pillow tumbling down a flight of stairs.

She thinks that perhaps she made a mistake. Perhaps her father is
just sleeping. She returns to the bedroom, but nothing has changed.
Her father lies open-eyed on the bed. For a long time, she huddles
beside his body, clinging to his hand.

He is the only person she has ever known. He is her father, her
teacher, her friend. She cannot leave him alone.

The afternoon sun blazes through the window, and still Aaron does
not move. The room grows dark, but Rachel does not turn on the lights.
She is waiting for Aaron to wake up. When the moon rises, its silver light
shines through the window to cast a bright rectangle on the far wall.

Outside, somewhere in the barren rocky land surrounding the
ranch house, a coyote lifts its head to the rising moon and wails, a thin
sound that is as lonely as a train whistling through an abandoned station. Rachel joins in with a desolate howl of loneliness and grief. Aaron
lies still and Rachel knows that he is dead.

When Rachel was younger, she had a favorite bedtime story.—Where
did I come from? she would ask Aaron, using the abbreviated gestures
of ASL, American Sign Language.—Tell me again.

"You're too old for bedtime stories," Aaron would say.

—Please, she'd sign.—Tell me the story.

In the end, he always relented and told her. "Once upon a time,
there was a little girl named Rachel," he said. "She was a pretty girl,
with long golden hair like a princess in a fairy tale. She lived with her
father and her mother and they were all very happy."

Rachel would snuggle contentedly beneath her blankets. The
story, like any good fairy tale, had elements of tragedy. In the story,
Rachel's father worked at a university, studying the workings of the
brain and charting the electric fields that the nervous impulses of an
active brain produced. But the other researchers at the university
didn't understand Rachel's father; they distrusted his research and cut

off his funding. (During this portion of the story, Aaron's voice took on a bitter edge.) So he left the university and took his wife and daughter to the desert, where he could work in peace.

He continued his research and determined that each individual brain produced its own unique pattern of fields, as characteristic as a fingerprint. (Rachel found this part of the story quite dull, but Aaron insisted on including it.) The shape of this "Electric Mind," as he called it, was determined by habitual patterns of thoughts and emotions. Record the Electric Mind, he postulated, and you could capture an individual's personality.

Then one sunny day, the doctor's wife and beautiful daughter went for a drive. A truck barreling down a winding cliffside road lost its brakes and met the car head-on, killing both the girl and her mother. (Rachel clung to Aaron's hand during this part of the story, frightened by the sudden evil twist of fortune.)

But though Rachel's body had died, all was not lost. In his desert lab, the doctor had recorded the electrical patterns produced by his daughter's brain. The doctor had been experimenting with the use of external magnetic fields to impose the patterns from one animal onto the brain of another. From an animal supply house, he obtained a young chimpanzee. He used a mixture of norepinephrin-based transmitter substances to boost the speed of neural processing in the chimp's brain, and then he imposed the pattern of his daughter's mind upon the brain of this young chimp, combining the two after his own fashion, saving his daughter in his own way. In the chimp's brain was all that remained of Rachel Jacobs.

The doctor named the chimp Rachel and raised her as his own daughter. Since the limitations of the chimpanzee larynx made speech very difficult, he instructed her in ASL. He taught her to read and to write. They were good friends, the best of companions.

By this point in the story, Rachel was usually asleep. But it didn't matter—she knew the ending. The doctor, whose name was Aaron Jacobs, and the chimp named Rachel lived happily ever after.

Rachel likes fairy tales and she likes happy endings. She has the mind of a teenage girl, but the innocent heart of a young chimp.

Sometimes, when Rachel looks at her gnarled brown fingers, they seem alien, wrong, out of place. She remembers having small, pale, delicate hands. Memories lie upon memories, layers upon layers, like the sedimentary rocks of the desert buttes.

Rachel remembers a blonde-haired fair-skinned woman who smelled sweetly of perfume. On a Halloween long ago, this woman (who was, in these memories, Rachel's mother) painted Rachel's fingernails bright red because Rachel was dressed as a gypsy and gypsies liked red. Rachel remembers the woman's hands: white hands with faintly blue veins hidden just beneath the skin, neatly clipped nails painted rose pink.

But Rachel also remembers another mother and another time. Her mother was dark and hairy and smelled sweetly of overripe fruit. She and Rachel lived in a wire cage in a room filled with chimps and she hugged Rachel to her hairy breast whenever any people came into the room. Rachel's mother groomed Rachel constantly, picking delicately through her fur in search of lice that she never found.

Memories upon memories: jumbled and confused, like random pictures clipped from magazines, a bright collage that makes no sense. Rachel remembers cages: cold wire mesh beneath her feet, the smell of fear around her. A man in a white lab coat took her from the arms of her hairy mother and pricked her with needles. She could hear her mother howling, but she could not escape from the man.

Rachel remembers a junior high school dance where she wore a new dress: she stood in a dark corner of the gym for hours, pretending to admire the crepe paper decorations because she felt too shy to search among the crowd for her friends.

She remembers when she was a young chimp: she huddled with five other adolescent chimps in the stuffy freight compartment of a train, frightened by the alien smells and sounds.

She remembers gym class: gray lockers and ugly gym suits that revealed her skinny legs. The teacher made everyone play softball, even Rachel who was unathletic and painfully shy. Rachel at bat, standing at the plate, was terrified to be the center of attention. "Easy out," said the catcher, a hard-edged girl who ran with the wrong crowd and always smelled of cigarette smoke. When Rachel swung at the ball and missed, the outfielders filled the air with malicious laughter.

Rachel's memories are as delicate and elusive as the dusty moths and butterflies that dance among the rabbit brush and sage. Memories of her girlhood never linger; they land for an instant, then take flight, leaving Rachel feeling abandoned and alone.

Rachel leaves Aaron's body where it is, but closes his eyes and pulls the sheet up over his head. She does not know what else to do. Each day she waters the garden and picks some greens for the rabbits. Each day, she cares for the animals in the lab, bringing them food and refilling their water bottles. The weather is cool, and Aaron's body does not smell too bad, though by the end of the week, a wide line of ants runs from the bed to the open window.

At the end of the first week, on a moonlit evening, Rachel decides to let the animals go free. She releases the rabbits one by one, climbing on a stepladder to reach down into the cage and lift each placid bunny out. She carries each one to the back door, holding it for a moment and stroking the soft warm fur. Then she sets the animal down and nudges it in the direction of the green grass that grows around the perimeter of the fenced garden.

The rats are more difficult to deal with. She manages to wrestle the large rat cage off the shelf, but it is heavier than she thought it would be. Though she slows its fall, it lands on the floor with a crash and the rats scurry to and fro within. She shoves the cage across the linoleum floor, sliding it down the hall, over the doorsill, and onto the back patio. When she opens the cage door, rats burst out like popcorn from a popper, white in the moonlight and dashing in all directions.

Once, while Aaron was taking a nap, Rachel walked along the dirt track that led to the main highway. She hadn't planned on going far. She just wanted to see what the highway looked like, maybe hide near the mailbox and watch a car drive past. She was curious about the outside world and her fleeting fragmentary memories did not satisfy that curiosity.

She was halfway to the mailbox when Aaron came roaring up in his old jeep. "Get in the car," he shouted at her. "Right now!" Rachel had never seen him so angry. She cowered in the jeep's passenger seat, covered with dust from the road, unhappy that Aaron was so upset. He didn't speak until they got back to the ranch house, and then he spoke in a low voice, filled with bitterness and suppressed rage.

"You don't want to go out there," he said. "You wouldn't like it out there. The world is filled with petty, narrow-minded, stupid people. They wouldn't understand you. And anyone they don't understand, they want to hurt. They hurt anyone who's different. If they know that you're different, they punish you, hurt you. They'd lock you up and never let you go."

He looked straight ahead, staring through the dirty windshield. "It's not like the shows on TV, Rachel," he said in a softer tone. "It's not like the stories in books."

He looked at her then and she gestured frantically. —I'm sorry. I'm sorry.

"I can't protect you out there," he said. "I can't keep you safe."

Rachel took his hand in both of hers. He relented then, stroking her head. "Never do that again," he said. "Never."

Aaron's fear was contagious. Rachel never again walked along the dirt track and sometimes she had dreams about bad people who wanted to lock her in a cage.

*   *   *

Two weeks after Aaron's death, a black-and-white police car drives slowly up to the house. When the policemen knock on the door, Rachel hides behind the couch in the living room. They knock again, try the knob, then open the door, which she had left unlocked.

Suddenly frightened, Rachel bolts from behind the couch, bounding toward the back door. Behind her, she hears one man yell, "My God! It's a gorilla!"

By the time he pulls his gun, Rachel has run out the back door and away into the hills. From the hills she watches as an ambulance drives up and two men in white take Aaron's body away. Even after the ambulance and the police car drive away, Rachel is afraid to go back to the house. Only after sunset does she return.

Just before dawn the next morning, she wakens to the sound of a truck jouncing down the dirt road. She peers out the window to see a pale green pickup. Sloppily stenciled in white on the door are the words: PRIMATE RESEARCH CENTER. Rachel hesitates as the truck pulls up in front of the house. By the time she has decided to flee, two men are getting out of the truck. One of them carries a rifle.

She runs out the back door and heads for the hills, but she is only halfway to hiding when she hears a sound like a sharp intake of breath and feels a painful jolt in her shoulder. Suddenly, her legs give way and she is tumbling backward down the sandy slope, dust coating her red-brown fur, her howl becoming a whimper, then fading to nothing at all. She falls into the blackness of sleep.

The sun is up. Rachel lies in a cage in the back of the pickup truck. She is partially conscious and she feels a tingling in her hands and feet. Nausea grips her stomach and bowels. Her body aches.

Rachel can blink, but otherwise she can't move. From where she lies, she can see only the wire mesh of the cage and the side of the truck. When she tries to turn her head, the burning in her skin intensifies. She lies still, wanting to cry out, but unable to make a sound. She can only blink slowly, trying to close out the pain. But the burning and nausea stay.

The truck jounces down a dirt road, then stops. It rocks as the men get out. The doors slam. Rachel hears the tailgate open.

A woman's voice: "Is that the animal the County Sheriff wanted us to pick up?" A woman peers into the cage. She wears a white lab coat and her brown hair is tied back in a single braid. Around her eyes, Rachel can see small wrinkles, etched by years of living in the desert. The woman doesn't look evil. Rachel hopes that the woman will save her from the men in the truck.

"Yeah. It should be knocked out for at least another half hour. Where do you want it?"

"Bring it into the lab where we had the rhesus monkeys. I'll keep it there until I have an empty cage in the breeding area."

Rachel's cage scrapes across the bed of the pickup. She feels each bump and jar as a new pain. The man swings the cage onto a cart and the woman pushes the cart down a concrete corridor. Rachel watches the walls pass just a few inches from her nose.

The lab contains rows of cages in which small animals sleepily move. In the sudden stark light of the overhead fluorescent bulbs, the eyes of white rats gleam red.

With the help of one of the men from the truck, the woman man-handles Rachel onto a lab table. The metal surface is cold and hard, painful against Rachel's skin. Rachel's body is not under her control; her limbs will not respond. She is still frozen by the tranquilizer, able to watch, but that is all. She cannot protest or plead for mercy.

Rachel watches with growing terror as the woman pulls on rubber gloves and fills a hypodermic needle with a clear solution. "Mark down that I'm giving her the standard test for tuberculosis; this eyelid should be checked before she's moved in with the others. I'll add thiabendazole to her feed for the next few days to clean out any intestinal worms. And I suppose we might as well de-flea her as well," the woman says. The man grunts in response.

Expertly, the woman closes one of Rachel's eyes. With her open eye, Rachel watches the hypodermic needle approach. She feels a sharp pain in her eyelid. In her mind, she is howling, but the only sound she can manage is a breathy sigh.

The woman sets the hypodermic aside and begins methodically spraying Rachel's fur with a cold, foul-smelling liquid. A drop strikes Rachel's eye and burns. Rachel blinks, but she cannot lift a hand to rub her eye. The woman treats Rachel with casual indifference, chatting with the man as she spreads Rachel's legs and sprays her genitals. "Looks healthy enough. Good breeding stock."

Rachel moans, but neither person notices. At last, they finish their torture, put her in a cage, and leave the room. She closes her eyes, and the darkness returns.

Rachel dreams. She is back at home in the ranch house. It is night and she is alone. Outside, coyotes yip and howl. The coyote is the voice of the desert, wailing as the wind wails when it stretches itself thin to squeeze through a crack between two boulders. The people native to this land tell tales of Coyote, a god who was a trickster, unreliable, changeable, mercurial.

Rachel is restless, anxious, unnerved by the howling of the coyotes. She is looking for Aaron. In the dream, she knows he is not dead, and she searches the house for him, wandering from his cluttered bedroom to her small room to the linoleum-tiled lab.

She is in the lab when she hears something tapping: a small dry scratching, like a wind-blown branch against the window, though no tree grows near the house and the night is still. Cautiously, she lifts the curtain to look out.

She looks into her own reflection: a pale oval face, long blonde hair. The hand that holds the curtain aside is smooth and white with carefully clipped fingernails. But something is wrong. Superimposed on the reflection is another face peering through the glass: a pair of dark brown eyes, a chimp face with red-brown hair and jug-handle ears. She sees her own reflection and she sees the outsider; the two images merge and blur. She is afraid, but she can't drop the curtain and shut the ape face out.

She is a chimp looking in through the cold, bright windowpane; she is a girl looking out; she is a girl looking in; she is an ape looking out. She is afraid and the coyotes are howling all around.

Rachel opens her eyes and blinks until the world comes into focus. The pain and tingling has retreated, but she still feels a little sick. Her left eye aches. When she rubs it, she feels a raised lump on the eyelid where the woman pricked her. She lies on the floor of a wire mesh cage. The room is hot and the air is thick with the smell of animals.

In the cage beside her is another chimp, an older animal with scruffy dark brown fur. He sits with his arms wrapped around his knees, rocking back and forth, back and forth. His head is down. As he rocks, he murmurs to himself, a meaningless cooing that goes on and on. On his scalp, Rachel can see a gleam of metal: a permanently implanted electrode protrudes from a shaven patch. Rachel makes a soft questioning sound, but the other chimp will not look up.

Rachel's own cage is just a few feet square. In one corner is a bowl of monkey pellets. A water bottle hangs on the side of the cage. Rachel ignores the food, but drinks thirstily.

Sunlight streams through the windows, sliced into small sections by the wire mesh that covers the glass. She tests her cage door, rattling it gently at first, then harder. It is securely latched. The gaps in the mesh are too small to admit her hand. She can't reach out to work the latch.

The other chimp continues to rock back and forth. When Rachel rattles the mesh of her cage and howls, he lifts his head wearily and looks at her. His red-rimmed eyes are unfocused; she can't be sure he sees her.

—Hello, she gestures tentatively.—What's wrong?

He blinks at her in the dim light. —Hurt, he signs in ASL. He reaches up to touch the electrode, fingering skin that is already raw from repeated rubbing.

—Who hurt you? she asks. He stares at her blankly and she repeats the question. —Who?

—Men, he signs.

As if on cue, there is the click of a latch and the door to the lab opens. A bearded man in a white coat steps in, followed by a clean-shaven man in a suit. The bearded man seems to be showing the other man around the lab. ". . . only preliminary testing, so far," the bearded man is saying. "We've been hampered by a shortage of chimps trained in ASL." The two men stop in front of the old chimp's cage. "This old fellow is from the Oregon center. Funding for the language program was cut back and some of the animals were dispersed to other programs." The old chimp huddles at the back of the cage, eyeing the bearded man with suspicion.

—Hungry? the bearded man signs to the old chimp. He holds up an orange where the old chimp can see it.

—Give orange, the old chimp gestures. He holds out his hand, but comes no nearer to the wire mesh than he must to reach the orange. With the fruit in hand, he retreats to the back of his cage.

The bearded man continues, "This project will provide us with the first solid data on neural activity during use of sign language. But we really need greater access to chimps with advanced language skills. People are so damn protective of their animals."

"Is this one of yours?" the clean-shaven man asks, pointing to Rachel. She cowers in the back of the cage, as far from the wire mesh as she can get.

"No, not mine. She was someone's household pet, apparently. The county sheriff had us pick her up." The bearded man peers into her cage. Rachel does not move; she is terrified that he will somehow guess that she knows ASL. She stares at his hands and thinks about those hands putting an electrode through her skull. "I think she'll be put in breeding stock," the man says as he turns away.

Rachel watches them go, wondering at what terrible people these are. Aaron was right: they want to punish her, put an electrode in her head.

After the men are gone, she tries to draw the old chimp into conversation, but he will not reply. He ignores her as he eats his orange. Then he returns to his former posture, hiding his head and rocking himself back and forth.

Rachel, hungry despite herself, samples one of the food pellets. It has a strange medicinal taste, and she puts it back in the bowl. She needs to pee, but there is no toilet and she cannot escape the cage. At last, unable to hold it, she pees in one corner of the cage. The urine flows through the wire mesh to soak the litter below, and the smell of warm piss fills her cage. Humiliated, frightened, her head aching, her skin itchy from the flea spray, Rachel watches as the sunlight creeps across the room.

The day wears on. Rachel samples her food again, but rejects it, preferring hunger to the strange taste. A black man comes and cleans the cages of the rabbits and rats. Rachel cowers in her cage and watches him warily, afraid that he will hurt her, too.

When night comes, she is not tired. Outside, coyotes howl. Moonlight filters in through the high windows. She draws her legs up toward her body, then rests with her arms wrapped around her knees. Her father is dead, and she is a captive in a strange place. For a time, she whimpers softly, hoping to awaken from this nightmare and find herself at home in bed. When she hears the click of a key in the door to the room, she hugs herself more tightly.

A man in green coveralls pushes a cart filled with cleaning supplies into the room. He takes a broom from the cart, and begins sweeping the concrete floor. Over the rows of cages, she can see the top of his head bobbing in time with his sweeping. He works slowly and methodically, bending down to sweep carefully under each row of cages, making a neat pile of dust, dung, and food scraps in the center of the aisle.

The janitor's name is Jake. He is a middle-aged deaf man who has been employed by the Primate Research Center for the past seven years. He works night shift. The personnel director at the Primate Research Center likes Jake because he fills the federal quota for handicapped employees, and because he has not asked for a raise in five years. There have been some complaints about Jake—his work is often sloppy—but never enough to merit firing the man.

Jake is an unambitious, somewhat slow-witted man. He likes the Primate Research Center because he works alone, which allows him to drink on the job. He is an easy-going man, and he likes the animals. Sometimes, he brings treats for them. Once, a lab assistant caught him feeding an apple to a pregnant rhesus monkey. The monkey was part of an experiment on the effect of dietary restrictions on fetal brain development, and the lab assistant warned Jake that he would be fired if he was ever caught interfering with the animals again. Jake still feeds the animals, but he is more careful about when he does it, and he has never been caught again.

As Rachel watches, the old chimp gestures to Jake. —Give banana, the chimp signs. —Please banana. Jake stops sweeping for a minute and reaches down to the bottom shelf of his cleaning cart. He returns with a banana and offers it to the old chimp. The chimp accepts the banana and leans against the mesh while Jake scratches his fur.

When Jake turns back to his sweeping, he catches sight of Rachel and sees that she is watching him. Emboldened by his kindness to the old chimp, Rachel timidly gestures to him. —Help me.

Jake hesitates, then peers at her more closely. Both his eyes are shot with a fine lacework of red. His nose displays the broken blood vessels of someone who has been friends with the bottle for too many years. He needs a shave. But when he leans close, Rachel catches the scent of whiskey and tobacco. The smells remind her of Aaron and give her courage.

—Please help me, Rachel signs. —I don't belong here.

For the last hour, Jake has been drinking steadily. His view of the world is somewhat fuzzy. He stares at her blearily.

Rachel's fear that he will hurt her is replaced by the fear that he will leave her locked up and alone. Desperately she signs again. —Please please please. Help me. I don't belong here. Please help me go home.

He watches her, considering the situation. Rachel does not move. She is afraid that any movement will make him leave. With a majestic speed dictated by his inebriation, Jake leans his broom on the row of cages behind him and steps toward Rachel's cage again. —You talk? he signs.

—I talk, she signs.

—Where did you come from?

—From my father's house, she signs. —Two men came and shot me and put me here. I don't know why. I don't know why they locked me in jail.

Jake looks around, willing to be sympathetic, but puzzled by her talk of jail. —This isn't jail, he signs. —This is a place where scientists raise monkeys.

Rachel is indignant. —I am not a monkey, she signs. —I am a girl.

Jake studies her hairy body and her jug-handle ears. —You look like a monkey.

Rachel shakes her head. —No. I am a girl.

Rachel runs her hands back over her head, a very human gesture of annoyance and unhappiness. She signs sadly, —I don't belong here. Please let me out.

Jake shifts his weight from foot to foot, wondering what to do. —I can't let you out. I'll get in big trouble.

—Just for a little while? Please?

Jake glances at his cart of supplies. He has to finish off this room and two corridors of offices before he can relax for the night.

—Don't go, Rachel signs, guessing his thoughts.

—I have work to do.

She looks at the cart, then suggests eagerly, —Let me out and I'll help you work.

Jake frowns. —If I let you out, you will run away.

—No, I won't run. I will help. Please let me out.

—You promise to go back?

Rachel nods.

Warily he unlatches the cage. Rachel bounds out, grabs a whisk broom from the cart, and begins industriously sweeping bits of food and droppings from beneath the row of cages. —Come on, she signs to Jake from the end of the aisle. —I will help.

When Jake pushes the cart from the room filled with cages, Rachel follows him closely. The rubber wheels of the cleaning cart rumble softly on the linoleum floor. They pass through a metal door into a corridor where the floor is carpeted and the air smells of chalk dust and paper.

Offices let off the corridor, each one a small room furnished with a desk, bookshelves, and a blackboard. Jake shows Rachel how to empty the wastebaskets into a garbage bag. While he cleans the blackboards, she wanders from office to office, trailing the trash-filled garbage bag.

At first, Jake keeps a close eye on Rachel. But after cleaning each blackboard, he pauses to refill a cup from the whiskey bottle that he keeps wedged between the Saniflush and the window cleaner. By the time he is halfway through the second cup; he is treating her like an old friend, telling her to hurry up so that they can eat dinner.

Rachel works quickly, but she stops sometimes to gaze out the office windows. Outside, moonlight shines on a sandy plain, dotted here and there with scrubby clumps of rabbit brush.

At the end of the corridor is a larger room in which there are several desks and typewriters. In one of the wastebaskets, buried beneath memos and candybar wrappers, she finds a magazine. The title is *Love Confessions* and the cover has a picture of a man and woman kissing. Rachel studies the cover, then takes the magazine, tucking it on the bottom shelf of the cart.

Jake pours himself another cup of whiskey and pushes the cart to another hallway. Jake is working slower now, and as he works he makes humming noises, tuneless sounds that he feels only as pleasant vibrations. The last few blackboards are sloppily done, and Rachel, finished with the wastebaskets, cleans the places that Jake missed.

They eat dinner in the janitor's storeroom, a stuffy windowless room furnished with an ancient grease-stained couch, a battered black-and-white television, and shelves of cleaning supplies. From a shelf,

Jake takes the paper bag that holds his lunch: a baloney sandwich, a bag of barbecued potato chips, and a box of vanilla wafers. From behind the gallon jugs of liquid cleanser, he takes a magazine. He lights a cigarette, pours himself another cup of whiskey, and settles down on the couch. After a moment's hesitation, he offers Rachel a drink, pouring a shot of whiskey into a chipped ceramic cup.

Aaron never let Rachel drink whiskey, and she samples it carefully. At first the smell makes her sneeze, but she is fascinated by the way that the drink warms her throat, and she sips some more.

As they drink, Rachel tells Jake about the men who shot her and the woman who pricked her with a needle, and he nods. —The people here are crazy, he signs.

—I know, she says, thinking of the old chimp with the electrode in his head. —You won't tell them I can talk, will you?

Jake nods. —I won't tell them anything.

—They treat me like I'm not real, Rachel signs sadly. Then she hugs her knees, frightened at the thought of being held captive by crazy people. She considers planning her escape: she is out of the cage and she is sure she could outrun Jake. As she wonders about it, she finishes her cup of whiskey. The alcohol takes the edge off her fear. She sits close beside Jake on the couch, and the smell of his cigarette smoke reminds her of Aaron. For the first time since Aaron's death she feels warm and happy.

She shares Jake's cookies and potato chips and looks at the *Love Confessions* magazine that she took from the trash. The first story that she reads is about a woman named Alice. The headline reads: "I became a Go-go dancer to pay off my husband's gambling debts, and now he wants me to sell my body."

Rachel sympathizes with Alice's loneliness and suffering. Alice, like Rachel, is alone and misunderstood. As Rachel slowly reads, she sips her second cup of whiskey. The story reminds her of a fairy tale: the nice man who rescues Alice from her terrible husband replaces the handsome prince who rescued the princess. Rachel glances at Jake and wonders if he will rescue her from the wicked people who locked her in the cage.

She has finished the second cup of whiskey and eaten half Jake's cookies when Jake says that she must go back to her cage. She goes reluctantly, taking the magazine with her. He promises that he will come for her again the next night, and with that she must be content. She puts the magazine in one corner of the cage and curls up to sleep.

She wakes early in the afternoon. A man in a white coat is wheeling a low cart into the lab.

Rachel's head aches with hangover and she feels sick. As she crouches in one corner of her cage, he stops the cart beside her cage and then locks the wheels. "Hold on there," he mutters to her, then slides her cage onto the cart.

The man wheels her through long corridors, where the walls are cement blocks, painted institutional green. Rachel huddles unhappily in the cage, wondering where she is going and whether Jake will ever be able to find her.

At the end of a long corridor, the man opens a thick metal door and a wave of warm air strikes Rachel. It stinks of chimpanzees, excrement, and rotting food. On either side of the corridor are metal bars and wire mesh. Behind the mesh, Rachel can see dark hairy shadows. In one cage, five adolescent chimps swing and play. In another, two females huddle together, grooming each other. The man slows as he passes a cage in which a big male is banging on the wire with his fist, making the mesh rattle and ring.

"Now, Johnson," says the man. "Cool it. Be nice. I'm bringing you a new little girlfriend."

With a series of hooks, the man links Rachel's cage with the cage next to Johnson's and opens the doors. "Go on, girl," he says. "See the nice fruit." In the cage is a bowl of sliced apples with an attendant swarm of fruit flies.

At first, Rachel will not move into the new cage. She crouches in the cage on the cart, hoping that the man will decide to take her back to the lab. She watches him get a hose and attach it to a water faucet. But she does not understand his intention until he turns the stream of water on her. A cold blast strikes her on the back and she howls, fleeing into the new cage to avoid the cold water. Then the man closes the doors, unhooks the cage, and hurries away.

The floor is bare cement. Her cage is at one end of the corridor and two walls are cement block. A door in one of the cement block walls leads to an outside run. The other two walls are wire mesh: one facing the corridor; the other, Johnson's cage.

Johnson, quiet now that the man has left, is sniffing around the door in the wire mesh wall that joins their cages. Rachel watches him anxiously. Her memories of other chimps are distant, softened by time. She remembers her mother; she vaguely remembers playing with other chimps her age. But she does not know how to react to Johnson when he stares at her with great intensity and makes a loud huffing sound. She gestures to him in ASL, but he only stares harder and huffs again. Beyond Johnson, she can see other cages and other chimps, so many that the wire mesh blurs her vision and she cannot see the other end of the corridor.

To escape Johnson's scrutiny, she ducks through the door into the outside run, a wire mesh cage on a white concrete foundation. Outside there is barren ground and rabbit brush. The afternoon sun is hot and all the other runs are deserted until Johnson appears in the run beside hers. His attention disturbs her and she goes back inside.

She retreats to the side of the cage farthest from Johnson. A crudely built wooden platform provides her with a place to sit. Wrapping her arms around her knees, she tries to relax and ignore Johnson. She dozes off for a while, but wakes to a commotion across the corridor.

In the cage across the way is a female chimp in heat. Rachel recognizes the smell from her own times in heat. Two keepers are opening the door that separates the female's cage from the adjoining cage, where a male stands, watching with great interest. Johnson is shaking the wire mesh and howling as he watches.

"Mike here is a virgin, but Susie knows what she's doing," one keeper was saying to the other. "So it should go smoothly. But keep the hose ready."

"Yeah?"

"Sometimes they fight. We only use the hose to break it up if it gets real bad. Generally, they do okay."

Mike stalks into Susie's cage. The keepers lower the cage door, trapping both chimps in the same cage. Susie seems unalarmed. She continues eating a slice of orange while Mike sniffs at her genitals with every indication of great interest. She bends over to let Mike finger her pink bottom, the sign of estrus.

Rachel finds herself standing at the wire mesh, making low moaning noises. She can see Mike's erection, hear his grunting cries. He squats on the floor of Susie's cage, gesturing to the female. Rachel's feelings are mixed: she is fascinated, fearful, confused. She keeps thinking of the description of sex in the *Love Confessions* story: When Alice feels Danny's lips on hers, she is swept away by the passion of the moment. He takes her in his arms and her skin tingles as if she were consumed by an inner fire.

Susie bends down and Mike penetrates her with a loud grunt, thrusting violently with his hips. Susie cries out shrilly and suddenly leaps up, knocking Mike away. Rachel watches, overcome with fascination. Mike, his penis now limp, follows Susie slowly to the corner of the cage, where he begins grooming her carefully. Rachel finds that the wire mesh has cut her hands where she gripped it too tightly.

It is night, and the door at the end of the corridor creaks open. Rachel is immediately alert, peering through the wire mesh and trying to see down to the end of the corridor. She bangs on the wire mesh. As Jake comes closer, she waves a greeting.

When Jake reaches for the lever that will raise the door to Rachel's cage, Johnson charges toward him, howling and waving his arms above his head. He hammers on the wire mesh with his fists, howling and grimacing at Jake. Rachel ignores Johnson and hurries after Jake.

Again Rachel helps Jake clean. In the laboratory, she greets the old chimp, but the animal is more interested in the banana that Jake has brought than in conversation. The chimp will not reply to her questions, and after several tries, she gives up.

While Jake vacuums the carpeted corridors, Rachel empties the trash, finding a magazine called *Modern Romance* in the same wastebasket that had provided *Love Confessions*.

Later, in the janitor's lounge, Jake smokes a cigarette, sips whiskey, and flips through one of his own magazines. Rachel reads love stories in *Modern Romance*.

Every once in a while, she looks over Jake's shoulder at grainy pictures of naked women with their legs spread wide apart. Jake looks for a long time at a picture of a blonde woman with big breasts, red fingernails, and purple-painted eyelids. The woman lies on her back and smiles as she strokes the pinkness between her legs. The picture on the next page shows her caressing her own breasts, pinching the dark nipples. The final picture shows her looking back over her shoulder. She is in the position that Susie took when she was ready to be mounted.

Rachel looks over Jake's shoulder at the magazine, but she does not ask questions. Jake's smell began to change as soon as he opened the magazine; the scent of nervous sweat mingles with the aromas of tobacco and whiskey. Rachel suspects that questions would not be welcome just now.

At Jake's insistence, she goes back to her cage before dawn.

Over the next week, she listens to the conversations of the men who come and go, bringing food and hosing out the cages. From the men's conversation, she learns that the Primate Research Center is primarily a breeding facility that supplies researchers with domestically bred apes and monkeys of several species. It also maintains its own research staff. In indifferent tones, the men talk of horrible things. The adolescent chimps at the end of the corridor are being fed a diet high in cholesterol to determine cholesterol's effects on the circulatory system. A group of pregnant females are being injected with male hormones to determine how that will affect the female offspring. A group of infants is being fed a low protein diet to determine adverse effects on their brain development.

The men look through her as if she were not real, as if she were a part of the wall, as if she were no one at all. She cannot speak to them; she cannot trust them.

Each night, Jake lets her out of her cage and she helps him clean. He brings treats: barbequed potato chips, fresh fruit, chocolate bars, and cookies. He treats her fondly, as one would treat a precocious child. And he talks to her.

At night, when she is with Jake, Rachel can almost forget the terror of the cage, the anxiety of watching Johnson pace to and fro, the sense of unreality that accompanies the simplest act. She would be content to stay with Jake forever, eating snack food and reading confessions magazines. He seems to like her company. But each morning, Jake insists that she must go back to the cage and the terror. By the end of the first week, she has begun plotting her escape.

Whenever Jake falls asleep over his whiskey, something that happens three nights out of five, Rachel prowls the center alone, surreptitiously gathering things that she will need to survive in the desert: a plastic jug filled with water, a plastic bag of food pellets, a large beach towel that will serve as a blanket on the cool desert nights, a discarded plastic shopping bag in which she can carry the other things. Her best find is a road map on which the Primate Center is marked in red. She knows the address of Aaron's ranch and finds it on the map. She studies the roads and plots a route home. Cross country, assuming that she does not get lost, she will have to travel about fifty miles to reach the ranch. She hides these things behind one of the shelves in the janitor's storeroom.

Her plans to run away and go home are disrupted by the idea that she is in love with Jake, a notion that comes to her slowly, fed by the stories in the confessions magazines. When Jake absent-mindedly strokes her, she is filled with a strange excitement. She longs for his company and misses him on the weekends when he is away. She is happy only when she is with him, following him through the halls of the center, sniffing the aroma of tobacco and whiskey that is his own perfume. She steals a cigarette from his pack and hides it in her cage, where she can savor the smell of it at her leisure.

She loves him, but she does not know how to make him love her back. Rachel knows little about love: she remembers a high school crush where she mooned after a boy with a locker near hers, but that came to nothing. She reads the confessions magazines and Ann Landers' column in the newspaper that Jake brings with him each night, and from these sources, she learns about romance. One night, after

Jake falls asleep, she types a badly punctuated, ungrammatical letter to Ann. In the letter, she explains her situation and asks for advice on how to make Jake love her. She slips the letter into a sack labeled "Outgoing Mail," and for the next week she reads Ann's column with increased interest. But her letter never appears.

Rachel searches for answers in the magazine pictures that seem to fascinate Jake. She studies the naked women, especially the big-breasted woman with the purple smudges around her eyes.

One night, in a secretary's desk, she finds a plastic case of eyeshadow. She steals it and takes it back to her cage. The next evening, as soon as the Center is quiet, she upturns her metal food dish and regards her reflection in the shiny bottom. Squatting, she balances the eye shadow case on one knee and examines its contents: a tiny makeup brush and three shades of eye shadow—INDIAN BLUE, FOREST GREEN, and WILDLY VIOLET. Rachel chooses the shade labeled WILDLY VIOLET.

Using one finger to hold her right eye closed, she dabs her eyelid carefully with the makeup brush, leaving a gaudy orchid-colored smudge on her brown skin. She studies the smudge critically, then adds to it, smearing the color beyond the corner of her eyelid until it disappears in her brown fur. The color gives her eye a carnival brightness, a lunatic gaiety. Working with great care, she matches the effect on the other side, then smiles at herself in the glass, blinking coquettishly.

In the other cage, Johnson bares his teeth and shakes the wire mesh. She ignores him.

When Jake comes to let her out, he frowns at her eyes. —Did you hurt yourself? he asks.

—No, she says. Then, after a pause, —Don't you like it?

Jake squats beside her and stares at her eyes. Rachel puts a hand on his knee and her heart pounds at her own boldness. —You are a very strange monkey, he signs.

Rachel is afraid to move. Her hand on his knee closes into a fist; her face folds in on itself, puckering around the eyes.

Then, straightening up, he signs, —I liked your eyes better before.

He likes her eyes. She nods without taking her eyes from his face. Later, she washes her face in the women's restroom, leaving dark smudges the color of bruises on a series of paper towels.

Rachel is dreaming. She is walking through the Painted Desert with her hairy brown mother, following a red rock canyon that Rachel somehow knows will lead her to the Primate Research Center. Her mother is lagging behind: she does not want to go to the center; she is afraid. In the shadow of a rock outcropping, Rachel stops to explain to her mother that they must go to the center because Jake is at the center.

Rachel's mother does not understand sign language. She watches Rachel with mournful eyes, then scrambles up the canyon wall, leaving Rachel behind. Rachel climbs after her mother, pulling herself over the edge in time to see the other chimp loping away across the wind-blown red cinder-rock and sand.

Rachel bounds after her mother, and as she runs she howls like an abandoned infant chimp, wailing her distress. The figure of her mother wavers in the distance, shimmering in the heat that rises from the sand. The figure changes. Running away across the red sands is a pale blonde woman wearing a purple sweatsuit and jogging shoes, the sweet-smelling mother that Rachel remembers. The woman looks back and smiles at Rachel. "Don't howl like an ape, daughter," she calls. "Say Mama."

Rachel runs silently, dream running that takes her nowhere. The sand burns her feet and the sun beats down on her head. The blonde woman vanishes in the distance, and Rachel is alone. She collapses on the sand, whimpering because she is alone and afraid.

She feels the gentle touch of fingers grooming her fur, and for a moment, still half asleep, she believes that her hairy mother has returned to her. She opens her eyes and looks into a pair of dark brown eyes, separated from her by wire mesh. Johnson. He has reached through a gap in the fence to groom her. As he sorts through her fur, he makes soft cooing sounds, gentle comforting noises.

Still half asleep, she gazes at him and wonders why she was so fearful. He does not seem so bad. He grooms her for a time, and then sits nearby, watching her through the mesh. She brings a slice of apple from her dish of food and offers it to him. With her free hand, she makes the sign for apple. When he takes it, she signs again: apple. He is not a particularly quick student, but she has time and many slices of apple.

All Rachel's preparations are done, but she cannot bring herself to leave the center. Leaving the center means leaving Jake, leaving potato chips and whiskey, leaving security. To Rachel, the thought of love is always accompanied by the warm taste of whiskey and potato chips.

Some nights, after Jake is asleep, she goes to the big glass doors that lead to the outside. She opens the doors and stands on the steps, looking down into the desert. Sometimes a jackrabbit sits on its haunches in the rectangles of light that shine through the glass doors. Sometimes she sees kangaroo rats, hopping through the moonlight like rubber balls bouncing on hard pavement. Once, a coyote trots by, casting a contemptuous glance in her direction.

The desert is a lonely place. Empty. Cold. She thinks of Jake snoring softly in the janitor's lounge. And always she closes the door and returns to him.

Rachel leads a double life: janitor's assistant by night, prisoner and teacher by day. She spends her afternoons drowsing in the sun and teaching Johnson new signs.

On a warm afternoon, Rachel sits in the outside run, basking in the sunlight. Johnson is inside, and the other chimps are quiet. She can almost imagine she is back at her father's ranch, sitting in her own yard. She naps and dreams of Jake.

She dreams that she is sitting in his lap on the battered old couch. Her hand is on his chest: a smooth pale hand with red-painted fingernails. When she looks at the dark screen of the television set, she can see her reflection. She is a thin teenager with blonde hair and blue eyes. She is naked.

Jake is looking at her and smiling. He runs a hand down her back and she closes her eyes in ecstacy.

But something changes when she closes her eyes. Jake is grooming her as her mother used to groom her, sorting through her hair in search of fleas. She opens her eyes and sees Johnson, his diligent fingers searching through her fur, his intent brown eyes watching her. The reflection on the television screen shows two chimps, tangled in each others' arms.

Rachel wakes to find that she is in heat for the first time since she came to the center. The skin surrounding her genitals is swollen and pink.

For the rest of the day, she is restless, pacing to and fro in her cage. On his side of the wire mesh wall, Johnson is equally restless, following her when she goes outside, sniffing long and hard at the edge of the barrier that separates him from her.

That night, Rachel goes eagerly to help Jake clean. She follows him closely, never letting him get far from her. When he is sweeping, she trots after him with the dustpan and he almost trips over her twice. She keeps waiting for him to notice her condition, but he seems oblivious.

As she works, she sips from a cup of whiskey. Excited, she drinks more than usual, finishing two full cups. The liquor leaves her a little disoriented, and she sways as she follows Jake to the janitor's lounge. She curls up close beside him on the couch. He relaxes with his arms resting on the back of the couch, his legs stretching out before him. She moves so that she presses against him.

He stretches, yawns, and rubs the back of his neck as if trying to rub away stiffness. Rachel reaches around behind him and begins to gently rub his neck, reveling in the feel of his skin, his hair against the

backs of her hands. The thoughts that hop and skip through her mind
are confusing. Sometimes it seems that the hair that tickles her hands
is Johnson's; sometimes, she knows it is Jake's. And sometimes it
doesn't seem to matter. Are they really so different? They are not so
different.

She rubs his neck, not knowing what to do next. In the confessions magazines, this is where the man crushes the woman in his arms.
Rachel climbs into Jake's lap and hugs him, waiting for him to crush
her in his arms. He blinks at her sleepily. Half asleep, he strokes her,
and his moving hand brushes near her genitals. She presses herself
against him, making a soft sound in her throat. She rubs her hip against
his crotch, aware now of a slight change in his smell, in the tempo of
his breathing. He blinks at her again, a little more awake now. She
bares her teeth in a smile and tilts her head back to lick his neck. She
can feel his hands on her shoulders, pushing her away, and she knows
what he wants. She slides from his lap and turns, presenting him with
her pink genitals, ready to be mounted, ready to have him penetrate
her. She moans in anticipation, a low inviting sound.

He does not come to her. She looks over her shoulder and he is
still sitting on the couch, watching her through half-closed eyes. He
reaches over and picks up a magazine filled with pictures of naked
women. His other hand drops to his crotch and he is lost in his own
world.

Rachel howls like an infant who has lost its mother, but he does
not look up. He is staring at the picture of the blonde woman.

Rachel runs down dark corridors to her cage, the only home she
has. When she reaches her corridor, she is breathing hard and making
small lonely whimpering noises. In the dimly lit corridor, she hesitates
for a moment, staring into Johnson's cage. The male chimp is asleep.
She remembers the touch of his hands when he groomed her.

From the corridor, she lifts the gate that leads into Johnson's cage
and enters. He wakes at the sound of the door and sniffs the air. When
he sees Rachel, he stalks toward her, sniffing eagerly. She lets him finger her genitals, sniff deeply of her scent. His penis is erect and he
grunts in excitement. She turns and presents herself to him and he
mounts her, thrusting deep inside. As he penetrates, she thinks, for a
moment, of Jake and of the thin blonde teenage girl named Rachel, but
then the moment passes. Almost against her will she cries out, a shrill
exclamation of welcoming and loss.

After he withdraws his penis, Johnson grooms her gently, sniffing
her genitals and softly stroking her fur. She is sleepy and content, but
she knows that she cannot delay.

Johnson is reluctant to leave his cage, but Rachel takes him by the
hand and leads him to the janitor's lounge. His presence gives her

courage. She listens at the door and hears Jake's soft breathing. Leaving Johnson in the hall, she slips into the room. Jake is lying on the couch, the magazine draped over his legs. Rachel takes the equipment that she has gathered and stands for a moment, staring at the sleeping man. His baseball cap hangs on the arm of a broken chair, and she takes that to remember him by.

Rachel leads Johnson through the empty halls. A kangaroo rat, collecting seeds in the dried grass near the glass doors, looks up curiously as Rachel leads Johnson down the steps. Rachel carries the plastic shopping bag slung over her shoulder. Somewhere in the distance, a coyote howls, a long yapping wail. His cry is joined by others, a chorus in the moonlight.

Rachel takes Johnson by the hand and leads him into the desert.

A cocktail waitress, driving from her job in Flagstaff to her home in Winslow, sees two apes dart across the road, hurrying away from the bright beams of her headlights. After wrestling with her conscience (she does not want to be accused of drinking on the job), she notifies the county sheriff.

A local newspaper reporter, an eager young man fresh out of journalism school, picks up the story from the police report and interviews the waitress. Flattered by his enthusiasm for her story and delighted to find a receptive ear, she tells him details that she failed to mention to the police: one of the apes was wearing a baseball cap and carrying what looked like a shopping bag.

The reporter writes up a quick humorous story for the morning edition, and begins researching a feature article to be run later in the week. He knows that the newspaper, eager for news in a slow season, will play a human-interest story up big—kind of *Lassie, Come Home* with chimps.

Just before dawn, a light rain begins to fall, the first rain of spring. Rachel searches for shelter and finds a small cave formed by three tumbled boulders. It will keep off the rain and hide them from casual observers. She shares her food and water with Johnson. He has followed her closely all night, seemingly intimidated by the darkness and the howling of distant coyotes. She feels protective toward him. At the same time, having him with her gives her courage. He knows only a few gestures in ASL, but he does not need to speak. His presence is comfort enough.

Johnson curls up in the back of the cave and falls asleep quickly. Rachel sits in the opening and watches dawnlight wash the stars from the sky. The rain rattles against the sand, a comforting sound. She thinks about Jake. The baseball cap on her head still smells of his cigarettes, but she does not miss him. Not really. She fingers the cap and wonders why she thought she loved Jake.

The rain lets up. The clouds rise like fairy castles in the distance and the rising sun tints them pink and gold and gives them flaming red banners. Rachel remembers when she was younger and Aaron read her the story of Pinnochio, the little puppet who wanted to be a real boy. At the end of his adventures, Pinnochio, who has been brave and kind, gets his wish. He becomes a real boy.

Rachel had cried at the end of the story and when Aaron asked why, she had rubbed her eyes on the backs of her hairy hands.—I want to be a real girl, she signed to him. —A real girl.

"You are a real girl," Aaron had told her, but somehow she had never believed him.

The sun rises higher and illuminates the broken rock turrets of the desert. There is a magic in this barren land of unassuming grandeur. Some cultures send their young people to the desert to seek visions and guidance, searching for true thinking spawned by the openness of the place, the loneliness, the beauty of emptiness.

Rachel drowses in the warm sun and dreams a vision that has the clarity of truth. In the dream, her father comes to her. "Rachel," he says to her, "it doesn't matter what anyone thinks of you. You're my daughter."

—I want to be a real girl, she signs.

"You *are* real," her father says. "And you don't need some two-bit drunken janitor to prove it to you." She knows she is dreaming, but she also knows that her father speaks the truth. She is warm and happy and she doesn't need Jake at all. The sunlight warms her and a lizard watches her from a rock, scurrying for cover when she moves. She picks up a bit of loose rock that lies on the floor of the cave. Idly, she scratches on the dark red sandstone wall of the cave. A lopsided heart shape. Within it, awkwardly printed: Rachel and Johnson. Between them, a plus sign. She goes over the letters again and again, leaving scores of fine lines on the smooth rock surface. Then, late in the morning, soothed by the warmth of the day, she sleeps.

Shortly after dark, an elderly rancher in a pickup truck spots two apes in a remote corner of his ranch. They run away and lose him in the rocks, but not until he has a good look at them. He calls the police, the newspaper, and the Primate Center.

The reporter arrives first thing the next morning, interviews the rancher, and follows the men from the Primate Center as they search for evidence of the chimps. They find monkey shit near the cave, confirming that the runaways were indeed nearby. The news reporter, an eager and curious young man, squirms on his belly into the cave and finds the names scratched on the cave wall. He peers at it. He might have dismissed them as the idle scratchings of kids, except that the names match the names of the missing chimps. "Hey," he called to his photographer, "Take a look at this."

The next morning's newspaper displays Rachel's crudely scratched letters. In a brief interview, the rancher mentioned that the chimps were carrying bags. "Looked like supplies," he said. "They looked like they were in for a long haul."

On the third day, Rachel's water runs out. She heads toward a small town, marked on the map. They reach it in the early morning—thirst forces them to travel by day. Beside an isolated ranch house, she finds a faucet. She is filling her bottle when Johnson grunts in alarm.

A dark-haired woman watches from the porch of the house. She does not move toward the apes, and Rachel continues filling the bottle. "It's all right, Rachel," the woman, who has been following the story in the papers, calls out. "Drink all you want."

Startled, but still suspicious, Rachel caps the bottle and, keeping her eyes on the woman, drinks from the faucet. The woman steps back into the house. Rachel motions Johnson to do the same, signaling for him to hurry and drink. She turns off the faucet when he is done.

They are turning to go when the woman emerges from the house carrying a plate of tortillas and a bowl of apples. She sets them on the edge of the porch and says, "These are for you."

The woman watches through the window as Rachel packs the food into her bag. Rachel puts away the last apple and gestures her thanks to the woman. When the woman fails to respond to the sign language, Rachel picks up a stick and writes in the sand of the yard. "THANK YOU," Rachel scratches, then waves good-bye and sets out across the desert. She is puzzled, but happy.

The next morning's newspaper includes an interview with the dark-haired woman. She describes how Rachel turned on the faucet and turned it off when she was through, how the chimp packed the apples neatly in her bag and wrote in the dirt with a stick.

The reporter also interviews the director of the Primate Research Center. "These are animals," the director explains angrily. "But people want to treat them like they're small hairy people." He describes the Center as "primarily a breeding center with some facilities for medical research." The reporter asks some pointed questions about their acquisition of Rachel.

But the biggest story is an investigative piece. The reporter reveals that he has tracked down Aaron Jacobs' lawyer and learned that Jacobs left a will. In this will, he bequeathed all his possessions— including his house and surrounding land—to "Rachel, the chimp I acknowledge as my daughter."

The reporter makes friends with one of the young women in the typing pool at the research center, and she tells him the office scuttlebutt: people suspect that the chimps may have been released by a deaf and drunken janitor, who was subsequently fired for negligence. The reporter, accompanied by a friend who can communicate in sign language, finds Jake in his apartment in downtown Flagstaff.

Jake, who has been drinking steadily since he was fired, feels betrayed by Rachel, by the Primate Center, by the world. He complains at length about Rachel: they had been friends, and then she took his baseball cap and ran away. He just didn't understand why she had run away like that.

"You mean she could talk?" the reporter asks through his interpreter.

—Of course she can talk, Jake signs impatiently. —She is a smart monkey.

The headlines read: "Intelligent chimp inherits fortune!" Of course, Aaron's bequest isn't really a fortune and she isn't just a chimp, but close enough. Animal rights activists rise up in Rachel's defense. The case is discussed on the national news. Ann Landers reports receiving a letter from a chimp named Rachel; she had thought it was a hoax perpetrated by the boys at Yale. The American Civil Liberties Union assigns a lawyer to the case.

By day, Rachel and Johnson sleep in whatever hiding places they can find: a cave; a shelter built for range cattle; the shell of an abandoned car, rusted from long years in a desert gully. Sometimes Rachel dreams of jungle darkness, and the coyotes in the distance become a part of her dreams, their howling becomes the cries of fellow apes.

The desert and the journey have changed her. She is wiser, having passed through the white-hot love of adolescence and emerged on the other side. She dreams, one day, of the ranch house. In the dream, she has long blonde hair and pale white skin. Her eyes are red from crying and she wanders the house restlessly, searching for something that she has lost. When she hears coyotes howling, she looks through a window at the darkness outside. The face that looks in at her has jug-handle ears and shaggy hair. When she sees the face, she cries out in recognition and opens the window to let herself in.

By night, they travel. The rocks and sands are cool beneath Rachel's feet as she walks toward her ranch. On television, scientists and politicians discuss the ramifications of her case, describe the technology uncovered by investigation of Aaron Jacobs' files. Their debates do not affect her steady progress toward her ranch or the stars that sprinkle the sky above her.

It is night when Rachel and Johnson approach the ranchhouse. Rachel sniffs the wind and smells automobile exhaust and strange humans. From the hills, she can see a small camp beside a white van marked with the name of a local television station. She hesitates, considering returning to the safety of the desert. Then she takes Johnson by the hand and starts down the hill. Rachel is going home.

WHY I LEFT HARRY'S ALL-NIGHT HAMBURGERS

by LAWRENCE WATT-EVANS

"Why I Left Harry's All-Night Hamburgers," Lawrence Watt-Evans's heart-warming story about the nightlife at a local restaurant, won the Hugo Award and the *Asimov's* Readers' Award poll when it was published in the magazine's July 1987 issue. Lawrence Watt-Evans is now the author of some two dozen novels and fourscore short stories in the fields of science fiction, fantasy, and horror. His most recent major work is the Three Worlds trilogy: *Out of This World*, *In the Empire of Shadow*, and *The Reign of the Brown Magician*. He lives in Maryland with his wife, two kids, two cats, a hamster, and a parakeet.

Harry's was a nice place—probably still is. I haven't been back lately. It's a couple of miles off I-79, a few exits north of Charleston, near a place called Sutton. Used to do a pretty fair business until they finished building the Interstate out from Charleston and made it worthwhile for some fast-food joints to move in right next to the cloverleaf; nobody wanted to drive the extra miles to Harry's after that. Folks used to wonder how old Harry stayed in business, as a matter of fact, but he did all right even without the Interstate trade. I found out when I worked there.

Why did I work there, instead of at one of the fast-food joints? Because my folks lived in a little house just around the corner from Harry's, out in the middle of nowhere—not in Sutton itself, just out there on the road. Wasn't anything around except our house and Harry's place. He lived out back of his restaurant. That was about the only thing I could walk to in under an hour, and I didn't have a car.

This was when I was sixteen. I needed a job, because my dad was out of work again and if I was gonna do anything I needed my own money. Mom didn't mind my using her car—so long as it came back with a full tank of gas and I didn't keep it too long. That was the rule. So I needed some work, and Harry's All-Night Hamburgers was the only thing within walking distance. Harry said he had all the help he needed—two cooks and two people working the counter, besides himself. The others worked days, two to a shift, and Harry did the late night stretch all by himself. I hung out there a little, since I didn't have anywhere else, and it looked like pretty easy work—there was hardly any business, and those guys mostly sat around telling dirty jokes. So I figured it was perfect.

Harry, though, said that he didn't need any help.

I figured that was probably true, but I wasn't going to let logic keep me out of driving my mother's car. I did some serious begging, and after I'd made his life miserable for a week or two, Harry said he'd take a chance and give me a shot, working the graveyard shift, midnight to eight A.M., as his counterman, busboy, and janitor all in one.

I talked him down to 7:30, so I could still get to school, and we had us a deal. I didn't care about school so much myself, but my parents wanted me to go, and it was a good place to see my friends, y'know? Meet girls and so on.

So I started working at Harry's nights. I showed up at midnight the first night, and Harry gave me an apron and a little hat, like something from a diner in an old movie, same as he wore himself. I was supposed to wait tables and clean up, not cook, so I don't know why he wanted me to wear them, but he gave them to me, and I needed the bucks, so I put them on and pretended I didn't notice that the apron was all stiff with grease and smelled like something nasty had died on it a few weeks back. And Harry—he's a funny old guy, always looked fifty-ish, as far back as I can remember. Never young, but never getting really old, either, you know? Some people do that, they just seem to go on forever. Anyway, he showed me where everything was in the kitchen and back room, told me to keep busy cleaning up whatever looked like it wanted cleaning, and told me, over and over again, like he was really worried that I was going to cause trouble, "Don't bother the customers. Just take their orders, bring them their food, and don't bother them. You got that?"

"Sure," I said, "I got it."

"Good," he said. "We get some funny guys in here at night, but they're good customers, most of them, so don't you screw up with anyone. One customer complains, one customer stiffs you for the check, and you're out of work, you got that?"

"Sure," I said, though I've gotta admit I was wondering what to do if some cheapskate skipped without paying. I tried to figure how much of a meal would be worth paying for in order to keep the job, but with taxes and all it got too tricky for me to work out, and I decided to wait until the time came, if it ever did.

Then Harry went back in the kitchen, and I got a broom and swept up out front a little until a couple of truckers came in and ordered burgers and coffee.

I was pretty awkward at first, but I got the hang of it after a little bit. Guys would come in, women, too, one or two at a time, and they'd order something, and Harry'd have it ready faster than you can say "cheese," practically, and they'd eat it, and wipe their mouths, and go use the john, and drive off, and none of them said a damn thing to me except their orders, and I didn't say anything back except "Yes, sir," or "Yes, ma'am," or "Thank you, come again." I figured they were all just truckers who didn't like the fast-food places.

That was what it was like at first, anyway, from midnight to about one, one-thirty, but then things would slow down. Even the truckers were off the roads by then, I guess, or they didn't want to get that far off the Interstate, or they'd all had lunch, or something. Anyway, by about two that first night I was thinking it was pretty clear why Harry didn't think he needed help on this shift, when the door opened and the little bell rang.

I jumped a bit; that bell startled me, and I turned around, but then I turned back to look at Harry, 'cause I'd seen him out of the corner of my eye, you know, and he'd got this worried look on his face, and *he* was watching *me;* he wasn't looking at the customer at all.

About then I realized that the reason the bell had startled me was that I hadn't heard anyone drive up, and who the hell was going to be out walking to Harry's place at two in the morning in the West Virginia mountains? The way Harry was looking at me, I knew this must be one of those special customers he didn't want me to scare away.

So I turned around, and there was this short little guy in a really heavy coat, all zipped up, made of that shiny silver fabric you see race-car drivers wear in the cigarette ads, you know? And he had on padded ski pants of the same stuff, with pockets all over the place, and he was just putting down a hood, and he had on big thick goggles like he'd been out in a blizzard, but it was April and there hadn't been any snow in weeks and it was about fifty, sixty degrees out.

Well, I didn't want to blow it, so I pretended I didn't notice, I just said, "Hello, sir; may I take your order?"

He looked at me funny and said, "I suppose so."

"Would you like to see a menu?" I said, trying to be on my best behavior—hell, I was probably overdoing it; I'd let the truckers find their own menus.

"I suppose so," he said again, and I handed him the menu.

He looked it over, pointed to a picture of a cheeseburger that looked about as much like anything from Harry's grill as Sly Stallone looks like me, and I wrote it down and passed the slip back to Harry, and he hissed at me, "Don't bother the guy!"

I took the hint, and went back to sweeping until the burger was up, and as I was handing the plate to the guy there was a sound out front like a shotgun going off, and this green light flashed in through the window, so I nearly dropped the thing, but I couldn't go look because the customer was digging through his pockets for money, to pay for the burger.

"You can pay after you've eaten, sir," I said.

"I will pay first," he said, real formal. "I may need to depart quickly. My money may not be good here."

The guy hadn't got any accent, but with that about the money I figured he was a foreigner, so I waited, and he hauled out a handful of weird coins, and I told him, "I'll need to check with the manager." He gave me the coins, and while I was taking them back to Harry and trying to see out the window, through the curtain, to see where that green light came from, the door opened and these three women came in, and where the first guy was all wrapped up like an Eskimo, these people weren't wearing anything but jeans. Women, remember, and it was only April.

Hey, I was just sixteen, so I tried real hard not to stare and I went running back to the kitchen and tried to tell Harry what was going on, but the money and the green light and the half-naked women all got tangled up and I didn't make much sense.

"I *told* you I get some strange customers, kid," he said. "Let's see the money." So I gave him the coins, and he said, "Yeah, we'll take these," and made change—I don't know how, because the writing on the coins looked like Russian to me, and I couldn't figure out what any of them were. He gave me the change, and then looked me in the eye and said, "Can you handle those women, boy? It's part of the job; I wasn't expecting them tonight, but we get strange people in here, I told you that. You think you can handle it without losing me any customers, or do you want to call it a night and find another job?"

I really wanted that paycheck; I gritted my teeth and said, "No problem!"

When you were sixteen, did you ever try to wait tables with six bare boobs right there in front of you? Those three were laughing and joking in some foreign language I'd never heard before, and I think only one of them spoke English, because she did all the ordering. I managed somehow, and by the time they left Harry was almost smiling at me.

Around four things slowed down again, and around four-thirty or five the breakfast crowd began to trickle in, but between two and four there were about half a dozen customers, I guess; I don't remember who they all were any more, most of them weren't that strange, but that first little guy and the three women, them I remember. Maybe some of the others were pretty strange, too, maybe stranger than the first guy, but he was the *first*, which makes a difference, and then those women—well, that's gonna really make an impression on a sixteen-year-old, y'know? It's not that they were particularly beautiful or anything, because they weren't, they were just women, and I wasn't used to seeing women with no shirts.

When I got off at seven-thirty, I was all mixed up; I didn't know what the hell was going on. I was beginning to think maybe I imagined it all.

I went home and changed clothes and caught the bus to school, and what with not really having adjusted to working nights, and being tired, and having to think about schoolwork, I was pretty much convinced that the whole thing had been some weird dream. So I came home, slept through until about eleven, then got up and went to work again.

And damn, it was almost the same, except that there weren't any half-naked women this time. The normal truckers and the rest came in first, then they faded out, and the weirdos starting turning up.

At sixteen, you know, you think you can cope with anything. At least, I did. So I didn't let the customers bother me, not even the ones who didn't look like they were exactly human beings to begin with. Harry got used to me being there, and I did make it a lot easier on him, so after the first couple of weeks it was pretty much settled that I could stay on for as long as I liked.

And I liked it fine, really, once I got used to the weird hours. I didn't have much of a social life during the week, but I never had, living where I did, and I could afford to do the weekends up in style with what Harry paid me and the tips I got. Some of those tips I had to take to the jewelers in Charleston, different ones so nobody would notice that one guy was bringing in all these weird coins and trinkets, but Harry gave me some pointers—he'd been doing the same thing for years, except that he'd gone through every jeweler in Charleston and Huntington and Wheeling and Washington, PA., and was halfway through Pittsburgh.

It was fun, really, seeing just what would turn up there and order a burger. I think my favorite was the guy who walked in, no car, no lights, no nothing, wearing this electric blue hunter's vest with wires all over it, and these medieval tights with what Harry called a codpiece, with snow and some kind of sticky goop all over his vest and in his hair, shivering like it was the Arctic out there, when it was the middle of July. He had some kind of little animal crawling around under that vest, but he wouldn't let me get a look at it; from the shape of the bulge it made it might have been a weasel or something. He had the strangest damn accent you ever heard, but he acted right at home and ordered without looking at the menu.

Harry admitted, when I'd been there awhile, that he figured anyone else would mess things up for him somehow. I might have thought I was going nuts, or I might have called the cops, or I might have spread a lot of strange stories around, but I didn't, and Harry appreciated that.

Hey, that was easy. If these people didn't bother Harry, I figured, why should they bother me? And it wasn't anybody else's business, either. When people asked, I used to tell them that sure, we got weirdos in the place late at night—but I never said just how weird.

And I never got as cool about it as Harry was; I mean, a flying saucer in the parking lot wouldn't make Harry blink. *I* blinked, when we got 'em—we did, but not very often, and I had to really work not to stare at them. Most of the customers had more sense; if they came in something strange they hid it in the woods or something. But there were always a few who couldn't be bothered. If any state cops ever cruised past there and saw those things, I guess they didn't dare report them. No one would've believed them anyway.

I asked Harry once if all these guys came from the same place.

"Damned if I know," he said. He'd never asked, and he didn't want me to, either.

Except he was wrong about thinking that would scare them away. Sometimes you can tell when someone wants to talk, and some of these people did. So I talked to them.

I think I was seventeen by the time someone told me what was really going on, though.

Before you ask any stupid questions, no, they weren't any of them Martians or monsters from outer space or anything like that. Some of them were from West Virginia, in fact. Just not *our* West Virginia. Lots of different West Virginias, instead. What the science fiction writers called "parallel worlds." That's one name, anyway. Other dimensions, alternate realities, they had lots of different names for it.

It all makes sense, really. A couple of them explained it to me. See, everything that ever could possibly have happened, in the entire history of the universe right from the Big Bang up until now, *did* happen—somewhere. And *every* possible difference means a different universe. Not just if Napoleon lost at Waterloo, or won, or whatever he didn't do here; what does Napoleon matter to the *universe*, anyway? Betelgeuse doesn't give a flying damn for all of Europe, past, present, or future. But every single atom or particle or whatever, whenever it had a chance to do something—break up or stay together, or move one direction instead of another, whatever—it did *all* of them, but all in different universes. They didn't branch off, either—all the universes were always there, there just wasn't any difference between them until this particular event came along. And that means that there are millions and millions of identical universes, too, where the differences haven't happened yet. There's an infinite number of universes—more than that, an infinity of infinities. I mean, you can't really comprehend it; if you think you're close, then multiply that a few zillion times. *Everything* is out there.

And that means that in a lot of those universes, people figured out how to travel from one to another. Apparently it's not that hard; there are lots of different ways to do it, too, which is why we got everything from guys in street clothes to people in spacesuits and flying saucers.

But there's one thing about it—with an infinite number of universes, I mean really infinite, how can you find just one? Particularly the first time out? Fact is, you can't. It's just not possible. So the explorers go out, but they don't come back. Maybe if some *did* come back, they could look at what they did and where it took them and figure out how to measure and aim and all that, but so far as any of the ones I've talked to know, nobody has ever done it. When you go out, that's it, you're out there. You can go on hopping from one world to the next, or you can settle down in one forever, but like the books say, you *really* can't go home again. You can get close, maybe—one way I found out a lot of this was in exchange for telling this poor old geezer a lot about the world outside Harry's. He was pretty happy about it when I was talking about what I'd seen on TV, and naming all the presidents I could think of, but then he asked me something about some religion I'd never heard of that he said he belonged to, and when I said I'd never heard of it he almost broke down. I guess he was looking for a world like his own, and ours was, you know, close, but not close enough. He said something about what he called a "random walk principle"—if you go wandering around at random you keep coming back close to where you started, but you'll never have your feet in *exactly* the original place, they'll always be a little bit off to one side or the other.

So there are millions of these people out there drifting from world to world, looking for whatever they're looking for, sometimes millions of them identical to each other, too, and they run into each other. They know what to look for, see. So they trade information, and some of them tell me they're working on figuring out how to *really* navigate whatever it is they do, and they've figured out some of it already, so they can steer a little.

I wondered out loud why so many of them turn up at Harry's, and this woman with blue-grey skin—from some kind of medication, she told me—tried to explain it. West Virginia is one of the best places to travel between worlds, particularly up in the mountains around Sutton, because it's a pretty central location for eastern North America, but there isn't anything there. I mean, there aren't any big cities, or big military bases, or anything, so that if there's an atomic war or something—and apparently there have been a *lot* of atomic wars, or wars with even worse weapons, in different worlds—nobody's very likely to heave any missiles at Sutton, West Virginia. Even in the realities where the Europeans never found America and it's the Chinese or somebody building the cities, there just isn't any reason to build anything near

Sutton. And there's something in particular that makes it an easy place to travel between worlds, too; I didn't follow the explanation. She said something about the Earth's magnetic field, but I didn't catch whether that was part of the explanation or just a comparison of some kind.

The mountains and forests make it easy to hide, too, which is why our area is better than out in the desert someplace.

Anyway, right around Sutton it's pretty safe and easy to travel between worlds, so lots of people do.

The strange thing, though, is that for some reason that nobody really seemed very clear on, Harry's, or something like it, is in just about the same place in millions of different realities. More than millions; infinities, really. It's not always exactly Harry's All-Night Hamburgers; one customer kept calling Harry Sal, for instance. It's *there*, though, or something like it, and one thing that doesn't seem to change much is that travelers can eat there without causing trouble. Word gets around that Harry's is a nice, quiet place, with decent burgers, where nobody's going to hassle them about anything, and they can pay in gold or silver if they haven't got the local money, or in trade goods or whatever they've got that Harry can use. It's easy to find, because it's in a lot of universes, relatively—as I said, this little area isn't one that varies a whole lot from universe to universe, unless you start moving long distances. Or maybe not *easy* to find, but it can be found. One guy told me that Harry's seems to be in more universes than Washington, D.C. He'd even seen one of my doubles before, last time he stopped in, and he thought he might have actually gotten back to the same place until I swore I'd never seen him before. He had these really funny eyes, so I was sure I'd have remembered him.

We never actually got repeat business from other worlds, y'know, not once, not ever; nobody could ever find the way back to exactly our world. What we got were people who had heard about Harry's from other people, in some other reality. Oh, maybe it wasn't exactly the same Harry's they'd heard about, but they'd heard that there was usually a good place to eat and swap stories in about that spot.

That's a weird thought, you know, that every time I served someone a burger a zillion of me were serving burgers to a zillion others—not all of them the same, either.

So they come to Harry's to eat, and they trade information with each other there, or in the parking lot, and they take a break from whatever they're doing.

They came there, and they talked to me about all those other universes, and I was seventeen years old, man. It was like those Navy recruiting ads on TV, see the world—except it was see the *worlds*, all of them, not just one. I listened to everything those guys said. I heard them talk about the worlds where zeppelins strafed Cincinnati in a

Third World War, about places the dinosaurs never died out and mammals never evolved any higher than rats, about cities built of colored glass or dug miles underground, about worlds where all the men were dead, or all the women, or both, from biological warfare. Any story you ever heard, anything you ever read, those guys could top it. Worlds where speaking aloud could get you the death penalty—not what you said, just saying *anything* out loud. Worlds with spaceships fighting a war against Arcturus. Beautiful women, strange places, everything you could ever want, out there *somewhere*, but it might take forever to find it.

I listened to those stories for months. I graduated from high school, but there wasn't anyway I could go to college, so I just stayed on with Harry—it paid enough to live on, anyway. I talked to those people from other worlds, even got inside some of their ships, or time machines, or whatever you want to call them, and I thought about how great it would be to just go roaming from world to world. Any time you don't like the way things are going, just pop! And the whole world is different! I could be a white god to the Indians in a world where the Europeans and Asians never reached America, I figured, or find a world where machines do all the work and people just relax and party.

When my eighteenth birthday came and went without any sign I'd ever get out of West Virginia, I began to really think about it, you know? I started asking customers about it. A lot of them told me not to be stupid; a lot just wouldn't talk about it. Some, though, some of them thought it was a great idea.

There was one guy, this one night—well, first, it was September, but it was still hot as the middle of summer, even in the middle of the night. Most of my friends were gone—they'd gone off to college, or gotten jobs somewhere, or gotten married, or maybe two out of the three. My dad was drinking a lot. The other kids were back in school. I'd started sleeping days, from eight in the morning until about four P.M., instead of evenings. Harry's air conditioner was busted, and I really wanted to just leave it all behind and go find myself a better world. So when I heard these two guys talking at one table about whether one of them had extra room in his machine, I sort of listened, when I could, when I wasn't fetching burgers and Cokes.

Now, one of these two I'd seen before—he'd been coming in every so often ever since I started working at Harry's. He looked like an ordinary guy, but he came in about three in the morning and talked to the weirdos like they were all old buddies, so I figured he had to be from some other world originally himself, even if he stayed put in ours now. He'd come in about every night for a week or two, then disappear for months, then start turning up again, and I had sort of wondered whether he might have licked the navigation problem all those other people had talked about. But then I figured, probably not, either he'd stopped jumping from one world to the next, or else it was just a bunch of parallel people coming in, and it probably wasn't ever the same guy at all, really. Usually, when that happened, we'd get two or three at a time, looking like identical twins or something, but there was only just one of this guy, every time, so I figured, like I said, either he hadn't been changing worlds at all, or he'd figured out how to navigate better than anyone else, or something.

The guy he was talking to was new; I'd never seen him before. He was big, maybe six-four and heavy. He'd come in shaking snow and soot off a plastic coverall of some kind, given me a big grin, and ordered two of Harry's biggest burgers, with everything. Five minutes later the regular customer sat down across the table from him, and now he was telling the regular that he had plenty of room in his ship for anything anyone might want him to haul cross-time.

I figured this was my chance, so when I brought the burgers I said something real polite, like, "Excuse me, sir, but I couldn't help over-hearing; d'you think you'd have room for a passenger?"

The big guy laughed and said, "Sure, kid! I was just telling Joe here that I could haul him and all his freight, and there'd be room for you, too, if you make it worth my trouble!"

I said, "I've got money; I've been saving up. What'll it take?"

The big guy gave me a big grin again, but before he could say anything Joe interrupted.

"Sid," he said, "could you excuse me for a minute? I want to talk to this young fellow for a minute, before he makes a big mistake."

The big guy, Sid, said, "Sure, sure, I don't mind." So Joe got up, and he yelled to Harry, "Okay if I borrow your counterman for a few minutes?"

Harry yelled back that it was okay. I didn't know what the hell was going on, but I went along, and the two of us went out to this guy's car to talk.

And it really was a car, too—an old Ford van. It was customized, with velvet and bubble windows and stuff, and there was a lot of stuff piled in the back, camping gear and clothes and things, but no sign of machinery or anything. I still wasn't sure, you know, because some of these guys did a really good job of disguising their ships, or time machines, or whatever, but it sure *looked* like an ordinary van, and that's what Joe said it was. He got into the driver's seat, and I got into the passenger seat, and we swiveled around to face each other.

"So," he said. "Do you know who all these people are? I mean people like Sid?"

"Sure," I said. "They're from other dimensions, parallel worlds and like that."

He leaned back and looked at me hard, and said, "You know that, huh? Did you know that none of them can ever get home?"

"Yes, I knew that," I told him, acting pretty cocky.

"And you still want to go with Sid to other universes? Even when you know you'll never come home to this universe again?"

"That's right, Mister," I told him. "I'm sick of this one. I don't have anything here but a nothing job in a diner; I want to *see* some of the stuff these people talk about, instead of just hearing about it."

"You want to see wonders and marvels, huh?"

"Yes!"

"You want to see buildings a hundred stories high? Cities of strange temples? Oceans thousands of miles wide? Mountains miles high? Prairies, and cities, and strange animals and stranger people?"

Well, that was just exactly what I wanted, better than I could have said it myself. "Yes," I said. "You got it, Mister."

"You lived here all your life?"

"You mean this world? Of course I have."

"No, I meant here in Sutton. You lived here all your life?"

"Well, yeah," I admitted. "Just about."

He sat forward and put his hands together, and his voice got intense, like he wanted to impress me with how serious he was. "Kid," he said, "I don't blame you a bit for wanting something different; I sure as hell wouldn't want to spend my entire life in these hills. But you're going about it the wrong way. You don't want to hitch with Sid."

"Oh, yeah?" I said. "Why not? Am I supposed to build my own machine? Hell, I can't even fix my mother's carburetor."

"No, that's not what I meant. But kid, you can see those buildings a thousand feet high in New York, or in Chicago. You've got oceans here in your own world as good as anything you'll find anywhere. You've got the mountains, and the seas, and the prairies, and all the rest of it. I've been in your world for eight years now, checking back here at Harry's every so often to see if anyone's figured out how to steer in no-space and get me home, and it's one hell of a big, interesting place."

"But," I said, "what about the spaceships, and . . ."

He interrupted me, and said, "You want to see spaceships? You go to Florida and watch a shuttle launch. Man, that's a spaceship. It may not go to other worlds, but that *is* a spaceship. You want strange animals? You go to Australia or Brazil. You want strange people? Go to New York or Los Angeles, or almost anywhere. You want a city carved out of a mountain top? It's called Machu Picchu, in Peru, I think. You want ancient, mysterious ruins? They're all over Greece and Italy and North Africa. Strange temples? Visit India; there are supposed to be over a thousand temples in Benares alone. See Angkor Wat, or the pyramids—not just the Egyptian ones, but the Mayan ones, too. And the great thing about all of these places, kid, is that afterwards, if you want to, you can come home. You don't *have* to, but you *can*. Who knows? You might get homesick some day. Most people do. *I* did. I wish to hell I'd seen more of my own world before I volunteered to try any others."

I kind of stared at him for a while. "I don't know," I said. I mean, it seemed so easy to just hop in Sid's machine and be gone forever, I thought, but New York was five hundred miles away—and then I realized how stupid that was.

"Hey," he said, "don't forget, if you decide I was wrong, you can always come back to Harry's and bum a ride with someone. It won't be Sid, he'll be gone forever, but you'll find someone. Most world-hoppers are lonely, kid; they've left behind everyone they ever knew. You won't have any trouble getting a lift."

Well, that decided it, because, you know, he was obviously right about that, as soon as I thought about it. I told him so.

"Well, good!" he said. "Now, you go pack your stuff and apologize to Harry and all that, and I'll give you a lift to Pittsburgh. You've got money to travel with from there, right? These idiots still haven't figured out how to steer, so I'm going back home—not my *real* home, but where I live in your world—and I wouldn't mind a passenger." And he smiled at me, and I smiled back, and we had to wait until the bank opened the next morning, but he didn't really mind. All the way to Pittsburgh he was singing these hymns and war-songs from his home world, where there was a second civil war in the nineteen-twenties because of some fundamentalist preacher trying to overthrow the Constitution and set up a church government; he hadn't had anyone he could sing them to in years, he said.

That was six years ago, and I haven't gone back to Harry's since.

So that was what got me started traveling. What brings *you* to Benares?

RIPPLES IN THE DIRAC SEA

by GEOFFREY A. LANDIS

Geoffrey A. Landis wrote his Nebula-Award-winning short story, "Ripples in the Dirac Sea," while working toward his doctorate in physics at Brown University. He has since received his Ph.D., and is now a scientific researcher at the Ohio Aerospace Institute at NASA Lewis Research Center. Geoff Landis's wide range of work projects include designing scientific instruments to fly on unmanned probes to Mars, inventing new concepts for high-efficiency solar cells, and doing research on advanced concepts for space propulsion, solar power satellites, and electronic materials.

Three years after "Ripples in the Dirac Sea" appeared in *Asimov's* October 1988 issue, the author published his Hugo-Award-winning short story, "A Walk in the Sun," in the October 1991 issue of the same magazine.

M y death looms over me like a tidal wave, rushing toward me with an inexorable slow-motion majesty. And yet I flee, pointless though it may be.

I depart, and my ripples diverge to infinity, like waves smoothing out the footprints of forgotten travelers.

We were so careful to avoid any paradox, the day we first tested my machine. We pasted a duct-tape cross onto the concrete floor of a windowless lab, placed an alarm clock on the mark, and locked the door. An hour later we came back, removed the clock, and put the experimental machine in the room with a super-eight camera set in the coils. I aimed the camera at the X, and one of my grad students programmed the machine to send the camera back half an hour, stay in the past five minutes, then return. It left and returned without even a flicker. When we developed the film, the time on the clock was half an hour before we loaded the camera. We'd succeeded in opening the door into the past. We celebrated with coffee and champagne.

Now that I know a lot more about time, I understand our mistake, that we had not thought to put a movie camera in the room with the clock to photograph the machine as it arrived from the future. But what is obvious to me now was not obvious then.

I arrive, and the ripples converge to the instant *now* from the vastness of the infinite sea.

To San Francisco, June 8, 1965. A warm breeze riffles across dandelion-speckled grass, while puffy white clouds form strange and wondrous shapes for our entertainment. Yet so very few people pause to enjoy it. They scurry about, diligently preoccupied, believing that if they act busy enough, they must be important. "They hurry so," I say. "Why can't they slow down, sit back, enjoy the day?"

"They're trapped in the illusion of time," says Dancer. He lies on his back and blows a soap bubble, his hair flopping back long and brown in a time when "long" hair meant anything below the ear. A puff of breeze takes the bubble down the hill and into the stream of pedestrians. They uniformly ignore it. "They're caught in the belief that what they do is important to some future goal." The bubble pops against a briefcase, and Dancer blows another. "You and I, we know how false an illusion that is. There is no past, no future, only the now, eternal."

He was right, more right than he could have possibly imagined. Once I, too, was preoccupied and self-important. Once I was brilliant and ambitious. I was twenty-eight years old, and I'd made the greatest discovery in the world.

From my hiding place I watched him come up the service elevator. He was thin almost to the point of starvation, a nervous man with stringy blonde hair and an armless white T-shirt. He looked up and down the hall, but failed to see me hidden in the janitor's closet. Under each arm was a two-gallon can of gasoline, in each hand another. He put down three of the cans and turned the last one upside down, then walked down the hall, spreading a pungent trail of gasoline. His face was blank. When he started on the second can, I figured it was about enough. As he passed my hiding spot, I walloped him over the head with a wrench, and called hotel security. Then I went back to the closet and let the ripples of time converge.

I arrived in a burning room, flames licking forth at me, the heat almost too much to bear. I gasped for breath—a mistake—and punched at the keypad.

NOTES ON THE THEORY AND PRACTICE
OF TIME TRAVEL:

1) Travel is possible only into the past.
2) The object transported will return to exactly the time and place of departure.
3) It is not possible to bring objects from the past to the present.
4) Actions in the past cannot change the present.

One time I tried jumping back a hundred million years, to the Cretaceous, to see dinosaurs. All the picture books show the landscape as being covered with dinosaurs. I spent three days wandering around a swamp—in my new tweed suit—before catching even a glimpse of any dinosaur larger than a basset hound. That one—a theropod of some sort, I don't know which—skittered away as soon as it caught a whiff of me. Quite a disappointment.

My professor in transfinite math used to tell stories about a hotel with an infinite number of rooms. One day all the rooms are full, and another guest arrives. "No problem," says the desk clerk. He moves the person in room one into room two, the person in room two into room three, and so on. Presto! A vacant room.

A little later, an infinite number of guests arrive. "No problem," says the dauntless desk clerk. He moves the person in room one into room two, the person in room two into room four, the person in room three into room six, and so on. Presto! An infinite number of rooms vacant.

My time machine works on just that principle.

Again I return to 1965, the fixed point, the strange attractor to my chaotic trajectory. In years of wandering I've met countless people, but Daniel Ranien—Dancer—was the only one who truly had his head together. He had a soft, easy smile, a battered secondhand guitar, and as much wisdom as it has taken me a hundred lifetimes to learn. I've known him in good times and bad, in summer days with blue skies that we swore would last a thousand years, in days of winter blizzards with drifted snow piled high over our heads. In happier times we have laid roses into the barrels of rifles, we laid our bodies across the city streets in the midst of riots, and not been hurt. And I have been with him when he died, once, twice, a hundred times over.

He died on February 8, 1969, a month into the reign of King Richard the Trickster and his court fool Spiro, a year before Kent State and Altamont and the secret war in Cambodia slowly strangled the summer of dreams. He died, and there was—is—nothing I can do. The last time he died I dragged him to a hospital, where I screamed and ranted until finally I convinced them to admit him for observation, though nothing seemed wrong with him. With X-rays and arteriograms and radioactive tracers, they found the incipient bubble in his brain; they drugged him, shaved his beautiful long brown hair, and operated on him, cutting out the offending capillary and tying it off neatly. When the anesthetic wore off, I sat in the hospital room and held his hand. There were big purple blotches under his eyes. He gripped my hand and stared, silent, into space. Visiting hours or no, I didn't let them throw me out of the room. He just stared. In the grey hours just before dawn he sighed softly and died. There was nothing at all that I could do.

Time travel is subject to two constraints: conservation of energy, and causality. The energy to appear in the past is only borrowed from the Dirac sea, and since ripples in the Dirac sea propagate in the negative t direction, transport is only into the past. Energy is conserved in the present as long as the object transported returns with zero time delay, and the principle of causality assures that actions in the past cannot change the present. For example, what if you went in the past and killed your father? Who, then, would invent the time machine?

Once I tried to commit suicide by murdering my father, before he met my mother, twenty three years before I was born. It changed nothing, of course, and even when I did it I knew it would change nothing. But you have to try these things. How else could I know for sure?

Next we tried sending a rat back. It made the trip through the Dirac sea and back undamaged. Then we tried a trained rat, one we borrowed from the psychology lab across the green without telling them what we wanted it for. Before its little trip it had been taught to run through a maze to get a piece of bacon. Afterwards, it ran the maze as fast as ever.

We still had to try it on a human. I volunteered myself and didn't allow anyone to talk me out of it. By trying it on myself, I dodged the University regulations about experimenting on humans.

The dive into the negative energy sea felt like nothing at all. One moment I stood in the center of the loop of Renselz coils, watched by my two grad students and a technician; the next I was alone, and the clock had jumped back exactly one hour. Alone in a locked room with nothing but a camera and a clock, that moment was the high point of my life.

The moment when I first met Dancer was the low point. I was in Berkeley, a bar called "Trishia's," slowly getting trashed. I'd been doing that a lot, caught between omnipotence and despair. It was 1967. 'Frisco then—it was the middle of the hippie era—seemed somehow appropriate.

There was a girl, sitting at a table with a group from the university. I walked over to her table and invited myself to sit down. I told her she didn't exist, that her whole world didn't exist, it was all created by the fact that I was watching, and would disappear back into the sea of unreality as soon as I stopped looking. Her name was Lisa, and she argued back. Her friends, bored, wandered off, and in a while Lisa realized just how drunk I was. She dropped a bill on the table and walked out into the foggy night.

I followed her out. When she saw me following, she clutched her purse and bolted.

He was suddenly there under the streetlight. For a second I thought he was a girl. He had bright blue eyes and straight brown hair down to his shoulders. He wore an embroidered Indian shirt, with a silver and turquoise medallion around his neck and a guitar slung across his back. He was lean, almost stringy, and moved like a dancer or a karate master. But it didn't occur to me to be afraid of him.

He looked me over. "That won't solve your problem, you know," he said.

And instantly I was ashamed. I was no longer sure exactly what I'd had in mind or why I'd followed her. It had been years since I'd first fled my death, and I had come to think of others as unreal, since nothing I could do would permanently affect them. My head was spinning. I slid down the wall and sat down, hard, on the sidewalk. What had I come to?

He helped me back into the bar, fed me orange juice and pretzels, and got me to talk. I told him everything. Why not, since I could unsay anything I said, undo anything I did? But I had no urge to. He listened to it all, saying nothing. No one else had ever listened to the whole story before. I can't explain the effect it had on me. For uncountable years I'd been alone, and then, if only for a moment . . . it hit me with the intensity of a tab of acid. If only for a moment, I was not alone.

We left arm in arm. Half a block away, Dancer stopped, in front of an alley. It was dark.

"Something not quite right here." His voice had a puzzled tone.

I pulled him back. "Hold on. You don't want to go down there—" He pulled free and walked in. After a slight hesitation, I followed.

The alley smelled of old beer, mixed with garbage and stale vomit. In a moment, my eyes became adjusted to the dark.

Lisa was cringing in a corner behind some trash cans. Her clothes had been cut away with a knife, and lay scattered around. Blood showed dark on her thighs and one arm. She didn't seem to see us. Dancer squatted down next to her and said something soft. She didn't respond. He pulled off his shirt and wrapped it around her, then cradled her in his arms and picked her up. "Help me get her to my apartment."

"Apartment, hell. We'd better call the police," I said.

"Call the pigs? Are you crazy? You want them to rape her, too?"

I'd forgotten; this was the sixties. Between the two of us, we got her to Dancer's VW bug and took her to his apartment in The Hash-bury. He explained it to me quietly as we drove, a dark side of the summer of love that I'd not seen before. It was greasers, he said. They come down to Berkeley because they heard that hippie chicks gave it away free, and get nasty when they met one who thought otherwise.

Her wounds were mostly superficial. Dancer cleaned her, put her in bed, and stayed up all night beside her, talking and crooning and making little reassuring noises. I slept on one of the mattresses in the hall. When I woke up in the morning, they were both in his bed. She was sleeping quietly. Dancer was awake, holding her. I was aware enough to realize that that was all he was doing, holding her, but still I felt a sharp pang of jealousy, and didn't know which one of them it was that I was jealous of.

NOTES FOR A LECTURE ON TIME TRAVEL

The beginning of the twentieth century was a time of intellectual giants, whose likes will perhaps never again be equaled. Einstein had just invented relativity, Heisenberg and Schrodinger quantum mechanics, but nobody yet knew how to make the two theories consistent with each other. In 1930, a new person tackled the problem. His name was Paul Dirac. He was twenty-eight years old. He succeeded where the others had failed.

His theory was an unprecedented success, except for one small detail. According to Dirac's theory, a particle could have either positive or negative energy. What did this mean, a particle of negative energy? How could something have negative energy? And why don't ordinary—positive energy—particles fall down into these negative energy states, releasing a lot of free energy in the process?

You or I might have merely stipulated that it was impossible for an ordinary positive energy particle to make a transition to negative energy. But Dirac was not an ordinary man. He was a genius, the greatest physicist of all, and he had an answer. If every possible negative energy state was already occupied, a particle couldn't drop into a negative energy state. Ah ha! So Dirac postulated that the entire universe is entirely filled with negative energy particles. They surround us, permeate us, in the vacuum of outer space and in the center of the earth, every possible place a particle could be. An infinitely dense "sea" of negative energy particles. The Dirac sea.

His argument had holes in it, but that comes later.

Once I went to visit the crucifixion. I took a jet from Santa Cruz to Tel Aviv, and a bus from Tel Aviv to Jerusalem. On a hill outside the city, I dove through the Dirac sea.

I arrived in my three-piece suit. No way to help that, unless I wanted to travel naked. The land was surprisingly green and fertile, more so than I'd expected. The hill was now a farm, covered with grape arbors and olive trees. I hid the coils behind some rocks and walked down to the road. I didn't get far. Five minutes on the road, I ran into a group of people. They had dark hair, dark skin, and wore clean white tunics. Romans? Jews? Egyptians? How could I tell? They spoke to me, but I couldn't understand a word. After a while two of them held me, while a third searched me. Were they robbers, searching for money? Romans, searching for some kind of identity papers? I realized how naïve I'd been to think I could just find appropriate dress and somehow blend in with the crowds. Finding nothing, the one who'd done the search carefully and methodically beat me up. At last he pushed me face down in the dirt. While the other two held me down, he pulled out a dagger and slashed through the tendons on the back of each leg. They were merciful, I guess. They left me with my life. Laughing and talking incomprehensibly among themselves, they walked away.

My legs were useless. One of my arms was broken. It took me four hours to crawl back up the hill, dragging myself with my good arm. Occasionally people would pass by on the road, studiously ignoring me. Once I reached the hiding place, pulling out the Renselz coils and wrapping them around me was pure agony. By the time I entered return on the keypad I was wavering in and out of consciousness. I finally managed to get it entered. From the Dirac sea the ripples converged

and I was in my hotel room in Santa Cruz. The ceiling had started to fall in where the girders had burned through. Fire alarms shrieked and wailed, but there was no place to run. The room was filled with a dense, acrid smoke. Trying not to breathe, I punched out a code on the keypad, somewhen, anywhen other than that one instant

and I was in the hotel room, five days before. I gasped for breath. The woman in the hotel bed shrieked and tried to pull the covers up. The man screwing her was too busy to pay any mind. They weren't real anyway. I ignored them and paid a little more attention to where to go next. Back to '65, I figured. I punched in the combo

and was standing in an empty room on the thirtieth floor of a hotel just under construction. A full moon gleamed on the silhouettes of silent construction cranes. I flexed my legs experimentally. Already the memory of the pain was beginning to fade. That was reasonable, because it had never happened. Time travel. It's not immortality, but it's got to be the next best thing.

You can't change the past, no matter how you try.

* * *

In the morning I explored Dancer's pad. It was crazy, a small third floor apartment a block off Haight Ashbury that had been converted into something from another planet. The floor of the apartment had been completely covered with old mattresses, on top of which was a jumbled confusion of quilts, pillows, Indian blankets, stuffed animals. You took off your shoes before coming in—Dancer always wore sandals, leather ones from Mexico with soles cut from old tires. The radiators, which didn't work anyway, were spray painted in dayglo colors. The walls were plastered with posters: Peter Max prints, brightly colored Eschers, poems by Allen Ginsberg, record album covers, peace rally posters, a "Haight is Love" sign, FBI ten-most-wanted posters torn down from a post office with the photos of famous antiwar activists circled in magic marker, a huge peace symbol in passion-pink. Some of the posters were illuminated with black light and luminesced in impossible colors. The air was musty with incense and the banana-sweet smell of dope. In one corner a record player played "Sergeant Pepper's Lonely Hearts Club Band" on infinite repeat. Whenever one copy of the album got too scratchy, inevitably one of Dancer's friends would bring in another.

He never locked the door. "Somebody wants to rip me off, well, hey, they probably need it more than I do anyway, okay? It's cool." People dropped by any time of day or night.

I let my hair grow long. Dancer and Lisa and I spent that summer together, laughing, playing guitar, making love, writing silly poems and sillier songs, experimenting with drugs. That was when LSD was blooming onto the scene like sunflowers, when people were still unafraid of the strange and beautiful world on the other side of reality. That was a time to live. I knew that it was Dancer that Lisa truly loved, not me, but in those days free love was in the air like the scent of poppies, and it didn't matter. Not much, anyway.

NOTES FOR A LECTURE ON TIME TRAVEL (continued)

Having postulated that all of space was filled with an infinitely dense sea of negative energy particles, Dirac went on further and asked if we, in the positive-energy universe, could interact with this negative energy sea. What would happen, say, if you added enough energy to an electron to take it out of the negative energy sea? Two things: first, you would create an electron, seemingly out of nowhere. Second, you would leave behind a "hole" in the sea. The hole, Dirac realized, would act as if it were a particle itself, a particle exactly like an electron except for one thing: it would have the opposite charge. But if the hole ever encountered an electron, the electron would fall back into the Dirac sea, annihilating both electron and hole in a bright burst of energy.

Eventually they gave the hole in the Dirac sea a name of its own: "positron." When Anderson discovered the positron two years later to vindicate Dirac's theory, it was almost an anticlimax.

And over the next fifty years, the reality of the Dirac sea was almost ignored by physicists. Antimatter, the holes in the sea, was the important feature of the theory; the rest was merely a mathematical artifact.

Seventy years later, I remembered the story my transfinite math teacher told and put it together with Dirac's theory. Like putting an extra guest into a hotel with an infinite number of rooms, I figured out how to borrow energy from the Dirac sea. Or, to put it another way: I learned how to make waves.

And waves on the Dirac sea travel backward in time.

Next we had to try something more ambitious. We had to send a human back farther into history, and obtain proof of the trip. Still we were afraid to make alterations in the past, even though the mathematics stated that the present could not be changed.

We pulled out our movie camera and chose our destinations carefully.

In September of 1853 a traveler named William Hapland and his family crossed the Sierra Nevadas to reach the California coast. His daughter Sarah kept a journal, and in it she recorded how, as they reached the crest of Parker's ridge, she caught her first glimpse of the distant Pacific ocean exactly as the sun touched the horizon, "in a blays of cryms'n glorie," as she wrote. The journal still exists. It was easy enough for us to conceal ourselves and a movie camera in a cleft of rocks above the pass, to photograph the weary travelers in their ox-drawn wagon as they crossed.

The second target was the great San Francisco earthquake of 1906. From a deserted warehouse that would survive the quake—but not the following fire—we watched and took movies as buildings tumbled down around us and embattled firemen in horse-drawn firetrucks strove in vain to quench a hundred blazes. Moments before the fire reached our building, we fled into the present.

The films were spectacular.

We were ready to tell the world.

There was a meeting of the AAAS in Santa Cruz in a month. I called the program chairman and wangled a spot as an invited speaker without revealing just what we'd accomplished to date. I planned to show those films at the talk. They were to make us instantly famous.

* * *

The day that Dancer died we had a going-away party, just Lisa and Dancer and I. He knew he was going to die; I'd told him and somehow he believed me. He always believed me. We stayed up all night, playing Dancer's second-hand mandolin, painting psychedelic designs on each other's bodies with grease-paint, competing against each other in a marathon game of cut-throat Monopoly, doing a hundred silly, ordinary things that took meaning only from the fact that it was the last time. About four in the morning, as the glimmer of false-dawn began to show in the sky, we went down to the bay and, huddling together for warmth, went tripping. Dancer took the largest dose, since he wasn't going to return. The last thing he said, he told us not to let our dreams die; to stay together.

We buried Dancer, at city expense, in a welfare grave. We split up three days later.

I kept in touch with Lisa, vaguely. In the late seventies she went back to school, first for an MBA, then law school. I think she was married for a while. We wrote each other cards on Christmas for a while, then I lost track of her. Years later, I got a letter from her. She said that she was finally able to forgive me for causing Dan's death.

It was a cold and foggy February day, but I knew I could find warmth in 1965. The ripples converged.

Anticipated questions from the audience:

Q (old, stodgy professor): It seems to me this proposed temporal jump of yours violates the law of conservation of mass/energy. For example, when a transported object is transported into the past, a quantity of mass will appear to vanish from the present, in clear violation of the conservation law.

A (me): Since the return is to the exact time of departure, the mass present is constant.

Q: Very well, but what about the arrival in the past? Doesn't this violate the conservation law?

A: No. The energy needed is taken from the Dirac sea, by the mechanism I explain in detail in the *Phys Rev* paper. When the object returns to the "future," the energy is restored to the sea.

Q (intense young physicist): Then doesn't Heisenberg uncertainty limit the amount of time that can be spent in the past?

A: A good question. The answer is yes, but because we borrow an infinitesimal amount of energy from an infinite number of particles, the amount of time spent in the past can be arbitrarily large. The only limitation is that you must leave the past an instant before you depart from the present.

* * *

In half an hour I was scheduled to present the paper that would rank my name with Newton's and Galileo's—and Dirac's. I was twenty-eight years old, the same age that Dirac was when he announced his theory. I was a firebrand, preparing to set the world aflame. I was nervous, rehearsing the speech in my hotel room. I took a swig out of an old Coke that one of my grad students had left sitting on top of the television. The evening news team was babbling on, but I wasn't listening.

I never delivered that talk. The hotel had already started to burn; my death was already foreordained. Tie neat, I inspected myself in the mirror, then walked to the door. The doorknob was warm. I opened it onto a sheet of fire. Flame burst through the opened door like a ravening dragon. I stumbled backward, staring at the flames in amazed fascination.

Somewhere in the hotel I heard a scream, and all at once I broke free of my spell. I was on the thirtieth story; there was no way out. My thought was for my machine. I rushed across the room and threw open the case holding the time machine. With swift, sure fingers I pulled out the Renselz coils and wrapped them around my body. The carpet had caught on fire, a sheet of flame between me and any possible escape. Holding my breath to avoid suffocation, I punched an entry into the keyboard and dove into time.

I return to that moment again and again. When I hit the final key, the air was already nearly unbreathable with smoke. I had about thirty seconds left to live, then. Over the years I've nibbled away my time down to ten seconds or less.

I live on borrowed time. So do we all, perhaps. But I know when and where my debt will fall due.

Dancer died on February 9, 1969. It was a dim, foggy day. In the morning he said he had a headache. That was unusual, for Dancer. He never had headaches. We decided to go for a walk through the fog. It was beautiful, as if we were alone in a strange, formless world. I'd forgotten about his headache altogether, until, looking out across the sea of fog from the park over the bay, he fell over. He was dead before the ambulance came. He died with a secret smile on his face. I've never understood that smile. Maybe he was smiling because the pain was gone.

Lisa committed suicide two days later.

You ordinary people, you have the chance to change the future. You can father children, write novels, sign petitions, invent new machines, go to cocktail parties, run for president. You affect the future with everything you do. No matter what I do, I cannot. It is too late for that, for me. My actions are written in flowing water. And having no effect, I have no responsibilities. It makes no difference what I do, not at all.

When I first fled the fire into the past, I tried everything I could to change it. I stopped the arsonist, I argued with mayors, I even went to my own house and told myself not to go to the conference.

But that's not how time works. No matter what I do, talk to a governor or dynamite the hotel, when I reach that critical moment—the present, my destiny, the moment I left—I vanish from whenever I was, and return to the hotel room, the fire approaching ever closer. I have about ten seconds left. Every time I dive through the Dirac sea, everything I changed in the past vanishes. Sometimes I pretend that the changes I make in the past create new futures, though I know this is not the case. When I return to the present, all the changes are wiped out by the ripples of the converging wave, like erasing a blackboard after a class.

Someday I will return and meet my destiny. But for now, I live in the past. It's a good life, I suppose. You get used to the fact that nothing you do will ever have any effect on the world. It gives you a feeling of freedom. I've been places no one has ever been, seen things no one alive has ever seen. I've given up physics, of course. Nothing I discover could endure past that fatal night in Santa Cruz. Maybe some people would continue for the sheer joy of knowledge. For me, the point is missing.

But there are compensations. Whenever I return to the hotel room, nothing is changed but my memories. I am again twenty-eight, again wearing the same three-piece suit, again have the fuzzy taste of stale cola in my mouth. Every time I return, I use up a little bit of time. One day I will have no time left.

Dancer, too, will never die. I won't let him. Every time I get to that final February morning, the day he died, I return to 1965, to that perfect day in June. He doesn't know me, he never knows me. But we meet on that hill, the only two willing to enjoy the day doing nothing. He lies on his back, idly fingering chords on his guitar, blowing bubbles and staring into the clouded blue sky. Later I will introduce him to Lisa. She won't know us either, but that's okay. We've got plenty of time.

"Time," I say to Dancer, lying in the park on the hill. "There's so much time."

"All the time there is," he says.

BOOBS

by SUZY MCKEE CHARNAS

Suzy McKee Charnas's darkly comic look at the cruelty and tur-moil of youth, "Boobs" (*Asimov's*, July 1989), picked up the 1990 Hugo Award for best short story. This completely original look at the teenage werewolf—an established horror theme—provided a bookend to her brilliant vampire novella, "Unicorn Tapestry," which won the 1980 Nebula Award. That story became part of her book, *The Vampire Tapestry*, and it was produced in San Francisco as a play called *Vampire Dreams*. The author's other books include *Walk to the End of the World*, *Motherlines*, and *The Furies*. She lives in Albuquerque, New Mexico, with her husband, Stephen.

The thing is, it's like your brain wants to go on thinking about the miserable history mid-term you have to take tomorrow, but your body takes over. And what a body! You can see in the dark and run like the wind and leap parked cars in a single bound.

Of course you pay for it next morning (but it's worth it). I always wake up stiff and sore, with dirty hands and feet and face, and I have to jump in the shower fast so Hilda won't see me like that.

Not that she would know what it was about, but why take chances? So I pretend it's the other thing that's bothering me. So she goes, "Come on, sweetie, everybody gets cramps, that's no reason to go around moaning and groaning. What are you doing, trying to get out of school just because you've got your period?"

If I didn't like Hilda, which I do even though she is only a step-mother instead of my real mother, I would show her something that would keep me out of school forever, and it's not fake, either.

But there are plenty of people I'd rather show that to.

I already showed that dork Billy Linden.

"Hey, Boobs!" he goes, in the hall right outside Homeroom. A lot of kids laughed, naturally, though Rita Frye called him an asshole.

Billy is the one that started it, sort of, because he always started everything, him with his big mouth. At the beginning of term, he came barreling down on me hollering, "Hey, look at Bornstein, something musta happened to her over the summer! What happened, Bornstein? Hey, everybody, look at Boobs Bornstein!"

He made a grab at my chest, and I socked him in the shoulder, and he punched me in the face, which made me dizzy and shocked and made me cry, too, in front of everybody.

I mean, I always used to wrestle and fight with the boys, being that I was strong for a girl. All of a sudden it was different. He hit me hard, to really hurt, and the shock sort of got me in the pit of my stomach and made me feel nauseous, too, as well as mad and embarrassed to death.

I had to go home with a bloody nose and lie with my head back and ice wrapped in a towel on my face and dripping down into my hair.

Hilda sat on the couch next to me and patted me. She goes, "I'm sorry about this, honey, but really, you have to learn it sometime. You're all growing up and the boys are getting stronger than you'll ever be. If you fight with boys, you're bound to get hurt. You have to find other ways to handle them."

To make things worse, the next morning I started to bleed down there, which Hilda had explained carefully to me a couple of times, so at least I knew what was going on. Hilda really tried extra hard without being icky about it, but I hated when she talked about how it was all part of these exciting changes in my body that are so important and how terrific it is to "become a young woman."

Sure. The whole thing was so messy and disgusting, worse than she had said, worse than I could imagine, with these black clots of gunk coming out in a smear of pink blood—I thought I would throw up. That's just the lining of your uterus, Hilda said. Big deal. It was still gross.

And plus, the *smell*.

Hilda tried to make me feel better, she really did. She said we should "mark the occasion" like primitive people do, so it's something special, not just a nasty thing that just sort of falls on you.

So we decided to put poor old Pinkie away, my stuffed dog that I've slept with since I was three. Pinkie is bald and sort of hard and lumpy, since he got put in the washing machine by mistake, and you would never know he was all soft plush when he was new, or even that he was pink.

Last time my friend Gerry-Anne came over, before the summer, she saw Pinky laying on my pillow and though she didn't say anything, I could tell she was thinking that was kind of babyish. So I'd been thinking about not keeping Pinky around anymore.

Hilda and I made him this nice box lined with pretty scraps from her quilting class, and I thanked him out loud for being my friend for so many years, and we put him up in the closet, on the top shelf.

I felt terrible, but if Gerry-Anne decided I was too babyish to be friends with anymore, I could end up with no friends at all. When you have never been popular since the time you were skinny and fast and everybody wanted you on their team, you have that kind of thing on your mind.

Hilda and Dad made me go to school the next morning so nobody would think I was scared of Billy Linden (which I was) or that I would let him keep me away just by being such a dork.

Everybody kept sneaking funny looks at me and whispering, and I was sure it was because I couldn't help walking funny with the pad between my legs and because they could smell what was happening, which as far as I knew hadn't happened to anybody else in Eight A yet. Just like nobody else in the whole grade had anything real in their stupid training bras except me, thanks a lot.

Anyway I stayed away from everybody as much as I could and wouldn't talk to Gerry-Anne, even, because I was scared she would ask me why I walked funny and smelled bad.

Billy Linden avoided me just like everybody else, except one of his stupid buddies purposely bumped into me so I stumbled into Billy on the lunch-line. Billy turns around and he goes, real loud, "Hey, Boobs, when did you start wearing black and blue make-up?"

I didn't give him the satisfaction of knowing that he had actually broken my nose, which the doctor said. Good thing they don't have to bandage you up for that. Billy would be hollering up a storm about how I had my nose in a sling as well as my boobs.

That night I got up after I was supposed to be asleep and took off my underpants and T-shirt that I sleep in and stood looking at myself in the mirror. I didn't need to turn a light on. The moon was full and it was shining right into my bedroom through the big dormer window.

I crossed my arms and pinched myself hard to sort of punish my body for what it was doing to me.

As if that could make it stop.

No wonder Edie Siler had starved herself to death in the tenth grade! I understood her perfectly. She was trying to keep her body down, keep it normal-looking, thin and strong, like I was too, back when I looked like a person, not a cartoon that somebody would call "Boobs."

And then something warm trickled in a little line down the inside of my leg, and I knew it was blood and I couldn't stand it anymore. I pressed my thighs together and shut my eyes hard, and I did something.

I mean I felt it happening. I felt myself shrink down to a hard core of sort of cold fire inside my bones, and all the flesh part, the muscles and the squishy insides and the skin, went sort of glowing and free-floating, all shining with moonlight, and I felt a sort of shifting and balance-changing going on.

I thought I was fainting on account of my stupid period. So I turned around and threw myself on my bed, only by the time I hit it, I knew something was seriously wrong.

For one thing, my nose and my head were crammed with these crazy, rich sensations that it took me a second to even figure out were smells, they were so much stronger than any smells I'd ever smelled. And they were—I don't know—*interesting* instead of just stinky, even the rotten ones.

I opened my mouth to get the smells a little better, and heard myself panting in a funny way as if I'd been running, which I hadn't, and then there was this long part of my face sticking out and something moving there—my tongue.

I was licking my chops.

Well, there was this moment of complete and utter panic. I tore around the room whining and panting and hearing my toenails clicking on the floorboards, and then I huddled down and crouched in the corner because I was scared Dad and Hilda would hear me and come to find out what was making all this racket.

Because I could hear them. I could hear their bed creak when one of them turned over, and Dad's breath whistling a little in an almost snore, and I could smell them too, each one with a perfectly clear bunch of smells, kind of like those desserts of mixed ice cream they call a medley.

My body was twitching and jumping with fear and energy, and my room—it's a converted attic-space, wide but with a ceiling that's low in places—my room felt like a jail. And plus, I was terrified of catching a glimpse of myself in the mirror. I had a pretty good idea of what I would see, and I didn't want to see it.

Besides, I had to pee, and I couldn't face trying to deal with the toilet in the state I was in.

So I eased the bedroom door open with my shoulder and nearly fell down the stairs trying to work them with four legs and thinking about it, instead of letting my body just do it. I put my hands on the front door to open it, but my hands weren't hands, they were paws with long knobby toes covered with fur, and the toes had thick black claws sticking out of the ends of them.

The pit of my stomach sort of exploded with horror, and I yelled. It came out this wavery "wooo" noise that echoed eerily in my skull-bones. Upstairs, Hilda goes, "Jack, what was that?" I bolted for the basement as I heard Dad hit the floor of their bedroom.

The basement door slips its latch all the time, so I just shoved it open and down I went, doing better on the stairs this time because I was too scared to think. I spent the rest of the night down there, moaning to myself (which meant whining through my nose, really) and trotting around rubbing against the walls trying to rub off this crazy shape I had, or just moving around because I couldn't sit still. The place was thick with stinks and these slow-swirling currents of hot and cold air. I couldn't handle all the input.

As for having to pee, in the end I managed to sort of hike my butt up over the edge of the slop-sink by Dad's workbench and let go in there. The only problem was that I couldn't turn the taps on to rinse out the smell because of my paws.

Then about three A.M. I woke up from a doze curled up in a bare place on the floor where the spiders weren't so likely to walk, and I couldn't see a thing or smell anything either, so I knew I was okay again even before I checked and found fingers on my hands again instead of claws.

I zipped upstairs and stood under the shower so long that Hilda yelled at me for using up the hot water when she had a load of wash to do that morning. I was only trying to steam some of the stiffness out of my muscles, but I couldn't tell her that.

It was real weird to just dress and go to school after a night like that. One good thing, I had stopped bleeding after only one day, which Hilda said wasn't so strange for the first time. So it had to be the huge greenish bruise on my face from Billy's punch that everybody was staring at.

That and the usual thing, of course. Well, why not? *They* didn't know I'd spent the night as a wolf.

So Fat Joey grabbed my book bag in the hallway outside science class and tossed it to some kid from Eight B. I had to run after them to get it back, which of course was set up so the boys could cheer the jouncing of my boobs under my shirt.

I was so mad I almost caught Fat Joey, except I was afraid if I grabbed him, maybe he would sock me like Billy had.

Dad had told me, Don't let it get you, kid, all boys are jerks at that age.

Hilda had been saying all summer, Look, it doesn't do any good to walk around all hunched up with your arms crossed, you should just throw your shoulders back and walk like a proud person who's pleased that she's growing up. You're just a little early, that's all, and I bet the other girls are secretly envious of you, with their cute little training bras, for Chrissake, as if there was something that needed to be *trained*.

It's okay for her, she's not in school, she doesn't remember what it's like.

So I quit running and walked after Joey until the bell rang, and then I got my book bag back from the bushes outside where he threw it. I was crying a little, and I ducked into the girls' room.

Stacey Buhl was in there doing her lipstick like usual and wouldn't talk to me like usual, but Rita came bustling in and said somebody should off that dumb dork Joey, except of course it was really Billy that put him up to it. Like usual.

Rita is okay except she's an outsider herself, being that her kid brother has AIDS, and lots of kids' parents don't think she should even be in the school. So I don't hang around with her a lot. I've got enough trouble, and anyway I was late for Math.

I had to talk to somebody, though. After school I told Gerry-Anne, who's been my best friend on and off since fourth grade. She was off at the moment, but I found her in the library and I told her I'd had a weird dream about being a wolf. She wants to be a psychiatrist like her mother, so of course she listened.

She told me I was nuts. That was a big help.

That night I made sure the back door wasn't exactly closed, and then I got in bed with no clothes on—imagine turning into a wolf in your underpants and T-shirt—and just shivered, waiting for something to happen.

The moon came up and shone in my window, and I changed again, just like before, which is not one bit like how it is in the movies—all struggling and screaming and bones snapping out with horrible cracking and tearing noises, just the way I guess you would imagine it to be, if you knew it had to be done by building special machines to do that for the camera and make it look real: if you were a special effects man, instead of a werewolf.

For me, it didn't have to look real, it was real. It was this melting and drifting thing, which I got sort of excited by this time. I mean it felt—interesting. Like something I was doing, instead of just another dumb body-mess happening to me because some brainless hormones said so.

I must have made a noise. Hilda came upstairs to the door of my bedroom, but luckily she didn't come in. She's tall, and my ceiling is low for her, so she often talks to me from the landing.

Anyway I'd heard her coming, so I was in my bed with my whole head shoved under my pillow, praying frantically that nothing showed.

I could smell her, it was the wildest thing—her own smell, sort of sweaty but sweet, and then on top of it her perfume, like an ice-pick stuck in my nose. I didn't actually hear a word she said, I was too scared, and also I had this ripply shaking feeling inside me, a high that was only partly terror.

See, I realized all of a sudden, with this big blossom of surprise, that I didn't have to be scared of Hilda, or anybody. I was strong, my wolf-body was strong, and anyhow one clear look at me and she would drop dead.

What a relief, though, when she went away. I was dying to get out from under the weight of the covers, and besides I had to sneeze.

Also I recognized that part of the energy roaring around inside me was hunger.

They went to bed—I heard their voices even in their bedroom, though not exactly what they said, which was fine. The words weren't important anymore, I could tell more from the tone of what they were saying.

Like I knew they were going to do it, and I was right. I could hear them messing around right through the walls, which was also something new, and I have never been so embarrassed in my life. I couldn't even put my hands over my ears, because my hands were paws.

So while I was waiting for them to go to sleep, I looked myself over in the big mirror on my closet door.

There was this big wolf head with a long slim muzzle and a thick ruff around my neck. The ruff stood up as I growled and backed up a little.

Which was silly of course, there was no wolf in the bedroom but me. But I was all strung out, I guess, and one wolf, me in my wolf body, was as much as I could handle the idea of, let alone two wolves, me and my reflection.

After that first shock, it was great. I kept turning one way and another for different views.

I was thin, with these long, slender legs but strong, you could see the muscles, and feet a little bigger than I would have picked. But I'll take four big feet over two big boobs any day.

My face was terrific, with jaggedy white ripsaw teeth and eyes that were small and clear and gleaming in the moonlight. The tail was a little bizarre, but I got used to it, and actually it had a nice plumy shape. My shoulders were big and covered with long, glossy-looking fur, and I had this neat coloring, dark on the back and a sort of melting silver on my front and underparts.

The thing was, though, my tongue, hanging out. I had a lot of trouble with that, it looked gross and silly at the same time. I mean, that was *my tongue*, about a foot long and neatly draped over the points of my bottom canines. That was when I realized that I didn't have a whole lot of expressions to use, not with that face, which was more like a mask.

But it was alive, it was my face, those were my own long black lips that my tongue licked.

No doubt about it, this was *me*. I was a werewolf, like in the movies they showed over Halloween weekend. But it wasn't anything like your ugly movie werewolf that's just some guy loaded up with pounds and pounds of make-up. I was *gorgeous*.

I didn't want to just hang around admiring myself in the mirror, though. I couldn't stand being cooped up in that stuffy, smell-crowded room.

When everything settled down and I could hear Dad and Hilda breathing the way they do when they're sleeping, I snuck out.

The dark wasn't very dark to me, and the cold felt sharp like vinegar, but not in a hurting way. Everyplace I went, there were these currents like waves in the air, and I could draw them in through my long wolf nose and roll the smell of them over the back of my tongue. It was like a whole different world, with bright sounds everywhere and rich, strong smells.

And I could run.

I started running because a car came by while I was sniffing at the garbage bags on the curb, and I was really scared of being seen in the headlights. So I took off down the dirt alley between our house and the Morrisons' next door, and holy cow, I could tear along with hardly a sound, I could jump their picket fence without even thinking about it. My back legs were like steel springs and I came down solid and square on four legs with almost no shock at all, let alone worrying about losing my balance or twisting an ankle.

Man, I could run through that chilly air all thick and moisty with smells, I could almost fly. It was like last year, when I didn't have boobs bouncing and yanking in front even when I'm only walking fast.

Just two rows of neat little bumps down the curve of my belly. I sat down and looked.

I tore open garbage bags to find out about the smells in them, but I didn't eat anything from them. I wasn't about to chow down on other people's stale hotdog-ends and pizza crusts and fat and bones scraped off their plates and all mixed in with mashed potatoes and stuff.

When I found places where dogs had stopped and made their mark, I squatted down and pissed there too, right on top, I just wiped them *out*.

I bounded across that enormous lawn around the Wanscombe place, where nobody but the Oriental gardener ever sets foot, and walked up the back and over the top of their BMW, leaving big fat pawprints all over it. Nobody saw me, nobody heard me, I was a shadow.

Well, except for the dogs, of course.

There was a lot of barking when I went by, real hysterics, which at first I was really scared about. But then I popped out of an alley up on Ridge Road, where the big houses are, right in front of about six dogs that run together. Their owners let them out all night and don't care if they get hit by a car.

They'd been trotting along with the wind behind them, checking out all the garbage bags set out for pickup the next morning. When they saw me, one of them let out a yelp of surprise, and they all skidded to a stop.

Six of them. I was scared. I growled.

The dogs turned fast, banging into each other in their hurry, and trotted away.

I don't know what they would have done if they met a real wolf, but I was something special, I guess.

I followed them.

They scattered and ran.

Well, I ran too, and this was a different kind of running. I mean, I stretched, and I raced, and there was this joy. I chased one of them.

Zig, zag, this little terrier-kind of dog tried to cut left and dive under the gate of somebody's front walk, all without a sound—he was running too hard to yell, and I was happy running quiet.

Just before he could ooze under the gate, I caught up with him and without thinking I grabbed the back of his neck and pulled him off his feet and gave him a shake as hard as I could, from side to side.

I felt his neck crack, the sound vibrated through all the bones of my face.

I picked him up in my mouth, and it was like he hardly weighed a thing. I trotted away holding him up off the ground, and under a bush in Baker's Park I held him down with my paws and I bit into his belly, that was still warm and quivering.

Like I said, I was hungry.

The blood gave me this rush like you wouldn't believe. I stood there a minute looking around and licking my lips, just sort of panting and tasting the taste because I was stunned by it, it was like eating honey or the best chocolate malted you ever had.

So I put my head down and chomped that little dog, like shoving your face into a pizza and inhaling it. God, I was *starved*, so I didn't mind that the meat was tough and rank-tasting after that first wonderful bite. I even licked blood off the ground after, never mind the grit mixed in.

I ate two more dogs that night, one that was tied up on a clothesline in a cruddy yard full of rusted-out car parts down on the South side, and one fat old yellow dog out snuffling around on his own and way too slow. He tasted pretty bad, and by then I was feeling full, so I left a lot.

I strolled around the park, shoving the swings with my big black wolf nose, and I found the bench where Mr. Granby sits and feeds the pigeons every day, never mind that nobody else wants the dirty birds around crapping on their cars. I took a dump there, right where he sits.

Then I gave the setting moon a goodnight, which came out quavery and wild, "Loo-loo-loo!" And I loped toward home, springing off the thick pads of my paws and letting my tongue loll out and feeling generally super.

I slipped inside and trotted upstairs, and in my room I stopped to look at myself in the mirror.

As gorgeous as before, and only a few dabs of blood on me, which I took time to lick off. I did get a little worried—I mean, suppose that was it, suppose having killed and eaten what I'd killed in my wolf shape, I was stuck in this shape forever? Like, if you wander into a fairy castle and eat or drink anything, that's it, you can't ever leave. Suppose when the morning came I didn't change back?

Well, there wasn't much I could do about that one way or the other, and to tell the truth, I felt like I wouldn't mind; it had been worth it.

When I was nice and clean, including licking off my own bottom which seemed like a perfectly normal and nice thing to do at the time, I jumped up on the bed, curled up, and corked right off. When I woke up with the sun in my eyes, there I was, my own self again.

It was very strange, grabbing breakfast and wearing my old sweatshirt that wallowed all over me so I didn't stick out so much, while Hilda yawned and shuffled around in her robe and slippers and acted like her and Dad hadn't been doing it last night, which I knew different.

And plus, it was perfectly clear that she didn't have a clue about what *I* had been doing, which gave me a strange feeling.

One of the things about growing up which they're careful not to tell you is, you start having more things you don't talk to your parents about. And I had a doozie.

Hilda goes, "What's the matter, are you off Sugar Pops now? Honestly, Kelsey, I can't keep up with you! And why can't you wear something nicer than that old shirt to school? Oh, I get it: disguise, right?"

She sighed and looked at me kind of sad but smiling, her hands on her hips. "Kelsey, Kelsey," she goes, "if only I'd had half of what you've got when *I* was a girl—I was flat as an ironing board, and it made me so miserable, I can't tell you."

She's still real thin and neat-looking, so what does she know about it? But she meant well, and anyhow I was feeling so good I didn't argue.

I didn't change my shirt, though.

That night I didn't turn into a wolf. I laid there waiting, but though the moon came up, nothing happened no matter how hard I tried, and after a while I went and looked out the window and realized that the moon wasn't really full anymore, it was getting smaller.

I wasn't so much relieved as sorry. I bought a calendar at the school book sale two weeks later, and I checked the full moon nights coming up and waited anxiously to see what would happen.

Meantime, things rolled along as usual. I got a rash of zits on my chin. I would look in the mirror and think about my wolf-face, that had beautiful sleek fur instead of zits.

Zits and all I went to Angela Durkin's party, and next day Billy Linden told everybody that I went in one of the bedrooms at Angela's and made out with him, which I did not. But since no grown-ups were home and Fat Joey brought grass to the party, most of the kids were stoned and didn't know who did what or where anyhow.

As a matter of fact, Billy once actually did get a girl in Seven B high one time out in his parents' garage, and him and two of his friends did it to her while she was zonked out of her mind, or anyway they said they did, and she was too embarrassed to say anything one way or the other, and a little while later she changed schools.

How I know about it is the same way everybody else does, which is because Billy was the biggest boaster in the whole school, and you could never tell if he was lying or not.

So I guess it wasn't so surprising that some people believed what Billy said about me. Gerry-Anne quit talking to me after that. Meantime Hilda got pregnant.

This turned into a huge discussion about how Hilda had been worried about her biological clock so she and Dad had decided to have a kid, and I shouldn't mind, it would be fun for me and good preparation for being a mother myself later on, when I found some nice guy and got married.

Sure. Great preparation. Like Mary O'Hare in my class, who gets to change her youngest baby sister's diapers all the time, yick. She jokes about it, but you can tell she really hates it. Now it looked like it was my turn coming up, as usual.

The only thing that made life bearable was my secret.

"You're laid back today," Devon Brown said to me in the lunchroom one day after Billy had been specially obnoxious, trying to flick rolled up pieces of bread from his table so they would land on my chest. Devon was sitting with me because he was bad at French, my only good subject, and I was helping him out with some verbs. I guess he wanted to know why I wasn't upset because of Billy picking on me. He goes, "How come?"

"That's a secret," I said, thinking about what Devon would say if he knew a werewolf was helping him with his French: *loup. Manger.*

He goes, "What secret?" Devon has freckles and is actually kind of cute-looking.

"*A secret,*" I go, "so I can't tell you, dummy."

He looks real superior and he goes, "Well, it can't be much of a secret, because girls can't keep secrets, everybody knows that."

Sure, like that kid Sara in Eight B who it turned out her own father had been molesting her for years, but she never told anybody until some psychologist caught on from some tests we all had to take in seventh grade. Up till then, Sara kept her secret fine.

And I kept mine, marking off the days on the calendar. The only part I didn't look forward to was having a period again, which last time came right before the change.

When the time came, I got crampy and more zits popped out on my face, but I didn't have a period.

I changed, though.

The next morning they were talking in school about a couple of prize miniature Schnauzers at the Wanscombes that had been hauled out of their yard by somebody and killed, and almost nothing left of them.

Well, my stomach turned a little when I heard some kids describing what Mr. Wanscombe had found over in Baker's Park, "the remains," as people said. I felt a little guilty, too, because Mrs. Wanscombe had really loved those little dogs, which somehow I didn't think about at all when I was a wolf the night before, trotting around hungry in the moonlight.

I knew those Schnauzers personally, so I was sorry, even if they were irritating little mutts that made a lot of noise.

But heck, the Wanscombes shouldn't have left them out all night in the cold. Anyhow, they were rich, they could buy new ones if they wanted.

Still and all, though. I mean, dogs are just dumb animals. If they're mean, it's because they're wired that way or somebody made them mean, they can't help it. They can't just decide to be nice, like a person can. And plus, they don't taste so great, I think because they put so much junk in commercial dog-foods—anti-worm medicine and ashes and ground up fish, stuff like that. Ick.

In fact after the second schnauzer I had felt sort of sick and I didn't sleep real well that night. So I was not in a great mood to start with; and that was the day that my new brassiere disappeared while I was in gym. Later on I got passed a note telling me where to find it: stapled to the bulletin board outside the Principal's office, where everybody could see that I was trying a bra with an underwire.

Naturally, it had to be Stacey Buhl that grabbed my bra while I was changing for gym and my back was turned, since she was now hanging out with Billy and his friends.

Billy went around all day making bets at the top of his lungs on how soon I would be wearing a D-cup.

Stacey didn't matter, she was just a jerk. Billy mattered. He had wrecked me in that school forever, with his nasty mind and his big, fat mouth. I was past crying or fighting and getting punched out. I was boiling, I had had enough crap from him, and I had an idea.

I followed Billy home and waited on his porch until his mom came home and she made him come down and talk to me. He stood in the doorway and talked through the screen door, eating a banana and lounging around like he didn't have a care in the world.

So he goes, "Whatcha want, Boobs?"

I stammered a lot, being I was so nervous about telling such big lies, but that probably made me sound more believable.

I told him that I would make a deal with him: I would meet him that night in Baker's Park, late, and take off my shirt and bra and let him do whatever he wanted with my boobs if that would satisfy his curiosity and he would find somebody else to pick on and leave me alone.

"What?" he said, staring at my chest with his mouth open. His voice squeaked and he was practically drooling on the floor. He couldn't believe his good luck.

I said the same thing over again.

He almost came out onto the porch to try it right then and there. "Well, shit," he goes, lowering his voice a lot, "why didn't you say something before? You really mean it?"

I go, "Sure," though I couldn't look at him.

After a minute he goes, "Okay, it's a deal. Listen, Kelsey, if you like it, can we, uh, do it again, you know?"

I go, "Sure. But Billy, one thing: this is a secret, between just you and me. If you tell anybody, if there's one other person hanging around out there tonight—"

"Oh no," he goes, real fast, "I won't say a thing to anybody, honest. Not a word, I promise!"

Not until afterward, of course, was what he meant, which if there was one thing Billy Linden couldn't do, it was to keep quiet if he knew something bad about another person.

"You're gonna like it, I know you are," he goes, speaking strictly for himself as usual. "Jeez. I can't believe this!"

But he did, the dork.

I couldn't eat much for dinner that night, I was too excited, and I went upstairs early to do homework, I told Dad and Hilda.

Then I waited for the moon, and when it came, I changed.

Billy was in the park. I caught a whiff of him, very sweaty and excited, but I stayed cool. I snuck around for a while, as quiet as I could—which was real quiet—making sure none of his stupid friends were lurking around. I mean, I wouldn't have trusted just his promise for a million dollars.

I passed up half a hamburger lying in the gutter where somebody had parked for lunch next to Baker's Park. My mouth watered, but I didn't want to spoil my appetite. I was hungry and happy, sort of singing inside my own head, "Shoo, fly, pie, and an apple-pan-dowdie . . ."

Without any sound, of course.

Billy had been sitting on a bench, his hands in his pockets, twisting around to look this way and that way, watching for me—for my human self—to come join him. He had a jacket on, being it was very chilly out.

Which he didn't stop to think that maybe a sane person wouldn't be crazy enough to sit out there and take off her top leaving her naked skin bare to the breeze. But that was Billy all right, totally fixed on his own greedy self and without a single thought for somebody else. I bet all he could think about was what a great scam this was, to feel up old Boobs in the park and then crow about it all over school.

Now he was walking around the park, kicking at the sprinkler-heads and glancing up every once in a while, frowning and looking sulky.

I could see he was starting to think that I might stand him up. Maybe he even suspected that old Boobs was lurking around watching him and laughing to herself because he had fallen for a trick. Maybe old Boobs had even brought some kids from school with her to see what a jerk he was.

Actually that would have been pretty good, except Billy probably would have broken my nose for me again, or worse, if I'd tried it.

"Kelsey?" he goes, sounding mad.

I didn't want him stomping off home in a huff. I moved up closer, and I let the bushes swish a little around my shoulders.

He goes, "Hey, Kelse, it's late, where've you been?"

I listened to the words, but mostly I listened to the little thread of worry flickering in his voice, low and high, high and low, as he tried to figure out what was going on.

I let out the whisper of a growl.

He stood real still, staring at the bushes, and he goes, "That you, Kelse? Answer me."

I was wild inside. I couldn't wait another second. I tore through the bushes and leaped for him, flying.

He stumbled backward with a squawk—"What!"—jerking his hands up in front of his face, and he was just sucking in a big breath to yell with when I hit him like a demo-derby truck.

I jammed my nose past his feeble claws and chomped down hard on his face.

No sound came out of him except this wet, thick gurgle, which I could more taste than hear because the sound came right into my mouth with the gush of his blood and the hot mess of meat and skin that I tore away and swallowed.

He thrashed around, hitting at me, but I hardly felt anything through my fur. I mean, he wasn't so big and strong laying there on the ground with me straddling him all lean and wiry with wolf-muscle. And plus, he was in shock. I got a strong whiff from below as he let go of everything right into his pants.

Dogs were barking, but so many people around Baker's Park have dogs to keep out burglars, and the dogs make such a racket all the time, that nobody pays any attention. I wasn't worried. Anyway, I was too busy to care.

I nosed in under what was left of Billy's jaw and I bit his throat out.

Now let him go around telling lies about people.

His clothes were a lot of trouble and I really missed having hands. I managed to drag his shirt out of his belt with my teeth, though, and it was easy to tear his belly open. Pretty messy, but once I got in there, it was better than Thanksgiving dinner. Who would think that somebody as horrible as Billy Linden could taste so *good?*

He was barely moving by then, and I quit thinking about him as Billy Linden anymore. I quit thinking at all, I just pushed my head in and pulled out delicious steaming chunks and ate until I was picking at tidbits, and everything was getting cold.

On the way home I saw a police car cruising the neighborhood the way they do sometimes. I hid in the shadows and of course they never saw me.

There was a lot of washing up to do in the morning, and when Hilda saw my sheets she shook her head and she goes, "You should be more careful about keeping track of your period so as not to get caught by surprise."

Everybody in school knew something had happened to Billy Linden, but it wasn't until the day after that that they got the word. Kids stood around in little huddles trading rumors about how some wild animal had chewed Billy up. I would walk up and listen in and add a really gross remark or two, like part of the game of thrilling each other green and nauseous with made-up details to see who would upchuck first.

Not me, that's for sure. I mean, when somebody went on about how Billy's whole head was gnawed down to the skull and they didn't even know who he was except from the bus pass in his wallet, I got a little urpy. It's amazing the things people will dream up. But when I thought about what I had actually done to Billy, I had to smile.

It felt totally wonderful to walk through the halls without having anybody yelling, "Hey, Boobs!"

Even my social life is looking up. Gerry-Anne is not only talking to me again, she invited me out on a double-date with her. Some guy she met at a party asked her to go to the movies with him next weekend, and he has a friend. They're both from Fawcett Junior High across town, which will be a change. I was nervous when she asked me, but finally I said yes. My first real date!

I am still pretty nervous, to tell the truth. I have to keep promising myself that I will not worry about my chest, I will not be self-conscious, even if the guy stares.

Actually things at school are not completely hunky-dory. Hilda says "That's Life" when I complain about things, and I am beginning to believe her. Fat Joey somehow got to be my lab-partner in Science, and if he doesn't quit trying to grab a feel whenever we have to stand close together to do an experiment, he is going to be sorry.

He doesn't know it, but he's got until the next full moon.

THE MANAMOUKI

by **MIKE RESNICK**

In 1988 Mike Resnick won the Hugo award for his novelette "Kirinyaga"—the initial story in a highly regarded series about a tribe of Kikuyu who try to reclaim their past on a satellite engineered to resemble pre-colonial Kenya. Since then, these stories have become one of the most-honored story-cycles in science fiction history. Midway through the series, "The Manamouki" (July 1990), picked up another Hugo award, and the penultimate tale, "When the Old Gods Die" (April 1995), was a recent finalist for the same award.

In addition to these laurels, Resnick recently won the Nebula Award for his brilliant, and unrelated, novella about "Seven Views of Olduvai Gorge." The author's numerous books include the anthology, *Future Earths: Under African Skies*, which he co-edited with Gardner Dozois, and his latest novel, *A Miracle of Rare Design*.

Many eons ago, the children of Gikuyu, who was himself the first Kikuyu, lived on the slopes of the holy mountain Kirinyaga, which men now call Mount Kenya.

There were many serpents on the mountain, but the sons and grandsons of Gikuyu found them repulsive, and they soon killed all but one.

Then one day the last serpent entered their village and killed and ate a young child. The children of Gikuyu sought out their *mundumugu*—their witch doctor—and asked him to destroy the menace.

The *mundumugu* rolled the bones and sacrificed a goat, and finally he created a poison that would kill the serpent. He slit open the belly of another goat, and placed the poison inside it, and left it beneath a tree, and the very next day the serpent swallowed the goat and died.

"Now," said the *mundumugu*, "you must cut the serpent into one hundred pieces and scatter them on the holy mountain, so that no demon can breathe life back into its body."

The children of Gikuyu did as they were instructed, and scattered the hundred pieces of the serpent across the slopes of Kirinyaga. But during the night, each piece came to life and became a new serpent, and soon the Kikuyu were afraid to leave their *bomas*.

The *mundumugu* ascended the mountain, and when he neared the highest peak, he addressed Ngai.

"We are besieged by serpents," he said. "If you do not slay them, then the Kikuyu shall surely die as a people."

"I made the serpent, just as I made the Kikuyu and all other things," answered Ngai, who sat on His golden throne atop Kirinyaga. "And anything that I made, be it a man or a serpent or a tree or even an idea, is not repellent in My eyes. I will save you this one time, because you are young and ignorant, but you must never forget that you cannot destroy that which you find repulsive—for if you try to destroy it, it will always return one hundred times greater than before."

This is one of the reasons why the Kikuyu chose to till the soil rather than hunt the beasts of the jungle like the Wakamba, or make war on their neighbors like the Maasai, for they had no wish to see that which they destroyed return to plague them. It is a lesson taught by every *mundumugu* to his people, even after we left Kenya and emigrated to the terraformed world of Kirinyaga.

In the entire history of our tribe, only one *mundumugu* ever forgot the lesson that Ngai taught atop the holy mountain on that distant day.

And that *mundumugu* was myself.

When I awoke, I found hyena dung within the thorn enclosure of my *boma*. That alone should have warned me that the day carried a curse, for there is no worse omen. Also the breeze, hot and dry and filled with dust, came from the west, and all good winds come from the east.

It was the day that our first immigrants were due to arrive. We had argued long and hard against allowing any newcomers to settle on Kirinyaga, for we were dedicated to the old ways of our people, and we wanted no outside influences corrupting the society that we had created. But our charter clearly stated that any Kikuyu who pledged to obey our laws and made the necessary payments to the Eutopian Council could emigrate from Kenya, and after postponing the inevitable for as long as we could, we finally agreed to accept Thomas Nkobe and his wife.

Of all the candidates for immigration, Nkobe had seemed the best. He had been born in Kenya, had grown up in the shadow of the holy mountain, and after going abroad for his schooling, had returned and run the large farm his family had purchased from one of the last European residents. Most important of all, he was a direct descendant of Jomo Kenyatta, the great Burning Spear of Kenya, who had led us to independence.

I trudged out across the hot, arid savannah to the tiny landing field at Haven to greet our new arrivals, accompanied only by Ndemi, my youthful assistant. Twice buffalo blocked our path, and once Ndemi had to hurl some stones to frighten a hyena away, but eventually we reached our destination, only to discover that the Maintenance ship which was carrying Nkobe and his wife had not yet arrived. I squatted down in the shade of an acacia tree, and a moment later Ndemi crouched down beside me.

"They are late," he said, peering into the cloudless sky. "Perhaps they will not come at all."

"They will come," I said. "The signs all point to it."

"But they are bad signs, and Nkobe may be a good man."

"There are many good men," I replied. "Not all of them belong on Kirinyaga."

"You are worried, Koriba?" asked Ndemi as a pair of crested cranes walked through the dry, brittle grass.

"I am concerned," I said.

"Why?"

"Because I do not know why he wants to live here."

"Why shouldn't he?" asked Ndemi, picking up a dry twig and methodically breaking it into tiny pieces. "Is it not Utopia?"

"There are many different notions of Utopia," I replied. "Kirinyaga is the Kikuyus'."

"And Nkobe is a Kikuyu, so this is where he belongs," said Ndemi decisively.

"I wonder."

"Why?"

"Because he is almost forty years old. Why did he wait so long to come here?"

"Perhaps he could not afford to come sooner."

I shook my head. "He comes from a very wealthy family."

"They have many cattle?" asked Ndemi.

"Many," I said.

"And goats?"

I nodded.

"Will he bring them with him?"

"No. He will come empty-handed, as we all did." I paused, frowning. "Why would a man who owned a large farm and had many tractors and men to do his work turn his back on all that he possessed? That is what troubles me."

"You make it sound like the way he lived on Earth was better," said Ndemi.

"Not better, just different."

He paused for a moment. "Koriba, what *is* a tractor?"

"A machine that does the work of many men in the fields."

"It sounds truly wonderful," offered Ndemi.

"It makes deep wounds in the ground and stinks of gasoline," I said, making no effort to hide my contempt.

We sat in silence for another moment. Then the Maintenance ship came into view, its descent creating a huge cloud of dust and causing a great screeching and squawking by the birds and monkeys in the nearby trees. "Well," I said, "we shall soon have our answer."

I remained in the shade until the ship had touched down and Thomas Nkobe and his wife emerged from its interior. He was a tall, well-built man dressed in casual Western clothes; she was slender and graceful, her hair elegantly braided, her khaki slacks and hunting jacket exquisitely tailored.

"Hello!" said Nkobe in English as I approached him. "I was afraid we might have to find our way to the village ourselves."

"*Jambo*," I replied in Swahili. "Welcome to Kirinyaga."

"*Jambo*," he amended, switching to Swahili. "Are you Koinnage?"

"No," I answered. "Koinnage is our paramount chief. You will live in his village."

"And you are?"

"I am Koriba," I said.

"He is the *mundumugu*," added Ndemi proudly. "I am Ndemi." He paused. "Someday I will be a *mundumugu* too."

Nkobe smiled down at him. "I'm sure you will." Suddenly he remembered his wife. "And this is Wanda."

She stepped forward, smiled, and extended her hand. "A true *mundumugu!*" she said in heavily-accented Swahili. "I'm thrilled to meet you!"

"I hope you will enjoy your new life on Kirinyaga," I said, shaking her hand.

"Oh, I'm certain I will," she replied enthusiastically, as the ship disgorged their baggage and promptly took off again. She looked around at the dry savannah, and saw a trio of maribou storks and a jackal patiently waiting for a hyena to finish gorging itself on the wildebeest calf it had killed earlier in the morning. "I love it already!" She paused, then added confidentially, "I'm really the one who got Tom to agree to come here."

"Oh?"

She nodded her head. "I just couldn't stand what Kenya has become. All those factories, all that pollution! Ever since I learned about Kirinyaga, I've wanted to move here, to come back to Nature and live the way we were meant to live." She inhaled deeply. "Smell that air, Tom! It will add ten years to your life."

"You don't have to sell me any more," he said with a smile. "I'm here, aren't I?"

I turned to Wanda Nkobe. "You yourself are not Kikuyu, are you?"

"I am now," she replied. "Ever since I married Tom. But to answer your question, no, I was born and raised in Oregon."

"Oregon?" repeated Ndemi, brushing some flies away from his face with his hand.

"That's in America," she explained. She paused. "By the way, why are we speaking Swahili rather than Kikuyu?"

"Kikuyu is a dead language," I said. "Most of our people no longer know it."

"I had rather hoped it would still be spoken here," she said, obviously disappointed. "I've been studying it for months."

"If you had moved to Italy, you would not speak Latin," I replied. "We still use a few Kikuyu words, just as the Italians use a few Latin words."

She was silent for a moment, then shrugged. "At least I'll have the opportunity to improve my Swahili."

"I am surprised that you are willing to forego the amenities of America for Kirinyaga," I said, studying her closely.

"I was willing years ago," she answered. "It was Tom who had to be convinced, not me." She paused. "Besides, I gave up most of those so-called amenities when I left America and moved to Kenya."

"Even Kenya has certain luxuries," I noted. "We have no electricity here, no running water, no—"

"We camp out whenever we can," she said, and I placed a hand on Ndemi's shoulder before he could chide her for interrupting the *mundumugu*. "I'm used to roughing it."

"But you have always had a home to return to."

She stared at me, an amused smile on her face. "Are you trying to talk me out of moving here?"

"No," I replied. "But I wish to point out that nothing is immutable. Any member of our society who is unhappy and wishes to leave need only inform Maintenance of the fact and a ship will arrive at Haven an hour later."

"Not us," she said. "We're in for the long haul."

"The long haul?" I repeated.

"She means that we're here to stay," explained Nkobe, putting an arm around his wife's shoulders.

A hot breeze sent the dust swirling around us.

"I think I should take you to the village," I said, shielding my eyes. "You are doubtless tired and will wish to rest."

"Not at all," said Wanda Nkobe. "This is a brand-new world. I want to look around." Her gaze fell upon Ndemi, who was staring at her intently. "Is something wrong?" she asked.

"You are very strong and sturdy," said Ndemi approvingly. "That is good. You will bear many children."

"I certainly hope not," she said. "If there's one thing Kenya has more than enough of, it's children."

"This is not Kenya," said Ndemi.

"I will find other ways to contribute to the society."

Ndemi studied her for a moment. "Well," he said at last, "I suppose you can carry firewood."

"I'm glad I meet with your approval," she said.

"But you will need a new name," continued Ndemi. "Wanda is a European name."

"It is just a name," I said. "Changing it will not make her more of a Kikuyu."

"I have no objection," she interjected. "I'm starting a new life; I *ought* to have a new name."

I shrugged. "Which name will you take as your own?"

She smiled at Ndemi. "You choose one," she said.

He furrowed his brow for a long moment, then looked up at her. "My mother's sister, who died in childbirth last year, was named Mwange, and now there is no one in the village of that name."

"Then Mwange it shall be," she said. "Mwange wa Ndemi."

"But I am not your father," said Ndemi.

She smiled at him. "You are the father of my new name."

Ndemi puffed his chest up proudly.

"Well, now that *that's* settled," said Nkobe, "what about our luggage?"

"You will not need it," I said.

"Yes we will," said Mwange.

"You were told to bring nothing of Kenya with you."

"I've brought some *kikois* that I made myself," she said. "Surely that must be permissible, since I will be expected to weave my own fabrics and make my own clothes on Kirinyaga."

I considered her explanation for a moment, then nodded my consent. "I will send one of the village children for the bags."

"It's not that heavy," said Nkobe. "I can carry it myself."

"Kikuyu men do not fetch and carry," said Ndemi.

"What about Kikuyu women?" asked Mwange, obviously reluctant to leave the luggage behind.

"They carry firewood and grain, not bags of clothing," responded Ndemi. "*Those*," he said, pointing contemptuously toward the two leather bags, "are for children."

"Then we might as well start walking," said Mwange. "There are no children here."

Ndemi beamed with pride and strutted forward.

"Let Ndemi go first," I said. "His eyes are young and clear. He will be able to see any snakes or hyenas hiding in the tall grass."

"Do you have poisonous snakes here?" asked Nkobe.

"A few."

"Why don't you kill them?"

"Because this is not Kenya," I replied.

I walked directly behind Ndemi, and Nkobe and Mwange followed us, remarking upon the scenery and the animals to each other. After about half a mile we came to an impala ram standing directly in our path.

"Isn't he beautiful?" whispered Mwange. "Look at the horns on him!"

"I wish I had my camera with me!" said Nkobe.

"We do not permit cameras on Kirinyaga," I said.

"I know," said Nkobe. "But to be perfectly honest, I can't see how something as simple as a camera could be a corrupting influence to your society."

"To have a camera, one needs film, and one must therefore have a factory that manufactures both cameras and films. To develop the film, one needs chemicals, and then one must find a place to dump those chemicals that haven't been used. To print the pictures, one needs photographic paper, and we have barely enough wood to burn in our fires." I paused. "Kirinyaga supplies us with all of our desires. That is why we came here."

"Kirinyaga supplies you with all of your *needs*," said Mwange. "That is not quite the same thing."

Suddenly Ndemi stopped walking and turned to her.

"This is your first day here, so you are to be forgiven your ignorance," he explained. "But no *manamouki* may argue with the *mundumugu*."

"*Manamouki?*" she repeated. "What is a *manamouki?*"

"*You* are," said Ndemi.

"I've heard that word before," said Nkobe. "I think it means *wife*."

"You are wrong," I said. "A *manamouki* is a female."

"You mean a woman?" asked Mwange.

I shook my head. "*Any* female property," I said. "A woman, a cow, a sow, a bitch, a ewe."

"And Ndemi thinks I'm some kind of property?"

"You are Nkobe's *manamouki*," said Ndemi.

She considered it for a moment, then shrugged with amusement. "What the hell," she said in English. "If Wanda was only a name, *manamouki* is only a word. I can live with it."

"I hope so," I replied in Swahili, "for you will have to."

She turned to me. "I know we are the first immigrants to come to Kirinyaga, and that you must have your doubts about us—but this is the life I've always wanted. I'm going to be the best damned *manamouki* you ever saw."

"I hope so," I said, but I noticed that the wind still blew from the west.

* * *

I introduced Nkobe and Mwange to their neighbors, showed them their *shamba* where they would grow their food, pointed out their six cattle and ten goats and recommended that they lock them in their *boma* at night to protect them from the hyenas, told them how to reach the river to procure water, and left them at the entrance to their hut. Mwange seemed enthused about everything, and was soon engaged in animated conversation with the women who came by to look at her strange outfit.

"She is very nice," commented Ndemi as I walked through the fields, blessing the scarecrows. "Perhaps the omens you read were wrong."

"Perhaps," I said.

He stared at me. "But you do not think so."

"No."

"Well, *I* like her," he said.

"That is your right."

"Do you dislike her, then?"

I paused as I considered my answer.

"No," I said at last. "I fear her."

"But she is just a *manamouki!*" he protested. "She can do no harm."

"Under the proper circumstances, anything can do harm."

"I do not believe it," said Ndemi.

"Do you doubt your *mundumugu's* word?" I asked.

"No," he said uncomfortably. "If you say something, then it must be true. But I cannot understand how."

I smiled wryly. "That is because you are not yet a *mundumugu*."

He stopped and pointed to a spot some three hundred yards away, where a group of impala does were grazing.

"Can even *they* do harm?" he asked.

"Yes."

"But how?" he asked, frowning. "When danger appears, they do not confront it, but run away from it. Ngai has not blessed them with horns, so they cannot defend themselves. They are not large enough to destroy our crops. They cannot even kick an enemy, as can the zebra. I do not understand."

"I shall tell you the tale of the Ugly Buffalo, and then you will understand," I said.

Ndemi smiled happily, for he loved stories above all things, and I led him to the shade of a thorn tree, where we both squatted down, facing each other.

"One day a cow buffalo was wandering through the savannah," I began. "The hyenas had recently taken her first calf, and she was very sad. Then she came upon a newborn impala, whose mother had been killed by hyenas that very morning.

" 'I would like to take you home with me,' said the buffalo, 'for I am very lonely, and have much love in my heart. But you are not a buffalo.'

" 'I, too, am very lonely,' said the impala. 'And if you leave me here, alone and unprotected, I surely will not survive the night.'

" 'There is a problem,' said the buffalo. 'You are an impala, and we are buffalo. You do not belong with us.'

" 'I will become the best buffalo of all,' promised the impala. 'I will eat what you eat, drink what you drink, go where you go.'

" 'How can you become a buffalo? You cannot even grow horns.'

" 'Then I will wear the branches of a tree upon my head.'

" 'You do not wallow in the mud to protect your skin from parasites,' noted the buffalo.

" 'Take me home with you and I will cover myself with more mud than any other buffalo,' said the impala.

"For every objection the buffalo raised, the impala had an answer, and finally the buffalo agreed to take the impala back with her. Most of the members of the herd thought that the impala was the ugliest buffalo they had ever seen"—Ndemi chuckled at that—"but because the impala tried so hard to act like a buffalo, they allowed her to remain.

"Then one day a number of young buffalo were grazing some distance from the herd, and they came to a deep mud wallow that blocked their way.

" 'We must return to the herd,' said one of the young buffalo.

" 'Why?' asked the impala. 'There is fresh grass on the other side of the wallow.'

" 'Because we have been warned that a deep wallow such as this can suck us down beneath the surface and kill us.'

" 'I do not believe it,' said the impala, and, bolder than her companions, she walked out to the center of the mud wallow.

" 'You see?' she said. 'I have not been sucked beneath the surface. It is perfectly safe.'

"Soon three of the young buffalo ventured out across the mud wallow, and each in turn was sucked beneath the surface and drowned.

" 'It is the ugly buffalo's fault,' said the king of the herd. 'It was she who told them to cross the mud wallow.'

" 'But she meant no harm,' said her foster mother. 'And what she told them was true: the wallow was safe for her. All she wants is to live with the herd and be a buffalo; please do not punish her."

"The king was blessed with more generosity than wisdom, and so he forgave the ugly buffalo.

"Then, a week later, the ugly buffalo, who could leap as high as a tall bush, jumped up in the air and saw a pack of hyenas lurking in the grass. She waited until they were almost close enough to catch her, and then cried out a warning. All the buffalo began running, but the hyenas were able to catch the ugly buffalo's foster mother, and they pulled her down and killed her.

"Most of the other buffalo were grateful to the ugly buffalo for warning them, but during the intervening week there had been a new king, and this one was wiser than the previous one.

" 'It is the ugly buffalo's fault,' he said.

" 'How can it be her fault?' asked one of the older buffalo. 'It was she who warned us of the hyenas.'

" 'But she only warned you when it was too late,' said the king. 'Had she warned you when she first saw the hyenas, her mother would still be among us. But she forgot that we cannot run as fast as she can, and so her mother is dead.'

"And the new king, though his heart was sad, decreed that the ugly buffalo must leave the herd, for there is a great difference between being a buffalo and *wanting* to be a buffalo."

I leaned back against the tree, my story completed.

"Did the ugly buffalo survive?" asked Ndemi.

I shrugged and brushed a crawling insect from my forearm. "That is another story."

"She meant no harm."

"But she caused harm nonetheless."

Ndemi traced patterns in the dirt with his finger as he considered my answer, then looked up at me. "But if she had not been with the herd, the hyenas would have killed her mother anyway."

"Perhaps."

"Then it was not her fault."

"If I fall asleep against this tree, and you see a black mamba slithering through the grass toward me, and you make no attempt to wake me, and the mamba kills me, would you be to blame for my death?" I asked.

"Yes."

"Even though it would certainly have killed me had you not been here?"

Ndemi frowned. "It is a difficult problem."

"Yes, it is."

"The mud wallow was much easier," he said. "That was surely the ugly buffalo's fault, for without her urging, the other buffalo would never have entered it."

"That is true," I said.

Ndemi remained motionless for a few moments, still wrestling with the nuances of the story.

"You are saying that there are many different ways to cause harm," he announced.

"Yes."

"And that it takes wisdom to understand who is to blame, for the foolish king did not recognize the harm of the ugly buffalo's action, while the wise king knew that she was to blame for her inaction."

I nodded my head.

"I see," said Ndemi.

"And what has this to do with the *manamouki?*" I asked.

He paused again. "If harm comes to the village, you must use your wisdom to decide whether Mwange, who wants nothing more than to be a Kikuyu, is responsible for it."

"That is correct," I said, getting to my feet.

"But I still do not know what harm she can do."

"Neither do I," I answered.

"Will you know it when you see it?" he asked. "Or will it seem like a good deed, such as warning the herd that hyenas are near?"

I made no reply.

"Why are you silent, Koriba?" asked Ndemi at last.

I sighed heavily. "Because there are some questions that even a *mundumugu* cannot answer."

Ndemi was waiting for me, as usual, when I emerged from my hut five mornings later.

"*Jambo*, Koriba," he said.

I grunted a greeting and walked over to the fire that he had built, sitting cross-legged next to it until it removed the chill from my aging bones.

"What is today's lesson?" he asked at last.

"Today I will teach you how to ask Ngai for a fruitful harvest," I answered.

"But we did that last week."

"And we will do it next week, and many more weeks as well," I answered.

"When will I learn how to make ointments to cure the sick, or how to turn an enemy into an insect so that I may step on him?"

"When you are older," I said.

"I am already old."

"And more mature."

"How will you know when I am more mature?" he persisted.

"I will know because you will have gone an entire month without asking about ointments or magic, for patience is one of the most important virtues a *mundumugu* can possess." I got to my feet. "Now take my gourds to the river and fill them with water," I said, indicating two empty water gourds.

"Yes, Koriba," he said dejectedly.

While I was waiting for him, I went into my hut, activated my computer, and instructed Maintenance to make a minor orbital adjustment that would bring rain and cooler air to the western plains.

This done, I slung my pouch around my neck and went back out into my *boma* to see if Ndemi had returned, but instead of my youthful apprentice, I found Wambu, Koinnage's senior wife, waiting for me, bristling with barely controlled fury.

"*Jambo*, Wambu," I said.

"*Jambo*, Koriba," she replied.

"You wish to speak to me?"

She nodded. "It is about the Kenyan woman."

"Oh?"

"Yes," said Wambu. "You must make her leave!"

"What has Mwange done?" I asked.

"I am the senior wife of the paramount chief, am I not?" demanded Wambu.

"That is true."

"She does not treat me with the respect that is my due."

"In what way?" I asked.

"In *all* ways!"

"For example?"

"Her *khanga* is much more beautiful than mine. The colors are brighter, the designs more intricate, the fabric softer."

"She wove her *khanga* on her own loom, in the old way," I said.

"What difference does *that* make?" snapped Wambu.

I frowned. "Do you wish me to make her give you the *khanga*?" I asked, trying to understand her rage.

"No!"

"Then I do not understand," I said.

"You are no different than Koinnage!" she said, obviously frustrated that I could not comprehend her complaint. "You may be a *mundumugu*, but you are still a man!"

"Perhaps if you told me more," I suggested.

"Kibo was as silly as a child," she said, referring to Koinnage's youngest wife, "but I was training her to be a good wife. Now she wants to be like the Kenyan woman."

"But the Kenyan woman," I said, using her terminology, "wants to be like *you*."

"She cannot be like me!" Wambu practically shouted at me. "I am Koinnage's senior wife!"

"I mean that she wants to be a member of the village."

"Impossible!" scoffed Wambu. "She speaks of many strange things."

"Such as?"

"It does not matter! You must make her leave!"

"For wearing a pretty *khanga* and making a good impression on Kibo?" I said.

"Bah!" she snapped. "You are just like Koinnage! You pretend not to understand, but you know she must go!"

"I truly do not understand," I said.

"You are *my mundumugu*, not hers. I will pay you two fat goats to place a *thahu* on her."

"I will not place a curse on Mwange for the reasons you gave me," I said firmly.

She glared at me for a long moment, then spat on the ground, turned on her heel and walked back down the winding path to the village, muttering furiously to herself, practically knocking Ndemi down as he returned with my water gourds.

I spent the next two hours instructing Ndemi in the harvest prayer, then told him to go into the village and bring Mwange back. An hour later Mwange, resplendent in her *khanga*, climbed up my hill, accompanied by Ndemi, and entered my *boma*.

"*Jambo,*" I greeted her.

"*Jambo,* Koriba," she replied. "Ndemi says that you wish to speak to me."

I nodded. "That is true."

"The other women seemed to think I should be frightened."

"I cannot imagine why," I said.

"Perhaps it is because you can call down the lightning, and change hyenas into insects, and kill your enemies from miles away," suggested Ndemi helpfully.

"Perhaps," I said.

"Why have you sent for me?" asked Mwange.

I paused for a moment, trying to think of how best to approach the subject. "There is a problem with your clothing," I said at last.

"But I am wearing a *khanga* that I wove on my own loom," she said, obviously puzzled.

"I know," I responded. "But the quality of the fabric and the subtlety of the colors, have caused a certain . . ." I searched for the proper word.

"Resentment?" she suggested.

"Precisely," I answered, grateful that she so quickly comprehended the situation. "I think it would be best if you were to weave some less colorful garments."

I half-expected her to protest, but she surprised me by agreeing immediately.

"Certainly," she said. "I have no wish to offend my neighbors. May I ask who objected to my *khanga*?"

"Why?"

"I'd like to make her a present of it."

"It was Wambu," I said.

"I should have realized the effect my clothing would have. I am truly sorry, Koriba."

"Anyone may make a mistake," I said. "As long as it is corrected, no lasting harm will be done."

"I hope you're right," she said sincerely.

"He is the *mundumugu*," said Ndemi. "He is always right."

"I don't want the women to be resentful of me," continued Mwange. "Perhaps I could find some way to show my good intentions." She paused. "What if I were to offer to teach them to speak Kikuyu?"

"No *manamouki* may be a teacher," I explained. "Only the chiefs and the *mundumugu* may instruct our people."

"That's not very efficient," she said. "It may very well be that someone besides yourself and the chiefs has something to offer."

"It is possible," I agreed. "Now let me ask you a question."

"What is it?"

"Did you come to Kirinyaga to be efficient?"

She sighed. "No," she admitted. She paused for a moment. "Is there anything else?"

"No."

"Then I think I'd better go back and begin weaving my new fabric."

I nodded my approval, and she walked back down the long, winding path to the village.

"When I become *mundumugu*," said Ndemi, watching her retreating figure, "I will not allow any *manamoukis* to argue with *me*."

"A *mundumugu* must also show understanding," I said. "Mwange is new here, and has much to learn."

"About Kirinyaga?"

I shook my head. "About *manamoukis*."

Life proceeded smoothly and uneventfully for almost six weeks, until just after the short rains. Then one morning, just as I was preparing to go down into the village to bless the scarecrows, three of the women came up the path to my *boma*.

There was Sabo, the widow of old Kadamu, and Bori, the second wife of Sabana, and Wambu.

"We must speak with you, *mundumugu*," said Wambu.

I sat down, cross-legged, in front of my hut, and waited for them to seat themselves opposite me.

"You may speak," I said.

"It is about the Kenyan woman," said Wambu.

"Oh?" I said. "I thought the problem was solved."

"It is not."

"Did she not present you with her *khanga* as a gift?" I asked.

"Yes."

"You are not wearing it," I noted.

"It does not fit," said Wambu.

"It is only a piece of cloth," I said. "How can it not fit?"

"It does not fit," she repeated adamantly.

I shrugged. "What is this new problem?"

"She flaunts the traditions of the Kikuyu," said Wambu.

I turned to the other women. "Is this true?" I asked.

Sabo nodded. "She is a married woman, and she has not shaved her head."

"And she keeps flowers in her hut," added Bori.

"It is not the custom for Kenyan women to shave their heads," I replied. "I will instruct her to do so. As for the flowers, they are not in violation of our laws."

"But *why* does she keep them?" persisted Bori.

"Perhaps she thinks they are pleasing to the eye," I suggested.

"But now my daughter wants to grow flowers, and she answers with disrespect when I tell it her is more important to grow food to eat."

"And now the Kenyan woman has made a throne for her husband, Nkobe," put in Sabo.

"A throne?" I repeated.

"She put a back and arms on his sitting stool," said Sabo. "What man besides a chief sits upon a throne? Does she think Nkobe will replace Koinnage?"

"*Never!*" snarled Wambu.

"And she has made another throne for herself," continued Sabo. "Even Wambu does not sit atop a throne."

"These are not thrones, but chairs," I said.

"Why can she not use stools, like all the other members of the village?" demanded Sabu.

"I think she is a witch," said Wambu.

"Why do you say that?" I asked.

"Just look at her," said Wambu. "She has seen the long rains come and go thirty-five times, and yet her back is not bent, and her skin is not wrinkled, and she has all her teeth."

"Her vegetables grow better than ours," added Sabo, "and yet she spends less time planting and tending to them than we do." She paused. "I think she *must* be a witch."

"And although she carries with her the worst of all *thahus*, that of barrenness, she acts as if she is not cursed at all," said Bori.

"And her new garments are still more beautiful than ours," muttered Sabo sullenly.

"That is true," agreed Bori. "Now Sabana is displeased with me because his *kikoi* is not so bright and soft as Nkobe's."

"And my daughters all want thrones instead of sitting stools," added Sabo. "I tell them that we have scarcely enough wood for the fire, and they say that this is more important. She has turned their heads. They no longer respect their elders."

"The young women all listen to her, as if *she* were the wife of a chief instead of a barren *manamouki*," complained Wambu. "You must send her away, Koriba."

"Are you giving me an order, Wambu?" I asked softly, and the other two women immediately fell silent.

"She is an evil witch, and she must go," insisted Wambu, her outrage overcoming her fear of disobeying her *mundumugu*.

"She is not a witch," I said, "for if she were, then I, your *mundumugu*, would certainly know it. She is just a *manamouki* who is trying to learn our ways, and who, as you note, carries the terrible *thahu* of barrenness with her."

"If she is less than a witch, she is still more than a *manamouki*," said Sabo.

"More in what way?" I asked.

"Just more," she answered with a sullen expression.

Which totally summed up the problem.

"I will speak to her again," I said.

"And you will make her shave her head?" demanded Wambu.

"Yes."

"And remove the flowers from her hut?"

"I will discuss it."

"Perhaps you can tell Nkobe to beat her from time to time," added Sabo. "Then she would not act so much like a chief's wife."

"I feel very sorry for him," said Bori.

"For Nkobe?" I asked.

Bori nodded. "To be cursed with such a wife, and further, to have no children."

"He is a good man," agreed Sabo. "He deserves better than the Kenyan woman."

"It is my understanding that he is perfectly happy with Mwange," I said.

"That is all the more reason to pity him, for being so foolish," said Wambu.

"Have you come here to talk about Mwange or Nkobe?" I asked.

"We have said what we have come to say," replied Wambu, getting to her feet. "You must do something, *mundumugu*."

"I will look into the matter," I said.

She walked down the path to the village, followed by Sabo. Bori, her back bent from carrying firewood all her life, her stomach distended from producing three sons and five daughters, all but nine of her teeth missing, her legs permanently bowed from some childhood disease, Bori, who had seen but thirty-four long rains, stood before me for a moment.

"She really *is* a witch, Koriba," she said. "You have only to look at her to know it."

Then she, too, left my hill and returned to the village.

Once again I summoned Mwange to my *boma*.

She came up the path with the graceful stride of a young girl, lithe and lean and filled with energy.

"How old are you, Mwange?" I asked as she approached me.

"Thirty-eight," she replied. "I usually tell people that I'm thirty-five, though," she added with a smile. She stood still for a moment. "Is that why you asked me to come here? To talk about my age?"

"No," I said. "Sit down, Mwange."

She seated herself on the dirt by the ashes of my morning fire, and I squatted across from her.

"How are you adjusting to your new life on Kirinyaga?" I asked at last.

"Very well," she said enthusiastically. "I've made many friends, and I find that I don't miss the amenities of Kenya at all."

"Then you are happy here?"

"Very."

"Tell me about your friends."

"Well, my closest friend is Kibo, Koinnage's youngest wife, and I have helped Sumi and Kalena with their gardens, and—"

"Have you no friends among the older women?" I interrupted.

"Not really," she admitted.

"Why should that be?" I asked. "They are women of your own age."

"We don't seem to have anything to talk about."

"Do you find them unfriendly?" I asked.

She considered the question. "Ndemi's mother has always been very kind to me. The others could be a little friendlier, I suppose, but. I imagine that's just because most of them are senior wives and are very busy running their households."

"Did it ever occur to you that there could be some other reason why they are not friendly?" I suggested.

"What are you getting at?" she asked, suddenly alert.

"There is a problem," I said.

"Oh?"

"Some of the older women resent your presence."

"Because I'm an immigrant?" she asked.

I shook my head. "No."

"Then why?" she persisted, genuinely puzzled.

"It is because we have a very rigid social order here, and you have not yet fit in."

"I thought I was fitting in very well," she said defensively.

"You were mistaken."

"Give me an example."

I looked at her. "You know that Kikuyu wives must shave their heads, and yet you have not done so."

She sighed and touched her hair. "I know," she replied. "I've been meaning to, but I'm very fond of it. I'll shave my head tonight." She seemed visibly relieved. "Is that what this is all about?"

"No," I said. "That is merely an outward sign of the problem."

"Then I don't understand."

"It is difficult to explain," I said. "Your *khangas* are more pleasing to the eye than theirs. Your garden grows better. You are as old as Wambu, but appear younger than her daughters. In their minds, these things set you apart from them and make you more than a *manamouki*. The corollary, which they have not yet voiced but must surely feel, is that if you are somehow *more*, then this makes them somehow *less*."

"What do you expect me to do?" she asked. "Wear rags and let my gardens go to seed?"

"No," I said. "I do not expect that."

"Then what can I do?" she continued. "You're telling me that they feel threatened because I am competent." She paused. "*You* are a competent man, Koriba. You have been schooled in Europe and America, you can read and write and work a computer. And yet I notice that you feel no need to hide your talents."

"I am a *mundumugu*," I said. "I live alone on my hill, removed from the village, and I am viewed with awe and fear by my people. This is the function of a *mundumugu*. It is not the function of a *manamouki*, who must live in the village and find her place in the social order of the tribe."

"That's what I am trying to do," she said in frustration.

"Do not try so hard."

"If you're not telling me to be incompetent, then I *still* don't understand."

"One does not fit in by being different," I said. "For example, I know that you bring flowers into your house. Doubtless they are fragrant and pleasing to the eye, but no other woman in the village decorates her hut with flowers."

"That's not true," she said defensively. "Sumi does."

"If so, then she does it because *you* do it," I pointed out. "Can you see that this is even more threatening to the older women than if you alone kept flowers, for it challenges their authority?"

She stared at me, trying to comprehend.

"They have spent their entire lives achieving their positions within the tribe," I continued, "and now you have come here and taken a position entirely outside of their order. We have a new world to populate: You are barren, but far from feeling shame or grief, you act as though this is not a terrible *thahu*. Such an attitude is contrary to their experience, just as decorating your house with flowers or creating *khangas* with intricate patterns is contrary to their experience, and thus they feel threatened."

"I still don't see what I can do about it," she protested. "I gave my original *khangas* to Wambu, but she refuses to wear them. And I have offered to show Bori how to get a greater yield from her gardens, but she won't listen."

"Of course not," I replied. "Senior wives will not accept advice from a *manamouki*, any more than a chief would accept advice from a newly circumcised young man. You must simply"—here I switched to English, for there is no comparable term in Swahili—"maintain a low profile. If you do so, in time the problems will go away."

She paused for a moment, considering what I had told her.

"I'll try," she said at last.

"And if you *must* do something that will call attention to yourself," I continued, reverting to Swahili, "try to do it in a way that will not offend."

"I didn't even know I *was* offending," she said. "How am I to avoid it if I'm calling attention to myself?"

"There are ways," I answered. "Take, for example, the chair that you built."

"Tom has had back spasms for years," she said. "I built the chair because he couldn't get enough support from a stool. Am I supposed to let my husband suffer because some of the women don't believe in chairs?"

"No," I said. "But you can tell the younger women that Nkobe ordered you to build the chair, and thus the stigma will not be upon you."

"Then it will be upon him."

I shook my head. "Men have far greater leeway here than women. There will be no stigma upon him for ordering his *manamouki* to see to his comfort." I paused long enough for the thought to sink in. "Do you understand?"

She sighed. "Yes."

"And you will do as I suggest?"

"If I'm to live in peace with my neighbors, I suppose I must."

"There is always an alternative," I said.

She shook her head vigorously. "I've dreamed of a place like this all my life, and nobody is going to make me leave it now that I'm here. I'll do whatever I have to do."

"Good," I said, getting to my feet to signify that the interview was over. "Then the problem will soon be solved."

But, of course, it wasn't.

I spent the next two weeks visiting a neighboring village whose chief had died quite suddenly. He had no sons and no brothers, and the line of succession was in doubt. I listened to all the applicants to the throne, discussed the situation with the Council of Elders until there was unanimity, presided at the ceremony that installed the new chief in his ceremonial robes and headdress, and finally returned to my own village.

As I climbed the path to my *boma*, I saw a female figure sitting just outside my hut. I drew closer and saw that it was Shima, Ndemi's mother.

"*Jambo*, Koriba," she said.

"*Jambo*, Shima," I responded.

"You are well, I trust."

"As well as an old man can feel after walking for most of the day," I responded, sitting down opposite her. I looked around my *boma*. "I do not see Ndemi."

"I sent him to the village for the afternoon, because I wished to speak to you alone."

"Does this concern Ndemi?" I asked.

She shook her head. "It is about Mwange."

I sighed wearily. "Proceed."

"I am not like the other women, Koriba," she began. "I have always been good to the Mwange."

"So she has told me."

"Her ways do not bother me," she continued. "After all, someday I shall be the mother of the *mundumugu*, and while there can be many senior wives, there can be only one *mundumugu* and one *mundumugu's* mother."

"This is true," I said, waiting for her to get to the point of her visit.

"Therefore, I have befriended Mwange, and have shown her many kindnesses, and she has responded in kind."

"I am pleased to hear it."

"And because I have befriended her," continued Shima, "I have felt great compassion for her, because as you know she carries the *thahu* of barrenness. And it seemed to me that, since Nkobe is such a wealthy man, that he should take another wife to help Mwange with the work on the *shamba* and to produce sons and daughters." She paused. "My daughter Shuni, as you know, will be circumcised before the short rains come, and so I approached Mwange as a friend, and as the mother of the future *mundumugu*, to suggest that Nkobe pay the bride price for Shuni." Here she paused again, and frowned. "She got very mad and yelled at me. You must speak to her, Koriba. A rich man like Nkobe should not be forced to live with only a barren wife."

"Why do you keep calling Nkobe a rich man?" I asked. "His *shamba* is small, and he has only six cattle."

"His family is rich," she stated. "Ndemi told me that they have many men and machines to do their planting and harvesting."

Thank you for nothing, little Ndemi, I thought irritably. Aloud I said: "All that is back on Earth. Here Nkobe is a poor man."

"Even if he is poor," said Shima, "he will not remain poor, for grain and vegetables grow for Mwange as for no one else, as if this is Ngai's blessing to make up for His *thahu* of barrenness." She stared at me. "You must talk to her, Koriba. This would be a good thing. Shuni is very obedient and hard-working, and she already likes Mwange very much. We will not demand a large bride price, for we know that the *mundumugu's* family will never go hungry."

"Why did you not wait for Nkobe to approach you, as is the custom?" I asked.

"I thought if I explained my idea to Mwange, she would see the wisdom of it and speak to Nkobe herself, for he listens to her more than most husbands listen to their wives, and surely the thought of a fertile woman who would share her chores would appeal to her."

"Well, you have presented your idea to her," I said. "Now it is up to Nkobe to make the offer or choose not to."

"But she says that she will permit him to marry no one else," answered Shima, more puzzled than outraged, "as if a *manamouki* could stop her husband from buying another wife. She is ignorant of our ways, Koriba, and for this reason you must speak with her. You must point out that she should be grateful to have another woman with whom to speak and share the work, and she should not want Nkobe to die without having fathered any children just because *she* has been cursed." She hesitated for a moment, and then concluded: "And you should remind her that Shuni will someday be sister to the *mundumugu*."

"I am glad that you are so concerned about Mwange's future," I said at last.

She caught the trace of sarcasm in my voice.

"Is it so wrong to be concerned about my little Shuni as well?" she demanded.

"No," I admitted. "No, it is not wrong."

"Oh!" said Shima, as if she had suddenly remembered something important. "When you speak to Mwange, remind her that she is named for my sister."

"I do not intend to speak to Mwange at all."

"Oh?"

"No," I said. "As you yourself pointed out, this is not her concern. I will speak to Nkobe."

"And you will mention Shuni?" she persisted.

"I will speak to Nkobe," I answered noncommittally.

She got to her feet and prepared to leave.

"You can do me a favor, Shima," I said.

"Oh?"

I nodded. "Have Ndemi come to my *boma* immediately. I have many tasks for him to do here."

"How can you be sure, since you have only just returned?"

"I am sure," I said adamantly.

She looked across my *boma*, still the protective mother. "I can see no chores that have been left undone."

"Then I will find some," I said.

I went down to the village in the afternoon, for old Siboki needed ointments to keep the pain from his joints, and Koinnage had asked me to help him settle a dispute between Njoro and Sangora concerning the ownership of a calf that their jointly owned cow had just produced.

When I had finished my business there, I placed charms on some of the scarecrows, and then, in midafternoon, I walked over to Nkobe's *shamba*, where I found him herding his cattle.

"*Jambo*, Koriba!" he greeted me, waving his hand.

"*Jambo*, Nkobe," I replied, approaching him.

"Would you like to come into my hut for some *pombe?*" he offered. "Mwange just brewed it yesterday."

"Thank you for the offer, but I do not care to drink warm *pombe* on a hot afternoon like this."

"It's actually quite cool," he said. "She buries the gourd in the ground to keep it that way."

"Then I will have some," I acquiesced, falling into step beside him as he drove his cattle toward his *boma*.

Mwange was waiting for us, and she invited us into the cool interior of the hut and poured our *pombe* for us, then began to leave, for *manamoukis* do not listen to the conversation of men.

"Stay here, Mwange," I said.

"You're sure?" she said.

"Yes."

She shrugged and sat on the floor, with her back propped up against a wall of the hut.

"What brings you here, Koriba?" asked Nkobe, sitting gingerly upon his chair, and I could see that his back was troubling him. "You have not paid us a visit before."

"The *mundumugu* rarely visits those who are healthy enough to visit him," I replied.

"Then this is a special occasion," said Nkobe.

"Yes," I replied, sipping my *pombe*. "This is a special occasion."

"What is it this time?" asked Mwange warily.

"What do you mean, 'this time'?" said Nkobe sharply.

"There have been some minor problems," I answered, "none of which concern you."

"Anything that affects Mwange concerns me," responded Nkobe. "I am not blind or deaf, Koriba. I know that the older women have refused to accept her—and I'm getting more than a little bit angry about it. She has gone out of her way to fit in here, and has met them more than halfway."

"I did not come here to discuss Mwange with you," I said.

"Oh?" he said suspiciously.

"Are you saying we have a problem that concerns *him?*" demanded Mwange.

"It concerns both of you," I replied. "That is why I have come here."

"All right, Koriba—what is it?" said Nkobe.

"You have made a good effort to fit into the community and to live as a Kikuyu, Nkobe," I said. "And yet there is one more thing that you will be expected to do, and it is this that I have come to discuss with you."

"And what is that?"

"Sooner or later, you will be expected to take another wife."

"I knew it!" said Mwange.

"I'm very happy with the wife I have," said Nkobe with unconcealed hostility.

"That may be," I said, draining the last of my *pombe*, "but you have no children, and as Mwange gets older she will need someone to help her with her duties."

"Now you listen to me!" snapped Nkobe. "I came here because I thought it would make Mwange happy. So far she's been ostracized and shunned and gossiped about, and now you're telling me that I have to take another wife into my house so that Mwange can keep being spat on by the other women? We don't need this, Koriba! I was just as happy on my farm in Kenya. I can go back there any time I want."

"If that is the way you feel, then perhaps you should return to Kenya," I said.

"*Tom*," said Mwange, staring at him, and he fell silent.

"It is true that you do not have to stay," I continued. "But you are Kikuyus, living on a Kikuyu world, and if you do stay, you will be expected to act as Kikuyus."

"There's no law that says a Kikuyu man must take a second wife," said Nkobe sullenly.

"No, there is no such law," I admitted. "Nor is there a law that says a Kikuyu man must father children. But these are our traditions, and you will be expected to abide by them."

"To hell with them!" he muttered in English.

Mwange laid a restraining hand on his arm. "There is a coterie of young warriors who live beyond the forest," she said. "Why don't *they* marry some of the young women? Why should the men of the village monopolize them all?"

"They cannot afford wives," I said. "That is why they live alone."

"That's *their* problem," said Nkobe.

"I've made many sacrifices in the name of communal harmony," said Mwange, "but this is asking too much, Koriba. We are happy just the way we are, and we intend to stay this way."

"You will not remain happy."

"What does that mean?" she demanded.

"Next month is the circumcision ritual," I said. "When it is over, there will be many girls eligible for marriage, and since you are barren, it is only reasonable to suppose that a number of their families will suggest that Nkobe pay the bride price for their daughters. He may refuse once, he may refuse twice, but if he continues to refuse, he will offend most of the village. They will assume that because he comes from Kenya he feels their women are not good enough for him, and they will be further offended by the fact that he refuses to have children with which to populate our empty planet."

"Then I'll explain my reasons to them," said Nkobe.

"They will not understand," I answered.

"No, they will not understand," agreed Mwange unhappily.

"Then they will have to learn to live with it," said Nkobe firmly.

"And you will have to learn to live with silence and animosity," I said. "Is this the life you envisioned when you came to Kirinyaga?"

"Of course not!" snapped Nkobe. "But nothing can make me—"

"We will think about it, Koriba," interrupted Mwange.

Nkobe turned to his wife, stunned. "What are you saying?"

"I am saying that we will think about it," repeated Mwange.

"That is all that I ask," I said, getting to my feet and walking to the door of the hut.

"You demand a lot, Koriba," said Mwange bitterly.

"I demand nothing," I replied. "I merely suggest."

"Coming from the *mundumugu*, is there a difference?"

I did not answer her, because in truth there was no difference whatsoever.

"You seem unhappy, Koriba," said Ndemi.

He had just finished feeding my chickens and my goats, and now he sat down beside me in the shade of my acacia tree.

"I am," I said.

"Mwange," he said, nodding his head.

"Mwange," I agreed.

Two weeks had passed since I had visited her and Nkobe.

"I saw her this morning, when I went to the river to fill your gourds," said Ndemi. "She, too, seems unhappy."

"She is," I said. "And there is nothing that I can do about it."

"But you are the *mundumugu*."

"I know."

"You are the most powerful of men," continued Ndemi. "Surely you can put an end to her sorrow."

I sighed. "The *mundumugu* is both the most powerful and the weakest of men. In Mwange's case, I am the weakest."

"I do not understand."

"The *mundumugu* is the most powerful of men when it comes to interpreting the law," I said. "But he is also the weakest of men, for it is he, of all men, who must be bound by that law, no matter what else happens." I paused. "I should allow her to be what she can be, instead of being merely a *manamouki*. And failing that, I should make her leave Kirinyaga and return to Kenya." I sighed again. "But she must behave like a *manamouki* if she is to have a life here, and she has broken no law that would allow me to force her to leave."

Ndemi frowned. "Being a *mundumugu* can be more difficult than I thought."

I smiled at him and placed a hand upon his head. "Tomorrow I will begin to teach you to make the ointments that cure the sick."

"Really?" he said, his face brightening.

I nodded. "Your last statement tells me that you are no longer a child."

"I have not been a child for many rains," he protested.

"Do not say any more," I told him with a wry smile, "or we will do more harvest prayers instead."

He immediately fell silent, and I looked out across the distant savannah, where a swirling tower of dust raced across the arid plain, and wondered, for perhaps the thousandth time, what to do about Mwange.

How long I sat thus, motionless, I do not know, but eventually I felt Ndemi tugging at the blanket I had wrapped around my shoulders.

"Women," he whispered.

"What?" I said, not comprehending.

"From the village," he said, gesturing toward the path that led to my *boma*.

I looked where he indicated and saw four of the village women approaching. There was Wambu, and Sabo, and Bori, and with them this time was Morina, the second wife of Kimoda.

"Should I leave?" asked Ndemi.

I shook my head. "If you are to become a *mundumugu*, it is time you started listening to a *mundumugu's* problems."

The four women stopped perhaps ten feet away from me.

"*Jambo*," I said, staring at them.

"The Kenyan witch must leave!" said Wambu.

"We have been through this before," I said.

"But now she has broken the law," said Wambu.

"Oh?" I said. "In what way?"

Wambu grabbed Morina by the arm and shoved her even closer to me. "Tell him," she said triumphantly.

"She has bewitched my daughter," said Morina, obviously uneasy in my presence.

"How has Mwange bewitched your daughter?" I asked.

"My Muri was a good, obedient child," said Morina. "She always helped me grind the grain, and she dutifully cared for her two younger brothers when I was working in the fields, and she never left the thorn gate open at night so that hyenas could enter our *boma* and kill our goats and cattle." She paused, and I could see that she was trying very hard not to cry. "All she could talk about since the last long rains was her forthcoming circumcision ceremony, and who she hoped would pay the bride price for her. She was a perfect daughter, a daughter any mother would be proud of." Now a tear trickled down her cheek. "And then the Kenyan woman came, and Muri spent her time with her, and now—" suddenly the single tear became a veritable flood "—now she tells me that she refuses to be circumcised. She will never marry and she will die an old, barren woman!"

Morina could speak no more, and began beating her breasts with her clenched fists.

"That is not all," added Wambu. "The reason Muri does not wish to be circumcised is because the Kenyan woman herself has not been circumcised. And yet the Kenyan woman has married a Kikuyu man, and has tried to live among us as his *manamouki*." She glared at me. "She has broken the law, Koriba! We must cast her out!"

"I am the *mundumugu*," I replied sternly. "I will decide what must be done."

"You *know* what must be done!" said Wambu furiously.

"That is all," I said. "I will hear no more."

Wambu glared at me, but did not dare to disobey me, and finally, turning on her heel, she stalked back down the path to the village, followed by Sabo and the still-wailing Morina.

Bori stood where she was for an extra moment, then turned to me.

"It is as I told you before, Koriba," she said, almost apologetically. "She really *is* a witch."

Then she, too, began walking back to the village.

"What will you do, Koriba?" asked Ndemi.

"The law is clear," I said wearily. "No uncircumcised woman may live with a Kikuyu man as his wife."

"Then you will make her leave Kirinyaga?"

"I will offer her a choice," I said, "and I will hope that she chooses to leave."

"It is too bad," said Ndemi. "She has tried very hard to be a good *manamouki*."

"I know," I said.

"Then why is Ngai visiting her with such unhappiness?"

"Because sometimes trying is not enough."

We stood at Haven—Mwange, Nkobe, and I—awaiting the Maintenance ship's arrival.

"I am truly sorry that things did not work out," I said sincerely.

Nkobe glared at me, but said nothing.

"It didn't have to end this way," said Mwange bitterly.

"We had no choice," I said. "If we are to create our Utopia here on Kirinyaga, we must be bound by its rules."

"The fact that a rule exists does not make it right, Koriba," she said. "I gave up almost everything to live here, but I will not let them mutilate me in the name of some foolish custom."

"Without our traditions, we are not Kikuyu, but only Kenyans who live on another world," I pointed out.

"There is a difference between tradition and stagnation, Koriba," she said. "If you stifle every variation in taste and behavior in the name of the former, you achieve only the latter." She paused. "I would have been a good member of the community."

"But a poor *manamouki*," I said. "The leopard may be a stealthy hunter and fearsome killer, but he does not belong among a pride of lions."

"Lions and leopards have been extinct for a long time, Koriba," she said. "We are talking about human beings, not animals, and no matter how many rules you make and no matter how many traditions you invoke, you cannot make all human being think and feel and act alike."

"It's coming," announced Nkobe as the Maintenance ship broke through the thin cloud cover.

"*Kwaheri*, Nkobe," I said, extending my hand.

He looked contemptuously at my hand for a moment, then turned his back and continued watching the Maintenance ship.

I turned to Mwange.

"I tried, Koriba," she said. "I really did."

"No one ever tried harder," I said. "*Kwaheri*, Mwange."

She stared at me, her face suddenly an emotionless mask.

"Good-bye, Koriba," she said in English. "And my name is Wanda."

The next morning Shima came to me to complain that Shuni had rejected the suitor that had been arranged for her.

Two days later Wambu complained to me that Kibo, Koinnage's youngest wife, had decorated her hut with colorful ribbons, and was beginning to let her hair grow.

And the morning after that, Kimi, who had only one son, announced that she wanted no more children.

"I thought it had ended," I said with a sigh as I watched Sangora, Kimi's distressed husband, walk back down the path to the village.

"That is because you made a mistake, Koriba."

"Why do you say that?"

"You believed the wrong story," answered Ndemi with the confidence of youth.

"Oh?"

He nodded. "You believed the story about the Ugly Buffalo."

"And which story should I have believed?"

"The story of the *mundumugu* and the serpent."

"Why do you think one story is more worthy of belief than the other?" I asked him.

"Does not the story of the *mundumugu* and the serpent tell us that we cannot be rid of that which Ngai created simply because we find it repugnant or unsettling?"

"That is true," I said.

Ndemi smiled and held up three fingers. "Shuni, Kibo, Kimi," he said, counting them off. "Three serpents have returned already. There are ninety-seven yet to come."

And suddenly I had the awful premonition that he was right.

BEARS DISCOVER FIRE

by **TERRY BISSON**

Terry Bisson's sad and funny and thoroughly engaging short story, "Bears Discover Fire," took the science fiction community by storm. It was published in the August 1990 issue of *Asimov's*, and it went on to win the Hugo, the Nebula, the Theodore Sturgeon Memorial Award, and the magazine's Readers' Award Poll. The author created "The No-Frills Books" in 1981. His other best known works are *Talking Man*, *Fire on the Mountain*, *Voyage to the Red Planet*, and *Car Talk with Click and Clack, the Tappet Brothers*—a book he co-wrote with Tom and Ray Magliozzi. A native of Kentucky, Terry now resides in New York City.

I was driving with my brother, the preacher, and my nephew, the preacher's son, on I-65 just north of Bowling Green when we got a flat. It was Sunday night and we had been to visit Mother at the Home. We were in my car. The flat caused what you might call knowing groans since, as the old-fashioned one in my family (so they tell me), I fix my own tires, and my brother is always telling me to get radials and quit buying old tires.

But if you know how to mount and fix tires yourself, you can pick them up for almost nothing.

Since it was a left rear tire, I pulled over left, onto the median grass. The way my Caddy stumbled to a stop, I figured the tire was ruined. "I guess there's no need asking if you have any of that *FlatFix* in the trunk," said Wallace.

"Here, son, hold the light," I said to Wallace Jr. He's old enough to want to help and not old enough (yet) to think he knows it all. If I'd married and had kids, he's the kind I'd have wanted.

An old Caddy has a big trunk that tends to fill up like a shed. Mine's a '56. Wallace was wearing his Sunday shirt, so he didn't offer to help while I pulled magazines, fishing tackle, a wooden tool box, some old clothes, a comealong wrapped in a grass sack, and a tobacco sprayer out of the way, looking for my jack. The spare looked a little soft.

The light went out. "Shake it, son," I said.

It went back on. The bumper jack was long gone, but I carry a little ¼ ton hydraulic. I finally found it under Mother's old *Southern Livings*, 1978–1986. I had been meaning to drop them at the dump. If Wallace hadn't been along, I'd have let Wallace Jr. position the jack under the axle, but I got on my knees and did it myself. There's nothing wrong with a boy learning to change a tire. Even if you're not going to fix and mount them, you're still going to have to change a few in this life. The light went off again before I had the wheel off the ground. I was surprised at how dark the night was already. It was late October and beginning to get cool. "Shake it again, son," I said.

It went back on but it was weak. Flickery.

"With radials you just don't *have* flats," Wallace explained in that voice he uses when he's talking to a number of people at once; in this case, Wallace Jr. and myself. "And even when you *do*, you just squirt them with this stuff called *FlatFix* and you just drive on: $3.95 the can."

"Uncle Bobby can fix a tire hisself," said Wallace Jr., out of loyalty I presume.

"*Him*self," I said from halfway under the car. If it was up to Wallace, the boy would talk like what Mother used to call "a helock from the gorges of the mountains." But drive on radials.

"Shake that light again," I said. It was about gone. I spun the lugs off into the hubcap and pulled the wheel. The tire had blown out along the sidewall. "Won't be fixing this one," I said. Not that I cared. I have a pile as tall as a man out by the barn.

The light went out again, then came back better than ever as I was fitting the spare over the lugs. "Much better," I said. There was a flood of dim orange flickery light. But when I turned to find the lug nuts, I was surprised to see that the flashlight the boy was holding was dead. The light was coming from two bears at the edge of the trees, holding torches. They were big, three-hundred pounders, standing about five feet tall. Wallace Jr. and his father had seen them and were standing perfectly still. It's best not to alarm bears.

I fished the lug nuts out of the hubcap and spun them on. I usually like to put a little oil on them, but this time I let it go. I reached under the car and let the jack down and pulled it out. I was relieved to see that the spare was high enough to drive on. I put the jack and the lug wrench and the flat into the trunk. Instead of replacing the hubcap, I put it in there too. All this time, the bears never made a move. They just held the torches up, whether out of curiosity or helpfulness, there was no way of knowing. It looked like there may have been more bears behind them, in the trees.

Opening three doors at once, we got into the car and drove off. Wallace was the first to speak. "Looks like bears have discovered fire," he said.

When we first took Mother to the Home, almost four years (forty-seven months) ago, she told Wallace and me she was ready to die. "Don't worry about me, boys," she whispered, pulling us both down so the nurse wouldn't hear. "I've drove a million miles and I'm ready to pass over to the other shore. I won't have long to linger here." She drove a consolidated school bus for thirty-nine years. Later, after Wallace left, she told me about her dream. A bunch of doctors were sitting around in a circle discussing her case. One said, "We've done all we can for her, boys, let's let her go." They all turned their hands up and smiled. When she didn't die that fall, she seemed disappointed, though as spring came she forgot about it, as old people will.

In addition to taking Wallace and Wallace Jr. to see Mother on Sunday nights, I go myself on Tuesdays and Thursdays. I usually find her sitting in front of the TV, even though she doesn't watch it. The nurses keep it on all the time. They say the old folks like the flickering. It soothes them down.

"What's this I hear about bears discovering fire?" she said on Tuesday. "It's true," I told her as I combed her long white hair with the shell comb Wallace had bought her from Florida. Monday there had been a story in the Louisville *Courier-Journal*, and Tuesday one on NBC or CBS Nightly News. People were seeing bears all over the state, and in Virginia as well. They had quit hibernating, and were apparently planning to spend the winter in the medians of the interstates. There have always been bears in the mountains of Virginia, but not here in western Kentucky, not for almost a hundred years. The last one was killed when Mother was a girl. The theory in the *Courier-Journal* was that they were following I-65 down from the forests of Michigan and Canada, but one old man from Allen County (interviewed on nationwide TV) said that there had always been a few bears left back in the hills, and they had come out to join the others now that they had discovered fire.

"They don't hibernate any more," I said. "They make a fire and keep it going all winter."

"I declare," Mother said. "What'll they think of next!" The nurse came to take her tobacco away, which is the signal for bedtime.

Every October, Wallace Jr. stays with me while his parents go to camp. I realize how backward that sounds, but there it is. My brother is a minister (House of the Righteous Way, Reformed), but he makes two thirds of his living in real estate. He and Elizabeth go to a Christian Success Retreat in South Carolina, where people from all over the country practice selling things to one another. I know what it's like not because they've ever bothered to tell me, but because I've seen the Revolving Equity Success Plan ads late at night on TV.

The schoolbus let Wallace Jr. off at my house on Wednesday, the day they left. The boy doesn't have to pack much of a bag when he stays with me. He has his own room here. As the eldest of our family, I hung onto the old home place near Smiths Grove. It's getting run down, but Wallace Jr. and I don't mind. He has his own room in Bowling Green, too, but since Wallace and Elizabeth move to a different house every three months (part of the Plan), he keeps his .22 and his comics, the stuff that's important to a boy his age, in his room here at the home place. It's the room his dad and I used to share.

Wallace Jr. is twelve. I found him sitting on the back porch that overlooks the interstate when I got home from work. I sell crop insurance.

After I changed clothes, I showed him how to break the bead on a tire two ways, with a hammer and by backing a car over it. Like making sorghum, fixing tires by hand is a dying art. The boy caught on fast, though. "Tomorrow I'll show you how to mount your tire with the hammer and a tire iron," I said.

"What I wish is I could see the bears," he said. He was looking across the field to I-65, where the northbound lanes cut off the corner of our field. From the house at night, sometimes the traffic sounds like a waterfall.

"Can't see their fire in the daytime," I said. "But wait till tonight." That night CBS or NBC (I forget which is which) did a special on the bears, which were becoming a story of nationwide interest. They were seen in Kentucky, West Virginia, Missouri, Illinois (southern), and, of course, Virginia. There have always been bears in Virginia. Some characters there were even talking about hunting them. A scientist said they were heading into the states where there is some snow but not too much, and where there is enough timber in the medians for firewood. He had gone in with a video camera, but his shots were just blurry figures sitting around a fire. Another scientist said the bears were attracted by the berries on a new bush that grew only in the medians of the interstates. He claimed this berry was the first new species in recent history, brought about by the mixing of seeds along the highway. He ate one on TV, making a face, and called it a "newberry." A climatic ecologist said that the warm winters (there was no snow last winter in Nashville, and only one flurry in Louisville) had changed the bears' hibernation cycle, and now they were able to remember things from year to year. "Bears may have discovered fire centuries ago," he said, "but forgot it." Another theory was that they had discovered (or remembered) fire when Yellowstone burned, several years ago.

The TV showed more guys talking about bears than it showed bears, and Wallace Jr. and I lost interest. After the supper dishes were done I took the boy out behind the house and down to our fence. Across the interstate and through the trees, we could see the light of the bears' fire. Wallace Jr. wanted to go back to the house and get his

.22 and go shoot one, and I explained why that would be wrong. "Besides," I said, "a .22 wouldn't do much more to a bear than make it mad."

"Besides," I added, "It's illegal to hunt in the medians."

The only trick to mounting a tire by hand, once you have beaten or pried it onto the rim, is setting the bead. You do this by setting the tire upright, sitting on it, and bouncing it up and down between your legs while the air goes in. When the bead sets on the rim, it makes a satis-fying "pop." On Thursday, I kept Wallace Jr. home from school and showed him how to do this until he got it right. Then we climbed our fence and crossed the field to get a look at the bears.

In northern Virginia, according to "Good Morning America," the bears were keeping their fires going all day long. Here in western Kentucky, though, it was still warm for late October and they only stayed around the fires at night. Where they went and what they did in the daytime, I don't know. Maybe they were watching from the new-berry bushes as Wallace Jr. and I climbed the government fence and crossed the northbound lanes. I carried an axe and Wallace Jr. brought his .22, not because he wanted to kill a bear but because a boy likes to carry some kind of a gun. The median was all tangled with brush and vines under the maples, oaks, and sycamores. Even though we were only a hundred yards from the house, I had never been there, and nei-ther had anyone else that I knew of. It was like a created country. We found a path in the center and followed it down across a slow, short stream that flowed out of one grate and into another. The tracks in the gray mud were the first bear signs we saw. There was a musty but not really unpleasant smell. In a clearing under a big hollow beech, where the fire had been, we found nothing but ashes. Logs were drawn up in a rough circle and the smell was stronger. I stirred the ashes and found enough coals left to start a new flame, so I banked them back the way they had been left.

I cut a little firewood and stacked it to one side, just to be neigh-borly.

Maybe the bears were watching us from the bushes even then. There's no way to know. I tasted one of the newberries and spit it out. It was so sweet it was sour, just the sort of thing you would imagine a bear would like.

That evening after supper, I asked Wallace Jr. if he might want to go with me to visit Mother. I wasn't surprised when he said "yes." Kids have more consideration than folks give them credit for. We found her sitting on the concrete front porch of the Home, watching the cars go by on I-65. The nurse said she had been agitated all day. I wasn't surprised by that, either. Every fall as the leaves change, she gets restless, maybe the word is hopeful, again. I brought her into the dayroom and combed her long white hair. "Nothing but bears on TV anymore," the nurse complained, flipping the channels. Wallace Jr. picked up the remote after the nurse left, and we watched a CBS or NBC Special Report about some hunters in Virginia who had gotten their houses torched. The TV interviewed a hunter and his wife whose $117,500 Shenandoah Valley home had burned. She blamed the bears. He didn't blame the bears, but he was suing for compensation from the state since he had a valid hunting license. The state hunting commissioner came on and said that possession of a hunting license didn't prohibit (enjoin, I think, was the word he used) *the hunted* from striking back. I thought that was a pretty liberal view for a state commissioner. Of course, he had a vested interest in not paying off. I'm not a hunter myself.

"Don't bother coming on Sunday," Mother told Wallace Jr. with a wink. "I've drove a million miles and I've got one hand on the gate." I'm used to her saying stuff like that, especially in the fall, but I was afraid it would upset the boy. In fact, he looked worried after we left and I asked him what was wrong.

"How could she have drove a million miles?" he asked. She had told him 48 miles a day for 39 years, and he had worked it out on his calculator to be 336,960 miles.

"Have *driven*," I said. "And it's forty-eight in the morning and forty-eight in the afternoon. Plus there were the football trips. Plus, old folks exaggerate a little." Mother was the first woman school bus driver in the state. She did it every day and raised a family, too. Dad just farmed.

I usually get off the interstate at Smiths Grove, but that night I drove north all the way to Horse Cave and doubled back so Wallace Jr. and I could see the bears' fires. There were not as many as you would think from the TV—one every six or seven miles, hidden back in a clump of trees or under a rocky ledge. Probably they look for water as well as wood. Wallace Jr. wanted to stop, but it's against the law to stop on the interstate and I was afraid the state police would run us off.

There was a card from Wallace in the mailbox. He and Elizabeth were doing fine and having a wonderful time. Not a word about Wallace Jr., but the boy didn't seem to mind. Like most kids his age, he doesn't really enjoy going places with his parents.

* * *

On Saturday afternoon, the Home called my office (Burley Belt Drought & Hail) and left word that Mother was gone. I was on the road. I work Saturdays. It's the only day a lot of part-time farmers are home. My heart literally skipped a beat when I called in and got the message, but only a beat. I had long been prepared. "It's a blessing," I said when I got the nurse on the phone.

"You don't understand" the nurse said. "Not *passed* away, gone. *Ran* away, gone. Your mother has escaped." Mother had gone through the door at the end of the corridor when no one was looking, wedging the door with her comb and taking a bedspread which belonged to the Home. What about her tobacco? I asked. It was gone. That was a sure sign she was planning to stay away. I was in Franklin, and it took me less than an hour to get to the Home on I-65. The nurse told me that Mother had been acting more and more confused lately. Of course they are going to say that. We looked around the grounds, which is only an acre with no trees between the interstate and a soybean field. Then they had me leave a message at the Sheriff's office. I would have to keep paying for her care until she was officially listed as Missing, which would be Monday.

It was dark by the time I got back to the house, and Wallace Jr. was fixing supper. This just involves opening a few cans, already selected and grouped together with a rubber band. I told him his grandmother had gone, and he nodded, saying, "She told us she would be." I called Florida and left a message. There was nothing more to be done. I sat down and tried to watch TV, but there was nothing on. Then, I looked out the back door, and saw the firelight twinkling through the trees across the northbound lane of I-65, and realized I just might know where she had gone to find her.

It was definitely getting colder, so I got my jacket. I told the boy to wait by the phone in case the Sheriff called, but when I looked back, halfway across the field, there he was behind me. He didn't have a jacket. I let him catch up. He was carrying his .22, and I made him leave it leaning against our fence. It was harder climbing the government fence in the dark, at my age, than it had been in the daylight. I am sixty-one. The highway was busy with cars heading south and trucks heading north.

Crossing the shoulder, I got my pants cuffs wet on the long grass, already wet with dew. It is actually bluegrass.

The first few feet into the trees it was pitch black and the boy grabbed my hand. Then it got lighter. At first I thought it was the

moon, but it was the high beams shining like moonlight into the tree-
tops, allowing Wallace Jr. and me to pick our way through the brush.
We soon found the path and its familiar bear smell.

I was wary of approaching the bears at night. If we stayed on the
path we might run into one in the dark, but if we went through the
bushes we might be seen as intruders. I wondered if maybe we
shouldn't have brought the gun.

We stayed on the path. The light seemed to drip down from the
canopy of the woods like rain. The going was easy, especially if we
didn't try to look at the path but let our feet find their own way.

Then through the trees I saw their fire.

The fire was mostly of sycamore and beech branches, the kind of fire
that puts out very little heat or light and lots of smoke. The bears
hadn't learned the ins and outs of wood yet. They did okay at tending
it, though. A large cinnamon brown northern-looking bear was poking
the fire with a stick, adding a branch now and then from a pile at his
side. The others sat around in a loose circle on the logs. Most were
smaller black or honey bears, one was a mother with cubs. Some were
eating berries from a hubcap. Not eating, but just watching the fire,
my mother sat among them with the bedspread from the Home
around her shoulders.

If the bears noticed us, they didn't let on. Mother patted a spot
right next to her on the log and I sat down. A bear moved over to let
Wallace Jr. sit on her other side.

The bear smell is rank but not unpleasant, once you get used to
it. It's not like a barn smell, but wilder. I leaned over to whisper something to Mother and she shook her head. *It would be rude to whisper
around these creatures that don't possess the power of speech*, she let me know
without speaking. Wallace Jr. was silent too. Mother shared the bedspread with us and we sat for what seemed hours, looking into the fire.

The big bear tended the fire, breaking up the dry branches by
holding one end and stepping on them, like people do. He was good at
keeping it going at the same level. Another bear poked the fire from
time to time, but the others left it alone. It looked like only a few of the
bears knew how to use fire, and were carrying the others along. But isn't
that how it is with everything? Every once in a while, a smaller bear
walked into the circle of firelight with an armload of wood and dropped
it onto the pile. Median wood has a silvery cast, like driftwood.

Wallace Jr. isn't fidgety like a lot of kids. I found it pleasant to sit
and stare into the fire. I took a little piece of Mother's *Red Man*, though
I don't generally chew. It was no different from visiting her at the
Home, only more interesting, because of the bears. There were about

eight or ten of them. Inside the fire itself, things weren't so dull, either: little dramas were being played out as fiery chambers were created and then destroyed in a crashing of sparks. My imagination ran wild. I looked around the circle at the bears and wondered what *they* saw. Some had their eyes closed. Though they were gathered together, their spirits still seemed solitary, as if each bear was sitting alone in front of its own fire.

The hubcap came around and we all took some newberries. I don't know about Mother, but I just pretended to eat mine. Wallace Jr. made a face and spit his out. When he went to sleep, I wrapped the bedspread around all three of us. It was getting colder and we were not provided, like the bears, with fur. I was ready to go home, but not Mother. She pointed up toward the canopy of trees, where a light was spreading, and then pointed to herself. Did she think it was angels approaching from on high? It was only the high beams of some southbound truck, but she seemed mighty pleased. Holding her hand, I felt it grow colder and colder in mine.

Wallace Jr. woke me up by tapping on my knee. It was past dawn, and his grandmother had died sitting on the log between us. The fire was banked up and the bears were gone and someone was crashing straight through the woods, ignoring the path. It was Wallace. Two state troopers were right behind him. He was wearing a white shirt, and I realized it was Sunday morning. Underneath his sadness on learning of Mother's death, he looked peeved.

The troopers were sniffing the air and nodding. The bear smell was still strong. Wallace and I wrapped Mother in the bedspread and started with her body back out to the highway. The troopers stayed behind and scattered the bears' fire ashes and flung their firewood away into the bushes. It seemed a petty thing to do. They were like bears themselves, each one solitary in his own uniform.

There was Wallace's Olds 98 on the median, with its radial tires looking squashed on the grass. In front of it there was a police car with a trooper standing beside it, and behind it a funeral home hearse, also an Olds 98.

"First report we've had of them bothering old folks," the trooper said to Wallace. "That's not hardly what happened at all," I said, but nobody asked me to explain. They have their own procedures. Two men in suits got out of the hearse and opened the rear door. That to me was the point at which Mother departed this life. After we put her in, I put my arms around the boy. He was shivering even though it wasn't that cold. Sometimes death will do that, especially at dawn, with the police around and the grass wet, even when it comes as a friend.

We stood for a minute watching the cars pass. "It's a blessing," Wallace said. It's surprising how much traffic there is at 6:22 A.M.

That afternoon, I went back to the median and cut a little firewood to replace what the troopers had flung away. I could see the fire through the trees that night.

I went back two nights later, after the funeral. The fire was going and it was the same bunch of bears, as far as I could tell. I sat around with them a while but it seemed to make them nervous, so I went home. I had taken a handful of newberries from the hubcap, and on Sunday I went with the boy and arranged them on Mother's grave. I tried again, but it's no use, you can't eat them.

Unless you're a bear.

BEGGARS IN SPAIN

by NANCY KRESS

Nancy Kress is the author of ten books: three fantasy novels, four science fiction novels, two collections of short stories, and a book on writing fiction, *Beginnings, Middles, and Ends.* Her most recent novel is *Beggars and Choosers* (Tor 1994), the sequel to *Beggars in Spain* (Avon/Nova 1993). The 1993 book was based on the following powerful novella about a future where babies can be made to order. The story was published in the April 1991 issue of *Asimov's*, and took the SF field by storm. It won the Hugo, the Nebula, and the magazine's own Readers' Award.

The author's fiction has appeared regularly in *Omni, Asimov's,* and other major SF publications. In 1985, she was awarded her first Nebula for the short story, "Out of All Them Bright Stars." Nancy Kress teaches the art of writing at various university workshops, and she is the monthly "Fiction" columnist for *Writer's Digest.* In a former life that still occasionally revives itself, she was a copywriter for Xerox, Bausch & Lomb, Kodak, and various other corporations. Kress lives with her two children, Kevin and Brian, in upstate New York.

"With energy and sleepless vigilance go forward and give us victories."
—Abraham Lincoln, to Major General Joseph Hooker, 1863

1

They sat stiffly on his antique Eames chairs, two people who didn't want to be here, or one person who didn't want to and one who resented the other's reluctance. Dr. Ong had seen this before. Within two minutes he was sure: the woman was the silently furious resister. She would lose. The man would pay for it later, in little ways, for a long time.

"I presume you've performed the necessary credit checks already," Roger Camden said pleasantly, "so let's get right on to details, shall we, doctor?"

"Certainly," Ong said. "Why don't we start by your telling me all the genetic modifications you're interested in for the baby."

The woman shifted suddenly on her chair. She was in her late twenties—clearly a second wife—but already had a faded look, as if keeping up with Roger Camden was wearing her out. Ong could easily believe that. Mrs. Camden's hair was brown, her eyes were brown, her skin had a brown tinge that might have been pretty if her cheeks had had any color. She wore a brown coat, neither fashionable nor cheap, and shoes that looked vaguely orthopedic. Ong glanced at his records for her name: Elizabeth. He would bet people forgot it often.

Next to her, Roger Camden radiated nervous vitality, a man in late middle age whose bullet-shaped head did not match his careful haircut and Italian-silk business suit. Ong did not need to consult his file to recall anything about Camden. A caricature of the bullet-shaped head had been the leading graphic of yesterday's on-line edition of the

Wall Street Journal: Camden had led a major coup in cross-border data-atoll investment. Ong was not sure what cross-border data-atoll investment was.

"A girl," Elizabeth Camden said. Ong hadn't expected her to speak first. Her voice was another surprise: upper-class British. "Blonde. Green eyes. Tall. Slender."

Ong smiled. "Appearance factors are the easiest to achieve, as I'm sure you already know. But all we can do about 'slenderness' is give her a genetic disposition in that direction. How you feed the child will naturally—"

"Yes, yes," Roger Camden said, "that's obvious. Now: intelligence. *High* intelligence. And a sense of daring."

"I'm sorry, Mr. Camden—personality factors are not yet understood well enough to allow genet—"

"Just testing," Camden said, with a smile that Ong thought was probably supposed to be light-hearted.

Elizabeth Camden said, "Musical ability."

"Again, Mrs. Camden, a disposition to be musical is all we can guarantee."

"Good enough," Camden said. "The full array of corrections for any potential gene-linked health problem, of course."

"Of course," Dr. Ong said. Neither client spoke. So far theirs was a fairly modest list, given Camden's money; most clients had to be argued out of contradictory genetic tendencies, alteration overload, or unrealistic expectations. Ong waited. Tension prickled in the room like heat.

"And," Camden said, "no need to sleep."

Elizabeth Camden jerked her head sideways to look out the window.

Ong picked a paper magnet off his desk. He made his voice pleasant. "May I ask how you learned whether that genetic-modification program exists?"

Camden grinned. "You're not denying it exists. I give you full credit for that, Doctor."

Ong held onto his temper. "May I ask how you learned whether the program exists?"

Camden reached into an inner pocket of his suit. The silk crinkled and pulled; body and suit came from different social classes. Camden was, Ong remembered, a Yagaiist, a personal friend of Kenzo Yagai himself. Camden handed Ong hard copy: program specifications.

"Don't bother hunting down the security leak in your data banks, Doctor—you won't find it. But if it's any consolation, neither will anybody else. Now." He leaned suddenly forward. His tone changed. "I know that you've created twenty children so far who don't need to sleep at all. That so far nineteen are healthy, intelligent, and psychologically normal. In fact, better than normal—they're all unusually precocious. The oldest is already four years old and can read in two languages. I know you're thinking of offering this genetic modification on the open market in a few years. All I want is a chance to buy it for my daughter *now*. At whatever price you name."

Ong stood. "I can't possibly discuss this with you unilaterally, Mr. Camden. Neither the theft of our data—"

"Which wasn't a theft—your system developed a spontaneous bubble regurgitation into a public gate, have a hell of a time proving otherwise—"

"—*nor* the offer to purchase this particular genetic modification lies in my sole area of authority. Both have to be discussed with the Institute's Board of Directors."

"By all means, by all means. When can I talk to them, too?"

"You?"

Camden, still seated, looked at him. It occurred to Ong that there were few men who could look so confident eighteen inches below eye level. "Certainly. I'd like the chance to present my offer to whoever has the actual authority to accept it. That's only good business."

"This isn't solely a business transaction, Mr. Camden."

"It isn't solely pure scientific research, either," Camden retorted. "You're a for-profit corporation here. *With* certain tax breaks available only to firms meeting certain fair-practice laws."

For a minute Ong couldn't think what Camden meant. "Fair-practice laws . . ."

". . . are designed to protect minorities who are suppliers. I know, it hasn't ever been tested in the case of customers, except for red-lining in Y-energy installations. But it could be tested, Doctor Ong. Minorities are entitled to the same product offerings as non-minorities. I know the Institute would not welcome a court case, Doctor. None of your twenty genetic beta-test families are either Black or Jewish."

"A court . . . but you're not Black *or* Jewish!"

"I'm a different minority. Polish-American. The name was Kaminsky." Camden finally stood. And smiled warmly. "Look, it is preposterous. You know that, and I know that, and we both know what a grand time journalists would have with it anyway. And you know that I don't want to sue you with a preposterous case, just to use the threat of premature and adverse publicity to get what I want. I don't want to make threats at all, believe me I don't. I just want this marvelous advancement you've come up with for my daughter." His face changed, to an expression Ong wouldn't have believed possible on those particular features: wistfulness. "Doctor—do you know how much more I could have accomplished if I hadn't had to *sleep* all my life?"

Elizabeth Camden said harshly, "You hardly sleep now."

Camden looked down at her as if he had forgotten she was there. "Well, no, my dear, not now. But when I was young . . . college, I might have been able to finish college and still support . . . well. None of that matters now. What matters, Doctor, is that you and I and your board come to an agreement."

"Mr. Camden, please leave my office now."

"You mean before you lose your temper at my presumptuousness? You wouldn't be the first. I'll expect to have a meeting set up by the end of next week, whenever and wherever you say, of course. Just let my personal secretary, Diane Clavers, know the details. Anytime that's best for you."

Ong did not accompany them to the door. Pressure throbbed behind his temples. In the doorway Elizabeth Camden turned. "What happened to the twentieth one?"

"What?"

"The twentieth baby. My husband said nineteen of them are healthy and normal. What happened to the twentieth?"

The pressure grew stronger, hotter. Ong knew that he should not answer; that Camden probably already knew the answer even if his wife didn't; that he, Ong, was going to answer anyway; that he would regret the lack of self-control, bitterly, later.

"The twentieth baby is dead. His parents turned out to be unstable. They separated during the pregnancy, and his mother could not bear the twenty-four-hour crying of a baby who never sleeps."

Elizabeth Camden's eyes widened. "She killed it?"

"By mistake," Camden said shortly. "Shook the little thing too hard." He frowned at Ong. "Nurses, Doctor. In shifts. You should have picked only parents wealthy enough to afford nurses in shifts."

"That's horrible!" Mrs. Camden burst out, and Ong could not tell if she meant the child's death, the lack of nurses, or the Institute's carelessness. Ong closed his eyes.

When they had gone, he took ten milligrams of cyclobenzaprine-III. For his back—it was solely for his back. The old injury hurting again. Afterward he stood for a long time at the window, still holding the paper magnet, feeling the pressure recede from his temples, feeling himself calm down. Below him Lake Michigan lapped peacefully at the shore; the police had driven away the homeless in another raid just last night, and they hadn't yet had time to return. Only their debris remained, thrown into the bushes of the lakeshore park: tattered blankets, newspapers, plastic bags like pathetic trampled standards. It was illegal to sleep in the park, illegal to enter it without a resident's permit, illegal to be homeless and without a residence. As Ong watched, uniformed park attendants began methodically spearing newspapers and shoving them into clean self-propelled receptacles.

Ong picked up the phone to call the President of Biotech Institute's Board of Directors.

Four men and three women sat around the polished mahogany table of the conference room. *Doctor, lawyer, Indian chief*, thought Susan Melling, looking from Ong to Sullivan to Camden. She smiled. Ong caught the smile and looked frosty. Pompous ass. Judy Sullivan, the Institute lawyer, turned to speak in a low voice to Camden's lawyer, a thin nervous man with the look of being owned. The owner, Roger Camden, the Indian chief himself, was the happiest-looking person in the room. The lethal little man—what did it take to become that rich, starting from nothing? She, Susan, would certainly never know—radiated excitement. He beamed, he glowed, so unlike the usual parents-to-be that Susan was intrigued. Usually the prospective daddies and mommies—especially the daddies—sat there looking as if they were at a corporate merger. Camden looked as if he were at a birthday party.

Which, of course, he was. Susan grinned at him, and was pleased when he grinned back. Wolfish, but with a sort of delight that could only be called innocent—what would he be like in bed? Ong frowned majestically and rose to speak.

"Ladies and gentlemen, I think we're ready to start. Perhaps introductions are in order. Mr. Roger Camden, Mrs. Camden, are of course our clients. Mr. John Jaworski, Mr. Camden's lawyer. Mr. Camden, this is Judith Sullivan, the Institute's head of Legal; Samuel Krenshaw, representing Institute Director Dr. Brad Marsteiner, who unfortunately couldn't be here today; and Dr. Susan Melling, who developed the genetic modification affecting sleep. A few legal points of interest to both parties—"

"Forget the contracts for a minute," Camden interrupted. "Let's talk about the sleep thing. I'd like to ask a few questions."

Susan said, "What would you like to know?" Camden's eyes were very blue in his blunt-featured face; he wasn't what she had expected. Mrs. Camden, who apparently lacked both a first name and a lawyer, since Jaworski had been introduced as her husband's but not hers, looked either sullen or scared, it was difficult to tell which.

Ong said sourly, "Then perhaps we should start with a short presentation by Dr. Melling."

Susan would have preferred a Q&A, to see what Camden would ask. But she had annoyed Ong enough for one session. Obediently she rose.

"Let me start with a brief description of sleep. Researchers have known for a long time that there are actually three kinds of sleep. One is 'slow-wave sleep,' characterized on an EEG by delta waves. One is 'rapid-eye-movement sleep,' or REM sleep, which is much lighter sleep and contains most dreaming. Together these two make up 'core sleep.' The third type of sleep is 'optional sleep,' so-called because people seem to get along without it with no ill effects, and some short sleepers don't do it at all, sleeping naturally only 3 or 4 hours a night."

"That's me," Camden said. "I trained myself into it. Couldn't everybody do that?"

Apparently they were going to have a Q&A after all. "No. The actual sleep mechanism has some flexibility, but not the same amount for every person. The raphe nuclei on the brain stem—"

Ong said, "I don't think we need that level of detail, Susan. Let's stick to basics."

Camden said, "The raphe nuclei regulate the balance among neurotransmitters and peptides that lead to a pressure to sleep, don't they?"

Susan couldn't help it; she grinned. Camden, the laser-sharp ruthless financier, sat trying to look solemn, a third-grader waiting to have his homework praised. Ong looked sour. Mrs. Camden looked away, out the window.

"Yes, that's correct, Mr. Camden. You've done your research."

Camden said, "This is my *daughter*," and Susan caught her breath. When was the last time she had heard that note of reverence in anyone's voice? But no one in the room seemed to notice.

"Well, then," Susan said, "you already know that the reason people sleep is because a pressure to sleep builds up in the brain. Over the last twenty years, research has determined that's the *only* reason. Neither slow-wave sleep nor REM sleep serve functions that can't be carried on while the body and brain are awake. A lot goes on during sleep, but it can go on awake just as well, if other hormonal adjustments are made.

"Sleep once served an important evolutionary function. Once Clem Pre-Mammal was done filling his stomach and squirting his sperm around, sleep kept him immobile and away from predators. Sleep was an aid to survival. But now it's a left-over mechanism, like the appendix. It switches on every night, but the need is gone. So we turn off the switch at its source, in the genes."

Ong winced. He hated it when she oversimplified like that. Or maybe it was the light-heartedness he hated. If Marsteiner were making this presentation, there'd be no Clem Pre-Mammal.

Camden said, "What about the need to dream?"

"Not necessary. A left-over bombardment of the cortex to keep it on semi-alert in case a predator attacked during sleep. Wakefulness does that better."

"Why not have wakefulness instead then? From the start of the evolution?"

He was testing her. Susan gave him a full, lavish smile, enjoying his brass. "I told you. Safety from predators. But when a modern predator attacks—say, a cross-border data atoll investor—it's safer to be awake."

Camden shot at her, "What about the high percentage of REM sleep in fetuses and babies?"

"Still an evolutionary hangover. Cerebrum develops perfectly well without it."

"What about neural repair during slow-wave sleep?"

"That does go on. But it can go on during wakefulness, if the DNA is programmed to do so. No loss of neural efficiency, as far as we know."

"What about the release of human growth enzyme in such large concentrations during slow-wave sleep?"

Susan looked at him admiringly. "Goes on without the sleep. Genetic adjustments tie it to other changes in the pineal gland."

"What about the—"

"The *side effects?*" Mrs. Camden said. Her mouth turned down. "What about the bloody side effects?"

Susan turned to Elizabeth Camden. She had forgotten she was there. The younger woman stared at Susan, mouth turned down at the corners.

"I'm glad you asked that, Mrs. Camden. Because there *are* side effects." Susan paused; she was enjoying herself. "Compared to their age mates, the non-sleep children—who have *not* had IQ genetic manipulation—are more intelligent, better at problem-solving, and more joyous."

Camden took out a cigarette. The archaic, filthy habit surprised Susan. Then she saw that it was deliberate: Roger Camden drawing attention to an ostentatious display to draw attention away from what he was feeling. His cigarette lighter was gold, monogrammed, innocently gaudy.

"Let me explain," Susan said. "REM sleep bombards the cerebral cortex with random neural firings from the brainstem; dreaming occurs because the poor besieged cortex tries so hard to make sense of the activated images and memories. It spends a lot of energy doing that. Without that energy expenditure, non-sleep cerebrums save the wear-and-tear and do better at coordinating real-life input. Thus— greater intelligence and problem-solving.

"Also, doctors have known for sixty years that antidepressants, which lift the mood of depressed patients, also suppress REM sleep entirely. What they have proved in the last ten years is that the reverse is equally true: suppress REM sleep and people don't *get* depressed.

The non-sleep kids are cheerful, outgoing . . . *joyous*. There's no other word for it."

"At what cost?" Mrs. Camden said. She held her neck rigid, but the corners of her jaw worked.

"No cost. No negative side effects at all."

"So far," Mrs. Camden shot back.

Susan shrugged. "So far."

"They're only four years old! At the most!"

Ong and Krenshaw were studying her closely. Susan saw the moment the Camden woman realized it; she sank back into her chair, drawing her fur coat around her, her face blank.

Camden did not look at his wife. He blew a cloud of cigarette smoke. "Everything has costs, Dr. Melling."

She liked the way he said her name. "Ordinarily, yes. Especially in genetic modification. But we honestly have not been able to find any here, despite looking." She smiled directly into Camden's eyes. "Is it too much to believe that just once the universe has given us something wholly good, wholly a step forward, wholly beneficial? Without hidden penalties?"

"Not the universe. The intelligence of people like you," Camden said, surprising Susan more than anything else that had gone before. His eyes held hers. She felt her chest tighten.

"I think," Dr. Ong said dryly, "that the philosophy of the universe may be beyond our concerns here. Mr. Camden, if you have no further medical questions, perhaps we can return to the legal points Ms. Sullivan and Mr. Jaworski have raised. Thank you, Dr. Melling."

Susan nodded. She didn't look again at Camden. But she knew what he said, how he looked, that he was there.

The house was about what she had expected, a huge mock Tudor on Lake Michigan north of Chicago. The land heavily wooded between the gate and the house, open between the house and the surging water. Patches of snow dotted the dormant grass. Biotech had been working with the Camdens for four months, but this was the first time Susan had driven to their home.

As she walked toward the house, another car drove up behind her. No, a truck, continuing around the curved driveway to a service entry at the side of the house. One man rang the service bell; a second began to unload a plastic-wrapped playpen from the back of the truck. White, with pink and yellow bunnies. Susan briefly closed her eyes.

Camden opened the door himself. She could see the effort not to look worried. "You didn't have to drive out, Susan—I'd have come into the city!"

"No, I didn't want you to do that, Roger. Mrs. Camden is here?"

"In the living room." Camden led her into a large room with a stone fireplace. English country-house furniture; prints of dogs or boats, all hung eighteen inches too high: Elizabeth Camden must have done the decorating. She did not rise from her wing chair as Susan entered.

"Let me be concise and fast," Susan said, "I don't want to make this any more drawn-out for you than I have to. We have all the amniocentesis, ultrasound, and Langston test results. The fetus is fine, developing normally for two weeks, no problems with the implant on the uterus wall. But a complication has developed."

"What?" Camden said. He took out a cigarette, looked at his wife, put it back unlit.

Susan said quietly, "Mrs. Camden, by sheer chance both your ovaries released eggs last month. We removed one for the gene surgery. By more sheer chance the second fertilized and implanted. You're carrying two fetuses."

Elizabeth Camden grew still. "Twins?"

"No," Susan said. Then she realized what she had said. "I mean, yes. They're twins, but non-identical. Only one has been genetically altered. The other will be no more similar to her than any two siblings. It's a so-called 'normal' baby. And I know you didn't want a so-called normal baby."

Camden said, "No. I didn't."

Elizabeth Camden said, "I did."

Camden shot her a fierce look that Susan couldn't read. He took out the cigarette again, lit it. His face was in profile to Susan, thinking intently; she doubted he knew the cigarette was there, or that he was lighting it. "Is the baby being affected by the other one's being there?"

"No," Susan said. "No, of course not. They're just . . . co-existing."

"Can you abort it?"

"Not without risk of aborting both of them. Removing the unaltered fetus might cause changes in the uterus lining that could lead to a spontaneous miscarriage of the other." She drew a deep breath. "There's that option, of course. We can start the whole process over again. But as I told you at the time, you were very lucky to have the in vitro fertilization take on only the second try. Some couples take eight or ten tries. If we started all over, the process could be a lengthy one."

Camden said, "Is the presence of this second fetus harming my daughter? Taking away nutrients or anything? Or will it change anything for her later on in the pregnancy?"

"No. Except that there is a chance of premature birth. Two fetuses take up a lot more room in the womb, and if it gets too crowded, birth can be premature. But the—"

"How premature? Enough to threaten survival?"

"Most probably not."

Camden went on smoking. A man appeared at the door. "Sir, London calling. James Kendall for Mr. Yagai."

"I'll take it." Camden rose. Susan watched him study his wife's face.

When he spoke, it was to her. "All right, Elizabeth. All right." He left the room.

For a long moment the two women sat in silence. Susan was aware of disappointment; this was not the Camden she had expected to see. She became aware of Elizabeth Camden watching her with amusement.

"Oh, yes, Doctor. He's like that."

Susan said nothing.

"Completely overbearing. But not this time." She laughed softly, with excitement. "Two. Do you . . . do you know what sex the other one is?"

"Both fetuses are female."

"I wanted a girl, you know. And now I'll have one."

"Then you'll go ahead with the pregnancy."

"Oh, yes. Thank you for coming, Doctor."

She was dismissed. No one saw her out. But as she was getting into her car, Camden rushed out of the house, coatless. "Susan! I wanted to thank you. For coming all the way out here to tell us yourself."

"You already thanked me."

"Yes. Well. You're sure the second fetus is no threat to my daughter?"

Susan said deliberately, "Nor is the genetically altered fetus a threat to the naturally conceived one."

He smiled. His voice was low and wistful. "And you think that should matter to me just as much. But it doesn't. And why should I fake what I feel? Especially to you?"

Susan opened her car door. She wasn't ready for this, or she had changed her mind, or something. But then Camden leaned over to close the door, and his manner held no trace of flirtatiousness, no smarmy ingratiation. "I better order a second playpen."

"Yes."

"And a second car seat."

"Yes."

"But not a second night-shift nurse."

"That's up to you."

"And you." Abruptly he leaned over and kissed her, a kiss so polite and respectful that Susan was shocked. Neither lust nor conquest would have shocked her; this did. Camden didn't give her a chance to react; he closed the car door and turned back toward the house. Susan drove toward the gate, her hands shaky on the wheel until amusement replaced shock: It *had* been a deliberately distant, respectful kiss, an engineered enigma. And nothing else could have guaranteed so well that there would have to be another.

She wondered what the Camdens would name their daughters.

Dr. Ong strode the hospital corridor, which had been dimmed to half-light. From the nurse's station in Maternity a nurse stepped forward as if to stop him—it was the middle of the night, long past visiting hours—got a good look at his face, and faded back into her station. Around a corner was the viewing glass to the nursery. To Ong's annoyance, Susan Melling stood pressed against the glass. To his further annoyance, she was crying.

Ong realized that he had never liked the woman. Maybe not any women. Even those with superior minds could not seem to refrain from being made damn fools by their emotions.

"Look," Susan said, laughing a little, swiping at her face. "Doctor—*look.*"

Behind the glass Roger Camden, gowned and masked, was holding up a baby in white undershirt and pink blanket. Camden's blue eyes—theatrically blue, a man really should not have such garish eyes—glowed. The baby had a head covered with blond fuzz, wide eyes, pink skin. Camden's eyes above the mask said that no other child had ever had these attributes.

Ong said, "An uncomplicated birth?"

"Yes," Susan Melling sobbed. "Perfectly straightforward. Elizabeth is fine. She's asleep. Isn't she beautiful? He has the most adventurous spirit I've ever known." She wiped her nose on her sleeve; Ong realized that she was drunk. "Did I ever tell you that I was engaged once? Fifteen years ago, in med school? I broke it off because he grew to seem so ordinary, so boring. Oh, God, I shouldn't be telling you all this I'm sorry I'm sorry."

Ong moved away from her. Behind the glass Roger Camden laid the baby in a small wheeled crib. The nameplate said BABY GIRL CAMDEN #1. 5.9 POUNDS. A night nurse watched indulgently.

Ong did not wait to see Camden emerge from the nursery or to hear Susan Melling say to him whatever she was going to say. Ong went to have the OB paged. Melling's report was not, under the circumstances, to be trusted. A perfect, unprecedented chance to record every detail of gene-alteration with a non-altered control, and Melling was more interested in her own sloppy emotions. Ong would obviously have to do the report himself, after talking to the OB. He was hungry for every detail. And not just about the pink-cheeked baby in Camden's arms. He wanted to know everything about the birth of the child in the other glass-sided crib: BABY GIRL CAMDEN #2. 5.1 POUNDS. The dark-haired baby with the mottled red features, lying scrunched down in her pink blanket, asleep.

2

Leisha's earliest memory was of flowing lines that were not there. She knew they were not there because when she reached out her fist to touch them, her fist was empty. Later she realized that the flowing lines were light: sunshine slanting in bars between curtains in her room, between the wooden blinds in the dining room, between the criss-cross lattices in the conservatory. The day she realized the golden flow was light she laughed out loud with the sheer joy of discovery, and Daddy turned from putting flowers in pots and smiled at her.

The whole house was full of light. Light bounded off the lake, streamed across the high white ceilings, puddled on the shining wooden floors. She and Alice moved continually through light, and sometimes Leisha would stop and tip back her head and let it flow over her face. She could feel it, like water.

The best light, of course, was in the conservatory. That's where Daddy liked to be when he was home from making money. Daddy potted plants and watered trees, humming, and Leisha and Alice ran between the wooden tables of flowers with their wonderful earthy smells, running from the dark side of the conservatory where the big purple flowers grew to the sunshine side with sprays of yellow flowers, running back and forth, in and out of the light. "Growth," Daddy said to her, "flowers all fulfilling their promise. Alice, be careful! You almost knocked over that orchid!" Alice, obedient, would stop running for a while. Daddy never told Leisha to stop running.

After a while the light would go away. Alice and Leisha would have their baths, and then Alice would get quiet, or cranky. She wouldn't play nice with Leisha, even when Leisha let her choose the game or even have all the best dolls. Then Nanny would take Alice to "bed," and Leisha would talk with Daddy some more until Daddy said he had to work in his study with the papers that made money. Leisha always felt a moment of regret that he had to go do that, but the moment never lasted very long because Mamselle would arrive and start Leisha's lessons, which she liked. Learning things was so interesting! She could already sing twenty songs and write all the letters in the alphabet and count to fifty. And by the time lessons were done, the light had come back, and it was time for breakfast.

Breakfast was the only time Leisha didn't like. Daddy had gone to the office, and Leisha and Alice had breakfast with Mommy in the big dining room. Mommy sat in a red robe, which Leisha liked, and she didn't smell funny or talk funny the way she would later in the day, but still breakfast wasn't fun. Mommy always started with The Question.

"Alice, sweetheart, how did you sleep?"

"Fine, Mommy."

"Did you have any nice dreams?"

For a long time Alice said no. Then one day she said, "I dreamed about a horse. I was riding him." Mommy clapped her hands and kissed Alice and gave her an extra sticky bun. After that Alice always had a dream to tell Mommy.

Once Leisha said, "I had a dream, too. I dreamed light was coming in the window and it wrapped all around me like a blanket and then it kissed me on my eyes."

Mommy put down her coffee cup so hard that coffee sloshed out of it. "Don't lie to me, Leisha. You did not have a dream."

"Yes, I did," Leisha said.

"Only children who sleep can have dreams. Don't lie to me. You did not have a dream."

"Yes I did! I did!" Leisha shouted. She could see it, almost: The light streaming in the window and wrapping around her like a golden blanket.

"I will not tolerate a child who is a liar! Do you hear me, Leisha— I won't tolerate it!"

"You're a liar!" Leisha shouted, knowing the words weren't true, hating herself because they weren't true but hating Mommy more and that was wrong, too, and there sat Alice stiff and frozen with her eyes wide, Alice was scared and it was Leisha's fault.

Mommy called sharply, "Nanny! Nanny! Take Leisha to her room at once. She can't sit with civilized people if she can't refrain from telling lies!"

Leisha started to cry. Nanny carried her out of the room. Leisha hadn't even had her breakfast. But she didn't care about that; all she could see while she cried was Alice's eyes, scared like that, reflecting broken bits of light.

But Leisha didn't cry long. Nanny read her a story, and then played Data Jump with her, and then Alice came up and Nanny drove them both into Chicago to the zoo where there were wonderful animals to see, animals Leisha could not have dreamed—nor Alice *either*. And by the time they came back Mommy had gone to her room and Leisha knew that she would stay there with the glasses of funny-smelling stuff the rest of the day and Leisha would not have to see her.

But that night, she went to her mother's room.

"I have to go to the bathroom," she told Mamselle. Mamselle said, "Do you need any help?" maybe because Alice still needed help in the bathroom. But Leisha didn't, and she thanked Mamselle. Then she sat on the toilet for a minute even though nothing came, so that what she had told Mamselle wouldn't be a lie.

Leisha tiptoed down the hall. She went first into Alice's room. A little light in a wall socket burned near the "crib." There was no crib in Leisha's room. Leisha looked at her sister through the bars. Alice lay on her side, with her eyes closed. The lids of the eyes fluttered quickly, like curtains blowing in the wind. Alice's chin and neck looked loose.

Leisha closed the door very carefully and went to her parents' room.

They didn't "sleep" in a crib but in a huge enormous "bed," with enough room between them for more people. Mommy's eyelids weren't fluttering; she lay on her back making a hrrr-hrrr sound through her nose. The funny smell was strong on her. Leisha backed away and tiptoed over to Daddy. He looked like Alice, except that his neck and chin looked even looser, folds of skin collapsed like the tent that had fallen down in the backyard. It scared Leisha to see him like that. Then Daddy's eyes flew open so suddenly that Leisha screamed.

Daddy rolled out of bed and picked her up, looking quickly at Mommy. But she didn't move. Daddy was wearing only his underpants. He carried Leisha out into the hall, where Mamselle came rushing up saying, "Oh, sir, I'm sorry, she just said she was going to the bathroom—"

"It's all right," Daddy said. "I'll take her with me."

"No!" Leisha screamed, because Daddy was only in his underpants and his neck had looked all funny and the room smelled bad because of Mommy. But Daddy carried her into the conservatory, set her down on a bench, wrapped himself in a piece of green plastic that was supposed to cover up plants, and sat down next to her.

"Now, what happened, Leisha? What were you doing?"

Leisha didn't answer.

"You were looking at people sleeping, weren't you?" Daddy said, and because his voice was softer Leisha mumbled, "Yes." She immediately felt better; it felt good not to lie.

"You were looking at people sleeping because you don't sleep and you were curious, weren't you? Like Curious George in your book?"

"Yes," Leisha said. "I thought you said you made money in your study all night!"

Daddy smiled. "Not all night. Some of it. But then I sleep, although not very much." He took Leisha on his lap. "I don't need much sleep, so I get a lot more done at night than most people. Different people need different amounts of sleep. And a few, a very few, are like you. You don't need any."

"Why not?"

"Because you're special. Better than other people. Before you were born, I had some doctors help make you that way."

"Why?"

"So you could do anything you want to and make manifest your own individuality."

Leisha twisted in his arms to stare at him; the words meant nothing. Daddy reached over and touched a single flower growing on a tall potted tree. The flower had thick white petals like the cream he put in coffee, and the center was a light pink.

"See, Leisha—this tree made this flower. Because it *can*. Only this tree can make this kind of wonderful flower. That plant hanging up there can't, and those can't either. Only this tree. Therefore the most important thing in the world for this tree to do is grow this flower. The flower is the tree's individuality—that means just *it*, and nothing else—made manifest. Nothing else matters."

"I don't understand, Daddy."

"You will. Someday."

"But I want to understand *now*," Leisha said, and Daddy laughed with pure delight and hugged her. The hug felt good, but Leisha still wanted to understand.

"When you make money, is that your indiv . . . that thing?"

"Yes," Daddy said happily.

"Then nobody else can make money? Like only that tree can make that flower?"

"Nobody else can make it just the way I do."

"What do you do with the money?"

"I buy things for you. This house, your dresses, Mamselle to teach you, the car to ride in."

"What does the tree do with the flower?"

"Glories in it," Daddy said, which made no sense. "Excellence is what counts, Leisha. Excellence supported by individual effort. And that's *all* that counts."

"I'm cold, Daddy."

"Then I better bring you back to Mamselle."

Leisha didn't move. She touched the flower with one finger. "I want to sleep, Daddy."

"No, you don't, sweetheart. Sleep is just lost time, wasted life. It's a little death."

"Alice sleeps."

"Alice isn't like you."

"Alice isn't special?"

"No. You are."

"Why didn't you make Alice special, too?"

"Alice made herself. I didn't have a chance to make her special."

The whole thing was too hard. Leisha stopped stroking the flower and slipped off Daddy's lap. He smiled at her. "My little questioner. When you grow up, you'll find your own excellence, and it will be a new order, a specialness the world hasn't ever seen before. You might even be like Kenzo Yagai. He made the Yagai generator that powers the world."

"Daddy, you look funny wrapped in the flower plastic." Leisha laughed. Daddy did, too. But then she said, "When I grow up, I'll make my specialness find a way to make Alice special, too," and Daddy stopped laughing.

He took her back to Mamselle, who taught her to write her name, which was so exciting she forget about the puzzling talk with Daddy. There were six letters, all different, and together they were *her name*. Leisha wrote it over and over, laughing, and Mamselle laughed too. But later, in the morning, Leisha thought again about the talk with Daddy. She thought of it often, turning the unfamiliar words over and over in her mind like small hard stones, but the part she thought about most wasn't a word. It was the frown on Daddy's face when she told him she would use her specialness to make Alice special, too.

Every week Dr. Melling came to see Leisha and Alice, sometimes alone, sometimes with other people. Leisha and Alice both liked Dr. Melling, who laughed a lot and whose eyes were bright and warm. Often Daddy was there, too. Dr. Melling played games with them, first with Alice and Leisha separately and then together. She took their pictures and weighed them. She made them lie down on a table and stuck little metal things to their temples, which sounded scary but wasn't because there were so many machines to watch, all making interesting noises, while you were lying there. Dr. Melling was as good at answering questions as Daddy. Once Leisha said, "Is Dr. Melling a special person? Like Kenzo Yagai?" And Daddy laughed and glanced at Dr. Melling and said, "Oh, yes, indeed."

When Leisha was five she and Alice started school. Daddy's driver took them every day into Chicago. They were in different rooms, which disappointed Leisha. The kids in Leisha's room were all older. But from the first day she adored school, with its fascinating science equipment and electronic drawers full of math puzzlers and other children to find countries on the map with. In half a year she had been moved to yet a different room, where the kids were still older, but they were nonetheless nice to her. Leisha started to learn Japanese. She loved drawing the beautiful characters on thick white paper. "The Sauley School was a good choice," Daddy said.

But Alice didn't like the Sauley School. She wanted to go to school on the same yellow bus as Cook's daughter. She cried and threw her paints on the floor at the Sauley School. Then Mommy came out of her room—Leisha hadn't seen her for a few weeks, although she knew Alice had—and threw some candlesticks from the mantlepiece on the floor. The candlesticks, which were china, broke. Leisha ran to pick up the pieces while Mommy and Daddy screamed at each other in the hall by the big staircase.

"She's my daughter, too! And I say she can go!"

"You don't have the right to say anything about it! A weepy drunk, the most rotten role model possible for both of them . . . and I thought I was getting a fine English aristocrat!"

"You got what you paid for! Nothing! Not that you ever needed anything from me or anybody else!"

"Stop it!" Leisha cried. "Stop it!" and there was silence in the hall. Leisha cut her fingers on the china; blood streamed onto the rug. Daddy rushed in and picked her up. "Stop it," Leisha sobbed, and didn't understand when Daddy said quietly, "*You* stop it, Leisha. Nothing *they* do should touch you at all. You have to be at least that strong."

Leisha buried her head in Daddy's shoulder. Alice transferred to Carl Sandburg Elementary School, riding there on the yellow school bus with Cook's daughter.

A few weeks later Daddy told them that Mommy was going away for a few weeks to a hospital, to stop drinking so much. When Mommy came out, he said, she was going to live somewhere else for a while. She and Daddy were not happy. Leisha and Alice would stay with Daddy and they would visit Mommy sometimes. He told them this very carefully, finding the right words for truth. Truth was very important, Leisha already knew. Truth was being true to your self, your specialness. Your individuality. An individual respected facts, and so always told the truth.

Mommy, Daddy did not say but Leisha knew, did not respect facts.

"I don't want Mommy to go away," Alice said. She started to cry. Leisha thought Daddy would pick Alice up, but he didn't. He just stood there looking at them both.

Leisha put her arms around Alice. "It's all right, Alice. It's all right! We'll make it all right! I'll play with you all the time we're not in school so you don't miss Mommy!"

Alice clung to Leisha. Leisha turned her head so she didn't have to see Daddy's face.

3

Kenzo Yagai was coming to the United States to lecture. The title of his talk, which he would give in New York, Los Angeles, Chicago, and Washington, with a repeat in Washington as a special address to Congress, was "The Further Political Implications of Inexpensive Power." Leisha Camden, eleven years old, was going to have a private introduction after the Chicago talk, arranged by her father.

She had studied the theory of cold fusion at school, and her Global Studies teacher had traced the changes in the world resulting from Yagai's patented, low-cost applications of what had, until him, been unworkable theory. The rising prosperity of the Third World, the last death throes of the old communist systems, the decline of the oil states, the renewed economic power of the United States. Her study group had written a news script, filmed with the school's professional-quality equipment, about how a 1985 American family lived with expensive energy costs and a belief in tax-supported help, while a 2019 family lived with cheap energy and a belief in the contract as the basis of civilization. Parts of her own research puzzled Leisha.

"Japan thinks Kenzo Yagai was a traitor to his own country," she said to Daddy at supper.

"No," Camden said, "*Some* Japanese think that. Watch out for generalizations, Leisha. Yagai patented and marketed Y-energy first in the United States because here there were at least the dying embers of individual enterprise. Because of his invention, our entire country has slowly swung back toward an individual meritocracy, and Japan has slowly been forced to follow."

"Your father held that belief all along," Susan said. "Eat your peas, Leisha." Leisha ate her peas. Susan and Daddy had only been married less than a year; it still felt a little strange to have her there. But nice. Daddy said Susan was a valuable addition to their household: intelligent, motivated, and cheerful. Like Leisha herself.

"Remember, Leisha," Camden said, "a man's worth to society and to himself doesn't rest on what he thinks other people should do or be or feel, but on himself. On what he can actually do, and do well. People trade what they do well, and everyone benefits. The basic tool of civilization is the contract. Contracts are voluntary and mutually beneficial. As opposed to coercion, which is wrong."

"The strong have no right to take anything from the weak by force," Susan said. "Alice, eat your peas, too, honey."

"Nor the weak to take anything by force from the strong," Camden said. "That's the basis of what you'll hear Kenzo Yagai discuss tonight, Leisha."

Alice said, "I don't like peas."

Camden said, "Your body does. They're good for you."

Alice smiled. Leisha felt her heart lift; Alice didn't smile much at dinner any more. "My body doesn't have a contract with the peas."

Camden said, a little impatiently, "Yes, it does. Your body benefits from them. Now eat."

Alice's smile vanished. Leisha looked down at her plate. Suddenly she saw a way out. "No, Daddy, look—Alice's body benefits, but the peas don't! It's not a mutually beneficial consideration—so there's no contract! Alice is right!"

Camden let out a shout of laughter. To Susan he said, "Eleven years old . . . *eleven*." Even Alice smiled, and Leisha waved her spoon triumphantly, light glinting off the bowl and dancing silver on the opposite wall.

But even so, Alice did not want to go hear Kenzo Yagai. She was going to sleep over at her friend Julie's house; they were going to curl their hair together. More surprisingly, Susan wasn't coming either. She and Daddy looked at each other a little funny at the front door, Leisha thought, but Leisha was too excited to think about this. She was going to hear *Kenzo Yagai*.

Yagai was a small man, dark and slim. Leisha liked his accent. She liked, too, something about him that took her a while to name. "Daddy," she whispered in the half-darkness of the auditorium, "he's a joyful man."

Daddy hugged her in the darkness.

Yagai spoke about spirituality and economics. "A man's spirituality—which is only his dignity as a man—rests on his own efforts. Dignity and worth are not automatically conferred by aristocratic birth—we have only to look at history to see that. Dignity and worth are not automatically conferred by inherited wealth—a great heir may be a thief, a wastrel, cruel, an exploiter, a person who leaves the world much poorer than he found it. Nor are dignity and worth automatically conferred by existence itself—a mass murderer exists, but is of negative worth to his society and possesses no dignity in his lust to kill.

"No, the only dignity, the only spirituality, rests on what a man can achieve with his own efforts. To rob a man of the chance to achieve, and to trade what he achieves with others, is to rob him of his spiritual dignity as a man. This is why communism has failed in our time. *All* coercion—all force to take from a man his own efforts to achieve—causes spiritual damage and weakens a society. Conscription, theft, fraud, violence, welfare, lack of legislative representation—*all* rob a man of his chance to choose, to achieve on his own, to trade the results of his achievement with others. Coercion is a cheat. It produces nothing new. Only freedom—the freedom to achieve, the freedom to trade freely the results of achievement—creates the environment proper to the dignity and spirituality of man."

Leisha applauded so hard her hands hurt. Going backstage with Daddy, she thought she could hardly breathe. Kenzo Yagai!

But backstage was more crowded than she had expected. There were cameras everywhere. Daddy said, "Mr. Yagai, may I present my daughter Leisha," and the cameras moved in close and fast—on *her*. A Japanese man whispered something in Kenzo Yagai's ear, and he looked more closely at Leisha. "Ah, yes."

"Look over here, Leisha," someone called, and she did. A robot camera zoomed so close to her face that Leisha stepped back, startled. Daddy spoke very sharply to someone, then to someone else. The cameras didn't move. A woman suddenly knelt in front of Leisha and thrust a microphone at her. "What does it feel like to never sleep, Leisha?"

"What?"

Someone laughed. The laugh was not kind. "Breeding geniuses . . ."

Leisha felt a hand on her shoulder. Kenzo Yagai gripped her very firmly, pulled her away from the cameras. Immediately, as if by magic, a line of Japanese men formed behind Yagai, parting only to let Daddy through. Behind the line, the three of them moved into a dressing room, and Kenzo Yagai shut the door.

"You must not let them bother you, Leisha," he said in his wonderful accent. "Not ever. There is an old Oriental proverb: 'The dogs bark but the caravan moves on.' You must never let your individual caravan be slowed by the barking of rude or envious dogs."

"I won't," Leisha breathed, not sure yet what the words really meant, knowing there was time later to sort them out, to talk about them with Daddy. For now she was dazzled by Kenzo Yagai, the actual man himself who was changing the world without force, without guns, with trading his special individual efforts. "We study your philosophy at my school, Mr. Yagai."

Kenzo Yagai looked at Daddy. Daddy said, "A private school. But Leisha's sister also studies it, although cursorily, in the public system. Slowly, Kenzo, but it comes. It comes." Leisha noticed that he did not say why Alice was not here tonight with them.

Back home, Leisha sat in her room for hours, thinking over everything that had happened. When Alice came home from Julie's the next morning, Leisha rushed toward her. But Alice seemed angry about something.

"Alice—what is it?"

"Don't you think I have enough to put up with at school already?" Alice shouted. "Everybody knows, but at least when you stayed quiet it didn't matter too much! They'd stopped teasing me! Why did you have to do it?"

"Do what?" Leisha said, bewildered.

Alice threw something at her: a hard-copy morning paper, on newsprint flimsier than the Camden system used. The paper dropped open at Leisha's feet. She stared at her own picture, three columns wide, with Kenzo Yagai. The headline said YAGAI AND THE FUTURE: ROOM FOR THE REST OF US? Y-ENERGY INVENTOR CONFERS WITH 'SLEEP-FREE' DAUGHTER OF MEGA-FINANCIER ROGER CAMDEN.

Alice kicked the paper. "It was on TV last night too—on *TV*. I work hard not to look stuck-up or creepy, and you go and do this! Now Julie probably won't even invite me to her slumber party next week!" She rushed up the broad curving stairs toward her room.

Leisha looked down at the paper. She heard Kenzo Yagai's voice in her head: "The dogs bark but the caravan moves on." She looked at the empty stairs. Aloud she said, "Alice—your hair looks really pretty curled like that."

4

"I want to meet the rest of them," Leisha said. "Why have you kept them from me this long?"

"I haven't kept them from you at all," Camden said. "Not offering is not the same as denial. Why shouldn't you be the one to do the asking? You're the one who now wants it."

Leisha looked at him. She was 15, in her last year at the Sauley School. "Why didn't you offer?"

"Why should I?"

"I don't know," Leisha said. "But you gave me everything else."

"Including the freedom to ask for what you want."

Leisha looked for the contradiction, and found it. "Most things that you provided for my education I didn't ask for, because I didn't know enough to ask and you, as the adult, did. But you've never offered the opportunity for me to meet any of the other sleepless mutants—"

"Don't use that word," Camden said sharply.

"—so you must either think it was not essential to my education or else you had another motive for not wanting me to meet them."

"Wrong," Camden said. "There's a third possibility. That I think meeting them is essential to your education, that I do want you to, but this issue provided a chance to further the education of your self-initiative by waiting for *you* to ask."

"All right," Leisha said, a little defiantly; there seemed to be a lot of defiance between them lately, for no good reason. She squared her shoulders. Her new breasts thrust forward. "I'm asking. How many of the Sleepless are there, who are they, and where are they?"

Camden said, "If you're using that term—'the Sleepless'—you've already done some reading on your own. So you probably know that there are 1,082 of you so far in the United States, a few more in foreign countries, most of them in major metropolitan areas. Seventy-nine are in Chicago, most of them still small children. Only nineteen anywhere are older than you."

Leisha didn't deny reading any of this. Camden leaned forward in his study chair to peer at her. Leisha wondered if he needed glasses. His hair was completely gray now, sparse and stiff, like lonely broom-straws. The *Wall Street Journal* listed him among the hundred richest men in America; *Women's Wear Daily* pointed out that he was the only billionaire in the country who did not move in the society of international parties, charity balls, and personal jets. Camden's jet ferried him to business meetings around the world, to the chairmanship of the Yagai Economics Institute, and to very little else. Over the years he had grown richer, more reclusive, and more cerebral. Leisha felt a rush of her old affection.

She threw herself sideways into a leather chair, her long slim legs dangling over the arm. Absently she scratched a mosquito bite on her thigh. "Well, then, I'd like to meet Richard Keller." He lived in Chicago and was the beta-test Sleepless closest to her own age. He was 17.

"Why ask me? Why not just go?"

Leisha thought there was a note of impatience in his voice. He liked her to explore things first, then report on them to him later. Both parts were important.

Leisha laughed. "You know what, Daddy? You're predictable."

Camden laughed, too. In the middle of the laugh Susan came in. "He certainly is not. Roger, what about that meeting in Buenos Aires Thursday? Is it on or off?" When he didn't answer, her voice grew shriller. "Roger? I'm talking to you!"

Leisha averted her eyes. Two years ago Susan had finally left genetic research to run Camden's house and schedule; before that she had tried hard to do both. Since she had left Biotech, it seemed to Leisha, Susan had changed. Her voice was tighter. She was more insistent that Cook and the gardener follow her directions exactly, without deviation. Her blonde braids had become stiff sculptured waves of platinum.

"It's on," Roger said.

"Well, thanks for at least answering. Am I going?"

"If you like."

"I like."

Susan left the room. Leisha rose and stretched. Her long legs rose on tiptoe. It felt good to reach, to stretch, to feel sunlight from the wide windows wash over her face. She smiled at her father, and found him watching her with an unexpected expression.

"Leisha—"

"What?"

"See Keller. But be careful."

"Of what?"

But Camden wouldn't answer.

The voice on the phone had been noncommital. "Leisha Camden? Yes, I know who you are. Three o'clock on Thursday?" The house was modest, a thirty-year-old Colonial on a quiet suburban street where small children on bicycles could be watched from the front window. Few roofs had more than one Y-energy cell. The trees, huge old sugar maples, were beautiful.

"Come in," Richard Keller said.

He was no taller than she, stocky, with a bad case of acne. Probably no genetic alterations except sleep, Leisha guessed. He had thick dark hair, a low forehead, and bushy black brows. Before he closed the door Leisha saw his stare at her car and driver, parked in the driveway next to a rusty ten-speed bike.

"I can't drive yet," she said. "I'm still fifteen."

"It's easy to learn," Keller said. "So, you want to tell me why you're here?"

Leisha liked his directness. "To meet some other Sleepless."

"You mean you never have? Not any of us?"

"You mean the rest of you know each other?" She hadn't expected that.

"Come to my room, Leisha."

She followed him to the back of the house. No one else seemed to be home. His room was large and airy, filled with computers and filing cabinets. A rowing machine sat in one corner. It looked like a shabbier version of the room of any bright classmate at the Sauley School, except there was more space without a bed. She walked over to the computer screen.

"Hey—you working on Boesc equations?"

"On an application of them."

"To what?"

"Fish migration patterns."

Leisha smiled. "Yeah—that would work. I never thought of that."

Keller seemed not to know what to do with her smile. He looked at the wall, then at her chin. "You interested in Gaea patterns? In the environment?"

"Well, no," Leisha confessed. "Not particularly. I'm going to study politics at Harvard. Pre-law. But of course we had Gaea patterns at school."

Keller's gaze finally came unstuck from her face. He ran a hand through his dark hair. "Sit down, if you want."

Leisha sat, looking appreciatively at the wall posters, shifting green on blue, like ocean currents. "I like those. Did you program them yourself?"

"You're not at all what I pictured," Keller said.

"How did you picture me?"

He didn't hesitate. "Stuck-up. Superior. Shallow, despite your IQ."

She was more hurt than she had expected to be.

Keller blurted, "You're the only one of the Sleepless who's really rich. But you already know that."

"No, I don't. I've never checked."

He took the chair beside her, stretching his stocky legs straight in front of him, in a slouch that had nothing to do with relaxation. "It makes sense, really. Rich people don't have their children genetically modified to be superior—they think any offspring of theirs is already superior. By their values. And poor people can't afford it. We Sleepless are upper-middle class, no more. Children of professors, scientists, people who value brains and time."

"My father values brains and time," Leisha said. "He's the biggest supporter of Kenzo Yagai."

"Oh, Leisha, do you think I don't already know that? Are you flashing me or what?"

Leisha said with great deliberateness, "I'm *talking* to you." But the next minute she could feel the hurt break through on her face.

"I'm sorry," Keller muttered. He shot off his chair and paced to the computer, back. "I *am* sorry. But I don't . . . I don't understand what you're doing here."

"I'm lonely," Leisha said, astonished at herself. She looked up at him. "It's true. I'm lonely. I am. I have friends and Daddy and Alice—but no one really knows, really understands—what? I don't know what I'm saying."

Keller smiled. The smile changed his whole face, opened up its dark planes to the light. "I do. Oh, do I. What do you do when they say, 'I had such a dream last night!'?"

"Yes!" Leisha said. "But that's even really minor—it's when *I* say, 'I'll look that up for you tonight' and they get that funny look on their face that means 'She'll do it while I'm asleep.' "

"But that's even really minor," Keller said. "It's when you're playing basketball in the gym after supper and then you go to the diner for food and then you say 'Let's have a walk by the lake' and they say 'I'm really tired. I'm going home to bed now.' "

"But that's really minor," Leisha said, jumping up. "It's when you really are absorbed by the movie and then you get the point and it's so goddamn beautiful you leap up and say 'Yes! Yes!' and Susan says 'Leisha, really—you'd think nobody but you ever enjoyed anything before.' "

"Who's Susan?" Keller said.

The mood was broken. But not really; Leisha could say "My stepmother" without much discomfort over what Susan had promised to be and what she had become. Keller stood inches from her, smiling that joyous smile, understanding, and suddenly relief washed over Leisha so strong that she walked straight into him and put her arms around his neck, only tightening them when she felt his startled jerk. She started to sob—she, Leisha, who never cried.

"Hey," Richard said. "Hey."

"Brilliant," Leisha said, laughing. "Brilliant remark."

She could feel his embarrassed smile. "Wanta see my fish migration curves instead?"

"No," Leisha sobbed, and he went on holding her, patting her back awkwardly, telling her without words that she was home.

Camden waited up for her, although it was past midnight. He had been smoking heavily. Through the blue air he said quietly, "Did you have a good time, Leisha?"

"Yes."

"I'm glad," he said, and put out his last cigarette, and climbed the stairs—slowly, stiffly, he was nearly seventy now—to bed.

They went everywhere together for nearly a year: swimming, dancing, to the museums, the theater, the library. Richard introduced her to the others, a group of twelve kids between fourteen and nineteen, all of them intelligent and eager. All Sleepless.

Leisha learned.

Tony's parents, like her own, had divorced. But Tony, fourteen, lived with his mother, who had not particularly wanted a Sleepless child, while his father, who had, acquired a red hovercar and a young girlfriend who designed ergonomic chairs in Paris. Tony was not allowed to tell anyone—relatives, schoolmates—that he was Sleepless.

"They'll think you're a freak," his mother said, eyes averted from her son's face. The one time Tony disobeyed her and told a friend that he never slept, his mother beat him. Then she moved the family to a new neighborhood. He was nine years old.

Jeanine, almost as long-legged and slim as Leisha, was training for the Olympics in ice skating. She practiced twelve hours a day, hours no Sleeper still in high school could ever have. So far the newspapers had not picked up the story. Jeanine was afraid that, if they did, they would somehow not let her compete.

Jack, like Leisha, would start college in September. Unlike Leisha, he had already started his career. The practice of law had to wait for law school; the practice of investment required only money. Jack didn't have much, but his precise financial analyses parlayed $600 saved from summer jobs to $3000 through stock-market investing, then to $10,000, and then he had enough to qualify for information-fund speculation. Jack was fifteen, not old enough to make legal investments; the transactions were all in the name of Kevin Baker, the oldest of the Sleepless, who lived in Austin. Jack told Leisha, "When I hit 84 percent profit over two consecutive quarters, the data analysts logged onto me. They were just sniffing. Well, that's their job, even when the overall amounts are actually small. It's the patterns they care about. If they take the trouble to cross-reference data banks and come up with the fact that Kevin is a Sleepless, will they try to stop us from investing somehow?"

"That's paranoid," Leisha said.

"No, it's not," Jeanine said. "Leisha, you don't *know*."

"You mean because I've been protected by my father's money and caring," Leisha said. No one grimaced; all of them confronted ideas openly, without shadowy allusions. Without dreams.

"Yes," Jeanine said. "Your father sounds terrific. And he raised you to think that achievement should not be fettered—Jesus Christ, he's a Yagaiist. Well, good. We're glad for you." She said it without sarcasm. Leisha nodded. "But the world isn't always like that. They hate us."

"That's too strong," Carol said. "Not hate."

"Well, maybe," Jeanine said. "But they're different from us. We're better, and they naturally resent that."

"I don't see what's natural about it," Tony said. "Why shouldn't it be just as natural to admire what's better? We do. Does any one of us resent Kenzo Yagai for his genius? Or Nelson Wade, the physicist? Or Catherine Raduski?"

"We don't resent them because we *are* better," Richard said. "Q.E.D."

"What we should do is have our own society," Tony said. "Why should we allow their regulations to restrict our natural, honest achievements? Why should Jeanine be barred from skating against them and Jack from investing on their same terms just because we're Sleepless? Some of them are brighter than others of them. Some have greater persistence. Well, we have greater concentration, more bio-chemical stability, and more time. All men are not created equal."

"Be fair, Jack—no one has been barred from anything yet," Jeanine said.

"But we will be."

"*Wait*," Leisha said. She was deeply troubled by the conversation. "I mean, yes, in many ways we're better. But you quoted out of context, Tony. The Declaration of Independence doesn't say all men are created equal in ability. It's talking about rights and power—it means that all are created equal *under the law*. We have no more right to a separate society or to being free of society's restrictions than anyone else does. There's no other way to freely trade one's efforts, unless the same contractual rules apply to all."

"Spoken like a true Yagaiist," Richard said, squeezing her hand.

"That's enough intellectual discussion for me," Carol said, laughing. "We've been at this for hours. We're at the beach, for Chrissake. Who wants to swim with me?"

"I do," Jeanine said. "Come on, Jack."

All of them rose, brushing sand off their suits, discarding sunglasses. Richard pulled Leisha to her feet. But just before they ran into the water, Tony put his skinny hand on her arm. "One more question, Leisha. Just to think about. If we achieve better than most other people, and we trade with the Sleepers when it's mutually beneficial, making no distinction there between the strong and the weak—what obligation do we have to those so weak they don't have anything to trade with us? We're already going to give more than we get—do we have to do it when we get nothing at all? Do we have to take care of their deformed and handicapped and sick and lazy and shiftless with the products of our work?"

"Do the Sleepers have to?" Leisha countered.

"Kenzo Yagai would say no. He's a Sleeper."

"He would say they would receive the benefits of contractual trade even if they aren't direct parties to the contract. The whole world is better-fed and healthier because of Y-energy."

"Come on!" Jeanine yelled. "Leisha, they're dunking me! Jack, you stop that! Leisha, help me!"

Leisha laughed. Just before she grabbed for Jeanine, she caught the look on Richard's face, on Tony's: Richard frankly lustful, Tony angry. At her. But why? What had she done, except argue in favor of dignity and trade?

Then Jack threw water on her, and Carol pushed Jack into the warm spray, and Richard was there with his arms around her, laughing.

When she got the water out of her eyes, Tony was gone.

Midnight. "Okay," Carol said. "Who's first?"

The six teenagers in the brambled clearing looked at each other. A Y-lamp, kept on low for atmosphere, cast weird shadows across their faces and over their bare legs. Around the clearing Roger Camden's trees stood thick and dark, a wall between them and the closest of the estate's outbuildings. It was very hot. August air hung heavy, sullen. They had voted against bringing an air-conditioned Y-field because this was a return to the primitive, the dangerous; let it be primitive.

Six pairs of eyes stared at the glass in Carol's hand.

"Come *on*," she said. "Who wants to drink up?" Her voice was jaunty, theatrically hard. "It was difficult enough to get this."

"How *did* you get it?" said Richard, the group member—except for Tony—with the least influential family contacts, the least money. "In a drinkable form like that?"

"My cousin Brian is a pharmaceutical supplier to the Biotech Institute. He's curious." Nods around the circle; except for Leisha, they were Sleepless precisely because they had relatives somehow connected to Biotech. And everyone was curious. The glass held interleukin-1, an immune system booster, one of many substances which as a side effect induced the brain to swift and deep sleep.

Leisha stared at the glass. A warm feeling crept through her lower belly, not unlike the feeling when she and Richard made love.

Tony said, "Give it to me!"

Carol did. "Remember—you only need a little sip."

Tony raised the glass to his mouth, stopped, looked at them over the rim from his fierce eyes. He drank.

Carol took back the glass. They all watched Tony. Within a minute he lay on the rough ground; within two, his eyes closed in sleep.

It wasn't like seeing parents sleep, siblings, friends. It was Tony. They looked away, didn't meet each other's eyes. Leisha felt the warmth between her legs tug and tingle, faintly obscene.

When it was her turn, she drank slowly, then passed the glass to Jeanine. Her head turned heavy, as if it were being stuffed with damp rags. The trees at the edge of the clearing blurred. The portable lamp blurred, too—it wasn't bright and clean anymore but squishy, blobby; if she touched it, it would smear. Then darkness swooped over her brain, taking it away: *Taking away her mind.* "Daddy!" She tried to call, to clutch for him, but then the darkness obliterated her.

Afterward, they all had headaches. Dragging themselves back through the woods in the thin morning light was torture, compounded by an odd shame. They didn't touch each other. Leisha walked as far away from Richard as she could. It was a whole day before the throbbing left the base of her skull, or the nausea her stomach.

There had not even been any dreams.

"I want you to come with me tonight," Leisha said, for the tenth or twelfth time. "We both leave for college in just two days; this is the last chance. I really want you to meet Richard."

Alice lay on her stomach across her bed. Her hair, brown and lusterless, fell around her face. She wore an expensive yellow jumpsuit, silk by Ann Patterson, which rucked up in wrinkles around her knees.

"Why? What do you care if I meet Richard or not?"

"Because you're my sister," Leisha said. She knew better than to say "my twin." Nothing got Alice angry faster.

"I don't want to." The next moment Alice's face changed. "Oh, I'm sorry, Leisha—I didn't mean to sound so snotty. But . . . but I don't want to."

"It won't be all of them. Just Richard. And just for an hour or so. Then you can come back here and pack for Northwestern."

"I'm not going to Northwestern."

Leisha stared at her.

Alice said, "I'm pregnant."

Leisha sat on the bed. Alice rolled onto her back, brushed the hair out of her eyes, and laughed. Leisha's ears closed against the sound. "Look at you," Alice said. "You'd think it was *you* who was pregnant. But you never would be, would you, Leisha? Not until it was the proper time. Not you."

"How?" Leisha said. "We both had our caps put in . . ."

"I had the cap removed," Alice said.

"You wanted to get pregnant?"

"Damn flash I did. And there's not a thing Daddy can do about it. Except, of course, cut off all credit completely, but I don't think he'll do that, do you?" She laughed again. "Even to me?"

"But Alice . . . why? Not just to anger Daddy!"

"No," Alice said. "Although you would think of that, wouldn't you? Because I want something to love. Something of my *own*. Something that has nothing to do with this house."

Leisha thought of her and Alice running through the conservatory, years ago, her and Alice, darting in and out of the sunlight. "It hasn't been so bad growing up in this house."

"Leisha, you're stupid. I don't know how anyone so smart can be so stupid. Get out of my room! Get out!"

"But Alice . . . a *baby* . . ."

"Get out!" Alice shrieked. "Go to Harvard! Go be successful! Just get out!"

Leisha jerked off the bed. "Gladly! You're irrational, Alice! You don't think ahead, you don't plan a *baby* . . ." But she could never sustain anger. It dribbled away, leaving her mind empty. She looked at Alice, who suddenly put out her arms. Leisha went into them.

"You're the baby," Alice said wonderingly. "You *are*. You're so . . . I don't know what. You're a baby."

Leisha said nothing. Alice's arms felt warm, felt whole, felt like two children running in and out of sunlight. "I'll help you, Alice. If Daddy won't."

Alice abruptly pushed her away. "I don't need your help."

Alice stood. Leisha rubbed her empty arms, fingertips scraping across opposite elbows. Alice kicked the empty, open trunk in which she was supposed to pack for Northwestern, and then abruptly smiled, a smile that made Leisha look away. She braced herself for more abuse. But what Alice said, very softly, was, "Have a good time at Harvard."

5

She loved it.

From the first sight of Massachusetts Hall, older than the United States by a half century, Leisha felt something that had been missing in Chicago: Age. Roots. Tradition. She touched the bricks of Widener Library, the glass cases in the Peabody Museum, as if they were the grail. She had never been particularly sensitive to myth or drama; the anguish of Juliet seemed to her artificial, that of Willy Loman merely wasteful. Only King Arthur, struggling to create a better social order, had interested her. But now, walking under the huge autumn trees, she suddenly caught a glimpse of a force that could span generations, fortunes left to endow learning and achievement the benefactors would never see, individual effort spanning and shaping centuries to come. She stopped, and looked at the sky through the leaves, at the buildings solid with purpose. At such moments she thought of Camden, bending the will of an entire genetic research Institute to create her in the image he wanted.

Within a month, she had forgotten all such mega-musings.

The work load was incredible, even for her. The Sauley School had encouraged individual exploration at her own pace; Harvard knew what it wanted from her, at its pace. In the last twenty years, under the academic leadership of a man who in his youth had watched Japanese

economic domination with dismay, Harvard had become the controversial leader of a return to hard-edged learning of facts, theories, applications, problem-solving, intellectual efficiency. The school accepted
one out of every two hundred applications from around the world. The
daughter of England's Prime Minister had flunked out her first year and
been sent home.

Leisha had a single room in a new dormitory, the dorm because
she had spent so many years isolated in Chicago and was hungry for
people, the single so she would not disturb anyone else when she
worked all night. Her second day a boy from down the hall sauntered
in and perched on the edge of her desk.

"So you're Leisha Camden."

"Yes."

"Sixteen years old."

"Almost seventeen."

"Going to out-perform us all, I understand, without even trying."

Leisha's smile faded. The boy stared at her from under lowered
downy brows. He was smiling, his eyes sharp. From Richard and Tony
and the others Leisha had learned to recognize the anger that presented itself as contempt.

"Yes," Leisha said coolly, "I am."

"Are you sure? With your pretty little-girl hair and your mutant
little-girl brain?"

"Oh, leave her alone, Hannaway," said another voice. A tall blond
boy, so thin his ribs looked like ripples in brown sand, stood in jeans
and bare feet, drying his wet hair. "Don't you ever get tired of walking
around being an asshole?"

"Do you?" Hannaway said. He heaved himself off the desk and
started toward the door. The blond moved out of his way. Leisha
moved into it.

"The reason I'm going to do better than you," she said evenly, "is
because I have certain advantages you don't. Including sleeplessness.
And then after I 'out-perform' you, I'll be glad to help you study for
your tests so that you can pass, too."

The blond, drying his ears, laughed. But Hannaway stood still,
and into his eyes came an expression that made Leisha back away. He
pushed past her and stormed out.

"Nice going, Camden," the blond said. "He deserved that."

"But I meant it," Leisha said. "I will help him study."

The blond lowered his towel and stared. "You did, didn't you?
You meant it."

"Yes! Why does everybody keep questioning that?"

"Well," the boy said, "I don't. You can help me if I get into trouble." Suddenly he smiled. "But I won't."

"Why not?"

"Because I'm just as good at anything as you are, Leisha Camden."
She studied him. "You're not one of us. Not Sleepless."

"Don't have to be. I know what I can do. Do, be, create, trade."

She said, delighted, "You're a Yagaiist!"

"Of course." He held out his hand. "Stewart Sutter. How about a
fishburger in the Yard?"

"Great," Leisha said. They walked out together, talking excitedly.
When people stared at her, she tried not to notice. She was here. At
Harvard. With space ahead of her, time to learn, and with people like
Stewart Sutter who accepted and challenged her.

All the hours he was awake.

She became totally absorbed in her classwork. Roger Camden drove
up once, walking the campus with her, listening, smiling. He was more
at home than Leisha would have expected: He knew Stewart Sutter's
father, Kate Addams' grandfather. They talked about Harvard, business, Harvard, the Yagaii Economics Institute, Harvard. "How's
Alice?" Leisha asked once, but Camden said that he didn't know, she
had moved out and did not want to see him. He made her an allowance
through his attorney. While he said this, his face remained serene.

Leisha went to the Homecoming Ball with Stewart, who was also
majoring in pre-law but was two years ahead of Leisha. She took a
weekend trip to Paris with Kate Addams and two other girlfriends, taking the Concorde III. She had a fight with Stewart over whether the
metaphor of superconductivity could apply to Yagaiism, a stupid fight
they both knew was stupid but had anyway, and afterward they became
lovers. After the fumbling sexual explorations with Richard, Stewart
was deft, experienced, smiling faintly as he taught her how to have an
orgasm both by herself and with him. Leisha was dazzled. "It's so *joyful*," she said, and Stewart looked at her with a tenderness she knew
was part disturbance but didn't know why.

At mid-semester she had the highest grades in the freshman class.
She got every answer right on every single question on her mid-terms.
She and Stewart went out for a beer to celebrate, and when they came
back Leisha's room had been destroyed. The computer was smashed,
the data banks wiped, hardcopies and books smoldering in a metal
wastebasket. Her clothes were ripped to pieces, her desk and bureau
hacked apart. The only thing untouched, pristine, was the bed.

Steward said, "There's no way this could have been done in
silence. Everyone on the floor—hell, on the floor *below*—had to know.
Someone will talk to the police." No one did. Leisha sat on the edge of

the bed, dazed, and looked at the remnants of her Homecoming gown. The next day Dave Hannaway gave her a long, wide smile.

Camden flew east again, taut with rage. He rented her an apartment in Cambridge with E-lock security and a bodyguard named Toshio. After he left, Leisha fired the bodyguard but kept the apartment. It gave her and Stewart more privacy, which they used to endlessly discuss the situation. It was Leisha who argued that it was an aberration, an immaturity.

"There have always been haters, Stewart. Hate Jews, hate Blacks, hate immigrants, hate Yagaiists who have more initiative and dignity than you do. I'm just the latest object of hatred. It's not new, it's not remarkable. It doesn't mean any basic kind of schism between the Sleepless and Sleepers."

Stewart sat up in bed and reached for the sandwiches on the night stand. "Doesn't it? Leisha, you're a different kind of person entirely. More evolutionarily fit, not only to survive but to prevail. Those other 'objects of hatred' you cite except Yagaiists—they were all powerless in their societies. They occupied *inferior* positions. You, on the other hand—all three Sleepless in Harvard Law are on the *Law Review*. All of them. Kevin Baker, your oldest, has already founded a successful bio-interface software firm and is making money, a lot of it. Every Sleepless is making superb grades, none have psychological problems, all are healthy—and most of you aren't even adults yet. How much hatred do you think you're going to encounter once you hit the big-stakes world of finance and business and scarce endowed chairs and national politics?"

"Give me a sandwich," Leisha said. "Here's my evidence you're wrong: You yourself. Kenzo Yagai. Kate Addams. Professor Lane. My father. Every Sleeper who inhabits the world of fair trade, mutually beneficial contracts. And that's most of you, or at least most of you who are worth considering. You believe that competition among the most capable leads to the most beneficial trades for everyone, strong and weak. Sleepless are making real and concrete contributions to society, in a lot of fields. That has to outweigh the discomfort we cause. We're *valuable* to you. You know that."

Stewart brushed crumbs off the sheets. "Yes. I do. Yagaiists do."

"Yagaiists run the business and financial and academic worlds. Or they will. In a meritocracy, they *should*. You underestimate the majority of people, Stew. Ethics aren't confined to the ones out front."

"I hope you're right," Steward said. "Because, you know, I'm in love with you."

Leisha put down her sandwich.

"Joy," Stewart mumbled into her breasts, "you are joy."

When Leisha went home for Thanksgiving, she told Richard about Stewart. He listened tight-lipped.

"A Sleeper."

"A *person*," Leisha said. "A good, intelligent, achieving person!"

"Do you know what your good intelligent achieving Sleepers have done, Leisha? Jeanine has been barred from Olympic skating. 'Genetic alteration, analogous to steroid abuse to create an unsportsmanlike advantage.' Chris Devereaux's left Stanford. They trashed his laboratory, destroyed two years' work in memory formation proteins. Kevin Baker's software company is fighting a nasty advertising campaign, all underground of course, about kids using software designed by 'non-human minds.' Corruption, mental slavery, satanic influences: the whole bag of witch-hunt tricks. Wake up, Leisha!"

They both heard his words. Moments dragged by. Richard stood like a boxer, forward on the balls of his feet, teeth clenched. Finally he said, very quietly, "Do you love him?"

"Yes," Leisha said. "I'm sorry."

"Your choice," Richard said coldly. "What do you do while he's asleep? Watch?"

"You make it sound like a perversion!"

Richard said nothing. Leisha drew a deep breath. She spoke rapidly but calmly, a controlled rush: "While Stewart is asleep I work. The same as you do. Richard—don't do this. I didn't mean to hurt you. And I don't want to lose the group. I believe the Sleepers are the same species as we are—are you going to punish me for that? Are you going to *add* to the hatred? Are you going to tell me that I can't belong to a wider world that includes all honest, worthwhile people whether they sleep or not? Are you going to tell me that the most important division is by genetics and not by economic spirituality? Are you going to force me into an artificial choice, 'us' or 'them'?"

Richard picked up a bracelet. Leisha recognized it: She had given it to him in the summer. His voice was quiet. "No. It's not a choice." He played with the gold links a minute, then looked up at her. "Not yet."

By spring break, Camden walked more slowly. He took medicine for his blood pressure, his heart. He and Susan, he told Leisha, were getting a divorce. "She changed, Leisha, after I married her. You saw that. She was independent and productive and happy, and then after a few years she stopped all that and became a shrew. A whining shrew." He shook his head in genuine bewilderment. "You saw the change."

Leisha had. A memory came to her: Susan leading her and Alice in "games" that were actually controlled cerebral-performance tests.

Susan's braids dancing around her sparkling eyes. Alice had loved Susan, then, as much as Leisha had.

"Dad, I want Alice's address."

"I told you up at Harvard, I don't have it," Camden said. He shifted in his chair, the impatient gesture of a body that never expected to wear out. In January Kenzo Yagai had died of pancreatic cancer; Camden had taken the news hard. "I make her allowance through an attorney. By her choice."

"Then I want the address of the attorney."

The attorney, however, refused to tell Leisha where Alice was. "She doesn't want to be found, Ms. Camden. She wanted a complete break."

"Not from me," Leisha said.

"Yes," the attorney said, and something flickered behind his eyes, something she had last seen in Dave Hannaway's face.

She flew to Austin before returning to Boston, making her a day late for classes. Kevin Baker saw her instantly, canceling a meeting with IBM. She told him what she needed, and he set his best data-net people on it, without telling them why. Within two hours she had Alice's address from the attorney's electronic files. It was the first time, she realized, that she had ever turned to one of the Sleepless for help, and it had been given instantly. Without trade.

Alice was in Pennsylvania. The next weekend Leisha rented a hovercar and driver—she had learned to drive, but only groundcars as yet—and went to High Ridge, in the Appalachian Mountains.

It was an isolated hamlet, twenty-five miles from the nearest hospital. Alice lived with a man named Ed, a silent carpenter twenty years older than she, in a cabin in the woods. The cabin had water and electricity but no news net. In the early spring light the earth was raw and bare, slashed with icy gullies. Alice and Ed apparently worked at nothing. Alice was eight months pregnant.

"I didn't want you here," she said to Leisha. "So why are you?"

"Because you're my sister."

"God, look at you. Is that what they're wearing at Harvard? Boots like that? When did you become fashionable, Leisha? You were always too busy being intellectual to care."

"What's this all about, Alice? Why here? What are you doing?"

"Living," Alice said. "Away from dear Daddy, away from Chicago, away from drunken broken Susan—did you know she drinks? Just like Mom. He does that to people. But not to me. I got out. I wonder if you ever will."

"Got out? To *this*?"

"I'm happy," Alice said angrily. "Isn't that what it's supposed to be about? Isn't that the aim of your great Kenzo Yagai—happiness through individual effort?"

Leisha thought of saying that Alice was making no efforts that she could see. She didn't say it. A chicken ran through the yard of the cabin. Behind, the Great Smoky Mountains rose in layers of blue haze. Leisha thought what this place must have been like in winter: cut off from the world where people strived towards goals, learned, changed.

"I'm glad you're happy, Alice."

"Are you?"

"Yes."

"Then I'm glad, too," Alice said, almost defiantly. The next moment she abruptly hugged Leisha, fiercely, the huge hard mound of her belly crushed between them. Alice's hair smelled sweet, like fresh grass in sunlight.

"I'll come see you again, Alice."

"Don't," Alice said.

6

SLEEPLESS MUTIE BEGS FOR REVERSAL OF GENE TAMPERING, screamed the headline in the Food Mart. "PLEASE LET ME SLEEP LIKE REAL PEOPLE!" CHILD PLEADS.

Leisha typed in her credit number and pressed the news kiosk for a print-out, although ordinarily she ignored the electronic tabloids. The headline went on circling the kiosk. A Food Mart employee stopped stacking boxes on shelves and watched her. Bruce, Leisha's bodyguard, watched the employee.

She was twenty-two, in her final year at Harvard Law, editor of the *Law Review*, ranked first in her class. The next three were Jonathan Cocchiara, Len Carter, and Martha Wentz. All Sleepless.

In her apartment she skimmed the print-out. Then she accessed the Groupnet run from Austin. The files had more news stories about the child, with comments from other Sleepless, but before she could call them up Kevin Baker came on-line himself, on voice.

"Leisha. I'm glad you called. I was going to call you."

"What's the situation with this Stella Bevington, Kev? Has anybody checked it out?"

"Randy Davies. He's from Chicago but I don't think you've met him, he's still in high school. He's in Park Ridge, Stella's in Skokie. Her parents wouldn't talk to him—were pretty abusive, in fact—but he got to see Stella face-to-face anyway. It doesn't look like an abuse case, just the usual stupidity: parents wanted a genius child, scrimped and saved, and now they can't handle that she *is* one. They scream at her to sleep, get emotionally abusive when she contradicts them, but so far no violence."

"Is the emotional abuse actionable?"

"I don't think we want to move on it yet. Two of us will keep in close touch with Stella—she does have a modem, and she hasn't told her parents about the net—and Randy will drive out weekly."

Leisha bit her lip. "A tabloid shitpiece said she's seven years old."

"Yes."

"Maybe she shouldn't be left there. I'm an Illinois resident, I can file an abuse grievance from here if Candy's got too much in her brief-case. . . ." *Seven years old.*

"No. Let it sit a while. Stella will probably be all right. You know that."

She did. Nearly all of the Sleepless stayed "all right," no matter how much opposition came from the stupid segment of society. And it was only the stupid segment, Leisha argued—a small if vocal minority. Most people could, and would, adjust to the growing presence of the Sleepless, when it became clear that that presence included not only growing power but growing benefits to the country as a whole.

Kevin Baker, now twenty-six, had made a fortune in micro-chips so revolutionary that Artificial Intelligence, once a debated dream, was yearly closer to reality. Carolyn Rizzolo had won the Pulitzer Prize in drama for her play *Morning Light.* She was twenty-four. Jeremy Robinson had done significant work in superconductivity applications while still a graduate student at Stanford. William Thaine, *Law Review* editor when Leisha first came to Harvard, was now in private practice. He had never lost a case. He was twenty-six, and the cases were becoming important. His clients valued his ability more than his age.

But not everyone reacted that way.

Kevin Baker and Richard Keller had started the datanet that bound the Sleepless into a tight group, constantly aware of each other's personal fights. Leisha Camden financed the legal battles, the educational costs of Sleepless whose parents were unable to meet them, the support of children in emotionally bad situations. Rhonda Lavelier got herself licensed as a foster mother in California, and whenever possible the Group maneuvered to have small Sleepless who were removed from their homes assigned to Rhonda. The Group now had three ABA lawyers; within the next year they would gain four more, licensed to practice in five different states.

The one time they had not been able to remove an abused Sleepless child legally, they kidnapped him.

Timmy DeMarzo, four years old. Leisha had been opposed to the action. She had argued the case morally and pragmatically—to her they were the same thing—thus: If they believed in their society, in its fundamental laws and in their ability to belong to it as free-trading productive individuals, they must remain bound by the society's contractual laws. The Sleepless were, for the most part, Yagaiists. They should already know this. And if the FBI caught them, the courts and press would crucify them.

They were not caught.

Timmy DeMarzo—not even old enough to call for help on the datanet, they had learned of the situation through the automatic police-record scan Kevin maintained through his company—was stolen from his own backyard in Wichita. He had lived the last year in an isolated trailer in North Dakota; no place was too isolated for a modem. He was cared for by a legally irreproachable foster mother who had lived there all her life. The foster mother was second cousin to a Sleepless, a broad cheerful woman with a much better brain than her appearance indicated. She was a Yagaiist. No record of the child's existence appeared in any data bank: not the IRS, not any school's, not even the local grocery store's computerized check-out slips. Food specifically for the child was shipped in monthly on a truck owned by a Sleepless in State College, Pennsylvania. Ten of the Group knew about the kidnapping, out of the total 3,428 born in the United States. Of that total, 2,691 were part of the Group via the net. Another 701 were as yet too young to use a modem. Only 36 Sleepless, for whatever reason, were not part of the Group.

The kidnapping had been arranged by Tony Indivino.

"It's Tony I wanted to talk to you about," Kevin said to Leisha. "He's started again. This time he means it. He's buying land."

She folded the tabloid very small and laid it carefully on the table. "Where?"

"Allegheny Mountains. In southern New York State. A lot of land. He's putting in the roads now. In the spring, the first buildings."

"Jennifer Sharifi still financing it?" She was the American-born daughter of an Arab prince who had wanted a Sleepless child. The prince was dead and Jennifer, dark-eyed and multilingual, was richer than Leisha would one day be.

"Yes. He's starting to get a following, Leisha."

"I know."

"Call him."

"I will. Keep me informed about Stella."

She worked until midnight at the *Law Review*, then until four A.M. preparing her classes. From four to five she handled legal matters for the Group. At five A.M. she called Tony, still in Chicago. He had finished high school, done one semester at Northwestern, and at Christmas vacation he had finally exploded at his mother for forcing him to live as a Sleeper. The explosion, it seemed to Leisha, had never ended.

"Tony? Leisha."

"The answer is yes, yes, no, and go to hell."

Leisha gritted her teeth. "Fine. Now tell me the questions."

"Are you really serious about the Sleepless withdrawing into their own self-sufficient society? Is Jennifer Sharifi willing to finance a project the size of building a small city? Don't you think that's a cheat of all that can be accomplished by patient integration of the Group into the mainstream? And what about the contradictions of living in an armed restricted city and still trading with the Outside?"

"I would never tell *you* to go to hell."

"Hooray for you," Tony said. After a moment he added, "I'm sorry. That sounds like one of *them*."

"It's wrong for us, Tony."

"Thanks for not saying I couldn't pull it off."

She wondered if he could. "We're not a separate species, Tony."

"Tell that to the Sleepers."

"You exaggerate. There are haters out there, there are *always* haters, but to give up . . ."

"We're not giving up. Whatever we create can be freely traded: software, hardware, novels, information, theories, legal counsel. We can travel in and out. But we'll have a safe place to return *to*. Without the leeches who think we owe them blood because we're better than they are."

"It isn't a matter of owing."

"Really?" Tony said. "Let's have this out, Leisha. All the way. You're a Yagaiist—what do you believe in?"

"Tony . . ."

"*Do it*," Tony said, and in his voice she heard the fourteen-year-old Richard had introduced her to. Simultaneously, she saw her father's face: not as he was now, since the by-pass, but as he had been when she was a little girl, holding her on his lap to explain that she was special.

"I believe in voluntary trade that is mutually beneficial. That spiritual dignity comes from supporting one's life through one's own efforts, and trading the results of those efforts in mutual cooperation throughout the society. That the symbol of this is the contract. And that we need each other for the fullest, most beneficial trade."

"Fine," Tony bit off. "Now what about the beggars in Spain?"

"The what?"

"You walk down a street in a poor country like Spain and you see a beggar. Do you give him a dollar?"

"Probably."

"Why? He's trading nothing with you. He has nothing to trade."

"I know. Out of kindness. Compassion."

"You see six beggars. Do you give them all a dollar?"

"Probably," Leisha said.

"You would. You see a hundred beggars and you haven't got Leisha Camden's money—do you give them each a dollar?"

"No."

"Why not?"

Leisha reached for patience. Few people could make her want to cut off a comm link; Tony was one of them. "Too draining on my own resources. My life has first claim on the resources I earn."

"All right. Now consider this. At Biotech Institute—where you and I began, dear pseudo-sister—Dr. Melling has just yesterday—"

"*Who?*"

"Dr. Susan Melling. Oh, God, I completely forgot—she used to be married to your father!"

"I lost track of her," Leisha said. "I didn't realize she'd gone back to research. Alice once said . . . never mind. What's going on at Biotech?"

"Two crucial items, just released. Carla Dutcher has had first-month fetal genetic analysis. Sleeplessness is a dominant gene. The next generation of the Group won't sleep either."

"We all knew that," Leisha said. Carla Dutcher was the world's first pregnant Sleepless. Her husband was a Sleeper. "The whole world expected that."

"But the press will have a windfall with it anyway. Just watch. Muties Breed! New Race Set To Dominate Next Generation of Children!"

Leisha didn't deny it. "And the second item?"

"It's sad, Leisha. We've just had our first death."

Her stomach tightened. "Who?"

"Bernie Kuhn. Seattle." She didn't know him. "A car accident. It looks pretty straightforward—he lost control on a steep curve when his brakes failed. He had only been driving a few months. He was seventeen. But the significance here is that his parents have donated his brain and body to Biotech, in conjunction with the pathology department at the Chicago Medical School. They're going to take him apart to get the first good look at what prolonged sleeplessness does to the body and brain."

"They should," Leisha said. "That poor kid. But what are you so afraid they'll find?"

"I don't know. I'm not a doctor. But whatever it is, if the haters can use it against us, they will."

"You're paranoid, Tony."

"Impossible. The Sleepless have personalities calmer and more reality-oriented than the norm. Don't you read the literature?"

"Tony—"

"What if you walk down that street in Spain and a hundred beggars each want a dollar and you say no and they have nothing to trade you but they're so rotten with anger about what you have that they knock you down and grab it and then beat you out of sheer envy and despair?"

Leisha didn't answer.

"Are you going to say that's not a human scenario, Leisha? That it never happens?"

"It happens," Leisha said evenly. "But not all that often."

"Bullshit. Read more history. Read more *newspapers*. But the point is: What do you owe the beggars then? What does a good Yagai-ist who believes in mutually beneficial contracts do with people who have nothing to trade and can only take?"

"You're not—"

"*What*, Leisha? In the most objective terms you can manage, what do we owe the grasping and non-productive needy?"

"What I said originally. Kindness. Compassion."

"Even if they don't trade it back? Why?"

"Because . . ." She stopped.

"Why? Why do law-abiding and productive human beings owe anything to those who neither produce very much nor abide by laws? What philosophical or economic or spiritual justification is there for owing them anything? Be as honest as I know you are."

Leisha put her head between her knees. The question gaped beneath her, but she didn't try to evade it. "I don't know. I just know we do."

"*Why?*"

She didn't answer. After a moment, Tony did. The intellectual challenge was gone from his voice. He said, almost tenderly, "Come down in the spring and see the site for Sanctuary. The buildings will be going up then."

"No," Leisha said.

"I'd like you to."

"No. Armed retreat is not the way."

Tony said, "The beggars are getting nastier, Leisha. As the Sleepless grow richer. And I don't mean in money."

"Tony—" she said, and stopped. She couldn't think what to say.

"Don't walk down too many streets armed with just the memory of Kenzo Yagai."

In March, a bitterly cold March of winds whipping down the Charles River, Richard Keller came to Cambridge. Leisha had not seen him for four years. He didn't send her word on the Groupnet that he was coming. She hurried up the walk to her townhouse, muffled to the eyes in a red wool scarf against the snowy cold, and he stood there blocking the doorway. Behind Leisha, her bodyguard tensed.

"Richard! Bruce, it's all right, this is an old friend."

"Hello, Leisha."

He was heavier, sturdier-looking, with a breadth of shoulder she didn't recognize. But the face was Richard's, older but unchanged: dark low brows, unruly dark hair. He had grown a beard.

"You look beautiful," he said.

She handed him a cup of coffee. "Are you here on business?" From the Groupnet she knew that he had finished his Master's and had done outstanding work in marine biology in the Caribbean, but had left that a year ago and disappeared from the net.

"No. Pleasure." He smiled suddenly, the old smile that opened up his dark face. "I almost forgot about that for a long time. Contentment, yes, we're all good at the contentment that comes from sustained work, but pleasure? Whim? Caprice? When was the last time you did something silly, Leisha?"

She smiled. "I ate cotton candy in the shower."

"Really? Why?"

"To see if it would dissolve in gooey pink patterns."

"Did it?"

"Yes. Lovely ones."

"And that was your last silly thing? When was it?"

"Last summer," Leisha said, and laughed.

"Well, mine is sooner than that. It's now. I'm in Boston for no other reason than the spontaneous pleasure of seeing you."

Leisha stopped laughing. "That's an intense tone for a spontaneous pleasure, Richard."

"Yup," he said, intensely. She laughed again. He didn't.

"I've been in India, Leisha. And China and Africa. Thinking, mostly. Watching. First I traveled like a Sleeper, attracting no attention. Then I set out to meet the Sleepless in India and China. There are a few, you know, whose parents were willing to come here for the operation. They pretty much are accepted and left alone. I tried to figure out why desperately poor countries—by our standards anyway, over there Y-energy is mostly available only in big cities—don't have any trouble accepting the superiority of Sleepless, whereas Americans, with more prosperity than any time in history, build in resentment more and more."

Leisha said, "Did you figure it out?"

"No. But I figured out something else, watching all those communes and villages and kampongs. We are too individualistic."

Disappointment swept Leisha. She saw her father's face: *Excellence is what counts, Leisha. Excellence supported by individual effort. . . .* She reached for Richard's cup. "More coffee?"

He caught her wrist and looked up into her face. "Don't misunderstand me, Leisha. I'm not talking about work. We are too much individuals in the rest of our lives. Too emotionally rational. Too much alone. Isolation kills more than the free flow of ideas. It kills joy."

He didn't let go of her wrist. She looked down into his eyes, into depths she hadn't seen before: It was the feeling of looking into a mine shaft, both giddy and frightening, knowing that at the bottom might be gold or darkness. Or both.

Richard said softly, "Stewart?"

"Over long ago. An undergraduate thing." Her voice didn't sound like her own.

"Kevin?"

"No, never—we're just friends."

"I wasn't sure. Anyone?"

"No."

He let go of her wrist. Leisha peered at him timidly. He suddenly laughed. "Joy, Leisha." An echo sounded in her mind, but she couldn't place it and then it was gone and she laughed too, a laugh airy and frothy as pink cotton candy in summer.

"Come home, Leisha. He's had another heart attack."

Susan Melling's voice on the phone was tired. Leisha said, "How bad?"

"The doctors aren't sure. Or say they're not sure. He wants to see you. Can you leave your studies?"

It was May, the last push toward her finals. The *Law Review* proofs were behind schedule. Richard had started a new business, marine consulting to Boston fishermen plagued with sudden inexplicable shifts in ocean currents, and was working twenty hours a day. "I'll come," Leisha said.

Chicago was colder than Boston. The trees were half-budded. On Lake Michigan, filling the huge east windows of her father's house, whitecaps tossed up cold spray. Leisha saw that Susan was living in the house: her brushes on Camden's dresser, her journals on the credenza in the foyer.

"Leisha," Camden said. He looked old. Gray skin, sunken cheeks, the fretful and bewildered look of men who accepted potency like air, indivisible from their lives. In the corner of the room, on a small eighteenth-century slipper chair, sat a short, stocky woman with brown braids.

"*Alice.*"

"Hello, Leisha."

"*Alice.* I've looked for you. . . ." The wrong thing to say. Leisha had looked, but not very hard, deterred by the knowledge that Alice had not wanted to be found. "How are you?"

"I'm fine," Alice said. She seemed remote, gentle, unlike the angry Alice of six years ago in the raw Pennsylvania hills. Camden moved painfully on the bed. He looked at Leisha with eyes which, she saw, were undimmed in their blue brightness.

"I asked Alice to come. And Susan. Susan came a while ago. I'm dying, Leisha."

No one contradicted him. Leisha, knowing his respect for facts, remained silent. Love hurt her chest.

"John Jaworski has my will. None of you can break it. But I wanted to tell you myself what's in it. The last few years I've been selling, liquidating. Most of my holdings are accessible now. I've left a tenth to Alice, a tenth to Susan, a tenth to Elizabeth, and the rest to you, Leisha, because you're the only one with the individual ability to use the money to its full potential for achievement."

Leisha looked wildly at Alice, who gazed back with her strange remote calm. "Elizabeth? My . . . mother? Is alive?"

"Yes," Camden said.

"You told me she was dead! Years and years ago!"

"Yes. I thought it was better for you that way. She didn't like what you were, was jealous of what you could become. And she had nothing to give you. She would only have caused you emotional harm."

Beggars in Spain . . .

"That was wrong, Dad. You were *wrong*. She's my *mother* . . ." She couldn't finish the sentence.

Camden didn't flinch. "I don't think I was. But you're an adult now. You can see her if you wish."

He went on looking at her from his bright, sunken eyes, while around Leisha the air heaved and snapped. Her father had lied to her. Susan watched her closely, a small smile on her lips. Was she glad to see Camden fall in his daughter's estimation? Had she all along been that jealous of their relationship, of Leisha . . .

She was thinking like Tony.

The thought steadied her a little. But she went on staring at Camden, who went on staring implacably back, unbudged, a man positive even on his death bed that he was right.

Alice's hand was on her elbow, Alice's voice so soft that no one but Leisha could hear. "He's done now, Leisha. And after a while you'll be all right."

* * *

Alice had left her son in California with her husband of two years, Beck Watrous, a building contractor she had met while waitressing in a resort on the Artificial Islands. Beck had adopted Jordan, Alice's son.

"Before Beck there was a real bad time," Alice said in her remote voice. "You know, when I was carrying Jordan I actually used to dream that he would be Sleepless? Like you. Every night I'd dream that, and every morning I'd wake up and have morning sickness with a baby that was only going to be a stupid nothing like me. I stayed with Ed—in Pennsylvania, remember? You came to see me there once—for two more years. When he beat me, I was glad. I wished Daddy could see. At least Ed was touching me."

Leisha made a sound in her throat.

"I finally left because I was afraid for Jordan. I went to California, did nothing but eat for a year. I got up to 190 pounds." Alice was, Leisha estimated, five-foot-four. "Then I came home to see Mother."

"You didn't tell me," Leisha said. "You knew she was alive and you didn't tell me."

"She's in a drying-out tank half the time," Alice said, with brutal simplicity. "She wouldn't see you if you wanted to. But she saw me, and she fell slobbering all over me as her 'real' daughter, and she threw up on my dress. And I backed away from her and looked at the dress and knew it *should* be thrown up on, it was so ugly. Deliberately ugly. She started screaming how Dad had ruined her life, ruined mine, all for *you*. And do you know what I did?"

"What?" Leisha said. Her voice was shaky.

"I flew home, burned all my clothes, got a job, started college, lost fifty pounds, and put Jordan in play therapy."

The sisters sat silent. Beyond the window the lake was dark, unlit by moon or stars. It was Leisha who suddenly shook, and Alice who patted her shoulder.

"Tell me . . ." Leisha couldn't think what she wanted to be told, except that she wanted to hear Alice's voice in the gloom, Alice's voice as it was now, gentle and remote, without damage any more from the damaging fact of Leisha's existence. Her very existence as damage. ". . . tell me about Jordan. He's five now? What's he like?"

Alice turned her head to look levelly into Leisha's eyes. "He's a happy, ordinary little boy. Completely ordinary."

Camden died a week later. After the funeral, Leisha tried to see her mother at the Brookfield Drug and Alcohol Abuse Center. Elizabeth Camden, she was told, saw no one except her only child, Alice Camden Watrous.

Susan Melling, dressed in black, drove Leisha to the airport. Susan talked deftly, determinedly, about Leisha's studies, about Harvard, about the *Review*. Leisha answered in monosyllables but Susan persisted, asking questions, quietly insisting on answers: When would Leisha take her bar exams? Where was she interviewing for jobs? Gradually Leisha began to lose the numbness she had felt since her father's casket was lowered into the ground. She realized that Susan's persistent questioning was a kindness.

"He sacrificed a lot of people," Leisha said suddenly.

"Not me," Susan said. She pulled the car into the airport parking lot. "Only for a while there, when I gave up my work to do his. Roger didn't respect sacrifice much."

"Was he wrong?" Leisha said. The question came out with a kind of desperation she hadn't intended.

Susan smiled sadly. "No. He wasn't wrong. I should never have left my research. It took me a long time to come back to myself after that."

He does that to people, Leisha heard inside her head. Susan? Or Alice? She couldn't, for once, remember clearly. She saw her father in the old conservatory, potting and repotting the dramatic exotic flowers he had loved.

She was tired. It was muscle fatigue from stress, she knew; twenty minutes of rest would restore her. Her eyes burned from unaccustomed tears. She leaned her head back against the car seat and closed them.

Susan pulled the car into the airport parking lot and turned off the ignition. "There's something I want to tell you, Leisha."

Leisha opened her eyes. "About the will?"

Susan smiled tightly. "No. You really don't have any problems with how he divided the estate, do you? It seems to you reasonable. But that's not it. The research team from Biotech and Chicago Medical has finished its analysis of Bernie Kuhn's brain."

Leisha turned to face Susan. She was startled by the complexity of Susan's expression. Determination, and satisfaction, and anger, and something else Leisha could not name.

Susan said, "We're going to publish next week, in the *New England Journal of Medicine*. Security has been unbelievably restricted—no leaks to the popular press. But I want to tell you now, myself, what we found. So you'll be prepared."

"Go on," Leisha said. Her chest felt tight.

"Do you remember when you and the other Sleepless kids took interleukin-1 to see what sleep was like? When you were sixteen?"

"How did you know about that?"

"You kids were watched a lot more closely than you think. Remember the headache you got?"

"Yes." She and Richard and Tony and Carol and Jeanine . . . after her rejection by the Olympic Committee, Jeanine had never skated again. She was a kindergarten teacher in Butte, Montana.

"Interleukin-1 is what I want to talk about. At least partly. It's one of a whole group of substances that boost the immune system. They stimulate the production of antibodies, the activity of white blood cells, and a host of other immunoenhancements. Normal people have surges of IL-1 released during the slow-wave phases of sleep. That means that they—we—are getting boosts to the immune system during sleep. One of the questions we researchers asked ourselves twenty-eight years ago was: Will Sleepless kids who don't get those surges of IL-1 get sick more often?"

"I've never been sick," Leisha said.

"Yes, you have. Chicken pox and three minor colds by the end of your fourth year," Susan said precisely. "But in general you were all a very healthy lot. So we researchers were left with the alternate theory of sleep-driven immunoenhancement: That the burst of immune activity existed as a counterpart to a greater vulnerability of the body in sleep to disease, probably in some way connected to the fluctuations in body temperature during REM sleep. In other words, sleep *caused* the immune vulnerability that endogenous pyrogens like IL-1 counteract. Sleep was the problem, immune system enhancements were the solution. Without sleep, there would be no problem. Are you following this?"

"Yes."

"Of course you are. Stupid question." Susan brushed her hair off her face. It was going gray at the temples. There was a tiny brown age spot beneath her right ear.

"Over the years we collected thousands—maybe hundreds of thousands—of Single Photon Emission Tomography scans of you and the other kids' brains, plus endless EEG's, samples of cerebrospinal fluid, and all the rest of it. But we couldn't really see inside your brains, really know what's going on in there. Until Bernie Kuhn hit that embankment."

"Susan," Leisha said, "give it to me straight. Without more build-up."

"You're not going to age."

"What?"

"Oh, cosmetically, yes. Gray hair, wrinkles, sags. But the absence of sleep peptides and all the rest of it affects the immune and tissue-restoration systems in ways we don't understand. Bernie Kuhn had a perfect liver. Perfect lungs, perfect heart, perfect lymph nodes, perfect pancreas, perfect medulla oblongata. Not just healthy, or young—*perfect*. There's a tissue regeneration enhancement that clearly derives from the operation of the immune system but is radically different from anything we ever suspected. Organs show no wear and tear—not even the minimal amount expected in a seventeen-year-old. They just repair themselves, perfectly, on and on . . . and on."

"For how long?" Leisha whispered.

"Who the hell knows? Bernie Kuhn was young—maybe there's some compensatory mechanism that cuts in at some point and you'll all just collapse, like an entire fucking gallery of Dorian Grays. But I don't think so. Neither do I think it can go on forever; no tissue regeneration can do that. But a long, long time."

Leisha stared at the blurred reflections in the car windshield. She saw her father's face against the blue satin of his casket, banked with white roses. His heart, unregenerated, had given out.

Susan said, "The future is all speculative at this point. We know that the peptide structures that build up the pressure to sleep in normal people resemble the components of bacterial cell walls. Maybe there's a connection between sleep and pathogen receptivity. We don't know. But ignorance never stopped the tabloids. I wanted to prepare you because you're going to get called supermen, *homo perfectus*, who-all-knows what. Immortal."

The two women sat in silence. Finally Leisha said, "I'm going to tell the others. On our datanet. Don't worry about the security. Kevin Baker designed Groupnet; nobody knows anything we don't want them to."

"You're that well organized already?"

"Yes."

Susan's mouth worked. She looked away from Leisha. "We better go in. You'll miss your flight."

"Susan . . ."

"What?"

"Thank you."

"You're welcome," Susan said, and in her voice Leisha heard the thing she had seen before in Susan's expression and not been able to name: It was longing.

Tissue regeneration. A long, long time, sang the blood in Leisha's ears on the flight to Boston. *Tissue regeneration*. And, eventually: *Immortal*. No, not that, she told herself severely. Not that. The blood didn't listen.

"You sure smile a lot," said the man next to her in first class, a business traveler who had not recognized Leisha. "You coming from a big party in Chicago?"

"No. From a funeral."

The man looked shocked, then disgusted. Leisha looked out the window at the ground far below. Rivers like micro-circuits, fields like neat index cards. And on the horizon, fluffy white clouds like masses of exotic flowers, blooms in a conservatory filled with light.

The letter was no thicker than any hard-copy mail, but hard-copy mail addressed by hand to either of them was so rare that Richard was nervous. "It might be explosive." Leisha looked at the letter on their hall credenza. MS. LIESHA CAMDEN. Block letters, misspelled.

"It looks like a child's writing," she said.

Richard stood with head lowered, legs braced apart. But his expression was only weary. "Perhaps deliberately like a child's. You'd be more open to a child's writing, they might have figured."

" 'They'? Richard, are we getting that paranoid?"

He didn't flinch from the question. "Yes. For the time being."

A week earlier the *New England Journal of Medicine* had published Susan's careful, sober article. An hour later the broadcast and datanet news had exploded in speculation, drama, outrage, and fear. Leisha and Richard, along with all the Sleepless on the Groupnet, had tracked and charted each of four components, looking for a dominant reaction: speculation ("The Sleepless may live for centuries, and this might lead to the following events . . ."); drama ("If a Sleepless marries only Sleepers, he may have lifetime enough for a dozen brides—and several dozen children, a bewildering blended family . . ."); outrage ("Tampering with the law of nature has only brought among us unnatural so-called people who will live with the unfair advantage of time: time to accumulate more kin, more power, more property than the rest of us could ever know. . . ."); and fear ("How soon before the Super-race takes over?")

"They're all fear, of one kind or another," Carolyn Rizzolo finally said, and the Groupnet stopped their differentiated tracking.

Leisha was taking the final exams of her last year of law school. Each day comments followed her to the campus, along the corridors and in the classroom; each day she forgot them in the grueling exam sessions, all students reduced to the same status of petitioner to the great university. Afterward, temporarily drained, she walked silently back home to Richard and the Groupnet, aware of the looks of people on the street, aware of her bodyguard Bruce striding between her and them.

"It will calm down," Leisha said. Richard didn't answer.

The town of Salt Springs, Texas, passed a local ordinance that no Sleepless could obtain a liquor license, on the grounds that civil rights statutes were built on the "all men were created equal" clause of the Constitution, and Sleepless clearly were not covered. There were no Sleepless within a hundred miles of Salt Springs and no one had applied for a new liquor license there for the past ten years, but the story was picked up by United Press and by Datanet News, and within twenty-four hours heated editorials appeared, on both sides of the issue, across the nation.

More local ordinances appeared. In Pollux, Pennsylvania, the Sleepless could be denied apartment rental on the grounds that their prolonged wakefulness would increase both wear-and-tear on the landlord's property and utility bills. In Cranston Estates, California, Sleepless were barred from operating twenty-four-hour businesses: "unfair competition." Iroquois County, New York, barred them from serving on county juries, arguing that a jury containing Sleepless, with their skewed idea of time, did not constitute "a jury of one's peers."

"All those statutes will be thrown out in superior courts," Leisha said. "But God! The waste of money and docket time to do it!" A part of her mind noticed that her tone as she said this was Roger Camden's.

The state of Georgia, in which some sex acts between consenting adults were still a crime, made sex between a Sleepless and a Sleeper a third-degree felony, classing it with bestiality.

Kevin Baker had designed software that scanned the newsnets at high speed, flagged all stories involving discrimination or attacks on Sleepless, and categorized them by type. The files were available on Groupnet. Leisha read through them, then called Kevin. "Can't you create a parallel program to flag defenses of us? We're getting a skewed picture."

"You're right," Kevin said, a little startled. "I didn't think of it."

"Think of it," Leisha said, grimly. Richard, watching her, said nothing.

She was most upset by the stories about Sleepless children. Shunning at school, verbal abuse by siblings, attacks by neighborhood bullies, confused resentment from parents who had wanted an exceptional child but had not bargained on one who might live centuries. The school board of Cold River, Iowa, voted to bar Sleepless children from conventional classrooms because their rapid learning "created feelings of inadequacy in others, interfering with their education." The board made funds available for Sleepless to have tutors at home. There were no volunteers among the teaching staff. Leisha started spending as much time on Groupnet with the kids, talking to them all night long, as she did studying for her bar exams, scheduled for July.

Stella Bevington stopped using her modem.

Kevin's second program catalogued editorials urging fairness towards Sleepless. The school board of Denver set aside funds for a program in which gifted children, including the Sleepless, could use their talents and build teamwork through tutoring even younger children. Rive Beau, Louisiana, elected Sleepless Danielle du Cherney to the City Council, although Danielle was twenty-two and technically too young to qualify. The prestigious medical research firm of Halley-Hall gave much publicity to their hiring of Christopher Amren, a Sleepless with a Ph.D. in cellular physics.

Dora Clarq, a Sleepless in Dallas, opened a letter addressed to her and a plastic explosive blew off her arm.

Leisha and Richard stared at the envelope on the hall credenza. The paper was thick, cream-colored, but not expensive: the kind of paper made of bulky newsprint dyed the shade of vellum. There was no return address. Richard called Liz Bishop, a Sleepless who was majoring in Criminal Justice in Michigan. He had never spoken with her before—neither had Leisha—but she came on Groupnet immediately and told them how to open it, or she could fly up and do it if they preferred. Richard and Leisha followed her directions for remote detonation in the basement of the townhouse. Nothing blew up. When the letter was open, they took it out and read it:

> Dear Ms. Camden,
> You been pretty good to me and I'm sorry to do this but I quit. They are making it pretty hot for me at the union not officially but you know how it is. If I was you I wouldn't go to the union for another bodyguard I'd try to find one privately. But be careful. Again I'm sorry but I have to live too.
>
> Bruce

"I don't know whether to laugh or cry," Leisha said. "The two of us getting all this equipment, spending hours on this set-up so an explosive won't detonate . . ."

"It's not as if I at least had a whole lot else to do," Richard said. Since the wave of anti-Sleepless sentiment, all but two of his marine-consultant clients, vulnerable to the marketplace and thus to public opinion, had canceled their accounts.

Groupnet, still up on Leisha's terminal, shrilled in emergency override. Leisha got there first. It was Tony.

"Leisha. I'll need your legal help, if you'll give it. They're trying to fight me on Sanctuary. Please fly down here."

* * *

Sanctuary was raw brown gashes in the late-spring earth. It was situated in the Allegheny Mountains of southern New York State, old hills rounded by age and covered with pine and hickory. A superb road led from the closest town, Belmont, to Sanctuary. Low, maintenance-free buildings, whose design was plain but graceful, stood in various stages of completion. Jennifer Sharifi, looking strained, met Leisha and Richard. "Tony wants to talk to you, but first he asked me to show you both around."

"What's wrong?" Leisha asked quietly. She had never met Jennifer before but no Sleepless looked like that—pinched, spent, *weary*— unless the stress level was enormous.

Jennifer didn't try to evade the question. "Later. First look at Sanctuary. Tony respects your opinion enormously, Leisha; he wants you to see everything."

The dormitories each held fifty, with communal rooms for cooking, dining, relaxing, and bathing, and a warren of separate offices and studios and labs for work. "We're calling them 'dorms' anyway, despite the etymology," Jennifer said, trying to smile. Leisha glanced at Richard. The smile was a failure.

She was impressed, despite herself, with the completeness of Tony's plans for lives that would be both communal and intensely private. There was a gym, a small hospital—"By the end of next year, we'll have eighteen AMA-certified doctors, you know, and four are thinking of coming here"—a daycare facility, a school, an intensive-crop farm. "Most of our food will come in from the outside, of course. So will most people's jobs, although they'll do as much of them as possible from here, over datanets. We're not cutting ourselves off from the world—only creating a safe place from which to trade with it." Leisha didn't answer.

Apart from the power facilities, self-supported Y-energy, she was most impressed with the human planning. Tony had Sleepless interested from virtually every field they would need both to care for themselves and to deal with the outside world. "Lawyers and accountants come first," Jennifer said. "That's our first line of defense in safeguarding ourselves. Tony recognizes that most modern battles for power are fought in the courtroom and boardroom."

But not all. Last, Jennifer showed them the plans for physical defense. She explained them with a mixture of defiance and pride: Every effort had been made to stop attackers without hurting them. Electronic surveillance completely circled the 150 square miles Jennifer had purchased—some *counties* were smaller than that, Leisha thought, dazed. When breached, a force field a half-mile within the E-gate activated, delivering electric shocks to anyone on foot—"But only on the *outside* of the field. We don't want any of our kids hurt." Unmanned penetration by vehicles or robots was identified by a system that located all moving metal above a certain mass within Sanctuary. Any moving metal that did not carry a special signaling device designed by Donna Pospula, a Sleepless who had patented important electronic components, was suspect.

"Of course, we're not set up for an air attack or an outright army assault," Jennifer said. "But we don't expect that. Only the haters in self-motivated hate." Her voice sagged.

Leisha touched the hard-copy of the security plans with one finger. They troubled her. "If we can't integrate ourselves into the world . . . free trade should imply free movement."

"Yeah. Well," Jennifer said, such an uncharacteristic Sleepless remark—both cynical and inarticulate—that Leisha looked up. "I have something to tell you, Leisha."

"What?"

"Tony isn't here."

"Where is he?"

"In Allegheny County jail. It's true we're having zoning battles about Sanctuary—zoning! In this isolated spot! But this is something else, something that just happened this morning. Tony's been arrested for the kidnapping of Timmy DeMarzo."

The room wavered. "FBI?"

"Yes."

"How . . . how did they find out?"

"Some agent eventually cracked the case. They didn't tell us how. Tony needs a lawyer, Leisha. Dana Monteiro has already agreed, but Tony wants you."

"Jennifer—I don't even take the bar exams until July!"

"He says he'll wait. Dana will act as his lawyer in the meantime. Will you pass the bar?"

"Of course. But I already have a job lined up with Morehouse, Kennedy, & Anderson in New York—" She stopped. Richard was looking at her hard, Jennifer gazing down at the floor. Leisha said quietly, "What will he plead?"

"Guilty," Jennifer said, "with—what is it called legally? Extenuating circumstances."

Leisha nodded. She had been afraid Tony would want to plead not guilty: more lies, subterfuge, ugly politics. Her mind ran swiftly over extenuating circumstances, precedents, tests to precedents. . . . They could use *Clements v. Voy* . . .

"Dana is at the jail now," Jennifer said. "Will you drive in with me?"

"Yes."

In Belmont, the county seat, they were not allowed to see Tony. Dana Monteiro, as his attorney, could go in and out freely. Leisha, not officially an attorney at all, could go nowhere. This was told them by a man in the D.A.'s office whose face stayed immobile while he spoke to them, and who spat on the ground behind their shoes when they turned to leave, even though this left him with a smear of spittle on his courthouse floor.

Richard and Leisha drove their rental car to the airport for the flight back to Boston. On the way Richard told Leisha he was leaving her. He was moving to Sanctuary, now, even before it was functional, to help with the planning and building.

She stayed most of the time in her townhouse, studying ferociously for the bar exams or checking on the Sleepless children through Group-net. She had not hired another bodyguard to replace Bruce, which made her reluctant to go outside very much; the reluctance in turn made her angry with herself. Once or twice a day she scanned Kevin's electronic news clippings.

There were signs of hope. The New York *Times* ran an editorial, widely reprinted on the electronic news services:

PROSPERITY AND HATRED:
A LOGIC CURVE WE'D RATHER NOT SEE

The United States has never been a country that much values calm, logic, rationality. We have, as a people, tended to label these things "cold." We have, as a people, tended to admire feeling and action: We exalt in our stories and our memorials; not the creation of the Constitution but its defense at Iwo Jima; not the intellectual achievements of a Stephen Hawkings but the heroic passion of a Charles Lindbergh; not the inventors of the monorails and computers that unite us but the composers of the angry songs of rebellion that divide us.

A peculiar aspect of this phenomenon is that it grows stronger in times of prosperity. The better off our citizenry, the greater their contempt for the calm reasoning that got them there, and the more passionate their indulgence in emotion. Consider, in the last century, the gaudy excesses of the Roaring Twenties and the anti-establishment contempt of the sixties. Consider, in our own century, the unprecedented prosperity brought about by Y-energy—and then consider that Kenzo Yagai, except to his followers, was seen as a greedy and bloodless logician, while our national adulation goes to neo-nihilist writer Stephen Castelli, to "feelie" actress Brenda Foss, and to daredevil gravity-well diver Jim Morse Luter.

But most of all, as you ponder this phenomenon in your Y-energy houses, consider the current outpouring of irrational feeling directed at the "Sleepless" since the publication of the joint findings of the Biotech Institute and the Chicago Medical School concerning Sleepless tissue regeneration.

Most of the Sleepless are intelligent. Most of them are calm, if you define that much-maligned word to mean directing one's energies into solving problems rather than to emoting about them. (Even Pulitzer Prize winner Carolyn Rizzolo gave us a stunning play of ideas, not of passions run amuck.) All of them show a natural bent toward achievement, a bent given a decided boost by the one-third more time in their days to achieve in. Their achievements lie, for the most part, in logical fields rather than emotional ones: Computers. Law. Finance. Physics. Medical research. They are rational, orderly, calm, intelligent, cheerful, young, and possibly very long-lived.

And, in our United States of unprecedented prosperity, increasingly hated.

Does the hatred that we have seen flower so fully over the last few months really grow, as many claim, from the "unfair advantage" the Sleepless have over the rest of us in securing jobs, promotions, money, success? Is it really envy over the Sleepless' good fortune? Or does it come from something more pernicious, rooted in our tradition of shoot-from-the-hip American action: Hatred of the logical, the calm, the considered? Hatred in fact of the superior mind?

If so, perhaps we should think deeply about the founders of this country: Jefferson, Washington, Paine, Adams—inhabitants of the Age of Reason, all. These men created our orderly and balanced system of laws precisely to protect the property and achievements created by the individual efforts of balanced and rational minds. The Sleepless may be our severest internal test yet of our own sober belief in law and order. No, the Sleepless were *not* "created equal," but our attitudes toward them should be examined with a care equal to our soberest jurisprudence. We may not like what we learn about our own motives, but our credibility as a people may depend on the rationality and intelligence of the examination.

Both have been in short supply in the public reaction to last month's research findings.

Law is not theater. Before we write laws reflecting gaudy and dramatic feelings, we must be very sure we understand the difference.

Leisha hugged herself, gazing in delight at the screen, smiling. She called the New York *Times:* Who had written the editorial? The receptionist, cordial when she answered the phone, grew brusque. The *Times* was not releasing that information, "prior to internal investigation."

It could not dampen her mood. She whirled around the apartment, after days of sitting at her desk or screen. Delight demanded physical action. She washed dishes, picked up books. There were gaps in the furniture patterns where Richard had taken pieces that belonged to him; a little quieter now, she moved the furniture to close the gaps.

Susan Melling called to tell her about the *Times* editorial; they talked warmly for a few minutes. When Susan hung up, the phone rang again.

"Leisha? Your voice still sounds the same. This is Stewart Sutter."

"Stewart." She had not seen him for years. Their romance had lasted two years and then dissolved, not from any painful issue so much as from the press of both their studies. Standing by the comm terminal, hearing his voice, Leisha suddenly felt again his hands on her breasts in the cramped dormitory bed: All those years before she had found a good use for a bed. The phantom hands became Richard's hands, and a sudden pain pierced her.

"Listen," Stewart said, "I'm calling because there's some information I think you should know. You take your bar exams next week, right? And then you have a tentative job with Morehouse, Kennedy, & Anderson."

"How do you know all that, Stewart?"

"Men's room gossip. Well, not as bad as that. But the New York legal community—that part of it, anyway—is smaller than you think. And you're a pretty visible figure."

"Yes," Leisha said neutrally.

"Nobody has the slightest doubt you'll be called to the bar. But there is some doubt about the job with Morehouse, Kennedy. You've got two senior partners, Alan Morehouse and Seth Brown, who have changed their minds since this . . . flap. 'Adverse publicity for the firm,' 'turning law into a circus,' blah blah blah. You know the drill. But you've also got two powerful champions, Ann Carlyle and Michael Kennedy, the old man himself. He's quite a mind. Anyway, I wanted you to know all this so you can recognize exactly what the situation is and know whom to count on in the in-fighting."

"Thank you," Leisha said. "Stew . . . why do you care if I get it or not? Why should it matter to you?"

There was a silence on the other end of the phone. Then Stewart said, very low, "We're not all noodleheads out here, Leisha. Justice does still matter to some of us. So does achievement."

Light rose in her, a bubble of buoyant light.

Stewart said, "You have a lot of support here for that stupid zoning fight over Sanctuary, too. You might not realize that, but you do. What the Parks Commission crowd is trying to pull is . . . but they're just being used as fronts. You know that. Anyway, when it gets as far as the courts, you'll have all the help you need."

"Sanctuary isn't my doing. At all."

"No? Well, I meant the plural you."

"Thank you. I mean that. How are you doing?"

"Fine. I'm a daddy now."

"Really! Boy or girl?"

"Girl. A beautiful little bitch, drives me crazy. I'd like you to meet my wife sometimes, Leisha."

"I'd like that," Leisha said.

She spent the rest of the night studying for her bar exams. The bubble stayed with her. She recognized exactly what it was: joy.

It was going to be all right. The contract, unwritten, between her and her society—Kenzo Yagai's society, Roger Camden's society—would hold. With dissent and strife and yes, some hatred: She suddenly thought of Tony's beggars in Spain, furious at the strong because they themselves were not. Yes. But it would hold.

She believed that.

She did.

7

Leisha took her bar exams in July. They did not seem hard to her. Afterward three classmates, two men and a woman, made a fakely casual point of talking to Leisha until she had climbed safely into a taxi whose driver obviously did not recognize her, or stop signs. The three were all Sleepers. A pair of undergraduates, clean-shaven blond men with the long faces and pointless arrogance of rich stupidity, eyed Leisha and sneered. Leisha's female classmate sneered back.

Leisha had a flight to Chicago the next morning. Alice was going to join her there. They had to clean out the big house on the lake, dispose of Roger's personal property, put the house on the market. Leisha had had no time to do it earlier.

She remembered her father in the conservatory, wearing an ancient flat-topped hat he had picked up somewhere, potting orchids and jasmine and passion flowers.

When the doorbell rang she was startled: she almost never had visitors. Eagerly, she turned on the outside camera—maybe it was Jonathan or Martha, back in Boston to surprise her, to celebrate—why hadn't she thought before about some sort of celebration?

Richard stood gazing up at the camera. He had been crying.

She tore open the door. Richard made no move to come in. Leisha saw that what the camera had registered as grief was actually something else: tears of rage.

"Tony's dead."

Leisha put out her hand, blindly. Richard did not take it.

"They killed him in prison. Not the authorities—the other prisoners. In the recreation yard. Murderers, rapists, looters, scum of the earth—and they thought they had the right to kill *him* because he was different."

Now Richard did grab her arm, so hard that something, some bone, shifted beneath the flesh and pressed on a nerve. "Not just different—*better*. Because he was better, because we all are, we goddamn just don't stand up and shout it out of some misplaced feeling for *their* feelings . . . God!"

Leisha pulled her arm free and rubbed it, numb, staring at Richard's contorted face.

"They beat him to death with a lead pipe. No one even knows how they got a lead pipe. They beat him on the back of the head and they rolled him over and—"

"Don't!" Leisha said. It came out a whimper.

Richard looked at her. Despite his shouting, his violent grip on her arm, Leisha had the confused impression that this was the first time he had actually seen her. She went on rubbing her arm, staring at him in terror.

He said quietly, "I've come to take you to Sanctuary, Leisha. Dan Walcott and Vernon Bulriss are in the car outside. The three of us will carry you out, if necessary. But you're coming. You see that, don't you? You're not safe here, with your high profile and your spectacular looks—you're a natural target if anyone is. Do we have to force you? Or do you finally see for yourself that we have no choice—the bastards have left us no choice—except Sanctuary?"

Leisha closed her eyes. Tony, at fourteen, at the beach. Tony, his eyes ferocious and alight, the first to reach out his hand for the glass of interleukin-1. Beggars in Spain.

"I'll come."

* * *

She had never known such anger. It scared her, coming in bouts throughout the long night, receding but always returning again. Richard held her in his arms, sitting with their backs against the wall of her library, and his holding made no difference at all. In the living room Dan and Vernon talked in low voices.

Sometimes the anger erupted in shouting, and Leisha heard herself and thought *I don't know you*. Sometimes it became crying, sometimes talking about Tony, about all of them. Not the shouting nor the crying nor the talking eased her at all.

Planning did, a little. In a cold dry voice she didn't recognize, Leisha told Richard about the trip to close the house in Chicago. She had to go; Alice was already there. If Richard and Dan and Vernon put Leisha on the plane, and Alice met her at the other end with union bodyguards, she should be safe enough. Then she would change her return ticket from Boston to Belmont and drive with Richard to Sanctuary.

"People are already arriving," Richard said. "Jennifer Sharifi is organizing it, greasing the Sleeper suppliers with so much money they can't resist. What about this townhouse here, Leisha? Your furniture and terminal and clothes?"

Leisha looked around her familiar office. Law books lined the walls, red and green and brown, although most of the same information was on-line. A coffee cup rested on a print-out on the desk. Beside it was the receipt she had requested from the taxi driver this afternoon, a giddy souvenir of the day she had passed her bar exams; she had thought of having it framed. Above the desk was a holographic portrait of Kenzo Yagai.

"Let it rot," Leisha said.

Richard's arm tightened around her.

"I've never seen you like this," Alice said, subdued. "It's more than just clearing out the house, isn't it?"

"Let's get on with it," Leisha said. She yanked a suit from her father's closet. "Do you want any of this stuff for your husband?"

"It wouldn't fit."

"The hats?"

"No," Alice said. "Leisha—what is it?"

"Let's just *do* it!" She yanked all the clothes from Camden's closet, piled them on the floor, scrawled FOR VOLUNTEER AGENCY on a piece of paper and dropped it on top of the pile. Silently, Alice started adding clothes from the dresser, which already bore a taped paper scrawled ESTATE AUCTION.

The curtains were already down throughout the house; Alice had done that yesterday. She had also rolled up the rugs. Sunset glared redly on the bare wooden floors.

"What about your old room?" Leisha said. "What do you want there?"

"I've already tagged it," Alice said. "A mover will come Thursday."

"Fine. What else?"

"The conservatory. Sanderson has been watering everything, but he didn't really know what needed how much, so some of the plants are—"

"Fire Sanderson," Leisha said curtly. "The exotics can die. Or have them sent to a hospital, if you'd rather. Just watch out for the ones that are poisonous. Come on, let's do the library."

Alice sat slowly on a rolled-up rug in the middle of Camden's bedroom. She had cut her hair; Leisha thought it looked ugly, jagged brown spikes around her broad face. She had also gained more weight. She was starting to look like their mother.

Alice said, "Do you remember the night I told you I was pregnant? Just before you left for Harvard?"

"Let's do the library!"

"Do you?" Alice said. "For God's sake, can't you just once listen to someone else, Leisha? Do you have to be so much like Daddy every single minute?"

"I'm not like Daddy!"

"The hell you're not. You're exactly what he made you. But that's not the point. Do you remember that night?"

Leisha walked over the rug and out the door. Alice simply sat. After a minute Leisha walked back in. "I remember."

"You were near tears," Alice said implacably. Her voice was quiet. "I don't even remember exactly why. Maybe because I wasn't going to college after all. But I put my arms around you, and for the first time in years—years, Leisha—I felt you really were my sister. Despite all of it—the roaming the halls all night and the show-off arguments with Daddy and the special school and the artificially long legs and golden hair—all that crap. You seemed to need me to hold you. You seemed to need me. You seemed to *need*."

"What are you saying?" Leisha demanded. "That you can only be close to someone if they're in trouble and need you? That you can only be a sister if I was in some kind of pain, open sores running? Is that the bond between you Sleepers? 'Protect me while I'm unconscious, I'm just as crippled as you are'?"

"No," Alice said. "I'm saying that *you* could be a sister only if you were in some kind of pain."

Leisha stared at her. "You're stupid, Alice."

Alice said calmly, "I know that. Compared to you, I am. I know that."

Leisha jerked her head angrily. She felt ashamed of what she had just said, and yet it was true, and they both knew it was true, and anger still lay in her like a dark void, formless and hot. It was the formless part that was the worst. Without shape, there could be no action; without action, the anger went on burning her, choking her.

Alice said, "When I was twelve Susan gave me a dress for our birthday. You were away somewhere, on one of those overnight field trips your fancy progressive school did all the time. The dress was silk, pale blue, with antique lace—very beautiful. I was thrilled, not only because it was beautiful but because Susan had gotten it for me and gotten software for you. The dress was mine. Was, I thought, *me*." In the gathering gloom Leisha could barely make out her broad, plain features. "The first time I wore it a boy said, 'Stole your sister's dress, Alice? Snitched it while she was *sleeping?*' Then he laughed like crazy, the way they always did.

"I threw the dress away. I didn't even explain to Susan, although I think she would have understood. Whatever was yours was yours, and whatever wasn't yours was yours, too. That's the way Daddy set it up. The way he hard-wired it into our genes."

"You, too?" Leisha said. "You're no different from the other envious beggars?"

Alice stood up from the rug. She did it slowly, leisurely, brushing dust off the back of her wrinkled skirt, smoothing the print fabric. Then she walked over and hit Leisha in the mouth.

"Now do you see me as real?" Alice asked quietly.

Leisha put her hand to her mouth. She felt blood. The phone rang, Camden's unlisted personal line. Alice walked over, picked it up, listened, and held it calmly out to Leisha. "It's for you."

Numb, Leisha took it.

"Leisha? This is Kevin. Listen, something's happened. Stella Bevington called me, on the phone not Groupnet, I think her parents took away her modem. I picked up the phone and she screamed, 'This is Stella! They're hitting me he's drunk—' and then the line went dead. Randy's gone to Sanctuary—hell, they've *all* gone. You're closest to her, she's still in Skokie. You better get there fast. Have you got bodyguards you trust?"

"Yes," Leisha said, although she hadn't. The anger—finally—took form. "I can handle it."

"I don't know how you'll get her out of there," Kevin said. "They'll recognize you, they know she called somebody, they might even have knocked her out . . ."

"I'll handle it," Leisha said.

"Handle what?" Alice said.

Leisha faced her. Even though she knew she shouldn't, she said, "What your people do. To one of ours. A seven-year-old kid who's getting beaten up by her parents because she's Sleepless—because she's *better* than you are—" She ran down the stairs and out to the rental car she had driven from the airport.

Alice ran right down with her. "Not your car, Leisha. They can trace a rental car just like that. My car."

Leisha screamed, "If you think you're—"

Alice yanked open the door of her battered Toyota, a model so old the Y-energy comes weren't even concealed but hung like drooping jowls on either side. She shoved Leisha into the passenger seat, slammed the door, and rammed herself behind the wheel. Her hands were steady. "Where?"

Blackness swooped over Leisha. She put her head down, as far between her knees as the cramped Toyota would allow. Two—no, three—days since she had eaten. Since the night before the bar exams. The faintness receded, swept over her again as soon as she raised her head.

She told Alice the address in Skokie.

"Stay way in the back," Alice said. "And there's a scarf in the glove compartment—put it on. Low, to hide as much of your face as possible."

Alice had stopped the car along Highway 42. Leisha said, "This isn't—"

"It's a union quick-guard place. We have to look like we have some protection, Leisha. We don't need to tell him anything. I'll hurry."

She was out in three minutes with a huge man in a cheap dark suit. He squeezed into the front seat beside Alice and said nothing at all. Alice did not introduce him.

The house was small, a little shabby, with lights on downstairs, none upstairs. The first stars shone in the north, away from Chicago. Alice said to the guard, "Get out of the car and stand here by the car door—no, more in the light—and don't do anything unless I'm attacked in some way." The man nodded. Alice started up the walk. Leisha scrambled out of the back seat and caught her sister two-thirds of the way to the plastic front door.

"Alice, what the hell are you doing? *I* have to—"

"Keep your voice down," Alice said, glancing at the guard. "Leisha, *think*. You'll be recognized. Here, near Chicago, with a Sleepless daughter—these people have looked at your picture in magazines for years. They've watched long-range holovids of you. They know you. They know you're going to be a lawyer. Me they've never seen. I'm nobody."

"Alice—"

"For Chrissake, get back in the car!" Alice hissed, and pounded on the front door.

Leisha drew off the walk, into the shadow of a willow tree. A man opened the door. His face was completely blank.

Alice said, "Child Protection Agency. We got a call from a little girl, this number. Let me in."

"There's no little girl here."

"This is an emergency, priority one," Alice said. "Child Protection Act 186. Let me in!"

The man, still blank-faced, glanced at the huge figure by the car. "You got a search warrant?"

"I don't need one in a priority-one child emergency. If you don't let me in, you're going to have legal snarls like you never bargained for."

Leisha clamped her lips together. No one would believe that, it was legal gobbledygook. . . . Her lip throbbed where Alice had hit her.

The man stood aside to let Alice enter.

The guard started forward. Leisha hesitated, then let him. He entered with Alice.

Leisha waited, alone, in the dark.

In three minutes they were out, the guard carrying a child. Alice's broad face gleamed pale in the porch light. Leisha sprang forward, opened the car door, and helped the guard ease the child inside. The guard was frowning, a slow puzzled frown shot with wariness.

Alice said, "Here. This is an extra hundred dollars. To get back to the city by yourself."

"Hey . . ." the guard said, but he took the money. He stood looking after them as Alice pulled away.

"He'll go straight to the police," Leisha said despairingly. "He has to, or risk his union membership."

"I know," Alice said. "But by that time we'll be out of the car."

"*Where?*"

"At the hospital," Alice said.

"Alice, we can't—" Leisha didn't finish. She turned to the back seat. "Stella? Are you conscious?"

"Yes," said the small voice.

Leisha groped until her fingers found the rear-seat illuminator. Stella lay stretched out on the back seat, her face distorted with pain. She cradled her left arm in her right. A single bruise colored her face, above the left eye.

"You're Leisha Camden," the child said, and started to cry.

"Her arm's broken," Alice said.

"Honey, can you . . ." Leisha's throat felt thick, she had trouble getting the words out ". . . can you hold on till we get you to a doctor?"

"Yes," Stella said. "Just don't take me back there!"

"We won't," Leisha said. "Ever." She glanced at Alice and saw Tony's face.

Alice said, "There's a community hospital about ten miles south of here."

"How do you know that?"

"I was there once. Drug overdose," Alice said briefly. She drove hunched over the wheel, with the face of someone thinking furiously. Leisha thought, too, trying to see a way around the legal charge of kidnapping. They probably couldn't say the child came willingly: Stella would undoubtedly cooperate but at her age and in her condition she was probably *non sui juris*, her word would have no legal weight . . .

"Alice, we can't even get her into the hospital without insurance information. Verifiable on-line."

"Listen," Alice said, not to Leisha but over her shoulder, toward the back seat, "here's what we're going to do, Stella. I'm going to tell them you're my daughter and you fell off a big rock you were climbing while we stopped for a snack at a roadside picnic area. We're driving from California to Philadelphia to see your grandmother. Your name is Jordan Watrous and you're five years old. Got that, honey?"

"I'm seven," Stella said. "Almost eight."

"You're a very large five. Your birthday is March 23. Can you do this, Stella?"

"Yes," the little girl said. Her voice was stronger.

Leisha stared at Alice. "Can *you* do this?"

"Of course I can," Alice said. "I'm Roger Camden's daughter."

Alice half-carried, half-supported Stella into the Emergency Room of the small community hospital. Leisha watched from the car: the short stocky woman, the child's thin body with the twisted arm. Then she drove Alice's car to the farthest corner of the parking lot, under the dubious cover of a skimpy maple, and locked it. She tied the scarf more securely around her face.

Alice's license plate number, and her name, would be in every police and rental-car databank by now. The medical banks were slower; often they uploaded from local precincts only once a day, resenting the governmental interference in what was still, despite a half-century of battle, a private-sector enterprise. Alice and Stella would probably be all right in the hospital. Probably. But Alice could not rent another car.

Leisha could.

But the data file that would flash to rental agencies on Alice Camden Watrous might or might not include that she was Leisha Camden's twin.

Leisha looked at the rows of cars in the lot. A flashy luxury Chrysler, an Ikeda van, a row of middle-class Toyotas and Mercedes, a vintage '99 Cadillac—she could imagine the owner's face if that were missing—ten or twelve cheap runabouts, a hovercar with the uniformed driver asleep at the wheel. And a battered farm truck.

Leisha walked over to the truck. A man sat at the wheel, smoking. She thought of her father.

"Hello," Leisha said.

The man rolled down his window but didn't answer. He had greasy brown hair.

"See that hovercar over there?" Leisha said. She made her voice sound young, high. The man glanced at it indifferently; from this angle you couldn't see that the driver was asleep. "That's my bodyguard. He thinks I'm in the hospital, the way my father told me to, getting this lip looked at." She could feel her mouth swollen from Alice's blow.

"So?"

Leisha stamped her foot. "So I don't want to be inside. He's a shit and so's Daddy. I want *out*. I'll give you 4,000 bank credits for your truck. Cash."

The man's eyes widened. He tossed away his cigarette, looked again at the hovercar. The driver's shoulders were broad, and the car was within easy screaming distance.

"All nice and legal," Leisha said, and tried to smirk. Her knees felt watery.

"Let me see the cash."

Leisha backed away from the truck, to where he could not reach her. She took the money from her arm clip. She was used to carrying a lot of cash; there had always been Bruce, or someone like Bruce. There had always been safety.

"Get out of the truck on the other side," Leisha said, "and lock the door behind you. Leave the keys on the seat, where I can see them from here. Then I'll put the money on the roof where you can see it."

The man laughed, a sound like gravel pouring. "Regular little Dabney Engh, aren't you? Is that what they teach you society debs at your fancy schools?"

Leisha had no idea who Dabney Engh was. She waited, watching the man try to think of a way to cheat her, and tried to hide her contempt. She thought of Tony.

"All right," he said, and slid out of the truck.

"Lock the door!"

He grinned, opened the door again, locked it. Leisha put the money on the roof, yanked open the driver's door, clambered in, locked the door, and powered up the window. The man laughed. She put the key into the ignition, started the truck, and drove toward the street. Her hands trembled.

She drove slowly around the block twice. When she came back, the man was gone, and the driver of the hovercar was still asleep. She had wondered if the man would wake him, out of sheer malice, but he had not. She parked the truck and waited.

An hour and a half later Alice and a nurse wheeled Stella out of the Emergency Entrance. Leisha leaped out of the truck and yelled, "Coming, Alice!" waving both her arms. It was too dark to see Alice's expression; Leisha could only hope that Alice showed no dismay at the battered truck, that she had not told the nurse to expect a red car.

Alice said, "This is Julie Bergadon, a friend that I called while you were setting Jordan's arm." The nurse nodded, uninterested. The two women helped Stella into the high truck cab; there was no back seat. Stella had a cast on her arm and looked drugged.

"How?" Alice said as they drove off.

Leisha didn't answer. She was watching a police hovercar land at the other end of the parking lot. Two officers got out and strode purposefully towards Alice's locked car under the skimpy maple.

"My God," Alice said. For the first time, she sounded frightened.

"They won't trace us," Leisha said. "Not to this truck. Count on it."

"Leisha." Alice's voice spiked with fear. "Stella's *asleep*."

Leisha glanced at the child, slumped against Alice's shoulder. "No, she's not. She's unconscious from painkillers."

"Is that all right? Normal? For . . . her?"

"We can black out. We can even experience substance-induced sleep." Tony and she and Richard and Jeanine in the midnight woods. . . . "Didn't you know that, Alice?"

"No."

"We don't know very much about each other, do we?"

They drove south in silence. Finally Alice said, "Where are we going to take her, Leisha?"

"I don't know. Any one of the Sleepless would be the first place the police would check—"

"You can't risk it. Not the way things are," Alice said. She sounded weary. "But all my friends are in California. I don't think we could drive this rust bucket that far before getting stopped."

"It wouldn't make it anyway."

"What should we do?"

"Let me think."

At an expressway exit stood a pay phone. It wouldn't be data-shielded, as Groupnet was. Would Kevin's open line be tapped? Probably.

There was no doubt the Sanctuary line would be.

Sanctuary. All of them going there or already there, Kevin had said. Holed up, trying to pull the worn Allegheny Mountains around them like a safe little den. Except for the children like Stella, who could not.

Where? With whom?

Leisha closed her eyes. The Sleepless were out; the police would find Stella within hours. Susan Melling? But she had been Alice's all-too-visible stepmother, and was co-beneficiary of Camden's will; they would question her almost immediately. It couldn't be anyone trace-able to Alice. It could only be a Sleeper that Leisha knew, and trusted, and why should anyone at all fit that description? Why should she risk so much on anyone who did? She stood a long time in the dark phone kiosk. Then she walked to the truck. Alice was asleep, her head thrown back against the seat. A tiny line of drool ran down her chin. Her face was white and drained in the bad light from the kiosk. Leisha walked back to the phone.

"Stewart? Stewart Sutter?"

"Yes?"

"This is Leisha Camden. Something has happened." She told the story tersely, in bald sentences. Stewart did not interrupt.

"Leisha—" Stewart said, and stopped.

"I need help, Stewart." *'I'll help you, Alice.' 'I don't need your help.'* A wind whistled over the dark field beside the kiosk and Leisha shivered. She heard in the wind the thin keen of a beggar. In the wind, in her own voice.

"All right," Stewart said, "this is what we'll do. I have a cousin in Ripley, New York, just over the state line from Pennsylvania the route you'll be driving east. It has to be in New York, I'm licensed in New York. Take the little girl there. I'll call my cousin and tell her you're coming. She's an elderly woman, was quite an activist in her youth, her name is Janet Patterson. The town is—"

"What makes you so sure she'll get involved? She could go to jail. And so could you."

"She's been in jail so many times you wouldn't believe it. Political protests going all the way back to Vietnam. But no one's going to jail. I'm now your attorney of record, I'm privileged. I'm going to get Stella declared a ward of the state. That shouldn't be too hard with the hospital records you established in Skokie. Then she can be transferred to a foster home in New York, I know just the place, people who are fair and kind. Then Alice—"

"She's resident in Illinois. You can't—"

"Yes, I can. Since those research findings about the Sleepless life span have come out, legislators have been railroaded by stupid constituents scared or jealous or just plain angry. The result is a body of so-called 'law' riddled with contradictions, absurdities, and loopholes. None of it will stand in the long run—or at least I hope not—but in the meantime it can all be exploited. I can use it to create the most goddamn convoluted case for Stella that anybody ever saw, and in the meantime she won't be returned home. But that won't work for Alice—she'll need an attorney licensed in Illinois."

"We have one," Leisha said. "Candace Holt."

"No, not a Sleepless. Trust me on this, Leisha. I'll find somebody good. There's a man in—are you crying?"

"No," Leisha said, crying.

"Ah, God," Stewart said. "Bastards. I'm sorry all this happened, Leisha."

"Don't be," Leisha said.

When she had directions to Stewart's cousin, she walked back to the truck. Alice was still asleep, Stella still unconscious. Leisha closed the truck door as quietly as possible. The engine balked and roared, but Alice didn't wake. There was a crowd of people with them in the narrow and darkened cab: Stewart Sutter, Tony Indivino, Susan Melling, Kenzo Yagai, Roger Camden.

To Stewart Sutter she said, You called to inform me about the situation at Morehouse, Kennedy. You are risking your career and your cousin for Stella. And you stand to gain nothing. Like Susan telling me in advance about Bernie Kuhn's brain. Susan, who lost her life to Daddy's dream and regained it by her own strength. A contract without consideration for each side is not a contract: Every first-year student knows that.

To Kenzo Yagai she said, Trade isn't always linear. You missed that. If Stewart gives me something, and I give Stella something, and ten years from now Stella is a different person because of that and gives something to someone else as yet unknown—it's an ecology. An *ecology* of trade, yes, each niche needed, even if they're not contractually bound. Does a horse need a fish? *Yes.*

To Tony she said, Yes, there are beggars in Spain who trade nothing, give nothing, do nothing. But there are *more* than beggars in Spain. Withdraw from the beggars, you withdraw from the whole damn country. And you withdraw from the possibility of the ecology of help. That's what Alice wanted, all those years ago in her bedroom. Pregnant, scared, angry, jealous, she wanted to help *me*, and I wouldn't let her because I didn't need it. But I do now. And she did then. Beggars need to help as well as be helped.

And finally, there was only Daddy left. She could *see* him, bright-eyed, holding thick-leaved exotic flowers in his strong hands. To Camden she said, You were wrong. Alice *is* special. Oh, Daddy—the specialness of Alice! You were *wrong*.

As soon as she thought this, lightness filled her. Not the buoyant bubble of joy, not the hard clarity of examination, but something else: sunshine, soft through the conservatory glass, where two children ran in and out. She suddenly felt light herself, not buoyant but translucent, a medium for the sunshine to pass clear through, on its way to somewhere else.

She drove the sleeping woman and the wounded child through the night, east, toward the state line.

Barnacle Bill
The Spacer

by LUCIUS SHEPARD

Lucius Shepard's Hugo-Award-winning tale about the triumph and tragedy of "Barnacle Bill the Spacer" appeared in the July 1992 issue of *Asimov's*. This tremendously moving story also won the *Asimov's* Readers' Award Poll for Best Novella. An earlier, Nebula-Award-winning novella, "R&R" (*Asimov's*, April 1986), became the first part of his acclaimed novel, *Life During Wartime*. According to all reliable sources, the novel is soon to be a major motion picture. The author's upcoming projects include an untitled trilogy and a novel called *The 'Velt*. He is also working on short stories for a mainstream collection to be entitled *What Dogs Want*, and he is putting together a genre collection of original novellas tentatively titled, *The Sewers of Mars*.

Lucius Shepard has set his exotic tales on space stations, in Central American jungles, and against the magical backdrop of a giant dragon. He currently lives in Seattle, Washington, but tells me his heart's in the Far East. He hopes to do some more traveling there in the coming year.

The way things happen, not the great movements of time but the ordinary things that make us what we are, the savage accidents of our births, the simple lusts that because of whimsy or a challenge to one's pride become transformed into complex tragedies of love, the heartless operations of change, the wild sweetness of other souls that intersect the orbits of our lives, travel along the same course for a while, then angle off into oblivion, leaving no formal shape for us to consider, no easily comprehensible pattern from which we may derive enlightenment . . . I often wonder why it is when stories are contrived from such materials as these, the storyteller is generally persuaded to perfume the raw stink of life, to replace bloody loss with talk of noble sacrifice, to reduce the grievous to the wistfully sad. Most people, I suppose, want their truth served with a side of sentiment; the perilous uncertainty of the world dismays them, and they wish to avoid being brought hard against it. Yet by this act of avoidance they neglect the profound sadness that can arise from a contemplation of the human spirit *in extremis* and blind themselves to beauty. That beauty, I mean, which is the iron of our existence. The beauty that enters through a wound, that whispers a black word in our ears at funerals, a word that causes us to shrug off our griever's weakness and say, No more, never again. The beauty that inspires anger, not regret, and provokes struggle, not the idle aesthetic of a beholder. That, to my mind, lies at the core of the only stories worth telling. And that is the fundamental purpose of the storyteller's art, to illumine such beauty, to declare its central importance and make it shine forth from the inevitable wreckage of our hopes and the sorry matter of our decline.

This, then, is the most beautiful story I know.

* * *

It all happened not so along ago on Solitaire Station, out beyond the orbit of Mars, where the lightships are assembled and launched, vanishing in thousand-mile-long shatterings, and it happened to a man by the name of William Stamey, otherwise known as Barnacle Bill.

Wait now, many of you are saying, I've heard that story. It's been told and retold and told again. What use could there be in repeating it?

But what have you heard, really?

That Bill was a sweet, balmy lad, I would imagine. That he was a carefree sort with a special golden spark of the Creator in his breast and the fey look of the hereafter in his eye, a friend to all who knew him. That he was touched not retarded, moonstruck and not sick at heart, ill-fated rather than violated, tormented, sinned against.

If that's the case, then you would do well to give a listen, for there were both man and boy in Bill, neither of them in the least carefree, and the things he did and how he did them are ultimately of less consequence than why he was so moved and how this reflects upon the spiritual paucity and desperation of our age.

Of all that, I would suspect, you have heard next to nothing.

Bill was thirty-two years old at the time of my story, a shambling, sour-smelling, unkempt fellow with a receding hairline and a daft, mooney face whose features—weak-looking blue eyes and Cupid's bow mouth and snub nose—were much too small for it, leaving the better part of a vast round area unexploited. His hands were always dirty, his station jumpsuit mapped with stains, and he was rarely without a little cloth bag in which he carried, among other items, a trove of candy and pornographic VR crystals. It was his taste for candy and pornography that frequently brought us together—the woman with whom I lived, Arlie Quires, operated the commissary outlet where Bill would go to replenish his supplies, and on occasion, when my duties with Security Section permitted, I would help Arlie out at the counter. Whenever Bill came in, he would prefer to have me wait on him; he was, you understand, intimidated by everyone he encountered, but by pretty women most of all. And Arlie, lithe and brown and clever of feature, was not only pretty but had a sharp mouth that put him off even more.

There was one instance in particular that should both serve to illustrate Bill's basic circumstance and provide a background for all that later transpired. It happened one day about six months before the return of the lightship *Perseverance*. The shift had just changed over on the assembly platforms, and the commissary bar was filled with workers. Arlie had run off somewhere, leaving me in charge, and from my vantage behind the counter, located in an ante-room whose walls were covered by a holographic photomural of a blue sky day in the now-defunct Alaskan wilderness, and furnished with metal tables and chairs, all empty at that juncture, I could see colored lights playing back and forth within the bar, and hear the insistent rhythms of a pulse group. Bill, as was his habit, peeked in from the corridor to make sure none of his enemies were about, then shuffled on in, glancing left and right, ducking his head, hunching his shoulders, the very image of a guilty party. He shoved his moneymaker at me, three green telltales winking on the slim metal cylinder, signifying the amount of credit he was releasing to the commissary, and demanded in that grating, adenoidal voice of his that I give him "new stuff," meaning by this new VR crystals.

"I've nothing new for you," I told him.

"A ship came in." He gave me a look of fierce suspicion. "I saw it. I was outside, and I saw it!"

Arlie and I had been quarreling that morning, a petty difference concerning whose turn it was to use the priority lines to speak with relatives in London that had subsequently built into a major battle; I was in no mood for this sort of exchange. "Don't be an ass," I said. "You know they won't have unloaded the cargo yet."

His suspicious look flickered, but did not fade. "They unloaded already," he said. "Sleds were going back and forth." His eyes went a bit dreamy and his head wobbled, as if he were imagining himself back out on the skin of the station, watching the sleds drifting in and out of the cargo bays; but he was, I realized, fixed upon a section of the holographic mural in which a brown bear had just ambled out of the woods and was sniffing about a pile of branches and sapling trunks at the edge of a stream that might have been a beaver dam. Though he had never seen a real one, the notion of animals fascinated Bill, and when unable to think of anything salient to say, he would recite facts about giraffes and elephants, kangaroos and whales, and beasts even more exotic, all now receded into legend.

"Bloody hell!" I said. "Even if they've unloaded, with processing and inventory, it'll be a week or more before we see anything from it. If you want something, give me a specific order. Don't just stroll in here and say"—I tried to imitate his delivery—" 'Gimme some new stuff.' "

Two men and a woman stepped in from the corridor as I was speaking; they fell into line, keeping a good distance between themselves and Bill, and on hearing me berating him, they established eye contact with me, letting me know by their complicitors' grins that they supported my harsh response. That made me ashamed of having yelled at him.

"Look here," I said, knowing that he would never be able to manage the specific. "Shall I pick you out something? I can probably find one or two you haven't done."

He hung his great head and nodded, bullied into submissiveness. I could tell by his body language that he wanted to turn and see whether the people behind him had witnessed his humiliation, but he could not bring himself to do so. He twitched and quivered as if their stares were pricking him, and his hands gripped the edge of the counter, fingers kneading the slick surface.

By the time I returned from the stockroom several more people had filtered in from the corridor, and half-a-dozen men and women were lounging about the entrance to the bar, laughing and talking, among them Braulio Menzies, perhaps the most dedicated of Bill's tormentors, a big, balding, sallow man with sleek black hair and thick shoulders and immense forearms and a Mephistophilean salt-and-pepper goatee that lent his generous features a thoroughly menacing aspect. He had left seven children, a wife and a mother behind in São Paolo to take a position as foreman in charge of a metalworkers unit, and the better part of his wages were sent directly to his family, leaving him little to spend on entertainment; if he was drinking, and it was apparent he had been, I could think of nothing that would have moved him to this end other than news from home. As he did not look to be in a cheerful mood, chances were the news had not been good.

Hostility was thick as cheap perfume in the room. Bill was still standing with his head hung down, hands gripping the counter, but he was no longer passively maintaining that attitude—he had gone rigid, his neck was corded, his fingers squeezed the plastic, recognizing himself to be the target of every disparaging whisper and snide laugh. He seemed about to explode, he was so tightly held. Braulio stared at him with undisguised loathing, and as I set Bill's goods down on the counter, the skinny blond girl who was clinging to Braulio's arm sang, "He can't get no woman, least not one that's human, he's Barnacle Bill the Spacer."

There was a general outburst of laughter, and Bill's face grew flushed; an ugly, broken noise issued from his throat. The girl, her smallish breasts half-spilling out from a skimpy dress of bright blue plastic, began to sing more of her cruel song.

"Oh, that's brilliant, that is!" I said. "The creative mind never ceases to amaze!" But my sarcasm had no effect upon her.

I pushed three VR crystals and a double handful of hard candy, Bill's favorite, across to him. "There you are," I said, doing my best to speak in a kindly tone, yet at the same time hoping to convey the urgency of the situation. "Don't be hanging about, now."

He gave a start. His eyelids fluttered open, and he lifted his gaze to meet mine. Anger crept into his expression, hardening the simple terrain of his face. He needed anger, I suppose, to maintain some fleeting sense of dignity, to hide from the terror growing inside him, and there was no one else whom he dared confront.

"No!" he said, swatting at the candy, scattering much of it onto the floor. "You cheated! I want more!"

"Gon' mek you a pathway, boog man!" said a gangly black man, leaning in over Bill's shoulder. "Den you best travel!" Others echoed him, and one gave Bill a push toward the corridor.

Bill's eyes were locked on mine. "You cheated me, you give me some more! You owe me more!"

"Right!" I said, my temper fraying. "I'm a thoroughly dishonest human being. I live to swindle yits like yourself." I added a few pieces of candy to his pile and made to shoo him away. Braulio came forward, swaying, his eyes none too clear.

"Let the son'beetch stay, man," he said, his voice burred with rage. "I wan' talk to heem."

I came out from behind the counter and took a stand between Braulio and Bill. My actions were not due to any affection for Bill—though I did not wish him ill, neither did I wish him well; I suppose I perceived him as less a person than an unwholesome problem. In part, I was still motivated by the residue of anger from my argument with Arlie, and of course it was my duty as an officer in the Security Section to maintain order. But I think the actual reason I came to his defense was that I was bored. We were all of us bored on Solitaire. Bored and bad-tempered and despairing, afflicted with the sort of feverish malaise that springs from a sense of futility.

"That's it," I said wearily to Braulio. "That's enough from all of you. Bugger off."

"I don't wan' hort you, John," said Braulio, weaving a bit as he tried to focus on me. "Joos' you step aside."

A couple of his co-workers came to stand beside him. Jammers with silver nubs protruding from their crewcut scalps, the tips of receivers that channeled radio waves, solar energy, any type of signal, into their various brain centers, producing a euphoric kinaesthesia. I had a philosophical bias against jamming, no doubt partially the result of some vestigial Christian reflex. The sight of them refined my annoyance.

"You poor sods are tuned to a dark channel," I said. "No saved by the bell. Not today. No happy endings."

The jammers smiled at one another. God only knows what insane jangle was responsible for their sense of well-being. I smiled, too. Then I kicked the nearer one in the head, aiming at but missing his silver stub; I did for his friend with a smartly delivered backfist. They lay motionless, their smiles still in place. Perhaps, I thought, the jamming had turned the beating into a stroll through the park. Braulio faded a step and adopted a defensive posture. The onlookers edged away. The throb of music from the bar seemed to be giving a readout of the tension in the room.

There remained a need in me for violent release, but I was not eager to mix it with Braulio; even drunk, he would be formidable, and in any case, no matter how compelling my urge to do injury, I was required by duty to make a show of restraint.

"Violence," I said, affecting a comical lower class accent, hoping to defuse the situation. "The wine of the fucking underclass. It's like me father used to say, son, 'e'd say, when you're bereft of reason and the wife's sucked up all the cooking sherry, just amble on down to the pub and have a piss in somebody's face. There's nothing so sweetly logical as an elbow to the throat, no argument so poignant as that made by grinding somebody's teeth beneath your heel. The very cracking of bones is in itself a philosophical language. And when you've captioned someone's beezer with a nice scar, it provides them a pleasant 'omily to read each time they look in the mirror. Aristotle, Plato, Einstein. All the great minds got their start brawling in the pubs. Groin punches. Elbows to the throat. These are often a first step toward the expression of the most subtle mathematical concepts. It's a fantastic intellectual experience we're embarking upon 'ere, and I for one, ladies and gents, am exhilarated by the challenge."

Among the onlookers there was a general slackening of expression and a few titters. Braulio, however, remained focused, his eyes pinned on Bill.

"This is ridiculous," I said to him. "Come on, friend. Do me the favor and shut it down."

He shook his head, slowly, awkwardly, like a bear bothered by a bee.

"What's the point of it all, man?" I nodded at Bill. "He only wants to vanish. Why don't you let him?"

The blond girl shrilled, "Way you huffin' this bombo's shit, you two gotta be flatbackin', man!"

"I didn't catch your name, darling," I said. "Tarantula, was it? You'd do well to feed her more often, Braulio. Couple of extra flies a day ought to make her more docile."

I ignored her curses, watching Braulio's shoulders; when the right one dropped a fraction, I tried a round kick; but he ducked under it and rolled away, coming up into the fluid, swaying stance of a *capoeirista*. We circled one another, looking for an opening. The crowd cleared a space around us. Then someone—Bill, I think—brushed against me. Braulio started what appeared to be a cartwheel, but as he braced on one hand at the mid-point of the move, his long left leg whipped out and caught me a glancing blow on the temple. Dazed, I reeled backward, took a harder blow on the side of my neck and slammed into the counter. If he had been sober, that would have done for me; but he was slow to follow, and as he moved in, I kicked him in the liver. He doubled over, and I drove a knee into his face, then swept his legs from under him. He fell heavily, and I was on him, no longer using my techniques, but punching in a frenzy like a streetfighter, venting all my ulcerated emotions. Somebody was clawing at my neck, my face. The blond girl. She was screaming, sobbing, saying, "No, no, stop it, you're killin' him." Then somebody else grabbed me from behind, pinned my arms, and I saw what I had wrought. Braulio's cheekbone was crushed, one eye was swollen shut, his upper lip had been smashed into a pulp.

"He's grievin', man!" The blond girl dropped to her knees beside him. "That's all he be doin'! Grievin' his little ones!" Her hands fluttered about his face. Most of the others stood expressionless, mute, as if the sight of violence had mollified their resentments.

I wrenched free of the man holding me.

"Fuckin' Security bitch!" said the blond. "All he's doin's grievin'."

"I don't give a fat damn what he was doing. There's no law says"—I labored for breath—"says he can exorcise it this way. Is there now?"

This last I addressed to those who had been watching, and though some refused to meet my eyes, from many I received nods and a grumbling assent. They cared nothing about my fate or Braulio's; they had been willing to witness whatever end we might have reached. But now I understood that something had happened to Braulio's children, and I understood too why he had chosen Bill to stand in for those who were truly culpable, and I felt sore in my heart for what I had done.

"Take him to the infirmary," I said, and then gestured at the jammers, who were still down, eyes closed, their smiles in place. "Them, too." I put a hand to my neck; a lump had materialized underneath my right ear and was throbbing away nicely.

Bill moved up beside me, clutching his little cloth sack. His smell and his softness and his witling ways, every facet of his being annoyed me. I think he was about to say something, but I had no wish to hear it; I saw in him then what Braulio must have seen: a pudgy monstrosity, a uselessness with two legs.

"Get out of here!" I said, disgusted with myself for having interceded on his behalf. "Go back to your goddamn crawl and stay there."

His shoulders hitched as if he were expecting a blow, and he started pushing his way through the press at the door. Just before he went off along the corridor, he turned back. I believe he may have still wanted to say something, perhaps to offer thanks or—just as likely—to drive home the point that he was dissatisfied with the quantity of his goods. In his face was a mixture of petulant defiance and fear, but that gave me no clue to his intent. It was his usual expression, one that had been thirty-two years in the making, for due to his peculiar history, he had every cause to be defiant and afraid.

Bill's mother had been a medical technician assigned to the station by the Seguin Corporation, which owned the development contract for the lightship program, and so, when his prenatal scan displayed evidence of severe retardation, she was able to use her position to alter computer records in order to disguise his condition; otherwise, by station law—in effect, the law of the corporation—the foetus would have been aborted. Why she did this, and why she then committed suicide seventeen months after Bill's birth, remain a mystery, though it is assumed that her irrational actions revolved around the probability that Bill's father, a colonist aboard the lightship *Perseverence*, would never more be returning.

The discovery that Bill was retarded incited a fierce controversy. A considerable plurality of the station's work force insisted that the infant be executed, claiming that since living space was at a premium, to allow this worthless creature to survive would be an affront to all those who had made great personal sacrifices in order to come to Solitaire. This group consisted in the main of those whose lives had been shaped by or whose duty it was to uphold the quota system: childless women and administrators and—the largest element of the plurality and of the population in general—people who, like Braulio, had won a job aboard the station and thus succeeded in escaping the crushing poverty and pollution of Earth, but who had not been sufficiently important to have their families sent along, and so had been forced to abandon them. In opposition stood a vocal minority comprised of those whose religious or philosophical bias would not permit such a callous act of violence; but this was, I believe, a stance founded almost entirely on principle, and I doubt that many of those involved were enthusiastic about Bill in the specific. Standing apart from the fray was a sizeable group who, for various social and political reasons, maintained neutrality; yet I would guess that at least half of them would, if asked, have expressed their distaste for the prospect of Bill's continued existence. Fistfights and shouting matches soon became the order of the day. Meetings were held; demands made; ultimatums presented. Finally, though, it was not politics or threats of force or calls to reason that settled the issue, but rather a corporate decision.

Among Seguin's enormous holdings was a company that supplied evolved animals to various industries and government agencies, where they were utilized in environments that had been deemed too stressful or physically challenging for human workers. The difficulty with such animals lay in maintaining control over them—the new nanotechnologies were considered untrustworthy and too expensive, and computer implants, though serviceable, inevitably failed. There were a number of ongoing research programs whose aim it was to perfect the implants, and thus Seguin, seeing an opportunity for a rigorous test, not to mention a minor public relations coup that would speak to the deeply humane concerns of the corporation, decided—in a reversal of traditional scientific methodology—to test on Bill a new implant that would eventually be used to govern the behavior of chimpanzees and dogs and the like.

The implant, a disc of black alloy about the size of a soy wafer, contained a personality designed to entertain and jolly and converse with its host; it was embedded just beneath the skin behind the ear, and it monitored emotional levels, stimulating appropriate activity by means of electrical charges capable of bestowing both pleasure and pain. According to Bill, his implant was named Mister C, and it was— also according to Bill—his best friend, this despite the fact that it would hurt him whenever he was slow to obey its commands. I could always tell when Mister C was talking to him. His face would empty, and his eyes dart about as if trying to see the person who was speaking, and his hands would clench and unclench. Not a pleasant thing to watch. Still I suppose that Mister C was, indeed, the closest thing Bill had to a friend. Certainly it was attentive to him and was never too busy to hold a conversation; more importantly, it enabled him to perform the menial chores that had been set him; janitorial duties, fetch and carry, and, once he had reached the age of fifteen, the job that eventually earned him the name Barnacle Bill. But none of this assuaged the ill feeling toward him that prevailed throughout the station, a sentiment that grew more pronounced following the incident with Braulio. Two of Braulio's sons had been killed by a death squad who had mistaken them for members of a gang, and this tragedy caused people to begin talking about what an injustice it was that Bill should have so privileged an existence while others more worthy should be condemned to hell on Earth. Before long, the question of Bill's status was raised once again, and the issue was seized upon by Menckyn Samuelson, one of Solitaire's leading lights and—to my shame, because he was such a germ—a fellow Londoner. Samuelson had emigrated to the station as a low temperature physicist and since had insinuated himself into a position of importance in the administration. I did not understand what he stood to gain from hounding Bill— he had, I assumed, some hidden political agenda—but he flogged the matter at every opportunity to whomever would listen and succeeded in stirring up a fiercely negative reaction toward Bill. Opinion came to be almost equally divided between the options of executing him, officially or otherwise, and shipping him back to an asylum on Earth, which—as everyone knew—was only a slower and more expensive form of the first option.

There was a second development resulting from my fight with Braulio, one that had a poignant effect on my personal life, this being that Bill and I began spending a good deal of time together.

It seemed the old Chinese proverb had come into play, the one that states if you save somebody's life you become responsible for them. I had not saved his life, perhaps, but I had certainly spared him grievous injury; thus he came to view me as his protector, and I . . . well, initially I had no desire to be either his protector or his apologist, but I was forced to adopt both these roles. Bill was terrified. Everywhere he went he was cursed or cuffed or ill-treated in some fashion, a drastic escalation of the abuse he had always suffered. And then there was the blond girl's song: "Barnacle Bill the Spacer." Scarcely a day passed when I did not hear a new verse or two. Everyone was writing them. Whenever Bill passed in a corridor or entered a room people would start to sing. It harrowed him from place to place, that song. He woke to it and fell asleep to it, and whatever self-esteem he had possessed was soon reduced to ashes.

When he first began hanging about me, dogging me on my rounds, I tried to put him off, but I could not manage it. I held myself partly to blame for the escalation of feeling against him; if I had not been so vicious in my handling of Braulio, I thought, Bill might not have come to this pass. But there was another, more significant reason behind my tolerance. I had, it appeared, developed a conscience. Or at least so I chose to interpret my growing concern for him. I have had cause to wonder if those protective feelings that emerged from some corner of my spirit were not merely a form of perversity, if I were using my relationship with Bill to demonstrate to the rest of the station that I had more power than most, that I could walk a contrary path without fear of retribution; but I remain convinced that the compassion I came to feel toward him was the product of a renewal of the ideals I had learned in the safe harbor of my family's home back in Chelsea, conceptions of personal honor and trust and responsibility that I had long believed to be as extinct as the tiger and the dove. It may be there was a premonitory force at work in me, for it occurs to me now that the rebirth of my personal hopes was the harbinger of a more general rebirth; and yet because of all that has happened, because of how my hopes were served, I have also had reason to doubt the validity of every hope, every renewal, and to consider whether the rebirth of hope is truly possible for such diffuse, heartless, and unruly creatures as ourselves.

One day, returning from my rounds with Bill shuffling along at my shoulder, I found a black crescent moon with a red star tipping its lower horn painted on the door of Bill's quarters: the symbol used by the Strange Magnificence, the most prominent of the gang religions flourishing back on Earth, to mark their intended victims. I doubt that Bill was aware of its significance. Yet he seemed to know instinctively the symbol was a threat, and no ordinary one at that. He clung to my arm, begging me to stay with him, and when I told him I had to leave, he threw a tantrum, rolling about on the floor, whimpering, leaking tears, wailing that bad things were going to happen. I assured him that I would have no trouble in determining who had painted the symbol; I could not believe that there were more than a handful of people on Solitaire with ties to the Magnificence. But this did nothing to soothe him. Finally, though I realized it might be a mistake, I told him he could spend the night in my quarters.

"Just this once," I said. "And you'd better keep damn quiet, or you'll be out on your bum."

He nodded, beaming at me, shifting his feet, atremble with eagerness. Had he a tail he would have wagged it. But by the time we reached my quarters, his mood had been disrupted by the dozens of stares and curses directed his way. He sat on a cushion, rocking back and forth, making a keening noise, completely unmindful of the decor, which had knocked me back a pace on opening the door. Arlie was apparently in a less than sunny mood herself, for she had slotted in a holographic interior of dark greens and browns, with heavy chairs and a sofa and tables whose wood had been worked into dragons' heads and clawed feet and such; the walls were adorned with brass light fixtures shaped like bestial masks with glowing eyes, and the rear of the room had been transformed into a receding perspective of sequentially smaller, square segments of black delineated by white lines, like a geometric tunnel into nowhere, still leading, I trusted, to something resembling a bedroom. The overall atmosphere was one of derangement, of a cramped magical lair through whose rear wall a hole had been punched into some negative dimension. Given this, I doubted that she would look kindly upon Bill's presence, but when she appeared in the far reaches of the tunnel—her chestnut hair done up, wearing a white Grecian-style robe, walking through an infinite black depth, looking minute at first, then growing larger by half with each successive segment she entered—she favored him with a cursory nod and turned her attention to me.

"'Ave you eaten?" she asked, and before I could answer she told me she wasn't hungry, there were some sandwiches, or I could do for myself, whatever I wanted, all in the most dispirited of tones. She was, as I have said, a pretty woman, with a feline cast of feature and sleek, muscular limbs; having too many interesting lines in her face, perhaps, to suit the prevailing standards of beauty, but sensual to a fault. Ordinarily, sexual potential surrounded her like an aura. That day, however, her face had settled into a dolorous mask, her shoulders had slumped and she seemed altogether drab.

"What's the matter?" I asked.

She shook her head. "Nuffin'."

"Nothing?" I said. "Right! You look like the Queen just died, and the place is fixed up like the death of philosophy. But everything's just bloody marvelous, right?"

"Do you mind?" she snapped. "It's personal!"

"Personal, is it? Well, excuse me. I certainly wouldn't want to be getting *personal* with you. What the hell's the matter? You been struck by the monthlies?"

She pinned me with a venomous stare. "God, you're disgustin'! What is it? You 'aven't broken any 'eads today, so you've decided to bash me around a bit?"

"All right, all right," I said. "I'm sorry."

"Nao," she said. "G'wan with it. Oi fuckin' love it when you're masterful. Really, Oi do!" She turned and started back along the tunnel. "Oi'll just await your pleasure, shall Oi?" she called over her shoulder. "Oi mean, you will let me know what more Oi can do to serve?"

"Christ!" I said, watching her ass twitching beneath the white cloth, thinking that I would have to make a heartfelt act of contrition before I laid hands on it again. I knew, of course, why I had baited her. It was for the same reason that had brought on her depression, that provoked the vast majority of our aberrant behaviors. Frustration, anger, despair, all feelings that—no matter their immediate causes—in some way arose from the fact that Solitaire had proved to be an abject failure. Of the twenty-seven ships assembled and launched, three had thus far returned. Two of the ships had reported no hospitable environments found. The crew of the third ship had been unable to report anything, being every one of them dead, apparently by each others' hands.

We had gotten a late start on the colonization of space, far too late to save the home planet, and it was unclear whether the piddling colonies on Mars and Europa and in the asteroids would allow us to survive. Perhaps it should have been clear, perhaps we should have realized that despite the horror and chaos of Earth, the brush wars, the almost weekly collapse of governments, our flimsy grasp of the new technologies, despite the failure of Solitaire and everything else . . . perhaps it should have been more than clear that our species possessed a root stubbornness capable of withstanding all but the most dire of cataclysms, and that eventually our colonies would thrive. But they would never be able to absorb the desperate population of Earth, and the knowledge that our brothers and sisters and parents were doomed to a life of diminishing expectations, to famines and wars and accidents of industry that would ultimately kill off billions, caused those of us fortunate enough to have escaped to become dazed and badly weighted in our heads, too heavy with a sense of responsibility to comprehend the true moral requisites of our good fortune. Even if successful the lightship program would only bleed off a tiny percentage of Earth's population, and most, I assumed, would be personnel attached to the Seguin Corporation and those whom the corporation or else some corrupt government agency deemed worthy; yet we came to perceive ourselves as the common people's last, best hope, and each successive failure struck at our hearts and left us so crucially dismayed, we developed astonishing talents for self-destruction. Like neurotic Prometheans, we gnawed at our own livers and sought to despoil every happy thing that fell to us. And when we grew too enervated to practice active self-destruction, we sank into clinical depression, as Arlie was doing now.

I sat thinking of these things for a long while, watching Bill rock back and forth, now and then popping a piece of hard candy into his mouth, muttering, and I reached no new conclusions, unless an evolution of distaste for the corporation and the world and the universe could be considered new and conclusive. At length, weary of the repetitive circuit of my thoughts, I decided it was time I tried to make my peace with Arlie. I doubted I had the energy for prolonged apology, but I hoped that intensity would do the trick.

"You can sleep on the couch," I said to Bill, getting to my feet. "The bathroom"—I pointed off along the corridor—"is down there somewhere."

He bobbed his head, but as he kept his eyes on the floor, I could not tell if it had been a response or simply a random movement.

"Did you hear me?" I asked.

"I gotta do somethin'," he said.

"Down there." I pointed again. "The bathroom."

"They gonna kill me 'less I do somethin'."

He was not, I realized, referring to his bodily functions.

"What do you mean?"

His eyes flicked up to me, then away. "'Less I do somethin' good, *really* good, they gonna kill me."

"Who's going to kill you?"

"The men," he said.

The men, I thought, sweet Jesus! I felt unutterably sad for him.

"I gotta find somethin'," he said with increased emphasis. "Somethin' good, somethin' makes 'em like me."

I had it now—he had seized on the notion that by some good deed or valuable service he could change people's opinion of him.

"You can't do anything, Bill. You just have to keep doing your job, and this will all wash away, I promise you."

"Mmn-mn." He shook his head vehemently like a child in denial. "I gotta find somethin' good to do."

"Look," I said. "Anything you try is very likely to backfire. Do you understand me? If you do something and you bugger it, people are going to be more angry at you than ever."

He tucked his lower lip beneath the upper and narrowed his eyes and maintained a stubborn silence.

"What does Mister C say about this?" I asked.

That was, apparently, a new thought. He blinked; the tightness left his face. "I don't know."

"Well, ask him. That's what he's there for . . . to help you with your problems."

"He doesn't always help. Sometimes he doesn't know stuff."

"Try, will you? Just give it a try."

He did not seem sure of this tactic, but after a moment he pawed at his head, running his palm along the crewcut stubble, then squeezed his eyes shut and began to mumble, long pattering phrases interrupted by pauses for breath, like a child saying his prayers as fast as he can. I guessed that he was outlining the entire situation for Mister C. After a minute his face went blank, the tip of his tongue pushed out between his lips, and I imagined the cartoonish voice—thus I had been told the implant's voice would manifest—speaking to him in rhymes, in silly patter. Then, after another few seconds, his eyes snapped open and he beamed at me.

"Mister C says good deeds are always good," he announced proudly, obviously satisfied that he had been proven right, and popped another piece of candy into his mouth.

I cursed the simplicity of the implant's programming, sat back down, and for the next half-hour or so I attempted to persuade Bill that his best course lay in doing absolutely nothing, in keeping a low profile. If he did, I told him, eventually the dust would settle and things would return to normal. He nodded and said, yes, yes, uh-huh, yet I could not be certain that my words were having an effect. I knew how resistant he could be to logic, and it was quite possible that he was only humoring me. But as I stood to take my leave of him, he did something that went some ways toward convincing me that I had made an impression: he reached out and caught my hand, held it for a second, only a second, but one during which I thought I felt the sorry hits of his life, the dim vibrations of all those sour loveless nights and lonely ejaculations. When he released my hand he turned away, appearing to be embarrassed. I was embarrassed myself. Embarrassed and, I must admit, a bit repelled at having this ungainly lump display affection toward me. Yet I was also moved, and trapped between those two poles of feeling, I hovered above him, not sure what to do or say. There was, however, no need for me to deliberate the matter. Before I could summon speech he began mumbling once again, lost in a chat with Mister C.

"Good night, Bill," I said.

He gave no response, as still as a Buddha on his cushion.

I stood beside him for a while, less observing him than cataloguing my emotions, then, puzzling more than a little over their complexity, I left him to his candy and his terror and his inner voices.

Apology was not so prickly a chore as I had feared. Arlie knew as well as I the demons that possessed us, and once I had submitted to a token humiliation, she relented and we made love. She was demanding in the act, wild and noisy, her teeth marked my shoulder, my neck; but as we lay together afterward in the dark, some trivial, gentle music trickling in from the speakers above us, she was tender and calm and seemed genuinely interested in the concerns of my day.

"God 'elp us!" she said. "You don't actually fink the Magnificence is at work 'ere, do you?"

"Christ, no!" I said. "Some miserable dwight's actin' on mad impulse, that's all. Probably done it 'cause his nanny wiped his bum too hard when he's a babe."

"Oi 'ope not," she said. "Oi've seen their work back 'ome too many toimes to ever want to see it again."

"You never told me you'd had dealings with the Magnificence."

"Oi never 'ad what you'd call dealin's with 'em, but they was all over our piece of 'eaven, they were. 'Alf the bloody houses sported some kind of daft mark. It was a bleedin' fertile field for 'em, with nobody 'avin' a job and the lads just 'angin' about on the corners and smokin' gannie. 'Twas a rare day the Bills didn't come 'round to scrape up some yobbo wearing his guts for a necktie and the mark of his crime carved into his fore'ead. Nights you'd hear 'em chantin' down by the stadium. 'Orrid stuff they was singin'. Wearin' that cheap black satin gear and those awrful masks. But it 'ad its appeal. All the senile old 'ooligans were diggin' out their jackboots and razors, and wantin' to go marchin' again. And in the pubs the soaks would be sayin', yes, yes, they do the odd bad thing, the Magnificence, but they've got the public good to 'eart. The odd bad thing! Jesus! Oi've seen messages written on the pavement in 'uman bones. Colored girls with their 'ips broken and their legs lashed back behind their necks. Still breathin' and starin' at you with them 'ollow eyes, loike they were mad to die. You were lucky, John, to be living up in Chelsea."

"Lucky enough, I suppose," I said stiffly, leery of drawing such distinctions; the old British class wars, though somewhat muted on Solitaire, were far from dormant, and even between lovers, class could be a dicey subject. "Chelsea's not exactly the Elysian Fields."

"Oi don't mean nuffin' by it, luv. You don't have to tell me the 'ole damn world's gone rotten long ago. Oi remember how just a black scrap of a life looked loike a brilliant career when Oi was livin' there. Now Oi don't know how Oi stood it."

I pulled her close against me and we lay without speaking for a long while. Finally Arlie said, "You know, it's 'alf nice 'avin' 'im 'ere."

"Bill, you mean?"

"Yeah, Bill."

"I hope you'll still feel that way if he can't find the loo," I said.

Arlie giggled. "Nao, I'm serious. It's loike 'avin' family again. The feel of somebody snorin' away in the next room. That's the thing we miss 'avin' here. We're all so bloody isolated. Two's a crowd and all that. We're missin' the warmth."

"I suppose you're right."

I touched her breasts, smoothed my hand along the swell of her hip, and soon we were involved again, more gently than before, more giving to the other, as if what Arlie had said about family had created a resonance in our bodies. Afterward I was so fatigued, the darkness seemed to be slowly circulating around us, pricked by tiny bursts of actinic light, the way a djinn must circulate within its prison bottle, a murky cloud of genius and magic. I was at peace lying there, yet I felt strangely excited to be so peaceful and my thoughts, too, were strange, soft, almost formless, the kind of thoughts I recalled having had as a child when it had not yet dawned on me that all my dreams would eventually be hammered flat and cut into steely dies so they could withstand the dreadful pressures of a dreamless world.

Arlie snuggled closer to me, her hand sought mine, clasped it tightly. "Ah, Johnny," she said. "Toimes loike this, Oi fink Oi was born to forget it all."

The next day I was able to track down the villain who had painted the menacing symbol on Bill's door. The cameras in the corridor outside his door had malfunctioned, permitting the act of vandalism to go unobserved; but this was hardly surprising—the damned things were always failing, and should they not fail on their own, it was no great feat to knock them out by using an electromagnet. Lacking a video record, I focused my attention on the personnel files. Only nine people on Solitaire proved to have had even minimal ties with the Strange Magnificence; by process of elimination I was able to reduce the number of possible culprits to three. The first of them I interviewed, Roger Thirwell, a pale, rabbity polymath in his mid-twenties who had emigrated from Manchester just the year before, admitted his guilt before I had scarcely begun his interrogation.

"I was only tryin' to do the wise and righteous," he said, squaring his shoulders and puffing out his meager chest. "Samuelson's been tellin' us we shouldn't sit back and allow things to just happen. We should let our voices be heard. Solitaire's our home. We should be the ones decide how it's run."

"And so, naturally," I said, "when it came time to let your majestic voice resound, the most compelling topic you could find upon which to make a statement was the fate of a halfwit."

"It's not that simple and you know it. His case speaks to a larger issue. Samuelson says. . . ."

"Fuck you," I said. "And fuck Samuelson." I was sick of him, sick of his Midlands accent, sick especially of his references to Samuelson. What possible service, I wondered, could a dwight such as he have provided for the Magnificence? Something to do with logistics, probably. Anticipating police strategies or solving computer defenses. Yet from what I knew of the Magnificence, it was hard to imagine them putting up with this nit for very long. They would find a hard use for him and then let him fall off the edge of the world.

"Why in hell's name did you paint that thing on his door?" I asked. "And don't tell me Samuelson ordered you to do it."

The light of hope came into his face, and I would have sworn he was about to create some fantasy concerning Samuelson and himself in order to shift the guilt to broader shoulders. But all he said was, "I wanted to scare him."

"You could have achieved that with a bloody stick figure," I said.

"Yeah, but no one else would have understood it. Samuelson says we ought to try to influence as many people as possible whenever we state our cause, no matter how limited our aims. That way we enlist others in our dialogue."

I was starting to have some idea of what Samuelson's agenda might be, but I did not believe Thirwell could further enlighten me on the subject. "All you've succeeded in doing," I told him, "is to frighten other people. Or is it your opinion that there are those here who would welcome a chapter of the Magnificence?"

He ducked his eyes and made no reply.

"If you're homesick for them, I can easily arrange for you to take a trip back to Manchester," I said.

This elicited from Thirwell a babble of pleas and promises. I saw that I would get no more out of him, and I cautioned him that if he were ever to trouble Bill again I would not hesitate to make good on my threat. I then sent him on his way and headed off to pay a call on Menckyn Samuelson.

Samuelson's apartment, like those belonging to most corporate regals, was situated in a large module adjoining the even larger module that housed the station's propulsion controls, and was furnished with antiques and pictures that would have fetched a dear price back on Earth, but here were absolutely priceless, less evidence of wealth than emblems of faith . . . the faith we were all taught to embrace, that one day life would be as once it had been, a vista of endless potential and possibility. The problem with Samuelson's digs, however, was that his taste was abysmally bad; he had assembled a motley collection of items, Guilford chests and blond Finnish chairs, a Jefferson corner cabinet and freeform video sculptures, Victorian sideboard and fiber-optic chandelier, that altogether created the impression one had stumbled into a pawn shop catering to millionaires. It may be that my amuse-ment at this appalling display showed in my face, for though he pre-sented a smile and an outstretched hand, I sensed a certain stiffness in his manner. Nevertheless, the politician in him brought him through that awkward moment. Soon he was nattering away, pouring me a glass of whiskey, ushering me to an easy chair, plopping himself down into another, giving out with an expansive sigh, and saying, "I'm so awfully glad you've come, John. I've been meaning to have you in for a cup of reminiscence, you know. Two old Londoners like ourselves, we can probably find a few choice topics to bang around."

He lifted his chin, beaming blandly, eyes half-lidded, as if expecting something pleasant to be dashed into his face. It was such a thespian pose, such a clichéd take on upper class manners, so redolent of someone trying to put on airs, I had to restrain a laugh. Everything about him struck me as being just the slightest bit off. He was a lean, middle-aged man, dressed in a loose cotton shirt and moleskin trousers, alert in manner, almost handsome, but the nose was a tad sharp, the eyes set a fraction too close together, the cheekbones not sufficiently prominent, the chin a touch insubstantial, too much fore-head and not enough hair. He had the essential features of good breeding, yet none of the charming detail, like the runt of a pedigreed litter.

"Yes," I said, "we must do that sometime. However, today I've come on station business."

"I see." He leaned back, crossed his legs, cradled his whiskey in his lap. "Then p'rhaps after we've concluded your business, there'll be time for a chat, eh?"

"Perhaps." I had a swallow of whiskey, savored the smoky flavor. "I'd like to talk with you about William Stamey."

"Ah, yes. Old Barnacle Bill." Samuelson's brow was creased by a single furrow, the sort of line a cartoonist would use to indicate a gently rolling sea. "A bothersome matter."

"It might be considerably less bothersome if you left it alone."

Not a crack in the veneer. He smiled, shook his head. "I should dearly love to, old fellow. But I'm afraid you've rather a short-sighted view of the situation. The question we must settle is not the question of Bill *per se*, but of general policy. We must develop clear guide. . . ."

"Come on! Give it up!" I said. "I'm not one of your damned pint and kidney pie boys who get all narky and start to drool at the thought of their rights being abused. Their rights! Jesus Christ! The poor scuts have been buggered more times than a Sydney whore, and they still think it feels good. You wouldn't waste a second on this if it were merely a question of policy. I want to know what you're really after."

"Oh my God," Samuelson said, bemused. "You're not going to be an easy lay, are you?"

"Not for you, darling. I'm saving myself for the one I love."

"And just who is that, I wonder." He swirled the whiskey in his glass, watched it settle. "What do you think I'm after?"

"Power. What else is it makes your toby stiffen?"

He made a dry noise. "A simplistic answer. Not inaccurate, I'll admit. But simplistic all the same."

"I'm here for an education," I told him, "not to give a lecture."

"And I may enlighten you," Samuelson said. "I very well may. But let me ask you something first. What's your interest in all this?"

"I'm looking after Bill's interests."

He arched an eyebrow. "Surely there's more to it than that."

"That's the sum of it. Aside from the odd deep-seated psychological motive, of course."

"Of course." His smile could have sliced an onion; when it vanished, his cheeks hollowed. "I should imagine there's an element of *noblesse oblige* involved."

"Call it what you like. The fact remains, I'm on the case."

"For now," he said. "These things have a way of changing."

"Is that a threat? Don't waste your time. I'm the oldest slut on the station, Samuelson. I know where all the big balls have been dragging, and I've made certain I'm protected. Should anything happen to me or mine, it's your superiors who're going to start squealing. They'll be most perturbed with you."

"You've nothing on me." This said with, I thought, forced confidence.

"True enough," I said. "But I'm working on it, don't you worry."

Samuelson drained his glass, got to his feet, went to the sideboard and poured himself a fresh whiskey. He held up the bottle, gave me an inquiring look.

"Why not?" I let him fill my glass, which I then lifted in a toast. "To England. May the seas wash over her and make her clean."

He gave an amused snort. "England," he said, and drank. He sat back down, adjusted his bottom. "You're an amazing fellow, John. I've been told as much, but now, having had some firsthand experience, I believe my informants may have underestimated you." He pinched the crease of one trouserleg. "Let me put something to you. Not as a threat, but as an item for discussion. You do understand, don't you, that the sort of protection you've developed is not proof against every circumstance?"

"Absolutely. In the end it all comes down to a question of who's got the biggest guns and the will to use them. Naturally I'm prepared along those lines."

"I don't doubt it. But you're not seeking a war, are you?"

I knocked back half my whiskey, rested the glass on my lap. "Look here, I'm quite willing to live as one with you, no matter. Until lately, you've done nothing to interfere with my agenda. But this dust-up over Bill, and now this bit with your man Thirwell and his paint gun, I won't have it. Too many people here, Brits and Yanks alike, have a tendency to soil their nappy when they catch a scent of the Magnificence. I've no quarrel with you making a power play. And that's what you're doing, old boy. You're stirring up the groundlings, throwing a few scraps to the hounds so they'll be eager for the sound of your voice. You're after taking over the administrative end of things, and you've decided to give climbing the ladder of success a pass in favor of scaling the castle walls. A bloodless coup, perhaps. Or maybe a spot of blood thrown in to slake the fiercest appetites. Well, that's fine. I don't give a fuck who's sitting in the big chair, and I don't much care how they get there, so long as we maintain the status quo. But one thing I won't have is you frightening people."

"People are forever being frightened," he said. "Whether there's a cause for fear or not. But that's not my intent."

"Perhaps not. But you've frightened the bejesus out of Bill, and now you've frightened a good many others by bringing the Magnificence into the picture."

"Thirwell's not my responsibility."

"The hell he's not! He's the walking Book of Samuelson. Every other sentence begins, 'Samuelson says. . . .' Give him a pretty smile, and he'll be your leg-humper for life."

"Leg-humper?" Samuelson looked bewildered.

"A little dog," I said impatiently. "You know the kind. Randy all the time. Jumps up on you and goes to having his honeymoon with your calf."

"I've never heard the term. Not British, is it?"

"American, I think. I heard it somewhere. I don't know."

"Marvelous expression. I'll have to remember it."

"Remember this, too," I said, trying to pick up the beat of my tirade. "I'm holding you responsible for any whisper I hear of the Magnificence. Before we had this heart-to-heart I was inclined to believe you had no part in what Thirwell did. Now I'm not altogether sure. I think you're quite capable of using fear to manipulate the public. I think you may have known something of Thirwell's history and given him a nudge."

"Even if that were true," he said, "I don't understand the depth of your reaction. We're a long way from the Magnificence here. A daub of paint or two can't have much effect."

My jaw dropped a fraction on hearing that. "You're not from London. You couldn't be and still say that."

"Oh, I'm from London all right," he said coldly. "And I'm no virgin where the Magnificence is concerned. They left my brother stretched on King's Road one morning with the Equation of Undying Love scrawled in his own blood on the sidewalk beneath him. They mailed his private parts to his wife in a plastic container. But I've come a very long way from those days and those places. I'd be terrified of the Magnificence if they were here. But they're not here, and I'll be damned if I'll treat them like the bogeyman just because some sad little twit with too much brain and the social skills of a ferret paints the Magelantic Exorcism on somebody's door."

His statement rang true, but nevertheless I made a mental note to check on his brother. "Wonderful," I said. "It's good you've come to terms with all that. But not everyone here has managed to put as much distance between themselves and their old fears as you seem to have done."

"That may be, but I'm. . . ." He broke off, clicked his tongue against his teeth. "All right. I see your point." He tapped his fingers on the arm of his chair. "Let's see if we can't reach an accord. It's not in my interests at the moment to break off my campaign against Bill, but"— he held up a hand to stop me from interrupting—"but I will acknowledge that I've no real ax to grind where he's concerned. He's serving a strictly utilitarian purpose. So here's what I'll do. I will not allow him to be shipped back to Earth. At a certain juncture, I'll defuse the campaign. Perhaps I'll even make a public apology. That should help return him to grace. In addition, I'll do what I can to prevent further incidents involving the Magnificence. Frankly I very much doubt there'll be further problems. If there are, it won't be because I'm encouraging them."

"All well and good," I said. "Very magnanimous, I'm sure. But nothing you've promised guarantees Bill's safety during the interim."

"You'll have to be his guarantee. I'll try to maintain the temper of the station at a simmer. The rest is up to you."

"Up to me? No, you're not going to avoid responsibility that way. I'll do my best to keep him from harm, but if he gets hurt, I'll hurt you. That much I can guarantee."

"Then let's hope that nothing happens to him, shall we? For both our sakes." His smile was so thin, such a sideways stretching of the lip muscles, I thought it must be making his gums ache. "Funny. I can't decide whether we've established a working relationship or declared war."

"I don't think it matters," I said.

"No, probably not." He stood, straightened the fall of his trousers, and again gave me that bland, beaming, expectant look. "Well, I won't keep you any longer. Do drop around once the dust has settled. We'll have that chat."

"About London."

"Right." He moved to the door.

"I don't know as I'd have very much to say about London," I told him. "Nothing fit for reminiscence, at any rate."

"Really?" he said, ushering me out into the corridor. "The old girl's petticoats have gotten a trifle bloody, I'll admit. Terrible, the things that go on nowadays. The hunting parties, hive systems, knife dances. And of course, the Magnificence. But here, you know"—he patted his chest—"in her heart, I firmly believe there's still a bit of all right. Or maybe it's just I'm the sentimental sort. Like the song says, 'call 'er a satan, call 'er a whore, she'll always be Mother to me'."

Unlike Samuelson, I no longer thought of London as mother or home, or in any framework that smacked of the wholesome. Even "satan" would have been a euphemism. London for me was a flurry of night visions: a silhouetted figure standing in the window of a burning building, not waving its arms, not leaning out, but calm, waiting to be taken by the flames; men and women in tight black satin, white silk masks all stamped with the same feral, exultant expression, running through the streets, singing; moonlight painting the eddies of the Thames into silk, water lapping at a stone pier, and floating just beyond the shadow of the pier, the enormous bulk of a man I had shot only a minute before, nearly four hundred pounds of strangler, rapist, cannibal, brought down by a bullet weighing no more than one of his teeth; the flash of a shotgun from around a dark corner, like the flash of heat lightning; the charge of poisonous light flowing along the blade of a bloody macro-knife just removed from the body of a fellow detective; a garbage bag resting on a steel table that contained the neatly butchered remains of seven infants; the façade of St. Paul's dyed into a grooved chaos of ver-million, green, and purple by stone-destroying bacteria released by the artist, Miralda Hate; the wardrobe of clothing sewn of human skin and embroidered in gilt and glitter with verses from William Blake that we found in a vacant Brixton flat; the blind man who begged each evening on St. Martin's Lane, spiders crawling in the hollow globes of his glass eyes; the plague of saints, young men and women afflicted by a drug that bred in them the artificial personalities of Biblical characters and inspired them to martyr themselves during certain phases of the moon; the eyes of wild dogs in Hyde Park gleaming in the beam of my torch like the flat discs of highway reflectors; those and a thousand equally blighted memories, that was my London. Nightmare, grief, and end-less fever.

It was Solitaire that was home and mother to me, and I treated it with the appropriate respect. Though I was an investigative officer, not a section guard, I spent a portion of nearly every day patrolling various areas, searching less for crime than for symptoms of London, inci-dences of infection that might produce London-like effects. The sta-tion was not one place, but many: one hundred and forty-three modules, several of which were larger than any of the Earth orbit sta-tions, connected by corridors encased in pressure shells that could be disengaged by means of the Central Propulsion Control and—as each module was outfitted with engines—moved to a new position in the complex, or even to a new orbit; should the Central Propulsion Con-trol (CPC) be destroyed or severely damaged, disengagement was automatic, and the modules would boost into pre-programmed orbits. I hardly ever bothered to include places such as the labs, tank farms, infirmaries, data management centers, fusion modules, and such on my unofficial rounds; nor did I include the surface of the station, the elec-tronic and solar arrays, radiator panels, communications and tracking equipment; those areas were well maintained and had no need of a watchman. I generally limited myself to entertainment and dwelling modules like East Louie, where Bill's quarters and mine were located, idiosyncratic environments decorated with holographic scenarios so ancient that they had blanked out in patches and you would often see a coded designation or a stretch of metal wall interrupting the pattern of, say, a hieroglyphic mural; and from time to time I also inspected those sections of the station that were rarely visited and were only monitored via recordings several times a day—storage bays and transport hangars and the CPC (the cameras in those areas were supposed to transmit automatic alarms whenever anyone entered, but the alarm system was on the fritz at least half the time, and due to depleted staff and lack of materials, repairs such as that were not a high priority).

The CPC was an immense, white, portless room situated, as I've said, in the module adjoining that which housed Samuelson's digs and the rest of the corporate dwelling units. The room was segmented by plastic panels into work stations, contained banks of terminals and control panels, and was of little interest to me; but Bill, once he learned its function, was fascinated by the notion that his world could separate into dozens of smaller worlds and arrow off into the nothing, and each time we visited it, he would sit at the main panel and ask questions about its operation. There was never anyone else about, and I saw no harm in answering the questions. Bill did not have sufficient mental capacity to understand the concept of launch codes, let alone to program a computer so it would accept them. Solitaire was the only world he would ever know, and he was eager to accumulate as much knowledge about it as possible. Thus I encouraged his curiosity and showed him how to call up pertinent information on his own computer.

Due to Arlie's sympathetic response, Bill took to sleeping in our front room nearly every night, this in addition to tagging along on my rounds, and therefore it was inevitable that we became closer; however, closeness is not a term I happily apply to the relationship. Suffice it to say that he grew less defiant and petulant, somewhat more open and, as a consequence, more demanding of attention. Because his behavior had been modified to some degree, I found his demands more tolerable. He continued to cling to the notion that in order to save himself he would have to perform some valuable service to the community, but he never insisted that I help him in this; he appeared satisfied merely to hang about and do things with me. And to my surprise I found there were some things I actually enjoyed doing with him. I took especial pleasure in going outside with him, in accompanying him on *his* rounds and watching as he cleared barnacles away from communications equipment and other delicate mechanisms.

Sauter's Barnacle was, of course, not a true barnacle, yet it possessed certain similarities to its namesake, the most observable of which was a supporting structure that consisted of a hard exoskeleton divided into plates so as to allow movement. They bore a passing resemblance to unopened buds, the largest about the size of a man's fist, and they were variously colored, some streaked with metallic shades of red, green, gold, and silver (their coloration depended to a great extent on the nature of the substrate and their nutrient sources), so that when you saw a colony of them from a distance, spreading over the surface of a module—and all the modules were covered by hundreds of thousands of them—they had the look of glittering beds of moss or lichen. I knew almost nothing about them, only that they fed on dust, that they were sensitive to changes in light, that they were not found within the orbit of Mars, and that wherever there was a space station, they were, as my immediate superior, the Chief of Security, Gerald Sessions, put it, "thick as flies on shit." Once it had been learned that they did no harm, that, indeed, their excretions served to strengthen the outer shells of the modules, interest in them had fallen off sharply. There was, I believe, some ongoing research into their physical characteristics, but it was not of high priority.

Except with Bill.

To Bill the barnacles were purpose, a reason for being. They were, apart from Mister C, the most important creatures in the universe, and he was obsessive in his attentiveness toward them. Watching him stump about over the skin of the station, huge and clumsy in his pressure suit, a monstrous figure made to appear even more monstrous by the light spraying up around him from this or that port, hosing offending clumps of barnacles with bursts of oxygen from the tank that floated alongside him, sending them drifting up from their perches, I had the impression not of someone performing a menial task, but of a gardener tending his prize roses or—more aptly—a shepherd his flock. And though according to the best information, the barnacles were mindless things, incapable of any activity more sophisticated than obeying the basic urges of feeding and reproduction, it seemed they responded to him; even after he had chased them away they would wobble about him like strange pets, bumping against his faceplate and sometimes settling on him briefly, vivid against the white material of the pressure suit, making it appear that he was wearing jeweled rosettes on his back and shoulders. (I did not understand at the time that these were females which, unable to effect true mobility, had been stimulated to detach from the station by the oxygen and now were unable to reattach to the colony.)

With Bill's example before me, I was no longer able to take the barnacles for granted, and I began reading about them whenever I had a spare moment. I discovered that the exoskeleton was an organic-inorganic matrix composed of carbon compounds and silicate minerals, primarily olivine, pyroxene, and magnetite, substances commonly found in meteorites. Changes in light intensity were registered by iridescent photophores that dotted the plates; even the finest spray of dust passing between the barnacle and a light source would trigger neurological activity and stimulate the opening of aperture plates, permitting the egress of what Jacob Sauter (the barnacles' Linnaeus, an amateur at biology) had called the "tongue," an organ utilized both in feeding and in the transmission of seminal material from the male to the female. I learned that only the males could move about the colony, and that they did so by first attaching to the substrate with their tongues, which were coated with adhesive material, then detaching at one of their upper plate segments, and finally re-attaching to the colony with the stubby segmented stalks that depended from their bottom plates. "In effect," Sauter had written, "they are doing cartwheels."

The most profound thing I discovered, however, had nothing to do with the barnacles, or rather had only peripherally to do with them, and was essentially a rediscovery, a rewakening of my wonderment at the bleak majesty surrounding us. The cold diamond chaos of the stars, shining so brightly they might have just been finished that day; the sun, old god grown small and tolerable to the naked eye; the surreal brilliance and solidity that even the most mundane object acquired against the backdrop of that black, unvarying distance; that blackness itself, somehow managing to seem both ominous and serene, absence and presence, metal-hard and soft as illusion, like a fold in God's mag-isterial robe; the station with its spidery complexes of interconnecting corridors and modules, all coated with the rainbow swirls and streaks of the barnacles' glittering colors, and beams of light spearing out from it at every angle, like some mad, gay, rickety toy, the sight of which made me expect to hear calliope music; the Earth transport vessels, gray and bulky as whales, berthed in the geometric webs of their docks; the remote white islands of the assembly platforms, and still more remote, made visible by setting one's faceplate for maximum visual enhancement, the tiny silver needle we were soon to hurl into the haystack of the unknown. It was glorious, that vista. It made a compre-hensible map of our endeavors and led me to understand that we had not botched it completely. Not yet. I had seen it all before, but Bill's devotion to the barnacles had rekindled the embers of my soul, restored my cognizance of the scope of our adventure, and looking out over the station, I would think I could feel the entire blast and spin of creation inside my head, the flood of particles from a trillion suns, the crackling conversations of electric clouds to whom the frozen seas of ammonia above which they drifted were repositories of nostalgia, the endless fall of matter through the less-than-nothing of a pure anomaly, the white face of Christ blurred and streaming within the frost-colored fire of a comet's head, the quasars not yet congealed into dragons and their centuries, the unerring persistence of meteors that travel for uncounted millennia through the zero dark to scoot and burn across the skies onto the exposure plates of mild astronomers and populate the legends of a summer night and tumble into cinders over the ghosted peaks of the Karakorum and then are blown onto the back porches of men who have never turned their faces to the sky and into the dreams of children. I would have a plunderous sense of my own destiny, and would imagine myself hurling through the plenum at the speed of thought, of wish, accumulating a momentum that was in itself a charge to go, to witness, to take, and I was so enlivened I would believe for an instant that, like a hero returning from war, I could lift my hand and let shine a blessing down upon everyone around me, enabling them to see and feel all I had seen and felt, to know as I knew that despite everything we were closer to heaven than we had ever been before.

It was difficult for me to regain my ordinary take on life following these excursions, but after the departure of the lightship *Sojourner,* an event that Bill and I observed together from a catwalk atop the solar array in East Louie, it was thrust hard upon me that I had best set a limit on my woolgathering and concentrate on the matters at hand, for it was coming more and more to look as if the Strange Magnificence had gained a foothold on Solitaire. Scraps of black satin had been found tied to several crates in one of the storage bays, one of them containing drugs; copies of *The Book of Inexhaustible Delirium* began turning up; and while I was on rounds with Bill one day, I discovered a cache of packet charges in the magnetism lab, each about half the size of a flattened soccer ball, any one of which would have been sufficient to destroy a module; Gerald Sessions and I divided them up and stored them in our apartments, not trusting our staff with the knowledge of their existence. Perhaps the most troubling thing of all, the basic question of whether or not the Magnificence had the common good to heart was being debated in every quarter of the station, an argument inspired by fear and fear alone, and leading to bloody fights and an increase in racial tension and perversion of every sort. The power of the Strange Magnificence, you see, lay in the subversive nihilism of their doctrine, which put forward the idea that it was man's duty to express all his urges, no matter how dark or violent, and that from the universal exorcism of these black secrets would ultimately derive a pure consensus, a vast averaging of all possible behaviors that would in turn reveal the true character of God and the manifest destiny of the race. Thus the leaders of the Magnificence saw nothing contradictory in funding a group in York, say, devoted to the expulsion of Pakistanis from Britain by whatever means necessary while simultaneously supporting a Sufi cult. They had no moral or philosophical problem with anything because according to them the ultimate morality was a work-in-progress. Their tracts were utter tripe, quasi-intellectual homily dressed up in the kind of adjective-heavy, gothic prose once used to give weight to stories of ghosts and ancient evil; their anthems were even less artful, but the style suited the product, and the product was an easy sell to the disenfranchised, the desperate and the mad, categories into one of which almost everyone alive would fit to some extent, and definitely were one or another descriptive of everyone on Solitaire. As I had promised him, once these symptoms started to manifest, I approached Samuelson again, but he gave every evidence of being as concerned about the Magnificence as was I, and though I was not certain I believed his pose, I was too busy with my official duties and my unofficial one—protecting Bill, who had become the target of increased abuse—to devote much time to him. Then came the day of the launch.

It was beautiful, of course. First a tiny stream of fire, like a scratch made on a wall painted black, revealing a white undercoat. This grew smaller and smaller, and eventually disappeared; but mere seconds after its disappearance, what looked to be an iridescent crack began to spread across the blackness, reaching from the place where *Sojourner* had gone superluminal to its point of departure, widening to a finger's breadth, then a hand's, and more, like an all-colored piece of lightning hardened into a great jagged sword that was sundering the void, and as it swung toward us, widening still, I thought I saw in it intimations of faces and forms and things written, as one sees the images of circuitry and patterns such as might be found on the skin of animals when staring at the grain of a varnished board, and the sight of these half-glimpsed faces and the rest, not quite decipherable yet familiar in the way a vast and complex sky with beams of sunlight shafting down through dark clouds appears to express a familiar glory . . . those sights were accompanied by a feeling of instability, a shivery apprehension of my own insubstantiality which, although it shook me to my soul, disabling any attempt to reject it, was also curiously exalting, and I yearned for that sword to swing through me, to bear me away into a thundering genesis where I would achieve completion, and afterward, after it had faded, leaving me bereft and confused, my focus upon it had been so intent, I felt I had witnessed not an exercise of intricate technology but a simple magical act of the sort used to summon demons from the ready rooms of Hell or to wake a white spirit in the depths of an underground lake. I turned to Bill. His faceplate was awash in reflected light, and what I could make out of his face was colored an eerie green by the read-outs inside his helmet. His mouth was opened, his eyes wide. I spoke to him, saying I can't recall what, but wanting him to second my amazement at the wonderful thing we had seen.

"Somethin's wrong," he said.

I realized then that he was gazing in another direction; he might have seen *Sojourner's* departure, but only out of the corner of his eye. His attention was fixed upon one of the modules—the avionics lab, I believe—from which a large number of barnacles had detached and were drifting off into space.

"Why're they doin' that?" he asked. "Why're they leavin'?"

"They're probably sick of it here," I said, disgruntled by his lack of sensitivity. "Like the rest of us."

"No," he said. "No, must be somethin' wrong. They wouldn't leave 'less somethin's wrong."

"Fine," I said. "Something's wrong. Let's go back in."

He followed me reluctantly into the airlock, and once we had shucked off our suits, he talked about the barnacles all the way back to my quarters, insisting that they would not have vacated the station if there had been nothing wrong.

"They like it here," he said. "There's lots of dust, and nobody bothers 'em much. And they. . . ."

"Christ!" I said. "If something's wrong, figure it out and tell me! Don't just blither on!"

"I can't." He ducked his eyes, swung his arms in exaggerated fashion, as if he were getting ready to skip. "I don't know how to figure it out."

"Ask Mister C." We had reached my door, and I punched out the entry code.

"He doesn't care." Bill pushed out his lower lip to cover the upper, and he shook his head back and forth, actually not shaking it so much as swinging it in great slow arcs. "He thinks it's stupid."

"What?" The door cycled open, the front room was pitch-dark.

"The barnacles," Bill said. "He thinks everything I like is stupid. The barnacles and the CPC and. . . ."

Just then I heard Arlie scream, and somebody came hurtling out of the dark, knocking me into a chair and down onto the floor. In the spill of light from the corridor, I saw Arlie getting to her feet, covering her breasts with her arms. Her blouse was hanging in tatters about her waist; her jeans were pushed down past her hips; her mouth was bloody. She tried to speak, but only managed a sob.

Sickened and terrified at the sight of her, I scrambled out into the corridor. A man dressed all in black was sprinting away, just turning off into one of the common rooms. I ran after him. Each step spiked the boil of my emotions with rage, and by the time I entered the common room, done up as the VR version of a pub, with dart boards and dusty, dark wood, and a few fraudulent old red-cheeked men slumped at corner tables, there was murder in my heart. I yelled at people taking their ease to call Security, then raced into the next corridor.

Not a sign of the man in black.

The corridor was ranged by about twenty doors, the panel of light above most showing blue, signalling that no one was within. I was about to try one of the occupied apartments when I noticed that the telltale beside the airlock hatch was winking red. I went over to the hatch, switched on the closed circuit camera. On the screen above the control panel appeared a grainy black-and-white picture of the air-lock's interior; the man I had been chasing was pacing back and forth, making an erratic humming noise. A pale, twitchy young man with a malnourished look and bones that seemed as frail as a bird's, the prod-uct of some row-house madonna and her pimply king, of not enough veggies and too many cigarettes, of centuries of a type of ignorance as peculiarly British as the hand-rolled lawns of family estates. I recog-nized him at once. Roger Thirwell. I also recognized his clothes. The tight black satin trousers and shirt of the Strange Magnificence, dotted with badges proclaiming levels of spiritual attainment and attendance at this or that function.

"Hello, Roger," I said into the intercom. "Lovely day for a rape, isn't it, you filthy bastard?"

He glanced around, then up to the monitor. Fear came into his face, then was washed away by hostility, which in turn was replaced by a sort of sneering happiness. "Send me to Manchester, will you?" he said. "Send me down the tube to bloody Manchester! I think not! Per-haps you realize now I'm not the sort to take threats lying down."

"Yeah, you're a fucking hero! Why don't you come out and show me how much of a man you are."

He appeared distracted, as if he had not heard me. I began to sus-pect that he was drugged, but drugged or not, I hated him.

"Come on out of there!" I said. "I swear to God, I'll be gentle."

"I'll show you," he said. "You want to see the man I am, I'll show you."

But he made no move.

"I had her in the mouth," he said quietly. "She's got a lovely, lovely mouth."

I didn't believe him, but the words afflicted me nevertheless. I pounded on the hatch. "You beady-eyed piece of shit! Come out, damn you!"

Voices talking excitedly behind me, then somebody put an arm on my shoulder and said in a carefully enunciated baritone, "Let me handle this one, John."

It was Gerald Sessions, my superior, a spindly black man with a handsome, open face and freckly light complexion and spidery arms that possessed inordinate strength. He was a quiet, private sort, not given to displays of emotion, understated in all ways, possessed of the glum manner of someone who continually feels themselves put upon; yet because of our years together, he was a man for whom I had devel-oped some affection, and though I trusted no one completely, he was one of the few people whom I was willing to let watch my back. Stand-

ing beside him were four guards, among them his bodyguard and lover,
Ernesto Carbajal, a little fume of a fellow with thick, oily yet well-
tended black hair and a prissy cast to his features; and behind them, at
a remove, was a grave-looking Menckyn Samuelson, nattily attired in
dinner jacket and white trousers. Apparently he had been called away
from a social occasion.

"No, thank you," I told Gerald. "I plan to hurt the son of a bitch.
Send someone round to check on Arlie, will you?"

"It's been taken care of." He studied me a moment. "All right.
Just don't kill him."

I turned back to the screen just as Thirwell, who had moved to
the outer hatch and was gazing at the control panel, burst into song.

> "*Night, my brother, gather round me,*
> *Breed the reign of violence,*
> *And with temptations of the spi-i-rit*
> *Blight the curse of innocence.*
> *Oh, supple daughters of the twilight,*
> *Will we have all our pleasures spent,*
> *when God emerges from the shadows,*
> *blinding in his Strange Magni-i-fi-i-cence . . ."*

He broke off and let out a weak chuckle. I was so astounded by
this behavior that my anger was muted and my investigative sensibili-
ties engaged.

"Who're your contacts on Solitaire?" I asked. "Talk to me, and
maybe things will go easier for you."

Thirwell continued staring at the panel, seemingly transfixed by it.

"Give it up, Roger," I said. "Tell us about the Magnificence. You
help us, and we'll do right by you, I swear."

He lifted his face to the ceiling and, in a shattered tone, verging
on tears, said, "Oh, God!"

"I may be wrong," I said, "but I don't believe he's going to answer
you. You'd best brace it up in there, get your head clear."

"I don't know," he said.

"Sure you do. You know. It was your brains got you here. Now
use them. Think. You have to make the best of this you can." It was
hard to make promises of leniency to this little grout who'd had his
hands on Arlie, but the rectitude of the job provided me a framework
in which I was able to function. "Look here, I can't predict what's
going to happen, but I can give you this much. You tell us what you
know, chapter and verse, and I'll speak up for you. There could be mitigating circumstances. Drugs. Coercion. Blackmail. That strike a

chord, Roger? Hasn't someone been pushing you into this? Yeah, yeah, I thought so. Mitigating circumstances. That being the case, it's likely the corporation will go lightly with you. And one thing I can promise for certain sure. We'll keep you safe from the Magnificence."

Thirwell turned to the monitor. From the working of his mouth and the darting of his eyes, I could see he was close to falling apart.

"That's it, there's the lad. Come along home."

"The Magnificence." He glanced about, as if concerned that someone might be eavesdropping. "They told me . . . uh . . . I. . . ." He swallowed hard and peered at the camera as if trying to see through to the other side of the lens. "I'm frightened," he said in a whispery, conspiratorial tone.

"We're all frightened, Roger. It's shit like the Magnificence keeps us frightened. Time to stop being afraid, don't you think. Maybe that's the only way to stop. Just to do it, I mean. Just to say, the hell with this! I'm. . . ."

"P'rhaps if I had a word with him," said Samuelson, leaning in over my shoulder. "You said I had some influence with the boy. P'rhaps. . . ."

I shoved him against the wall; Gerald caught him on the rebound and slung him along the corridor, holding a finger up to his lips, indicating that Samuelson should keep very quiet. But the damage was done. Thirwell had turned back to the control panel and was punching in the code that would break the seal on the outer hatch.

"Don't be an ass!" I said. "That way's no good for anyone."

He finished punching in the code and stood staring at the stud that would cycle the lock open. The Danger lights above the inner hatch were winking, and a computer voice had begun repeating, Warning, Warning, The outer hatch has been unsealed, the airlock has not been depressurized, Warning, Warning. . . .

"Don't do it, Roger!"

"I have to," he said. "I realize that now. I was confused, but now it's okay. I can do it."

"Nobody wants this to happen, Roger."

"I do, I want it."

"Listen to me!"

Thirwell's hand went falteringly toward the stud. "Lord of the alley mouths," he said, "Lord of the rifles, Lord of the inflamed, Thou who hath committed every vileness. . . ."

"For Christ's sake, man!" I said. "Nobody's going to hurt you. Not the Magnificence, not anyone. I'll guarantee your safety."

". . . every sin, every violence, stand with me now, help me shape this dying into an undying love. . . ." His voice dropped in volume, becoming too low to hear.

"Goddamn it, Thirwell! You silly bastard. Will you stop jabbering that nonsense! Don't give in to it! Don't listen to what they've taught you. It's all utter rot!"

Thirwell looked up at the camera, at me. Terror warped his features for a moment, but then the lines of tension softened and he giggled. "He's right," he said. "The man's dead on right. You'll never understand."

"Who's right? What won't I understand?"

"Watch," said Thirwell gleefully. "Watch my face."

I kept silent, trying to think of the perfect thing to say, something to foil his demented impulse.

"Are you watching?"

"I want to understand," I said. "I want you to help me understand. Will you help me, Roger? Will you tell me about the Magnificence?"

"I can't. I can't explain it." He drew a deep breath, let it out slowly. "But I'll show you."

He smiled blissfully at the camera as he pushed the stud.

Explosive decompression, even when viewed on a black-and-white-monitor, is not a good thing to see. I looked away. Inadvertently, my eyes went to Samuelson. He was standing about fifteen feet away, hands behind his back, expressionless, like a minister composing himself before delivering his sermon; but there was something else evident in that lean, blank face, something happening beneath the surface, some slight engorgement, and I knew, *knew*, that he was not distressed in the least by the death, that he was pleased by it. No one of his position, I thought, would be so ingenuous as to interrupt a security man trying to talk in a potential suicide. And if what he had done to Thirwell had been intentional, a poorly disguised threat, if he had that much power and menace at his command, then he might well be responsible for what Thirwell had done to Arlie.

I strolled over to him. His eyes tracked my movements. I stopped about four feet away and studied him, searching for signs of guilt, for hints of a black satin past, of torchlight and blood and group sing-alongs. There was weakness in his face, but was it a weakness bred by perversion and brutality, or was it simply a product of fear? I decided that for Arlie's sake, for Thirwell's, I should assume the worst. "Guess what I'm going to do next?" I asked him. Before he could answer I kicked him in the pit of the stomach, and as he crumpled, I struck him a chopping left to the jaw that twisted his head a quarter-turn. Two of the guards started toward me, but I warned them back. Carbajal fixed me with a look of prim disapproval.

"That was a stupid damn thing to do," said Gerald, ambling over and gazing down at Samuelson, who was moaning, stirring.

"He deserves worse," I said. "Thirwell was coming out. I'm certain of it. And then this bastard opened his mouth."

"Yeah." Gerald leaned against the wall, crossed his legs. "So how come you figure he did it?"

"Why don't you ask him? Be interesting to see how he responds."

Gerald let out a sardonic laugh. "Man's an altruist. He was trying to help." He picked at a rough place on one of his knuckles. "The real question I got is how deep he's in it. Whether he's involved with the Magnificence, or if he's just trying to convince everyone he is, I need to know so I can make an informed decision."

I did not much care for the edge of coldness in his voice. "And what decision is that, pray?"

Carbajal, staring at me over his shoulder, flashed me a knowing smile.

"He already don't like you, John," said Gerald. "Man told me so. Now he's gonna want your ass on a plaque. And I have to decide whether or not I should let him have you."

"Oh, really?"

"This is some serious crap, man. I defy Samuelson, we're gonna have us one helluva situation. Security lined up against Administration."

Samuelson was trying to sit up; his jaw was swollen and discolored. I hoped it was broken.

"We could be talkin' about a war," Gerald said.

"I think you're exaggerating," I said. "Even so, a civil war wouldn't be the worst thing that could happen, not so long as the right side won. There are a number of assholes on station who would make splendid casualties."

Gerald said, "No comment."

Samuelson had managed to prop himself up on an elbow. "I want you to arrest him," he said to Gerald.

I looked at Gerald. "Might I have a few words with him before you decide?"

He met my eyes for a few beats, then shook his head in dismay. "Aw, fuck it," he said.

"Thanks, friend," I said.

"Fuck you, too," he said; he walked a couple of paces away and stood gazing off along the corridor; Carbajal went with him, whispered in his ear and rubbed his shoulders.

"Did you hear what I told you?" Samuelson heaved himself up into a sitting position, cupping his jaw. "Arrest him. Now!"

"Here, let me help you up." I grabbed a fistful of Samuelson's jacket, hauled him to his feet, and slammed him into the wall. "There. All better, are we?"

Samuelson's eyes darted left to right, hoping for allies. I bashed his head against the wall to get his attention, and he struggled against my hold.

"Such a tragedy," I said in my best upper crust accent. "The death of young Thirwell, what?"

The fight went out of him; his eyes held on mine.

"That was as calculated a bit of murder as I've seen in many a year," I told him.

"I haven't the foggiest notion what you're talking about!"

"Oh, yes you do! I had him walking the tightrope back. Then you popped in and reminded him of the consequences he'd be facing should he betray the Magnificence. God only knows what he thought you had in store for him."

"I did no such thing! I was. . . ."

I dug the fingers of my left hand in behind his windpipe; I would have liked to squeeze until thumb and fingers touched, but I only applied enough force to make him squeak. "Shut your gob! I'm not finished." I adjusted my grip to give him more air. "You're dirty, Samuelson. You're the germ that's causing all the pale looks around here. I don't know how you got past the screens, but that's not important. Sooner or later I'm going to have your balls for breakfast. And when I've cleaned my plate, I'll send what's left of you to the same place you chased Thirwell. Of course you could tell me the names of everyone on Solitaire who's involved with the Magnificence. That might weaken my resolve. But don't be too long about it, because I am fucking lusting for you. I can scarcely wait for you to thwart me. My saliva gets all thick and ropy when I think of the times we could have together." I gave him a shake, listened to him gurgle. "I know what you are, and I know what you want. You've got a dream, don't you? A vast, splendid dream of men in black satin populating the stars. New planets to befoul. Well, it's just not going to happen. If it ever comes to pass that a ship returns with good news, you won't be on it, son. Nor will any of your tribe. You'll be floating out there in the black grip of Jesus, with your blood all frozen in sprays around you and your hearts stuffed in your fucking mouths." I released him, gave him a cheerful wink. "All right. Go ahead. Your innings."

Samuelson scooted away along the wall, holding his throat. "You're mad!" He glanced over at Gerald. "The both of you!"

Gerald shrugged, spread his hands. "It's part of the job description."

"May we take it," I said to Samuelson, "that you're not intending to confess at this time?"

Samuelson noticed, as had I, that a number of people had come out of the common room and were watching the proceedings. "I'll tell you what I intend," he said, pulling himself erect in an attempt to look impressive. "I intend to make a detailed report concerning your disregard for authority and your abuse of position."

"Now, now," Gerald said, walking toward him. "Let's have no threats. Otherwise somebody"—his voice built into a shout—"somebody might lose their temper!" He accompanied the shout by slapping his palm against the wall, and this sent Samuelson staggering back another dozen feet or so.

Several of the gathering laughed.

"Come clean, man," I said to Samuelson. "Do the right thing. I'm told it's better than sex once those horrid secrets start spilling out."

"If it'll make you feel any easier, you can dress up in your black satins first," Gerald said. "Having that smooth stuff next to your skin, that'll put a nice wiggle on things."

"You know, Gerald," I said. "Maybe these poofs are onto something. Maybe the Magnificence has a great deal to offer."

"I'm always interested in upgrading my pleasure potential," he said. "Why don't you give us the sales pitch, Samuelson?"

"Yeah," I said. "Let's hear about all the snarky quivers you get from twisting the arms off a virgin."

The laughter swelled in volume, inspired by Samuelson's expression of foolish impotence.

"You don't understand who you're dealing with," he said. "But you will, I promise."

There, I said to myself, there's his confession. Not enough to bring into court, but for a moment it was there in his face, all the sick hauteur and corrupted passion of his tribe.

"I bet you're a real important man with the Magnificence," said Gerald. "Bet you even got a title."

"Minister of Scum and Delirium," I suggested.

"I like it," said Gerald. "How 'bout Secretary of the Inferior?"

"Grand High Salamander," said Carbajal, and tittered.

"Master of the Excremental."

"Stop it," said Samuelson, clenching his fists; he looked ready to stamp his foot and cry.

Several other titular suggestions came from the crowd of onlookers, and Gerald offered, "Queen of the Shitlickers."

"I'm warning you," said Samuelson, then he shouted, "I am warning you!" He was flushed, trembling. All the twitchy material of his inner core exposed. It had been fun bashing him about, but now I wanted to put my heel on him, feel him crunch underfoot.

"Go on," Gerald said. "Get along home. You've done all you can here."

Samuelson shot him an unsteady look, as if not sure what Gerald was telling him.

Gerald waved him off. "We'll talk soon."

"Yes," said Samuelson, straightening his jacket, trying to muster a shred of dignity. "Yes, indeed, we most certainly will." He delivered what I suppose he hoped was a withering stare and stalked off along the corridor.

"There goes an asshole on a mission," said Gerald, watching him round the bend.

"Not a doubt in my mind," I said.

"Trouble." Gerald scuffed his heel against the steel floor, glanced down as if expecting to see a mark. "No shit, the man's trouble."

"So are we," I said.

"Yeah, uh-huh." He sounded unconvinced.

We exchanged a quick glance. We had been through a lot together, Gerald and I, and I knew by the tilt of his head, the wry set of his mouth, that he was very worried. I was about to make a stab at boosting his spirits when I remembered something more pressing.

"Oh, Christ!" I said. "Arlie! I've got to get back."

"Forgot about her, huh?" He nodded gloomily, as if my forgetfulness were something he had long decried. "You know you're an asshole, don't you? You know you don't deserve the love of woman or the friendship of man."

"Yeah, yeah," I said. "Can you handle things here?"

He made a gesture of dismissal. Another morose nod. "Just so you know," he said.

There were no seasons on Solitaire, no quick lapses into cold, dark weather, no sudden transformations into flowers and greenery; yet it seemed that in those days after Thirwell's suicide the station passed through an autumnal dimming, one lacking changes in foliage and temperature, but having in their stead a flourishing of black satin ribbons and ugly rumors, a gradual decaying of the spirit of the place into an oppressive atmosphere of sullen wariness, and the slow occlusion of all the visible brightness of our lives, a slump of patronage in the bars, the common rooms standing empty, incidences of decline that reminded me in sum of the stubborn resistance of the English oaks to their inevitable change, their profuse and solemn green surrendering bit by bit to the sparse imperatives of winter, like a strong man's will gradually being eroded by grief.

War did not come immediately, as Gerald had predicted, but the sporadic violences continued, along with the arguments concerning the true intentions and nature of the Strange Magnificence, and few of us doubted that war, or something akin to it, was in the offing. Everyone went about their duties hurriedly, grimly—everyone, that is, except for Bill. He was so absorbed by his own difficulties, I doubt he noticed any of this, and though the focus of hostility had shifted away from him to an extent, becoming more diffuse and general, he grew increasingly agitated and continued to prattle on about having to "do something" and—this a new chord in his simple symphony—that something must be terribly wrong because the barnacles were leaving.

That they were leaving was undeniable. Every hour saw the migration of thousands more, and large areas of the station's surface had been laid bare. Not completely bare, mind you. There remained a layer of the substrate laid down by the females, greenish silver in color, but nonetheless it was a shock to see the station so denuded. I gave no real credence to Bill's contention that we were in danger, but neither did I totally disregard it, and so, partly to calm him, to reassure him that the matter was being investigated, I went back to Jacob Sauter's notes to learn if such migrations were to be expected.

According to the notes, pre-adult barnacles—Sauter called them "larvae"—free-floated in space, each encapsulated in its own segment of a tube whose ends had been annealed so as to form a ring. Like the adult barnacle, the exterior of the ring was dotted with light-sensitive photophores, and when a suitable place for attachment was sensed, the ring colony was able to orient itself by means of excretions sprayed through pores in the skin of the tube, a method not dissimilar to that utilized by orbital vessels when aligning themselves for re-entry. The slightest change in forward momentum induced secretions to occur along the edge of the colony oriented for imminent attachment, and ultimately the colony stuck to its new home, whereupon the females excreted an acidic substrate that bonded with the metal. The barnacles were hermaphroditic, and the initial metamorphitosis always resulted in female barnacles alone. Once the female colony grew dense, some of the females would become male. When the colony reached a certain density it reproduced *en masse*. As the larval tubes were secreted, they sometimes intertwined, and this would result in braided ring colonies, which helped insure variation in the gene pool. And that was all I could find on the subject of migration. If Sauter were to be believed, by giving up their purchase on the station, the barnacles were essentially placing their fate in the hands of God, taking the chance—and given the vastness of space, the absence of ring secretions, it was an extremely slim chance—that they would happen to bump into something and be able to cling long enough to attach themselves. If one were to judge their actions in human terms, it would appear that they must be terrified of something, otherwise they would stay where they were; but it would require an immense logical leap for me to judge them according to those standards and I had no idea what was responsible for their exodus.

Following my examination of Sauter's notes I persuaded Gerald to accompany me on an inspection tour of Solitaire's surface. I thought seeing the migration for himself might affect him more profoundly than had the camera views, and that he might then join me in entertaining the suspicion that—as unlikely a prospect as it was—Bill had stumbled onto something. But Gerald was not moved to agreement.

"Man, I don't know," he said as we stood on the surface of East Louie, looking out toward the CPC and the administration module. There were a few sparse patches of barnacles around us, creatures that for whatever reason—impaired sensitivity, some form of silicate stubbornness—had not abandoned the station. Now and then one or several would drift up toward the glittering clouds of their fellows that shone against the blackness like outcroppings of mica in anthracite. "What do I know about these damn things! They could be doing anything. Could be they ran out of food, and that's why they're moving. Shit! You giving the idiot way too much credit! He's got his own reasons for wanting this to mean something."

I could not argue with him. It would be entirely consistent with Bill's character for him to view the migration as part of his personal apocalypse, and his growing agitation might stem from the fact that he saw his world being whittled down, his usefulness reduced, and thus his existence menaced all the more.

"Still," I said, "it seems odd."

" 'Odd' ain't enough. Weird, now, that might carry some weight. Crazy. Run amok. They qualify for my attention. But 'odd' I can live with. You want to worry about this, I can't stop you. Me, I got more important things to do. And so do you."

"I'm doing my job, don't you worry."

"Okay. Tell me about it."

Through the glaze of reflection on his faceplate, I could only make out his eyes and his forehead, and these gave no clue to his mood.

"There's not very much to tell. As far as I can determine Samuelson's pure through and through. There's a curious lack of depth to the background material, a few dead ends in the investigative reports. Deceased informants. Vanished employers. That sort of thing. It doesn't feel quite right to me, but it's nothing I could bring to the corporation. And it does appear that his elder brother was murdered by the Magnificence, which establishes at least one of his *bona fides*."

"If Samuelson's part of the Magnificence, I. . . ."

" 'If,' my ass!" I said. "You know damned well he is."

"I was going to say, his brother's murder is just the kind of tactic they like to use in order to draw suspicion away from one of their own. Hell, he may have hated his brother."

"Or he may have loved him and wanted the pain."

Gerald grunted.

"I've isolated fourteen files that have a sketchiness reminiscent of Samuelson's," I said. "Of course that doesn't prove anything. Most of them are administration and most are relatively new on Solitaire. But only a couple are his close associates."

"That makes it more likely they're all dirty. They don't believe in bunching up. I'll check into it." I heard a burst of static over my earphones, which meant that he had let out a heavy sigh. "The damn thing is," he went on, "Samuelson might not be the lead dog. Whoever's running things might be keeping in the shadows for now."

"No, not a chance," I said. "Samuelson's too lovely in the part."

A construction sled, a boxy thing of silver struts powered by a man in a rocket pack, went arcing up from the zero physics lab and boosted toward one of the assembly platforms; all manner of objects were lashed to the struts, some of them—mostly tools, vacuum welders and such—trailing along in its wake, giving the sled a raggedy, gypsy look.

"Those explosives you got stashed," Gerald said, staring after the sled.

"They're safe."

"I hope so. We didn't have 'em, they might have moved on us by now. Done a hostage thing. Or maybe just blown something up. I'm pretty sure nothing else has been brought on station, so you just keep a close watch on that shit. That's our hole card."

"I don't like waiting for them to make the first move."

"I know you don't. Was up to you, we'd be stiffening citizens right and left, and figuring out later if they guilty or not. That's how come you got the teeth, and I'm holding the leash."

Though his face was hidden, I knew he was not smiling.

"Your way's not always the right of it, Gerald," I said. "Sometimes my way's the most effective, the most secure."

"Yeah, maybe. But not this time. This is too bullshit, this mess. Too many upper level people involved. We scratch the wrong number off the page, we be down the tube in a fucking flash. You don't want to be scuffling around back on Earth, do you? I sure as hell don't."

"I'd prefer it to having my lungs sucked out through my mouth like Thirwell."

"Would you, now? Me, I'm not so sure. I want a life that's more than just gnawing bones, John. I ain't up to that kind of hustle no more. And I don't believe you are, either."

We stood without speaking for a minute or so. It was getting near time for a shift change, and everywhere bits of silver were lifting from the blotched surface of the station, flocking together in the brilliant beams of light shooting from the transport bays, their movements as quick and fitful as the play of dust in sunlight.

"You're thinking too much these days, man," Gerald said. "You're not sniffing the air, you're not feeling things here." He made a slow, ungainly patting motion above his gut.

"That's rot!"

"Is it? Listen to this. 'Life has meaning but no theme. There is no truth we can assign to it that does not in some way lessen the bright flash of being that is its essential matter. There is no lesson learned that does not signal a misapprehension of our stars. There is no moral to this darkness.' That's some nice shit. Extremely profound. But the man who wrote that, he's not watching the water for sharks. He's too busy thinking."

"I'm so pleased," I said, "you've been able to access my computer once again. I know the childlike joy it brings you. And I'm quite sure Ernesto is absolutely thrilled at having a peek."

"Practice makes perfect."

"Any further conclusions you've drawn from poking around in my personal files?"

"You got one helluva fantasy life. Or else that Arlie, man, she's about half some kind of beast. How come you write all that sex stuff down?"

"Prurience," I said. "Damn! I don't know why I put up with this shit from you."

"Well, I do. I'm the luckiest Chief of Security in the system, see, 'cause I've got me a big, bad dog who's smart and loyal, and"—he lifted one finger of his gauntleted hand to signify that this was key—"who has no ambition to take my job."

"Don't be too sure."

"No, man, you don't want my job. I mean, you'd accept it if it was handed to you, but you like things the way they are. You always running wild and me trying to cover your ass."

"I hope you're not suggesting that I'm irresponsible."

"You're responsible, all right. You just wouldn't want the kind of responsibility I've got. It'd interfere with your style. The way you move around the station, talking bullshit to the people, everything's smooth, then all of a sudden you go Bam! Bam!, and take somebody down, then the next second you're talking about Degas or some shit, and then, Bam!, somebody else on the floor, you say, Oops, shit, I guess I messed up, will you please forgive me, did I ever tell you 'bout Paris in the springtime when all the poets turn into cherryblossoms, Bam!

It's fucking beautiful, man. You got half the people so scared they crawl under the damn rug when they see you coming, and the other half loves you to death, and most all of 'em would swear you're some kind of Robin Hood, you whip 'em 'cause you love 'em and it's your duty, and you only use your powers for goodness and truth. They don't understand you like I do. They don't see you're just a dangerous, amoral son of a bitch."

"Is this the sort of babble that goes into your personnel reports?"

"Not hardly. I present you as a real citizen. A model of integrity and courage and resourcefulness."

"Thanks for that," I said coldly.

"Just don't ever change, man. Don't ever change."

The sleds that had lifted from the station had all disappeared, but others were materializing from the blackness, tiny points of silver and light coming home from the assembly platforms, looking no more substantial than the clouds of barnacles. Finally Gerald said, "I got things to take care of." He waved at the barnacles. "Leave this shit alone, will you? After everything else gets settled, maybe then we'll look into it. Right now all you doing is wasting my fucking time."

I watched him moving off along the curve of the module toward the airlock, feeling somewhat put off by his brusque reaction and his analysis. I respected him a great deal as a professional, and his clinical assessment of my abilities made me doubt that his respect for me was so unqualified.

There was a faint click against the side of my helmet. I reached up and plucked off a barnacle. Lying in the palm of my gauntlet, its plates closed, its olive surface threaded with gold and crimson, it seemed cryptic, magical, rare, like something one would find after a search lasting half a lifetime, a relic buried with a wizard king, lying in his ribcage in place of a heart. I had shifted my position so that the light from the port behind me cast my shadow over the surface, and, a neurological change having been triggered by the shift in light intensity, some of the barnacles in the shadow were opening their plates and probing the vacuum with stubby gray "tongues," trying to feed. It was an uncanny sight, the way their "tongues" moved, stiffly, jerkily, like bad animation, like creatures in a grotesque garden hallucinated by Hawthorne or Baudelaire, and standing there among them, with the technological hodgepodge of the station stretching away in every direction, I felt as if I were stranded in a pool of primitive time, looking out onto the future. It was, I realized, a feeling akin to that I'd had in London whenever I thought about the space colonies, the outposts strung across the system.

Gnawing bones.

As my old Classics professor would have said, Gerald's metaphor was "a happy choice."

And now I had time to consider, I realized that Gerald was right: after all the years on Solitaire, I would be ill-suited for life in London, my instincts rusty, incapable of readjusting to the city's rabid intensity. But I did not believe he was right to wait for Samuelson to move against us. Once the Magnificence set their sights on a goal, they were not inclined to use half-measures. I was too disciplined to break ranks with Gerald, but there was nothing to prevent me from preparing myself for the day of judgment. Samuelson might bring us down, I told myself, but I would see to it that he would not outlive us. I was not aware, however, that judgment day was almost at hand.

Perhaps it was the trouble of those days that brought Arlie and I closer together, that reawakened us to the sweetness of our bodies and the sharp mesh of our souls, to all those things we had come to take for granted. And perhaps Bill had something to do with it. As dismal an item as he was, it may be his presence served—as Arlie had suggested—to supply us with some missing essential of warmth or heart. But whatever the cause, it was a great good time for us, and I came once again to perceive her not merely as someone who could cure a hurt or make me stop thinking for a while, but as the embodiment of my hopes. After everything I had witnessed, all the shabby, bloody evidence I had been presented of our kind's pettiness and greed, that I could feel anything so pure for another human being. . . . Christ, it astounded me! And if that much could happen, then why not the fulfillment of other, more improbable hopes? For instance, suppose a ship were to return with news of a habitable world. I pictured the two of us boarding, flying away, landing, being washed clean in the struggle of a stern and simple life. Foolishness, I told myself. Wild ignorance. Yet each time I fell into bed with Arlie, though the darkness that covered us seemed always imbued with a touch of black satin, with the sickly patina of the Strange Magnificence, I would sense in the back of my mind that in touching her I was flying away again, and in entering her I was making landfall on some perfect blue-green sphere. There came a night, however, when to entertain such thoughts seemed not mere folly but the height of indulgence.

It was close upon half-eleven, and the three of us, Bill, Arlie, and I, were sitting in the living room, the walls playing a holographic scenario of a white-capped sea and Alps of towering cumulus, with whales breeching and a three-masted schooner coasting on the wind, vanishing whenever it reached a corner, then reappearing on the adjoining wall. Bill and Arlie were on the sofa, and she was telling him stories about Earth, lies about the wonderful animals that lived there, trying to distract him from his obsessive nattering about the barnacles. I had just brought out several of the packet charges that Gerald and I had hidden away, and I was working at reshaping them into smaller units, a project that had occupied me for several nights. Bill had previously seemed frightened by them and had never mentioned them. That night, however, he pointed at the charges and said, "'Splosives?"

"Very good," I said. "The ones we found, you and I. The ones I was working with yesterday. Remember?"

"Uh-huh." He watched me re-insert a timer into one of the charges and then asked what I was doing.

"Making some presents," I told him.

"Birthday presents?"

"More like Guy Fawkes Day presents."

He had no clue as to the identity of Guy Fawkes, but he nodded sagely as though he had. "Is one for Gerald?"

"You might say they're all for Gerald."

He watched me a while longer, then said, "Why is it presents? Don't 'splosives hurt?"

"'E's just havin' a joke," Arlie said.

Bill sat quietly for a minute or so, his eyes tracking my fingers, and at last he said, "Why won't you talk to Gerald about the barnacles? You should tell him it's important."

"Give it a rest, Billy," Arlie said, patting his arm.

"What do you expect Gerald to do?" I said. "Even if he agreed with you, there's nothing to be done."

"Leave," he said. "Like the barnacles."

"What a marvelous idea! We'll just pick up and abandon the place."

"No, no!" he shrilled. "CPC! CPC!"

"Listen 'ere," said Arlie. "There's not a chance in 'ell the corporation's goin' to authorize usin' the CPC for somethin' loike that. So put it from mind, dear, won't you?"

"Don't need the corporation," Bill said in a whiney tone.

"He's got the CPC on the brain," I said. "Every night I come in here and find him running the file."

Arlie shushed me and asked, "What's that you said, Bill?"

He clamped his lips together, leaned back against the wall, his head making a dark, ominous-looking interruption in the path of the schooner; a wave of bright water appeared to crash over him, sending up a white spray.

"You 'ave somethin' to tell us, dear?"

"Be grateful for the silence," I said.

A few seconds later Bill began to weep, to wail that it wasn't fair, that everyone hated him.

We did our best to soothe him, but to no avail. He scrambled to his feet and went to beating his fists against his thighs, hopping up and down, shrieking at the top of his voice, his face gone as red as a squalling infant's. Then of a sudden he clutched the sides of his head. His legs stiffened, his neck cabled. He fell back on the sofa, twitching, screaming, clawing at the lump behind his ear. Mister C had intervened and was punishing him with electric shocks. It was a hideous thing to see, this enormous, babyish man jolted by internal lightnings, strings of drool braiding his chin, the animation ebbing from his face, his protests growing ever more feeble, until at last he sat staring blankly into nowhere, an ugly, outsized doll in a stained white jumpsuit.

Arlie moved close to him, mopped his face with a tissue. Her mouth thinned; the lines bracketing the corners of her lips deepened. "God, 'e's a disgustin' object," she said. "I don't know what it is about 'im touches me so."

"Perhaps he reminds you of your uncle."

"I realize this is hard toimes for you, luv," she said, continuing to mop Bill's face. "But do you really find it necessary to treat me so sarcastic, loike I was one of your culprits?"

"Sorry," I said.

She gave an almost imperceptible shrug. Something shifted in her face, as if an opaque mask had slid aside, revealing her newly vulnerable. "What you fink's goin' to 'appen to 'im?"

"Same as'll happen to us, probably. It appears our fates have become intertwined." I picked up another charge. "Anyway, what's it matter, the poor droob? His best pal is a little black bean that zaps him whenever he throws a wobbler. He's universally loathed, and his idea of a happy time is to pop a crystal and flog the bishop all night long. As far as I can tell, his fate's already bottomed out."

She clicked her tongue against her teeth. "Maybe it's us Oi see in 'im."

"You and me? That's a laugh."

"Nao, I mean all of us. Don't it seem sometimes we're all 'elpless loike 'im? Just big, loopy animals without a proper sense of things."

"I don't choose to think that way."

Displeasure came into her face, but before she could voice it, a loud buzzer went off in the bedroom—Gerald's private alarm, a device he would only use if unable to communicate with me openly. I jumped to my feet and grabbed a hand laser from a drawer in the table beside the sofa.

"Don't let anyone in," I told Arlie. "Not under any circumstances."

She nodded, gave me a brisk hug. "You 'urry back."

The corridors of East Louie were thronged, hundreds of people milling about the entrances of the common rooms and the commissaries. I smelled hashish, perfume, pheromone sprays. Desperate with worry, I pushed and elbowed my way through the crowds toward Gerald's quarters, which lay at the opposite end of the module. When I reached his door, I found it partway open and the concerned brown face of Ernesto Carbajal, peering out at me. He pulled me into the foyer. The room beyond was dark; a slant of light fell across the carpet from the bedroom door, which was open a foot or so; but I could make out nothing within.

"Where's Gerald?" I asked.

Carbajal's hands made delicate, ineffectual gestures in the air, as if trying to find a safe hold on something with a lot of sharp edges. "I didn't know what to do," he said. "I didn't know . . . I. . . ."

I watched him flutter and spew. He was Gerald's man, and Gerald claimed he was trustworthy. For my part, I had never formed an opinion. Now, however, I saw nothing that made me want to turn my back on him. And so, of course, I determined that I would do exactly that as soon as a suitable opportunity presented itself.

"You gave the alarm?" I asked him.

"Yes, I didn't want anyone to hear . . . the intercom. You know, it . . . I. . . ."

"Yeah, yeah, I know. Calm down!" I pushed him against the wall, kept my hand flat against his chest. "Where's Gerald?"

His eyes flicked toward the bedroom; for an instant the flesh of his face seemed to sag away from the bone, to lose all its firmness. "There," he said. "Back there. Oh, God!"

It was at that moment I knew Gerald was dead, but I refused to let the knowledge affect me. No matter how terrible the scene in the bedroom, Carbajal's reactions—though nicely done—were too flighty for a professional; even considering his involvement with Gerald, he should have been able to manage a more businesslike façade.

"Let's have a look, shall we?"

"No, I don't want to go back in there!"

"All right, then," I said. "You wait here."

I crossed to the bedroom, keeping an ear out for movement behind me. I swallowed, held my breath. The surface of the door seemed hot to the touch, and when I slid it open, I had the thought that the heat must be real, that all the glare off the slick red surfaces within had permeated the metal. Gerald was lying on the bed, the great crimson hollow of his stomach and chest exposed and empty, unbelievably empty, cave empty, with things like glistening, pulpy red fruit resting by his head, hands and feet; but I did not admit to the sight, I kept a distant focus. I heard a step behind me and turned, throwing up my guard as Carbajal, his face distorted by a grimace, struck at me with a knife. I caught his knife arm, bent the elbow backward against the doorframe; I heard it crack as he screamed and shoved him back into the living room. He staggered off-balance, but did not fall. He righted himself, began to move in a stealthy crouch, keeping his shattered elbow toward me, willing to accept more pain in order to protect his good left hand. Disabled or not, he was still very fast, dangerous with his kicks. But I knew I had him so long as I was careful, and I chose to play him rather than end it with the laser. The more I punished him, I thought, the less resistant he would be to interrogation. I feinted, and when he jumped back, I saw him wince. A chalky wash spread across his skin. Every move he made was going to hurt him.

"You might as well hazard it all on one throw, Ernesto," I told him. "If you don't, you're probably going to fall over before I knock you down."

He continued to circle me, unwilling to waste energy on a response; his eyes looked all dark, brimming with concentrated rage. Passing through the spill of light from the bedroom, he seemed ablaze with fury, a slim little devil with a crooked arm.

"It's not your karate let you down, Ernesto. It's that ridiculous drama queen style of acting. Absolutely vile! I thought you might start beating your breast and crying out to Jesus for succor. Of course that's the weakness all you yobbos in the Magnificence seem to have. You're so damned arrogant, you think you can fool everyone with the most rudimentary tactics. I wonder why that is. Never mind. In a moment I'm going to let you tell me all about it."

I gave him an opening, a good angle of attack. I'm certain he knew it was a trap, but he was in so much pain, so eager to stop the pain, that his body reacted toward the opening before his mind could cancel the order. He swung his right leg in a vicious arc, I stepped inside the kick, executed a hip throw; as he flew into the air and down, I wrenched his good arm out of the socket with a quick twist. He gave a cry, but wriggled out of my reach and bridged to his feet, both arms dangling. I took him back down with a leg sweep and smashed his right kneecap with my heel. Once his screaming had subsided I sat down on the edge of a coffee table and showed him the laser.

"Now we can talk undisturbed," I said brightly. "I hope you feel like talking, because otherwise. . . ."

He cursed in Spanish, spat toward me.

"I can see there's no fooling you, Ernesto. You obviously know you're not leaving here alive, not after what you've done. But you do have one life choice remaining that might be of some interest. Quickly"—I flourished the laser—"or slowly. What's your pleasure?"

He lay without moving, his chest heaving, blinking from time to time, a neutral expression on his face, perhaps trying to think of something he could tell me that would raise the stakes. His breath whistled in his throat; sweat beaded his forehead. My thoughts kept pulling me back into that red room, and as I sat there the pull became irresistible. I saw it clearly this time. The heart lying on the pillow above Gerald's head, the other organs arranged neatly beside his hands and feet; the darkly crimson hollow with its pale flaps. Things written in blood on the wall. It made me weary to see it, and the most wearisome thing of all was the fact that I was numb, that I felt almost nothing. I knew I would have to rouse myself from this spiritual malaise and go after Samuelson. I could trust no one to help me wage a campaign—quick retaliation was the best chance I had. Perhaps the only chance. The Magnificence had a number of shortcomings. Their arrogance, a crudeness of tactics, an infrastructure that allowed unstable personalities to rise to power. To be truthful, the fear and ignorance of their victims was their greatest strength. But their most pertinent flaw was that they tended to give their subordinates too little autonomy. With Samuelson out of the picture, the rest might very well scatter. And then I realized there was something I could do that would leave nothing to chance.

"Ernesto," I said, "now I've considered it, there's really not a thing you can tell me that I want to know."

"No," he said. "No, I have something. Please!"

I shrugged. "All right. Let's hear it."

"The bosses," he said. "I know where they are."

"The Magnificence, you mean? Those bosses?"

A nod. "Administration. They're all there."

"They're there right this moment?"

Something must have given a twinge, for he winced and said, "Dios!" When he recovered he added, "Yes. They're waiting. . . ." Another pain took him away for a moment.

"Waiting for the revolution to be won?" I suggested.

"Yes."

"And just how many bosses are we speaking about?"

"Twenty. Almost twenty, I think."

Christ, I thought, nearly half of the administration gone to black satin and nightmare.

I got to my feet, pocketed the laser.

"Wha. . . ." Ernesto said, and swallowed; his pallor had increased, and I realized he was going into shock. His dark eyes searched my face.

"I'm going, Ernesto," I said. "I don't have the time to treat you as you did Gerald. But my fervent hope is that someone else with more time on their hands will find you. Perhaps one of your brothers in the Magnificence. Or one of Gerald's friends. Neither, I suspect, will view your situation in a favorable light. And should no one come upon you in the forseeable future, I suppose I shall have to be satisfied with knowing you died a lingering death." I bent to him. "Getting cold, isn't it? You've had the sweet bit, Ernesto. There'll be no more pretending you've a pretty pair of charlies and playing sweet angelina to the hard boys. No more gobble offs for you, dearie. It's all fucking over."

I would have loved to hurt him some more, but I did not believe I would have been able to stop once I got started. I blew him a kiss, told him that if the pain got too bad he could always swallow his tongue, and left him to what would almost certainly be the first of his final misgivings.

When I returned to my quarters Arlie threw her arms about me and held me tight while I gave her the news about Gerald. I still felt nothing. Telling her was like hearing my own voice delivering a news summary.

"I've got work to do," I said. "I can't protect you here. They're liable to pay a visit while I'm away. You'll have to come with me."

She nodded, her face buried in my shoulder.

"We have to go outside," I said. "We can use one of the sleds. Just a short hop over to Administration, a few minutes there, and we're done. Can you manage?"

Arlie liked having something solid underfoot; going outside was a dread prospect for her, but she made no objection.

"What are you intendin'?" she asked, watching me gather the packet charges I had left scattered about the floor.

"Nothing nice," I said, peering under the sofa; I was, it appeared, short four charges. "Don't worry about it."

"Don't you get cheeky with me! Oi'm not some low-heel Sharon you've only just met. Oi've a right to know what you're about."

"I'm going to blow up the damned place," I said, moving the sofa away from the wall.

She stared at me, open-mouthed. "You're plannin' to blow up Admin? 'Ave you done your crust? What you finkin' of?"

I told her about the suspicious files and what Ernesto had said, but this did little to soothe her.

"There's twenty other people livin' in there!" she said. "What about them?"

"Maybe they won't be at home." I pushed the sofa back against the wall. "I'm missing four charges here. You seen 'em?"

"It's almost one o'clock. Some of 'em might be out, Oi grant you. But whether it's twenty or fifteen, you're talkin' about the murder of innocent people."

"Look here," I said, continuing my search, heaving chairs about to bleed off my anger. "First of all, they're not people. They're corporation deadlegs. Using the word 'innocent' to describe them makes as much sense as using the word 'dainty' to describe a pig's eating habits. At one time or another they've every one put the drill to some poor Joey's backside and made it bleed. And they'd do it again in a flicker, because that's all they fucking know how to do. Secondly, if they were in my shoes, if they had a chance to rid the station of the Magnificence with only twenty lives lost, they wouldn't hesitate. Thirdly"—I flipped up the cushions on the sofa—"and most importantly, I don't have a bloody choice! Do you understand me? There's no one I can trust to help. I don't have a loyal force with which to lay siege to them. This is the only way I can settle things. I'm not thrilled with the idea of murdering—as you say—twenty people in order to do what's necessary. And I realize it allows you to feel morally superior to think of me as a villain. But if I don't do something soon there'll be hearts and livers strewn about the station like party favors, and twenty dead is going to seem like nothing!" I hurled a cushion into the corner. "Shit! Where are they?"

Arlie was still staring at me, but the outrage had drained from her face. "Oi 'aven't seen 'em."

"Bill," I said, struck by a notion. "Where he'd get to?"

"Bill?"

"Yeah, Bill. The fuckwit. Where is he?"

"'E's away somewhere," she said. "'E was in the loo for a while, then Oi went in the bedroom, and when Oi come out 'e was gone."

I crossed to the bathroom, hoping to find the charges there. But when the door slid open, I saw only that the floor was spattered with bright, tacky blood; there was more blood in the sink, along with a kitchen knife, matted hair, handfuls of wadded, becrimsoned paper towels. And something else: a thin black disc about the size of a soy wafer. It took me a while to absorb all this, to put it together with Bill's recent obsessions, and even after I had done so, my conclusion was difficult to credit. Yet I could think of no other explanation that would satisfy the conditions.

"Arlie," I called. "You seen this?"

"Nao, what?" she said, coming up behind me; then: "Holy Christ!"

"That's his implant, isn't it?" I said, pointing to the disc.

"Yeah, I s'pose it is. My God! Why'd he do that?" She put a hand to her mouth. "You don't fink 'e took the charges. . . ."

"The CPC," I said. "He knew he couldn't do anything with Mister C along for the ride, so he cut the bastard out. And now he's gone for the CPC. Jesus! That's just what we needed, isn't it! Another fucking maniac on the loose!"

"It must 'ave 'urt 'im somethin' fierce!" Arlie said wonderingly. "I mean, he 'ad to 'ave done it quick and savage, or else Mister C would 'ave 'ad time to stop 'im. And I never heard a peep."

"I wouldn't worry about Bill if I were you. You think twenty dead's a tragedy? Think what'll happen if he blows the CPC. How many do you reckon will be walking between modules when they disengage? How many others will be killed by falling things? By other sorts of accidents?"

I went back into the living room, shouldered my pack; I handed Arlie a laser. "If you see anyone coming after us, use it. Burn them low if that's all you can bear, but burn them. All right?"

She gave a tight, anxious nod and looked down at the weapon in her hand.

"Come on," I said. "Once we get to the airlock we'll be fine."

But I was none too confident of our chances. Thanks to the greed of madmen and the single-mindedness of our resident idiot, it seemed that the chances of everyone on Solitaire were growing slimmer by the second.

I suppose some of you will say at this juncture that I should have known bad things were going to happen, and further will claim that many of the things that did happen might have been forestalled had I taken a few basic precautions and shown the slightest good sense. What possessed me, you might ask, to run out of my quarters leaving explosives scattered about the floor where Bill could easily appropriate them? And couldn't I have seen that his fascination with the CPC might lead to some perilous circumstance? And why had I not perceived his potential for destructiveness? Well, what had possessed me was concern for a friend, the closest to a friend that I had ever known. And as to Bill, his dangerous potentials, he had never displayed any sign that he was capable of enduring the kind of pain he must have endured, or of employing logic sufficiently well so as to plan even such a simple act as he perpetrated. It was desperation, I'm certain, that fathered the plan, and how was I to factor in desperation with the IQ of a biscuit and come up with the sum of that event? No, I reject guilt and credit both. My part in things was simpler than demanded by that complex twist of fate. I was only there, it seems, to finish things, to stamp out a few last fires, and—in the end—to give a name to the demons of that place and time. And yet perhaps there was something in that whole fury of moments that was mine. Perhaps I saw an opportunity to take a step away from the past, albeit a violent step, and moved by a signal of some sort, one too slight to register except in my cells, I took it. I would like to think I had a higher purpose in mind, and was not merely acting out the imperatives of some fierce vanity.

We docked the sled next to an airlock in the administration module, my reasoning being that if we were forced to flee, it would take less time to run back to administration than it would to cycle the CPC airlock; but instead of entering there, we walked along the top of the corridor that connected administration and the CPC, working our way along molded troughs of plastic covered with the greenish silver substrate left by the barnacles, past an electric array, beneath a tree of radiator panels thirty times as tall as a man, and entered the emergency lock at its nether end. There was a sled docked beside it, and realizing that Bill must have used it, I thought how terrified he must have been to cross even that much of the void without Mister C to lend him guidance. Before entering, I set the timer of one of the charges in the pack to a half-second delay and stuck it in the hip pouch of my pressure suit. I would be able to trigger the switch with just the touch of my palm against the pouch. A worst case eventuality.

The cameras inside the CPC were functioning, but since there were no security personnel in evidence, I had to assume that the automatic alarms had failed and that—as usual—no one was bothered to monitor the screens. We had not gone twenty feet into the main room when we saw Bill, dressed in a pressure suit, helmet in hand, emerge from behind a plastic partition, one of many which—as I have said— divided the cavernous white space into a maze of work stations. He looked stunned, lost, and when he noticed us he gave no sign of recognition; the side of his neck was covered with dried blood, and he held his head tipped to that side, as one might when trying to muffle pain by applying pressure to the injured spot. His mouth hung open, his posture was slack, and his eyes were bleary. Under the trays of cold light his complexion was splotchy and dappled with the angry red spots of pimples just coming up.

"The explosives," I said. "Where are they? Where'd you put them?"

His eyes wandered up, grazed my face, twitched toward Arlie, and then lowered to the floor. His breath made an ugly glutinous noise.

He was a pitiable sight, but I could not afford pity; I was enraged at him for having betrayed my trust. "You miserable fucking stain!" I said. "Tell me where they are!" I palmed the back of his head with my left hand; with my right I knuckled the ragged wound behind his ear. He tried to twist away, letting out a wail; he put his hands up to his chest and pushed feebly at me. Tears leaked from his eyes. "Don't!" he bawled. "Don't! It hurts!"

"Tell me where the explosives are," I said, "or I'll hurt you worse. I swear to Christ, I won't ever stop hurting you."

"I don't remember!" he whined.

"I take you into my house," I said. "I protect you, I feed you, I wash your messes up. And what do you do? You steal from me." I slapped him, eliciting a shriek. "Now tell me where they are!"

Arlie was watching me, a hard light in her eyes; but she said nothing.

I nodded toward the labyrinth of partitions. "Have a fucking look round, will you? We don't have much time!"

She went off, and I turned again to Bill.

"Tell me," I said, and began cuffing him about the face, not hard, but hurtful, driving him back with the flurries, setting him to stagger and wail and weep. He fetched up against a partition, eyes popped, that tiny pink mouth pursed in a moue. "Tell me," I repeated, and then said it again, said it every time I hit him, "Tell me, tell me, tell me, tell me . . .", until he dropped to his knees, cowering, shielding his head with his arms, and yelled, "Over there! It's over there!"

"Where?" I said, hauling him to his feet. "Take me to it."

I pushed him ahead of me, keeping hold of the neck ring of his suit, yanking, jerking, not wanting to give him a second to gather himself, to make up a lie. He yelped, grunted, pleaded, saying, "Don't!", "Stop it!", until at last he bumped and spun round a corner, and there, resting atop a computer terminal, was one of the charges, a red light winking on the timer, signaling that it had been activated. I picked it up and punched in the deactivation code. The read-out showed that fifty-eight seconds had remained before detonation.

"Arlie!" I shouted. "Get back here! Now!"

I grabbed Bill by the neck ring, pulled him close. "Did you set all the timers the same?"

He gazed at me, uncomprehending.

"Answer me, damn you! How did you set the timers?"

He opened his mouth, made a scratchy noise in the back of his throat; runners of saliva bridged between his upper and lower teeth.

My interior clock was ticking down, 53, 52, 51. . . . Given the size of the room, there was no hope of locating the other three charges in less than a minute. I would have risked a goodly sum on the proposition that Bill had been inconsistent, but I was not willing to risk my life.

Arlie came trotting up and smiled. "You found one!"

"We've got fifty seconds," I told her. "Or less. Run!"

I cannot be certain how long it took us to negotiate the distance between where we had stood and the hatch of the administration module; it seemed an endless time, and I kept expecting to feel the corridor shake and sway and tear loose from its fittings, and to go whirling out into the vacuum. Having to drag Bill along slowed us considerably, and I spent perhaps ten seconds longer opening the hatch with my pass key; but altogether, I would guess we came very near to the fifty second limit. And I *am* certain that as I sealed the hatch behind us, that limit was exceeded. Bill had, indeed, proved inconsistent.

As I stepped in through the inner hatch, I found that Admin had been transformed into a holographic rendering of a beautiful starfield spread across a velvety black depth in which—an oddly charming incongruity—fifteen or twenty doors were visible, a couple of them open, slants of white light spilling out, it seemed, from God's office space behind the walls of space and time. We were walking on gas clouds, nebulae, and constellate beings. Then I noticed the body of a woman lying some thirty feet away, blood pooled wide as a table beneath her. No one else was in sight, but as we proceeded toward the airlock, the outlines of the hatch barely perceptible beneath the astronomical display, three men in black gear stepped out from a doorway farther along the passage. I fired at them, as did Arlie, but our aim was off. Strikes of ruby light smoked the starry expanse beside them as they ducked back into cover. I heard shouts, then shouted answers. The next second, as I fumbled with the hatch, laser fire needled from several doorways, pinning us down. Whoever was firing could have killed us easily, but they satisfied themselves by scoring near misses. Above Bill's frightened cries and the sizzle of burning metal, I could hear laughter. I tossed my laser aside and told Arlie to do the same. I touched the charge in my hip pouch. I believed if necessary I would be able to detonate it, but the thought made me cold.

A group of men and women, some ten or eleven strong, came along the corridor toward us, Samuelson in the lead. Like the rest, he wore black satin trousers and a blouse of the same material adorned with badges. Creatures, it appeared, wrought from the same mystic stuff as the black walls and ceiling and floor. He was smiling broadly and nodding, as if our invasion were a delightful interlude that he had been long awaiting.

"How kind of you to do your dying with us, John," he said as we came to our feet; they gathered in a semi-circle around us, hemming us in against the hatch. "I never expected to have this opportunity. And with your lady, too. We're going to have such fun together."

"Bet she's a real groaner," said a muscular, black-haired man at his shoulder.

"Well, we'll find out soon enough, won't we?" said Samuelson.

"Try it," said Arlie, "and Oi'll squeeze you off at the knackers!"

Samuelson beamed at her, then glanced at Bill. "And how are you today, sir? What brings you along, I wonder, on this merry outing?"

Bill returned a look of bewilderment that after a moment, infected by Samuelson's happy countenance, turned into a perplexed smile.

"Do me a favor," I said to Samuelson, moving my hand so that the palm was almost touching the switch of the charge at my hip. "There's something I've been yearning to know. Does that gear of yours come with matching underwear? I'd imagine it must. Bunch of ginger-looking poofs and lizzies like you got behind you, I suppose wearing black nasties is *de rigueur.*"

"For somebody who's 'bout to major in high-pitched screams," said a woman at the edge of the group, a heavyset blonde with a thick American accent and an indecipherable tattoo on her bicep, "you gotta helluva mouth on you, I give ya that."

"That's just John's unfortunate manner," Samuelson said. "He's not very good at defeat, you see. It should be interesting to watch him explore the boundaries of this particular defeat."

My hand had begun to tremble on the switch; I found myself unable to control it.

"What is it with you, Samuelson?" said the blonde woman. "Every time you chop someone, you gotta play Dracula? Let's just do 'em and get on with business."

There was a brief argument concerning the right of the woman to speak her mind, the propriety of mentally preparing the victim, of "tasting the experience," and other assorted drivel. Under different circumstances, I would have laughed to see how ludicrous and inept a bunch were these demons; I might have thought how their ineptitude spoke to the terminal disarray back on Earth, that such a feeble lot could have gained so much power. But I was absorbed by the trembling of my hand, the sweat trickling down my belly, and the jellied weakness of my legs. I imagined I could feel the cold mass of explosives turning, giving a kick, like a dark and fatal child striving to break free of the womb. Before long I would have to reveal the presence of the charge and force a conclusion, one way or another, and I was not sure I was up to it. My hand wanted to slap the switch, pushed against, it seemed, by all the weighty detritus of my violent life.

Finally Samuelson brought an end to the argument. "This is my show, Amy. I'll do as I please. If you want to discuss method during Retreat, I'll be happy to satisfy. Until then, I'd appreciate your full cooperation."

He said all this with the mild ultra-sincerity of a priest settling a squabble among the Ladies Auxiliary concerning a jumble sale; but when he turned to me, all the anger that he must have repressed came spewing forth.

"You naff little scrote!" he shouted. "I'm sick to death of you getting on my tits! When I've done working over your slippery and that great dozy blot beside you, I'm going to paint you red on red."

I did not see what happened at that moment with Arlie. Somebody tried to fondle her, I believe, and there was a commotion beside me, too brief to call a struggle, and then she had a laser in her hand and was firing. A beam of crimson light no thicker than a knitting needle spat from the muzzle and punched its way through the temple of a compact graying man, exiting through the top of his skull, dropping him in a heap. Another beam spitted the shoulder of the blonde woman. All this at close quarters, people shrieking, stumbling, pushing together, nudging me, nearly causing me to set off the charge. Then the laser was knocked from Arlie's hand, and she was thrown to the floor. Samuelson came to stand astraddle her, his laser aimed at her chest.

"Carve the bitch up!" said the blonde woman, holding her shoulder.

"Splendid idea," Samuelson said, adjusting the setting of his laser. "I'll just do a little writing to begin with. Start with an inspirational saying, don't you think? Or maybe"—he chuckled—"John Loves Arlie."

"No," I said, my nerves steadied by this frontal assault; I pulled out the packet charge. "No, you're not going to do that. Because unless you do the right thing, in about two seconds the best part of you is going to be sliding all greasylike down the walls. I'll give you to three to put down your weapons." I drew a breath and tried to feel Arlie beside me. "One." I stared at Samuelson, coming hard at him with all the fire left in me. "You best tell 'em how mad I am for you." I squared my shoulders; I prayed I had the guts to press the switch on three. "That's two."

"Do it!" he said to his people. "Do it now!"

They let their weapons fall.

"Back it off," I said, feeling relief, but also a ghostly momentum as if the count had continued on in some alternate probability and I was now blowing away in fire and ruin. I picked up my pack, grabbed Samuelson by the shirtfront as the rest retreated along the corridor. "Open the hatch," I told Arlie, who had scrambled up from the floor.

I heard her punching out the code, and a moment later, I heard the hatch swing open. I backed around the door, slung Samuelson into the airlock, slamming him up against Bill, who had wandered in on his own. At that precise moment, the CPC exploded.

The sound of the explosion was immense, a great wallop of pressure and noise that sent me reeling into the airlock, reeling and floating up, the artificial gravity systems no longer operative; but what was truly terrifying was the vented hiss that followed the explosion, signaling disengagement from the connecting corridors, and the sickening sway of the floor, and then the roar of ignition as the module's engines transformed what had been a habitat into a ship. I pictured the whole of Solitaire coming apart piece by piece, each one igniting and moving off into the nothing, little glowing bits, like the break-up of an electric reef.

Arlie had snatched up one of the lasers and she was now training it at Samuelson, urging him into his pressure suit—a difficult chore considering the acceleration. But he was managing. I helped Bill on with his helmet and fitted mine in place just as the boost ended and we drifted free. Then I broke the seal on the outer hatch, started the lock cycling.

Once the lock had opened, I told Arlie she would have to drive the sled. I watched as she fitted herself into the harness of the rocket pack, then I lashed Samuelson to one of the metal struts, Bill to another. I set the charge I had been carrying on the surface of the station, took two more out of the pack. I set the timers for ninety seconds. I had no thought in my head as I was doing this; I might have been a technician stripping a wire, a welder joining a seam. Yet as I prepared to activate the charges, I realized that I was not merely ridding the station of the Strange Magnificence, but of the corporation's personnel. I had, of course, known this before, but I had not understood what it meant. Within a month, probably considerably less, the various elements of the station would reunite, and when they did, for the first time in our history, Solitaire would be a free place, without a corporate presence to strike the fear of God and Planet Earth into the hearts and minds of the workers. Oh, it was true, some corporates might have been in other modules when the explosion occurred, but most of them were gone, and the survivors would not be able to wield much power; it would be six months at least before their replacements arrived and a new administration could be installed. A lot could happen in that time. My comprehension of this was much less linear than I am reporting; it came to me as a passion, a hope, and as I activated the timers, I had a wild sense of freedom that, though I did not fathom it then, seems now to have been premonitory and inspired.

I lashed and locked myself on to a strut close to Arlie and told her to get the hell gone, pointing out as a destination the web of a transport dock that we were passing. I did not see the explosion, but I saw the white flare of it in Arlie's faceplace as she turned to watch; I kept my eyes fixed for a time on the bits and pieces of Solitaire passing silently around us, and when I turned to her, as the reflected fire died away and her eyes were revealed, wide and lovely and dark, I saw no hatred in her, no disgust. Perhaps she had already forgiven me for being the man I was. Not kindly, and yet not without kindness. Merely someone who had learned to do the necessary and to live with it. Someone whose past had burned a shadow that stretched across his future.

I told her to reverse the thrusters and stop the sled. There was one thing left to do, though I was not so eager to have done with it as once I had been. Out in the dark, in the nothing, with all those stars pointing their hot eyes at you and trying to spear your mind with their secret colors, out in that absolute desert the questions of villainy and heroism grow remote. The most terrible of sins and the sweetest virtues often become compressed in the midst of all that sunless cold; compared to the terrible inhumanity of space, they both seem warmly human and comprehensible. And thus when I approached the matter of ending Samuelson's life I did so without relish, without the vindictive spirit that I might have expressed had we been back on Solitaire.

I inched my way back to where I had tied him and locked on to a strut; I trained the laser on the plastic rope that lashed him to the sled and burned it through. His legs floated up, and he held on to a strut with his gauntleted hands.

"Please, God! Don't!" he said, the panic in his voice made tinny and comical by my helmet speaker; he stared down through the struts that sectioned off the void into which he was about to travel—silver frames each enclosing a rectangle of unrelieved black, some containing a few scraps of billion-year-old light. "Please!"

"What do you expect from me?" I asked. "What do you expect from life? Mercy? Or the accolade? Here." I pointed at the sweep of stars and poetry, the iron puzzle of the dock beginning to loom, to swell into a massive crosshatching of girders, each strung with white lights, with Mars a phantom crescent below and the sun a yellow coal. "You longed for God, didn't you? Where is He if not here? Here's your strange magnificence." I gestured with the laser. "Push off. Hard. If you don't push hard enough, we'll come after you and give you a nudge. You can open your faceplate whenever you want it to end."

He began to plead, to bargain. "I can make you wealthy," he said. "I can get you back to Earth. Not London. Nova Sibersk. One of the towers."

"Of course you can," I said. "And I would be a wise man, indeed, to trust that promise, now wouldn't I?"

"There are ways," Samuelson said. "Ways to guarantee it. It's not that difficult. Really. I can. . . ."

"Thirwell smiled at me," I reminded him. "He sang. Are your beliefs so shallow you won't even favor us with a tune?"

"Do you want me to sing? Do you want me to be humiliated? If that's what it'll take to get you to listen to me, I'll do it. I'll do anything."

"No," I said. "That's not what I want."

His eyes were big with the idea of death. I knew what he was feeling: all his life was suddenly thrilling, precious, new; and he was almost made innocent by the size and intensity of his fear, almost cleansed and converted by the knowledge that all this sensey splendor was about to go on forever and ever without him. It was a hard moment, and he did not do well by it.

When he began to weep I burned a hole in his radio housing to silence him. He put a hand up to shield his face, fearing I would burn the helmet; I kicked his other hand loose from the sled, sending him spinning away slowly, head over heels toward the sun, a bulky white figure growing toylike and clever against the black ground of his future, like one of those little mechanical monkeys that spins round and round on a plastic bar. I knew he would never open his faceplate—the greater the villain, the greater their inability to accept fate. He would be a long time dying.

I checked on Bill—he was sleeping!—and returned to my place beside Arlie. We boosted again toward the dock. I thought about Gerald, about the scattered station, about Bill, but I could not concentrate on them. It was as if what I saw before me had gone inside my skull, and my mind was no longer a storm of electric impulse, but an immense black emptiness lit by tiny stars and populated by four souls, one of whom was only now beginning to know the terrible loneliness of his absent god.

We entrusted Bill to the captain of the docked transport, *Steel City*, a hideous name for a hideous vessel, pitted and gray and ungainly in form, like a sad leviathan. There was no going back to Solitaire for Bill. They had checked the recordings taken in the CPC, and they knew who had been responsible for the break-up of the station, for the nearly one hundred and thirty lives that had been lost, for the billions in credit blown away. Even under happier circumstances, without Mister C to guide him, he would not be able to survive. Nor would he survive on Earth. But there he would at least have a slight chance. The corporation had no particular interest in punishing him. They were not altogether dissatisfied with the situation, being pleased to learn that their failsafe system worked, and they would, they assured us, see to it that he was given institutional care. I knew what that portended. Shunted off to some vast dark building with a Catholic statue centering a seedy garden out front, and misplaced, lost among the howling damned and terminally feeble, and eventually, for want of any reason to do otherwise, going dark himself, lying down and breathing, perhaps feeding from time to time, for a while, and then, one day, simply giving up, giving out, going away on a rattle of dishes on the dinner cart or a wild cry ghosting up from some nether region or a shiver of winter light on a cracked linoleum floor, some little piece of brightness to which he could attach himself and let go of the rest. It was horrible to contemplate, but we had no choice. Back on the station he would have been torn apart.

The *Steel City* was six hours from launching inbound when Arlie and I last saw Bill. He was in a cell lit by a bilious yellow tray of light set in the ceiling, wearing a gray ship's jumpsuit; his wound had been dressed, and he was clean, and he was terrified. He tried to hold us, he pleaded with us to take him back home, and when we told him that was impossible, he sat cross-legged on the floor, rocking back and forth, humming a tune that I recognized as "Barnacle Bill the Spacer." He had apparently forgotten its context and the cruel words. Arlie kneeled beside him and told stories of the animals he would soon be seeing. There were tigers sleek as fire, she said, and elephants bigger than small towns, and birds faster than rain, and wolves with mysterious lights in their eyes. There were serpents too, she said, green ones with ruby tongues that told the most beautiful stories in the world, and cries so musical had been heard in the Mountains of the Moon that no one dared seek out the creature who had uttered them for fear of being immolated by the sight of such beauty, and the wind, she said, the wind was also an animal, and to those who listened carefully to it, it would whisper its name and give them a ride around the world in a single day. Birds as bright as the moon, great lizards who roared when it thundered as if answering questions, white bears with golden claws and magical destinies. It was a wonderland to which he was traveling, and she expected him to call and tell us all the amazing things that he would do and see.

Watching them, I had a clearer sense of him than ever before. I knew he did not believe Arlie, that he was only playing at belief, and I saw in this his courage, the stubborn, clean drive to live that had been buried under years of abuse and denial. He was not physically courageous, not in the least, but I for one knew how easy that sort of courage was to sustain, requiring only a certain careless view of life and a few tricks to inspire a red madness. And I doubted I could have withstood all he had suffered, the incessant badgering and humiliation, the sharp rejection, the sexual defeats, the monstrous loneliness. Years of it. Decades. God knows, he had committed an abysmal stupidity, but we had driven him to it, we had menaced and tormented him, and in return—an act of selfishness and desperation, I admit, yet selfishness in its most refined form, desperation in its most gentle incarnation—he had tried to save us, to make us love him.

It is little enough to know of a man or a woman, that he or she has courage. Perhaps there might have been more to know about Bill had we allowed him to flourish, had we given his strength levers against which to test itself and thus increase. But at the moment knowing what I knew seemed more than enough, and it opened me to all the feelings I had been repressing, to thoughts of Gerald in particular. I saw that my relationship with him—in fact most of my relationships—were similar to the one I'd had with Bill; I had shied away from real knowledge, real intimacy. I felt like weeping, but the pity of it was, I would only be weeping for myself.

Finally it was time for us to leave. Bill pawed us, gave us clumsy hugs, clung to us, but not so desperately as he might have; he realized, I am fairly certain, that there would be no reprieve. And, too, he may not have thought he deserved one. He was ashamed, he believed he had done wrong, and so it was with a shameful attitude, not at all demanding, that he asked me if they would give him another implant, if I would help him get one.

"Yeah, sure, Bill," I said. "I'll do my best."

He sat back down on the floor, touched the wound on his neck. "I wish he was here," he said.

"Mister C?" said Arlie, who had been talking to a young officer; he had just come along to lead us back to our sled. "Is that who you're talkin' about, dear?"

He nodded, eyes on the floor.

"Don't you fret, luv. You'll get another friend back 'ome. A better one than Mister C. One what won't 'urt you."

"I don't mind he hurts me," Bill said. "Sometimes I do things wrong."

"We all of us do wrong, luv. But it ain't always necessary for us to be 'urt for it."

He stared up at her as if she were off her nut, as if he could not imagine a circumstance in which wrong was not followed by hurt.

"That's the gospel," said the officer. "And I promise, we'll be takin' good care of you, Bill." He had been eyefucking Arlie, the officer had, and he was only saying this to impress her with his humanity. Chances were, as soon as we were out of sight, he would go to kicking and yelling at Bill. Arlie was not fooled by him.

"Goodbye, Bill," she said, taking his hand, but he did not return her pressure, and his hand slipped out of her grasp, flopped onto his knee; he was already retreating from us, receding into his private misery, no longer able to manufacture a brave front. And as the door closed on him, that first of many doors, leaving him alone in that sickly yellow space, he put his hands to the sides of his head as if his skull could not contain some terrible pain, and began rocking back and forth, and saying, almost chanting the words, like a bitter monk his hopeless litany, "Oh, no . . . oh, no . . . oh, no. . . ."

Some seventy-nine hours after the destruction of the CPC and the dispersal of Solitaire, the lightship *Perseverance* came home . . . came home with such uncanny accuracy, that had the station been situated where it should have been, the energies released by the ship's re-entry from the supraluminal would have annihilated the entire facility and all on board. The barnacles, perhaps sensing some vast overload of light through their photophores . . . the barnacles and an idiot man had proved wiser than the rest of us. And this was no ordinary homecoming in yet another way, for it turned out that the voyage of the *Perseverance* had been successful. There was a new world waiting on the other side of the nothing, unspoiled, a garden of possibility, a challenge to our hearts and a beacon to our souls.

I contacted the corporation. They, of course, had heard the news, and they also recognized that had Bill not acted the *Perseverance* and all aboard her would have been destroyed along with Solitaire. He was, they were delighted to attest, a hero, and they would treat him as such. How's that, I asked. Promotions, news specials, celebrations, parades, was their answer. What he really wants, I told them, is to come back to Solitaire. Well, of course, they said, we'll see what we can do. When it's time, they said. We'll do right by him, don't you worry. How about another implant, I asked. Absolutely, no problem, anything he needs. By the time I broke contact, I understood that Bill's fate would be little different now he was a hero than it would have been when he was a mere fool and a villain. They would use him, milk his story for all the good it could do them, and then he would be discarded, misplaced, lost, dropped down to circulate among the swirling masses of the useless, the doomed and the forgotten.

Though I had already—in concert with others—formed a plan of action, it was this duplicity on the corporation's part that hardened me against them, and thereafter I threw myself into the implementation of the plan. A few weeks from now, the *Perseverance* and three other starships soon to be completed will launch for the new world. Aboard will be the population of Solitaire, minus a few unsympathetic personnel who have been rendered lifeless, and the populations of other, smaller stations in the asteroid belt and orbiting Mars. Solitaire itself, and the other stations, will be destroyed. It will take the corporation decades, perhaps a century, to rebuild what has been lost, and by the time they are able to reach us, we hope to have grown strong, to have fabricated a society free of corporations and Strange Magnificences, composed of those who have learned to survive without the quotas and the dread consolations of the Earth. It is an old dream, this desire to say, No more, Never again, to build a society cleansed of the old compulsions and corruptions, the ancient, vicious ways, and perhaps it is a futile one, perhaps the fact that men like myself, violent men, men who will do the necessary, who will protect against all enemies with no thought for moral fall-out, must be included on the roster, perhaps this pre-ordains that it will fail. Nevertheless, it needs to be dreamed every so often, and we are prepared to be the dreamers.

So that is the story of Barnacle Bill. My story, and Arlie's as well, yet his most of all, though his real part in it, the stuff of his thoughts and hopes, the pain he suffered and the fear he overcame, those things can never be told. Perhaps you have seen him recently on the HV, or even in person, riding in an open car at the end of a parade with men in suits, eating an ice and smiling, but in truth he is already gone into history, already part of the past, already half-forgotten, and when the final door has closed on him, it may be that his role in all this will be reduced to a mere footnote or simply a mention of his name, the slightest token of a life. But I will remember him, not in memorial grace, not as a hero, but as he was, in all his graceless ways and pitiable form. It is of absolute importance to remember him thus, because that, I have come to realize, the raw and the deformed, the ugly, the miser-able miracles of our days, the unalloyed baseness of existence, that is what we must learn to love, to accept, to embrace, if we are to cease the denials that weaken us, if we are ever to admit our dismal frailty and to confront the natural terror and heartbreak weather of our lives and live like a strong light across the sky instead of retreating into darkness.

The barnacles have returned to Solitaire. Or rather, new colonies of barnacles have attached to the newly re-united station, not covering it completely, but dressing it up in patches. I have taken to walking among them, weeding them as Bill once did; I have become interested in them, curious as to how they perceived a ship coming from light years away, and I intend to carry some along with us on the voyage and make an attempt at a study. Yet what compels me to take these walks is less scientific curiosity than a kind of furious nostalgia, a desire to remember and hold the center of those moments that have so changed the direction of our lives, to think about Bill and how it must have been for him, a frightened lump of a man with a clever voice in his ear, alone in all that daunting immensity, fixing his eyes on the bright clots of life at his feet. Just today Arlie joined me on such a walk, and it seemed we were passing along the rim of an infinite dark eye flecked with a trillion bits of color, and that everything of our souls and of every other soul could be seen in that eye, that I could look down to Earth through the haze and scum of the ocean air and see Bill where he stood looking up and trying to find us in that mottled sky, and I felt all the eerie connections a man feels when he needs to believe in something more than what he knows is real, and I tried to tell myself he was all right, walking in his garden in Nova Sibersk, taking the air with an idiot woman so beautiful it nearly made him wise. But I could not sustain the fantasy. I could only mourn, and I had no right to mourn, having never loved him—or if I did, even in the puniest of ways, it was never his person I loved, but what I had from him, the things awakened in me by what had happened. Just the thought that I could have loved him, maybe that was all I owned of right.

We were heading back toward the East Louie airlock, when Arlie stooped and plucked up a male barnacle. Dark green as an emerald, it was, except for its stubby appendage. Glowing like magic, alive with threads of color like a potter's glaze.

"That's a rare one," I said. "Never saw one that color before."

"Bill would 'ave fancied it," she said.

"Fancied, hell. He would have hung the damned thing about his neck."

She set it back down, and we watched as it began working its way across the surface of the barnacle patch, doing its slow, ungainly cartwheels, wobbling off-true, lurching in flight, nearly missing its landing, but somehow making it, somehow getting there. It landed in the shadow of some communications gear, stuck out its tongue and tried to feed. We watched it for a long, long while, with no more words spoken, but somehow there was a little truth hanging in the space between us, in the silence, a poor thing not worth naming, and maybe not even having a name, it was such an infinitesimal slice of what was, and we let it nourish us as much as it could, we took its luster and added it to our own. We sucked it dry, we had its every flavor, and then we went back inside arm in arm, to rejoin the lie of the world.

DANNY GOES TO MARS

by PAMELA SARGENT

Pamela Sargent's Nebula-Award-winning novelette, "Danny Goes to Mars," appeared in the October 1992 issue of *Asimov's*. It may seem as though it takes place in an alternate timeline now, but it continues to be a fresh and intriguing look at America's space program. The author's best known works include *Venus of Dreams; Venus of Shadows; The Shore of Women;* and her historical novel about Genghis Khan, *Ruler of the Sky.* Two new anthologies, *Women of Wonder, The Classic Years: Science Fiction by Women from the 1940s to the 1970s* and *Women of Wonder, The Contemporary Years: Science Fiction by Women from the 1970s to the 1990s,* have just been published by Harcourt Brace & Company.

Sargent has a master's degree in philosophy from the State University of New York at Binghamton. She resides in upstate New York.

> "Mars is essentially in the same orbit [as Earth]. Mars is somewhat the same distance from the sun, which is very important. We have seen pictures where there are canals, we believe, and water. If there is water, that means there is oxygen. If oxygen, that means we can breathe."
> —J. Danforth Quayle, Vice-President of the United States, as quoted in *Mother Jones*, January 1990

The Vice-President had known that this White House lunch would be different. For one thing, the President's voice kept shifting from his Mr. Rogers pitch to his John Wayne tone, and that always made Dan nervous. For another, the former Chief of Staff was there as a guest, and that bothered him.

John Sununu might have mouthed off in public about how much Dan had learned on the job, but away from the cameras, his big M.I.T. brain couldn't be bothered with even saying hello to the Vice-President. Not that it really mattered, since Nunu, as most of the White House staff called him behind his back, had pretty much treated everybody that way, except when he was having a temper tantrum. Almost everyone had been relieved when the former Chief of Staff had been eased out of that position.

Now, here he was in the White House again, sitting around at this intimate lunch as if he still had the President's full confidence. Maybe the President needed Big John's help on some scientific deal or other; Dan hoped it was that, and not something political. He squinted slightly, thinking of Robert Stack. That was the ticket, putting on that Robert Stack I'm-a-nice-guy-but-don't-mess-with-me kind of expression.

"A squeaker," the President said, "a real squeaker. Almost didn't pull it out. The Democrats—bad. Attack from the right—even worse. Got something up our sleeve, though—they'll say, Never saw *that* coming."

The Vice-President tried to look attentive. Sometimes he couldn't figure out what the President was talking about. Once he had worried about that, before discovering that many members of the White House staff had the same problem.

"Council on Competitiveness, and, uh, the space thing, too— you're our man there," the President was saying now. Marilyn had guessed that the President might be toying with the idea of a space spectacular, and Big John, whatever his lacks in the political arena, was one of the few advisors who could understand the scientific ins and outs. It made sense, what with that big breakthrough in developing an engine for space travel. Dan didn't know exactly how it worked, but it could get a ship to the Moon almost overnight—if there was an "overnight" in space.

"Mars," the president said. "About time."

"Mars?" Dan sat up. That was an even better idea than going to the Moon.

"We're sending out feelers." The former Chief of Staff adjusted his glasses, looking as if this project was his idea. Maybe it was; maybe that was how he had gotten back into the President's good graces. "The Japanese have hinted they might foot most of the bill if one of their people is among the astronauts. The Saudis'll pick up the rest if we get one of their men on board. The Russians would do almost anything to take their people's minds off the mess over there, and we can use one of those long-term habitat modules they've developed for the crew's quarters. Putting a cosmonaut on the crew in return for that would be a hell of a lot cheaper than sending more aid down that rathole."

"Impressive," the President said. "Won't cost us."

"We can get this going before the mid-term elections," Big John muttered. "America's reaching for the stars again—that should play pretty goddamned well, and you can use the brotherhood angle, too." He shifted his stocky body in his chair. "A crash program for building the ship will create jobs. The crew can be trained, and the ship ready to go, by the summer of '95. Two weeks or less to Mars, depending on where it is in relation to Earth's orbit, and back in plenty of time for the presidential primaries."

"With the new nuclear fission-to-fusion pulse engine," Dan said, "that's possible." He'd picked up a few things during his meetings with the Space Council. He was a little annoyed that no one had even hinted at the possibility of a Mars trip, but then he was usually the last guy to find anything out. "With that kind of engine, we could cross from, say, Mercury to Jupiter in less than a hundred days." He had heard one of the NASA boys say that. Or had it been less than thirty days? Not that it made that much difference, at least to him.

The former Chief of Staff lifted his brows in surprise. Sununu had a habit of looking at him like that sometimes, the way Dan's high school teachers and college professors had looked at him when he actually managed to come up with a correct answer.

"But you know," the Vice-President continued, "you could take longer to train the crew, and have this whole Mars deal going on during the primary season. That might actually help me more, having it happen right while I'm running."

"Two terms," the President said, sounding a lot more like John Wayne than Mr. Rogers this time. "Straight line from nineteen-eighty. I want a Republican in the White House in two-thousand-and-one. Maybe the Navy band could play that music at the inauguration, you know, the piece in that movie—"

"*Also Sprach Zarathustra,*" the former Chief of Staff said, then turned toward the Vice-President. "The theme from *2001.*" He had that funny smile on his face, the one that made his eyes seem even colder.

"What I was thinking, though," Dan said, "is that people have short memories." That was a piece of political wisdom he had picked up, partly because his own memory wasn't so great. "So it might make more sense to have a ship on Mars right in the middle of the primaries. It'd sure be a help to be able to make speeches about that, and—"

"Unless something goes wrong. That could really fuck up the campaign, a big space disaster." Big John folded his arms over his broad chest. "But we'll just have to see that doesn't happen. Besides, that sucker has to be back before the primaries." His smile faded. "See, the thing is—"

"On the crew, Dan," the President interrupted. "Still young, and you're in good shape—think it'll work."

The Vice-President set down his fork. "What would work?"

The former Chief of Staff unfolded his arms. "The President is saying that he'd like you to go to Mars."

Dan was too stunned to speak.

"If you'll volunteer, that is," the President said.

The Vice-President steadied himself, hoping his eyes had not widened into his Bambi-caught-in-the-headlights look. Big John might be willing to shove him aboard a ship heading for Mars just to get back in the good graces of the White House, but the President, for a guy without a whole lot of principles, was a gentleman. A man who never forgot to write thank-you notes wasn't the kind of person to force his Veep on a risky space mission.

"Well." Dan frowned. "Do I really have to do this?"

Big John said, "It may be the only way we can get you elected. It sure as hell would give you an edge, and you're going to need one. The President was getting it from the right, but you're going to be getting it from the moderate Republicans." He sneered. "We're only talking a two or three week trip, hardly more than a space shuttle flight. Come back from Mars, and you wouldn't just be the Vice-President—you'd be a hero." He said the words as if he didn't quite believe them.

"Hard to run against a hero," the President said. He pressed his hands together, then flung them out to his sides. "Moderates—trouble. But it's up to you, Dan. Think you can handle this Mars thing—make sure there's good people on the crew with you—but you gotta decide."

The Vice-President swallowed, trying for his Robert Stack look once more. He was about to say he would have to talk it over with Marilyn, but Big John would give him one of his funny looks if he said that.

"I'll consider it very seriously," he said. If Marilyn thought this was a good idea, he might have to go along with it.

"You do that," the former Chief of Staff said quietly.

He explained it all to his wife after dinner. There would be the months of training, but a house would be provided for him, and the family could visit him in Houston. They could even move there temporarily, but Dan wasn't about to insist on that. His son Tucker was in college, so it wouldn't much matter to him where they lived, but the move might be disruptive for Corinne and Ben.

"I can see it, in a way," he said. "If I do this, I might be unbeatable. On the other hand, it didn't work for John Glenn."

"But this is *Mars*, honey," Marilyn said. "John Glenn didn't go to Mars." She brushed back a lock of brown hair, then frowned. Dan had the sinking feeling that this whole business had already been decided. Whatever his fears about the journey, he was more afraid of facing the President and telling him he had decided not to volunteer. Besides, this space stuff might finally put an end to all the mockery. Maybe there wouldn't be any more jokes about his lousy grades and his golf trips and being on beer duty during his stint in the National Guard. Maybe that bastard Garry Trudeau would finally stop depicting him as a feather in his *Doonesbury* comic strip.

"I'd miss you a lot," Marilyn said.

"I'd miss you, too." He slipped an arm over her shoulders. "But it isn't like it's going to be one of those three-year-round-trip deals. If that's what it was, I would have said no right on the spot. They said it would be safe."

She rested her head against his chest. "Nobody could top this, you know. I doubt you'd have any challengers in the primaries afterwards, and the Democrats won't have the easy time they expected against you. Even then—"

He owed it to Marilyn. He wouldn't have gotten this far without her; in a way, it was too bad she couldn't go to Mars with him. She'd had to give up her law practice in Indiana when he was first elected to Congress, and later, her hopes of finding a job when he was running for Vice-President. She had wised him up after his election to the Senate, after the story about his colleague Tom Evans and that Parkinson babe broke; if he had listened to Marilyn in the first place, he wouldn't have been in Palm Beach with them that weekend. She had given him good advice and sacrificed plenty for him. The least he could do was make her First Lady. "What should I do?" he asked.

Marilyn drew away from him and sat up. "There's only one thing to do," she murmured. "This is too big for us to decide by ourselves, so we have to put it in God's hands. He'll show us what's right."

He folded his hands, bowed his head, and tried to summon up a prayer. He definitely needed the Lord's help on this one, but had the feeling that God was likely to agree with the President.

When Dan agreed to become an astronaut, it seemed that a great weight was lifted from his shoulders. The announcement brought the expected press and television coverage, along with varying reactions from stunned commentators, but the conventional wisdom was that he could probably handle his Vice-Presidential duties as well in Houston or on Mars as he could anywhere else.

There was a press conference to endure with his four fellow crew members, and the interviews, but he got through them all without any major gaffes, except for calling the moons of Mars Photos and Zenith. That snotty nerd George Will had tried to get him on some old remarks he had made about the Red Planet having canals, but Dan had muddied the waters with a bunch of memorized statistics he had mastered in the years since, along with a comment about having been under the spell of some Ray Bradbury stories. It was smart of his staff to feed him that stuff about Bradbury's *Martian Chronicles* along with the other information. Dan had not only made Will look like a bully, but had also given viewers the impression that the Vice-President actually read books.

In Houston, at least, he would not have to do many interviews, on the grounds that they might interfere with his training. This did not keep some reporters from trying to get leaked information about his progress.

There was little for them to discover. Surprisingly, the training was not nearly as rigorous as he had expected. The other American on the crew, Ashana Washington, was both a physicist and an experienced pilot; she would technically be in command of the expedition. Prince Ahmed was also a pilot, although the ship itself would be piloted automatically during the voyage. Sergei Vavilov and Kiichi Taranaga each had a string of degrees in various subjects requiring big brains, and since they, like Prince Ahmed, spoke fluent English, the Vice-President, to his great relief, would not have to try to learn a foreign language.

Basically, Dan knew, he would be little more than a passenger. Learning about the Mars vessel and its capacities was more interesting than Cabinet meetings, and messing around with the NASA computers was a little like those video games he had sometimes played with Tucker and Ben. The crew had to be in good shape, but he had always jogged and played a fair amount of tennis. He often missed Marilyn and the kids, but they had been apart for extended periods during political campaigns in the past, and their weekends together more than made up for it. He didn't have to talk to reporters, although occasionally he didn't mind posing for photographers in his NASA garb with a Robert Redford grin on his face. Once a week, some of his staffers and the President's would fly down to brief him on various matters, but Washington often seemed far away.

He had wondered if his fellow astronauts would take to him, since they would have to spend at least a couple of weeks in isolation with him—longer if NASA decided they should remain in a Martian base camp for a while, which they might have to do if they found anything really interesting. Within three weeks after his arrival in Houston, however, he was golfing twice a week with Kiichi, jogging in the mornings with Prince Ahmed after the Saudi's morning prayers, and playing tennis with Sergei, who, despite his small size, had one hell of a backhand.

Only Ashana had intimidated him just a little. The tall, good-looking black woman was too damned brainy and formal for him to regard her as a real babe—not that he, as a married man and a future Presidential candidate, was inclined to dwell on her apparent babe qualities anyway. Maybe Ashana thought that she was commanding this expedition for the same reason Clarence Thomas was on the Supreme Court. That was another reason to keep his distance. It wouldn't help his chances for the White House if Ashana turned into another Anita Hill.

He might have gone on being distantly polite to her, if, a month and a half into his training, he hadn't been drawn into a pick-up basketball game with a few of the NASA officers. Ashana came by, and before he knew it, she was giving him some good advice on how to improve his jump shots.

Basketball was the glue that sealed their friendship, but Dan had nearly blown it when Ashana had come to his house one weekend to meet his family and watch a game. "I should have known," he said as he settled into his chair, "that you'd be a hoop fan."

Ashana's face suddenly got very stiff. Next to her on the sofa, Marilyn was rolling her eyes and giving him her I-don't-believe-you-just-said-that look.

"Exactly why should you have known?" Ashana asked in a small but kind of scary voice.

"In your official biography—I mean, you grew up in Indiana, didn't you? Everybody's a fan there."

Ashana relaxed, but he didn't quite understand why she had laughed so hard afterward.

He admitted it to himself; if he had to be a hero to win the election, this was the way to do it. His crewmates were the real experts, so he could leave all the major decisions to them. He would, of course, do his best to be helpful. Sergei would use him as a subject in some medical experiments, and he could also help Kiichi sort his soil samples. That would be great, if they actually found life on Mars, even if it was only something like the mildew that sometimes showed up in the Vice-Presidential residence.

People were really getting psyched about this mission. After all the economic bad news of recent years, putting people to work on the ship, now called the *Edgar Rice Burroughs,* and its systems, as well as expanding the size of the Russian and American space stations to house those who had to work on the *Burroughs* in orbit, had given the economy a boost. Part of that was the new jobs, but most of it was simply that the country was regaining its confidence. This Mars thing would propel him into the White House on a wave of good feeling, and he would lead the country into the next century during his second term. By then, the economy would be booming along under the impetus of a revived space program. Dan wasn't exactly sure how this would happen, but would let his advisors figure that out when it was time for them to write his speeches.

It was, when he thought about it, amazing that the Mars mission had won such widespread support. There were, of course, some people who had to bitch, like those protestors who showed up at the Johnson Space Center or Cape Canaveral to protest the ship's technology, but they were the kind who panicked whenever they saw the word "fission," especially if "fusion" was sitting right next to it. A comedian on David Letterman's show had said something about how a dopehead must have thought of putting the Vice-President aboard, and so maybe they should have called the ship the *William S. Burroughs*. Dan didn't see what was so funny about that, but it didn't really matter. Most of the clippings Marilyn brought to him on her visits had optimistic words about the mission and comments from various people about his bravery and increasing maturity.

Almost before he knew it, he and his fellow astronauts were being flown to Florida, where they would spend their final days before liftoff; a space shuttle would carry them to the *Burroughs*. The President would be there, along with several ambassadors and any other dignitaries who had managed to wangle an invitation. A whole contingent of family and friends were coming in from Indiana to view the launch, which would be covered by camera teams and reporters from just about everywhere. Everything had gone basically without a hitch so far, although they were going to be late taking off for the *Burroughs*; the shuttle launch had been postponed until October, what with a few small delays on construction and testing. Still, the Mars ship and its systems had passed every test with flying colors, and this had inspired a number of articles contending, basically, that American workers had finally gotten their shit together again. More kids were deciding to take science and math courses in school. There was a rumor that *Time* magazine had decided early that Dan would have to be their Man of the Year.

Only one dark spot marred his impending triumph. That creep Garry Trudeau was now depicting him as a feather floating inside a space helmet and referring to him as "the candidate from Mars."

The *Burroughs* wasn't exactly the kind of sleek ship Dan had seen in movies about space. Its frame held two heavily shielded habitat modules, the lander, and the Mars base assembly. The large metallic bowl that housed the pulse engine was attached to the end of the frame. The whole thing reminded him a little of a giant Tootsie Roll with a big dish at one end, but he felt confident as he floated into the crew's quarters through an open lock. The President and Barbara had wished him well, and Marilyn and the kids had looked so proud of him. If he had known that being courageous was this simple, maybe he would have tried it sooner.

Inside the large barrel of this habitat, five seats near wall screens had been bolted to what would be the floor during acceleration. He propelled himself toward a seat and strapped himself in without a qualm. The *Burroughs* circled the Earth, then took off like a dream;

Dan, pressed against his seat, watched in awe as the globe on the screen shrank to the size of a marble.

The ship would take a little while to reach one g, at which point the crew could get up and move around. The *Burroughs* would continue to accelerate until they were halfway to Mars, at which point it would begin to decelerate. The faster the ship boosted, the more gravity it would have; at least that was how Dan understood the matter. Even though it might have been kind of fun to float around the *Burroughs*, he had been a bit queasy during the shuttle flight, and was just as happy that they wouldn't have to endure weightlessness during the voyage. He had heard too many stories about space sickness and the effects of weightlessness on gas; he didn't want to puke and fart all the way to Mars.

Dan had little time to glance at the viewscreens when he finally rose from his seat. The others were already messing around with the computers and setting up experiments and generally doing whatever they were supposed to do; his job now was to monitor any transmissions from Earth.

He sent back greetings, having rehearsed the words during the last few days. He didn't have anything really eloquent to say about actually being out in space at last, but a lot of astronauts weren't great talkers. When he was about to sign off, the NASA CapCom patched him through to Marilyn.

She had cut out James J. Kilpatrick's latest column to read to him. The columnist had written: "Lloyd Bentsen once said of the Vice-President, 'You're no Jack Kennedy.' This has been verified in a way Senator Bentsen could never have predicted. This man is no Jack Kennedy. Instead, he has donned the mantle of Columbus and the other great explorers of the past."

That was the kind of thing that could really make a guy feel great.

There was little privacy on the *Burroughs*. What with the shielding, the engine, the Mars lander they would use when they reached their destination, and the base camp assembly that would be sent to the Martian surface if NASA deemed a longer stay worthwhile, there wasn't exactly an abundance of space for the crew in the habitat modules. The next ship, which was already being built, would have the additional luxuries of a recreational module, along with separate sleeping compartments, but NASA had cut a few corners on this one.

The bathroom, toilet and shower included, was the size of a small closet; their beds, which had to be pulled out from the walls, were in the adjoining module, with no partitions. The whole place smelled like a locker room, maybe because the modules had been part of the Russian space station before being recycled for use in this mission. The food tasted even worse than some of the stuff Dan had eaten in the Deke house at DePauw.

But their comfort was not entirely overlooked; the *Burroughs* had a small library of CDs, videodiscs, and books stored on microdot. Within twenty-four hours, Dan and his companions had worked out a schedule so that each of them would have some time alone in the bed compartment to read, listen to music, or take a nap. There was no sense getting on one another's nerves during this voyage, and some solitude would ease any tensions.

Dan went to the sleeping quarters during his scheduled time on the third day out, meaning to watch one of his favorite movies, *Ferris Bueller's Day Off*. He could stretch out on one of the beds and still see the screen on the wall in the back. He nodded off just as Ferris Bueller, played by Matthew Broderick, was calling up his friend Cameron on the phone; he woke up to the sounds of "Twist and Shout." Matthew Broderick was gyrating on a float in the middle of a Chicago parade.

Dan had missed most of the movie. He must have been more tired than he realized, even though he didn't have as much to do as the rest of the crew. Sergei had said something about doing some medical tests on him. He looked at his watch, set on Eastern Standard Time, which they were keeping aboard ship, and noticed that it was past 8:00 P.M. He stared at the screen, not understanding why the movie was still on until he realized that the player had gone back to the beginning of the disk and started running the film again. It was Ahmed's time to use the compartment now, so why wasn't the Prince here bugging him about it? On top of that, nobody had come to get him for dinner.

He sat up slowly. A weird feeling came over him, a little like the nervousness he had felt before calling his father about trying to get into the Guard. He got to his feet and climbed the ladder through the passageway that connected this module to the next.

The hatch at the end of the short passage was open as he came up. His shipmates were slumped over the table where they usually ate, their faces in their trays. Dan crept toward them, wondering if this was some kind of joke. "Okay, guys," he said, "you can cut it out now." They were awfully still, and Sergei had written something on the table in Cyrillic letters with his fingers and some gravy. "Okay, you faked me out. Come on." Dan stopped behind Kiichi and nudged him, then saw that the Japanese had stopped breathing. Very slowly, he moved around the table, taking each person's pulse in turn. The arms were flaccid, the bodies cold.

"Oh, my God," he said. "Oh, my God." He sank to the floor, covered his face with his hands, and sat there for a long time until a voice called out to him from the com.

"Houston to *Burroughs*. Houston to *Burroughs*." He got up and stumbled toward the com. "Come in, *Burroughs*." He sat down and turned on the com screen.

Sallie Werfel, the CapCom, stared out at him from the screen.

"They're dead," he blurted out. "They're all dead." Not until after he had said it did he remember that NASA had planned a live broadcast for that evening. "Oh, my God."

Sallie gazed back at him with a big smile on her face; it would take a while for his words to reach her, since signals had to work harder to get through all that space. Then her smile disappeared, and she was suddenly shouting to somebody else before turning to the screen once more.

"We're off the air," she said. "All right, what the hell do you mean about—"

"They're all dead," he replied. "At the table. Turn on the cameras and take a look. Sergei wrote something next to his tray, but it's in Russian."

Sallie was whispering to a man near her. Some more time passed. "All right, Dan," she said very quietly. "I want you to stay right where you are for the moment. We've got the cameras on the others now. You're absolutely sure they're, uh, gone."

"Yeah."

A few more minutes passed. "We're looking at Sergei's message. A couple of our people here know Russian, so we should have a translation in just a little bit. While we're waiting, I want to know exactly what you were doing during the last few hours."

"Not much," he said. "I mean, it was my turn for some private time—we had, like, a schedule for times to be alone, you know? So I went to the other module thinking I'd catch a movie." He was about to say he had been watching *Ferris Bueller's Day Off*, but thought better of it. "What I remember is that Ashana was on the treadmill working out, and Sergei and Ahmed were checking some numbers or something. Kiichi was in the can—er, bathroom. I fell asleep, and when I woke up and looked at the time, it was past dinner. Then I came out and—" He swallowed hard. "Oh, my God." He waited.

"Take it easy, Dan," she said finally. "We're opening up a line to the White House right now."

An alien, he thought. Some creepy blob thing, the kind of creature they showed in old sci-fi movies, had somehow found its way aboard the ship. He imagined it oozing out to kill his companions during dinner, then concealing itself somewhere aboard the *Burroughs* to wait for him. Except that it wouldn't find too many places it could hide in the crew's quarters. Maybe the alien was concealed in the Mars lander by now, waiting for him. He shuddered. It couldn't be an alien. There wasn't any way for one to get aboard.

"We've got a translation," Sallie was saying. Dan forced his attention back to the screen. "We know what Sergei wrote." Her eyes glistened; he held his breath. "Not the food. Fever. Feels like flu."

"What?" He waited.

"Flu. Influenza." She lifted a hand to her temples. "He's telling us it wasn't anything in the food, that it felt as if they were coming down with something."

Everything had happened awfully fast. The whole business might be some sort of weird assassination attempt; maybe someone had figured out a way to poison the main module's air system. It was pure chance that he had not been sitting there with the others. But why would anyone want to assassinate him? Only the Democrats had anything to gain from that, and they had so many loose cannons that somebody would have leaked such a plot by now.

He didn't know whether to be relieved or not when Sallie contacted him an hour later and gave him NASA's hypothesis. They suspected that his comrades had been the victims of an extremely virulent but short-lived virus—virulent because the others had died so quickly, and short-lived because Dan, in the same module breathing the same air, was still alive. They had come up with this explanation after consulting with the Russians, who had admitted that milder viruses had occasionally afflicted their cosmonauts. The closed ecologies of their modules had never been perfect. What that meant was that things could get kind of scuzzy in there.

The next order of business was to dispose of the bodies. Dan put on his spacesuit and tried not to look at the foodstained faces of his dead comrades as he dragged them one by one into the airlock.

They deserved a prayer. The only ones he knew were Christian prayers, but maybe Kiichi and Ahmed wouldn't mind, and he suspected Sergei was more religious than he let on. He whispered the Lord's Prayer, and then another he had often used at prayer breakfasts. Too late, he realized that a prayer said at meals might not be the most appropriate thing, given that his companions had died over their chow.

He looked up from the bodies as the outside door slid slowly open to reveal the blackness of space. His comrades deserved a few more words before he consigned them to the darkness.

"You guys," he whispered, "you were some of the best friends I ever had. You were definitely the smartest."

It took a while to get the bodies outside. As he watched them drift away from the ship, tears rose to his eyes. He was really going to miss them.

Sallie contacted Dan an hour before the President was to address the nation and the world. The most important thing now was for Dan to seem in control of himself when it was time for his own broadcast. The NASA scientists were fairly certain that Dan wouldn't suffer the fate of the others; there was only a slight chance that the mysterious virus would reappear to infect him. He didn't find this very consoling, since there had been only a slight chance of such a thing happening in the first place.

"Do me a favor, Sallie," Dan said. "If I do kick off, don't let the media have tapes of it or anything. I mean, I don't want Marilyn and my kids watching that stuff on CNN or something." He waited. The time for roundtrip signals was growing longer.

"You got it, Dano."

The President made his announcement, and Dan went on an hour later to show that he was still able to function. He had no prepared speech, but the most important thing was to look calm and not hysterical. He succeeded in that, mostly because he felt too stunned and empty to crack up in front of the hundreds of millions who would be viewing him from Earth.

Sallie spoke to him after his appearance. Ashana Washington's parents and brother had already retained counsel, and there was talk of massive lawsuits. He might have known that the lawyers would get in on this immediately.

"The most important thing now," Sallie said, "is to bring you home as fast as possible. You'll reach your destination four days from now." She narrowed her eyes. "The *Burroughs* is already programmed to orbit Mars automatically, so all we have to do is let it swing around and head back to Earth. You can get back in—"

"I'm not going to land?" he asked, and waited even longer.

Sallie sat up. "Land?"

"I want to land, Sallie. Don't you understand? I have to now. The others would have expected me to—I've got to do it for them." He searched for another phrase. "It means they won't have died in vain. I can do it—you can program the lander, and I can go down to the surface. Maybe I can't do the experiments and stuff they were going to, but I can set up the cameras and bring back soil samples. It wouldn't be right not to try. And if I'm going to die, I might as well die doing something."

He waited for his words to reach her. "Dan," she said at last, "you surprise me."

It would probably surprise the hell out of the President, too. "I've got to do it, Sallie." He frowned, struggling with the effort of all this thinking. "Look, if I land, it'll inspire the world to bigger and better space triumphs. We'll get that bigger space station built and the more advanced ships, too. But if you just bring me back, all the nuts will start whining again about what a waste all this was and how four people died for nothing." He waited.

"I'll do what I can, Dan." She shook her head. "I don't have much to say about this, but I can speak up for you. In the end, though, it's probably going to be up to the President."

"Then put me through to him now."

He hashed it out with the President in the slow motion of radio delay, listened to the objections, and replied by invoking the memory of his dead comrades. When the President, looking tense and even more hyper than usual, signed off by saying he would have to consult with his advisors, Dan was certain he had won. He felt no surprise when word came twelve hours later that he would be allowed to undertake the landing.

After all, if the President didn't let him go ahead, it was like admitting publicly that he had put an incompetent without adequate training aboard the *Burroughs*. The President, having finally salvaged his place in history, wasn't about to go down in the record books as a doofus.

David Bowie was singing about Major Tom and Ground Control. Kiichi had been a David Bowie fan, so a lot of Bowie's music, everything from his Ziggy Stardust phase up through Tin Machine, was in the *Burroughs*'s music collection. Dan had never been into David Bowie, who struck him as being kind of fruity, but now he felt as if he understood this particular song.

Sometimes, during his work with the President's Council on Space, Dan had wondered why some early astronauts had gotten kind of flaky after returning to Earth. These were macho test pilot guys, not the kind of men anyone would expect to get mystical or weirded out. But as he moved around the ship, which was usually silent except for the low throbbing hum of the engine and an occasional beep from the consoles, he was beginning to feel a bit odd himself, as if his mind had somehow moved outside of his body.

He had never thought all that much about God. He had, of course, never doubted that God was out there going about His business; he had simply never thought about the Lord that much, except when he was in church or saying a prayer. When he was a boy, he had imagined a God something like his grandfather Pulliam, an angry old man ready to smite all those liberal Democrats, Communists, and other forces of darkness. Later on, when he was older and more mature, God had seemed more like a sort of basketball coach or golf pro.

Now, when he gazed at the image of Mars on his screen, a rust-red dot surrounded by blackness, he had the strangest feeling that he had never really understood the Lord at all. God had created all this, the planets and the space between them and the stars that were so far away he could not even comprehend the distance. God, in some ways, was a lot like the NASA computers, but there was even more to Him than that. Dan wasn't quite sure how to put it; things like that were hard to explain. He supposed that was what it meant to be mystical—having weird feelings you couldn't quite put into words. And faith was believing what no one in his right mind would believe even though it was true.

NASA kept him busy during his waking hours programming the Mars lander and checking out its systems. After supper, he usually worked on his speech, with some suggestions NASA was passing along from his speechwriters. They had given him another speech earlier, but he couldn't use that one now. With what had happened, this one would have to be really inspiring.

Yet he still had his moments of solitude, the times when he felt, for the first time in his life, what it was like to be utterly alone. He couldn't actually be alone, he supposed, since God had to be some-where in the vicinity, but there were times when it seemed that the emptiness of space had seeped into him.

Mars swelled until it filled the screen, and then his ship was falling around the planet. There was no way to avoid weightlessness now; the *Burroughs* had begun to decelerate after the halfway point of the journey, and its engine had finally shut down. Dan put on his spacesuit and floated through the tunnel that connected the crew's quarters with the module holding the base assembly. He wouldn't be setting up a Mars base, though, since NASA didn't want him fooling around down there for very long. He entered the last module, which held the lander.

He pressed his hand against the lander's door; it slid open. The lander had food, a small lavatory, and equipment for experiments. There was even a Mars rover on board so that he could ride around on the surface. He wouldn't be doing much, though, except for shooting a bunch of stuff with the cameras and gathering soil samples. The important thing was to land, make his speech, mess around for a little while, catch some shut-eye, and then get back to the *Burroughs*.

He strapped himself into one of the chairs. The four empty seats made him feel as if the ghosts of the others were with him. NASA had allowed each of the astronauts to bring along a small personal possession to take down to the Martian surface, and Dan had his companions' choices with him in the lander. Ahmed had brought a Koran, Kiichi a vintage Louisville Slugger with Joe DiMaggio's signature engraved on it, Sergei a set of nested Russian dolls, and Ashana a pair of Nikes personally autographed by Michael Jordan. A lump rose in his throat.

The doors to the outside were opening; he tensed. The President had spoken to him just a couple of hours ago, telling him that everyone in the world would be waiting for his first transmission from the surface. In spite of the tragedy, Dan's determination to carry out the landing had inspired everybody in the country. Having come so far, humankind would not be discouraged by this setback; the Vice-President had shown the way. Construction of the next ship was moving along; it would probably be spaceworthy by spring, and a follow-up Mars mission would give an even bigger boost to Dan's candidacy. At this point, he would probably carry all the states, and even D.C., in the general election.

"Asteroids," the President had said. "Lotta resources there. Just get one of those things in Earth orbit, where we can go into, uh, a mining mode, and supply-side economics can work." It was nice for Dan to think that, when he finally became President, things might be moving along so well that he'd have plenty of time for golf, the way Eisenhower had.

The lander glided forward toward the new world below.

Mars filled his screen. Dan, pressed against his seat, braced himself. He had known what to expect; his training had included maneuvers with a model of the Mars rover in areas much like the Martian surface. Yet actually seeing it this close up still awed him. It looked, he thought, like the biggest sand trap in the universe.

His chair trembled under him as he landed. Dan waited, wanting to make sure everything was all right before he got up. Time to contact Earth, but in the excitement of actually being on Mars, he had forgotten what he was supposed to say.

He cleared his throat. "Guys," he said, "I'm down." That ought to do the job.

Over four minutes passed before he heard what sounded like cheers at the other end. Sallie was saying something, but he couldn't make out the words. By then, he was rummaging through the compartments of his spacesuit looking for the cards that held his speech.

"—all ecstatic," Sallie's voice said. "Congratulations, and God bless you—you don't know how much—"

He sighed, realizing at last that he had forgotten the cards. He might have known that, during the most important moment of his life, he would have to ad lib.

Dan waited in the small airlock until the door slid open. Above him was the pinkish-red sky of an alien world. A rust-colored barren landscape stretched to the horizon, which, he noticed, seemed closer than it should be, then he remembered that Mars was smaller than Earth. He felt a lot lighter, too, since Mars, being a smaller place, didn't have as much gravity.

He made his way down the ladder to the surface, then inhaled slowly. "Whoa," he said aloud, overcome with awe at the immensity of this accomplishment and sorrow that his dead comrades could not share the moment with him. "Jeez." He pressed his lips together, suddenly realizing that history would record man's first words on the surface of Mars as "Whoa" and "Jeez."

"Well, here I am," he said, knowing he would have to wing it. "I almost can't believe I'm here. Man, if anybody had told me when I was a kid that I'd go to Mars, I would have thought—" He paused. "Anyway, the thing is, I wish the others were here with me, because they're the ones who really deserved to make this trip. What I mean is, I'm really going to miss them, but I can tell you all I'm not ever going to forget them. It's why I'm here, because of them. In other words, I figured I had to come down and stand here for them." He remembered that he was supposed to plant the United Nations flag about now, and took the pole out from under his arm. "Now we'll go forward." The words he had planned to say at this point were something like that. "And someday, other people will come here and turn into Martians." Dan cleared his throat. "Guess I'll show you around a little now."

He scanned the landscape with a camera, then went back to the lander. By then, the President had given him his congratulations, and Marilyn had gotten on to talk to him after that. He was happy to hear his wife's voice, even though, what with having to wait a few minutes until she heard him and could reply, it wasn't actually possible to have what he would call a real conversation. This far from Earth, the signals had to work even harder to reach him.

The rover had been lowered from another side of the lander on a platform. Since about all he could do was take pictures and gather soil samples, NASA wanted him to drive around and take them in different places. They didn't want him to go too far or take any unnecessary risks, and maybe, now that he'd given a speech of sorts, he could let the images of the Martian surface speak for themselves.

He rode around, careful not to drive too fast since there were some nasty-looking rocks and rims of small craters nearby, until the orange sky grew darker. By the time he got back to the lander with his samples, the sky was nearly black and the sun a bright swirl on the horizon.

I actually got here, he thought, then remembered the others with a pang.

He slept well, then got up to say his farewells to the Red Planet—although Rusty Planet might be a better name for it. Another ride, some more pictures and samples, and he was ready to go. He hoped the NASA scientists weren't too unhappy with his answers to their questions about what unusual things he might have observed. Hell, *everything* seemed pretty unusual here, when he stopped to think about it.

He went inside, then strapped in. "Ready to go," he said. There were just a couple of buttons to push, and he had practiced a lot during the last days aboard the *Burroughs* to be sure he didn't make a mistake. He pressed one, waited for it to light up, then hit the next. For a few moments, he wondered why he couldn't feel the lander taking off, then realized that it wasn't moving.

"Uh, Mars to Houston," he said, then waited until he heard Sallie's voice respond. "I hate to say this, but I'm not going anywhere. Should I hit those whosits again, or what?"

Nearly ten minutes later, he heard Sallie's reply. Her first word was, "Shit."

No matter how many times he activated the controls, nothing happened. Mission Control had various theories about what might be wrong, none of which were doing him any good. Gradually it dawned on him that he might be stranded. Twenty-four hours after he reached that conclusion, Sallie confirmed it. They could not pinpoint the problem at that distance. They did not want to take any risks with the lander. He was reminded of which buttons to push in order to bring down the Mars base assembly.

It could have been worse, he told himself. There were enough provisions in the lander alone to last him more than a month, since his companions weren't there to share them. With the supplies the base assembly had, he could survive until a rescue mission arrived.

There would be such a mission. The President assured him of that, as did Sallie. Another ship would be on its way to him within a few months. The wonderful thing was that his mission, despite the tragedy, was in its own way a success, even if he wasn't in the best position to appreciate that fact. A man had made it to Mars and was now on its surface, and the fate of his fellow astronauts had only temporarily stemmed the rising tide of optimism and hope. Humankind would return to the Moon and reach out to the other planets. Dan, who had insisted on landing instead of turning back, would be remembered by future generations of space explorers.

How his present predicament might affect the elections was not discussed. The President had said something vague about getting him back there in time for the convention. Now that Dan was a true hero, it didn't look as though there would be any opposition in the Republican primaries anyway.

Dan tried to feel comforted by this, but the campaign, and everything else, seemed awfully far away.

A distant object shaped like a shuttlecock dropped toward the cratered plain. Its engines fired; the object landed two kilometers away.

Dan sighed with relief at the sight of the base assembly. He had been worrying that something might go wrong at this point; one disadvantage of being a hero was that sometimes it required you to be dead. Now he would be safe, and could keep busy making observations, watching movies, working out, and in general keeping himself together until the rescue mission arrived. It was sort of depressing to know he'd miss Thanksgiving and Christmas, although fortunately there were some turkey dinners among the provisions, and Mission Control had promised to sing carols for him.

He climbed into the rover and started toward the barrels of the base assembly; he'd check it out first, then come back another time to load up whatever he might need from the lander. His staff had promised to transmit the text for the official announcement of his candidacy in a few days, and he supposed they would want him to make some speeches from Mars later, during the primaries. Maybe being on Mars, whatever the disadvantages, was better than having to trudge through New Hampshire.

He had to admit it; life in the somewhat more spacious quarters of the Mars base wasn't too bad in some ways. He was getting used to the desolate orange landscape and the way the sun set so suddenly. There were movies and records enough to keep him occupied, although he was beginning to see that there were limits to how many times he could watch some movies, even ones as great as *Ferris Bueller's Day Off*.

But there were times when the solitude, even with all the messages NASA was relaying from Earth, really got to him. There wasn't a whole lot a guy could do all alone, except for stuff it was better not to think about too much. He had spoken to Marilyn and the kids a couple of times, but having to speak and then wait long minutes for the response made him realize how far he was from everything he knew.

Maybe things would pick up when he really got into his campaign. There was plenty he could do, even out here. His staff was already trying to set him up for a *Nightline* appearance, which would probably have to be taped so that the delay between Ted Koppel's questions and his answers could be deleted. His staff should be transmitting the text for the official announcement of his candidacy any day now.

Dan had finished struggling into his spacesuit and was about to put on his helmet when the com started beeping at him. Maybe his speechwriters had finally gotten their act together. He sat down and turned on the screen.

The President's face stared out at him. "Uh, hello, Mr. President," Dan said. "I was just about to take a drive over to the lander—there's some stuff I want to move here."

"I don't know how to tell you this, Dan," the President said. "Something's gone, well, a bit awry. Might have known the Democrats would think of some devious—see, we're going to have to postpone your announcement for a while."

"But why?"

He waited a long time for the President's answer. "The Democrats—they're saying you have to be on Earth to make your announcement. Somebody found some loophole or other in the law, and they're arguing that you can't declare and run for president while you're on Mars. Got our guys working on it—think they can beat those bastards in court—but by the time they do, it may be too late to file and get you on primary ballots. Could try to get write-ins, but the rules are, uh, different in every state."

Dan tried to recall if there was something in the law the Democrats could use to pull a stunt like this. He couldn't think of anything, but then he hadn't been exactly the biggest brain in law school. Maybe the Democrats would drag out John Glenn, however old he was, to run this time. They'd probably use Ashana's family in the campaign, too; they had plenty of reason to be pissed off at the Administration.

"You said I could get back by the convention," Dan murmured. "I mean, aren't the delegates free to switch their votes if they want?"

The minutes passed. "Well, you're right on the money there, and no question they'd turn to you, but—see, NASA's got sort of a little problem with the new ship. Nothing for you to worry about, just some bitty technical thing they can definitely iron out, but they're certain they can have you back here next fall."

Dan was beginning to see more problems. The Democrats might use his predicament against the Republicans. They would say he wouldn't be stranded there if the Administration had thought more about real science and space exploration and less about politics and publicity stunts, if they hadn't been rushing to put him on another planet. He wouldn't be on the campaign trail to inspire people and to invoke the names of his comrades; he would be only a distant voice and grainy image from Mars. The whole business might turn into as big a bummer as the end of the Gulf War.

"What are we going to do?" Dan asked.

When the President replied, he said, "Well, there's a lotta sentiment here to make Marilyn our candidate."

That figured. The idea was so perfect that Dan was surprised he hadn't thought of it himself. The Democrats would look mean-spirited slinging mud at a hero's wife, one waiting and praying for her husband to return safely.

"All I can say," Dan said quietly, "is that she has my full support."

Dan finished loading the rover, climbed in and drove slowly toward the scattered Tootsie Rolls of his base. He had not had to talk to Marilyn very long to convince her to run; in fact, he had expected her to object a lot more to the idea. She would make a pretty good president, though—maybe a better one than he would have been.

He had packed up the personal items of his comrades—Ashana's Nikes, Ahmed's Koran, Kiichi's bat, and Sergei's dolls—feeling that he wanted his dead friends' things with him. He had also brought his golf balls and his favorite wood. The club, which had a persimmon head, had cost him a pretty penny, but he liked a driver with a solid hardwood head.

An inspiration came to him. He stopped the rover, climbed down, then took out one of his balls and the wood. Stepping over a small crater, he set down the ball, then gripped his club. Getting in a smooth swing was going to be rough with his spacesuit on, but he thought he could manage it. Alan Shepard might be the first guy to tee off on the Moon, but Dan would be the first to do so on another planet.

He swung his club and knew the head's sweet spot had met the ball. The small white orb arched above the orange cratered landscape and soared toward the distant pink sky.

THE NUTCRACKER COUP

by JANET KAGAN

Janet Kagan is one of *Asimov's* most popular authors. Year after year, the stories that eventually made up her novel, *Mirabile* (Tor 1991), were the recipients of the *Asimov's* Readers' Award. Although her delightful Hugo-Award-winning novelette about "The Nutcracker Coup" (December 1992) is not a part of that series, it, too, is one of the magazine's Readers' Award winners. Janet Kagan's other novels include *Uhura's Song* (*Star Trek* #21) and *Hellspark*. She and her husband, Ricky, share their Lincoln Park, New Jersey home with several gracious cats.

Marianne Tedesco had "The Nutcracker Suite" turned up full blast for inspiration, and as she whittled she now and then raised her knife to conduct Tchaikovsky. That was what she was doing when one of the locals poked his delicate snout around the corner of the door to her office. She nudged the sound down to a whisper in the background and beckoned him in.

It was Tatep, of course. After almost a year on Rejoicing (that was the literal translation of the world's name), she still had a bit of trouble recognizing the Rejoicers by snout alone, but the three white quills in Tatep's ruff had made him the first real "individual" to her. Helluva thing for a junior diplomat *not* to be able to tell one local from another—but there it was. Marianne was desperately trying to learn the snout shapes that distinguished the Rejoicers to each other.

"Good morning, Tatep. What can I do for you?"

"Share?" said Tatep.

"Of course. Shall I turn the music off?" Marianne knew that *The Nutcracker Suite* was as alien to him as the rattling and scraping of his music was to her. She was beginning to like pieces here and there of the Rejoicer style, but she didn't know if Tatep felt the same way about Tchaikovsky.

"Please, leave it on," he said. "You've played it every day this week—am I right? And now I find you waving your knife to the beat. Will you share the reason?"

She *had* played it every day this week, she realized. "I'll try to explain. It's a little silly, really, and it shouldn't be taken as characteristic of humans. Just as characteristic of Marianne."

"Understood." He climbed the stepstool she'd cobbled together her first month on Rejoicing and settled himself on his haunches comfortably to listen. At rest, the wicked quills adorning his ruff and tail seemed just that: adornments. By local standards, Tatep was a handsome male.

He was also a quadruped, and human chairs weren't the least bit of use to him. The stepstool let him lounge on its broad upper platform or sit upright on the step below that—in either case, it put a Rejoicer eye to eye with Marianne. This had been so successful an innovation in the embassy that they had hired a local artisan to make several for each office. Chornian's stepstools were a more elaborate affair, but Chornian himself had refused to make one to replace "the very first." A fine sense of tradition, these Rejoicers.

That was, of course, the best way to explain the Tchaikovsky. "Have you noticed, Tatep, that the further away from home you go, the more important it becomes to keep traditions?"

"Yes," he said. He drew a small piece of sweetwood from his pouch and seemed to consider it thoughtfully. "Ah! I hadn't thought how very strongly you must need tradition! You're very far from home indeed. Some thirty light years, is it not?" He bit into the wood, shaving a delicate curl from it with one corner of his razor sharp front tooth. The curl he swallowed, then he said, "Please, go on."

The control he had always fascinated Marianne—she would have preferred to watch him carve, but she spoke instead. "My family tradition is to celebrate a holiday called Christmas."

He swallowed another shaving and repeated, "Christmas."

"For some humans Christmas is a religious holiday. For my family, it was more of . . . a turning of the seasons. Now, Esperanza and I couldn't agree on a date—her homeworld's calendar runs differently than mine—but we both agreed on a need to celebrate Christmas once a year. So, since it's a solstice festival, I asked Muhammed what was the shortest day of the year on Rejoicing. He says that's Tamemb Nap Ohd."

Tatep bristled his ruff forward, confirming Muhammed's date.

"So I have decided to celebrate Christmas Eve on Tamemb Nap Ohd and to celebrate Christmas Day on Tememb Nap Chorr."

"Christmas is a revival, then? An awakening?"

"Yes, something like that. A renewal. A promise of spring to come."

"Yes, we have an Awakening on Tememb Nap Chorr as well."

Marianne nodded. "Many peoples do. Anyhow, I mentioned that I wanted to celebrate and a number of other people at the embassy decided it was a good idea. So, we're trying to put together something that resembles a Christmas celebration—mostly from local materials."

She gestured toward the player. "That piece of music is generally associated with Christmas. I've been playing it because it—gives me an anticipation of the Awakening to come."

Tatep was doing fine finishing work now, and Marianne had to stop to watch. The bit of sweetwood was turning into a pair of tommets—the Embassy staff had dubbed them "notrabbits" for their sexual proclivities—engaged in their mating dance. Tatep rattled his spines, amused, and passed the carving into her hands. He waited quietly while she turned it this way and that, admiring the exquisite workmanship.

"You don't get the joke," he said, at last.

"No, Tatep. I'm afraid I don't. Can you share it?"

"Look closely at their teeth."

Marianne did, and got the joke. The creatures were tommets, yes, but the teeth they had were not tommet teeth. They were the same sort of teeth that Tatep had used to carve them. Apparently, "fucking like tommets" was a Rejoicer joke.

"It's a gift for Hapet and Achinto. They had *six* children! We're all pleased and amazed for them."

Four to a brood was the usual, but birthings were few and far between. A couple that had more than two birthings in a lifetime was considered unusually lucky.

"Congratulate them for me, if you think it appropriate," Marianne said. "Would it be proper for the embassy to send a gift?"

"Proper and most welcome. Hapet and Achinto will need help feeding that many."

"Would you help me choose? Something to make children grow healthy and strong, and something as well to delight their senses."

"I'd be glad to. Shall we go to the market or the wood?"

"Let's go chop our own, Tatep. I've been sitting behind this desk too damn long. I could use the exercise."

As Marianne rose, Tatep put his finished carving into his pouch and climbed down. "You will share more about Christmas with me while we work? You can talk and chop at the same time."

Marianne grinned. "I'll do better than that. You can help me choose something that we can use for a Christmas tree, as well. If it's something that is also edible when it has seasoned for a few weeks' time, that would be all the more to the spirit of the festival."

The two of them took a leisurely stroll down the narrow cobbled streets. Marianne shared more of her Christmas customs with Tatep and found her anticipation growing apace as she did.

At Tatep's suggestion they paused at Killim the glassblower's, where Tatep helped Marianne describe and order a dozen ornamental balls for the tree. Unaccustomed to the idea of purely ornamental glass objects, Killim was fascinated. "She says," reported Tatep when Marianne missed a few crucial words of her reply, "she'll make a number of samples and you'll return on Debem Op Chorr to choose the most proper."

Marianne nodded. Before she could thank Killim, however, she heard the door behind her open, heard a muffled squeak of surprise, and turned. Halemtat had ordered yet another of his subjects clipped—Marianne saw that much before the local beat a hasty retreat from the door and vanished.

"Oh, god," she said aloud. "Another one." That, she admitted to herself for the first time, was why she was making such an effort to recognize the individual Rejoicers by facial shape alone. She'd seen no less than fifty clipped in the year she'd been on Rejoicing. There was no doubt in her mind that this was a new one—the blunted tips of its quills had been bright and crisp. "Who is it this time, Tatep?"

Tatep ducked his head in shame. "Chornian," he said.

For once, Marianne couldn't restrain herself. "Why?" she asked, and she heard the unprofessional belligerence in her own voice.

"For saying something I dare not repeat, not even in your language," Tatep said, "unless I wish to have *my* quills clipped."

Marianne took a deep breath. "I apologize for asking, Tatep. It was stupid of me." Best thing to do would be to get the hell out and let Chornian complete his errand without being shamed in front of the two of them. "Though," she said aloud, not caring if it was professional or not, "it's Halemtat who should be shamed, not Chornian."

Tatep's eyes widened, and Marianne knew she'd gone too far. She thanked the glassblower politely in Rejoicer and promised to return on Debem Op Chorr to examine the samples.

As they left Killim's, Marianne heard the scurry behind them— Chornian entering the shop as quickly and as unobtrusively as possible. She set her mouth—her silence raging—and followed Tatep without a backward glance.

At last they reached the communal wood. Trying for some semblance of normalcy, Marianne asked Tatep for the particulars of an unfamiliar tree.

"*Huep,*" he said. "Very good for carving, but not very good for eating." He paused a moment, thoughtfully. "I think I've put that wrong. The flavor is *very* good, but it's very low in food value. It grows prodigiously, though, so a lot of people eat too much of it when they shouldn't."

"Junk food," said Marianne, nodding. She explained the term to Tatep and he concurred. "Youngsters are particularly fond of it—but it wouldn't be a good gift for Hapet and Achinto."

"Then let's concentrate on good *healthy* food for Hapet and Achinto," said Marianne.

Deeper in the wood, they found a stand of the trees the embassy staff had dubbed gnomewood for its gnarly, stunted appearance. Tatep proclaimed this perfect, and Marianne set about to chop the proper branches. Gathering food was more a matter of pruning than chopping down, she'd learned, and she followed Tatep's careful instructions so she did not damage the tree's productive capabilities in the process.

"Now this one—just here," he said. "See, Marianne? Above the bole, for new growth will spring from the bole soon after your Awakening. If you damage the bole, however, there will be no new growth on this branch again."

Marianne chopped with care. The chopping took some of the edge off her anger. Then she inspected the gnomewood and found a second possibility. "Here," she said. "Would this be the proper place?"

"Yes," said Tatep, obviously pleased that she'd caught on so quickly. "That's right." He waited until she had lopped off the second branch and properly chosen a third and then he said, "Chornian said Halemtat had the twining tricks of a *talemtat*. One of his children liked the rhyme and repeated it."

"*Talemtat* is the vine that strangles the tree it climbs, am I right?" She kept her voice very low.

Instead of answering aloud, Tatep nodded.

"Did Halemtat—did Halemtat order the child clipped as well?"

Tatep's eyelids shaded his pupils darkly. "The entire family. He ordered the entire family clipped."

So that was why Chornian was running the errands. He *would* risk his own shame to protect his family from the awful embarrassment— for a Rejoicer—of appearing in public with their quills clipped.

She took out her anger on yet another branch of the gnomewood. When the branch fell—on her foot, as luck would have it—she sat down of a heap, thinking to examine the bruise, then looked Tatep straight in the eye. "How long? How long does it take for the quills to grow out again?" After much of a year, she hadn't yet seen evidence that an adult's quills regenerated at all. "They do regrow?"

"After several Awakenings," he said. "The regrowth can be quickened by eating *welspeth*, but . . ."

But *welspeth* was a hot-house plant in this country. Too expensive for somebody like Chornian.

"I see," she said. "Thank you, Tatep."

"Be careful where you repeat what I've told you. Best you not repeat it at all." He cocked his head at her and added, with a rattle of quills, "I'm not sure where Halemtat would clip a human, or even if you'd feel shamed by a clipping, but I wouldn't like to be responsible for finding out."

Marianne couldn't help but grin. She ran a hand through her pale white hair. "I've had my head shaved—that was long ago and far away—and it was intended to shame me."

"Intended to?"

"I painted my naked scalp bright red and went about my business as usual. I set something of a new fashion and, in the end, it was the shaver who was—quite properly—shamed."

Tatep's eyelids once again shaded his eyes. "I must think about that," he said, at last. "We have enough branches for a proper gift now, Marianne. Shall we consider the question of your Christmas tree?"

"Yes," she said. She rose to her feet and gathered up the branches. "And another thing as well. . . . I'll need some more wood for carving. I'd like to carve some gifts for my friends, as well. That's another tradition of Christmas."

"Carving gifts? Marianne, you make Christmas sound as if it were a Rejoicing holiday!"

Marianne laughed. "It is, Tatep. I'll gladly share my Christmas with you."

Clarence Doggett was Super Plenipotentiary Representing Terra to Rejoicing and today he was dressed to live up to his extravagant title in striped silver tights and a purple silk weskit. No less than four hoops of office jangled from his belt. Marianne had, since meeting him, conceived the theory that the more stylishly outré his dress the more likely he was to say yes to the request of a subordinate. Scratch that theory. . . .

Clarence Doggett straightened his weskit with a tug and said, "We have no reason to write a letter of protest about Emperor Halemtat's treatment of Chornian. He's deprived us of a valuable worker, true, but . . ."

"Whatever happened to human rights?"

"They're not human, Marianne. They're aliens."

At least he hadn't called them "Pincushions" as he usually did, Marianne thought. Clarence Doggett was the unfortunate result of what the media had dubbed "the Grand Opening." One day humans had been alone in the galaxy, and the next they'd found themselves only a tiny fraction of the intelligent species. Setting up five hundred embassies in the space of a few years had strained the diplomatic service to the bursting point. Rejoicing, considered a backwater world, got the scrapings from the bottom of the barrel. Marianne was trying very hard not to be one of those scrapings, despite the example set by Clarence. She clamped her jaw shut very hard.

Clarence brushed at his fashionably large mustache and added, "It's not as if they'll *really* die of shame, after all."

"Sir," Marianne began.

He raised his hands. "The subject is closed. How are the plans coming for the Christmas bash?"

"Fine, sir," she said without enthusiasm. "Killim—she's the local glassblower—would like to arrange a trade for some dyes, by the way. Not just for the Christmas tree ornaments, I gather, but for some project of her own. I'm sending letters with Nick Minski to a number of glassblowers back home to find out what sort of dye is wanted."

"Good work. Any trade item that helps tie the Rejoicers into the galactic economy is a find. You're to be commended."

Marianne wasn't feeling very commended, but she said, "Thank you, sir."

"And keep up the good work—this Christmas idea of yours is turning out to be a big morale booster."

That was the dismissal. Marianne excused herself and, feet dragging, she headed back to her office. " 'They're not human,' " she muttered to herself. " 'They're aliens. It's not as if they'll *really* die of shame. . . .' " She slammed her door closed behind her and snarled aloud, "But Chornian can't keep up work and the kids can't play with their friends and his mate Chaylam can't go to the market. What if they starve?"

"They won't starve," said a firm voice.

Marianne jumped.

"It's just me," said Nick Minski. "I'm early." He leaned back in the chair and put his long legs up on her desk. "I've been watching how the neighbors behave. Friends—your friend Tatep included—take their leftovers to Chornian's family. They won't starve. At least, Chornian's family won't. I'm not sure what would happen to someone who is generally unpopular."

Nick was head of the ethnology team studying the Rejoicers. At least he had genuine observations to base his decisions on.

He tipped the chair to a precarious angle. "I can't begin to guess whether or not helping Chornian will land Tatep in the same hot water, so I can't reassure you there. I take it from your muttering that Clarence won't make a formal protest."

Marianne nodded.

He straightened the chair with a bang that made Marianne start. "Shit," he said. "Doggett's such a pissant."

Marianne grinned ruefully. "God, I'm going to miss you, Nick. Diplomats aren't permitted to speak in such matter-of-fact terms."

"I'll be back in a year. I'll bring you fireworks for your next Christmas." He grinned.

"We've been through that, Nick. Fireworks may be part of your family's Christmas tradition, but they're not part of mine. All that banging and flashing of light just wouldn't *feel* right to me, not on Christmas."

"Meanwhile," he went on, undeterred, "you think about my offer. You've learned more about Tatep and his people than half the folks on my staff; academic credentials or no, I can swing putting you on the ethnology team. We're short-handed as it is. I'd rather have skipped the rotation home this year, but . . . ."

"You can't get everything you want, either."

He laughed. "I think they're afraid we'll all go native if we don't go home one year in five." He preened and grinned suddenly. "How d'you think I'd look in quills?"

"Sharp," she said and drew a second burst of laughter from him.

There was a knock at the door. Marianne stretched out a toe and tapped the latch. Tatep stood on the threshold, his quills still bristling from the cold. "Hi, Tatep—you're just in time. Come share."

His laughter subsiding to a chuckle, Nick took his feet from the desk and greeted Tatep in high-formal Rejoicer. Tatep returned the favor, then added by way of explanation, "Marianne is sharing her Christmas with me."

Nick cocked his head at Marianne. "But it's not for some time yet. . . ."

"I know," said Marianne. She went to her desk and pulled out a wrapped package. "Tatep, Nick is my very good friend. Ordinarily, we exchange gifts on Christmas Day, but since Nick won't be here for Christmas, I'm going to give him his present now."

She held out the package. "Merry Christmas, Nick. A little too early, but—"

"You've hidden the gift in paper," said Tatep. "Is that also traditional?"

"Traditional but not necessary. Some of the pleasure is the surprise involved," Nick told the Rejoicer. With a sidelong glance and a smile at Marianne, he held the package to his ear and shook it. "And some of the pleasure is in trying to guess what's in the package." He shook it and listened again. "Nope, I haven't the faintest idea."

He laid the package in his lap.

Tatep flicked his tail in surprise. "Why don't you open it?"

"In my family, it's traditional to wait until Christmas Day to open your presents, even if they're wrapped and sitting under the Christmas tree in plain sight for three weeks or more."

Tatep clambered onto the stool to give him a stare of open astonishment from a more effective angle.

"Oh, no!" said Marianne. "Do you really mean it, Nick? You're *not* going to open it until Christmas Day?"

Nick laughed again. "I'm teasing." To Tatep, he said, "It's traditional in my family to wait—but it's also traditional to find some rationalization to open a gift the minute you lay hands on it. Marianne wants to see my expression; I think that takes precedence in this case."

His long fingers found a cranny in the paper wrapping and began to worry it ever so slightly. "Besides, our respective homeworlds can't agree on a date for Christmas. . . . On some world *today* must be Christmas, right?"

"Good rationalizing," said Marianne, with a sigh and a smile of relief. "Right!"

"Right," said Tatep, catching on. He leaned precariously from his perch to watch as Nick ripped open the wrapping paper.

"Tchaikovsky made me think of it," Marianne said. "Although, to be honest, Tchaikovsky's nutcracker wasn't particularly traditional. This one *is:* take a close look."

He did. He held up the brightly painted figure, took in its green weskit, its striped silver tights, its flamboyant mustache. Four metal loops jangled at its carved belt and Nick laughed aloud.

With a barely suppressed smile, Marianne handed him a "walnut" of the local variety.

Nick stopped laughing long enough to say, "You mean, this is a genuine, honest-to-god, *working* nutcracker?"

"Well, of course it is! My family's been making them for years." She made a motion with her hands to demonstrate. "Go ahead—crack that nut!"

Nick put the nut between the cracker's prominent jaws and, after a moment's hesitation, closed his eyes and went ahead. The nut gave with an audible and very satisfying craaack! and Nick began to laugh all over again.

"Share the joke," said Tatep.

"Gladly," said Marianne. "The Christmas nutcracker, of which that is a prime example, is traditionally carved to resemble an authority figure—particularly one nobody much likes. It's a way of getting back at the fraudulent, the pompous. Through the years they've poked fun at everybody from princes to policemen to"—Marianne waved a gracious hand at her own carved figure—"well, surely you recognize *him.*"

"Oh, my," said Tatep, his eyes widening. "Clarence Doggett, is it not?" When Marianne nodded, Tatep said, "Are you about to get your head shaved again?"

Marianne laughed enormously. "If I do, Tatep, this time I'll paint my scalp red and green—traditional Christmas colors—and hang one of Killim's glass ornaments from my ear. Not likely, though," she added, to be fair. "Clarence doesn't go in for head shaving." To Nick, who had clearly taken in Tatep's "again," she said, "I'll tell you about it sometime."

Nick nodded and stuck another nut between Clarence's jaws. This time he watched as the nut gave way with a explosive bang. Still laughing, he handed the nutmeat to Tatep, who ate it and rattled his quills in laughter of his own. Marianne was doubly glad she'd invited Tatep to share the occasion—now she knew exactly what to make *him* for Christmas.

Christmas Eve found Marianne at a loss—something was missing from her holiday and she hadn't been able to put her finger on precisely what that something was.

It wasn't the color of the tree Tatep had helped her choose. The tree was the perfect Christmas tree shape, and if its foliage was a red so deep it approached black, that didn't matter a bit. "Next year we'll have Killim make some green ornaments," Marianne said to Tatep, "for the proper contrast."

Tinsel—silver thread she'd bought from one of the Rejoicer weavers and cut to length—flew in all directions. All seven of the kids who'd come to Rejoicing with their ethnologist parents were showing the Rejoicers the "proper" way to hang tinsel, which meant more tinsel was making it onto the kids and the Rejoicers than onto the tree.

Just as well. She'd have to clean the tinsel off the tree before she passed it on to Hapet and Achinto—well-seasoned and just the thing for growing children.

Nick would really have enjoyed seeing this, Marianne thought. Esperanza was filming the whole party, but that just wasn't the same as being here.

Killim brought the glass ornaments herself. She'd made more than the commissioned dozen. The dozen glass balls she gave to Marianne. Each was a swirl of colors, each unique. Everyone ooohed and aaahed—but the best was yet to come. From her sidepack, Killim produced a second container. "Presents," she said. "A present for your Awakening Tree."

Inside the box was a menagerie of tiny, bright glass animals: notrabbits, fingerfish, wispwings. . . . Each one had a loop of glass at the top to allow them to be hung from the tree. Scarcely trusting herself with such delicate objects of art, Marianne passed them on to George to string and hang.

Later, she took Killim aside and, with Tatep's help, thanked her profusely for the gifts. "Though I'm not sure she should have. Tell her

I'll be glad to pay for them, Tatep. If she'd had them in her shop, I'd have snapped them up on the spot. I didn't know how badly our Christmas needed them until I saw her unwrap them."

Tatep spoke for a long time to Killim, who rattled all the while. Finally, Tatep rattled too. "Marianne, three humans have commissioned Killim to make animals for them to send home." Killim said something Marianne didn't catch. "Three humans in the last five minutes. She says, Think of this set as a—as an advertisement."

"No, you may not pay me for them," Killim said, still rattling. "I have gained something to trade for my dyes."

"She says," Tatep began.

"It's okay, Tatep. That I understood."

Marianne hung the wooden ornaments she'd carved and painted in bright colors, then she unsnagged a handful of tinsel from Tatep's ruff, divided it in half, and they both flung it onto the tree. Tatep's handful just barely missed Matsimoto, who was hanging strings of beads he'd bought in the bazaar, but Marianne's got Juliet, who was hanging chains of paper cranes it must have taken her the better part of the month to fold. Juliet laughed and pulled the tinsel from her hair to drape it—length by length and *neatly*—over the deep red branches.

Then Kelleb brought out the star. Made of silver wire delicately filigreed, it shone just the way a Christmas tree star should. He hoisted Juliet to his shoulders and she affixed it to the top of the tree and the entire company burst into cheers and applause.

Marianne sighed and wondered why that made her feel so down. "If Nick had been here," Tatep observed, "I believe he could have reached the top without an assistant."

"I think you're right," said Marianne. "I wish he *were* here. He'd enjoy this." Just for a moment, Marianne let herself realize that what was missing from this Christmas was Nick Minski.

"Next year," said Tatep.

"Next year," said Marianne. The prospect brightened her.

The tree glittered with its finery. For a moment they all stood back and admired it—then there was a scurry and a flurry as folks went to various bags and hiding places and brought out the brightly wrapped presents. Marianne excused herself from Tatep and Killim and brought out hers to heap at the bottom of the tree with the rest.

Again there was a moment's pause of appreciation. Then Clarence Doggett—of all people—raised his glass and said, "A toast! A Christmas toast! Here's to Marianne, for bringing Christmas thirty light years from old Earth!"

Marianne blushed as they raised their glasses to her. When they'd finished, she raised hers and found the right traditional response: "A Merry Christmas—and God bless us, every one!"

"Okay, Marianne. It's your call," said Esperanza. "Do we open the presents now or"—her voice turned to a mock whine—"do we *hafta* wait till tomorrow?"

Marianne glanced at Tatep. "What day is it now?" she asked. She knew enough about local time reckoning to know what answer he'd give.

"Why, today is Tememb Nap Chorr."

She grinned at the faces around her. "By Rejoicer reckoning, the day changes when the sun sets—it's been Christmas Day for an hour at least now. But stand back and let the kids find their presents first."

There was a great clamor and rustle of wrapping paper and whoops of delight as the kids dived into the pile of presents.

As Marianne watched with rising joy, Tatep touched her arm. "More guests," he said, and Marianne turned.

It was Chornian, his mate Chaylam, and their four children. Marianne's jaw dropped at the sight of them. She had invited the six with no hope of a response and here they were. "And all dressed up for Christmas!" she said aloud, though she knew Christmas was *not* the occasion. "You're as glittery as the Christmas tree itself," she told Chornian, her eyes gleaming with the reflection of it.

Ruff and tail, each and every one of Chornian's short-clipped quills was tipped by a brilliant red bead. "Glass?" she asked.

"Yes," said Chornian. "Killim made them for us."

"You look magnificent! Oh—how wonderful!" Chaylam's clipped quills had been dipped in gold; when she shifted shyly, her ruff and tail rippled with light. "You sparkle like sun on the water," Marianne told her. The children's ruffs and tails had been tipped in gold and candy pink and vivid yellow and—the last but certainly not the least—in beads every color of the rainbow.

"A kid after my own heart," said Marianne. "I think that would have been my choice too." She gave a closer look. "No two alike, am I right? Come—join the party. I was afraid I'd have to drop your presents by your house tomorrow. Now I get to watch you open them, to see if I chose correctly."

She escorted the four children to the tree and, thanking her lucky stars she'd had Tatep write their names on their packages, she left them to hunt for their presents. Those for their parents she brought back with her.

"It was difficult," Chornian said to Marianne. "It was difficult to walk through the streets with pride but—we did. And the children walked the proudest. They give us courage."

Chaylam said, "If only on their behalf."

"Yes," agreed Chornian. "Tomorrow I shall walk in the sunlight. I shall go to the bazaar. My clipped quills will glitter, and *I* will not be ashamed that I have spoken the truth about Halemtat."

That was all the Christmas gift Marianne needed, she thought to herself, and handed the wrapped package to Chornian. Tatep gave him a running commentary on the habits and rituals of the human Awakening as he opened the package. Chornian's eyes shaded and Tatep's running commentary ceased abruptly as they peered together into the box.

"Did I get it right?" said Marianne, suddenly afraid she'd committed some awful faux pas. She'd scoured the bazaar for *welspeth* shoots and, finding none, she'd pulled enough strings with the ethnology team to get some imported.

Tatep was the one who spoke. "You got it right," he said. "Chornian thanks you." Chornian spoke rapid-fire Rejoicer for a long time; Marianne couldn't follow the half of it. When he'd finished, Tatep said simply, "He regrets that he has no present to give you."

"It's not necessary. Seeing those kids all in spangles brightened up the party—that's present enough for me!"

"Nevertheless," said Tatep, speaking slowly so she wouldn't miss a word. "Chornian and I make you this present."

Marianne knew the present Tatep drew from his pouch was from Tatep alone, but she was happy enough to play along with the fiction if it made him happy. She hadn't expected a present from Tatep and she could scarcely wait to see what it was he felt appropriate to the occasion.

Still, she gave it the proper treatment—shaking it, very gently, beside her ear. If there was anything to hear, it was drowned out by the robust singing of carols from the other side of the room. "I can't begin to guess, Tatep," she told him happily.

"Then open it."

She did. Inside the paper, she found a carving, the rich wine-red of burgundy-wood, bitter to the taste and therefore rarely carved but treasured because none of the kids would gnaw on it as they tested their teeth. The style of carving was so utterly Rejoicer that it took her a long moment to recognize the subject, but once she did, she knew she'd treasure the gift for a lifetime.

It was unmistakeably Nick—but Nick as seen from Tatep's point of view, hence the unfamiliar perspective. It was Looking Up At Nick.

"Oh, Tatep!" And then she remembered just in time and added, "Oh, Chornian! Thank you both so very much. I can't *wait* to show it to Nick when he gets back. Whatever made you think of doing Nick?"

Tatep said, "He's your best *human* friend. I know you miss him. You have no pictures; I thought you would feel better with a likeness."

She hugged the sculpture to her. "Oh, I do. Thank you, both of you." Then she motioned, eyes shining. "Wait. Wait right here, Tatep. Don't go away."

She darted to the tree and, pushing aside wads of rustling paper, she found the gift she'd made for Tatep. Back she darted to where the Rejoicers were waiting.

"I waited," Tatep said solemnly.

She handed him the package. "I hope this is worth the wait."

Tatep shook the package. "I can't begin to guess," he said.

"Then open it. *I* can't stand the wait!"

He ripped away the paper as flamboyantly as Nick had—to expose the brightly colored nutcracker and a woven bag of nuts.

Marianne held her breath. The problem had been, of course, to adapt the nutcracker to a recognizable Rejoicer version. She'd made the Emperor Halemtat sit back on his haunches, which meant far less adaptation of the cracking mechanism. Overly plump, she'd made him, and spiky. In his right hand, he carried an oversized pair of scissors—of the sort his underlings used for clipping quills. In his left, he carried a sprig of *talemtat*, that unfortunate rhyme for his name.

Chornian's eyes widened. Again, he rattled off a spate of Rejoicer too fast for Marianne to follow . . . except that Chornian seemed anxious.

Only then did Marianne realize what she'd done. "Oh, my God, Tatep! He wouldn't clip your quills for *having* that, would he?"

Tatep's quills rattled and rattled. He put one of the nuts between Halemtat's jaws and cracked with a vengeance. The nutmeat he offered to Marianne, his quills still rattling. "If he does, Marianne, you'll come to Killim's to help me chose a good color for *my* glass beading!"

He cracked another nut and handed the meat to Chornian. The next thing Marianne knew, the two of them were rattling at each other—Chornian's glass beads adding a splendid tinkling to the merriment.

Much relieved, Marianne laughed with them. A few minutes later, Esperanza dashed out to buy more nuts—so Chornian's children could each take a turn at the cracking.

Marianne looked down at the image of Nick cradled in her arm. "I'm sorry you missed this," she told it, "but I promise I'll write everything down for you before I go to bed tonight. I'll try to remember every last bit of it for you."

"Dear Nick," Marianne wrote in another letter some months later. "You're not going to approve of this. I find I haven't been ethnologically correct—much less diplomatic. I'd only meant to share my

Christmas with Tatep and Chornian and, for that matter, whoever wanted to join in the festivities. To hear Clarence tell it, I've sent Rejoicing to hell in a handbasket.

"You see, it does Halemtat no good to clip quills these days. There are some seventy-five Rejoicers walking around town clipped and beaded—as gaudy and as shameless as you please. I even saw one newly male (teenager) with beads on the ends of his unclipped spines!

"Killim says thanks for the dyes, by the way. They're just what she had in mind. She's so busy, she's taken on two apprentices to help her. She makes 'Christmas ornaments' and half the art galleries in the known universe are after her for more and more. The apprentices make glass beads. One of them—one of Chornian's kids, by the way—hit upon the bright idea of making simple sets of beads that can be stuck on the ends of quills cold. Saves time and trouble over the hot glass method.

"What's more—

"Well, yesterday I stopped by to say 'hi' to Killim, when who should turn up but Koppen—you remember him? He's one of Halemtat's advisors? You'll never guess what he wanted: a set of quill tipping beads.

"No, he hadn't had his quills clipped. Nor was he buying them for a friend. He was planning, he told Killim, to tell Halemtat a thing or two—I missed the details because he went too fast—and he expected he'd be clipped for it, so he was planning ahead. Very expensive *blue* beads for him, if you please, Killim!

"I find myself unprofessionally pleased. There's a thing or two Halemtat *ought* to be told. . . .

"Meanwhile, Chornian has gone into the business of making nutcrackers. —All right, so sue me, I showed him how to make the actual cracker work. It was that or risk his taking Tatep's present apart to find out for himself.

"I'm sending holos—including a holo of the one I made—because you've got to see the transformation Chornian's worked on mine. The difference between a human-carved nutcracker and a Rejoicer-carved nutcracker is as unmistakable as the difference between Looking Up At Nick and . . . well, *looking up at Nick*.

"I still miss you, even if you do think fireworks are appropriate at Christmas.

"See you soon—if Clarence doesn't boil me in my own pudding and bury me with a stake of holly through my heart."

Marianne sat with her light pen poised over the screen for a long moment, then she added, "Love, Marianne," and saved it to the next outgoing Dirt-bound mail.

Rejoicing
Midsummer's Eve
(Rejoicer reckoning)

Dear Nick—

This time it's not my fault. This time it's Esperanza's doing. Esperanza decided, for *her* contribution to our round of holidays, to celebrate Martin Luther King Day. (All right—if I'd known about Martin Luther King I'd probably have suggested a celebration myself—but I didn't. Look him up; you'll like him.) And she invited a handful of the Rejoicers to attend as well.

Now, the final part of the celebration is that each person in turn "has a dream." This is not like wishes, Nick. This is more on the order of setting yourself a goal, even one that looks to all intents and purposes to be unattainable, but one you will strive to attain. Even Clarence got so into the occasion that he had a dream that he would stop thinking of the Rejoicers as "Pincushions" so he could start thinking of them as Rejoicers. Esperanza said later Clarence didn't quite get the point but for him she supposed that was a step in the right direction.

Well, after that, Tatep asked Esperanza, in his very polite fashion, if it would be proper for him to have a dream as well. There was some consultation over the proper phrasing—Esperanza says her report will tell you all about that—and then Tatep rose and said, "I have a dream . . . I have a dream that someday no one will get his quills clipped for speaking the truth."

(You'll see it on the tape. Everybody agreed that this was a good dream, indeed.)

After which, Esperanza had her dream "for human rights for all."

Following which, of course, we all took turns trying to explain the concept of "human rights" to a half-dozen Rejoicers. Esperanza ended up translating five different constitutions for them—*and* an entire book of speeches by Martin Luther King.

Oh, god. I just realized . . . maybe it *is* my fault. I'd forgotten till just now. Oh. You judge, Nick.

About a week later Tatep and I were out gathering wood for some carving he plans to do—for Christmas, he says, but he wanted to get a good start on it—and he stopped gnawing long enough to ask me, "Marianne, what's 'human'?"

"How do you mean?"

"I think when Clarence says 'human,' he means something different than you do."

"That's entirely possible. Humans use words pretty loosely at the best of times—there, I just did it myself."

"What do you mean when you say 'human'?"

"Sometimes I mean the species *homo sapiens*. When I say, Humans use words pretty loosely, I do. Rejoicers seem to be more particular about their speech, as a general rule."

"And when you say 'human rights,' what do you mean?"

"When I say 'human rights,' I mean *Homo sapiens* and *Rejoicing sapiens*. I mean any *sapiens*, in that context. I wouldn't guarantee that Clarence uses the word the same way in the same context."

"You think I'm human?"

"I *know* you're human. We're friends, aren't we? I couldn't be friends with—oh, a notrabbit—now, could I?"

He made that wonderful rattly sound he does when he's amused. "No, I can't imagine it. Then, if I'm human, I ought to have human rights."

"Yes," I said, "You bloody well ought to."

Maybe it is all my fault. Esperanza will tell you the rest—she's had Rejoicers all over her house for the past two weeks—they're watching every scrap of film she's got on Martin Luther King.

I don't know how this will all end up, but I wish to hell you were here to watch.

Love, Marianne

Marianne watched the Rejoicer child crack nuts with his Halemtat cracker and a cold, cold shiver went up her spine. That was the eleventh she'd seen this week. Chornian wasn't the only one making them, apparently; somebody else had gone into the nutcracker business as well. This was, however, the first time she'd seen a child cracking nuts with Halemtat's jaw.

"Hello," she said, stooping to meet the child's eyes. "What a pretty toy! Will you show me how it works?"

Rattling all the while, the child showed her, step by step. Then he (or she—it wasn't polite to ask before puberty) said, "Isn't it funny? It makes Mama laugh and laugh and laugh."

"And what's your mama's name?"

"Pilli," said the child. Then it added, "With the green and white beads on her quills."

Pilli—who'd been clipped for saying that Halemtat had been overcutting the imperial reserve so badly that the trees would never grow back properly.

And then she realized that, less than a year ago, no child would have admitted that its mama had been clipped. The very thought of it would have shamed both mother *and* child.

Come to think of it . . . she glanced around the bazaar and saw no less than four clipped Rejoicers shopping for dinner. Two of them she recognized as Chornian and one of his children, the other two were new to her. She tried to identify them by their snouts and failed utterly—she'd have to ask Chornian. She also noted, with utterly unprofessional satisfaction, that she *could* ask Chornian such a thing now. That too would have been unthinkable and shaming less than a year ago.

Less than a year ago. She was thinking in Dirt terms because of Nick. There wasn't any point dropping him a line; mail would cross in deep space at this late a date. He'd be here just in time for "Christmas." She wished like hell he was already here. He'd know what to make of all this, she was certain.

As Marianne thanked the child and got to her feet, three Rejoicers—all with the painted ruff of quills at their necks that identified them as Halemtat's guards—came waddling officiously up. "Here's one," said the largest. "Yes," said another. "Caught in the very act."

The largest squatted back on his haunches and said, "You will come with us, child. Halemtat decrees it."

Horror shot through Marianne's body.

The child cracked one last nut, rattled happily, and said, "I get my quills clipped?"

"Yes," said the largest Rejoicer. "You will have your quills clipped." Roughly, he separated child from nutcracker and began to tow the child away, each of them in that odd three-legged gait necessitated by the grip.

All Marianne could think to do was call after the child, "I'll tell Pilli what happened and where to find you!"

The child glanced over its shoulder, rattled again, and said, "Ask her could I have silver beads like Hortap!"

Marianne picked up the discarded nutcracker—lest some other child find it and meet the same fate—and ran full speed for Pilli's house.

At the corner, two children looked up from their own play and galloped along beside her until she skidded to a halt by Pilli's bakery. They followed her in, rattling happily to themselves over the race they'd run. Marianne's first thought was to shoo them off before she told Pilli what had happened, but Pilli greeted the two as if they were her own, and Marianne found herself blurting out the news.

Pilli gave a slow inclination of the head. "Yes," she said, pronouncing the words carefully so Marianne wouldn't miss them, "I expected that. Had it not been the nutcracker, it would have been words." She rattled. "That child is the most outspoken of my brood."

"But—" Marianne wanted to say, Aren't you afraid? but the question never surfaced.

Pilli gave a few coins to the other children and said, "Run to Killim's, my dears, and ask her to make a set of silver beads, if she doesn't already have one on hand. Then run tell your father what has happened."

The children were off in the scurry of excitement.

Pilli drew down the awning in front of her shop, then paused. "I think you are afraid for my child."

"Yes," said Marianne. Lying had never been her strong suit; maybe Nick was right—maybe diplomacy wasn't her field.

"You are kind," said Pilli. "But don't be afraid. Even Halemtat wouldn't dare to order a child *hashay*."

"I don't understand the term."

"*Hashay?*" Pilli flipped her tail around in front of her and held out a single quill. "Chippet will be clipped here," she said, drawing a finger across the quill about half-way up its length. "*Hashay* is to clip here." The finger slid inward, to a spot about a quarter of an inch from her skin. "Don't worry, Marianne. Even Halemtat wouldn't dare to *hashay* a child."

I'm supposed to be reassured, thought Marianne. "Good," she said aloud, "I'm relieved to hear that." In truth, she hadn't the slightest idea what Pilli was talking about—and she was considerably less than reassured by the ominous implications of the distinction. She'd never come across the term in any of the ethnologists' reports.

She was still holding the Halemtat nutcracker in her hands. Now she considered it carefully. Only in its broadest outlines did it resemble the one she'd made for Tatep. This nutcracker was purely Rejoicer in style and—she almost dropped it at the sudden realization—peculiarly *Tatep's* style of carving. Tatep was making them too?

If *she* could recognize Tatep's distinctive style, surely Halemtat could—what then?

Carefully, she tucked the nutcracker under the awning—let Pilli decide what to do with the object; Marianne couldn't make the decision for her—and set off at a quick pace for Tatep's house.

On the way, she passed yet another child with a Halemtat nutcracker. She paused, found the child's father and passed the news to him that Halemtat's guards were clipping Pilli's child for the "offense." The father thanked her for the information and, with much politeness, took the nutcracker from the child.

This one, Marianne saw, was *not* carved in Tatep's style or in Chornian's. This one was the work of an unfamiliar set of teeth.

Having shooed his child indoors, the Rejoicer squatted back on his haunches. In plain view of the street, he took up the bowl of nuts his child had left uncracked and began to crack them, one by one, with such deliberation that Marianne's jaw dropped.

She'd never seen an insolent Rejoicer but she would have bet money she was seeing one now. He even managed to make the crack of each nut resound like a gunshot. With the sound still ringing in her ears, Marianne quickened her steps toward Tatep's.

She found him at home, carving yet another nutcracker. He swallowed, then held out the nutcracker to her and said, "What do you think, Marianne? Do you approve of my portrayal?"

This one wasn't Halemtat, but his—for want of a better word—grand vizier, Corten. The grand vizier always looked to her as if he smirked. She knew the expression was due to a slightly malformed tooth but, to a human eye, the result was a smirk. Tatep's portrayal had the same smirk, only more so. Marianne couldn't help it . . . she giggled.

"Aha!" said Tatep, rattling up a rainstorm's worth of sound. "For once, you've shared the joke without the need of explanation!" He gave a long grave look at the nutcracker. "The grand vizier has earned his keep this once!"

Marianne laughed, and Tatep rattled. This time the sound of the quills sobered Marianne. "I think your work will get you clipped, Tatep," she said, and she told him about Pilli's child.

He made no response. Instead, he dropped to his feet and went to the chest in the corner, where he kept any number of carvings and other precious objects. From the chest, he drew out a box. Three-legged, he walked back to her. "Shake this! I'll bet you can guess what's inside."

Curious, she shook the box: it rattled. "A set of beads," she said.

"You see? I'm prepared. They rattle like a laugh, don't they?—a laugh at Halemtat. I asked Killim to make the beads red because that was the color you painted your scalp when you were clipped."

"I'm honored. . . ."

"But?"

"But I'm afraid for you. For *all* of you."

"Pilli's child wasn't afraid."

"No. No, Pilli's child wasn't afraid. Pilli said even Halemtat wouldn't dare *hashay* a child." Marianne took a deep breath and said, "But you're not a child." And I don't know what *hashaying* does to a Rejoicer, she wanted to add.

"I've swallowed a talpseed," Tatep said, as if that said it all.

"I don't understand."

"Ah! I'll share, then. A talpseed can't grow unless it has been through the"—he patted himself—"stomach? digestive system? of a Rejoicer. Sometimes they don't grow even then. To swallow a talpseed means to take a step toward the growth of something important. I swallowed a talpseed called 'human rights.' "

There was nothing Marianne could say to that but: "I understand."

Slowly, thoughtfully, Marianne made her way back to the embassy. Yes, she understood Tatep—hadn't she been screaming at Clarence for just the same reason? But she was terrified for Tatep—for them all.

Without consciously meaning to, she bypassed the embassy for the little clutch of domes that housed the ethnologists. Esperanza—it was Esperanza she had to see.

She was in luck. Esperanza was at home writing up one of her reports. She looked up and said, "Oh, good. It's time for a break!"

"Not a break, I'm afraid. A question that, I think, is right up your alley. Do you know much about the physiology of the Rejoicers?"

"I'm the expert," Esperanza said, leaning back in her chair. "As far as there is one in the group."

"What happens if you cut a Rejoicer's spine"—she held up her fingers—"*this* close to the skin?"

"Like a cat's claw, sort of. If you cut the tip, nothing happens. If you cut too far down, you hit the blood supply—and maybe the nerve. The quill would bleed most certainly. Might never grow back properly. And it'd hurt like hell, I'm sure—like gouging the base of your thumbnail."

She sat forward suddenly. "Marianne, you're shaking. What is it?"

Marianne took a deep breath but couldn't stop shaking. "What would happen if somebody did that to all of Ta"—she found she couldn't get the name out—"all of a Rejoicer's quills?"

"He'd bleed to death, Marianne." Esperanza took her hand and gave it a firm squeeze. "Now, I'm going to get you a good stiff drink and you are going to tell me all about it."

Fighting nausea, Marianne nodded. "Yes," she said with enormous effort. "Yes."

"Who the *hell* told the Pincushions about 'human rights'?" Clarence roared. Furious, he glowered down at Marianne and waited for her response.

Esperanza drew herself up to her full height and stepped between the two of them. "Martin Luther King told the *Rejoicers* about human rights. You were there when he did it. Though you seem to have forgotten *your* dream, obviously the Rejoicers haven't forgotten theirs."

"There's a goddamned revolution going on out there!" Clarence waved a hand vaguely in the direction of the center of town.

"That is certainly what it looks like," Juliet said mildly. "So why are we here instead of out there observing?"

"You're here because I'm responsible for your safety."

"Bull," said Matsimoto. "Halemtat isn't interested in clipping *us*."

"Besides," said Esperanza. "The supply ship will be landing in about five minutes. Somebody's got to go pick up the supplies—and Nick. Otherwise, he's going to step right into the thick of it. The last mail went out two months ago. Nick's had no warning that the situation has"—she frowned slightly, then brightened as she found the proper phrase—"changed *radically*."

Clarence glared again at Marianne. "As a member of the embassy staff, you are assigned the job. You will pick up the supplies and Nick."

Marianne, who'd been about to volunteer to do just that, suppressed the urge to say, "Thank you!" and said instead, "Yes, sir."

Once out of Clarence's sight, Marianne let herself breathe a sigh of relief. The supply transport was built like a tank. While Marianne wasn't any more afraid of Halemtat's wrath than the ethnologists, she was well aware that innocent *Dirt* bystanders might easily find themselves stuck—all too literally—in a mob of Rejoicers. When the Rejoicers fought, as she understood it, they used teeth and quills. She had no desire to get too close to a lashing tail-full. An unclipped quill was needle-sharp.

Belatedly, she caught the significance of the clipping Halemtat had instituted as punishment. Slapping a snout with a tail full of glass beads was not nearly as effective as slapping a snout with a morning-star made of spines.

She radioed the supply ship to tell them they'd all have to wait for transport before they came out. Captain's gonna love that, I'm sure, she thought, until she got a response from Captain Tertain. By reputation he'd never set foot on a world other than Dirt and certainly didn't intend to do so now. So she simply told Nick to stay put until she came for him.

Nick's cheery voice over the radio said only, "It's going to be a very special Christmas this year."

"Nick," she said, "You don't know the half of it."

She took a slight detour along the way, passing the narrow street that led to Tatep's house. She didn't dare to stop, but she could see from the awning that he wasn't home. In fact, nobody seemed to be home . . . even the bazaar was deserted.

The supply truck rolled on, and Marianne took a second slight detour. What Esperanza had dubbed "the Grande Allez" led directly to Halemtat's imperial residence. The courtyard was filled with Rejoicers. Well-spaced Rejoicers, she saw, for they were—each and every one—bristled to their fullest extent. She wished she dared go for a closer look, but Clarence would be livid if she took much more time than normal reaching the supply ship. And he'd be checking—she knew his habits well enough to know that.

She floored the accelerator and made her way to the improvised landing field in record time. Nick waved to her from the port and stepped out. Just like Nick, she thought. She'd told him to wait in the ship until she arrived; he'd obeyed to the letter. It was all she could do to keep from hugging him as she hit the ground beside him. With a grateful sigh of relief, she said, "We've got to move fast on the transfer, Nick. I'll fill you in as we load."

By the time the two of them had transferred all the supplies from the ship, she'd done just that.

He climbed into the seat beside her, gave her a long thoughtful look, and said, "So Clarence has restricted all of the *other* ethnologists to the embassy grounds, has he?" He shook his head in mock sadness and clicked his tongue. "I see I haven't trained my team in the proper response to embassy edicts." He grinned at Marianne. "So the embassy advises that I stay off the streets, does it?"

"Yes," said Marianne. She hated being the one to tell him but he'd asked her. "The Super Plenipotentiary Etc. has issued a full and formal Advisory to all non-governmental personnel. . . ."

"Okay," said Nick. "You've done your job: I've been Advised. Now I want to go have a look at this revolution-in-progress." He folded his arms across his chest and waited.

He was right. All Clarence could do was issue an Advisory; he had no power whatsoever to keep the ethnologists off the streets. And Marianne wanted to see the revolution as badly as Nick did.

"All right," she said. "I *am* responsible for your safety, though, so best we go in the transport. I don't want you stuck." She set the supply-transport into motion and headed back toward the Grande Allez.

Nick pressed his nose to the window and watched the streets as they went. He was humming cheerfully under his breath.

"Uh, Nick—if Clarence calls us . . ."

"We'll worry about that when it happens," he said.

Worry is right, thought Marianne, but she smiled. He'd been humming Christmas carols, like some excited child. Inappropriate as all hell, but she liked him all the more for it.

She pulled the supply-transport to a stop at the entrance to the palace courtyard and turned to ask Nick if he had a good enough view. He was already out the door and making his way carefully into the crowd of Rejoicers. "Hey!" she shouted—and she hit the ground running to catch up with him. "Nick!"

He paused long enough for her to catch his arm, then said, "I need to see this, Marianne. It's my *job*."

"It's *my* job to see you don't get hurt—"

He smiled. "Then you lead. I want to be over there where I can see and hear everything Halemtat and his advisors are up to."

Marianne harbored a brief fantasy about dragging him bodily back to the safety of the supply-transport, but he was twice her weight and, from his expression, not about to cooperate. Best she lead, then. Her only consolation was that, when Clarence tried to radio them, there'd be nobody to pick up and receive his orders.

"Hey, Marianne!" said Chornian from the crowd. "Over here! Good view from here!"

And safer too. Grateful for the invitation, Marianne gingerly headed in that direction. Several quilled Rejoicers eased aside to let the two of them safely through. Better to be surrounded by beaded Rejoicers.

"Welcome back, Nick," said Chornian. He and Chaylam stepped apart to create a space of safety for the two humans. "You're just in time."

"So I see. What's going on?"

"Halemtat just had Pilli's Chippet clipped for playing with a Halemtat cracker. Halemtat doesn't *like* the Halemtat crackers."

Beside him, a fully quilled Rejoicer said, "Halemtat doesn't like much of anything. I think a proper prince ought to rattle his spines once or twice a year at least."

Marianne frowned up at Nick, who grinned and said, "Roughly translated: Hapter thinks a proper prince ought to have a sense of humor, however minimal."

"Rattle your spines, Halemtat!" shouted a voice from the crowd. "Let's see if you can do it."

"Yes," came another voice—and Marianne realized it was Chornian's—"Rattle your spines, Great Prince of the Nutcrackers!"

All around them, like rain on a tin roof, came the sound of rattling spines. Marianne looked around—the laughter swept through the crowd, setting every Rejoicer in vibrant motion. Even the grand vizier rattled briefly, then caught himself, his ruff stiff with alarm.

Halemtat didn't rattle.

From his pouch, Chornian took a nutcracker and a nut. Placing the nut in the cracker's smirking mouth, Chornian made the bite cut through the rattling of the crowd like the sound of a shot. From somewhere to her right, a second crack resounded. Then a third. . . . Then the rattling took up a renewed life.

Marianne felt as if she were under water. All around her spines shifted and rattled. Chornian's beaded spines chattered as he cracked a second nut in the smirking face of the nutcracker.

Then one of Halemtat's guards ripped the nutcracker from Chornian's hands. The guard glared at Chornian, who rattled all the harder.

Looking over his shoulder to Halemtat, the guard called, "He's already clipped. What shall I do?"

"Bring me the nutcracker," said Halemtat. The guard glared again at Chornian, who had not stopped laughing, and loped back with the nutcracker in hand. Belatedly, Marianne recognized the smirk on the nutcracker's face.

The guard handed the nutcracker to the grand vizier—Marianne knew beyond a doubt that he recognized the smirk too.

"Whose teeth carved this?" demanded Halemtat.

An unclipped Rejoicer worked his way to the front of the crowd, sat proudly back on his haunches, and said, "Mine." To the grand vizier, he added, with a slight rasp of his quills that was a barely suppressed laugh, "What do you think of my work, Corten? Does it amuse you? You have a strong jaw."

Rattling swept the crowd again.

Halemtat sat up on his haunches. His bristles stood straight out. Marianne had never seen a Rejoicer bristle quite that way before. "Silence!" he bellowed.

Startled, either by the shout or by the electrified bristle of their ruler, the crowd spread itself thinner. The laughter had subsided only because each of the Rejoicers had gone as bristly as Halemtat. Chornian shifted slightly to keep Marianne and Nick near the protected cover of his beaded ruff.

"Marianne," said Nick softly, "That's Tatep."

"I know," she said. Without meaning to, she'd grabbed his arm for reassurance.

Tatep. . . . He sat back on his haunches, as if fully at ease—the only sleeked Rejoicer in the courtyard. He might have been sitting in Marianne's office discussing different grades of wood, for all the excitement he displayed.

Halemtat, rage quivering in every quill, turned to his guards and said, "Clip Tatep. *Hashay.*"

"*No!*" shouted Marianne, starting forward. As she realized she'd spoken Dirtside and opened her mouth to shout it again in Rejoicer, Nick grabbed her and clapped a hand over her mouth.

"*No!*" shouted Chornian, seeming to translate for her, but speaking his own mind.

Marianne fought Nick's grip in vain. Furious, she bit the hand he'd clapped over her mouth. When he yelped and removed it—still not letting her free—she said, "It'll kill him! He'll bleed to death! Let me *go.*" On the last word, she kicked him hard, but he didn't let go.

A guard produced the ritual scissors and handed them to the official in charge of clipping. She held the instrument aloft and made the ritual display, clipping the air three times. With each snap of the scissors, the crowd chanted, "No. No. No."

Taken aback, the official paused. Halemtat clicked at her and she abruptly remembered the rest of the ritual. She turned to make the three ritual clips in the air before Halemtat.

This time the voice of the crowd was stronger. "No. No. No," came the shout with each snap.

Marianne struggled harder as the official stepped toward Tatep. . . .

Then the grand vizier scuttled to intercept. "No," he told the official. Turning to Halemtat, he said, "The image is mine. *I* can laugh at the caricature. Why is it, I wonder, that you can't, Halemtat? Has some disease softened your spines so that they no longer rattle?"

Marianne was so surprised she stopped struggling against Nick's hold—and felt the hold ease. He didn't let go, but held her against him in what was almost an embrace. Marianne held her breath, waiting for Halemtat's reply.

Halemtat snatched the ritual scissors from the official and threw them at Corten's feet. "You," he said. "You will *hashay* Tatep."

"No," said Corten. "I won't. *My* spines are still stiff enough to rattle."

Chornian chose that moment to shout once more, "Rattle your spines, Halemtat! Let us hear you rattle your spines!"

And without so much as a by-your-leave the entire crowd suddenly took up the chant: "Rattle your spines! Rattle your spines!"

Halemtat looked wildly around. He couldn't have rattled if he'd wanted to—his spines were too bristled to touch one to another. He turned his glare on the official, as if willing her to pick up the scissors and proceed.

Instead, she said, in perfect cadence with the crowd, "Rattle your spines!"

Halemtat made an imperious gesture to his guard—and the guard said, "Rattle your spines!"

Halemtat turned and galloped full tilt into his palace. Behind him the chant continued—"Rattle your spines! Rattle your spines!"

Then, quite without warning, Tatep rattled his spines. The next thing Marianne knew, the entire crowd was laughing and laughing and laughing at their vanished ruler.

Marianne went limp against Nick. He gave her a suggestion of a hug, then let her go. Against the rattle of the crowd, he said, "I thought you were going to get yourself killed, you little idiot."

"I couldn't—I couldn't stand by and do *nothing*; they might have killed Tatep."

"I thought doing nothing was a diplomat's job."

"You're right; some diplomat I make. Well, after this little episode, I probably don't have a job anyhow."

"My offer's still open."

"Tell the truth, Nick. If I'd been a member of your team fifteen minutes ago, would you have let me go?"

He threw back his head and laughed. "Of course not," he said. "But at least I understand why you bit the hell out of my hand."

"Oh, god, Nick! I'm so sorry! Did I hurt you?"

"Yes," he said. "But I accept your apology—and next time I won't give you that option."

" 'Next time,' huh?"

Nick, still grinning, nodded.

Well, there was that to be said for Nick: he was realistic.

"Hi, Nick," said Tatep. "Welcome back."

"Hi, Tatep. Some show you folks laid on. What happens next?"

Tatep rattled the length of his body. "Your guess is as good as mine," he said. "I've never done anything like this before. Corten's still rattling. In fact, he asked me to make him a grand vizier nutcracker. I think I'll make him a present of it—for Christmas."

He turned to Marianne. "Share?" he said. "I was too busy to watch at the time. Were you and Nick mating? If you do it again, may I watch?"

Marianne turned a vivid shade of red, and Nick laughed entirely too much. "You explain it to him," Marianne told Nick firmly. "Mating habits are not within my diplomatic jurisdiction. And I'm still in the diplomatic corps—at least, until we get back to the embassy."

Tatep sat back on his haunches, eagerly awaiting Nick's explanation. Marianne shivered with relief and said hastily, "No, it wasn't mating, Tatep. I was so scared for you I was going to charge in and—well, I don't know what I was going to do after that—but I couldn't just stand by and let Halemtat hurt you." She scowled at Nick and finished, "Nick was afraid I'd get hurt myself and wouldn't let me go."

Tatep's eyes widened in surprise. "Marianne, you would have fought for me?"

"Yes. You're my friend."

"Thank you," he said solemnly. Then to Nick, he said, "You were right to hold her back. Rattling is a better way than fighting." He turned again to Marianne. "You surprise me," he said. "You showed us how to rattle at Halemtat."

He shook from snout to tail-tip, with a sound like a hundred snare drums. "Halemtat turned tail and *ran* from our rattling!"

"And now?" Nick asked him.

"Now I'm going to go home. It's almost dinner time and I'm hungry enough to eat an entire tree all by myself." Still rattling, he added,

"Too bad the hardwood I make the nutcrackers from is so bitter—though tonight I could almost make an exception and dine exclusively on bitter wood."

Tatep got down off his haunches and started for home. Most of the crowd had dispersed as well. It seemed oddly anticlimactic, until Marianne heard and saw the rattles of laughter ripple through the departing Rejoicers.

Beside the supply-transport, Tatep paused. "Nick, at your convenience—I really *would* like you to share about human mating. For friendship's sake, I should know when Marianne is fighting and when she's mating. Then I'd know whether she needs help or—or what kind of help she needs. After all, some trees need help to mate. . . ."

Marianne had turned scarlet again. Nick said, "I'll tell you all about it as soon as I get settled in again."

"Thank you." Tatep headed for home, for all the world as if nothing unusual had happened. In fact, the entire crowd, laughing as it was, might have been a crowd of picnickers off for home as the sun began to set.

A squawk from the radio brought Marianne back to business. No use putting it off. Time to bite the bullet and check in with Clarence—if nothing else, the rest of the staff would be worried about both of them.

Marianne climbed into the cab. Without prompting, Nick climbed in beside her. For a long moment, they listened to the diatribe that came over the radio, but Marianne made no move to reply. Instead, she watched the Rejoicers laughing their way home from the palace courtyard.

"Nick," she said. "Can you really laugh a dictator into submission?"

He cocked a thumb at the radio. "Give it a try," he said. "It's not worth cursing back at Clarence—you haven't his gift for bureaucratic invective."

Marianne also didn't have a job by the time she got back to the embassy. Clarence had tried to clap her onto the returning supply ship, but Nick stepped in to announce that Clarence had no business sending anybody from his ethnology staff home. In the end, Clarence's bureaucratic invective had failed him and the ethnologists simply disobeyed, as Nick had. All Clarence could do, after all, was issue a directive; if they chose to ignore it, the blame no longer fell on Clarence. Since that was all that worried Clarence, that was all right.

In the end, Marianne found that being an ethnologist was considerably more interesting than being a diplomat . . . especially during a revolution.

She and Nick, with Tatep, had taken time off from their mutual studies to chose this year's Christmas tree—from Halemtat's reserve. "Why," said Marianne, bemused at her own reaction, "do I feel like I'm cutting a Christmas tree with Thomas Jefferson?"

"Because you are," Nick said. "Even Thomas Jefferson did ordinary things once in a while. Chances are, he even hung out with his friends. . . ." He waved. "Hi, Tatep. How goes the revolution?"

For answer, Tatep rattled the length of his body.

"Good," said Nick.

"I may have good news to share with you at the Christmas party," added the Rejoicer.

"Then we look forward to the Christmas party even more than usual," said Marianne.

"And I brought a surprise for Marianne all the way from Dirt," Nick added. When Marianne lifted an eyebrow, he said, "No, no hints."

"Share?" said Tatep.

"Christmas Eve," Nick told him. "After you've shared your news, I think."

The tree-trimming party was in full swing. The newly formed Ad Hoc Christmas Chorus was singing Czech carols—a gift from Esperanza to everybody on both staffs. Clarence had gotten so mellow on the Christmas punch that he'd even offered Marianne her job back—if she was willing to be dropped a grade for insubordination. Marianne, equally mellow, said no but said it politely.

Nick had arrived at last, along with Tatep and Chornian and Chaylam and their kids. Surprisingly, Nick stepped in between verses to wave the Ad Hoc Christmas Chorus to silence. "Attention, please," he shouted over the hubbub. "Attention, *please!* Tatep has an announcement to make." When he'd finally gotten silence, Nick turned to Tatep and said, "You have the floor."

Tatep looked down, then looked up again at Nick.

"I mean," Nick said, "go ahead and speak. Marianne's not the only one who'll want to know your news, believe me."

But it was Marianne Tatep chose to address.

"We've all been to see Halemtat," he said. "And Halemtat has agreed: no one will be clipped again unless five people from the same village agree that the offense warrants that severe a punishment. *We* will chose the five, not Halemtat. Furthermore, from this day forward, anyone may say anything without fear of being clipped. Speaking one's mind is no longer to be punished."

The crowd broke into applause. Beside Tatep, Nick beamed.

Tatep took a piece of parchment from his pouch. "You see, Marianne? Halemtat signed it and put his bite to it."

"How did you get him to agree?"

"We laughed at him—and we cracked our nutcrackers in the palace courtyard for three days and three nights straight, until he agreed."

Chornian rattled. "He said he'd sign anything if we'd all just go away and let him sleep." He hefted the enormous package he'd brought with him and rattled again. "Look at all the shelled nuts we've brought for your Christmas party!"

Marianne almost found it in her heart to feel sorry for Halemtat. Grinning, she accepted the package and mounded the table with shelled nuts. "Those are almost too important to eat," she said, stepping back to admire their handiwork. "Are you sure they oughtn't to go into a museum?"

"The important thing," Tatep said, "is that I can say anything I want." He popped one of the nuts into his mouth and chewed it down. "Halemtat is a talemtat," he said, and rattled for the sheer joy of it.

"Corten looks like he's been eating too much briarwood," said Chornian—catching the spirit of the thing.

Not recognizing the expression, Marianne cast an eye at Nick, who said, "We'd say, 'Been eating a lemon.'"

One of Chornian's brood sat back on his/her haunches and said, "I'll show you Halemtat's guards—"

The child organized its siblings with much pomp and ceremony (except for the littlest who couldn't stop rattling) and marched them back and forth. After the second repetition, Marianne caught the rough import of their chant: "We're Halemtat's guards/We send our regards/We wish you nothing but ill/Clip! we cut off your quill!"

After three passes, one child stepped on another's tail and the whole troop dissolved into squabbling amongst themselves and insulting each other. "You look like Corten!" said one, for full effect. The adults rattled away at them. The littlest one, delighted to find that insults could be funny, turned to Marianne and said, "Marianne! You're spineless!"

Marianne laughed even harder. When she'd caught her breath, she explained to the child what the phrase meant when it was translated literally into Standard. "If you want a good Dirt insult," she said, mischievously, "I give you 'birdbrain.'" All the sounds in that were easy for a Rejoicer mouth to utter—and when Marianne explained why it was an insult, the children all agreed that it was a very good insult indeed.

"Marianne is a birdbrain," said the littlest.

"No," said Tatep. "*Halemtat* is a birdbrain, not Marianne."

"Let the kid alone, Tatep," said Marianne. "The kid can say anything it wants!"

"True," said Tatep. "True!"

They shooed the children off to look for their presents under the tree, and Tatep turned to Nick. "Share, Nick—your surprise for Marianne."

Nick reached under the table. After a moment's searching, he brought out a large bulky parcel and hoisted it onto the table beside the heap of Halemtat nuts. Marianne caught a double-handful before they spilled onto the floor.

Nick laid a protective hand atop the parcel. "Wait," he said. "I'd better explain. Tatep, every family has a slightly different Christmas tradition—the way you folks do for Awakening. This is part of my family's Christmas tradition. It's *not* part of Marianne's Christmas tradition—but, just this once, I'm betting she'll go along with me." He took his hand from the parcel and held it out to Marianne. "Now you can open it," he said.

Dropping the Halemtat nuts back onto their pile, Marianne reached for the parcel and ripped it open with enough verve to satisfy anybody's Christmas unwrapping tradition. Inside was a box, and inside the box a jumble of gaudy cardboard tubes—glittering in stars and stripes and polka dots and even an entire school of metallic green fish. "Fireworks!" said Marianne. "Oh, Nick. . . ."

He put his finger to her lips. "Before you say another word—you chose today to celebrate Christmas because it was the right time of the Rejoicer year. You, furthermore, said that holidays on Dirt and the other human worlds don't converge—"

Marianne nodded.

Nick let that slow smile spread across his face. "But they *do*. This year, back on Dirt, today is the Fourth of July. The dates won't coincide again in our lifetimes but, just this once, they do. So, just this once—fireworks. You do traditionally celebrate Independence Day with fireworks, don't you?"

The pure impudence in his eyes made Marianne duck her head and look away but, in turning, she found herself looking right into Tatep's bright expectant gaze. In fact, all of the Rejoicers were waiting to see what Nick had chosen for her and if he'd chosen right.

"Yes," she said, speaking to Tatep but turning to smile at Nick. "After all, today's Independence Day right here on Rejoicing, too. Come on, let's go shoot off fireworks!"

And so, for the next twenty minutes, the night sky of Rejoicing was alive with Roman candles, shooting stars and all the brightness of all the Christmases and all the Independence Days in Marianne's memory. In the streets, humans ooohed and aaahed and Rejoicers rattled. The pops and bangs even woke Halemtat, but all he could do was come out on his balcony and watch.

A day later Tatep reported the rumor that one of the palace guards even claimed to have heard Halemtat rattle. "I don't believe it for a minute," Nick added when he passed the tale on to Marianne.

"Me neither," she said, "but it's a good enough story that I'd *like* to believe it."

"A perfect Christmas tale, then. What would you like to bet that the story of The First Time Halemtat Rattled gets told every Christmas from now on?"

"Sucker bet," said Marianne. Then the wonder struck her. "Nick? Do traditions start that easily—that quickly?"

He laughed. "What kind of fireworks would you like to have *next* year?"

"One of each," she said. "And about five of those with the gold fish-like things that swirl down and then go *bam!* at you when you least expect it."

For a moment, she thought he'd changed the subject, then she realized he'd answered her question. Wherever she went, for the rest of her life, her Christmas tradition would include fireworks—not just any fireworks, but Fourth of July fireworks. She smiled. "Next year, maybe we should play Tchaikovsky's *1812 Overture* as well as *The Nutcracker Suite.*"

He shook his head. "No," he said, "*The Nutcracker Suite* has plenty enough fireworks all by itself—at least *your* version of it certainly did!"

ABOUT THE EDITOR

Sheila Williams is the executive editor of *Asimov's Science Fiction* magazine. She has been with the magazine for thirteen years.

Williams is also the editor, or co-editor, of a number of anthologies. These books include *Tales from Isaac Asimov's Science Fiction Magazine* (HBJ, 1986), *Why I Left Harry's All-Night Hamburgers, and Other Stories from IAsfm* (Delacorte, 1990), *The Loch Moose Monster: More Stories from IAsfm* (Delacorte, 1992), *Isaac Asimov's Skin Deep* (Ace, 1995), *Isaac Asimov's Cyberdreams* (Ace, 1994), and *Isaac Asimov's Robots* (Ace, 1991). In addition to these anthologies, Williams has co-edited *Writing Science Fiction and Fantasy* (St. Martin's Press, 1991) with the editors of *Asimov's* and *Analog*.

Williams received her bachelor's degree from Elmira College in Elmira, New York, and her master's from Washington University in St. Louis, Missouri. During her junior year she studied at the London School of Economics. She lives in New York City with her husband, David Bruce, and their daughter, Irene.